THE OTTOMANS

BOOK ONE

THE THRACIAN SUN

Murat Tuncel

Translated by Hande Eagle

THE THRACIAN SUN
by Murat Tuncel
Translated by Hande Eagle

© 2021 Murat Tuncel

ISBN 978-3-949197-54-3

Texianer Verlag
www.texianer.com

CHAPTER ONE

Seeing the unruly waves ease, Suleyman Pasha tilted his head and looked at the violet ripples surrounding the sun as they percolated towards the bosom of the evening as if he was embarrassed by the boundless serenity of the blue sky. "It's just like the flight of a bird over the sea," he muttered. From watching the beams of light lodge themselves into the blue crystal of the sky and playfully reach the earth, his eyes now gazed into the tired waves. He walked slowly on the shore and looked at the sun once again, did some sums in his head and removed his artless yellow-striped turban. After placing it on a large black rock sunken into the ash grey sands of the shore, he took a few more steps on the sand. He stopped when the water reached the toes of his Sarukhanid-made, double-stitched boots that snuggly wrapped his calves. He knelt, bending his toned yet bony legs at the knees. He plunged his ample hand into the cool water. After a pause, he submerged his other hand, too. He filled his cupped palms with water and repeatedly splashed his face, which soured as the saltwater from his temples rolled down to his prominent lips and into his mouth. As he dried his face with a white handkerchief he complained, "It's too salty."

Evrenos Bey had been watching him since their arrival, "My Bey, the seawater is too salty for us because we are used to freshwater. But according to myth, it's the tide from the Black Sea that makes the Aegean and the Dardanelles so salty."

Suleyman Pasha didn't like to talk about things he didn't know much about, so he didn't express an opinion on seawater. Without looking at Evrenos Bey's long face, a face that transformed its expression according to each situation, he turned and looked at the massive sun over his shoulder as it swiftly tried to blend into the horizon. "It's flowing down."

Unsure as to whether this was about the sun or the waters of the strait, Evrenos Bey decided to presume it was about the waters, those that coursed through the strait, "It is said that the surface current in the Dardanelles is channelled into the Aegean Sea and the undercurrent to the Black Sea My Bey, but no one knows how it really works. Perhaps this explanation is an epithet of the Genoese."

As Suleyman Pasha stood up, he turned towards Evrenos Bey and pointing to the sea he softly said, "Evrenos Bey, do you think it's calmed down now?"

Evrenos Bey smiled with the whole of his long face. He surveyed the strait in both directions, turning towards Suleyman Pasha to reply, "My Bey, whatever I might say it would be in vain. If I tell you that it has calmed down and it gets wild again by the power of the winds I would be ashamed. The local fishermen would know best."

Knowing that Evrenos Bey was good with his words, Suleyman Pasha didn't persist but as he turned towards the sea he was decided, "We've been here for many days—we've waited long enough. It'd be to our advantage if we didn't wait any longer."

With a tone of voice signalling his agreement, Evrenos Bey ruminated, "My Bey, you are indeed correct but the sea is not steady as the earth under our feet. Most of our *levends*[1] don't know how to swim. I'd say we have to be cautious. I'd rather set sail a day late but be safe."

Suleyman Pasha retorted, "You are also right, but we are tired of waiting."

Just as he continued, "You see, the shores across the sea are calling," he saw sailing ships arriving from the Sea of Marmara. He was alarmed. Realizing just how flustered Suleyman Pasha was getting, Evrenos Bey tried to comfort him, "My Bey, don't worry about how close to us they seem to be, they cannot see us that easily."

---

1   Translator's Note, *Levend* (old Turkish) meaning "naval soldier". At the end of the fifteenth century, it is possible to see an increase in the number of Ottoman pirates in the Mediterranean. Lots of pirates, none with official titles or positions, started to aid Ottoman maritime activities. These pirates were called *levends*.

Suleyman Pasha replied, "Still... We should be prudent."

Evrenos Bey placed his hand against his brow to block the sunlight and carefully surveyed the ship closest to them. He turned to Suleyman Pasha and said, "They are Venetian ships, My Bey. If it were the Genoese, we would have to hide, but we don't need to hide from the Venetians."

Suleyman Pasha laughed, showing his shining white teeth that seemed to brighten up his sunburnt tawny face. In a tone of voice akin to whistling, he asked, "Why?"

After gulping as if to swallow the smile spreading across his thin lips, Evrenos Bey explained, "Because it's said that the Venetians do not care much for those who are of no use to them. And when they do care, they first offer cold drinks before they sit and talk."

"I understand why they wouldn't care much for those who are of no use to them but what's this cold drink you speak of?"

"They say cold drinks 'don't numb the mind'."

Suleyman Pasha first looked at Evrenos Bey and then at the ships gliding towards them as he turned his large eyes and their swirling gaze from one ship to the other. He weighed Evrenos Bey's sentence in his mind. It was as if something lodged itself in his speech centre. He decided not to say what he was going to say. Taking his turban from the black stone he said, "We should still stand behind those bushes over there just to be cautious."

He walked behind the thick shrubs near him. He looked at Evrenos Bey standing next to him and asked, "How did you know that they are Venetian ships?"

Evrenos Bey appeared to resent the question, "My Bey, are you trying to tell me that I have grown old?"

"No, not at all! I was only curious as to how you could see the banner from such a distance."

"Their ships are very different from those of others. They can also be identified without catching sight of the banner."

"How is that so?"

"The bows of their ships are curved up as if they were sniffing the sky. Their starboards are also larger and more curved than others."

"Who is more superior on the seas? The Genoese or the Venetians?"

"The Venetians, My Bey. Though, it wouldn't be improper to say there is great rivalry between them."

Just as Suleyman Pasha was getting ready for another question, Hacı Ilbey approached with quickened steps. They both looked at him at the same time. Hacı Ilbey said, "We sought someone knowledgeable about the seas and everyone told us about the same fisherman, the one from yesterday. According to them, he is the most knowledgeable fisherman around here."

As Suleyman Pasha stroked his short beard he said, "If that's the case we'll take him with us..."

Evrenos Bey looked at them as if dreaming with eyes wide open, then wiped both his eyes with his forefingers simultaneously and looked at the Dardanelles. Seeing a ship sailing from the Aegean towards *Kostantiniyye*[2] he said, "That one is a Genoese ship. It'd be good if we kept out of sight."

As he knelt down he continued, referring to the Genoese, "It is said they can even see the ants walking on the land when they are at sea. I don't know how true that is, but it's best to hide from them."

Suleyman Pasha knelt down just as Hacı Ilbey and Evrenos Bey did, and asked, "Evrenos Bey, had you seen that fisherman before? Why did he seem so angry when he was looking at you yesterday? He also adamantly kept calling the strait 'Leander's Sea'."

Evrenos Bey replied, "I don't think I've ever seen him before, My

---

2   T.N. *Kostantiniyye* is the name by which the city came to be known in the Islamic world. It is an Arabic calqued form of Constantinople, with an Arabic ending meaning 'place of' instead of the Greek element '-polis'. After the Ottoman conquest of 1453, it was used as the most formal official name in Ottoman Turkish, and remained in use throughout most of the time up to the fall of the Empire in 1923. In the novel, Byzantine emperors refer to the city as 'Constantinople' while the Ottomans suitably refer to it as 'Kostantiniyye'.

Bey, but I think he somehow knows me. The things he speaks of aren't common knowledge. It's obvious that he was educated at a madrasah... If he has ever been to Bursa, he might know me from there. He doesn't like me but, to tell you the truth, I don't seem to get on with him either."

In his usual soft tone of voice, Hacı Ilbey said, "It doesn't matter who he is, he knows this place better than anyone..."

After a short silence spent looking at them both, Suleyman Pasha reminded them, "Can you believe that he wanted to tell us about the 'lament of Scamander who overflowed, unable to bear the pain of Troy' as if all he told us wasn't enough already."

As he straightened his back and stood up, with his eyes lowered to the ground, Evrenos Bey said, "I know the lament I'll tell him once he helps us cross to the other shore."

CHAPTER TWO

As Emperor John VI Kantakouzenos watched the waves of the blue Golden Horn through the window his wife Empress Irene Asanina walked into the room. Seeing the Emperor pensively watching the distant waves she approached him, swaying her body—a figure that had not lost any of its vitality with age. She moved in such a way it appeared that her top half may separate itself at the waistline. The Emperor was scratching his greying beard with his stubby fingers as she touched his shoulder and softly said, "John."

She waited for the distracted emperor to reply. He didn't so she called out once more, "John, you are absorbed again. I know it is very difficult to make a decision but you have to if you want to be calm. Whatever your decision maybe I will as always, be by your side."

As the Emperor turned his head towards his wife he explained, "It is truly not an easy thing to make a decision after all that has happened. Still, we must try to make rational decisions. If what I heard is correct, Empress Anna's mind is yet to win over her ambition. I suppose it's best to wait a bit longer."

Irene Asanina, who gained the title of consort empress since her husband shared the rule of the empire with their son-in-law John V Palaiologos, gazed at his bearded face and told him, "John, I do not desire anything more than that. I believe in the virtue of finding happiness in the small things in life. What I most desire is that you do the same. See, that sun and that moon as it set anew in the last few days unwittingly make us grow old. One of our daughters is in the palace of Orhan Bey and the other in the palace of your co-ruler. Our sons are happy in their castles. I'm afraid that wanting more than this could only bring unhappiness.

He gratefully looked at the greyish blue eyes of Empress Irene. She had managed to keep the love between them alive by demonstrating

her affections for him in different ways every day since their wedding, and the Emperor thought to himself, "My beloved Irene, I also
need peace and calm. That is what I've been searching for all along.
But that daughter of the Savoys, Empress Anna, has always made
heavy weather of everything. I wanted to teach her a lesson—I
wanted her to stop ignoring my efforts. If it wasn't so would I ever
want to be away from my Helena and my grandchildren?" Once he
finished his internal conversation, he continued in his deflated tone
of voice, "What I desired was also that peace you mention. But as
you see, it wasn't enough only for me to desire it. Just as I'd thought
that everything would be fine once the heart of Savoy's daughter was
softened, those from Theodosia afflicted us with that slovenly disease. Just as we got rid of that disease, the zealots of Thessaloniki
hung over our heads. As if these misfortunes were not enough our
fleet, stuck between the Venetians and the Genoese, suffered a set-
back. I do not find it strange that Anna of Savoy, like all other
empresses, wants to see her son as the sole emperor but I bitterly re-
sented her for seeing me as a rag she could use any way she saw fit.
As a matter of fact..."

His gaze swept the other coast before finishing. Empress Irene Asanina tried to encourage him by repeating, "As a matter of fact..."

The Emperor remained quiet. Moving her hand from her husband's shoulder to his waist, she asked him, "John, why do you keep
your eyes fixed in that one direction?"

As she fell quiet, the Emperor felt a shudder from the slow motion
of the empress's hand on his back. For a moment, he remained undecided. As he waited for that uneasy feeling within to subside, he
walked closer to the window and looked at the Genoese ship rocking
back and forth on the lathered waves of the Golden Horn and approaching the dock on the far side. In a troubled tone of voice, he
said, "That's the second today."

Empress Irene curiously asked, "What's the second?"

"That Genoese ship."

"Don't they always sail by? That might be the second, but it might also be the third. On some days aren't there four or five ships docking?"

The Emperor jerked as if a needle had pierced his thigh and continued, "What they did last really drew the line for me, more so than Kalekas and Apokaukos. Despite the fact that the Venetians have less revenue from customs, they pay in better time than the Genoese. They keep a foot in both camps but are keen to work behind my back. I am not sure whether they are on our side or Orhan's. He has also become like them lately. I cannot understand why as he is getting everything he wishes. If I could only know what he is after..."

As Empress Irene Asanina walked closer to her husband she replied, "I don't think he has any quarrel with you. Theodora is very happy with him. However, I think it's best for Byzantium if you stay away from Orhan."

As John VI Kantakouzenos turned towards the empress he continued, "My beautiful Irene, you should know that sovereignty is a succession of infinite desires, which is why the desires of rulers never end. That is why they want to change everything all the time. I don't know what news I will hear from my mesazōn[3] when I go to my throne room in a little while. Perhaps he will act as if he is voicing rumours again and make my blood boil by telling me that we are proponents in willingly giving up Constantinople to the Ottomans just as the feudal lord of Bursa did. If only our commanders were as loyal to us as the beys of the Ottomans are to them I would know what to do but all to no avail. My men do not respect each other nor do they feel any love for Byzantium. Do you remember that Orhan came all the way to Scutari when we returned to the palace? When Orhan agreed to my request to host their prince at the palace I re-

---

3   T.N, The *mesazōn* (meaning "intermediary" in Greek) was a high dignitary and official during the last centuries of the Byzantine Empire, who acted as the chief minister and principal aide of the Byzantine emperor.

joiced inside thinking that peace was at hand. However, their mutual passion and respect for each other intimidated me. After that day I thought about how I could attain that level of love and respect amongst my commanders. But I haven't been able to make any headway at all."

With a smile on her thin lips Irene replied, "Perhaps you have but because you want to have made more, you feel you have accomplished nothing."

John turned from the smiling lips of the empress to the Bosphorus and looked across at Scutari, "Perhaps you are right. Perhaps I cannot recognise my accomplishments because the transformation of those reckoning upon Rome and Avignon is very slow."

The Empress this time wetted her thin lips with her tongue. In a soft tone of voice emanating from the depths of her larynx she said, "Those before Andronicus also went to Rome and Avignon but, as you know, it takes more than a few buckets of water to turn the wheel in the mill."

"My dear Irene, your angel's mind is making you say much. Solomon says that "if you are hard done by, compromise—but if you are evil, protect yourself..." That is exactly the state of affairs in which we find ourselves today."

"What if the one who is evil is much more powerful than you? Did Solomon also say something about that?"

"I don't know if he said anything else on the subject but I do think that keeping patient and finding a logical solution is the best way to go about this."

"Surely you know well that your logical mind won't be of any use if all your sources of power have dried up?"

The Emperor first tried to enliven his eyes that had become empty as if there was nothing that could be done. Then he thought about what his wife was trying to tell him. After taking a few steps towards the door he turned back and looked at his wife's heaving chest.

Hearing no response, he uttered, "What's happening to me?" After praying for the emotional withers he felt inside to vanish, he whispered, "They say that 'New waters ever flow on those who step into the same rivers'."

Upon hearing what the Emperor said, Irene replied, "Surely the one at fault in this matter is water."

The Emperor, gazing at his wife, nodded as if expressing surprise at his wife's intelligence. He turned and looked out the window towards the Genoese quarter and said, "The third one has come into port, too."

CHAPTER THREE

A few northern clouds passed slowly in front of the moon and cast a shadow on the coast. The builders hiding behind the barrow nearest to the shore carried the foursquare beams that were reamed out at equal distances from one another along with the wooden drop siding they'd stowed behind some reeds to the coast. As some passed the siding from one to the other, others lined up the beams on the sandy ground spacing them equally once again. The broad-shouldered, average-height foreman standing in the middle repeatedly said, "Don't make a sound, and be quick!" The other builders listened to him and skilfully kept to their work. After watching them work for a while and seeing that all the wooden drop siding had been placed atop the beams, the foreman took the wooden pegs from a large pocket in his leather apron and passed them to the builders waiting around him. As he looked at the mallets in their hands he said, "It'll make noise if you nail the pegs in like that." Then, while trying to get better control of a mallet handle he decided, "Wrap the mallets in rags."

Just as the builders had begun to hammer the pegs into their places with their rag covered mallets the whisper of the sentry was heard, "Hide!"

Hearing the warning the builders hid behind the rocks and bushes. They turned their gaze to the sailing ship, rocking in the arms of the wind under the hazy moonlight, as it headed towards the mouth of the Dardanelles from the northeast. With their breaths held the builders looked on. Lit up by sailor's lanterns hanging from masts that resembled open arms, the ship was far enough away that the men returned to work. When the moonlight had become dimmed by the clouds, they fumbled but still managed to complete their endeavour in good time. The finished rafts were to be loaded with stores. The foreman had the men tightly fasten the rafts together with

bristle tethers in two pairs. Once secure the foreman got the builders to launch the large four-part raft. Just as it was in the water the
sound of the fishermen's oars came from along the coast. Four rowing boats pulled alongside the four corners of the raft and attached
thick tethers on each corner. The sonorous voice of the foreman
was heard when the guide fisherman's boat took its place at the
front, "Everything is ready, My Bey. We can now load the baskets
onto the rafts."

Hearing the voice of the foreman, the *levends* behind the barrow
carted the baskets bought from the villagers to the shore. The
builders, standing in water up to their waists, evenly loaded the
baskets onto the four-piece raft, and lashed them together with
tethers. Once they finished loading, the Karasid *levends* took their
positions at the oars, and then the beys and other *levends* got on
and seated themselves. Seeing that everyone had taken their place
Evrenos Bey moved from raft to raft and boarded the guide fisherman's boat. He sat right behind the guide whose face was dappled
with moonlight. He turned around and looked behind him once
again. Realising that everyone was waiting for them he lightly
tapped the guide on the shoulder and in the fisherman's language
said, "All right, let's go!"

The fisherman turned around and looked at his friends on the
coast. Then he turned his gaze to Evrenos Bey. As he signalled with
his hand the direction in which they had to row he said, in his own
language, "All right, let's go."

Evrenos Bey translated the fisherman's instructions and all the
rowers plunged their oars into the water. As the boats pulling the
large raft slowly departed from the coast, the builders and the owners of the fishing boats remaining on the shore watched them leave.
The guide fisherman was sculling the oars along with the Karasid
levends and repeating in Greek to Evrenos Bey who sat behind him,
"They must scull at the same time and in the same direction."

Evrenos Bey continually repeated what the fisherman said in Turkish so that all the men could hear.

The sea was now as calm as a millpond. The waves of the Dardanelles were tired of their daily struggle. This made the guide fisherman uneasy as the rowing boats advanced easily for a considerable period of time. Looking at Evrenos Bey he said, "It bodes no good that the sea is so calm but we should make use of this stillness and cover as much distance as possible."

Listening to the fisherman, whose eyes were shining under the hazy moonlight, Evrenos Bey muttered to himself, "I haven't trusted this demon since the first time I set eyes on him." Then in an angry tone of voice, he scolded him, "Heaven forbid!"

Thinking that there was nothing to be misunderstood in what he said the fisherman couldn't understand Evrenos Bey's anger. As he looked towards the moon that popped in and out of the clouds in the sky he said, "I only said so because I know the sea. There should have been a slight breeze right about now. It scares me that there is none."

This time Evrenos Bey raised his voice a little more, "Keep your thoughts to yourself—your job is to take us safely to the other side. I do not want to hear another word out of your mouth henceforth!"

The guide fisherman took advantage of the clouds again passing in front of the moon and grinned furtively. Evrenos Bey noticed this when the clouds suddenly cleared around the moon and swaying he looked at the rowing boats behind them. His gaze briefly searched for Suleyman Pasha and felt relief when he saw him. As he turned to the front and looked at the fisherman he thought, "I hope he hasn't forgotten that his family's life is in my hands," and whispered in a tone of voice only he could hear, "I should still keep an eye on him."

While Evrenos Bey was watching the guide fisherman closely, Suleyman Pasha was gazing at the play of the water's phosphorescence in the hazy light of the moon. As he pondered about the other day in the void filled by the splashing phosphorescence, the myth of Hero and Leander as told by Evrenos Bey came to his mind. He thought about Leander, the young, brave man, and looked on at the men rowing the boats. In a tone of voice that melded with the sound of the oars heaving in and out of the deep waters, he said, "We struggle even with all these rowers but he had to navigate these waters every night..."

Evrenos Bey sitting in the guiding rowing boat at the front turned back and peering at Suleyman Pasha asked, "My Bey, don't you think we could do this trip twice in a single day if we had Hero showing us the way across the sea with her lamp?"

Embarrassed that what he muttered to himself was overheard, "I thought I'd spoken quietly enough but..."

"My Bey, don't be fooled that the waters hide many things in their depths for they cannot hide anything above them. The waters carry everything ashore."

"I don't know the sea as well as you all do, I cannot say much of it but... perhaps if the waters cannot keep secrets, they are untrustworthy..."

In order to include Hacı Ilbey in the conversation, as he was sitting in the rowing boat behind the one Suleyman Pasha was in, Evrenos Bey said, "My Bey, you ought to listen to the myths of these shores from Hacı Ilbey, he tells them best."

As Hacı Ilbey looked at grey-haired Ece Bey who was sitting in the parallel boat he said, "Ece Bey knows the myths of these parts the best. He walked every square inch of these lands during the time of the Karasid. The only myth I know well is the myth of Abdurrahman and Semenderos[4] that I heard in Nicomedia.

Suleyman Pasha interrupted, "I've heard that one, too. I want to hear some new myths."

---

4 T.N, *Semenderos* was the daughter of a castle commander appointed near present-day Izmit (Nicomedia). One night, she dreamt of Abdurrahman and fell in love with him. When she saw him outside the castle walls the following day, she dangled a rope from the castle window and let him in. In turn, Abdurrahman opened the castle gate that night and let in Akçakoca's cavalry. Thus, the castle was easily besieged.

Just as Hacı Ilbey was about to reply, the screeching voice of the guide fisherman was heard, "Scull faster and at the same time."

Startled by the sudden screeching of the guide, Evrenos Bey realised that there may be danger ahead and loudly translated the guide's words, so that everyone could hear him.

Upon hearing what Evrenos Bey said, the rowers began to go even faster but they were late. Out of nowhere, mountainous waves were rolling towards them and about to career into the boats. Hacı Ilbey, more scared of the waves than anyone else, began to sing hymns out loud. The *levends* heard and joined him but when the sound of the waves splashing against their boats quickly drowned out their voices they all fell silent. As even the large rowing boats rocked like little bits of wood on the harsh waves, dolphins appeared around the boats from out of nowhere. As if to make fun of the boats they seemed to start competing with each other to see who could jump the highest. The guide fisherman burst into laughter at the sight. He laughed to his heart's content regardless of Evrenos Bey's teeth grinding behind him. He turned around, "They are the real owners of these waters."

Irritated by his burst of laughter Evrenos Bey replied, "Once we go ashore we can make you the real owner of the mainland."

Registering Evrenos Bey's rash reply, the guide realised he had gone too far and apologetically said, "I was only trying to say that there are living creatures in the sea other than us."

Evrenos Bey threateningly leaned towards the fisherman whose face could only be partially seen, "I just told you to keep your thoughts to yourself... If I hear your voice once more I'll cut out your tongue!"

CHAPTER FOUR

Dowager Empress Anna smiled as she looked at her son's sleepy eyes. A genteel smile poured from her gaze that reflected all shades of blue with the light filling the room from the window frame ensconced in the thick wall. She looked at the island-grown vegetables and the fresh Selymbria cheeses on the plates atop a table decorated with small glazed Antigone[5] tiles. She added the smile on her daughter-in-law Helena's vivacious rosebud lips to the one in her gaze and looked at her son. She muttered, "So young..." and let herself fall into a reverie.

Seeing his mother slip into a daydream, exiled Emperor John V Palaiologos tried to get rid of the sleep in his eyes and headed for the breakfast table the servants had prepared. For a while, his gaze switched between his mother Empress Anna and his wife, Empress Helena. He sat back down in his chair, looked at them both once again and uttered, "Enjoy your breakfast!" After eating quietly for a while he posed a question to his mother, "Mother, will you be going to the Genoese market today? I'd have liked to join you but I have too much to do. I will be receiving the envoys from the Aegean Sea. If it would please you I could delay some meetings until tomorrow. These committee meetings go on incessantly. It doesn't make much difference to them if they are received a day early or a day late."

Insistently, Dowager Empress Anna replied, "My son, it's fine. We can go by ourselves. You should take care of those who come to tell you of their allegiance. We can never know just what tomorrow may bring. You might need each and every one on your side."

Swallowing the bite that was in his mouth, John V Palaiologos replied, "Mother, don't fantasise about such intricate plans. The

---

5   T.N, The place mentioned here on as "Antigone" is currently referred to as the island of "Burgaz" located in the Marmara Sea. Demetrius I of Macedon, son of Antigonus I Monophthalmus (general and strap under Alexander the Great) named the island "Antigone" in order to keep his father's legacy alive.

truth is we are in exile on this island. My wish, for now, is to spend a
bit of time with you. Other affairs are dealt with whether I am here
or not. Alexius is far more adept at dealing with most matters than
I."

As Dowager Empress Anna watched the persistent smile that remained on her daughter-in-law's lips even while eating, she said to
her son, "Your father-in-law was a man who was raised and highly-
trusted by your father. He learnt what he had to from your father, as
did your father from him. Oh, how I only wish that I and the others
could have come to terms with him and none of this would have befallen Byzantium. I still trust in your father-in-law's wisdom and
reason. We cannot just hold him responsible for what has happened.
I suppose we are all to blame..."

Exiled Emperor John V Palaiologos looked at his wife Empress
Helena sitting in the chair beside him, still harbouring the smile on
her lips, "Dear mother, I believe in the reasoning of my father-in-law
just as much as you do. For some reason, there isn't of the slightest
doubt in my heart for his integrity. The fact that he still refers to me
as Co-Emperor feeds my hope. I believe that he will call us back to
Constantinople sooner or later. And if he doesn't, others surely
will..."

Once he finished speaking his train of thought he peered over at
his wife once again. Seeing that the smile Empress Helena habitually
carried on her lips had disappeared he exclaimed in a tender tone of
voice,, "Oh Helena, you misunderstood me!"

Helena, nicknamed the "little empress" by the servants, slowly
turned towards her husband and softly looked at Dowager Empress
Anna, "John, it doesn't matter to me one iota what you want to get
out of my father. Both our childhoods were spent amidst fighting
and fleeing. We are yet to overcome all that. Perhaps it pains you to
be far away from Constantinople now but believe me when I say I
am happy for my children's sake. I want to bring our baby into the

world on this peaceful island. Wouldn't it all be better if only you could make use of my father's experiences and he could benefit from your youth?"

As Empress Anna viewed Helena's small but scintillating body she thought to herself, "She is still so young but far more mature than we. When I was her age I couldn't stand it if Andronicus was away from Constantinople for a day, let alone being exiled to an island..."

Helena retired to her room after finishing breakfast in silence and Empress Anna continued to watch her son eat hungrily. As she watched his face, the round, droopy face of her husband appeared on that of her son. The way her son's mouth opened and closed was so similar to her husband. Without diverting her gaze from her son's face she leaned against the back of her chair. She took a sip of her warm drink and snarled, "Andronicus's mouth was more like that of an aged frog while John's is more like a younger one." She tried to remember the last time when her husband had eaten his breakfast with such an appetite. After blinking a couple of times she spoke aloud, "If my memory doesn't deceive me your father ate his breakfast with such vigour the day he was heading to Nicaea for the meeting of the seventh council."

Listening to his mother, John gulped several times as if the last mouthful he swallowed was stuck in his throat. Despite the fact that he wanted to speak, his voice wouldn't emerge from his lips. He drank the fruit juice in his wide-rimmed cup and finally managed to reply, "Mother it eases me that you always talk about my father but when I remember that Antigone was left undefended I can't help blaming him. I think that if my father hadn't pulled out of Antigone back then, none of this would have befallen us."

Empress Anna listened to her son's thoughts before clarifying his story, "The Ottomans laid siege to Antigone for many years even before your father's time. Your father never left that island undefended as you think. In fact, your father, anticipating the dangers that lay

ahead, told the participants of the seventh council that if they didn't
aid us in stopping the Ottomans in Anatolia they wouldn't be able to
stop them from later invading their own lands. The cardinal from
Avignon had at the time replied, 'Andronicus your suspicions are unfounded. Do not fear. The power of the Ottomans will dry up in
Anatolia and on earth in a few years and the same with the Seljuks.'
Your father was upset that his words carried no weight with the
members of the council. To console himself he would always say,
'Anna, they do not consider me as one of them. If they took what I
said seriously they would have long returned with their armies that
defeated the Seljuks.' Feeling his sadness in my veins, I remember
caressing his hair as he lay on my chest. Every time I would try to
console him and say, 'My dear Andronicus, don't you know that this
vast continent is like a wildfire? The kings have it in for one another
and meanwhile, the plague spreads from one city to the next. You
shall in due course see that once they are done with their own
troubles, both Avignon and Rome will run to your rescue.'"

As his mother spoke, the exiled emperor's mind was predisposed
with the question of what they were supposed to do about the Ottomans. Once she was done he rose from his chair and paced the large
dining room from one end to the other repeatedly. He paused to
watch his mother as she ate her breakfast and left for the morning
room. As he sat on the camel-leather stool and cast his gaze outside
the window his mother entered. He turned to her and said, "Mother,
won't you tell me of my father's time on the throne?"

Her age could only be determined by the wrinkles on her neck as
she looked deep into her son's eyes, "Son, when your father became
emperor the wounds caused by the Latins, whom your great-grand-
father rid Constantinople of with much trickery, were still fresh."

After falling silent for a short while, she was about to continue
when there was a knock at the door. A messenger entered the room.
After bowing and saluting them he said, "Your Majesty, they are

coming and in vast numbers."

The exiled emperor's face paled and he ran from the room without even thinking to ask who was coming. His mother followed him.

CHAPTER FIVE

T he dolphins had appeared out of nowhere and played around the rowing boats until the break of dawn. At which point they disappeared as suddenly as they had arrived, diving deep into the cool waters of the Dardanelles and out of sight amidst the first rays of sunlight. Upon seeing the dolphins leave and the shore emerge as a black line on the horizon Suleyman Pasha warned Evrenos Bey, "Evrenos Bey, we must reach the shore before sunrise."

Upon hearing the warning, the *levends* sculled harder and began to cover the distance as if it were a race.

As the rowing boats quickly approached the shore, Evrenos Bey frequently looked to Suleyman Pasha, waiting for a sign from him, but soon realised there was no sign coming and turned around to face the broad shoulders of the guide seated in front of him. Noticing that the guide was smiling insidiously he said, "You must be in the know about what's going on as you are now smiling so peculiarly —as if it wasn't enough that you made the *levends* row against the current all night."

Viewing the nearby shore, he muttered to himself, "If he jumps into the sea we won't be able to catch him." He slowly approached the guide from behind. The guide fisherman, lost in the view of the shore and with that evil grin on his face, didn't notice Evrenos Bey approach him. Evrenos Bey went down on his knees to grab the guide fisherman from behind and leaned over him as if preparing to smother him with his kaftan. He was startled at Evrenos Bey's warm breath on the nape of his neck. He tried to turn his head but Evrenos Bey grabbed and squeezed his throat like a pair of pliers with one hand while the other grasped for the mother-of-pearl hilt of his renowned thin, long dagger tucked into his waistband. Realising his fate, the fisherman looked at his socks embroidered like miniature tapestries, aimlessly expressing himself in a resigning tone of voice,

"No one from around here knits embroidered socks like this but my missus."

Unable to comprehend even half of what the guide fisherman said, Evrenos Bey, put his mouth right by the man's ear as he crouched over his shoulders like a nightmare in the twilight. After a few deep breaths, he spoke into the man's ear, "If for a moment I thought that you wouldn't jump into the sea to escape I wouldn't do this, but since the first moment I saw you have done nothing to earn my trust."

With those words, he buried the tip of his long dagger deep in the nape of the fisherman's neck. The thin blade of the dagger thrust through the soft flesh as if unsure which direction to take, not stopping until it met his brain. His eyes glassed over and he let himself go. Evrenos Bey hauled the fisherman from under his armpits and slowly pulled him to the side of the rowing boat. He pushed him overboard in the gap between two rowers, an ominous sound echoed as the body fell into the water. As it was buried by the darkness, Evrenos Bey looked at the spot where the man was buried, his long face slightly contorted. The fisherman seemed to appear above the cool waters once again. This time, his face opened and closed like an enormous mouth as he yelped, "Leandeeer!"

Evrenos Bey wiped his eyes and continued looking at the water, smiling bitterly that the image had disappeared. He whispered before sitting down once again, "Both Hero and your children are under my protection now."

Watching from the rowing boat just behind, Suleyman Pasha thought that there must be a good reason for Evrenos Bey's actions. As he looked at the guiding rowing boat their eyes met. Evrenos Bey shrugged his shoulders at the questioning gaze he was met by and loudly said, "It was for the sake of all of these lives!"

Unwilling to reply, Suleyman Pasha fell silent for a little while before quietly saying, "Let's hope for the best."

Unable to hear, Evrenos Bey stood up unperturbed by the fact that they no longer had a guide and pointed to the place the *levends* were to row to on the shore. Once he was done, he turned back and replied to Suleyman Pasha, whom he presumed had been looking at him for a while, "He was getting ready to escape as if it wasn't enough that he'd had us aimlessly rowing around the sea."

To offer him a sense of comfort and affirm that it may have been the correct decision Suleyman Pasha repeated himself but louder, "Let's just hope for the best."

Evrenos Bey turned towards the shore as if nothing of note had happened. He stood quietly until the rowing boats came in. Once the bow of the guiding boat grated against the sandy shore he told the men to get off.

He went to Suleyman Pasha once all the boats were ashore. "I couldn't wait for us to get to the beach because I knew that he was going to jump into the sea from the way he was smiling at the sight of land..."

Suleyman Pasha looked at Evrenos Bey's large bony hands with a slightly soured expression. He remembered the first time he saw the fisherman and how he had conversed with them to keep them distracted. He recalled how the fisherman said, "If you like I can tell you the lament of Scamander who overflowed, unable to bear the pain of Troy". As he lightly smiled he delivered his delayed reply to Evrenos Bey, "His family is under your safeguard now."

As Evrenos Bey prepared himself for a reply Hacı Ilbey appeared next to them, "The angels of Yunus[6] scared us quite a bit."

Gathering that the beys standing by him had no interest in conversing, he squinted and looked at the opposite shore. Evrenos Bey observed, "It looks so close, doesn't it?

---

6   T.N, Jonah, Jonas or as to referred to in Turkish "Yunus" is the name given in the Hebrew Bible (Old Testament) to a prophet of the northern kingdom of Israel in about the 8th century BC. He is the eponymous central character in the Book of Jonah, famous for being swallowed by a fish or a whale, depending on translation. The Biblical story of Jonah is repeated, with a few notable differences, in the Qur'an. In this instance, Hacı Ilbey refers to the dolphins as the "angels of Jonah".

Hacı Ilbey laughed, "I thought we would never set foot on land again!"

"We should have reached the shore long before the morning but he delayed our arrival by letting us fall into the path of the current twice."

As they talked amongst themselves Fazıl Bey was standing near the *levends* taking the oars from their holes, "Hide the oars in those bushes over there. Pull the rafts apart and pile the timbers so it looks like a pile of firewood."

Watching the *levends* quietly do their work together, Ece Bey and Balabancıkoğlu looked across the Dardanelles just as Hacı Ilbey did. Then, walking towards the other beys Akça Kocaoğlu approached them cheerfully, "Do you intend on crossing back again?"

Bursting into laughter Ece Bey replied, "I'm willing to ride a horse for ten years if I don't have to get in a small rowing boat again!"

Hearing their jolly chatter Evrenos Bey walked towards them and in his sonorous tone of voice Suleyman Pasha gathered them together.

"Gather round. Let's disguise ourselves and sit down for breakfast. After breakfast, we will wait for the villagers to begin to arrive at the castle. Meanwhile, we should delegate tasks."

None of the *levends* sitting around the hastily assembled breakfast floor tables felt like eating. While sitting down most of them felt as if they were still rocking back and forth on the boats. Realising that no one felt like eating, Suleyman Pasha turned to the beys and *levends* and told them his plan, "Those of you who feel fit enough should scout the area around the road. The others should rest until the castle gates are opened. When the villagers begin entering the castle we will scatter ourselves amongst them as they walk in. We must enter Tzympe before noon. Any later and we will draw attention to ourselves. Ece Bey, Fazıl Bey and Hasan Bey's men will be first to enter the castle, they will deal with the sentries in the bastions and secure the castle commander's mansion. After that, Akça Kocaoğlu and his *levends* will deal with the guards around and inside the gatehouses. Hacı Ilbey and Balabancıkoğlu with their *levends* will together take over the market and the streets. Last but not least, Evrenos Bey and I will enter the keep itself.

After explaining his intricate plan Suleyman Pasha fell quiet. Knowing he had said all he wanted to, Evrenos Bey added, "The Greek spoken in these quarters is nothing like that spoken across the strait. It's best if those who speak Greek do not speak at all."

He momentarily paused before exclaiming, "May our holy war be blessed!"

CHAPTER SIX

Emperor John VI Kantakouzenos leaned back on his throne. After casting his gaze around the large room a few times, he looked at the throne of his Co-Emperor and son-in-law John V Palaiologos, whom he had reluctantly sent on exile. He had still not been able to bring himself to order for the removal of the throne. He recalled the days when his Co-Emperor was still a child—long before the day he exiled him after definitively consolidating his power in Constantinople with the aid of Orhan Bey, his other son-in-law. A bitter smile appeared on his lips. As he looked at the empty throne, he remembered the past, reliving his memory of Emperor Palaiologos and he quietly talked to himself, "He got up from the throne he was sitting on with the vigour of his mother and walked towards the woven limestone wall. As he looked outside the window, on that first day he asked the mesazōn who entered the room, 'Were you able to determine the situation on the other side?'

"The mesazōn first looked at me in slight surprise and then as he extended the papers he had prepared towards him, he explained further, 'Orhan Bey has decided to support the Genoese by asserting that the Venetians whom he had previously supported against the Genoese during the past conflict on the Bosphorus did not hold up their end of the agreement. Surely this is of no concern to us, but the fact that the Genoese have promised to pay Orhan Bey part of the customs duty that they owe to us is our concern. Also, the fact that the Ottomans have taken Chalcedon, where the storehouses of Venetians are, will cause problems for us. What's direr is that the clergymen of the churches on the islands have sent missions to Orhan Bey saying 'Extend your just hand to our islands and free their people from Byzantine taxes.' Your Majesty, if we cannot accommodate the wishes of the feudal lord of the islands and prevent our subjects from inventing new taxes for their own gain, we will, in a short period of

time, be unable to prevent the inclusion of the islands within the territory of the Ottomans.'

"When my Co-Emperor turned his head, like a little ball covered
with curly hair, he saw me looking beyond the Genoese quarter from
the large window. Then, as if to imply I wasn't paying attention to
the matter, he spoke his mother's words, 'I wonder what my honourable Co-Emperor thinks about all this. I see it wasn't much help that
you married your daughter Theodora to Orhan Bey, despite the fact
that you did so for the sake of friendship and peace. After everything
he has stripped from us, what more does he want? It would be fitting
if you travelled to the other side as you did in the past to serve your
own needs, but this time you should do it for our Byzantium's sake.
If not, thanks to your son-in-law Orhan Bey our empire will not last.'

"Until the moment he said this I considered him as a little child,
but when I heard his words I understood that I was face to face with
someone who had begun to mature. However, I was still slightly distracted by the similarity he bore to his mother. As it always
happened when I felt nervous, my hand went directly to my beard,
'You are my son-in-law too, John. Just so that you know, Orhan only
pays as much heed to me as you do. Your father and I discussed the
invasion of our lands by the Ottomans a great deal before he passed
away. I suggested that we destroy them before they became powerful.
Alas, instead of having faith in our own power your father put this
trust in the Catalans from the west. He called Roger de Flor and his
men, who were returning from Malta, to our aid. However, before
long we realised that it was the idea of plunder that quenched the
thirst of the Catalans and the hunger of the other Latins. Perhaps
your mother has told you about all the evil the Catalans and Latins
inflicted on Byzantium when they came to our aid. Moreover, they
didn't return home but came and hovered around most of our castles
like night terrors. As if that wasn't enough, they invaded many of our
fortresses. Pigas was one of them. If the castle commander of Hadri-

anopolis hadn't trapped Roger de Flor and his commanders, they would have entered Constantinople on their return from the Balkans. At that time the dissolution of the Seljuks tantalised us so much but we had to fight with the remaining Catalans. During the period in which we drove them out towards Thessaly and Morea the fertile lands of Anatolia gave birth to the Ottomans. Befriending them was a decision that your father made. The reason I gave Theodora's hand in marriage to the Ottomans was so we could remain friends for the peace of Byzantium because, before me, your father had married Asporsha, who was at the time very young, to Orhan. Perhaps your mother has put it in your heart to find all this peculiar but your father sent his daughter to the Ottomans long before I did. Also we must not forget that it was first Umur Bey and then the Ottomans who stopped the Serbian king from attacking us when he went out of control after the troubles with Roger de Flor. There is nothing strange to be found in all that has been done.'

"Upon hearing what I had to say, my Co-Emperor replied with the impetuosity of his lineage, 'We have to find a way to drive them from our lands. They should stay in their own and we should remain within the bounds of ours.'

"I was quite staggered by his sudden reaction but I explained it all to him, 'Your Majesty, I think that because you are still young you are unable to see that Byzantium is losing power with every passing day. The Athenians have a saying though, 'Cold things warm, warm things cool, wet things dry and parched things get wet.' Our circumstances are exactly so. It is now time for us to get wet... We can only save Byzantium if we do not rot in the intensity of the wetness.'

"As Emperor John V Palaiologos looked at me with fascination, I asked him 'Or had your teachers not taught you this? I learnt these things from you, not from my teachers. But, despite the fact that you taught me these things, you keep repeating the same lesson and don't afford me any faith.'

"Embarking on this discussion about 'having faith in him', a point
we reached at the end of every conversation we had, I felt uneasy
and saddened, 'Let's not discuss this again, let's stay loyal to our co-
ruling agreement. You must also stop acting upon your mother's
words because we have no time to lose. I don't wish to waste time on
these meagre conversations while our castles, first turned into ruins
by the Latins and then by the Catalans, wait for immediate aid.'

"Child emperor Palaiologos in turn tried to lay it all on me as he
spoke without even looking me in the face, 'You know much more
than I do. In the future I won't discuss this matter, but we should do
whatever needs to be done for the sake of Byzantium and for our
Constantinople.'

"When I retorted, 'But, Your Majesty, when I place my big hands
under this rock you also have to place your small hands under it,' a
sense of shy lament was reflected in his child eyes. He shut his eyes
tight and said, 'My dear father-in-law, then we shall do everything in
our power to provide aid for Byzantium.'"

Emperor John VI Kantakouzenos continued muttering to himself
for a while longer as he stared at the empty throne of his exiled son-
in-law and his Co-Emperor Palaiologos V, just as he did every day.
When he was about to continue further, mesazōn Demetrios Saman-
dros returned after having left with mellifluous silence in the morning after delivering his daily report. Noticing that his face was
flushed, the Emperor said, "You must tell me, even if it is bad news,
Demetrios."

The mesazōn took an ancient map drawn on parchment from under his armchair and spread it on the table. He glanced towards the
Emperor and appeared to be alarmed, "Your Majesty, as you well
know, Proceratis and Scutari were seized by the Ottomans. As you
endeavour to regain them the devils in Constantinople are keeping
themselves busy..."

As the Emperor vacantly looked at his mesazōn's face showing no sign of having understood what he was being told, he suddenly uttered, "Who are you talking about Demetrios? I don't understand."

"Your Majesty, forgive me, but I am talking about Patriarch John Kalekas, Alexius's most trusted man in Constantinople. Just as he cannot accept you as emperor he is also trying to blacken your reputation by declaring you a 'usurper' emperor..."

Pummelling his hand against his forehead Kantakouzenos VI uttered, "There is no other person on earth who uses his knowledge to serve his hatred like he does. It's best to bring him here, to the palace, and sort him out..."

With that, the head messenger hastily entered the room, "Your Majesty, forgive me for I bring dire news."

He bowed and began to deliver his message...

CHAPTER SEVEN

Tzympe Castle, a small stronghold, had for centuries kept a watchful eye over the blue waters of Hellespont as they flowed into the estuary of the Dardanelles on one side, and on the other the salty twinkling of Melas, the blue tongue of the Aegean Sea that stretched to Thrace. She awoke from her slumber and cast her gaze on Abydos Castle, erected across the water. She smiled at the lovers meeting at Temaşalık and Çardak in the early hours of the morning. She felt sad when she couldn't see the dolphins that usually played the game of 'who can jump highest' during these early hours of the morning. Seeing the guards in her bastions change shifts just as they did at the same time every day she spoke to the wind, "They presume that today will not be any different." Shifting her gaze back towards the strait in the hope that she may see the dolphins playing, she could see not the dolphins or the fish that dally in the sparkle of the sea. Her stone walls shuddered. Searching for the reason she grumbled, "I wonder if it is the anniversary of the day that Hellē fell from the flying ram with the Golden Fleece into the sea and drowned." After pondering the thought for a while she decided, "No, today is not the anniversary of that." She surmised that her large chiselled stones, cold from the strong wind blowing from her bastions, were shaking. She whispered, "Today I will either crumble or I will find myself in the arms of a new life," and fell back into silence[7].

It had not been long since the castle welcomed the morning like a human being when Suleyman Pasha's men began entering through the gates, merging themselves with the crowds of villagers one by one. Even though the guards were chaotically checking those entering the castle the *levends* dressed in local attire with baskets on their backs aroused no suspicion. Suleyman Pasha was watching from an

---

7   T.N, In this section the author is referring to the earthquakes that had devastating effects on the region of Gallipoli in the years of 1357-58.

alcove in which he had hidden himself. He hurriedly scratched his
face as if an itch had manifested itself in the roots of his straggly
beard. A smile found its way to his lips. The timidity of the *levends*
as they stood beside him dressed in their local attire... He was engrossed in the smile when the question of how he looked himself
grabbed his thoughts. Assuming he also looked like his timid men he
flapped his hand as if to say he couldn't care. He shouldered the ve-
getable basket in which his sword was hidden, fresh produce and hay
masking its presence. He seized a comparatively quiet moment on
the road and set off. As he shuffled towards the castle he looked at
the villagers passing by on the back of a horse-drawn carriage. He
mixed into a group as they briskly walked past him, making sure to
keep his distance from the *serdengeçtis*[8] at the front. A man and a
woman in front of him were talking to each other. Every now and
again the woman was handing something to the man from the
pocket of her loincloth. The man kept quickly popping whatever it
was that she gave to him in his mouth. This game was continuously
repeated. Atop her long legs the buttocks of the broad shouldered
woman jiggled as she walked—her most noticeable feature. Her long
jet-black hair flowed down to her waist under her kerchief, her hair
swaying to and fro with the movement of her hips.

Suleyman Pasha arrived at the gates of Tzympe Castle having
taken turns watching the stride of the woman and keeping an eye on
the *serdengeçtis* at the front and back. The guards, dressed in brown
uniforms, were watching the castle gates standing with their backs to
those arriving. Suleyman Pasha nevertheless recognised the men of
Akça Kocaoğlu. "This was supposed to happen once we'd all entered
the castle," he thought as he saw Akça Kocaoğlu himself, the tallest
man amongst the beys. He was leaning against the interior wall and
sleepily sitting right across from the only gate that was open. Seeing

8   T.N, *Serdengeçti* was a military term used in the Ottoman Army. It was not a
    military class but a title given to soldiers who did heroic acts in the battlefield
    like assaulting heavily fortified positions, which generally ended with the death
    of the assaulters.

his relaxed posture Suleyman Pasha realised there was no cause for concern. He passed through the exterior gates after the last couple. He had difficulty holding his laughter when Akça Kocaoğlu stood up in his long robe, the same as those usually worn by men in that region. Noticing that he was also smiling back at him he uttered, "I suppose we all look as funny as the next man."

Akça Kocaoğlu peeked out from behind the villagers with their baskets and sacks passing through the gate and approached Suleyman Pasha, "We started a bit early because the guards at the gates were suspicious of one of our *levends* and took him to the guardsmen's cellar. I was concerned that if we'd waited for them to return they would have been more watchful."

Despite the fact that Suleyman Pasha tried so hard to disguise the excitement and joy spreading across his tawny face, he couldn't. As he smiled at Akça Kocaoğlu, who infused trust in all who saw his face, he gestured that it didn't matter and asked what happened to the guards who went to the cellar. Akça Kocaoğlu whispered, "They were silenced, My Bey."

Satisfied that there was nothing more to be done at the gate Suleyman Pasha quickly walked towards the market.

The stalls were set up on the cobbled road that led to the gate across and seemed to split the castle into two sections, north and south. Inside, the castle had modestly-sized yet grand houses standing against the walls and looking over towards the strait. A narrow road connecting the east and west gates of the castle to one another intersected this road of market stalls.

Seeing a large group of guards during his meandering amongst the sellers in the market, Suleyman Pasha signalled the *serdengeçtis* at the front to walk down the narrow path towards the east gate. As they advanced towards the east gate with no aim other than to pass time, the castle commander and his guards surveyed the marketplace while occasionally talking to the vendors. The commander abruptly turned and asked his ancillary, "Are there any barges that could go and inspect the ship waiting off-shore?"

The castle commander ancillary, standing in front of the guards in his dirty blue uniform with green marks on one of his sleeves replied, "There is one, sir."

The commander in return asked, "Is the one anchored off-shore a merchant ship?"

The ancillary replied, "It is said to be."

The commander angrily asked again, "What does that mean? Is it or isn't it?"

"Forgive me, sir, for being unable to provide a definitive answer. As usual we were not able to get much information from those that fly the flag of the Genoese... When we persist they tell us that they will inform only the Emperor of their cargoes and that they are not required to account for their actions to us..."

"Is that so? Then you should send a messenger to the captain summoning him to the castle... Tell them that if he doesn't his barges loaded with stores will not leave the docks."

"If they don't leave before we get to them..."

"Aren't they still purchasing goods?"

"I heard that they'll be setting sail today, sir."

"If they are getting ready to leave there is likely no one from the ship at the market now."

"I presume that to be the case, sir."

"If so then, why is the market so busy? Are there people coming in from the opposite shore?"

"A few fishermen's boats, sir..."

"But this crowd doesn't seem to be formed of the passengers of a few boats. Find out why the market is so busy as we need to know what's going on."

The ancillary, who stood straight as a nail as if to show off the coat of arms on his chest and the symbols on the sleeve of his dirty-blue uniform, lifted his arm and self-righteously said, "I presume a few people from each family came to the market today because it is harvest time."

Unconvinced by his ancillary's explanation the castle commander looked around with suspicious eyes and walked all the way to the north gate. After responding to the respectful salutations of a few villagers entering through the gates he immediately began to climb the stone stairs leading to the top of the castle walls. Once he had climbed to the top of the wall he made his way to the highest sentry tower. He first looked down at the narrow streets within the castle and then carefully inspected the shrubby gardens extending far outside the castle. Realising that the stone buildings within the castle and the gardens outside were just as peaceful as usual he grumbled at his pointless suspicion and descended the stairs as quickly as he had climbed them.

Evrenos Bey had been quietly keeping an eye on the commander since the moment he and his guards set out to inspect the market. Seeing the commander head towards the building down the cobbled market street he presumed to be the military quarters, he signalled for his *levends* scattered amongst the vendors to follow him. Right then, he saw Suleyman Pasha return after having walked towards to the east gates. When the commander neared the stone building that housed the military quarters, Suleyman Pasha with his sword hidden beneath his robe caught up with Evrenos Bey.

Evrenos Bey slowed right down as he neared the building the commander had entered. While looking at him, Suleyman Pasha tripped on a loose cobblestone, staggered and crashed into the stall he was walking past. The female stall-owner who saw him lose his balance caught him and let out a shriek. Still in shock, Suleyman Pasha pulled himself together having avoided hitting the ground and hastily saluted the woman in the Greek words his mother had taught him as a boy. The middle-aged woman, a stallholder for many years,

gawked at the large whites of Suleyman Pasha's bright eyes. She had
never seen him before. But Suleyman Pasha continued walking
briskly in the same direction as Evrenos Bey. In the meantime, the
castle commander had come to the door of the military quarters and
heard the woman shrieking but went on his way since he considered
this to be the ruckus of the marketplace. As soon as the castle commander entered his office at the end of the long corridor inside the
military quarters, he took off his armlet, wristlet and sword and hung
them in their usual place, in the built-in closet. At the same time
both Evrenos Bey and Suleyman Pasha arrived outside the military
quarters. The *serdengeçtis* who had been watching them from near
and far were preparing one by one. Just then, Suleyman Pasha felt an
excitement he had never known before course through his body.
When he realised that he could not overcome his excitement he hastily looked at Evrenos Bey and said, "It's time."

Evrenos Bey winked at him in approval and waved the large, white
handkerchief that he had pulled from the pocket of his vest, usually
worn by Thracian villagers, in a manner that could be seen from
afar. Standing guard, Ece Bey, Fazıl Bey, Kara Hasan Bey and Akça
Kocaoğlu signalled to their *levends* positioned in the towers and al-
coves of the castle. On receiving their long awaited signal, the
levends and *serdengeçtis* quietly escorted the guards out of the
towers and took them to the secluded cellars underneath. After stripping them and tying their hands and feet, the *levends* and *serdengeçtis* changed into their uniforms and went back to their positions.

Neither the market-sellers nor the shoppers in the marketplace had
yet noticed anything. However, the middle-aged woman, who had
gazed into the large whites of Suleyman Pasha's bright eyes, was
standing straight with her neck held up high and looking at Evrenos
Bey and Suleyman Pasha out of the corner of her eye. Just as they approached the door she rambled, "It's as if a bird has flown out of his

gaze and into my eyes." She looked at the door of the military quarters. When she could no longer see them there she too walked towards the military quarters as if she had forgotten she had a stall to
mind. Just as she had taken a few steps one of the other women stallholders shouted from behind, "Where're you going?"

When she heard the loud question the middle-aged woman came
back to her senses and returned to mind her display of goods. Her
feet had returned but her heart still kept asking, "What're you waiting for?"

CHAPTER EIGHT

J ohn VI Kantakouzenos, one of the two emperors of the double-headed Byzantium in Constantinople, was grieved by the news his mesazōn had delivered. However, recalling what he had been thinking about his eldest son Matthew for a long time, slightly assuaged the worry and sorrow on his face. His thoughts raced as he scratched his bearded round face with his large, plump fingers. When he looked at the throne of his Co-Emperor and son-in-law John V Palaiologos, he thought of his daughter Helena. His eyes filled with yearning. In a sentimental tone of voice, he said, "My God, give me the power to pull through this difficult time! You know I can't spare anyone. Please do not dissuade me from the decision I made! Please do not deaden the complaisance of my heart no matter what they do."

He wanted to delve into his thoughts for a moment as if he was ashamed of himself and what he had done up to now. He couldn't bear the flames of clear truth which for so long rose from the fires within him, and he roared, "I am not a man of war. I am wholly for peace. That's why I gave my daughter to a man of your age. Oh, Orhan! Why do you always call me to war when I do my best to invite you to friendship? You should know that the patience of Byzantium has its limits. I think you will deter me from these thoughts of friendship. Know that the power of Byzantium will be sufficient to bring you down."

Emperor John VI Kantakouzenos stood up with the last word that exited his lips. As he anxiously walked his study from wall to wall he muttered, "The power of Byzantium". He bit his thick bottom lip and grasped his beard. Then he began talking to himself as if he were in a heated argument, "Oh Kantakouzenos, you must think about everything carefully and weigh the situation. Look at the shore opposite. Only a few years ago Byzantine flags were waving from the turrets of the castles over there. Now, there are none. Let alone those, we have hardly any castles left on this side of the strait. Going to war under these circumstances will bring the end of both your empire and of Byzantium!"

After letting it all out he felt a slight sense of relief, but he still wanted to pour more out. As he searched for words to express his heart's heaviness he recalled Emperor Andronicus. He saw Andronicus around him, whirling around the chair he was seated in as if he hadn't died long ago. He looked at him and said, "Oh Andronicus, if you had just listened to what I said! Couldn't you have gotten on with the Ottomans? How am I going to stop them now that their daggers are plunged in blood? If they'd stayed put on the Asian shores it could've all been all right but now they are on this side too. I haven't yet been able to verify the truth behind all the news we've received but if they are planning on staying on this side of the Hellespont, they won't stop at Thrace either."

He felt tired as he walked from one corner of the room to the other. He sat on his throne. He looked down and fell quiet for a considerable period of time. When he tilted his head up his gaze fixed on the old throne, known as the Justinian throne which had passed from Andronicus III to his son John V Palaiologos. Then he remembered how one day he saw his son-in-law pick his nose with his slender fingers. As he wet his lips with his meaty tongue he said, "He could never overcome his suspicions. He always looked at me with fear not knowing that I pitied him." He remembered a conversation they once had. Then as if his son-in-law was sitting in the throne he asked, "Son of Andronicus, have you felt something in this room?"

The voice of exiled Emperor John V Palaiologos echoed, "No, only my seething heart."

"No my dear son, it is not your heart that seethes but the anger within you. It might seem natural to someone your age but you should know that anger is the scourge of men. Anger that comes in unison with greed is the worst."

Unable to grasp what he was saying John V Palaiologos repined, "I do not understand what you are trying to tell me. If you think you are humiliating me by sarcastically referring to me as the son of Andronicus, my venerable father-in-law, you are mistaken. It would be much better if you dropped this riddle and talked to me in a language I can understand."

John VI Kantakouzenos looked at his young Co-Emperor with a bitter smile. Then before weighing the possibility of an appropriate reply he said, "If you listen well you will understand, son of Andronicus, but I think you first need to learn to listen."

Angered by Kantakouzenos's unacceptance of him and his sarcastic remarks, John V Palaiologos looked at his father-in-law and said, "The day you stop treating me as the little boy who plays with your daughters and accept me as your Co-Emperor will be the day I listen to you whole-heartedly."

In return, John VI Kantakouzenos assumed a humble attitude in order to calm his young Co-Emperor and replied, "Fine, I won't call you son of Andronicus from now on. I will call you "Your Majesty" as the mesazōn does. Your Majesty, do not for a moment forget that we are face to face with a more powerful and formidable threat than the Romans[9] because these ones do not allow anyone to bear any hate in their hearts towards them..."

After rubbing his bony hands, which looked like two large sledgehammers extending from his wrists and did not suit the grace of his tall and slender physique, against each other, Palaiologos V replied, "Do not assume that I am not aware of the threat that we face. It is

---

9   T.N, Here the author is referring to a time when the King of Pergamon bestowed his kingdom to the Romans because he didn't have an heir. Not everyone in Pergamon accepted Rome's rule. Aristonicus, who claimed to be Attalus' brother as well as the son of Eumenes II, an earlier king, led a revolt among the lower classes with the help of Blossius. The revolt was put down in 129 BC, and Pergamon was divided among Rome, Pontus, and Cappadocia. Later, these lands played a central role in the establishment of the East Roman Empire.

not as if I am not thinking of a solution for the looming threat but everything is happening so fast that before I can remedy one situation, another one has arisen in the meantime.

Sensing that Palaiologos V was far too engrossed in the rumours circulating in the city and was about to take a wrong course of action he warned him, "I haven't uttered a word to you about the Ottomans until this day but it would be good if you knew that every single one of the stones of these deaf walls is an ear that only hears what it wants to hear. Until the death of your father those stones were only ears but after his death they also became tongues. Tongues that only want to make what they say heard. That is why it would be best if you would lend an ear to every tongue that speaks."

Andronicus's son replied without looking at his face, "If only you could do things that are as beneficial as your words..."

Kantakouzenos lost his temper completely and retorted, "Son of Andronicus, I suppose I won't be able to do anything beneficial as long as you and your mother keep testing my patience. But I will repeat this—we must find a way to get on well with the Ottomans..."

Noticing the curtness in his tone of voice Andronicus's son averted his eyes and said, "How would my venerable father-in-law like us to treat the Ottomans? I think it is high time that we met with the envoys of the noble Gattilusio family, who have just arrived from Aenus. Only the mercenaries of the noble Gattilusio family can stop the Ottomans now.

Kantakouzenos thought favourably of this idea. Then Palaiologos V laughed insidiously and looked out the window with an expression on his face that seemed to say, "I have one more idea but I'll share that with you later."

CHAPTER NINE

Hearing the sounds get louder and echo as they reverberated between the long corridor's stone walls, Tzympe castle commander Teleutias Sermanosidis looked up at the door opposite his desk. He cocked his ears, trying to figure out what the raucous sounds emanating from the corridor were. The sounds gradually became louder. He looked to his belt and scabbard on the wall and as the footsteps approached the door he grasped the hilt of his sword. The corridor fell silent. As he moved to unsheathe his weapon the door flew open and the cold blade of a dagger nestled against his neck. The soft yet authoritative voice of Evrenos Bey followed, "Take your hands off the sword and put your hands in the air."

The castle commander, breathing fire, was planning on turning around when he noticed a second blade pushing against his right side. His arms in the air, eight hands of four *serdengeçtis* grabbed his limbs and forced him face down on the floor. Misled by Evrenos Bey's speaking Greek, the castle commander spoke, trilling with rage, "I hope you know of the punishment for armed rebellion!"

He fell quiet for a short moment before roaring. "If this is a rebellion you're surely aware that you'll pay for it with your lives!"

A stout *serdengeçti*, enraged by the castle commander shouting at his bey, gave in to his anger and slapped him across the face. The castle commander had crusaded in numerous wars and was wounded innumerable times but he had never thought that a slap could hurt so much. As he tried to see the *serdengeçti* who slapped him he grimaced, Evrenos Bey scolded the *serdengeçti* in Turkish, "You know better than to hit a prisoner with tied hands!" Once he was done with the *serdengeçti* he spoke in Greek, "From this moment on, you are our prisoner. This is not a rebellion. We have come to take back our castle that was promised to us long ago. If you surrender it to us without causing trouble, we will not treat you as our prisoner. You can serve under one of our beys and continue your life with your family. In fact, you could return to Tzympe Castle after some time. But if you start trouble, we will have no choice but to take you and your family as prisoners. The choice is up to you. You will either serve the Ottomans as a free commander or you will work on the land of an Ottoman bey as a prisoner!

The castle commander, who hadn't understood anything he was told, felt the inside of his cheek bleeding and was possessed by a tangled sense of fear. He trembled with a chill that shook his entire body. Experiencing shock and consequential temporary memory loss, he gawped at the long-faced, tall man who had been waiting for his reply. As he tried to move his lips with the desire of saying something he noticed his tongue was swollen. The pain spread into his tongue. "I must have bitten it," he uttered. It felt as if his tongue was getting larger and larger. His eyes filled with tears. He could not understand why he felt the need to weep. It was as if someone had removed the nerves that stretched to every cell in his body—none of his organs were under the command of his brain. For a moment, he tried to get rid of the fog in his head but both his body and mind were in pieces. When he wanted to lift his head and look around a hand pushed him back onto the floor. Realising that he could only move if they allowed him, he had only just decided to stay put when the large hand that had slapped him and the others on his neck lifted him up to a standing position. Bewildered, the castle commander looked at the people in the room. Evrenos Bey smiled and looked at Suleyman Pasha standing right beside him while Suleyman Pasha looked into the terror-filled eyes of the castle commander. Suleyman Pasha had seen many eyes that opened wide with the fear of death in battle but he had never seen a person's eyes reflect fear as much as the castle commander's did. After silently watching his bewildered and fearful eyes, Suleyman Pasha said, "His fear is so visible, Evrenos Bey."

As the smile spread from his eyes down his long, thin face towards his lips Evrenos Bey replied, "It's obvious that he wasn't expecting anything of the sort."

"What?"

"That we would come to the castle. He is transitioning from one fear to another, My Bey."

"I don't understand what you mean."

For a split second, Evrenos Bey looked around wondering how he could explain himself. He wet his thin lips and continued, "It's like the disintegration of the mind, My Bey. Just like a transition from one thought to the other—it's a transition from one fear to another."

"So you suppose he will talk when the cycle is completed."

"Yes..."

"If a new wave of fear hits him..."

"Perhaps he will revert back to the beginning and recall everything that's happened..."

As soon as he was done speaking Suleyman Pasha pulled out his snake-like dagger and plunged it into the castle commander's calf. Squirming with surprise and the pain coursing through his leg, the castle commander returned to his senses. His gaze, previously vacant, brightened up. He faintly shut his eyes and tried to make sense of what had happened. As he looked at the people around him, he ascertained that they were from the foreign shore when he heard Suleyman Pasha's voice. The moment he figured out the situation tears poured from his eyes—eyes which previously appeared to be incapable of producing tears. The *serdengeçtis* had until then never seen a castle commander cry, in awe, they let go of him. Keeping his eye on the man Evrenos Bey said, "He is hysterical now. It'll pass in a little while... He couldn't conceive anything earlier because he was shut down by fear. Now that his consciousness is refreshed he understands what is happening here. Let's keep him under open arrests—you never know what he might do when he fully returns to his senses. We should go and take a look at the others. We will talk to this one shortly once he's calmed down.

He had just finished speaking when they heard the sounds coming from the corridor. They cocked their ears. The sounds were coming from the direction of the courtyard. The corridor, overlooking the sea from its small, battlement style windows, was extremely long. They ran and were out of breath when they finally reached the courtyard. About ten castle guards and a bulky man with a tangled beard and hair had been wounded by the swords of the *levends* and were lying on the ground. Evrenos Bey anxiously looked at Suleyman Pasha, who arrived in the courtyard moments after him. In a mellow tone of voice, Suleyman Pasha said, "Evrenos Bey, talk to these men. Find out who they are."

This time in his dialect of peninsula Greek, Evrenos Bey asked, "Gentlemen, who are you and what are you doing in Tzympe?"

The man with the tangled beard and hair smiled at Evrenos Bey, who had the same accent as him but the apprehension in his eyes did not disappear. He replied in a chesty tone of voice, "My name is Alki-asides. I am the owner of the harbour."

When Evrenos Bey translated what the man had said, the man's bearded, large and round face turned pale. Seeing the change in the man's complexion Evrenos Bey asked, "Well, what about these guards?"

The man made a move to stand up but one of the *levends* standing beside him immediately pushed him down by his shoulders. Evrenos Bey said to let him stand up. The man rose to his feet. After carefully looking at the faces of the men in the courtyard he said, "The castle commander sent for me and the captains of the ships that were anchored in the harbour last night..."

As the man fell quiet Evrenos Bey insisted, "Complete your sentence. What happened to these boats?"

"We were demanding their taxes."

"Does every ship that anchors here pay taxes to you?"

"Genoese and Venetian ships pay taxes when they carry cargo from our harbour."

Suleyman Pasha, trying to ease the fear in the man's face, jokingly said, "Evrenos Bey, tell him that from now on we will cut their taxes by half on one condition."

When Evrenos Bey translated what Suleyman Pasha had said, the bulky man rejoiced but his anxiety was still clear as daylight, "Gentlemen, I don't really understand what you are trying to hint but I have been paying our emperor his taxes in full for years. However, we have not been able to pay the taxes recently since some Genoese ships have not been paying us at all."

Hearing Evrenos Bey's translation of what the man had said, Suleyman Pasha replied, "From now on he will be paying his taxes to us."

Taking care not to scare the man Evrenos Bey spoke in a reassuring tone of voice, "This castle is now in the safekeeping of Orhan Ghazi, the Ottoman Bey. You will be paying your taxes to the Ottoman Beylik from now on."

Realising who he had been talking to the harbour owner scratched his chin with his long fingers and said, "Effendi, I am a loyal vassal to my emperor. Please do not ask this of me."

Suleyman Pasha replied, "We are also friends of your emperor. He previously told us that we could leave a small contingent of men here at the castle in return for the help we gave him. However, the castle commander took the *levends* we had stationed here and sent them to the other shore. It's not our custom to return a gift such as Tzympe Castle once given and so we wish it to be returned to our command. The effendi will also pay his taxes to us. If he also wants to pay taxes to his emperor, that's his business. We will not interfere with that."

Upon hearing Evrenos Bey's translation, the man scratched his head not knowing what to say. He looked at the guards lying face down in the courtyard. As the man kept quiet, Suleyman Pasha looked at his face and spoke in Greek, "I will ask you for one more thing if you want to keep managing the harbour."

Appearing to have swallowed his tongue, the man took a while to speak, "What would the effendi ask of me?"

This time Evrenos Bey didn't have to translate what the man said as Suleyman Pasha understood, "Here is my condition! You will rent the barges in the harbour to us."

The bulky man appeared to have finally understood that this situation was one he never thought he would encounter from the way he helplessly looked at the beys. In order to save him from his helplessness, Evrenos Bey showed him the Ottoman banner hung on the bastion of the castle by Fazıl Bey and Akça Kocaoğlu's me who had detained the castle guards during their shift change. Then Evrenos Bey said, "Effendi, Tzympe is now an Ottoman castle."

Just as the bulky man's face turned ashen, the castle commander's ancillary who was lying on the ground took advantage of the *levend*'s relaxed hand on his neck. He rolled onto his back and bit the *levend*'s hand. The *levend* recoiled with pain giving the ancillary the opportunity to leap to his feet. Within seconds, both of his hands were around Suleyman Pasha's throat.

CHAPTER TEN

Neither John V Palaiologos in exile in Tenedos nor his father-in-law, John VI Kantakouzenos, who had exiled him and was now known as "usurper emperor" in Constantinople had been able to sleep for days. They were both thinking about how to get rid of each other and how they would send the Ottomans, who had invaded the peninsula of Gallipoli, back across the Hellespont. They were also both rewriting the letter they'd addressed to Francesco Gattilusio, whom they'd appointed as the Duca of Aenus, in order to give more emphasis to matters that'd be to their benefit. What was so strange was that despite the fact that they were far from each other they were dealing with the same business almost at the same time of the day.

In the evening of one of those days, usurper Emperor John Kantakouzenos VI shut himself in the study of his palace and added the last lines to the letter he wrote to the Duca of Aenus, just as exiled Emperor John Palaiologos V did. He rolled the letter and placed it in a cylindrical box. After sealing the lid tightly and attaching the marker thread with wax he walked out of his study. He passed through his living room and into his bed-chamber as he swung the hem of his night robe that was becoming looser on him with every passing day. He wasn't even aware of the fact that his round face and forehead had turned red with the joy of finishing the letter. His wife, Empress Irene, noticing the strange look on his face as soon as he entered the oil lamp-lit bedroom, quickly approached him. John took a step backwards and said, "My dear Irene now is not the time..."

As Irene smiled and looked at her husband, she anxiously asked him, "John, why is your face red?"

Noticing his wife carefully observing his face, the Emperor became puzzled and in return asked, "What redness are you talking about?"

"I am talking about the redness on your face, John. Are you worried about something? Are you running a fever?"

"How could I not be running a fever under these circumstances? I wish that Genoese ship had never arrived..."

As if she hadn't understood anything, Irene spoke softly and slowly looking at her husband's face, "John, are you well? Genoese ships arrive every week, if not every day. Which Genoese ship are you talking about? You used to be concerned when the ships didn't come here. Why is it a problem now that they do? The other day you were bothered when you saw all the ships dropping anchor, why?"

Realising that his wife hadn't a clue about anything the Emperor forced a smile which then became glued to his lips, "Oh my Irene... Orhan's son has crossed the Hellespont. A Genoese ship that arrived earlier this afternoon brought us the news that an Ottoman banner flies from atop one of our castles. I'd heard a rumour that Orhan's son entered the castle a few days ago but I didn't want to believe it. I'd promised them that they could in time have a sentry in that castle but the castle commander sent the Ottoman guards back across the strait. I thought they'd forgotten about it since I didn't hear from Orhan for such a long time, but now I know that they hadn't."

"Perhaps Orhan doesn't know what his son has done."

"I don't know whether he does or doesn't but I'm certain that they'd never do anything without each other's knowledge."

"Perhaps some good will come out of it all, John. Orhan is our son-in-law... You can talk to him."

"Oh, Irene oh...! Don't you know that power gained always creates a desire for more? Once land is captured it is difficult to hand it back. Though, as you say, we must try to see the good in everything. I have been thinking about our son Matthew for some time. As you know, Andronicus's son never wanted him to gain any power. Today I vested the rule of Didymóteicho in addition to the command of Hadrianopolis castle to our son, my future Co-Emperor. In fact, I am considering other options as well. However, the situation in Constantinople has to be dealt with first. Many dynasties have come and gone. Why shouldn't there be a dynasty of the Kantakouzenos after the Palaiologos? I know you will be against this because you think about the safety of our Helena but if her brother becomes Co-Emperor, there will be no change in her life. I also want Andronicus's son to cooperate with our son and for both of them to become more powerful but it is difficult to have them in the same room let alone establish cooperation between them. I actually want to take them both under my wing and work with them but my son blames me for being soft and my son-in-law calls me usurper as I am his Co-Emperor. It is best if our family continues to rule the empire."

Seeing that the redness on her husband's face subsided as he talked and let all his worries out, the empress found it easier to breathe. As she gazed at him with slightly pitiful eyes, she took the Emperor's large and chubby hand between her soft palms, "Your hand is not hot. You are not running a fever..."

Feeling the subtle warmth of the empress move upwards in her body and flow into his through his hand as it lay in hers, the Emperor's gaze slowly shifted towards his wife's breasts, revealed by her nightdress. Empress Irene pushed her husband's hand away upon seeing the desire in his eyes and slowly walked to her bed.

In that same hour when Emperor Kantakouzenos walked towards his wife with flaming desire, exiled Emperor John V Palaiologos was viewing the beautiful body of his wife as she lay on her side in bed. No matter how much he wanted to extend his hand and caress her he couldn't overcome the reluctance within himself. Seeing the concern in his eyes, Helena asked, "John, is something bothering you? If you are afraid of my father starting another one of his games you shouldn't be worried. You will see, sooner or later he will call us back to Constantinople."

John V Palaiologos smiled as if wanting to get rid of his worries and replied, "Helena, I was thinking that until now no empress other than you had been driven away from being an empress by her own father. Don't you think so, too?"

"I think that my father will call us back to Constantinople when it's time. That's why I don't think I am being driven away from being an empress."

"I agree that we might be called back but you can never know these things for sure. If the rumours that he has appointed your brother Matthew as Co-Emperor are true, our return to Constantinople is a mere dream."

"In my opinion, your suspicions are unfounded. If my father had his heart set on the reign of Kantakouzenos he wouldn't have wanted us to get married. I do not think that my father has his eyes on your emperorship but I do think that he is seizing the day. One day you will rule the empire."

"That was what he said when he sent us here, to Tenedos."

"I know how it pains him to have had to make that decision but if we had stayed in Constantinople either you'd have killed him or he would have killed you... My father never does anything without prior consideration. If I hadn't seen how he suffered the day he sent my older sister Theodora to Orhan, I'd believe those who say he has a heart of stone. But I saw his sorrow with my own eyes. You needn't worry. My father isn't so selfish that he would want more than he already has."

Exiled Emperor John V Palaiologos wanted to touch the snowdrop that was Helena—her body was waiting for his attention. He shuffled towards her in the bed. He wanted to embrace her tightly but couldn't bring himself to it. He moved away. As he looked at her he spoke, failing to hide his anxieties, "I remembered something when you mentioned Orhan... In my letter to Gattilusio, which I finished writing earlier this evening to give to his envoys, I wrote that I was happy to hear that Aenus and its environs had been given into his control. But just in that moment, when I wrote that, a sense of bitterness sank inside me. I tried hard to get rid of that feeling of resentment but I could not. I had this strange feeling, as strange as it is peculiar, that I seem to have given up the empire to the Duca of Aenus. You see, everything we heard turned out to be true. Orhan's son has captured Tzympe."

Helena thought she understood the source of her husband's worries and consolingly said, "John, why are you always judging the past? Look to the future! Isn't it more important what you will do tomorrow than what our fathers did yesterday? I am not asking you not to question their mistakes, do—but all that is happening should contribute something to your own truths."

As the exiled emperor cast his gaze on the small mouth and the red rosy lips of his wife he said, "Oh Helena! I want to do all those things you say but since these men are not content with remaining on the other side of the strait they must be planning other moves. I suppose that's what worries me. I am yet to become a sole emperor but when I do this, it will probably be the biggest trouble I'll have hovering over my head.

CHAPTER ELEVEN

Seeing the large ship and all the barges departing one after another, the market stallholders left their goods and ran down to the harbour. No ship had left the harbour without ceremony and this quietly since the castle was built. It didn't matter so much that the ship was leaving but they wondered why the barges were following an empty ship. It surprised them and made them sad to think that they were deprived of the pleasure of seeing the ships depart. After all, it was their only entertainment. For a while, they all watched the ship and the barges quietly cross towards the other shore. With tall Xienos in the lead, they all headed back to their stalls. Seeing the armoured guards in front of the gate of the castle that led to the harbour, Xienos' slender throat roared angrily, "Did the castle commander make a new decision again without asking our opinion? Would you tell us what's going on?"

One of the castle guards lifted his spear into the air in order to hush the crowd and said, "We don't know what's going on either. The castle commander will shortly be delivering a speech from the main gate. If you head to the square in front you can find out what's happening."

They were even more puzzled after the guard's explanation and vigorously packed up their stalls to get to the square in front of the main gate. Arriving at the square, tall Xienos looked at the new flag waving from the bastion of the castle and suddenly shouted, "Has our castle been captured?"

Since he didn't receive an answer to his question, Xienos raised his voice and repeated himself.

At that point, the guards shut all the gates and encircled the people in the square. The locals and the market-sellers who had come to the castle from nearby villages were completely surrounded by guards. They had a strange feeling within the thick stone walls of this castle where they had always felt safe. The hearts of the people, who had grown up hearing about the invasions of the Latins and the Catalans, began to beat with excitement. Before that, their castle had only been taken by the sons of emperors who weren't Co-Emperors. However, this time the banner hanging from the bastion of the castle was one they did not recognise.

By now everyone in the castle had gathered in the main square. They were all curious about the new master of the castle and they all wanted the castle commander to climb on top of the wall above the main gate to provide an explanation as soon as possible.

Xienos, who until that day considered himself happy in his castle, gazed at the way the long hair of the plump woman in front of him drifted in the evening breeze. This image made him think, "In our castle, there is always a breeze that cools our chests. I hope that the news the castle commander delivers won't set a flame to it." He thought to himself, "I wonder where that undefeatable aura the castle commander always has is today. Why are all the guards, who go about their business without armour every day, wearing it today?" Then he asked the woman with swaying hair standing in front of him and wiping the sweat from her neck with her kerchief, "Agnasi have you understood anything about all this? Who has captured the castle without any combat?"

The woman replied reluctantly, "It could only be someone in cahoots with the castle commander..."

"He only gets on well with the Palaiologos. Since their only living representative John Palaiologos is Co-Emperor, those who have taken our castle must be someone else..."

"He is the Co-Emperor but he is currently in exile. I think he is sorting out his business with the commanders from here before he leaves Tenedos for Constantinople. He will probably do away with the Kantakouzenos when he gets there."

Xienos tried to dry the sweat on his neck while also looking at the woman who answered his question in the face, "I hope they'll provide an explanation before long."

Evrenos Bey soon appeared on top of the wall above the large main gate. He stood up straight and tall looking at the people gathered in the square, the beys and archers who had also climbed the stairs within the castle walls lined up next to him from both sides. Evrenos Bey first looked at Fazıl Bey standing to his right and then at Hacı Ilbey to his left before raising his hand in the air towards the people. Everyone standing in the square fell silent. Evrenos Bey subtly smiled and looked at the people who were trying impatiently to keep silent as they themselves looked at the guards on the walls of the castle. Speaking in Greek he began, "People of Tzympe, my brothers!"

He cast his glance on the square and tried to evaluate the effect his voice had on the crowd. They, on the other hand, were looking at him with their breaths held as they now understood that this man, whom they'd never seen before and who spoke their language in such a confident tone of voice had everything under his control. Seeing the confidence he evoked in the people of the castle, Evrenos Bey continued as he repeated his initial call, "People of Tzympe, my brothers! We arrived at your castle early this morning. After talking with your castle commander at length we have come to an agreement... As of this moment, your castle is under our protection. And, as of this day, you should know that your lives and goods are in our safekeeping. If you do not want anyone's nose to bleed you should follow our orders. We will show no mercy to anyone who makes a mistake."

The people in the square couldn't really understand what this tall, long-faced man who spoke their language better than they did was trying to explain. Xienos thought to ask where the castle commander was and voiced his question, "Where is our castle commander? We cannot see him beside you. If you are in agreement, then where is he?"

Taking courage from his questions, Agnasi raised her voice, "Xienos is right, where is our castle commander? Who are you? Why
should we do what you say? We've been living in this castle since
we were born and until today no ship departed from the harbour
without a farewell ceremony. But we now see ships depart without
ceremony, and a man we don't know is talking about our security
of life as if talking in riddles..."

Instantly realising that Agnasi's escalating rant would create
anxiety amongst the people gathered in the square Evrenos Bey signalled the archers of Hacı Ilbey to attention then raised his hand
and spoke again, "Lady, you speak well but be patient. If you listen
more, you'd find your answers sooner."

Agnasi screeched at the man on the wall who had interrupted her
and accused her of being too impatient, clearly trying to put him in
his place, "Do not try to silence me. I was born in this castle and I
will grow old here. This is the first time we have seen you. So I ask
again, who are you? Why are we surrounded by these guards? You
cannot occupy our castle by force. If you do, we will defend it in the
name of our emperor."

With one voice the crowd signalled agreement.

Before beginning to talk again Evrenos Bey smiled subtly as he
did before. Just as the nerves in his cheeks started twitching he suddenly put his hand up in the air and then down. This signalled Hacı
Ilbey to prepare his archers. They drew their bowstrings and aimed
their arrows at the crowd. Startled, the people in the square squatted on the ground in fear. The strange behaviour of the unknown
man scared Agnasi and everyone else senseless. She did not utter
another word but an old man at the front leaning on his cane
spoke in a manner that defied any fear of death, "My lords, first tell
us who you are. No one in this castle wants trouble. Thank God,
our castle hasn't been invaded since the Catalans. It is our wish

that it won't be taken in future. We are loyal children of the great Byzantine Emperors—we do not want anyone else in our castle."

Evrenos Bey looked at the man who had expressed all his quandaries succinctly and said, "My brothers... We wish to be listened to when we talk. No one, until now, has disobeyed us. But as I just observed, you are all very hasty... You put words into my mouth before I could finish explaining. There was no need for that. As of this moment you are under the safekeeping of Orhan Ghazi, son of Osman."

CHAPTER TWELVE

Emperor John VI Kantakouzenos looked at the old throne that he couldn't bring himself to have removed as he drank the warm drink served by the servant. It dated back to the Roman era of the empire and resided in the executive palace where the mesazōn also lived. He decided that it was indeed time to be rid of the throne, but he knew that if he did so, emptiness would flood the room and he would be left alone in the void. Thus, he instantly reversed the decision and smiled coyly uttering, "If I get it removed, I'll be left alone." As often, he looked at the throne picturing his son-in-law and Co-Emperor John V Palaiologos sitting there. His voice emanated rebuke and angered authority as it spoke to his imagined counterpart...

"My dear partner, the husband of my dear Helena... This is perhaps our last conversation. None of the messengers I have sent one after another to you has returned. It is as if there is a bottomless well in Tenedos and you're throwing them in there. Perhaps it's not important for you to return the messengers but picture the heat that rose from the witch's cauldron in Constantinople when they didn't return! That same cauldron was boiling profusely when you were here. I thought that if I distanced you everything would settle down but Orhan's son crossing the Hellespont brought it back to the boil. My only consolation in all this hopelessness is the news that comes from Gattilusio, the Duca of Aenus."

Co-Emperor John V Palaiologos, still in exile in Tenedos, smiled with such cunning that didn't suit his young age and said, "I see that our usurper Emperor, who believes he is as powerful as the Palaiologos, is rather alarmed. I wonder what could be the reason behind this foment."

Seeing the cunning edge pour forth between the thin lips of his son-in-law, Emperor John VI Kantakouzenos felt a breeze of bitterness tangled with sorrow course through his body. He felt a chill on his skin. Goose pimples rose on his skin. Gesturing towards his son-in-law's throne he angrily said, "Affairs of the state are no joking matter, son of Andronicus. If only your father had lived, we could have taken precautions against the Ottomans to counter all that's befalling us now. Don't you see that they've gained power as ours has turned to shreds? I hope you do. That is the reason for my rash ways and turmoil..."

Freed from adolescence, Palaiologos V's voice spread from the empty throne, "You are responsible for shredding our power, my honourable father-in-law... A youth like me bears no fault in this. If Byzantium has been incapacitated in its fight against the Ottomans in recent years, aren't you, my father-in-law sitting across from me, the chief architect of it? Last night I pondered on how Byzantium might be saved. In fact, I wrote to my brother-in-law Matthew with whom I know I will never in a million years be in agreement. Yet I still fear you and have my suspicions. I think it's time that you gave me back the throne you usurped and that you left Constantinople once and for all. What have you been able to fix since you sent me here? Did you bring peace to the streets? Has the Patriarch kept silent? Did the Genoese pay their taxes on time? Have you signed new agreements with the Venetians? I think that if you were to give me back my empire before it's too late you'll have done the greatest deed for Byzantium."

Emperor John V Kantakouzenos, who hadn't seen a moment of peace since he was left alone on the throne of the Byzantine Empire, angrily dealt a blow with his large hand to the table in front of him and raised his voice to the empty throne, "Son of Andronicus, cease talking about the same issues every day! You have a place in this empire because of your lineage. But I have a right to this throne not only through my mother but also because of all my hard work for the empire. Why should I let all my efforts go when you do not let go of your right to the throne passed on to you by your father? Moreover, I love Constantinople more than you do. I have seen many cities from the Vatican to Jerusalem, Damascus to Trebizond, and Hadrianopolis to Vindobona but none of them is as beautiful as Constantinople. And now you tell me to leave this beautiful city and go before it's too late. Tell me, where should I go?"

The voice of John V Palaiologos emanating from his empty throne persisted, "Oh my dear father-in-law, I know it's not pleasing to open the same subject every morning but I am trying to explain to you how each day that I spend in Tenedos pains me and I want you to leave Constantinople for all our sakes. Go wherever you wish but just go."

Kantakouzenos VI got angry at his son-in-law's persistence on the same matters. With the rage he felt inside he thought it was time he screamed the secret he had been holding in for days to his face, "Palaiologos! You foolish man! Your mother wanted me to send you there just as much as I did. Your mother, who spewed evil at me for years, said that it would be best for Byzantium if you left and wanted you to be sent to Tenedos. If you'd stayed here either you or I would have been done away with. When your mother finally comprehended the situation, she asked this of me for your sake. You shall remain there until you are mature enough to understand that not every waft of air is a wind."

Sustaining his vexation John V Palaiologos exclaimed, "My mother was probably deceived by you!"

Emperor John VI Kantakouzenos asserted himself as he was exasperated by the subject and did not want to start a new one, "If I wanted to trick her I would have done so the day your father died. That way neither you nor anyone else would hang over my head."

Knowing that his father-in-law was far too angry to keep talking, exiled Co-Emperor John V Palaiologos began to reminisce in his mind, "It was sunset when I felt very lonely the other day. I was looking towards the Hellespont from the window—I was lost in thought. My mother entered my room as if to chase the darkness that slowly seeped in. Noticing my thoughtfulness, she asked, 'Are you thinking about the journey to Constantinople, my son?'

"Ignoring the silence I gave in return for her question, she continued, 'You'll first have to make yourself believe that you'll return there. Then, you have to feel that you are adequately knowledgeable to go. Look, I put up with everything to raise you after your father died. Thank God that you are now of age and we can share our thoughts. It is now time to do everything and anything you want.'

"When I asked her, 'What are my chances of living and doing what I want to do now, dear mother?' She replied, 'I think you have plenty of time but you'll have to create your own chances.'

"Then I asked her 'How can I create my own chances when there is not even a single rowing boat left on this island, surrounded by nothing but water, dear mother?'

"She didn't explain but simply repeated herself, 'I told you, son if you want to prolong your life you'll have to create your own chances.'

"In order for her to illuminate me, I asked, 'How will that be, dear mother? If at least you were in Constantinople I would perhaps have a chance but we are both very far from that beautiful city.'

"My mother replied patiently and tried to make me understand the innocence of our exile 'The reason why I consented to this exile was to give you time to mature and to prevent further bloodshed in Constantinople. Both Kantakouzenos and I felt that the pain the city had endured was enough. It was best if you distanced yourself from her for some time. And, that was what we did. If we hadn't, either you or your father-in-law could have been found one night with a slit throat in bed. Don't ever presume that only Kantakouzenos's men are capable of betrayal, your own men are quite capable of that evil trait.'

"With persistence powered by my youth I replied, 'I hope we are not getting closer to another danger just as we think we pulled through this one.'

"My mother elucidated me once again, 'If you mean that we are getting close to Matthew you are wrong. The Duca of Aenus, the castle commander of Gallipoli and the commanders of the sailors sailing in the Aegean Sea have always been on your side. As long as they are on your side, no castle commander can defeat or arrest you even if his name is Matthew.'

"Before she left the room she advised in a motherly tone of voice, 'Now you should continue learning the affairs of the state by day and enriching your life by doing other things with your nights.'"

Kantakouzenos was surprised that he was talking to the old emperor throne, on which his son-in-law used to sit before he was exiled as if it were a human being, situated right across from his own. When he shook off his surprise he burst into laughter. While he laughed out loud, a messenger entered his room with a tray. The inside of the silver tray was covered with red velvet, and on the red velvet, there was a letter waiting to be opened.

Emperor John VI Kantakouzenos asked, "Who is the letter from?"

His messenger replied, "From the Empress, Your Majesty."

CHAPTER THIRTEEN

Suleyman Pasha stopped referring to the castle the way locals did and started calling it "Çimpe"[10] as it was easier for him. As he walked down the cobbled streets of the castle swaying his shoulders Evrenos Bey was walking beside him, looking at him and smiling. Seeing his bright eyes, Suleyman Pasha did not ponder on the reason for them. Looking at the ships sailing towards the shore in the twilight he said, "When we were on the rowing boats, our *levends* sculled almost all night in order to cross that strait, but those ships can get to those shores and back within the space of a few hours. If we want to own the seas, we must have ships like theirs."

After swallowing as if to gulp down his smile Evrenos Bey said, "Hacı Ilbey, Fazıl Bey and Ece Bey know the seas well because they travelled the Aegean Sea. That first night, our guide deliberately led us to where the currents were fast and prolonged our journey. As the captains of those ships and barges know the seas very well and as the vessels don't get affected by the currents much, due to their weight, they are able to cross the strait much faster. At certain points they let the current do the work without having to scull much."

Suleyman Pasha looked at Fazıl Bey, who hid a smile in his face even in the most difficult of times. He smiled at this jovial expression as it was slowly overtaken by the dark of night. When Fazıl Bey, paying no attention to his half-greyed goatee dancing in the cool breeze of the evening, turned his head towards Suleyman Pasha their eyes met. With content emanating from his bright eyes, Suleyman Pasha asked Fazıl Bey the question that had been on his mind since the moment he began looking at the ships but had not had the courage to pose, "What do you say Fazıl Bey? Will we also have sailing boats, barges, galleys and galleons that shall set sail into the seas?"

Ece Bey was a few years older than Fazıl Bey and had previously

10   T.N, In Turkish, the letter "ç" is read as "ch".

crossed the Aegean Sea with a small number of rowing boats and
barges belonging to the Karasid Beylik and a galley purchased from
Phocaean pirates. Smiling, he pointed at him and said, "Ece Bey
knows that best, My Bey. In recent times the Karasid armada was
under his safekeeping."

Ece Bey laughed as he looked at the men whose faces were shadowed by the evening. When he decided he'd let all his laughter out,
he said, "The Karasid armada..."

He couldn't hold himself back and laughed again as if to show his
white teeth to the dark. He kept quiet for some time before continuing, "My Bey, the only way to defeat Byzantium is to have absolute
control over the seas. That is why we must have a superior armada,
unlike the little fleet of the Karasid. If we have a fully equipped armada, the empire known as Byzantium will cease to exist."

A sense of worry spread across all their shadowed faces and none
of them felt like talking. Anticipating the languidness coursing
through their bodies and minds, Suleyman Pasha waived the idea of
talking and asking questions. As they walked silently upon the
cobbled ground of the narrow street with all their feet making the
same noise Suleyman Pasha saw the area at the end of the street that
the doors of the church opened onto. He remembered the first time
they went to that church. He recalled how the old priest with the vir-
tuous face anxiously welcomed them and addressed them wryly before falling silent, "Gentlemen, welcome to our castle. I hope you will
not deny your tolerance to anyone living within its walls. Just like the
other castles on this side of the Hellespont this is a nook of Sestos
and has been living with the guilt of not being able to stop the light
in Hero's hand from being blown out. My only wish is that the sorrowful mourning of Leander and Hero hovering over our castle will
come to an end as of now."

Then he remembered how the worry apparent in the priest's face
subsided when he replied, "Father, it is also our wish that no one in

this castle feels discontent, that there isn't any trouble. We want the people of the castle to continue to live their lives as they always have, today and tomorrow. If you could deliver this message to those attending your services or coming to the church to pray, we would be obliged. Also inform them that now they are under the safekeeping of Orhan Ghazi, son of Osman. Until now, none other than a few villagers who have attacked our guards and men, or resisted our *levends* in the castle have been taken prisoner. We hope that no one will prove troublesome in the future."

He muttered, "Thank God that with the aid of the priest the castle attained the peace we desired in a short time," then looking at Fazıl Bey as he walked beside him he asked, "Fazıl Bey, have all your cavalry managed to cross the strait?"

Fazıl Bey replied, "The last convoy arrived a short while ago."

Suleyman Pasha then gave his orders, "In that case make your move tonight, lay siege to Sestos. The forces of Balabancıkoğlu will follow you as soon as they have arrived on this shore. When you besiege the castle his forces can take control of the surrounding villages and come to your aid. If there are any ships in the harbour you can sequester them before Balabancıkoğlu's forces arrive."

Suleyman Pasha looked towards Çimpe Harbour through the open castle gate. As he gazed at the inbound ships and barges he continued detailing his plan to Ece Bey before walking out of the castle gate and silently heading towards the harbour, "Ece Bey, after Fazıl Bey's and Balabancıkoğlu's troops, yours should also cross to this side. As soon as your troops arrive you should set forth. You will be laying siege to Maydos. When Akça Kocaoğlu and Kara Hasanoğlu arrive on this side with their cavalry they will follow you. As we wait for favourable news from you, Hacı Ilbey and I will complete our business in Çimpe. When all our forces have crossed to this side we will leave the castle under the guidance of Hacı Ilbey and set forth towards Gallipoli with Evrenos Bey.

Once he's finished setting everything up here Hacı Ilbey will also follow us."

Hacı Ilbey was responsible for keeping order in the small castle of Çimpe. He placed the most courageous soldiers in the castle, in the bastions and at the gates in such a way that even a bird couldn't fly over the castle without permission, let alone a human get in or out unacknowledged. Moreover, he was paying great attention to ensure that castles in the surrounding area did not discover the events in Çimpe until a sufficient number of soldiers had crossed the strait to join them there. He let in those who arrived at the castle in but never let anyone leave. Up until then, order in the harbour had been maintained by Akça Kocaoğlu. However, as he was going to follow Fazıl Bey on his campaign, the duty of maintaining order at the harbour was passed to Hacı Ilbey.

With the light of the first moon drenched in dirty yellow dallying with the phosphorescence of the waves, the last of the cavalry disembarked from the last galley. Before Fazıl Bey and Balabancıkoğlu set out towards their troops' encampment, in preparation for the campaign, they wanted to receive Suleyman Pasha's blessing. When they approached him to bid farewell, Suleyman Pasha said, "In the name of my father Orhan Ghazi and our Beylik I speak, My Beys, you who always give me strength with your holy wars, may you all be courageous, cheerful, fruitful, and victorious in this journey you undertake alongside your brave men."

Then he bid farewell by embracing them one after another. As with every other time this ceremony had taken place, a subtle sorrowful sense of separation coursed through Suleyman Pasha's heart. For a while he gazed at the sea from where he was standing. Neither the waves dressed in the dirty moonlight, nor sight of the ships and barges decorated with colourful oil lamps sailing towards the opposite shore resolved that subtle sorrow he felt in his chest. When he turned around and walked towards the castle, that sorrow was constant. The feeling of separation lay heavy in his gut even after walking through the narrow streets lined with stone houses to reach Hacı Ilbey's headquarters in the castle commander's office.

Suleyman Pasha posed a question to Hacı Ilbey who was yet to sit down, "Hacı, what does your experience tell you? Will we be able to stay here?"

As if to comb out the sincere worries in Suleyman Pasha's voice, he replied, "Do not harbour any worry, My Bey. The campaigns and holy wars we undertake here will be less troublesome than we may have anticipated. For those living on the other shore, land is more valuable than life. For those living on this side, on the contrary, life is more valuable. If we can make the people living here understand that their lives are also valuable to us and that we will not interfere with what is theirs, our work here will be much easier."

Hacı Ilbey was once vizier to the Karasid Beylik. He was about to continue his reply with the maturity learned through his experience as a statesman when Kara Hasanoğlu entered the room through the half-open door. He put his hand on his chest and leaned forward to salute those in the room and looked at Suleyman Pasha, "My Bey, Ece Bey is about to complete his preparations. He wants to move out as soon as his last convoy arrives. He will be taking the counterweight trebuchets we have found in the cellars of the castle with him. However, he does not have carts or draught animals to carry them. If you allow it, he would like to commandeer draught animals from the people living in the castle."

Suleyman Pasha looked at Kara Hasanoğlu for a while. Then he turned to Hacı Ilbey and before he had a chance to open his mouth to speak Hacı Ilbey said, "This is a very important opportunity. I am going to send a messenger now to call those who have draught animals here and I will explain to them that we will rent their animals from them in return for a fee. In fact, I will tell them that we will hire those who are willing to carry the counterweight trebuchets with

their own oxcarts. We must immediately summon Evrenos Bey. He
will be able to explain to them our wishes much better than we."

Then he looked at Suleyman Pasha and said, "My Bey this is the
opportunity we have been waiting for."

Suleyman Pasha, who hadn't understood much of what Hacı Ilbey
said, looked at Kara Hasanoğlu. He too was looking back at him in
a way that suggested he hadn't gleaned much either. When he turned
his back to Hacı Ilbey he saw him scratching his round, bearded face.
Hacı Ilbey spoke his train of thought, "My Bey, when we pay them
for this work they will not only believe we are not after their goods
but that they can also profit by working for us. Think about how this
word of mouth will travel to all the surrounding areas... When everyone knows who we are our work will become much easier. These
people, who have never been able to earn any payment for all their
hard work, will understand that we are different from their previous
masters once we pay them for their work.

CHAPTER FOURTEEN

The letter Emperor John VI Kantakouzenos received from Dowager Empress Anna had turned his life upside down. The last two sentences of the letter kept appearing in his mind wherever he went. As long as they kept doing so, Emperor John VI Kantakouzenos surmised that he was judging himself in a court where he was the chancellor. Even though every time the words came to mind he told himself he was not to blame, he couldn't get rid of the feeling of guilt and thought that the court would eventually find him guilty. In the ebb and flow of these thoughts, he felt so weary that he couldn't find rest, even in sleep and consequently preferred staying awake.

He knew that the only way to get out of the situation was to decide upon their return. "My first order of business tomorrow will be to send the ships," he would vow when he awoke in the middle of the night but would change his mind with the first light of day. Even though he managed to keep himself occupied until lunchtime, the feelings of regret would once again rush from his mind to his heart as soon as the afternoon arrived. The rest of the day was spent either thinking about them or dwelling in the weariness that the regret had transformed itself into.

In the night, despite decisively telling himself that he would send the ships, it was not until daybreak's first rays of sun that he hesitated. He circled the indecision until breakfast. At some points during eating he wanted to say, "Irene, I am going to send a couple of ships and bring the Palaiologos back from the island." Afterwards, once in his royal carriage, this desire would be countered with the thought that they should stay a little longer in order for "...that pig-headed Anna and her mule of a son to come to their senses and not mistake every breeze for a wind..."

Kantakouzenos VI referred to his mansion as his 'peaceful palace'.

On this day he didn't question his decision until arriving in the executive palace when upon entering his study he was enveloped by regret. For a while, he paced the room from one end to the other, not
sure what to do with himself. From the wide window, he began
watching one of his ships cruising on the blue waters heading from
the Bosphorus across towards the Hellespont. He tenuously waved
his hand and weakly, like a breath leaving his lips said, "Give my
greetings to Empress Anna, to my Helena and my Co-Emperor." As
soon as the words left his mouth he was ashamed of what he had
said. He put his hands over his large and round face to hide his
shame. After standing in front of the window for a while he briskly
walked over to his desk and sat down. Angrily slamming the desk
with his fist he grieved, "My God! What sin have I committed that
you are leaving me head-to-head with such a predica..."

The study door was opened before he could finish his sentence. A
footman entered the room. He saluted him with a bow of his head
and asked, "My lord, did you want something?"

Staring at his fist the Emperor responded, "Bring me a drink!"

As soon as the footman shut the door, the gaze of Emperor
Kantakouzenos VI quickly shifted to the throne of John V Palaiologos, the position of which he switched with his own the previous day.
This time it wasn't Palaiologos V sitting on the throne but Empress
Anna. She was giggling as she looked at him. As her giggles gradually
turned into raucous laughter, she suddenly paused. Before she left
the room, she looked at Emperor Kantakouzenos VI and said, "It
would be best if you did not prolong this situation. I wanted to go
away with my son but I never thought I'd be away from Constantinople for so long. I too have limits to my patience and wit."

When she mixed into the light flooding into the spacious room and
disappeared from sight, Emperor Kantakouzenos VI recalled the last
visit of the empress to the study he used to share with Palaiologos V.
As his gaze became hostage to a nervous twitch he recounted that

day to himself, he recalled how embarrassed the son of Andronicus was to see his mother, the Empress, walk unannounced into his study. Without looking at her he'd tried to explain that she couldn't just walk into his study whenever she pleased, "Dear mother, I do wish you'd informed me of your arrival. You see, until now we have listened to the mesazōn and other officers and we will shortly be hearing what the messengers have to say... After they are finished we will hear from two other envoys."

Knowing the thoughts coursing through Empress Anna's head and how hurt she was by her son's words I intervened to pour oil on the troubled waters, "Son of Andronicus, you should know that Empress Anna is the mainmast of our empire. Do not, for a moment, forget that she has just as much right to speak on matters of the empire as we do. She has the right to enter into our study any time she pleases. Also, remember that no news from any messenger and no gifts from any envoy is more valuable than a word or two Empress Anna may wish to say. I do not mind her presence here at all. We can listen to what the messengers have to say in her presence.

When I finished speaking my thoughts John V Palaiologos cast his gaze on the floor, surprised that his mind had been read. Without a trace of his prior anger and hard attitude he replied in a dulcet tone, "As long as my revered father-in-law doesn't mind..."

As I fumbled with my beard, which I presumed to be in a mess, before he could finish his sentence I said, "Why would I mind at all? The Empress has the right to know what's going on in the empire. We do not have any secrets to keep from her.

My child Co-Emperor, who was relieved by my words, turned towards the door and spoke loudly, "Show the messengers in."

The messengers who arrived were the first ones we had sent to Gattilusio to inform him that we had approved his request to be the Duca of Aenus. They brought a letter informing us that Gattilusio had started work at once. He had written to us both separately.

When we both opened the letters and began to read quietly Empress Anna said, "Seeing as you are not reading your letters out loud, I should go."

Upon her rebuke, we both began to read the letters out loud. That was when we realised that Gattilusio had written words of praise to us both using the exact same words. Empress Anna burst into loud laughter as she listened to our identical letters. Once she had let all her laughter out she said, "You see my son, there is nothing in there that should remain as a secret of the empire."

In order to appease her, I replied, "My empress, what would you say to a stroll in the garden after we have had our drinks? I am sure that we can find something to talk about."

As Empress Anna looked at her son, she replied to my invitation by posing a question to him, "Would my emperor son mind if I left him alone for a while?"

After wavering between joy and despair at this decision that removed him from that moment of worry, my Co-Emperor Palaiologos V had said, "If you will not rebuke me later for leaving you alone with my father-in-law, you may go for a stroll, my dear mother. If I complete my business here I might later join you as well."

Upon hearing her son's words, Empress Anna replied, "I never thought that I would get an invitation to a stroll in the garden from two emperors after the death of my husband. I thought you were keeping me to one side but now I see that despite all the hurt between us neither emperor has forgotten about me."

After her last sentence, we both walked out into the rear garden where I told her, "Andronicus's son cannot yet fully trust either of us. I sometimes find his scepticism beneficial, but at other times when I see him abuse it selfishly I find it to be vulgar."

Empress Anna walked ahead of me on the path paved with white stone and shadowed by the plane trees but waited for me to catch up to her, and when I began walking beside her she said, "The only one he trusts is Helena..."

As I looked at her face I tried to figure out whether she had any motherly feelings of jealousy but I couldn't see any signs of it.

"Helena is intelligent. I think it's a good sign that he trusts her."

Empress Anna replied, "I think so too but Helena should not be left alone. John changes his mind quickly because he has just left childhood behind. My only desire is for him to mature and become a man."

I took courage from Empress Anna's sincere words and replied, "I am hopeful of this and I do not want to lose my hope. I know that if I do both the Kantakouzenos and the Palaiologos lines will cease to exist. Every chance I get I pray for our empire to regain its old strength and for my fears that began with the Ottomans of Bursa interfering in our land to subside. I wish that God would give us a bit of time for my prayers to come true. As you know, the reason why I sent my Theodora to Orhan Ghazi was so that we could gain time."

Empress Anna, taking courage from my heartfelt words, was about to start talking when a massive horse chestnut from one of the far branches of the tree planted between the old plane trees fell onto the path. We were both startled by the full sound of it hitting the stone and looked in its direction at the same time. The spiky case split due to the high fall and as it rolled on the stone surface I forgot that the empress was about to speak. Looking at it, I said, "That's all, my empress."

Empress Anna looked at the horse chestnut with eyes that asked whether it had no choice but to fall at that moment. She overcame the woeful anguish that often mixed into her voice and instead, in a sweet and yet sour tone, she told me, "Whatever you want to say, say it straight."

In that moment I kneeled down, took the thorny shell of the horse chestnut into my hand and I replied, as I showed it to her, "My

empress, what I wanted to tell you is that when it is time all shells
crack and fresh new life appears from them. But no one can know
whether that fresh life will last longer than the life of that old shell.
That is why we have to find a way to let Andronicus's son to mature."

Empress Anna looked at my face with a more serious expression
and replied, "Oh my dear friend! Time is as fine as a grain of sand
that can go through everyone's sieve of logic. That is why it determ-
ines the outcome of everything. We should now give him some time
and wait for him to process everything through his own sieve.
Though unfortunately, they don't let him be. That's why I say he
should stay away from Constantinople for a while."

In those days when I battled with the idea as to how I could get out
of this two-headed empire business, her suggestion sounded rather
rational to me. As Emperor Kantakouzenos thought, "It was she who
wanted to go away with her son but I am not sure what she meant by
her last letter," and leaned back in his chair as the door opened.

CHAPTER FIFTEEN

Fazıl Bey got off his horse and cast his gaze at Sestos Castle, muffled by the silence of the moonlight. The walls of the little castle were not very high, in fact in some places the walls were just a notch higher than the staircase that led to its bastions. Delighted by what he saw, Fazıl Bey looked at the tall bastions of the castle and thought to himself, "I suppose that at one time its walls were also tall, they seem to have been destroyed and rebuilt much lower." Then he realised—those same walls had once been viewed by the Macedonians, whose names the Athenians pronounced in a way that sounded as if they were spitting. He thought of the Persians, known as the 'sword of little Asia' roaming this area, the Romans and the warriors of many clans whose names have been lost. "Perhaps some of those who arrived before us did as we do now and attacked after the castle watchmen fell into a deep sleep. Or perhaps, the castle watchmen saw them coming and pretended to be asleep to trap them. Maybe those at the castle realised they couldn't fight against those arriving and resigned the castle over without any fuss. Or perhaps, none of these things that I imagine ever happened, and the walls of the castle were destroyed by the wear and tear of time."

After thinking all this Fazıl Bey looked at Sarı Suleyman Bey, known better as Suleyman of Pigas, one of the men standing beside him. The stillness in the whites of Suleyman Bey's eyes sparkling in the moonlight filled him with serenity. As he took deep breaths with the sense of serenity filling him inside, he looked around. He looked at the far end of the tree casting a shadow on where he was standing. He stood on tiptoes in his Bursa-made boots and held the closest branch of the tree. As he stood there on tiptoes he looked at Suleyman of Pigas once again. The stillness he felt when he looked into his eyes this time spread through his body. He muttered, "My mind is a field, and he is scattered to all four corners of that field like a seed." Before his thoughts slipped away from his mind, he somehow remembered the day Suleyman of Pigas entered his service. Fazıl Bey thought to himself, "Kalam Bey, whom I told that I wanted to train young officers in place of the old ones worn out by the passing of the years, had sent me some youths so I could choose a few. I was trying them out to choose the most resilient and invulnerable. Suleyman walked towards me confidently with the boldness of youth. When I gave him a chance to make the first move he was very surprised to see his sword suddenly fly out of his hand. But I recall his surprise didn't last long and he immediately went for the scimitar in his scabbard, hanging from his belt and tied to his sash. Trying to defend himself against a sword with a scimitar showed his bravery. I knew then that he was courageous. Once I was sure that I could trust him after proving himself through various try-outs and drills I told him to form his own troop. It was on one of the days when I got to the end of My Beylik try-outs that I decided to test him one last time. The Karasid province had been added to the Ottoman Beylik of Orhan Ghazi. We, along with all the other Karasid beys had joined the forces of Orhan Ghazi. Our first campaign together was to the Byzantine lands to the north. When we arrived near Nicomedia, Sinus[11] spread before us like a blue bedsheet. Orhan Ghazi sent us to aid the cunning Aygut Alp. A castle defended by John II Komnenos[12] was being laid siege by Aygut Alp. Referred to as "Koyunhisar" by Akça Koca, the castle walls were so tall that both the climbers and the *serdengeçti* had lost heart. Akça Koca, who had at that moment arrived beside Aygut Alp, looked at their *serdengeçti* who were being picked off by the arrows of Komnenos' defenders and said, "This is not a job for just anyone. I am looking for people to scale the castle walls." Kara Ali Bey, Aygut Alp's son, was the first to offer his service and following him was Suleyman of Pigas. At that moment when I looked

---

11 T.N, Referred to here as *Sinus* is "Astacenus/Olbianus Sinus."
12 T.N, Referred to as "Ioannis Kolo-Yani" in Turkish, and Ioannis Kaloïōannēs in Greek (meaning "John the Good/ "John the Beautiful"), John II Komnenos was the Byzantine Emperor from 1118 to 1143.

at him, I told myself, "If he returns alive from the castle I am going to make him a bey." I thought that they wouldn't return like those who'd left before but the darkness that descended upon the castle that night protected them. The defenders didn't see them climbing up the castle walls nor reaching the top. From there they were able to open the gates of the castle at dawn for the cavalry of Aygut Alp and Akça Koca. As the sun rose, he was the one who brought the head of Komnenos. Seeing his severed head from the castle, his sister Maria Palaiologos, Lady of Lesbos and wife of Francesco I Gattilusio, ceased defending the castle. I got that deep wound on my shoulder when we went in to clean out the castle. The moment I fell from my horse it was Suleyman of Pigas who came to save me. As the physician cleaned and wrapped my wound Orhan Ghazi came to speak to me, "It had for many years been our desire to take Nicomedia. My late father always said, "Son you must take Nicomedia after Bursa. If that castle is under our command, the first light of the day will shine on our courageous men from the north for the first time." Today, that first light has shone on our brave men with your aid and that of your beys. The most beautiful girls of Nicomedia will be given to the brave men who have opened the gates of Koyunhisar Castle as wives.

Then he had turned to Suleyman Pasha standing behind him and said, "As of today I entrust the honourable cavalry of Karasid, namely the troops of Fazıl Bey, Ece Bey and Hacı Ilbey to you. That day I appointed Suleyman of Pigas as a bey and in the evening I married him to one of the most beautiful captive girls of Nicomedia. Much time has passed by since then. His men have become much better at climbing castle walls. Now, these low walls will be child's play for them."

After this long train of thought, Fazıl Bey returned under the tree that stole shadow from the moonlight. When he strayed from thinking about Suleyman of Pigas and looked at the low walls of the

castle again he felt inclined to make a move. However, he changed
his mind and decided to wait for those still walking to reach the
castle. When he couldn't see a single light or a watchman in the
guard posts situated on the bastions of the castle the excitement in
his heart covered the thoughts on his mind. As he looked at the
castle he muttered, "Those in the castle must have gone to sleep
thinking tonight will be like any other night."

When his blood, pricking the excitement in his heart, really boiled
he turned to the beys beside him and said, "There is neither a light
nor a watchman within sight. I think they are fast asleep. If we wait
for those who are still walking we will miss this opportunity. It would
be good if we make a foray while they are fast asleep.

When he didn't get any reaction from his beys he asked them their
opinions one by one. When he comprehended that most of them believed making a foray would be the wise thing to do he decided it
was best to make a move as soon as possible. He began to delegate
tasks to his beys, "Suleyman of Pigas, you will be the first to make a
move with your climbers and men in charge of the scaling ladders.
Once the scaling ladders are set up and the *serdengeçtis* climb on top
of the walls your brave men will secure the gates and walls. The *serdengeçtis* at the front will force open the gates and you will clear any
opposition approaching from the gates and take hold of the streets.
Konduk Alp, you will stand by with your cavalry in front of the north
gate. Mihaloğlu, your archers will sneak up to the castle. Pasha Yiğit
Bey, you will approach the gate on the west with your cavalry. I will
be deployed in front of the main gate to the south. For now, we will
leave a small troop at the east gate. When Balabancıkoğlu arrives,
he can hold that gate. Our cue is the hoot of an owl. No one but the
climbers and *serdengeçtis* of Suleyman of Pigas should make a move
before they hear the owl sound—they should move towards the
castle walls slowly and quietly. Everyone will stay put and be ready
to move once I've reconnoitred all around the castle."

The castle sat between two gulfs and had truly been buried in the moonlit night. Fazıl Bey, riding his horse, genuinely thought that there was no one at the castle when he looked at it—though, the well-worn path on which he rode his horse instantly made him change his mind. His lightly trotting horse circled on the path that surrounded the castle and approached the point where they started. Then he prayed, "My God, please do not let me down in this endeavour." As soon as he arrived where his beys were waiting for him, he got off his horse and embraced them one by one. Then looking at them all he said, "May your holy war be blessed!"

Just then, the messengers informed him that Balabancıkoğlu and his cavalry were also approaching. Seeing that the castle was so quiet the forces he had with him seemed sufficient to take the castle but he decided to wait for Balabancıkoğlu's arrival. However, what he was really waiting for wasn't the arrival of Balabancıkoğlu but the dawn when even the moon fell silent. For in that moment, scared of the sun, the moon speedily advanced towards the horizon and the stars forgot about the earth while the earth itself became embarrassed of the birth pains of the dawn and hid in utter darkness. It was then that the unseen climbers hauled their bodies up the walls and the men in charge of the scaling ladders could easily prop their ladders against the walls. The courageous men reached the top of the walls of the castle bastions whilst keeping out of the sight of any sentries. In any case, the most difficult part of the job was to climb to the top of the walls.

Fazıl Bey waited silently for a while and when Balabancıkoğlu arrived he said, "Welcome" and told him his siege plans. Then looking at him and the others he gave strict orders, "No one other than those who fight you shall be killed. The castle commander and the watchmen will be taken captive, led outside the castle and entrusted to the cavalry of Balabancıkoğlu. Priests will not be harmed. May your holy war be blessed!"

He had just begun walking towards his horse when all the horses became restless and snorted. Then, a skylark took flight from the bushes near them and as it ascended into the sky it sang. Fazıl Bey took the restlessness of the horses and the skylark singing loudly and hovering over their heads as bad omens. He fell silent for a while but didn't change his mind about the attack. Seeing his decisiveness, the skylark sang for a while longer and suddenly glided towards the castle that looked like a tortoise drawn into its shell and disappeared from sight. As if the horses were also waiting for the skylark to fly away they relaxed their erect ears and abandoned their restlessness.

Wanting to make use of the brief silence that was created Balabancıkoğlu was just about to suggest, "My Bey, why don't we wait for the morning and ask the people of the castle to surrender then?" when one of the messengers of Kuloğlu Hasan Bey approached him and whispered in his ear. Kuloğlu Hasan Bey subtly bowed his large head shadowed by a tree and requested to speak, "My Bey, the artillerymen sent by Evrenos Bey will also be arriving shortly with their counterweight trebuchets and scaling ladders which will be of great use."

Once Kuloğlu Hasan Bey was done talking, Suleyman of Pigas, looking at his men, said, "My Bey, we should wait for their arrival. We can move ahead once we have shared the scaling ladders amongst the climbers and positioned the trebuchets amongst the men in charge of them.

Fazıl Bey, trying to see the faces of his men shadowed by the tree, thought to himself, "If we delay we will be just in time for the moment I've been waiting for and our attack can start" and then looked at Kuloğlu Hasan Bey and smiled. As he turned and gazed at the castle he thought, "He too was inexperienced and naïve when he first came under my service. But it was clear that he was using his sword with his mind. Despite all the years that have passed by his child-like face still remains. Always that same fair and smiling face decorated with black and bright eyes within the childish seriousness. It is time that I housed them in these castles. I will ask Suleyman Pasha to appoint one of them as *subaşı*[13] to Sestos. Somehow his mind that strayed away from thinking about his beys for a moment and travelled across the Dardanelles to visit the memory of the feminine beauty of Alaca Nergis Hatun whom he left in Bursa... He became startled when Kuloğlu addressed him as "My Bey" to inform him of the arrival of a messenger who got there after the horses became restless once again.

The image of the castle waiting for them became vivid in front of his eyes again. Yet it was strange that the castle seemed to have stripped its nightclothes off. As he shook his head he said, "How strange, I am seeing the castle as if she has taken her nightdress off." Then looking at Kuloğlu he loudly said, "My brave men! Until now you have made all the castles you approached in Anatolia kneel before you. Do you have any doubts that you cannot make this small castle do the same? Now share the equipment that has arrived amongst yourselves and take your positions in front of your troops. Our cue is the hoot of an owl. No one should leave their positions before hearing that hoot. The attack will begin with the hoot. Until then keep as quiet as possible. My brave men! May your holy war be blessed!"

---

13   T.N, *Subaşı* (Albanian, Subash, Bosnian, Subaša) was an Ottoman gubernatorial title used to describe different positions within Ottoman hierarchy, depending on the context. This title was given to sanjak-beys of Ottoman sanjaks that generated more than 15,000 aspers per annum or to the assistants of the sanjabey. The term was also used for commander of the town or castle in Ottoman Empire, an ancient version of the chief of police.

CHAPTER SIXTEEN

The only thing that entertained Emperor Kantakouzenos VI in those indecisive and sleepless days was the reception ceremonies for envoys. He occasionally included Empress Irene in these entertaining ceremonies and really enjoyed her presence. That day, when he completed his morning work and was sipping his wine with the empress to relieve their tiredness together an auxiliary came into the room and informed him that the envoys of Aenus were ready to present the gifts of the Duca. He got up and moved to his throne. After seating Empress Irene on the low chair beside him he ordered, "Tell the envoys of noble Gattilusio to enter."

The envoys of Gattilusio, Duca of Aenus, were walking slowly and swaying their double-stitched Thracian robes that were embroidered with Cretan motifs from side to side. As they walked they made sure to show off their golden crosses inlaid with black amber and hanging from wide silver chains on their chests. They took such measured steps that neither one of them walked even an inch ahead of the other. On their feet they wore handmade flat leather shoes unique to the Black Sea region with curved toes that resembled colourful Genoese rowing boats. On their heads they wore black Thracian kalpaks that looked as if they were cut in half. They'd tucked their green velvet narrow-legged, wide crotched salwars[14], visible from under their dark red robes, into their colourful embroidered socks. The men seemed to take their duties so seriously that anyone who looked at them would have thought that there possibly couldn't be a more serious task than theirs. Despite their endeavours to look so serious when Empress Kantakouzenos VI looked at them, he couldn't stop himself from thinking about the pandemonium house jesters who came to his mansion during his years in Didymóteicho.

---

14 T.N, These narrow-legged, wide crotched salwar are called *zıǧva* or *ziǧva* in Turkey.

Empress Irene, who joined her husband just before the envoys' arrival, was keenly observing four men carrying little single-shaded
walnut chests with lids decorated with gold bands all round that
were behind the envoys rather than the elaborate costumes that the
envoys wore. Now and then she caressed the cross hanging from the
gold necklace on top of her beige blouse that covered her fair chest.
Emperor Kantakouzenos VI gazed at his wife and whispered to himself between his smile that sat on his thick lips that looked like they
might have been cut out of paper, "It's good that I asked her to attend this reception ceremony." Then the imperial bellman spoke in
his high-pitched tone of voice to initiate the ceremony,

"Envoys of our noble Duca Gattilusio, appointed as the ruler of the
lands between Aenus and Tenedos by our Emperor, are delighted to
present the gifts they have brought with them to our Almighty Emperor."

Once he finished speaking, the Emperor's letter carrier presented
the letter to the Emperor brought by the envoys in a leather case and
written on silk paper to the Emperor placed on a silver tray. The
Emperor took the letter from the tray slowly and waited a while to
prolong the moment. Before he read the letter he looked at the envoys. As he looked at them, the head envoy said, "The same letter
has been sent to Co-Emperor Palaiologos V in Tenedos along with
gifts from Duca Gattilusio following Your Majesty's wishes."

Emperor John VI Kantakouzenos once again thought how both letters were written in exactly the same words. He began to read his letter but skipped the words of pompous compliments at the start, "I
am truly glad to accept the honourable duties you have bestowed
upon me with great kindness and inform you that I will protect the
peace in the environs of Aenus and Tenedos, Duca of Aenus and
Tenedos, Gattilusio..." An embossed seal decorated the space below
the name.

Once the letter was read it was time for the gift chests to be opened and their contents to be presented. Empress Irene, who didn't enjoy taking part in these ceremonies also didn't like to disappoint her husband. So, when she saw the subtle irony in her husband's eyes gazing at her she blushed. The Emperor, who saw how shy she was, said, "My Irene, empresses are considered to be half emperors", to ease her out of the difficult situation. Though Empress Irene felt she was even more crushed under the hidden weight of the words. As she directed her penetrating gaze at her husband she said, "I should have left earlier, I can't leave now" and decided to wait until the end of the ceremony.

Genoese nobleman Francesco Gattilusio, who understood commerce and had been a great trader with the empire for years had transported goods from the Aegean to the Balkans and from the Balkans to four corners of the world by way of the Aegean, had sent the Emperor incredible gifts in return for the title he had been bestowed with. In addition to those incredible gifts, he hadn't neglected to remember Empress Irene. He had sent her *kutni*[15] fabric, which she loved very much, and necklaces inlaid with precious stones. While Emperor Kantakouzenos VI thought about how much wealthier his treasury had become with the precious stones and metals, he had completely forgotten about the presence of the envoys. The envoys laughed up their sleeves seeing as how astonished the imperial couple were in the face of such dazzling gifts. Their gazes directed at the Emperor and the empress seemed to say, "Our Duca has many such trinkets... He can give you some of them every year and while you play with these toys, he can add the wealth from the Balkans on top of the greater wealth he acquires from the Aegean".

The Emperor didn't care much about who went to Aenus or what the envoys thought. He took pleasure in looking at his gifts and muttered to himself, "I wish these envoys would say what they have to say and leave as soon as possible." Now and then he looked at

---

15 T.N, *Kutni* fabric is a handmade fabric of patterned silk. It is currently mass produced mostly in India and Pakistan.

Empress Irene and wanted her to be as excited as he was. However, upon recalling that she never cared about such things he thought to himself, "If it was Empress Anna she would have screamed with joy at the sight of all this. I remember how happy she was when I gave her the Fergana turquoise necklace, given to me by that merchant who arrived from Persia and was heading towards Morea—I kept it aside in Didymóteicho for years thinking, "This will suit Empress Anna beautifully." He looked at Empress Irene once again. Seeing how unexcited she was he sighed briefly. When he turned his gaze at the gifts and the envoys once again, Empress Irene spoke, "Your Majesty, without wishing to lay down the law, I'd like to say that the envoys that travelled from such far lands should need time to rest."

As Emperor Kantakouzenos VI looked at Empress Irene with a cold expression on his face, he impatiently said, "You are right, my empress. We would like to thank noble Francesco Gattilusio, whom we have entrusted with the administrative duties of one of the most valuable areas of our empire, for the kindness he has shown. From now on, both the Castle of Aenus and the harbour of Tenedos will attain a level of peace previously unknown thanks to the reverend Duca. A letter to be addressed to the Duca in the name of the empire will be ready tomorrow. The respectable envoys can now rest in the guest house.

As he uttered that last sentence he looked at the mesazōn stand-ing by the door as if to tell him to escort the envoys to the guest house. When the envoys held their robes up and walked backwards to the door and left the room without turning their backs to the Emperor, the Emperor and the empress looked at one another. Em-peror Kantakouzenos VI assigned all the officers in the room, ex-cept the treasury officer with tasks so they would leave. This way the empress could examine the gifts they received in further detail. Then he looked at Empress Irene and seeing that his wife wasn't really looking forward to seeing the gifts he asked, "Does our Empress wish to retire to her chambers?"

"John, I hope that you didn't think I would grow impatient when I saw the gifts."

Emperor Kantakouzenos VI loved his wife's candour, he smiled and replied, "I would have liked the gifts to have excited you like they would anyone else. I thought that you were bothered about something when I couldn't see any trace of excitement in your eyes."

"You know that what I want is not gifts, but my children. I know that I can see my Theodora any time I wish but I cannot find a justifiable reason as to why I should be so far from my Helena..."

Noticing that Empress Irene had changed the subject to that unsavoury matter Emperor Kantakouzenos VI clapped his hands and called the servants who always waited outside the door into the room. He ordered the servants to carry the gift chests to the treasury room. As the chests were carried to the treasury he stamped the imperial crest under a few scripts that were placed in front of him. In the meantime, Empress Irene looked at a Genoese sailing boat dropping anchor in the harbour, visible from the window, across from the Golden Horn. As she watched the rough seas of the Bosphorus, her gaze stretching across the waters, she thought to herself, "Perhaps the waters carried by these waves will reach the coasts of Tenedos. If my Helena is taking a stroll by the shore perhaps these waters will slowly brush against her feet. She too will look at them as I do but she won't notice that I have sent her my gaze..." She smiled at the thought of this image. When she recalled her daughter Theodora she ended her train of thought with, "I shall send my loving gaze to my Theodora with the winds," without realising she had spoken out loud.

The Emperor turned to her and looking at her face said, "My Irene, I too miss my daughters very much."

"If that's so lift these thick walls you have erected between us! We have no chance of seeing one of them, so why keep the other so far from us?"

As Emperor Kantakouzenos VI turned his gaze towards the blue waters of the Bosphorus he replied, "Don't speak to me like I wanted all this... Empress Anna's greed, Andronicus's son's stubbornness, and the desires of Byzantine nobility, captives to their greed, have brought us to this point. But do not worry yourself, I will solve this problem in the best way possible."

"You always said that saying and doing are two different things. But I now see that you do not truly want to solve the problem that keeps you awake at night. I want this motherly yearning within me to come to an end. I cannot wait any longer."

Emperor Kantakouzenos VI made a wry face as he listened to his wife. He heaved a sigh as if to blow the stress within him out. Then he spoke loudly, "I hope that their men will not make a move before us and take her to the other shore as it has been rumoured. If they do, everything will become much more complicated."

After a brief silence he softly said, "Come, Irene, let's take a stroll in the garden."

CHAPTER SEVENTEEN

When Fazıl Bey and his *levends* entered Sestos Castle, Ece Bey set out toward Maydos with his cavalry. When the castle finally drew in sight in the early hours of the morning, he decided to wait for Akça Kocaoğlu who was bringing ancillary forces. He ordered the mobile headquarters to be erected and told his cavalrymen to rest out of sight of those in the castle. When Akça Kocaoğlu arrived at the headquarters with his advance cavalry Ece Bey told him, "I received news that Fazıl Bey entered Sestos Castle this morning. We have heard nothing since then. Now it is our turn. Sestos is a tiny little castle, Maydos isn't. It's best if we wait for the arrival of the large trebuchets. We can begin the siege once they arrive. How long will it be before the carriages arrive?"

"The artillerymen will be here in the afternoon but the oxcarts pulling the large trebuchets will only be able to get here by the evening."

"In that the case we should slowly surround the castle depending on the news from the advance cavalry and wait for the evening. While we wait we can determine where the trebuchets should be positioned. In the meantime, the cavalry can find out whether there are any ships in the harbour. If there are, you and your beys can raid the harbour as soon as evening falls. If there are none, the advance cavalry should keep the harbour under watch. And I will prepare laying siege to the castle."

Hanging on every word that Ece Bey uttered, Akça Kocaoğlu spoke his request, "My cavalry hasn't slept all night. It would be beneficial if they rested until the *yaya*[16] and the carts arrive."

Ece Bey authorised this request with a nod. Having quickly deleg-

---

16 T.N, The *yaya* (literally translated from Turkish as "pedestrian") were infantry military units of the Ottoman Empire and some other medieval Anatolian emirates.

ated tasks between themselves Ece Bey and Akça Kocaoğlu evalu-
ated the situation with their beys and in suitable ambush positions
began to wait for the evening.

As the evening neared, the horse carts, the *yayas*, and later the ox
and cow carts pulling the large counterweight trebuchets arrived. As
they slowly approached the castle, Ece Bey's cavalry units took control of all the roads leading to the castle. The units completed all the
preparations before it was evening, rested a short while and then
began to approach the castle step by step. The climbers and *serdengeçtis* were at the very front. The *yayas* advanced towards the
gates behind them while the cavalry was waiting ready near the
castle gate closest to them.

Ece Bey, waiting on his horse near the north gate of the castle,
looked at the sky and at the moon as it was seconds away from disappearing behind a black cloud and the castle. After dinner, which
he referred to as "the moment of drowse", he sent his messengers to
relay the order to attack to his beys who were surrounding all four
sides of the castle. As soon as he received the message, Akça Kocaoğlu commanded his very alert climbers and *serdengeçti* sergeants,
"May your holy war be blessed!"

Upon hearing his command, the sergeants immediately got to work.
The message was conveyed to all the climbers and *serdengeçtis*
around the castle as it was whispered from mouth to ear. First the
climbers reached the top of the wall with their ladders, and then they
hooked in ropes for the *serdengeçtis* and the *akıncı deliler*[17] who
climbed to the top of the walls after them. Akça Kocaoğlu had immense faith in his climbers and *serdengeçtis*, who joined his service
after his father Akça Koca died. He thought that they would very
quickly take out the watchmen on top of the walls and open the

---

17 T.N, *Akıncı* (literally translated from Turkish as "raider") were irregular light
cavalry, scout divisions (deli) and advance troops. Here, the author is referring
to a group of them known as *akıncı deliler* (literally meaning crazy raiders), who
were a special advance unit within the Ottoman army known for their cour-
ageousness and fearlessness.

gates, so he was waiting on his horse on the road between the castle and the harbour thinking how easy was going to be. However, what he thought somehow wasn't turning out to be true. The combat atop the walls continued and the castle gates were still shut tight. Completely out of humour, as he turned back and watched Ece Bey and his men approach the ships docked in the harbour, he heard a scream that suppressed all the shouts and cries on top of the castle walls. Startled, for a moment he didn't know what to do. When he came back to his senses he looked sceptically at Ese Bey's men approaching the shadow-like ship. Hearing the cries and screams of those atop the castle walls, the sailors ran to the deck lit by colourful oil lamps. Seeing this Ese Bey commanded his archers, "Release, now!" Once the taut strings of the archers' bows were released the screams from the decks of the ships mixed with the cries from walls. Just in that moment, the sea was set aflame just a little further from the ships on the harbour with Roman Fire[18], thrown from one of the bastions of the castle. The horses were scared of the noise and flames and began to neigh and rear up. As the cavalrymen tried to keep balance Akça Kocaoğlu got furious and shouted at the men in charge of the battering ram positioned in front of the *yayas,* "Break that gate down!"

While this was happening at the south gate that led to the harbour, Ece Bey was growing impatient at the north gate and so had ridden his horse all the way to the gate itself. He too had just commanded the men in charge of the battering ram to break down the gate when the *serdengeçti* sergeant Altunoğlu Süleyman and his men opened the gates. Mad with anger, Ece Bey rode his horse towards Altunoğlu who was holding a huge torch. Comprehending that his bey was enraged, Altunoğlu Suleyman quickly said, "My Bey, the castle only appears quiet from the outside. Inside it's boiling like a kettle. The nar-

---

18 T.N, *Roman Fire,* also known as Greek Fire, was an incendiary weapon used by the Byzantine Empire. The Byzantines typically used it in naval battles to great effect as it could continue burning while floating on water.

row streets are filled with traps. It is impossible for the cavalry to
enter into these. No one but the *yayas* is of any use. Koçan Agha is
trying to secure the headquarters..."

Ece Bey, who had shortly before sacrificed the *serdengeçti* sergeant
in order to quench his rage, calmed down when he heard what Altunoğlu Suleyman said. He quickly decided on a course of action and
commanded, "The *yayas* should go in first. The cavalrymen should
leave their horses outside and follow them in on foot."

He got off his horse and rushed into a dark and narrow street after
his *serdengeçtis* and *yayas*. Altunoğlu did not think that Ece Bey
would act so quickly. In an overwhelmed tone of voice, he said, "My
Bey, be careful."

Just then the doors of the buildings within the castle walls were
opened and boiling water was poured onto the *serdengeçtis* and
yayas. As they were scalded with the immense heat they screamed
and threw themselves on the ground. Ece Bey commanded,
"Retreat!"

As soon as he commanded the retreat, he also retreated together
with his unharmed *serdengeçtis*. As soon as they reached the square
in front of the north gate he ordered the *yayas*, "Get into the houses
by way of the bastions. Ensure that there isn't a single living being
left in them."

In the meantime, as Akça Kocaoğlu tried to get his *serdengeçtis* to
break down the south gate of the castle Ese Bey boarded the ships in
the harbour and told the captains that they were seized in the name
of Orhan Ghazi, the Ottoman Bey, and if they attempted to do anything their deckhands would be killed one by one. Akça Kocaoğlu
wanted to quickly finish with the ships and run to Ece Bey's aid.
However, as he could only communicate with the ship captains
through two interpreters his task was strung out. Impatient with this
finicky business, Akça Kocaoğlu was about to explode with rage. Ese
Bey, who brought the captain of the second ship with him, noticed

this in his face, tipped his head down and said, "My Bey, if you allow me I would like to speak to them."

Once Akça Kocaoğlu gave permission, he calmly said, "Your ships have been seized in the name of Orhan Ghazi, son of Osman."

Both captains calmed down and smiled once what he said was translated to them. Unable to make sense of the change in the captains' demeanour, Ese Bey put his anger aside and smiled. The captain of the first ship saw him smile meaningfully and said, "Our ships only carry the empire's orders when they enter Byzantine waters but our ships are Venetian. We are seafarers who work on this ship. We are people of commerce and we follow the orders given to us by the owners of the ships."

Hearing the translation of what the captain had said, Ese Bey replied, "Since you are not Byzantines and solely people of commerce you can certainly do business with us. If you transport our units from the opposite shore across to this side our bey will pay you for your services."

Upon hearing the interpreter's translation of Ese Bey's words, the captain said, "The only harbour that our ships can dock into on the other side is Pigas."

Ese Bey, speaking on behalf of Ece Bey and Akça Kocaoğlu, thought that the captain was swinging the lead and replied in a harsh tone of voice, "You, as the captains, have only two options. The first is, if they don't accept my offer their ships will be seized regardless of who owns them and the deckhands will become our captives. And the second, if they help us to transport our forces, they will be paid and can continue on their voyage."

Listening to the interpreter's translation, the captain's eyes, previously shining in the light of the oil lamps, became dim. They turned around with that tarnished look in their eyes and looked at their half-dressed men with their hands tied. After stroking his long moustache and beard, the first captain spoke in a trilling voice before looking at the second captain, "I side with their second offer."

The second captain was a twig-like man. His plain face was shaven and he seemed self-confident. As his lips caught on a strange smile he adamantly said, "Most of my men are from the villages that surround Maydos. They are currently off-duty. I cannot move my ship a single inch before they arrive."

Noticing the cunning smile on the captain's lips, Ese Bey replied, "We are not sailors... I am not certain what you mean. But what do you do when your men get sick at sea? How do you sail this massive ship then?"

Not expecting such a question, the captain of the second ship replied as if he knew that the rage in Ese Bey's voice was gradually increasing, "We have reserves over there—we usually continue the voyage with them."

Ese Bey moved one of his hands towards the dagger in his sash. The captain of the second ship was following the movement of his hand out of the corner of his eye, so he told the interpreter, "Please tell him that our deckhands will aid them with our barges."

Akça Kocaoğlu, who arrived on the deck at that moment, tried to withhold his anger and told Ese Bey, "Something must be going awry in the castle. I am going to the aid of Ece Bey with my cavalry. Both the ships and the men are under your control. If anyone disobeys you take them captive."

When Akça Kocaoğlu left with his *serdengeçtis* Ese Bey first distributed tasks amongst his men and then turned to the captains and said, "Since your oarsmen are off-duty, we will provide the sufficient number of oarsmen. There are small piers on the shores across where the barges can pull up to. You will, no matter what the cost, transport our cavalry and *yayas* to this side. Begin the preparations immediately."

As the captains looked at Ese Bey in desperation, Ese Bey addressed Yuvruca Hasan Bey who was standing beside him, "Hasan

Bey, I assign this task to you and the men under your command. You and your men are responsible for the voyage of the ships and for maintaining order at the piers. Get on with it."

Then he got off the ship with his *serdengeçti* and a few deckhands they took captive.

Quickly completing all preparations, the captains set sail with their ships and barges. Then a very loud noise erupted from the castle that swallowed all the noises of conflict and screams. When they heard that deafening noise, Ece Bey and Akça Kocaoğlu were looking at the half-burned *levends*, whose bodies were being carried to the square by the north gate of the castle. What the beys, whose sorrow was reflected on their faces, couldn't make sense of was how this attack had been achieved so quickly and how they hadn't even managed to catch one of the attackers. As they put forward ideas on the issue at hand, one of Akça Kocaoğlu's head sergeants approached them. After he bowed his head and saluted by placing his hand over his chest he reported, "My Bey, there are inner doors rising like the steps of a staircase, that connect the houses, to one another. Some of the doors are hidden in the walls of the houses and open to the tunnels under the castle. The tunnels lead to the guard's headquarters under the castle. The headquarters have just been cleared out. Our *levends* have killed everyone all the way to the cesspits under the castle walls. But we think that the heathens who poured boiling water on our *levends* in the streets made use of the dusk and escaped to the fields through the tunnels."

Hearing what the head sergeant said Ece Bey was defeated by his rage in a trice. No one expected him to roar, "We said we did not want anyone's nose to bleed. But they drowned our courageous men in pain. They have to account for this! Get all the captured guards to the square by the piers. Capture all suspicious-looking people in the castle and send them as captives back across to the shore opposite on the second voyage of the ships..."

Listening to him in awe Akça Kocaoğlu spoke as if to ask him for a favour, "My Bey, if you wish the houses can be searched. Any suspected men can be captured by our *yayas* without harming any of the women or children."

Ece Bey, knowing that Akça Kocaoğlu is a soft-hearted man despite his size, tough looks, and plain face, replied, "Fine, let it be so. Those who do obey should not be taken as captive. You should take a look at the ones already taken captive as well. Disregarding rank, send those who disobey you to Bursa."

As Akça Kocaoğlu bowed his head gratefully he said, "My Bey, I suppose it is time we informed Suleyman Pasha that the castle has fallen..."

Looking across to the injured Ece Bey replied, "You are right Akça Kocaoğlu. I forgot about that completely as I tried to control my fury. Send messengers this instant.

Gazing at Ece Bey's soft face decorated by his greyed beard, Akça Kocaoğlu recalled the walls of Nicomedia where he had encountered him for the first time, "Orhan Ghazi had told us to fulfil the wishes of his father and my father's will. We'd promised him so. Yet we somehow were unable to keep our promise, we could not seize Maria Palaiologos's castle. The more impatient I became, the more I wanted to attack, and the more I attacked, the harder I lost. I'd come to the end of my power and wits when he arrived in front of the castle with his forces. Seeing my cavalrymen's crestfallen faces, he walked me all the way to the headquarters and told me, 'Akça Kocaoğlu, you are only still outside that castle because your rage is getting the better of you. If you had defeated your rage, you'd long have entered.' Then he had helped us lay siege to the castle with great composure. We were able to keep fighting for a long time due to his calmness. Then Aygut Alp had come to our aid."

For a split second he turned his gaze towards the castle gate. As he looked at the thick, sturdy wooden gate he muttered, "But now he is about to be defeated by his rage." When he looked at Ece Bey again, he saw that he had arrived at the far end of the street. He'd just begun running after him, wondering how he'd run all the way there so quickly, when he heard the sound of brisk footsteps approaching him.

CHAPTER EIGHTEEN

Exiled Emperor John V Palaiologos in Tenedos, and usurper Emperor John VI Kantakouzenos in Constantinople had both finished writing their letters of thanks for the gifts he sent them to the Genoese nobleman Francesco Gattilusio whom they appointed as the Duca of Aenus. Soon afterwards they were both overcome by similar feelings and had, enveloped in deep thought, withdrawn to their studies. At the same time, messengers from the Gallipoli peninsula began arriving one after another. Regardless of which castle they were sent from they spoke using almost the exact same words. Somehow all that they had told the lone emperors behind the walls of their castles, was also heard immediately in the houses, monasteries, and palaces in all neighbourhoods of Constantinople. Though this situation did not affect exiled Emperor Palaiologos V much, it left Emperor Kantakouzenos VI residing in Constantinople in a dire situation. As if that wasn't enough, supporters of Palaiologos in Constantinople were holding meeting after meeting and spreading the rumours that Emperor Kantakouzenos VI had given the Gallipoli peninsula and some castles in Thrace to Orhan Ghazi as dowry for his daughter, Theodora. Moreover, Patriarch John XIV of Constantinople was visiting church after church delivering sermons against Kantakouzenos VI, repeating that he had usurped the throne of the Palaiologos.

Given the circumstances, Constantinople was simmering with anger and rage just as it had a few years before. Being informed of all that had been happening minute by minute, Emperor Kantakouzenos VI anticipated the approaching fires but he couldn't do anything to suppress the flames. Whomever he sent from his palace, messenger or envoy, they either did not return or they returned with unconvincing news. In fact, even the mesazōn whom he kept a close eye on couldn't believe the news, and most of the time he underhandedly sent Palaiologos reports about the situation in Constantinople. The latest news delivered to Emperor Kantakouzenos VI, who was already without hope, was worse than bad. Supporters of Palaiologos were spreading rumours that Tzympe Castle was not given to Suleyman Pasha, the son of Orhan Ghazi, so they could keep a sentry in the castle but rather so that he could invade the whole of Thrace. They said, "The Kantakouzenos are giving Gallipoli as their daughter's dowry but once the Ottomans have that they will want the whole of Thrace. We must do everything in our power to stop the Ottomans from possessing Gallipoli. If we lose it we will never be able to save Thrace from their grasp. That is why our army should be led by Emperor John V Palaiologos." Hearing such rumours infuriated usurper Emperor Kantakouzenos VI. After punishing anyone and everyone who appeared before him, he withdrew into his study and engaged in soliloquy.

A few days after he wrote and sent a letter to the Duca of Aenus, Emperor John VI Kantakouzenos experienced another fit of muttering to himself. He felt relieved as if he had got everything off his chest to someone else, but that deceptive moment did not last long. His worries seemed to begin accumulating instead of diminishing with time. Realising this, he became even more flustered. He looked for a way out to ease his worries and to relieve him, but, for a considerable amount of time, he couldn't find a solution. His thoughts became even more complicated and mangled. This new moment of worry added onto his already bewildering concern made him even angrier. He stood up with that anger, kicked every piece of furniture around him and then walked towards the window to look at the Golden Horn. When he saw a small Genoese sailboat decorated with tinselled banners, obviously carrying adventurous Genoese, sail towards the Bosphorus he thought to himself, "The Genoese are having fun and leading colourful lives while we, consumed with suspicion and worry, cannot even go out to the Golden Horn to get some air." Just then the devil coiled up around his tongue and he said, "They are leading colourful lives with the colours they stole from others." Feeling that the toils within him hadn't subsided in the slightest, he trotted back to his throne and sat down. He loudly uttered, "You were someone called John Kantakouzenos when you were standing in front of those windows. You could not find any solution to lessen your worries as John Kantakouzenos. Now you should think as Emperor John VI Kantakouzenos and drown the worries within you..." Then as if to explain the difference between the two Kantakouzenos he said, "We must urgently suggest an agreement to the Ottomans. I must convince them to return to their own shores before they spread further into Thrace..."

Emperor Kantakouzenos VI fell silent for a while, and after he wiped his eyes with the back of his hand he said, "Oh! If only they thought that we had the military might to attack them overland they wouldn't have had the courage to do this. If I send our sailors to fight on land they will be like fish washed ashore. How can I convince the Ottomans to go back to where they came from if we don't have the power to resist them? It is inconceivable that a castle was seized in one night, and more so that a few of the castles surrendered out of their own free will."

The Emperor then delved into an ocean of reticence. After a long and deep silence, he once again looked at the ancient throne of Palaiologos V, dating from the time of the Romans. He had switched its place with his own throne in his study at the palace, but he still couldn't bring himself to get it removed. His vacant gaze returning its ocean voyage became fixed on the imperial throne for a while. He momentarily wanted to turn his face and look into the distance but he couldn't turn his head. As the clever gaze of his whirling eyes, which were quite small in relation to his face, roamed the room, he walked towards his desk and sat in a chair that looked like the thrones behind him. For a while, he looked at the throne of Palaiologos and talked to himself, "My dear son-in-law, you are also like my son... Let me tell you something, you will never be able to rid your mind of. Critias says, 'There is nothing more definite than the fact that every living being born into this world will die and that those living will never be able to run away from that calamity.'"

After a short respite, he continued his commentary loudly, "Our castle commanders and guards, all of us and even Orhan will not be able to escape this end. But somehow, when all the sincerity runs out and the ambition of keeping one's rank dominates, the fact that we will all die is forgotten by every living soul. Look and you will see that the commanders, most of whom we handpicked together, are forgetting reality for the sake of their ambitions and are crossing over to the side of the Ottomans who promise much more than us. It doesn't even cross their minds that they will lose double in the future. But you should know that the Ottomans are making their moves in a very calculated manner. You should also know that the Ottomans will not let us be before they receive the mouthful they want from us. Also, the bite they want is quite big, so don't later tell me that I did not warn you."

Listening to his voice echo in the large stone room for a while, Kantakouzenos VI felt his ears ringing. He heard the voice of Palaiologos V, his exiled Co-Emperor, hidden in his own voice. Yet the voice he heard was very different from the heady and excitedly confident one he last heard before he was sent into exile. Palaiologos's voice had the tone of someone with no self-esteem, no power and no life. With that powerless voice, Palaiologos spoke to his father-in-law and Co-Emperor, Kantakouzenos VI, "Sincerity is surely important. As Critias says 'death is an indisputable end for humans' but is it, as you said, only our castle commanders who forget this fact."

"Surely it is not only they who forget this fact. We also often forget that inevitable end, but we are deceived. If only we could have come to realise that deceit sooner!"

"I don't know what I should make of the thoughts you convey by referring to the ideas of Critias but from your comments, I have come to the conclusion that we can get Orhan to change his mind about his secret plans by offering him a bigger mouthful."

"You understand fully... We have to do all we can to stop them in Thrace, or we will come to see our castles in Thrace as islands belonging to the Ottoman forces, as we have already done about the lands across the seas. The same is also true for Constantinople."

Palaiologos's voice transformed into a worrisome, sorrowful tone, "My dear father-in-law, let's do whatever you want to do. I am sure that your vast experience will be of much use at this time. I want you to go to your son-in-law Orhan and ask him to remove his forces from our castles. I already accept whatever you offer them in the negotiations in return for their retreat. If you wish, Empress Irene, my mother-in-law, can also accompany you on your journey to Bursa. This way, she will also get to see her daughter residing in Orhan's palace."

Kantakouzenos VI suddenly flared up and replied to the voice of his son-in-law as he roamed the room, "You want me to go on a family visit? Yes, the Ottomans would certainly like that but if I am going to go there to negotiate it is a matter of the state and cannot be like a family visit. I should not turn such meetings into an agreement between two families."

When replying to Emperor Kantakouzenos VI's voice, Palaiologos V's voice also came out angrily even if less so then his father-in-law's, "If you think so then you should inform your son-in-law of our terms in a letter. I am personally convinced that you should go there but do as you wish. Just make sure you hurry so we don't lose Thrace. If they do to Thrace what they did to Pantichium, Pelecanum and Nicomedia the situation will be irreversible. Especially if they get the Thracian clergy on their side, as they did in the islands, it will be too late to recover the situation."

As Emperor Kantakouzenos VI listened to his son-in-law, he bit his thick bottom lip so hard it could have bled. In agreement, he replied, "I like your opinions son of Andronicus. You didn't ponder on such things before but I now see that you have matured being with my Helena."

After a short silence he muttered as if the words were pouring out of his mouth, "If only we could have seen the importance of thinking together long ago..." He spoke loudly once again, "Son of Andronicus, it seems to me that you will give meaning to the throne you will sit on in the future. The last things you said aren't childish at all. What we now have to do is to stop being defeated by our separate ambitions and start working together. If not, black clouds will descend on Constantinople, she who keeps our empire alive."

Exiled Co-Emperor Palaiologos's voice trilled in the room, "Hush now! Heaven forbid! If only you didn't have such great ambitions and fears you wouldn't have made so many promises to the Ottomans. You are the only one to blame for what has befallen us!"

Patiently listening to his invisible yet sonorous son-in-law, usurper Emperor Kantakouzenos VI became angry and replied in irritation, "Son of Andronicus, make sure never to forget that what makes light what it is, is the dark. If it wasn't for that darkness you and your family cast on me, I would have perhaps never been able to see the light asyou."

Exiled Emperor John V Palaiologos thought that his malicious little comments did their job to warn his father-in-law. He decided not to give him a hard time and softened his echoing voice, "My Helena's father, what you mean to say is that this is a time for unity. A time for defeating the Ottomans and to do so, it is time we gave Orhan a bigger mouthful than he wishes for. These are intelligent desires, but I am here and you are there..."

Emperor Kantakouzenos VI took a deep breath during his son-in-law's last sentences. He held the letter that had been on the desk for a long time and looking at it he walked to his throne. As he sat down he sighed, "Oh, son of Andronicus, oh! You must know that no agreement is eternal. Yet, we should come to an agreement with Orhan. The conditions we state in the agreement have to satisfy his wishes and also gain us enough time. Just as the script of the agreement Anatolian Hittites made is carved on the walls of Egyptian cities, the script of the agreement we shall make should be carved on the walls of Ottoman castles."

Palaiologos V's gradually withering voice replied once again before disappearing completely, "I agree completely."

Coming back to his senses after his son-in-law disappeared from his mind's eye Kantakouzenos VI muttered to himself, "Whom was I talking to?" He bit his lips. He tried to settle himself by thinking he had dreamt with his eyes wide open and looked out from the wide windows of the room at the Genoese neighbourhood across the Golden Horn, "Has the Genoese population increased or are my eyes mistaking me? According to the rumours many people have moved to Sycae from inside the city walls, as it was during the last few years of the Romans. Apparently, a group of those who emigrated there settled and changed the name of our Sycae to Pera of their own accord."

CHAPTER NINETEEN

The happiness Suleyman Pasha felt the moment he sent gifts to his beys for all the good news their messengers had brought, specifically the news that the castles were now completely under their control, did not last long. Despite the fact that they were all in the same room and were conversing seated across from each other, he couldn't concentrate on Evrenos Bey or Hacı Ilbey's words no matter how hard he tried. He kept daydreaming, distancing himself from the room and from himself. Now and again he'd think to himself, "I was much more joyous just a few days ago when we took over the small castle. We now have hold of three castles. The joy in my heart grows faint whereas it should be growing stronger. My withering joy..." and before ending his thought he grumbled, "My father is right once more. He says one should never get hasty or underestimate anyone." Noticing that he was getting agitated and bothered, he voiced his thoughts out loud as he said, "We shouldn't have encountered such a great loss of manpower for these small castles. We should have also accounted for the losses we gave during combat that wasn't fought bravely," before walking out of the room. The spacious courtyard of the commander's mansion felt too small to take away the distress in his chest. He suddenly thought that if he walked down by the sea the wind blowing from the sea would take his worries with it. He quickly left the courtyard and walked towards the castle gate leading to the harbour. After a few days' break, the marketplace had been set up again. As he walked towards the castle gate looking at the stalls of the sellers, he noticed that the woman who had carefully looked at him on that first day with her greyish blue eyes was once again following him. A couple of times he hesitantly thought to pause and look back at the woman but instead, he walked even faster. When he reached the gate where the short slope leading to the harbour began, he changed his mind and headed towards the staircase leading to the highest tower of the castle walls.

Watching him out of the corner of her eye, the tall woman left her stall to her friend and hurried towards the staircase. As she walked after the man whom she didn't know, she was questioning why she was following him at all. Just then she realised that her heart was brimming with emotion for the first time in years. Her pace gained speed with that stirring sensation she felt in her chest. She at once squirmed out of the crowds of the marketplace and turned into the narrow street the man was walking down. He was about to reach the stairs at the end of the street, seemingly pushed between the houses on either side. The woman quickened her steps with the desire to reach him before she had to climb but as soon as she had taken just a few steps she was startled by footsteps behind her. When she turned she was face to face with two *serdengeçtis* who were so close to her she could feel their breath. She was briefly undecided between pursuing the man and going back to her stall. Then she decided that it would be best for her to return. She leaned against the wall to give way to the *serdengeçtis* who had their right hands on the hilts of their swords hanging from their waists. Her courage was renewed when she noticed that as they passed by her they weren't interested in her activity. Peeking out at them from behind, she saw that the man was on the last step of the stone-paved staircase. She bobbed her head to each side as she murmured, "The new owners of our castle."

Completely oblivious to the fact that the tall woman was following him, Suleyman Pasha climbed the stairs at the double and reached the top of the wide castle wall. He then continued walking briskly until he reached the highest bastion where the guardsmen were. When the breeze blowing from the top of the waves of the Dardanelles licked his sun-burnt and tawny face he exclaimed, "Pish!" in a tone that failed to scare away the breeze. He let the breeze lick his face for a while before he snarled, "All the *yayas* on the shore across must be transported here or the cavalrymen, unmatched by any other warrior in pitched battles, will be slain for no reason. If we manage to transport all our *yayas* to this shore they'll see that we mean business."

The guardsmen who had been watching Suleyman Pasha since the moment he climbed up to their tower were not able to figure out whom he was talking to, but Suleyman Pasha felt relief at the idea that sparked in his mind. In fact, feeling that his previous worries were replaced by joy, he looked down from the edge of the castle wall. There was an empty area between the foundations of the wall and the greenery further ahead. There was almost no empty space from the point where trees rose until the shore was licked by the waves. The tips of the lowest branches of the trees nearest to the shore looked as if they were emerging from the depths of the sea.

Tired of standing, Suleyman Pasha sat on top of the castle wall and watched the green mix into the blue. As he did so he dove into a boundless ocean of thought. Lost in the grasping scenery he had just about forgotten where he was when he heard footsteps at the tower entrance. He curiously turned his gaze towards the sound of the footsteps but couldn't see anyone around, so his hand involuntarily moved towards the small heirloom dagger hidden in his sash. As his hand grasped the mother-of-pearl inlaid hilt he tried to remember his father's large face with a goatee the day he gave it to him. Alas, the image of his father's face on that day had slipped from his mind filled with one too many memories. As he looked at the shores below, again surprised that he couldn't recall his father's face, he heard Hacı Ilbey's elderly messenger's voice. The moment he stood up on the wall he was sitting on, the elderly messenger bowed and said, "All the beys are waiting for you, My Prince."

The old man had been Hacı Ilbey's messenger since his time as vizier of the Karasid dynasty. Like the beys he also called Suleyman Pasha "My Prince" because Suleyman Pasha treated him as an equal most of the time. He even summoned him to his marquee on dark and long nights so the old man could tell him stories. He had grown used to this habit of listening to stories during his childhood when he was scared of rainy and pitch-black nights. Back in those days, it was always his mother who told him stories.

Suleyman Pasha walked back towards the military headquarters where his beys were gathered. As he walked between the market stalls he once again noticed that the tall, big-boned woman with greyish blue eyes was following him with her gaze. He paused momentarily and looked back at the woman until he heard the footsteps of the *serdengeçtis*. When the *serdengeçtis* approached him from behind he began to walk once again towards the headquarters. Though, the tall woman kept her gaze fixed on him and those walking beside him. She walked after them for a short while to find out where they were headed. Seeing them enter the old mansion of the castle commander, she stopped and returned to mind her stall.

The beys were gathered in Hacı Ilbey's office in the headquarters. They all stood up on Suleyman Pasha's entrance. Suleyman Pasha first hugged and congratulated Ece Bey, then Akça Kocaoğlu, Fazıl Bey and Balabancıkoğlu. As he sat down he spoke in a hurt, soft and slow tone of voice, "Welcome."

No one wanted to speak for a while due to the effect his emotional and soft tone of voice had. Knowing that his beys were waiting for him to speak Suleyman Pasha continued, "Beys, first of all I am grateful to you for this new beginning you have undertaken to show our permanence in these lands."

Then he turned to Fazıl Bey and said, "My condolences to you for the loss of Suleyman of Pigas. But don't forget that this is a pain we all share. The path we are on is such that none of us can ever know what is to befall any of us, where or when. And that fact will remain as long as we have brave men to take the places of those we have lost."

He tipped his head down and fell silent. Raising his head back up, he looked at Fazıl Bey and continued, "As of today Sestos Castle shall be remembered by the name of brave Suleyman of Pigas as suggested by Hacı Ilbey and Evrenos Bey."

He looked at Ece Bey and Akça Kocaoğlu's faces to see their reactions. Ece Bey replied, "That is fitting, My Prince."

Akça Kocaoğlu also showed his agreement with a nod of his head.

Fazıl Bey looked at the faces of each and every bey and then replied to Suleyman Pasha before falling silent, "Thank you, My Prince."

Anticipating that Fazıl Bey needed some inner peace and that it would be better if he was left alone Suleyman Pasha turned to Ece Bey and said, "Ece Bey, my condolences go to you too. I heard that many of your courageous men died of scalding. I hope that those who have caused you such pain have been punished in a just manner?"

Deep in thought, Ece Bey replied, "Of course, My Prince. All the culprits have been punished."

After a few deep breaths, he continued explaining,

"My Prince, the people living in the castle helped the castle guards both because they are sick and tired of the Byzantine taxes and also because they witnessed the cruelty of the Catalans. That is why we took care not to punish anyone unjustly. Only those who defended voluntarily have been taken captive together with the guards. Everything went more or less to plan, but because we failed to identify that there were tunnels opening out into the field outside the castle a few guards succeeded in escaping towards Gallipoli Fortress."

Evrenos Bey jumped up from his chair. His facial expression reflected his restlessness. Looking on, Suleyman Pasha tried to ease him, "Do not fret Evrenos Bey. Even if those guards hadn't slipped away Gallipoli would still have found out that we invaded the castles. It doesn't matter much if they heard the news a little earlier. Who cares if they inform the Emperor of what they heard. What of it?"

Upon hearing Prince Suleyman Pasha's train of thought Evrenos Bey replied, "My Prince, what worries me is not that their emperor will hear of our capture of their castles but that our *yayas* waiting to be transported here from the opposite shore will be caught defenceless at sea. The merchant ships carrying our *yayas* will not stand the Roman Fire that the Byzantine fleet may throw at them—they would burn to death in a few hours."

Gazing at Evrenos Bey's face, Suleyman Pasha fumblingly replied, "Evrenos Bey, your worries are my worries but there is nothing we can do at this stage..."

Then he turned to Hacı Ilbey for a bright idea. Aware of the heavy and dreary air in the room, Hacı Ilbey replied, "My Prince, we have finally set foot on these Rumelian lands which we viewed from the Anatolian shores for many years during the days of the Karasid dynasty. Our beys who bestowed us with such happiness have surely done all they could have. Alas, some of it went awry. We cannot allow the negatives to deter us. I think that Maydos Castle should be attributed to Ece Bey and be called 'Ece-Abad'."

Upon his opinion being accepted by the beys, Evrenos Bey's lacklustre gaze followed the faces of those in the room as if something had been forgotten. Shaking it off, he continued, "Those living in the castles built on the fertile land of Thrace have endured much pain until now. Thus, they might be very reactive. I think that we should make them feel that we are nothing like the Latins or the Catalans. Remember these Orthodox people were forced to convert to Catholicism when the westerners ruled the empire. They also lost everything they had to those pillagers. The people we talked to today told us that until our arrival two guards collected taxes every morning and every evening. The cruelty of the last Catalans also caused much suffering to the people here. This gives us an important opportunity. If we show them that we are different to those before us our work here will be smooth-sailing. In any case, from what we can see there is nothing Byzantine about this place but its name."

Looking at Balabancıkoğlu, who hadn't uttered a single word until then, Fazıl Bey addressed Suleyman Pasha, "My Prince..."

It was as if something had lodged itself in his throat—he couldn't speak. He paused and swallowed his spit a few times. After exhaling as if to clear the words stuck in his throat together with his breath, he continued, "My Prince, we've fallen into great sin by letting ourselves be overwhelmed with the rage of our sadness."

Trying to make sense of such a confessional sentence, Prince Suleyman Pasha and the other beys carefully inspected Fazıl Bey's round face. Meantime Balabancıkoğlu's gaze was stuck on the stone floors of the headquarters. Hacı Ilbey cut into the conversation, "Fazıl Bey, surely we are all too human. The fact that we are beys doesn't bestow us with additional divine powers. We can make mistakes and fall into sin because we are human. What's important is that we never forget that we are only human and to embody the virtue of understanding our mistakes. Would you like to tell us about your mistake that sorrows you so much and allow yourself to find peace of mind?"

Trying to hide the pale skin of his round face under his grey beard, Fazıl Bey said, "Before the old woman who poured boiling water on Suleyman of Pigas was beheaded, she said, 'I thought the Catalans had come back,' but because we couldn't understand what she was saying, she died in vain..."

CHAPTER TWENTY

Palaiologos V was scuttling up and down the shore with the precipitousness of his youth. Now and then when he stopped and turned towards the blue waters of the Aegean Sea, he shouted out, "What are you still waiting for Kantakouzenos? If the news we hear is correct we will also soon be hearing Ottoman footsteps in Constantinople. If you think that your son-in-law Orhan won't harm you, you are mistaken. Constantinople is a pearl that shines inside out. I suppose Orhan isn't so foolish as to not see that brightness, that beauty. You took advantage of my childhood and usurped my empire, but know this! There are also those who will usurp the empire from you!"

As he paced up and down the beach, he heard a sound coming from the water. For a while he couldn't figure out if the sound was emerging from the fear within him or the depths of the Aegean Sea. He sat down on a rock on the shore caressed by the blue waves. As he held his breath and carefully looked out into the distance shielding his gaze with his hand in order to figure out the origin of the sound, he saw a winged golden bull with Emperor Kantakouzenos VI on it, like Zeus, flying towards him over Mount Ida. Riding his bull-like horse Kantakouzenos replied to his son-in-law's previous lament, "Hey you! Son of Andronicus! We have begun our preparations but we don't know where to send our letter to Orhan as he is on a campaign. Among the news we received was a report that he is ill. Nevertheless, I will shortly be setting forth to Antigone to meet him. In Antigone, I will also make a pilgrimage to the small church of Saint Sophia, which has been host to the holy consul twice."

Exiled Emperor Palaiologos V replied to his father-in-law, on the back of his winged-creature, without moving an inch from the rock he was seated on, "Give my greetings to both Nicaea and Antigone..."

"You just think about my Helena's love for you, try to be worthy of it. Leave the business of greeting Nicaea and Antigone to me."

After speaking, Emperor Kantakouzenos VI kept his thunder-like voice in his chest and blended into the bluish clouds with his bull-like golden creature. Only after his departure did Palaiologos V realise that he was all alone on the shores of Tenedos. Realising that he had been talking to his fear he quickly stood up and began running towards his mansion with all his might. As he did so, in Constantinople Kantakouzenos VI had boarded the most magnificent imperial barge in all the empire and was cruising towards the Genoese neighbourhood across from the Golden Horn. After a short trip, the sound of the oars into water quietened as the magnificent boats landed. The mayor of Galata, the Genoese colony, was waiting for the Emperor on the shore. As soon as the Emperor and his entourage set foot on the shore, the musicians at the back began beating their snare drums with twiglike drumsticks. After greeting them Kantakouzenos VI slowly walked towards the carriages readied for the imperial family. The carriage of the mayor, who was showing the Emperor and statesmen to their carriages, was more decorated and magnificent than all the others. There were silverfish figures jumping into the water embellished on the decorative surfaces of the wheels.

There were armoured cavalrymen in front of the carriage in which Emperor Kantakouzenos VI was seated. The ceremonial cavalry of the Emperor had crossed the sea on barges in the early hours of the morning. The knights were so equipped and sat up so straight on their horses that anyone looking at them would have thought that Byzantine glory and power could not be any better embodied. The helmets on their heads and the armour on their bodies made them look particularly spectacular. The weapon they all held in their hands had a double-headed axe on one end and a spear on the other. It seemed to growl, "Whoever dares come a spear's length from me should accept their fate!"

After proceeding along the paved harbour road the horse carriages drew an arc to the left and began to climb up the slope, parallel to the road they'd come from. They made their way, taking many corners through the narrow streets lined with houses. Progress was slow as the procession had to give way to the single-horse carriages coming out of side streets. The knights at the front were becoming agitated but Emperor Kantakouzenos VI was still comfortably watching the Bosphorus from his carriage. In fact, he was making use of the delays, taking pleasure in being able to view his surroundings at leisure.

All three carriages stopped at the open space that led to the atrium of the tallest building in the Genoese neighbourhood overlooking the strait. The mayor ran towards the Emperor and escorted him inside. They all sat on the mattresses placed on top of stone benches in the most beautiful corner of the ministry that had a most delectable view of the Bosphorus as well as across the Golden Horn. In fact, where they sat was both the meeting hall of the mayor and a spacious gazebo where he welcomed his esteemed guests. When it was cold and wintry the windows were covered with woven bristle curtains that kept the cold and the rain out, and when it was warm and amiable, all four sides of the gazebo were kept open. Despite the fact that it was autumn it wasn't yet cold. The mellow breeze blowing from the Bosphorus was cooling those sitting in the gazebo without making them shiver. Now and then, the mayor entertained the rich merchants who arrived with their ships, and in return, the merchants presented the mayor with gifts of which one could not even dream. Almost every one of the Genoese merchants who frequented Constantinople was invited as the mayor's guest. When they came to participate in the festivities they brought their own servants and cooks along to help the Greek servants of the mayor. At the end of the night, those servants and cooks were left behind as gifts for the mayor. As a matter of fact, in those days the merchants made it a

habit to take such gifts wherever they went. Moreover, the wives of
the merchants bought concubines from the slave markets to use on
such days. The wives of Genoese merchants made such purchases
from the Venetian markets while the wives of Venetian merchants
did the same from Genoese ones. They never revealed the secret behind their preferences to anyone.

As soon as the mayor of the Genoese living in Galata found out
that the Emperor was going to visit the neighbourhood, he immediately commissioned two golden mermaids to be made in the style of
Alexandrian statues and got them decorated with Fergana emeralds.
He had taken great care to make sure that they were both made from
the same mould. John V Palaiologos, referred to as child emperor by
the Genoese, was far away but even so, the mayor, knowing that the
ears of emperors hear everything, had erred on the side of caution
and commissioned both mermaids to be made. The mayor didn't like
Kantakouzenos VI at all, not even as much as the dirt under his
nails, but the fact that he was the Emperor made it compulsory that
he served him to the best of his capabilities. Also, according to rumours, Kantakouzenos was the only one who opposed Andronicus
IV Palaiologos when he wrote to Roger de Flor to summon the
Catalans. The Catalans subsequently devoured everything the Genoese had. In the past, when Emperor Andronicus had told
Kantakouzenos that he would be punished for meddling in his decisions, Kantakouzenos had taken a great risk and told him, "Your
Majesty, it is easy to be covered in trouble head to toe, but it is not so
easy to stray from it. The Catalans invaded Sicily and gave it to the
French king because he wished it so, but later they scourged him too.

It must have been what Kantakouzenos had said that made him re-
consider and change his mind about punishing him. Nevertheless, he
was still mad that Kantakouzenos had meddled in his business, so he
replied, "Kantakouzenos as you well know the final decision in this
empire is that of the Emperor. I cannot give any meaning to your ac-

tions considering that you know this so well and you still defied me."

Kantakouzenos VI thought a loose thread is one that will soon snap and replied, "Your Majesty, I defied you because I thought you were going to cause greater harm to our empire while trying to stop the calamity that is the Ottomans. My master, forgive me if I failed to respect your authority."

After several deep breaths, Andronicus IV Palaiologos replied, "I think you are wrong. Everything aside, the Catalans share our beliefs and because they will be our mercenaries they will cause us no harm. We can get them to undertake monumental tasks with our smallest promises. Once they are finished doing our bidding we can ship them back home. Whereas, the Ottomans who have invaded our lands bit by bit are more dangerous than all the enemies Byzantium has had until now. No other power but the Catalans can deter them from taking swathes of our land."

Kantakouzenos, the Emperor's mesazōn, tipped his head down and replied, "I have nothing to say if they are going to save us like they did Sicily, but if they also try to plunder our Byzantium, our Constantinople like the Latins who participated in the Crusades, it will be near impossible for us to eradicate them."

Andronicus IV replied in a slightly angry tone of voice, "So are you trying to tell me that my decisions are wrong, Kantakouzenos?"

Knowing that the cost of replying "yes" would be too grave because of the Emperor's increasing anger, Kantakouzenos VI bowed his head forth and replied, "No, Your Majesty... You make the best decisions. Would we ever dare oppose you? However, if you allow me I have a humble suggestion."

In order to show the courtesy of listening to his minister, who hadn't strayed from his orders for years, Palaiologos IV replied, "All right, what is your suggestion? Let's hear it."

"It would be good if you keep them away from our Constantinople, Your Majesty."

"This suggestion of yours cannot be disregarded. In any case, I want to send them to fight the Ottomans immediately. If they dock in a port of the Karasid dynasty by the Anatolian shores of the Dardanelles we can easily send them to fight the Ottomans from there."

In the Genoese neighbourhood, it is a legend that Andronicus IV Palaiologos didn't let anyone other than Roger de Flor, the commander of the Catalans who sailed through the Dardanelles, enter Constantinople. If the Catalans had left their ships and set foot on Constantinople it would probably be almost impossible to get them out again. After settling in Constantinople they would have done the "cleaning up" they previously did in Sicily.

The mayor of the Genoese neighbourhood had thought about that while looking at Kantakouzenos VI as he just watched the Bosphorus like he had done from his horse carriage until the offering of the mayor's concubines began. He was quietly drinking his wine with a vacant mind when the concubines began their service together with the offerings. He instantly leapt to his feet as if he'd remembered something. Standing, he addressed the mayor, "The view of our Constantinople is very pleasant from your neighbourhood. If we were to climb up towards Pera I am sure the city would look even more beautiful."

The mayor replied in surprise, "Your Majesty should not make the effort to climb up the hill. Constantinople doesn't look any more beautiful from there than it does from here."

In order to make the mayor perceive that his walk had a purpose, Emperor Kantakouzenos VI replied in a disgruntled and reproachful tone of voice, "According to the rumours the people have been referring to, our dear Sykai under different names..."

The mayor, who couldn't properly say the name that was easy for the Byzantines to pronounce, usually referred to the neighbourhood of Sykai as Little Genoa. Yet, knowing that the Byzantines didn't like to change place names, he replied tactfully, "The people of our neighbourhood favour the name of Sykai but travelling merchants sometimes love to make up new names. As you may understand, the name Sykai is rather difficult to say for those travelling people."

Emperor Kantakouzenos VI did not utter another word as he walked towards the gate of the courtyard that led to the road. The mayor ran and caught up with him. Together they climbed up the hill and in a short while reached the peak. After walking side by side for some time, they reached the neighbourhood of Pera, established by Jews who were exiled from their neighbourhoods inside the walls of Constantinople during the reign of Emperor Theodosius II. Emperor John VI Kantakouzenos didn't look in the direction of the Jewish neighbourhood, as they hadn't been able to collect taxes from them due to the fact that they were banned from owning horses since the reign of Basil I. Instead, pointing to the new neighbourhood that the Genoese established next to Sykai, he asked, "Why haven't we been informed that this neighbourhood has been erected next to Sykai?"

Faced by silence from the mayor, he turned and began walking in the opposite direction. As he walked he authoritatively told the mayor, "A count of those living in these new houses will be done under the supervision of our guards. The new taxes will be determined according to the population."

CHAPTER TWENTY-ONE

Suleyman Pasha walked towards the harbour in his princely attire for the first time and descended the stairs two by two. When he saw the tall, big-boned woman appear before him from one of the side streets he stopped. His men who were following him saw that he had stopped, and ran to his side. The woman seemed to have locked her greyish blue eyes on the large black eyes and round nose of Suleyman inherited from his father. As he was about to be overcome by the effect of the tall woman's greyish blue gaze conveying an emotional light he pulled himself together. In order to find out what the woman, who had been observing him for days wanted, he looked at the Greek-speaking guard given to him by Evrenos Bey for reassurance and then, in the Greek his mother, Nilüfer Hatun, had taught him, he asked the woman, "Why are you following me?"

The long and fair-necked woman dressed in black, standing as if to assert that she was the Aphrodite of her times, tried to smile and took a step towards Suleyman Pasha. Suspicious of her movement, an alert guard immediately drew his sword and extended it towards the woman's neck. Looking at the sword, the woman took two steps back. Befitting of her long neck, looking at Suleyman Pasha she addressed him with the calm and flat voice of a crane,

"I have been watching you since the first day I saw you at the market. You are the new owner of our castle. I am a woman who was widowed by the last Catalans who left for Thessaly and Athens. If you allow me I would like to be in your service."

As Suleyman Pasha couldn't understand the long sentences spoken quickly, he turned to the guard given to him by Evrenos Bey and asked, "Can you translate what she said word by word?"

When the guard translated what the woman had said, Suleyman Pasha realised that the woman did not have any bad intentions by following him for days. He smiled and said, "I have much to do now.

Tell the lady I will summon her when we need her services. It's sufficient for her to show you her house for when I have need of her."

Then he speedily began descending the stairs again.

When the guard told the woman what Suleyman Pasha said, the
woman softly smiled with an obscure facial expression that conveyed
neither happiness nor sadness. She hastily walked towards the spot
from which her house could be easily seen. After showing the guard
walking behind her the house she turned into a narrow street. As she
walked home the guard turned back and walked quickly to catch up
with the *serdengeçtis* escorting Suleyman Pasha.

Suleyman Pasha had become quite frustrated with the woman who
suddenly appeared before him, as he was hurrying to the harbour to
see his Grey embark from a barge. When he saw his horse on the pier
he quickly forgot about his frustration and also the woman. In a
single breath, he approached his steed, the reins of which were held
by his groom. He was ecstatic to see his horse again. It was raised in
the stables of the Karasid and gifted to him by his father. It had
been a dear comrade to him in every battle throughout the years.
Caressing his horse's head and mane he muttered, "I wanted to welcome you as you were getting off the barge but I was delayed." The
Grey rubbed its nose against his shoulder as if to say, "What matters
is that you came to welcome me." For a moment their eyes met with
yearning. As the prince scratched his horse's neck he murmured,
"The woman also had a very pale neck." He looked around as if he
were ashamed of what he mumbled and was surprised that he remembered the woman he thought he had forgotten. For a moment
he couldn't make sense of why the woman had made a place in his
mind because until then, he had only thought about his horse when
he was with him. Wishing to remove the woman from his thoughts
he grouched, "I have plenty of men in my service!" He looked over at
the second barge by the pier. When the offloading of the horses from
the second barge started he told the groom, "Don't lead him up to

the castle by the stairs—I'd prefer him to be near my marquee with the other horses. We will be setting out tomorrow anyway."

Then he passed the reins back to the groom. Seeing that Hacı Ilbey was approaching him, he walked towards him. Hacı Ilbey had just welcomed his own black horse and was walking towards him. As he did so, he was muttering to himself, "He loves his Grey and I love my black horse. I suppose if we hadn't greeted our horses here we wouldn't feel at ease. He let me know how much he missed me with the way he put his head under my arm and rubbed against the side of my body." Seeing that Hacı Ilbey was now at speaking-distance from him, Suleyman Pasha said, "I see that you missed your horse as I did mine."

Hacı Ilbey smiled and said, "How could I not, My Prince? I haven't been separated from him for years until now. If you'd only seen the way he placed his head under my arm..."

"Mine was no less affectionate. He caressed my shoulder with his nose as if it wasn't enough for him to put his head against my shoulder."

"We hadn't fought in wars with our previous horses, but we have been in many battles with these ones. Somewhere, sometime we joined our fates with theirs. Perhaps that is why we dote on them so much."

"I think ours is more of a keenness for affection rather than a unity of fate..."

Hacı Ilbey looked at him smiling, "I suppose our interpretation of love has changed since we spent so much time with *ulema*[19]."

"You know what I'm like. I am a man with both an open mind and an open heart. Just as I was coming here, a lady appeared in front of me. Despite the fact that I only looked at her face for a few seconds, I noticed that I was thinking about her as I caressed my horse."

Hacı Ilbey looked at Suleyman Pasha, dressed in his princely attire

---

19 T.N, *Ulema*, refers to the educated class of Muslim legal scholars engaged in several fields of Islamic studies and Polymath.

and asked, "Did she appear in front of you intentionally or by coincidence?"

"I suppose this time she appeared before me intentionally."

"If she did so intentionally, she must have seen you before."

"She said she had been watching us since the day of our arrival..."

Hacı Ilbey then turned his head and looked at the guards standing a few steps back, "Did Evrenos Bey's man translate what the woman said?"

"Yes..."

"Did you find out where her house is?"

"I didn't prolong the conversation since I wanted to get to the harbour as soon as possible. I think Evrenos Bey's man found out about the location of her house."

Hacı Ilbey called Evrenos Bey's man, who was talking with the *serdengeçtis* standing a little further from them. After talking to him he turned to Suleyman Pasha and said, "We will find out about her and see what she wants."

Then, as if he had forgotten about all he had said, he walked towards the castle and began climbing the stairs. Suleyman Pasha also followed him. As he walked behind Hacı Ilbey, his heart suddenly filled with a childish sense of joy. A strange sound, like a whistle, came out from between his lips as he tried to give meaning to the joy in his heart. He burst into laughter upon hearing that sound. Hearing him laugh Hacı Ilbey turned around. He also burst into laughter when he saw the childish joy on the prince's face. Once they had quietened down, Hacı Ilbey spoke to Suleyman Pasha as they climbed up the stairs beside each other, "I don't know what you are laughing about, My Prince, but I haven't laughed so sweetly in a long time. Laughter is the source of enthusiasm. If only we could laugh more often!"

Suleyman Pasha replied in a manner implying that his laughter had nothing to do with the subject he mentioned previously, "Hacı I am yet neither as old nor as emotional as you are... I'd long forgotten about what I told you. The reason for my laughter is that the other day when I was viewing these lands from the other side, the castles looked so far and impossible to seize that I thought it would take us centuries to get here. Now we are promenading around here. What's more, is that some of what I once viewed from afar is under our command now. That's what seems strange to me and what really made me laugh."

Then in a soft tone of voice, he added, "I surely don't know yet if all this bodes well."

Hacı Ilbey responded, "My Prince, in my life of what I've seen and learned, is that life includes all things. No one can know what bodes well and doesn't. But, do not forget that the games of Byzantium will begin once they find out that we have seized their castles."

"I am really curious to see how old Byzantium, that is hardly capable of standing on his own two feet, will participate in such games."

"No need to be curious, My Prince. You shall soon see. Don't be fooled by its age, it will find a game to play regardless. When it comes to how easy it was for us to seize the castles, I suppose we owe it to the Latins and the Catalans to a certain extent. If they hadn't demoralised the people here so, seizing the castle wouldn't have been so easy. I don't know how much you know about the people of these lands but there are no other people who love their land as much as they do. We mustn't step on their toes. The fact that the bloodiest of wars happened here in the past shows their love. The Karasid dynasty had many aspirations for this area. That is why during the time of Aclan Bey an armada, small but nonetheless an armada, was put together to cross to this coastline. We weren't able to cope with the pirates of the Aegean Sea with those small ships but we never let them come near our coasts. It was Aclan Bey's greatest dream to reach this side of the strait. He protected his armada as if it was his own child. May he rest in peace—he couldn't live long enough to at-

tain his dream. Once Aclan Bey died, instead of keeping the land un-
divided, his sons decided to share it. That was when I'd understood
that the Karasids needed a more unifying force. What I mean to say
is that I felt these lands breathe when I was serving the Karasid dynasty. In fact, the first love stories I listened to were those based on
these lands."

"Are there other love stories from here except for the story of the
king's son and the nun that Evrenos Bey told me about?"

"Yes, My Bey. These lands have always been the setting of the most
heart-breaking love stories. We didn't know many of them back then,
but wherever we went to in the Karasid dynasty we were told a different love story. In fact, there are such sorrowful love stories that
resulted in wars. There is a place to the west of the Karasid dynasty.
The natives call it the place watered by Scamander. Once upon a
time in that place, the happiest community of Trojans lived in the
unattainable Castle of Troy under the reign of King Priam. The
youngest son of King Priam fell in love with a queen from one of the
distant shores of the Aegean Sea and brought her to Priam's Castle
of Troy. Troy looked much like the Castle of Afrasiab. So, the kings
of all the Greeks opposed their love so much that they sent an incredible number of ships—so many that when they all arrived on the
Trojan coastline the surface of the sea was hardly visible. During
that long war blood flowed instead of water in Scamander River. Unable to bear the wailing of the bodies flowing in its waters the river
begged Achilles to quell his rage. Filled with anger and unable to
bear the pain of losing Patroclus, Achilles stopped at nothing. That
was when Scamander ran out of patience and pursued Achilles by
coursing his waters wildly. When he couldn't catch up with Achilles
he called his neighbour, the Simoeis River, to his aid. Knowing that
he couldn't deal with the waters of both rivers, Achilles asked for
help from the gods. However, the gods were only able to protect him
until the arrow lodged into his heel..."

Intently listening to Hacı Ilbey, who conveyed the formidable fight with great mastery and a silver tongue, Suleyman Pasha replied, "To tell you the truth, I am very curious about Troy and the Scamander River now..."

"They may not be real... but maybe they existed once upon a time. Or perhaps their names were changed along the way."

"Fine, we can find out whether they were real or not later but are all the supposed deeds of the Catalans here real?"

"Of course they are. Just like the Latins, they supposedly came here to provide aid but when they saw the rich Byzantine castles, they began plundering everything thinking that 'all castles are bounties that can be plundered'. When their plundering turned into savagery the Emperor made an excuse and diverted them to the Balkans. The Co-Emperor in Hadrianopolis held a feast in honour of Roger de Flor, the chief of the Catalans, upon their return. During the feast he put the chief and his men to the sword. The remaining Catalans left nothing standing as they withdrew to the west and south of Thrace in order to find shelter. Some of them are currently at the Castle of Pigas where we have had a bone to pick with them since they arrived. I hope that God allows us to live long enough to settle our score."

Suleyman Pasha replied to Hacı Ilbey, whom he was looking at over his shoulder as they walked, "Once we control this side of the strait, the other side will be easy to attain. We can corner them at Pigas if we campaign there from here and Orhan Ghazi campaigns from Bursa. But we should first build a bridge across the Dardanelles."

Looking at Suleyman Pasha, Hacı Ilbey was not aware that the rays of the setting sun, like a round metal tray of İznik red, were also turning his white hair red. He turned towards Gallipoli. After measuring the Dardanelles with his gaze, he smiled and said, "My Prince, you can even bring the seas to heel if you wish to, just like Xerxes I of Persia."

Before walking towards his stone-walled headquarters, Suleyman Pasha said, "Understood—you are going to tell the legends of these lands all day. I'd heard the story that Xerxes came here from Aşık Pasha in Bursa, but I'd never heard that he brought the seas to heel."

CHAPTER TWENTY-TWO

When the flat-tailed barge with sails bearing the double-headed Byzantine eagle pulled up near Chrysopolis[20] pier its three imperial carriages pulled by eight journey horses were brought ashore one after another. The Emperor's carriage was the second to be unloaded. On one side it had a flag embroidered with the imperial badge and a white peace envoy flag on the other. The third carriage was accompanied by goods and servicemen needed for the journey. The guards in the carriages stood in their basket-like partitions and the armoured knights atop their horses accompanying the carriages looked like Byzantine monuments.

A few days after the return of the envoys, who informed Orhan Ghazi that Emperor Kantakouzenos VI wanted to meet him, to Constantinople, messengers were sent to the *subaşı* of Chrysopolis—renamed by the Turks. On hearing the information delivered by the messengers the *subaşı* of Chrysopolis made the necessary arrangements to be taken on the pier and on the roads the Emperor would travel. He'd also arranged for a cavalry unit to accompany the procession of Emperor to the next castle. The new settlers of Chrysopolis, who had seen the cavalry unit ready at the pier that morning, had grown curious and ran to the harbour. When the spectacular imperial carriage was transported onto the pier they'd greeted it with shouts and applause. Impressed by this unexpected welcome, the Emperor stood up in his carriage and saluted the enthusiastic crowds. In the meantime, the wide-eyed, jubilating crowds were looking at the spectacle as if it were the carriage of Afrasiab, told of in tales they'd heard. Despite the fact that the new immigrants were so curious, the natives of Chrysopolis were nowhere to be seen. No one knew if they were cross with the Byzantine emperor or if they were very content with their new masters, or simply that they were too

---

20 T.N, *Chrysopolis* is also known as Scutari, currently named Üsküdar.

scared. The curtains of the imperial carriage were drawn yet Kantakouzenos VI couldn't see the natives of Chrysopolis amongst the immigrants, whom he referred to as 'the half-nudes', so he muttered, "They were probably too scared to come." However, after a short while, when he saw that the natives of Chrysopolis who had been Byzantines for a long time, had come out to the pavements in groups to wave at him, he thought, "Perhaps it is not a matter of fear but one of resentment!" A short period of time later when he realised that those out on the streets hadn't come out to see him but rather his spectacular carriage, a sense of emptiness spread within him. He mumbled between his thick lips, "Haven't they got used to their new lives very quickly?" Just as his lips stopped moving, he felt a squirm inside, "Do our people, whom we have not been able to look after, have any other choice than to appear sweet to their new master?" As if to resent the sudden exit of this opportunist sentiment from his mouth he made a wry face and noticed the dryness of his lips. He turned around and asked the servant at the back of the carriage for water. He drank the water from a silver tankard extended to him from behind the curtain and vacantly continued looking outside.

As the well-fed horses harnessed to the carriage gained speed, Chrysopolis and the people standing on the pavements were left behind and the road became narrower as it ran between orchards stretching as far as the eye could see. Some of the fruit trees had long lost their leaves while some others still had some fruit and autumnal leaves. Looking at the fruit trees, decorated with hundreds of shades of colour, Kantakouzenos VI muttered, "If it was the olden days I'd have stopped the carriage and picked some fruit off the trees. I liked picking fruit even if I didn't eat it. In those days a sense of joy coursed through me from my fingertips as they touched the fruit. I used to make various excuses to prolong those joyous moments and lingered under the trees. But now, let alone touch the fruit, I don't even want to look at the orchards. In our youthful years, Andronicus and I used to visit these parts frequently. I never ate the fruit I picked back then either but I received great gratification from touching them."

After reminiscing about days of his youth for a while he realised that sweet slumber was encasing his body. He hopelessly tried to shake off the numbing effect of sleepiness but sleep embraced his body with its tender arms and pulled him to its cosy and warm bosom. He slept sweetly until their first stop, Pentikion[21].

When Emperor John VI Kantakouzenos stepped from his carriage he felt pins and needles in his legs. He smiled and thought, "Old age is pounding at my door. When we came here with Andronicus to hunt we used to spend the entire day on horseback but we never got pins and needles. Now I can't even stand travelling for a few hours." Seeing Aydos Hill to the north he mumbled, "I see that Aydos, through which wild cold waters flow, still hasn't stopped protecting the castle from the north wind. I wonder if Orhan knows he has much prey in these lands..." Just as he finished his train of thought, he heard a voice inviting him to listen. The man was speaking the Emperor's language. Kantakouzenos followed the man to his quarters where he would get some rest and when they arrived in front of the door to his quarters he turned around and told his servant, "We shall stay here for me to rest my knees for a bit. We can continue our journey in a while. The quicker we get there and back the better..."

As the Emperor entered the resting room of the guest house his servant ran to the commander of the Emperor's guard. He conveyed what the Emperor had told him and returned to the guest house and began waiting in front of the door of the room Kantakouzenos VI had just entered. Knowing that the Emperor liked his sleep the servant thought they would be there for a considerable amount of time, but that wasn't the case. The Emperor, who had gone into the room to rest, lost his sleepiness as soon as he lay on the wide bed and

---

21 T.N, Known as *Pentikion* or *Pantikion* during the Byzantine era, it is currently a district of Istanbul called Pendik.

changed his mind about taking a rest. He said, "I'd rather make way than lay around without sleeping," and left the room. He told his servant waiting for him in front of the door to tip the inn-keeper.

Then he ordered for everyone to set forth once again. The guards and the guides, who didn't like to wait on standby in places of rest, were happy to hear they were going to be on the move again. In actual fact, Emperor John VI Kantakouzenos neither wanted to leave Constantinople nor make this journey at all but he was forced to in order to escape the responsibility of Suleyman Pasha's crossing of the Dardanelles. He thought that if he met Orhan Ghazi face to face he would be able to solve this problem but he smelled a rat as soon as his imperial carriage left the city. His mind kept repeating the same thought, "What if they take advantage of my absence and make a move?" This same thought was what made him lose his drowsiness when he went into the resting room at the inn, and that was why he almost instantly left the room. He thought of telling his servant, "Come on, we are going back," but he had kept quiet because he was too embarrassed to say it. He knew very well that if he returned to the city he would have had to account for everything to his Co-Emperor John V Palaiologos and his arch-enemy in Constantinople, the Patriarch. Or perhaps, hearing of his return, Patriarch John XIV of Constantinople would come running to his palace to try to humiliate him by jeering and saying, "Has our beloved emperor returned so soon because he didn't have faith in us?"

Emperor Kantakouzenos could stand many things but he could never stand being mocked. He didn't want to return to the old contentious days again. Especially now that one of her daughters was in Bursa, belonging to the Ottomans, and the other in the palace of the Co-Emperor, his wife Irene was empress, his eldest son Matthew had become the governor of Hadrianopolis, thanks to an unexpected opportunity, and had also received the title of imperial co-partner. His younger son Manuel had become the Despotēs of Morea while his youngest son headed towards Thessaly. Empress Anna, who had made his life into hell after the death of Emperor Andronicus, had voluntarily distanced herself from Constantinople for now. His son-in-law and also Co-Emperor John V Palaiologos was gradually accepting his command. Thinking of all the advantages he had, Kantakouzenos put away the thought of returning and got back into his imperial carriage once again as he muttered, "Neither will I return nor will I let anyone mock me. It is only expected that there will be those who are jealous of the happiness I've been endowed with."

As the imperial carriage sped towards Nicomedia the Emperor continued similar internal monologues. He didn't want to but the same chain of thoughts kept appearing in his mind with the suspicions he had inside. Emperor Kantakouzenos VI didn't shut his mind to such thoughts believing that his suspicions might be assuaged but no matter what he did they weren't. The suspicions squeezed his heart tight in their grasp. He hadn't had breakfast in the morning to avoid being seasick and it was now afternoon and he still hadn't eaten anything. Before resuming their journey, his servant had made the taster try the food and brought it to him, but now the food was cold. At one point he looked out the open window of his carriage to distract himself and to flick away the suspicion he had inside like a ball of felt, but he failed. When he returned to his inner world once again, he realised that his decision should have been to return. Just as he reached out to pull the string of the small bell hanging next to his head servant, who was seated next to the driver, his daughter Helena, with the fairest face, appeared before his eyes. As his daughter looked at him with bulging, black, clever eyes and a crestfallen expression on her face she said, "Father, don't do this."

Hearing his daughter's face echoing from the depths of the world, Emperor Kantakouzenos VI tilted his head down as if he was ashamed of his thought of returning. His hand extending to the string of the small bell was left in the air. He stood up and held the handle on the ceiling of the carriage. As he stretched his legs to both sides to balance himself, he drew back the curtain from the window on the other side with his free hand. For a while, he watched the well-fed horses gallop as if they were racing with the wind. The speed of the horses momentarily made him feel the excitement of a race. He felt his suspicions shrink as that excitement he felt inside grew. After sitting down, assisting each movement of his body with a grip on the handles, he looked at the pewter lid of the food container on the low table by his knee. The moment he extended his hand and touched the lid of the container his hunger suppressed all his thoughts. He began eating his food. His servant, watching him eat through the gap in the curtain that separated the carriage from the rear section, tidied up everything quickly once he was finished and shut the curtain. The Emperor informed his servant that he did not want a drink and, caressing his stomach full of food, lay down on the sofa. As he looked out the window that extended from behind him, he heard the voice of the driver. Whenever they passed by a castle, he would announce the name of the castle out loud. This time the driver had announced, "Libyssa!"

The guides, consisting of Ottoman cavalrymen who were not used to this tradition, slowed down their horses just as they did every time the driver called the castle names, but seeing as the carriages were following them with great speed they spurred their horses on. Watching Libyssa Castle for a while, tiredness set in Kantakouzenos's eyes just as it had done in the morning, his body becoming heavy, he dropped into a deep sleep.

Emperor Kantakouzenos awoke when the sunlight filled the carriage through its back window. He crossed himself and sat up. He was mesmerised when he saw the red light percolating on the gulf to his right playing with the blue twinkle of the sea. When he realised that a crystalline twinkle such as this was seldom seen in the restless waters of the Bosphorus, he called out to the gulf, continuing to view its effervescent beauty, "Oh Astacus! You are truly more colourful than our Bosphorus and the Golden Horn. I now understand why John II Komnenos risked his head over you and why Maria Palaiologos didn't want to come to Constantinople. They must have both noticed your beauty before us. In any case, the princess didn't live long after she left this beauty—she couldn't bear the absence of it."

They arrived at the castle they called Nicomedia, which the Ottoman's referred to as the dormitory of Akça Kocain, in the late evening, but since Prince Halil was campaigning in the south of the Beylik with Orhan Ghazi at the time, Aygut Bey was the acting castle commander. Receiving the news that the imperial carriage was approaching the castle, Aygut Bey ordered the servants to prepare the large room that was once the quarters of Maria Palaiologos for Emperor Kantakouzenos VI. Despite the fact that the imperial carriage arrived at the castle much later than expected, a prosperous welcome was provided. A delicious breakfast was served in the morning and with magnificent ceremony, he was bid farewell on his way to Nicaea.

From the moment he set foot in the castle until the time of his departure, Byzantine emperor Kantakouzenos was surprised by the invisible yet respectful order at the castle. Their services were provided fully but no one had been seen around. Nor had he seen the castle commander except during the welcoming and the departure ceremonies. Despite the fact that he at first wanted to converse with him, the thought that an emperor can only converse with a sovereign who is his equal changed his mind about wanting to talk to him.

When the horses arrived at Praenetos after circling the cape of Astacus stretching towards the lake, the sun was yet to rise above the Samanlı Peaks to shed its light on the blue waters of Astacus. The waves slowly licking the shore seemed to lay the coolness of the morning on the wayside and call out for the heat of the sun. Listening to the sound made by the splash of the small waves on the shore for a while, Kantakouzenos VI emptied his mind of all thoughts as he looked at the serene vastness of the blue waters until he reached the Praenetos Castle, which was famed for its paper similar to Egyptian parchment. Regardless of the fact that the castle was now referred to by the Ottomans by the name of the first Ottoman bey who entered the castle, to him the castle overlooking Astacus was still Praenetos for the Byzantines.

Seeing that the priest standing next to the sanjak bey, who was welcoming the imperial carriage at the entrance of the castle was acting as interpreter, Emperor Kantakouzenos thought, "He certainly has learnt the language of the Ottomans quickly!" Despite the fact that the sanjak bey insisted they should rest for a while, the Emperor returned the kindness by declining gently, "Orhan Bey will be waiting for us at Nicaea... It would be best if we continue on our way, we wouldn't want to make him wait."

Once the guides of the sanjak bey of Praenetos Castle had taken their places, they immediately set forth again.

CHAPTER TWENTY-THREE

As the sun rose over the Dardanelles tearing the blue of the sky over the Mysian Olympus, Suleyman Pasha and his entourage were riding their horses towards the bay where their temporary marquees were set up. All the beys with whom he'd previously stepped foot on the Tzympe coastline were with him. Looking at the bay decorated with the prince's marquee set up by Balabancıkoğlu's men and the colourful tents for the beys, Suleyman Pasha addressed Evrenos Bey, "This should be the first stopover for our forces travelling across the sea."

Evrenos Bey looked at Hacı Ilbey, standing on the other side of Suleyman Pasha, as if seeking his support, "This location is good for a stopover for now, My Bey."

Hacı Ilbey sensed Evrenos Bey's plan. After a dry cough, he said, "Tomorrow is another day My Bey... If we transport the forces other than those currently across the shore to here, neither this bay nor this peninsula will be big enough to contain all of us. As you know the Genoese are constantly travelling between these shores to transport our forces. If it continues like this, we will have to ask for more infantry to be sent from Bursa..."

Evrenos Bey smiled and said, "We did well to offer a fee to the Genoese, knowing that they will receive their money they work day and night."

Suleyman Pasha replied, "If only we had the power to seize the other ships crossing the strait we could get them to transport a greater contingent of infantry and cavalryman from the opposite shore."

With his usual patient tone of voice, Hacı Ilbey assuaged Suleyman Pasha, "Don't worry, My Bey. Now that we have set foot on these lands, what can stop us from having control over the seas?"

Until they got off their horses, they quietly watched the Genoese

ships and barges sailing towards the opposite shore as if they had
been sprinkled upon the sea.

The Genoese, who had been waiting for villagers to bring goods to
stock their ships at Maydos harbour, knew that the opportunity they
had was a godsend and had immediately begun work. They were
restless and tireless with the idea that if they worked really hard they
could increase their fee with every trip they made. Since the fee for
their first trip was paid on time, they'd put their shoulder to the
wheel and were taking shifts in transporting the Ottoman infantry
and cavalryman from Abydos to Maydos. The only thing that made
their work hard was the insufficient number of piers to which the
barges could dock. Near Sestos, there was also a very old harbour
but since the pier was too damaged, the barges couldn't be moored
to them. According to some rumours, the harbour was turned into
ruins by the Byzantines in order to stop the Persians from approaching their castles. Others said it was to keep away Macedonians, while
others stated it was because the Byzantines were sick of the cruelty of
the Latins. Thus, the harbour was never used by the people of Sestos,
settled away from the shore. Even the fishermen of Sestos dropped
anchor at Maydos harbour. Even though the Genoese sailors who
looked after the old harbour deplored the situation, they just waited
their turn because there was nothing else to be done. Taking turns,
they moored their barges at the piers, emptied their cargo and
sculled their oars hard and sailed out towards Abydos straight away.
After watching the ardent work of the Genoese for a while with a
smile on his face, Suleyman Pasha walked into his newly set up marquee. Looking at the breakfast trays at the entrance of his marquee
with the same smile he said, "Beys, let's sit down for the breakfast we
have been waiting to enjoy for some time. Once we have eaten to our
heart's content we can talk over our plans."

The beys headed to pick up the breakfast trays in groups of three,
as if they knew what he was going to say and sat down on the floor

cross-legged. Suleyman Pasha, Evrenos Bey and Hacı Ilbey were sharing food from the same tray. Not paying heed to the orderly work carried out by footmen, Suleyman Pasha recalled the previous night while chewing his first bite. For some reason, he'd wanted to be alone for a while after hearing the bridge story of Xerxes I as told by Hacı Ilbey. He had retired to his room and begun to compare the great Persian king with his father's Beylik. While comparing them, he had also thought about the harem his mother established for him in Bursa. After a short while, he had heard a knock on his door and saw his messenger appear at the edge of the door, "Hacı Ilbey has sent a lady accompanied by Evrenos Bey's man to meet you, My Bey."

Dressed in his princely attire he felt as if he was a guest in the room. He replied, "Show them both in, the lady and Evrenos Bey's man."

The tall and fair woman with greyish-blue eyes, who had been watching him from a distance since the day he arrived at the castle, entered the room dressed in red garments that complemented both her complexion and figure. She bowed down and saluted the prince and in return, the prince showed her to her seat. And, as he sat down on the relatively higher divan he inhaled the spring-like scent of the woman. Gazing at her shapely body that suited her height, he addressed the interpreter, Evrenos Bey's man, "Ask her who she is and what she wants from me. She had also told me she had things to tell me when she appeared before me on the street. Ask her what she was going to tell me—I am all ears."

Having been referred to as bright as a button by Evrenos Bey, the interpreter conveyed what Suleyman Pasha said word by word. The woman felt relieved hearing the man's calm and reassuring voice. With her soft and flat voice emerging from her slender neck, she replied, "My name is Antiope Illonnai—I was given my mother's middle name. The people of the castle usually distance themselves from me. I have been living in this castle alone for many years. I make a living by selling the hand-made fabrics brought to me by villagers at the stall I set up every Sunday."

Upon Evrenos Bey's man's translation, Suleyman Pasha asked, "Why does she live alone, doesn't she have parents or a husband?"

The woman's bluish-grey gaze sunk in sorrow when Evrenos Bey's man translated Suleyman Pasha's question, but she managed to keep her voice neutral, "The Catalans killed my father before they left the castle and took my mother with them, who wasn't even twenty years of age. I was only a little baby then. The people of the castle consider me to be ill-boding because they think that the calamity that befell my family is related to my birth. I grew up under the protection of the church like so many others my age did in this castle. When I was old enough to marry, I married a young man who had grown up under the guardianship of the church, like me. My husband began to work on the Genoese ships. It must be that God didn't foreordain happiness to me that my husband, who travelled to distant provinces a few times didn't return from his last journey. Some said that the ship he worked on was captured by pirates and some others said the ship foundered off somewhere in a storm. I believed all the rumours, but despite them waited for my husband's return for years, but all the waiting was to no avail... This deemed me even more ill-boding to the people of the castle, which in turn made me even lonelier. There is no one I can talk to in this castle other than the villagers I buy goods from..."

As Suleyman Pasha listened to the woman's story through the interpreter's flat voice he was also casting his gaze on the beauty of the woman's fair neck. When the interpreter fell quiet, Suleyman Pasha suddenly said, "So, what does the lady want from me?"

The woman, listening to the translation of Suleyman Pasha's sentence, experienced the frustration of being unable to speak the words she had on her mind. Sensing the woman's frustration, Suleyman Pasha softened his voice and asked, "What can I do for her?"

Antiope's bluish-grey eyes sparkled upon comprehending that Suleyman Pasha softened his question intelligently from the way the interpreter repeated the question. Shrugging off her frustration, she replied to Evrenos Bey's man, "I am a capable woman. I see that the servants of your bey are yet to arrive. I would be happy to serve your bey until his servants arrive and if he likes my work, I would like to stay on as one of his servants."

Just as Suleyman Pasha figured out that the woman desired to be close to him for protection, he recognised also that the vibration of his heartstrings had changed. The gaze of the woman no longer resonated fear as it did in the initial moments of their meeting but was now penetrating his soul. Sensing that his heart was beating faster, Suleyman Pasha addressed the interpreter, "Tell the lady to go home now. I will inform her of my decision tomorrow."

As the interpreter translated the last sentence, the warmth in Antiope's gaze trickled down into Suleyman Pasha's heart and he couldn't stop thinking about her. Upon Hacı Ilbey's approval, with whom he discussed the matter early next morning, Suleyman Pasha accepted the woman into his service at his marquee.

While his beys heartily ate their breakfast, what made him delve into such thoughts was the decision that he had made. After almost finishing his breakfast he muttered, "I shouldn't have made this decision so hastily." And, as he swallowed his last bite, he had almost decided that the woman could wait a bit longer after all the lonesome years she spent but he heard voices emanating from the rear end of the marquee and got distracted. Wiping his hand with a damp cloth, he reverted back to his original decision and muttered, "It's too late now." He stood up and got out of the triangular door of the marquee with his head tilted down. He walked towards the marquee of the military quarters. Once everyone was seated cross-legged on the divans inside the military quarters Suleyman Pasha said, "My Beys, our next aim is to capture the Gallipoli Fortress."

Then, he observed their faces to assess their reactions.

Evrenos Bey replied, "That's the most important castle in all of the Dardanelles. If we take Gallipoli under our command, we will have absolute control over the Dardanelles. We must be cautious not to alert the ships docked at the harbour. The Genoese have transported a sufficient number of irregular light cavalry, infantries and cavalryman to lay siege on the castle from land, but in order to have full control over the harbour we need more *levends.*"

Hacı Ilbey agreed with Evrenos Bey, "We cannot leave before we capture Gallipoli. Evrenos Bey is right—first we have to seize the harbour in order to stop the news reaching Kostantiniyye and to deter the Byzantine troops from coming here. We should gather voluntary units of *levends* who previously participated in maritime invasions alongside Karasid raiders."

After the opinions of the other beys were respectively listened to, tasks were delegated amongst them in order to proceed with the siege of Gallipoli as well as to advance in Thrace. Fazıl Bey and Balabancıkoğlu were given the responsibility of managing communications with the new castle commanders and organising the irregular light cavalry. Akça Kocaoğlu and Evrenos Bey were given the responsibility of welcoming and transporting the forces brought in by ships and barges as well as the management of deployment to the Gallipoli pier while Hacı Ilbey was appointed as the infantry commander, and Ece Bey was to become the right-hand man of Suleyman Pasha. Suleyman Pasha also had the duty of commanding the cavalry. After being delegated with their duties, the beys bid farewell to each other as they usually did after every meeting. However, they were as happy as if they were going to see each other the next day.

In the afternoon of that day, as the small groups of irregular light cavalry headed out to block Byzantine armies from the north and the northwest, the infantry and cavalryman located at the military quarters completed their preparations and set forth to lay siege on the Gallipoli Fortress over land.

Suleyman Pasha, who was in close correspondence with the leading troops, had no idea why his horse, advancing under the dark yellow, honey-like light of the autumnal full moon like a white pheasant suddenly stopped. As he gazed around him, surprised by his horse's lasting pause, his glance focussed in the direction of the Byzantine Sea of Marmora. Watching the motion of the silvery phosphorescence on the waves, he mumbled, "It's as if the phosphorescence is riding the waves." He felt like getting off his horse and running towards the sea but his Grey, sensing his thoughts, turned his head to the east and walked. Suspicious of his horse's ill-temper, Suleyman Pasha carefully observed his surroundings and saw the steep cliff a few steps ahead. As he caressed the mane of his Grey, he heard footsteps approaching him.

CHAPTER TWENTY-FOUR

The horses pulling Emperor Kantakouzenos VI's imperial carriage diverted from the wide road by the lake, advancing down the path between endless vineyards and gardens, as if to race against the north wind blowing against their chests. The carriage was filled with the sweet scent of ripe fruit. Breathing in the fruit-scented air the Emperor thought, "I'd heard about the outstanding grapes of this region, but I had no idea that such a rich variety of fruit was being grown here." He put his head out of the open window and looked to the rear of the carriage. He gasped with astonishment when he saw the purplish colour reflected onto the sky from the lake, which he was able to catch a glimpse of now and then from between the tree branches. As he looked at the blue lake, which had still not shaken off its morning slumber, and the bright sun hovering above it, he mumbled, "This is a game of yours, too." Just then he came back to his senses because of the rocking carriage. He sat down on the settee holding the rails on either side. He mumbled, "The Ottomans are neither destroying the castles nor ruining the vineyards."

For a while, he idly sat. When he was tired of sitting he started looking at the colourful leaves decorating the branches of the sea of trees on either side of the road. The powerful horses harnessed to the carriage speedily advanced through the lowlands and the gardens decorating the hillside after the plains. He continued to look out of the window of his carriage until the horses began to gallop through the hills where a dense forest of Turkish pine trees was visible. Seeing that the conifer trees were relatively greener than the other trees, he deducted, "Broad-leaved trees are for cooling the plains, and conifer trees are for warming the cold breeze blowing from the mountains". He made a wry face as if he didn't like his train of thought. He glanced at the blueberry bushes, which

looked like baffled guests unsure of where they should sit amongst
the fir trees that seemed to get gradually taller as the imperial carriage advanced.

He saw Trikokia Castle situated atop the hill opposite him but the
scenery fell distant from his gaze as he continued watching the trees.
His gaze became distanced from himself as if it slid back into the
past and took him back to his youth. He recalled the time when he
and Co-Emperor Andronicus stood beside each other and read the
inscription on the interior of the castle wall that read, "Trikokia, the
Byzantine lantern extinguished by the Latins." His eyes filled with
tears. As he felt a wave of tears on the brink of rolling down from his
eyes, he looked at the zenith of Mount Gürle and repeated, "The Byzantine lantern extinguished by the Latins." As he continued his journey in the past, the carriage worming its way through the hills suddenly arrived at a valley decorated by a lush vastness of trees. The
bright green of the trees, initially viewed panoramically from the carriage, slowly mixed into the blue sky viewed from between trees.
Then, as the flora became denser the castle disappeared from sight.
The Emperor felt strange inside when the branches of the trees on
either side of the road formed a canopy. He felt claustrophobic and
tried to ease his nerves by consoling himself, "I've waited long
enough and I couldn't have waited any longer. Apparently, you were
in dispute with the Beylik of Dulkadir, and Orhan had to visit them
to straighten it out. If you didn't want to meet me, you shouldn't
have replied to my letter positively. I put my empire at risk and came
all the way here, where *you* wanted to meet me. If you had taken a
step towards me, we could have deliberated and come to an agreement. But you didn't show up. That means you don't want to meet
me and that you know about what's happening in Thrace. On my
way here I thought that you didn't know about it and that, in fact, if
we reached an agreement you could get your forces to retreat back to
Anatolia. Just the possibility of that was enough to ease my nerves.

But now I know that not only do you know about it all but you also want to stay in Thrace, just like your son. I set forth on this journey to solve our problems peacefully but by not showing up, you have lost your chance. I will now abandon any hope I had for peace as Antigone Castle and Lake Ascania disappear into the distance. As of now, we are forced to cooperate with those who don't want you there."

The carriage left the road with the dense forests on either side and began to advance down a road that was relatively brighter. Kantakouzenos spoke out loud, "I am the one with least blame even though I am returning empty-handed from this journey. I am at peace because I did all I could even if the Palaiologos won't see it that way because of their hollow Athenian pride." He had spoken out loud because he knew that the best way to suppress the distress he felt inside was to think out loud. He was just about to shout out, "Athenian pride" when the gods of Olympus came to his mind. While he thought about the gods he also thought about Nicaea. And, right then, he was reminded of how Dionysus knelt down before Nicaea and begged her. He was trying hard to muster up a cunning smile that looked out of place on his thick lips when he seemingly became very confused. Sitting in the carriage he bristly blurted another train of thought, "I saw red when the priest of Hagia Sophia, a small church, which witnessed council meetings that were previously never witnessed by any other church, met me and told me, 'We can comply with the Ottomans—if we can carry out the conditions of our religion as we wish and speak our own language, what else can we ask for? Bursa is not far from us and our co-religionists, as well as our clergymen are just as free as we are and can speak their own languages. There is an immense difference between what's said about the Ottomans and what they actually do. When the people of Bursa were under Byzantine rule, they only had enough money to get by after they paid all their taxes. Whereas now they pay the Ottomans their taxes in accordance with what they think would be fair. In the meantime, here, the face of poverty left behind from the times of the Latins is still visible on the walls of our castles.'"

He scowled with anger. Then he tried to watch the scenery in order to get rid of the troublesome thoughts in his head but he couldn't relax. His mind became more and more lucid. He likened himself to an old fir tree on the side of the road. As he looked at it he muttered, "The grandeur and shade of everything increases when it grows old." He got angry with himself for thinking so. He hastily mumbled, "The dark shadow above Byzantium is one that is cast by the Palaiologos." He took a few consecutive and deep breaths as if to shoo away the thoughts he thought of about himself and waved his hand as if to clear them away. He was still anxious. He took his walking stick leaning against the door of the carriage and grabbed its handle with both hands. He placed his chin on his hands and recited all the prayers he knew.

He thought he had found peace of mind when he blurted out once again, "The Ottomans know how to keep what they bring with themselves and what already exists in the places they go. Perhaps that is the reason behind their permanence." Byzantine Emperor Kantakouzenos VI's old body sunk with exhaustion after dealing with the ebb and flow of the thoughts in his mind. His eyelids became heavy. He lied down on the settee and delved into a deep sleep as he listened to the sound of wheels turning on dry leaves.

Kantakouzenos VI woke up when they arrived at the first rest stop on the north skirt of the mountain. Upon seeing the Gulf of Astacus begin where the plains decorated with orchards ended, he spoke in a soft yet forced tone of voice, "I see we have passed over the mountain."

His servant replied, "Yes, Your Majesty, we will be setting forth again after we allow the horses some rest by the springhead over there. According to your guarding commander, we will be in Praenetos in a few hours."

The skin on the Emperor's forehead became creased as he got out of the carriage—as if he found it difficult. As soon as he had alighted he shivered, as he was sweaty and there was a cold breeze blowing in his direction. Noticing that the Emperor was cold, the servant brought his coat and helped him put it on. Followed by his head servant, the Emperor walked to the water surrounded by fir trees. He drank the water served to him in a silver tankard. As he passed the tankard back to his servant he looked at him and said, "Oh Cronus, you are as noble and as powerful as your name... The air is cold but we must not set out before eating something by this spring."

Head servant Cronus, who had been in the Emperor's service for years and was the only person to ever serve him except when the Emperor was sick, did not want the Emperor to snack amongst the guards but he couldn't reject the Emperor's wishes. He ran to the servants' carriage. Left alone, Emperor Kantakouzenos VI recalled that he had never voiced such a request before and thought that perhaps his desire to be an emperor was waning. He felt strange because of the thoughts coursing through his mind. Unable to bear the weakness of his knees, which he bent so that neither the servants at the back nor the guards at the front could see just how fatigued he was, he leaned his back against a tree by the water and knelt down. The question, "What remains of my empire?" coursed through his mind as he knelt down and he was even more confused. He muttered, "What's happening to me?" as his cook brought him Nicaean flatbread, cooked over charcoal and dipped in honey. The Emperor ate the honey-dipped flatbread made with various fruits and flour with gusto, filled his silver tankard from the cold spring, and drank the cool water. As he handed his tankard to his servant he said, "Cronus, would you summon the guarding commander?"

The head servant ran to the guarding commander immediately.

When the commander appeared before the Emperor, Kantakouzenos looked at him and said, "Tell the guides that we will continue our journey without stopping at the castles en-route. I want to return to Constantinople at once. Send forth advance guards as a precaution and get them to deliver the news that we will not be stopping over at their castles to the castle commanders so that they can ready our guides before we arrive at their castles."

The commander instantly started carrying out the Emperor's orders. He first informed the guides of the change of plans and then sent the advance guards on their way. He told his men that they would continue travelling with short breaks. The horses were harnessed to the carriages once again. The Emperor saw the rampant waters of the Bosphorus from the hills of Chrysopolis two days after the horses set out with concerted steps. In a tired and reproachful tone of voice, the Emperor whispered, "So that is where our bad luck began."

CHAPTER TWENTY-FIVE

The sky had been closing in on the mountains, the knees of the earth, for days and asked the black clouds to help appease its children's tears, trailing like vines from the sky to the earth. The earth looked at the sky with sorrow, hiding a cunning smile in her eyes, and muttered in relief, "The more tears your children shed the more fertile I become." Unaware of the stalemate between the earth and the sky, Suleyman Pasha was sick and tired of being stuck in his quarters for days. He kept walking up and down the section of his marquee set up for gatherings and as he did so, he likened himself to an idle shadow. His broad and upright shoulders, which added grandeur to his appearance at all times, seemed to have weakened and sunken after the long wait. It was as if they were sinking deeper into his body with every step he took. He momentarily thought that alongside his sunken posture, his entire body was also being shred to pieces and that the shadow he thought he possessed was shattered to smithereens. He desperately turned his head to either side like a snared tiger. He lethargically decided to go and lie down on his bed when Hacı Ilbey entered the marquee with his impermeable coat made of felt. As he took his coat off he said, "My Bey, I thought it would be good to chat since we are both unable to sleep. I didn't send a messenger to you to inform you of my arrival as I decided to come on the spur of moment. But I think I can say that I do regret having left my quarters in the rain—it's raining as if the sky had been torn open.

Suleyman Pasha was pleasantly surprised at Hacı Ilbey's visit, especially because he was so bored. "Hacı, I have also been very bored. I have not been able to leave the marquee for two days. You are right —it's raining as if the sky had been torn open. However, it is not only the skies that have been causing us grief but also the seas—it's as if they were overflowing."

"The people of these lands refer to such days as the day on which
the daughter of the goddess of rain was taken by the sea. According
to myth, the sea is said to bang its head against the shores because of
the guilt it feels for taking the daughter of the goddess of rain."

With the relief of having someone to talk to, Suleyman Pasha sat
down on one of the mattresses situated in the spacious section of his
marquee. He looked at Hacı Ilbey's face glistening like beeswax in
the light of the oil lamps. They both looked like shadows in this dim
light. Surrounded by those colourful oil lamps, he listened to the
sound of the rain for a while. He blinked a few times and said, "It
seems that you'll be brightening our dark evening with your presence, Hacı Ilbey. When I was a child, my mother used to gather us all
in one room and tell us tales in Greek and Turkish when my father
was away on his campaigns. It was always Murad who first fell
asleep to my mother's tales. Despite the fact that he fell asleep, the
next day he was somehow always able to retell the story my mother
told us with only minor differences in the storyline. In any case, they
were just tales and they remain hidden in our childhood. The legends
you and Evrenos Bey tell truly appeal to me even if I don't believe
them to be real. Also, they seem to somehow rid me off my worries."

Hacı Ilbey inspected Suleyman Pasha's face and replied, "I am not
nearly as good a story-teller as your mother, Nilüfer Hatun, but if
the stories I tell help you forget your worries, then I am happy to tell
you more. If you allow me, tonight I shall tell you the legend of
Helle, which I heard at the Hüdavendigâr[22] headquarters many years
ago. According to this legend, many years before our time, these
lands were the heaven of the gods and goddesses created by people.
One of those gods was Athamas, the son of Aeolus who was the ruler
of winds, who married a cloud nymph named Nephele. The couple
who were under the protection of the other gods and goddesses had

22 T.N, The "Hüdavendigâr Vilayet" (Hüdavendigâr Province) was one of the
   provinces of the Ottoman Empire. Today this province is named Bursa, but in
   this instance the author uses the Ottoman name instead.

two children, a boy and a girl. They named their son Phrixus and, their daughter Helle. As the young couple raised their children in that heaven of the gods, one day, Athamas, the son of the ruler of winds proclaimed he wanted to swim in the sea and climbed down to the shore. Seeing him approach, the azure sea excitedly began rippling and calling the young man to swim in its waters. Athamas couldn't turn down such an invitation, so he undressed and walked into the cool waters. As his warm skin cooled down while swimming in the refreshing waters, his strokes became longer. With those long strokes, he dove into the waves and swam far into the sea. Ino, a sea goddess who had been watching him from the back of her horse of waves since the moment Athamas walked into the sea, saw how the young man was getting tired and rode her horse of waves towards him. Seeing her approach, the young man asked for help and Ino took him into her warm arms and brought him to her sandy beach. The young man lied down on the beach for some time before waking up to her kisses. Gaining consciousness, he realised that he had fallen in love with Ino. He told her that he could no longer return to his wife Nephele because he wanted to marry Ino. Overjoyed with his decision, she accepted his hand in marriage. Together, they had two children. Nephele, the Goddess of Clouds, was so saddened by what had happened and cried so much that let alone rain, not even a single drop of water remained in her clouds. And when she could no longer shed tears from her clouds, the earth got scorched with drought. Seeing that other living creatures were exhausted by the drought, Nephele felt an overwhelming sense of guilt, which caused her further sorrow. As she wandered the earthly paradise she was unable to care for her children. Ino turned this into her advantage and immediately acted. She told her husband about her terrifying plan which she devised long ago. She told her husband, Athamas that if the drought continued all earthly creatures would cease to exist. Noticing that he was also saddened by this possibility she urged him,

"Athamas, I know how hard it is for you but if you don't sacrifice your eldest son, Phrixus, the earth will never be rid of drought."

Unable to decide his son's fate, Athamas lamented for days. But Ino repeatedly tried to convince him to sacrifice Phrixus, of whom she was jealous since the beginning. Unable to bear the groans of the earthly creatures Athamas finally decided to sacrifice his son and headed out. However, Nephele, who despite all her sorrow had been observing from above the clouds, found out about Athamas' intentions with the help of her father-in-law, Aeolus. She immediately put her son and daughter on the back of a golden-fleeced flying ram and sent them to Colchis situated to the east of Hellespont. She also left with them so that she could stall her ex-husband Athamas. Seeing her approach, the earth Athamas ordered her to give him the children with all his rage. In turn, Nephele began crying again. Unable to bear the sorrow shed from her tears, the other clouds also began to weep by turning the steam they borrowed from the gods into drops of rain. In that moment, flying under a cloud, the ram with the golden fleece got wet. Helle slipped off the golden-fleece and began to fall down towards the earth. Seeing her fall, Ino quickly moved to where Helle would fall. The Hellespont and the Black Sea, both of whom knew Ino was malevolent and only intended to harm Helle, hastily reached out and held the hands of the Aegean Sea. The straits of our day were back then, their arms. The reason why they held hands was so that they could flood where Helle would fall and delay Ino from finding her. And as such, these straits have existed since then, and that's how Hellespont got its name.

Noticing that his body was relaxing as he listened to Hacı Ilbey, Suleyman Pasha said, "My mind felt at ease while listening to the legend but I got quite furious with Ino. Was Phrixus saved?"

"He arrived at Colchis on the back of the golden-fleeced ram and was able to escape the fate of Ino's terrifying plan when a gracious ruler hid him in the dark forests."

ne miners[24] were able to reach the castle walls. Since no one
he inner castle was sent out, the people of the castle couldn't
found out what was happening in the castle. In the meantime,
ve completed assembling the bases of the counterweight treb-
."

yman Pasha replied in a deep tone of voice, "Perhaps, as you
esterday, luck is on our side..."

Ilbey stood up and replied, "My Prince, God is also on our

re he put his felt coat on and left the marquee, he saluted Su-
n Pasha with his head and said, "Good night."

After smiling softly, Suleyman Pasha said, "This legend reminds me
a little of the plan to sacrifice Ishmael..."

In his softest tone of voice, Hacı Ilbey replied, "I assume that this
legend and others like it were told in these lands before the time of
Ishmael because they are also in holy books. When we were little,
Karesioğlu, the father of Alcan Bey, a bey of the Karasid Dynasty,
paid close attention to our education, monitored our breaks and conversed with us. When he was in service of the Seljuks, Alcan Bey travelled a lot, fought in many wars and witnessed a great deal his lifetime. One day, after our arithmetic lesson, our mullah of fiqh[23]
recited the surah of Ibrahim to us as a story. After we all listened to
him I enquired, 'I had heard similar stories when I went to Baghdad
where the Seljuk Dynasty flourished. Why are there so many similar
stories?' The mullah replied, 'It is because Ash'ari tribe who lived in
these lands before us told the legend according to their heart's will.'
Since then, whenever I listen to a legend or a tale I add my own interpretation to it and enrich it. So to say, I also do what Prince
Murad does, I tell the stories I previously listened to in my own way."

"So, Hacı Ilbey, what you mean to say is if we add our own interpretation to the story we will help the story to be passed down from
generation to generation."

"Yes, in a way. What's important is that our interpretation of the
story has to embrace the flow of the legend."

When Suleyman Pasha laughed his wheat-coloured facial skin became taut and his shapely teeth glinted in the citron light of the oil
lamp. As his laughter faded, he gently inhaled and continued, "I miss
my mother's tales but the legends you tell are also fine. Just as my
mother's tales did, your legends teach me that this land I briskly
walk on does not only have a cultivated surface. Also, when comparing the good and the bad with both the kindness and cruelty they em-

---

N, Referred to here as "miners" are the "lağımcı", who dug out tunnels under
e castle walls and laid them with gunpowder to collapse the walls.

---

23 T.N, Fiqh is Islamic jurisprudence. It is an expansion of the code of conduct
(Sharia) expounded in the Quran, often supplemented by tradition (Sunnah) and
implemented by the rulings and interpretations of Islamic jurists.

body, I am also trying to find where I stand through the legends you tell me. Perhaps I am not solely good, or bad. It's as if I am somewhere in the middle. As if I am delivering kindness to those awaiting kindness and cruelty to those awaiting bad news."

After listening to Suleyman Pasha's concise but poignant explanation, Hacı Ilbey replied, "My Prince, you described yourself so well. I assume you know Dursun Bey of the Karasids, who studied with you in Bursa. His temperament was the same as yours. May he live long, Orhan Ghazi treated him the way he treated you, as a son. When he completed his education and left I was in Balıkistri, the centre of our dynasty, in service of Demür Khan, Dursun Bey's older brother. We'd sent a messenger to Orhan Ghazi as soon as we found out about the trap Demür Khan had set up for him immediately after Dursun Bey's arrival at the castle. But we couldn't save Dursun Bey, we got there too late. I pray to God that I will never witness cruelty inflicted on a brother by his brother."

Suleyman Pasha noticed that Hacı Ilbey was grieving, so he decided to leave him alone even if it would only last for the blink of an eye. After casting his gaze on the oil lamps, he thought about Hacı Ilbey who told him legends now and then, with whom he went horse racing, and who at times lent a sympathetic ear to him. He muttered, "I hope that none of us will experience such cruelty." Then, he looked at Hacı Ilbey again. As their eyes met, the door of the marquee was opened ajar. First, a cold breeze roamed the interior, and then a burly *serdengeçti* leader wearing a felt overcoat entered the marquee. After saluting Suleyman Pasha and dulcetly bowing his head to Hacı Ilbey he said, "My Beys, Fazıl Bey's messengers have arrived."

Suleyman Pasha turned towards Hacı Ilbey and said, "It must be important, seeing as Fazıl Bey sent his messengers to us in this horrid weather."

Then he turned to the *serdengeçti* leader, and commanded, "Show them in immediately."

The *serdengeçti* turned back, put his head o[ut] door of the marquee and invited them in. It was [...] outside entered the marquee when the messeng[er...] The messengers bowed to the beys. As one of t[hem] beside the *serdengeçti* leader, the other approach[ed...] expressed salaam and knelt before him. Tilting [...] messenger said, "Fazıl Bey ordered us to inform [...] two Byzantine messengers en-route to Gallipoli."

After looking at the drenched messengers, Sule[yman...] to Hacı Ilbey, "Hacı Ilbey, what should our cours[e...]

"Fazıl Bey should interrogate the messengers [...] situation. Once he is certain that he has all [...] should offer the men to go in his service. If they [...] tion, he should get them to join his service units. [...] to serve him, he should tell them they will be [...] there is one thing he shouldn't do, it is to send tl[...] tium."

Suleyman Pasha expressed that he agreed with [...] it would be best if Fazıl Bey decided himself. Th[...] *serdengeçti* leader and said, "Balaban Agha, pro[...] the messengers."

Fazıl Bey's messengers explained that their b[...] them for news from Suleyman Pasha and that [...] back as soon as possible, but Suleyman Pasha w[...] decision. He repeated, "Balaban Agha, these men [...] to leave before they change into dry clothes."

As soon as Balaban Agha and Fazıl Bey's messe[...] quee the wind died down and the sound of rain b[...] ticing the change outside, Hacı Ilbey said, "My Pr[ince...] rain has done some good. The people settled in tl[...] outside the castle did not notice our forces appr[...]

and [...]
from [...]
have [...]
we h[...]
uche[...]
Sul[...]
said [...]
Ha[...]
side.[...]
Bef[...]
leym[...]

24 [...]
t[...]

After smiling softly, Suleyman Pasha said, "This legend reminds me a little of the plan to sacrifice Ishmael..."

In his softest tone of voice, Hacı Ilbey replied, "I assume that this legend and others like it were told in these lands before the time of Ishmael because they are also in holy books. When we were little, Karesioğlu, the father of Alcan Bey, a bey of the Karasid Dynasty, paid close attention to our education, monitored our breaks and conversed with us. When he was in service of the Seljuks, Alcan Bey travelled a lot, fought in many wars and witnessed a great deal his life-time. One day, after our arithmetic lesson, our mullah of fiqh[23] recited the surah of Ibrahim to us as a story. After we all listened to him I enquired, 'I had heard similar stories when I went to Baghdad where the Seljuk Dynasty flourished. Why are there so many similar stories?' The mullah replied, 'It is because Ash'ari tribe who lived in these lands before us told the legend according to their heart's will.' Since then, whenever I listen to a legend or a tale I add my own interpretation to it and enrich it. So to say, I also do what Prince Murad does, I tell the stories I previously listened to in my own way."

"So, Hacı Ilbey, what you mean to say is if we add our own interpretation to the story we will help the story to be passed down from generation to generation."

"Yes, in a way. What's important is that our interpretation of the story has to embrace the flow of the legend."

When Suleyman Pasha laughed his wheat-coloured facial skin became taut and his shapely teeth glinted in the citron light of the oil lamp. As his laughter faded, he gently inhaled and continued, "I miss my mother's tales but the legends you tell are also fine. Just as my mother's tales did, your legends teach me that this land I briskly walk on does not only have a cultivated surface. Also, when comparing the good and the bad with both the kindness and cruelty they em-

---

23 T.N, Fiqh is Islamic jurisprudence. It is an expansion of the code of conduct (Sharia) expounded in the Quran, often supplemented by tradition (Sunnah) and implemented by the rulings and interpretations of Islamic jurists.

body, I am also trying to find where I stand through the legends you tell me. Perhaps I am not solely good, or bad. It's as if I am somewhere in the middle. As if I am delivering kindness to those awaiting kindness and cruelty to those awaiting bad news."

After listening to Suleyman Pasha's concise but poignant explanation, Hacı Ilbey replied, "My Prince, you described yourself so well. I assume you know Dursun Bey of the Karasids, who studied with you in Bursa. His temperament was the same as yours. May he live long, Orhan Ghazi treated him the way he treated you, as a son. When he completed his education and left I was in Balıkistri, the centre of our dynasty, in service of Demür Khan, Dursun Bey's older brother. We'd sent a messenger to Orhan Ghazi as soon as we found out about the trap Demür Khan had set up for him immediately after Dursun Bey's arrival at the castle. But we couldn't save Dursun Bey, we got there too late. I pray to God that I will never witness cruelty inflicted on a brother by his brother."

Suleyman Pasha noticed that Hacı Ilbey was grieving, so he decided to leave him alone even if it would only last for the blink of an eye. After casting his gaze on the oil lamps, he thought about Hacı Ilbey who told him legends now and then, with whom he went horse racing, and who at times lent a sympathetic ear to him. He muttered, "I hope that none of us will experience such cruelty." Then, he looked at Hacı Ilbey again. As their eyes met, the door of the marquee was opened ajar. First, a cold breeze roamed the interior, and then a burly *serdengeçti* leader wearing a felt overcoat entered the marquee. After saluting Suleyman Pasha and dulcetly bowing his head to Hacı Ilbey he said, "My Beys, Fazıl Bey's messengers have arrived."

Suleyman Pasha turned towards Hacı Ilbey and said, "It must be important, seeing as Fazıl Bey sent his messengers to us in this horrid weather."

Then he turned to the *serdengeçti* leader, and commanded, "Show them in immediately."

The *serdengeçti* turned back, put his head out of the triangular door of the marquee and invited them in. It was almost as if the rain outside entered the marquee when the messengers stepped indoors. The messengers bowed to the beys. As one of the messengers stood beside the *serdengeçti* leader, the other approached Suleyman Pasha, expressed salaam and knelt before him. Tilting his head down, the messenger said, "Fazıl Bey ordered us to inform you that we caught two Byzantine messengers en-route to Gallipoli."

After looking at the drenched messengers, Suleyman Pasha turned to Hacı Ilbey, "Hacı Ilbey, what should our course of action be?"

"Fazıl Bey should interrogate the messengers depending on the situation. Once he is certain that he has all the information, he should offer the men to go in his service. If they accept this proposition, he should get them to join his service units. If they don't agree to serve him, he should tell them they will be taken prisoner... If there is one thing he shouldn't do, it is to send them back to Byzantium."

Suleyman Pasha expressed that he agreed with Hacı Ilbey but that it would be best if Fazıl Bey decided himself. Then he turned to the *serdengeçti* leader and said, "Balaban Agha, procure dry clothes for the messengers."

Fazıl Bey's messengers explained that their bey was waiting on them for news from Suleyman Pasha and that they wanted to get back as soon as possible, but Suleyman Pasha was adamant in his decision. He repeated, "Balaban Agha, these men will not be allowed to leave before they change into dry clothes."

As soon as Balaban Agha and Fazıl Bey's messengers left the marquee the wind died down and the sound of rain became quieter. Noticing the change outside, Hacı Ilbey said, "My Prince, in a way this rain has done some good. The people settled in the neighbourhoods outside the castle did not notice our forces approaching the castle, and the miners[24] were able to reach the castle walls. Since no one from the inner castle was sent out, the people of the castle couldn't have found out what was happening in the castle. In the meantime, we have completed assembling the bases of the counterweight treb-uchets."

Suleyman Pasha replied in a deep tone of voice, "Perhaps, as you said yesterday, luck is on our side..."

Hacı Ilbey stood up and replied, "My Prince, God is also on our side."

Before he put his felt coat on and left the marquee, he saluted Su-leyman Pasha with his head and said, "Good night."

---

24 T.N, Referred to here as "miners" are the "lağımcı", who dug out tunnels under the castle walls and laid them with gunpowder to collapse the walls.

CHAPTER TWENTY-SIX

Emperor Kantakouzenos VI and his entourage were able to reach the hillside of Chrysopolis three days after their departure from Nicaea due to the high performance of the carriage horses. After gazing at Chrysopolis situated on the coast, at Constantinople across the water and the treacle black clouds up above his head, the Emperor dryly spoke to his guarding commander and carriage driver, "It seems we are going have some bad weather. We should cross the water with the first barges we can find. Summon the *subaşı* so we can meet him at the pier."

Hearing the Emperor's orders, the guarding commander passed on the orders of the Emperor to the sergeant of the irregular light cavalry who had been guiding them since Nicomedia and who instantly sent two of his men to the *subaşı* of Chrysopolis to deliver the Emperor's message. Shortly after the departure of the messengers, both of whom were expert horse riders, the Emperor got back into his carriage and the procession headed towards Chrysopolis pier. They were quietly advancing when it started spitting with rain. Emperor Kantakouzenos VI mumbled, "This rain will cease too, just like those before" as he watched the rainfall from the open window of the carriage. He tilted up his head, decorated with the imperial crown that made him look more statuesque than he actually was, and saw that the grey clouds were turning darker and darker. Then he hastily said, "I suppose this time it will last", as if to take back his previous assertion. He turned his head and asked the driver, "Can't we go faster?"

The driver lifted his head too. He looked at the ever-darkening sky and cracked his whip on the horses' backs. The rain gained power from the errant wind blowing in the sky as if it was waiting for the whip to come down on the horses' backs, and the large and heavy drops of rain began to beat against the imperial carriage. Holding his crown with one hand, the Emperor immediately pulled his head back inside the carriage and quickly closed the window on the upper section of the carriage door. He had just sat back when the rain came pouring down. Unable to see where they were going, the horses became uneasy. The experienced driver readily handed the reins and the whip to the head servant sitting next to him, got off the carriage and slowly led the horses towards the pier. When they arrived at the pier the earth and the sky had become completely blurred. The *subaşı*, who arrived at the pier just before the imperial procession, looked at the enraged waves of the Bosphorus swelling up with the unyielding wind and the heavy downpour. He briskly walked towards the Emperor. Using his interpreter as intermediary he addressed the Emperor, "Your Majesty, you cannot cross these waters under such conditions. You shall be our guest until the wind eases and the sea calms down."

Considering the danger posed by the swollen waves more than the incessant rain, Emperor Kantakouzenos VI replied, "You are right. I suppose we have to wait until the rain ceases. We are sorry to trouble you."

Listening to the Emperor's reply through the words of his interpreter the *subaşı* turned his horse towards the guest mansion closest to the pier. The Emperor arrived at the guest mansion alongside his procession after the *subaşı*. He felt depleted because of being unable to set out for the opposite shore as he planned. The Emperor entered the large room reserved for him at the mansion. He didn't leave his room or talk to anyone until the rain had stopped. He only spoke out loud to himself every other hour as he gazed at his beloved Constantinople, visible from his chambers. He lamented, "I departed from you several times. There were times when I thought I'd never see you again. But I never thought I could be so far from you when I am so near you." He uttered no other words other than these.

The rain poured down at the same speed for two whole days before it finally stopped. Though, it must have been that the wind's wings hadn't tired as the mad waves of the strait continued beating the coastline for one more day. When the wind completely eased off, not a single trace of Chrysopolis pier remained to be seen. All the wooden planks that once formed the pier had been washed away by the waves and only the stakes nailed into the sea bed were visible.

The *subaşı* of Chrysopolis observed that the Emperor was very upset for he couldn't see any positive outcome in all the damage. The *subaşı* immediately gathered all the carpenters residing in the neighbourhood and commissioned them to rebuild the pier. The Emperor stayed with the toiling carpenters. Once the final plank of wood was nailed onto the pier he regained a sense of happiness. He spoke to the treasurer in an uplifted tone of voice, "Reward all the carpenters who worked on rebuilding the pier."

The treasurer, who guarded the Emperor's treasury more than the Emperor himself, reluctantly gave pouchfuls of Byzantine coins to the carpenters. In turn, the carpenters responded to this generous reward by cheering the Emperor in his own language, "Long live Byzantine Emperor John Kantakouzenos!"

The Emperor felt elated hearing the rhapsody of their voices. He interrupted his silence by giving orders to his guarding commander, "Prepare the carriages—we must set forth at once!"

The guarding commander helplessly looked at the Emperor, bowing his head he replied, "Your Majesty, the owners of the barges hauled them to sheltered bays. It is impossible for us to set forth now. The earliest we can leave is tomorrow morning."

Furious with his guarding commander for not arranging the necessary means for travel, the Emperor suddenly became bewildered. He began screaming at the commander as if he had gone mad. Not even a shadow of the Emperor's previous jovial state of mind remained. The carpenters were watching the situation, awestruck, from a distance. The *subaşı* of Chrysopolis came to the rescue of the commander. After finding out the reason for the Emperor's rage he attempted to calm him down, "Your Majesty, I will immediately send my men to find large barges to transport you across the sea at once."

Seeing some reason in the *subaşi's* efforts to ease his nerves, the angry emperor became ashamed of his sudden outrage. He tilted his head down and walked towards the guest mansion. As he walked, he felt an overwhelming sense of fatigue washed over him as it was the case in recent times when he suddenly got angry at something. He arduously retired to his room as soon as he stepped into the mansion.

The guarding commander awoke the Emperor past midnight and said, "Your Majesty, the barges are moored at the pier. If you like we can set forth immediately."

Still angry at his guarding commander, the Emperor replied in a weary tone, "Yes, we shall."

At daybreak, when the imperial carriage arrived at the stone-paved square situated between the Balati pier and the castle, Emperor John VI Kantakouzenos stepped out of his carriage. He took a few deep breaths as he first cast his gaze on the dawn and then on the castle gates. Wondering about the fate that would meet him behind the shut gates, he muttered, "Almost every day I made up a story for my return. I wonder which one of the last paragraphs I composed to my various stories will come to be true..." He stepped back in his carriage. He wanted to get rid of all those made-up stories that crowded his mind, as the horses trotted towards the colossal iron-gate. As he endeavoured to brush away his fears he thought, "They are all just stories created by my apprehensions." He also mumbled, "In any case, none of them has a conclusive last paragraph." He was trying to create reasons suited to console himself. Somehow, all the last paragraphs were rendered "null and void" by the stories he had made up in his mind that overflowed with thoughts. As he irately looked at the gate that was still shut, he mumbled, "Only one of them had a closing paragraph", in a final attempt to stop the fearful thoughts that swarmed his mind. To no avail, apprehension and fear won. The first story he had in his mind unravelled, "The castle gates will be shut as soon as the guards and carriages enter. As my leading guards slowly ride their horses amidst the guards positioned around the square by Palaiologos V, Palaiologos's guards will seize the perfect moment to separate us from each other. The commander of Palaiologos's guards, who will have severed the communication between me and my men, will open the door of my carriage and declare, 'I'm arresting you in the name of John V Palaiologos, son of Emperor Andronicus.' The servants standing behind me will understand what is happening and they will attack Palaiologos's guards in a last collective attempt to save me. I will interfere in order to prevent bloodshed because the men have been so loyal to me. However, the unbiddable guards will arrest me and my men. As they strangle and kill my men in the vaults under the castle they will take me to one of the dungeons of the Blacharnea Palace where once imprisoned, I would never see the light of day again. After waiting for days, I will be put on trial but the verdict won't change.

As I await death in the dungeons only three people will come to visit me. First, Empress Irene will come and while she bids farewell, her quiet tears will pour out into the darkness of the dungeons. My daughter, Empress Helena will be the second person to visit me. She will come and brighten the pitch-black dungeons as if to defy the whole world. She will turn a deaf ear to the rules her husband set. She will give me hope and strength. Before leaving, she will assure me, "My dear father, you will see that John will not let you be executed." Last but not least, Sole Empress Anna will arrive with all her hatred. As I scorn at her she will say, "Don't fear, I won't allow my son to kill you. Because it is more important for me to have you die a little inside each day, like all those days I suffered when I died a little inside every day." Then she will look at my face with pity and at length before muttering, "But don't get your hopes up, perhaps my son will not pay heed to my words." She will then walk away. The chain holding the large rocks in place will come loose as if it had been waiting for her to leave and the rock will speedily fall on me, the usurper emperor. As I think that my end has come I will howl, 'I never thought I'd die crushed between two rocks.'"

Every time the last paragraph of this first scenario appeared in his mind he was becoming ever-more exhausted with fear. That's why, the moment that last paragraph fell into his mind, he added a few sentences to this trail of thought in order to console himself, "I'll land on my feet. My son Matthew will be fuming when he hears I have been thrown into a dungeon. He will come to my aid when Sole Empress Anna is there in the dungeon with me. He will decapitate the dungeon guards with the help of his men and tie Empress Anna, who previously looked at me with pity from between the bars, and put her behind bars. Once I am freed and on the same side as his men, he will untie the chain holding the rocks and they will crush Empress Anna." Despite his attempts to find some relief, he could neither change the last paragraph of his self-manufactured scenario nor forget the last paragraphs of the other scenarios that lingered in his mind. As he tried to save himself from the weight of those terrifying paragraphs, the only thing he was capable of doing was to sweat profusely.

The horses slowly approached the castle gates. The Emperor was thinking about the last paragraphs of all his scenarios. When the castle gates were not opened, he became very frustrated and roared, "This god damn gate better be opened right now! Whatever shall happen, will happen!"

CHAPTER TWENTY-SEVEN

Before the rain came down, the sky was as blue as the sky of the evening when he first saw the sea sitting on the back of his Grey. Once again, the moon was hanging in the blue sky like a round tray, but the stars were distant from the moon as if they had fallen out with her.

The waves that were wildly beating against the shore just a few days ago were now as calm as soap foam. The Grey looked more like milk-white than grey under the yellow light of the moon and anticipated every single movement of the cavalry positioned on the shore, knowing exactly what he had to do when his reins were lightly pulled. So, he stopped and slowly turned his head towards the sea. He watched the phosphorescence on the sea blink, brightening and darkening with the refraction of the moonlight washing the slightly tumultuous surface of the sea. He tilted his head up and looked at the moon, during which his breathing became quicker. He neighed consecutively as he took interrupted breaths from both of his nostrils. Startled by his neighing horse, Suleyman Pasha tightened the reins of his horse. He spoke to his horse in such a scared tone of voice that he reproached himself, "Grey horse, the other day when you neighed only once we were caught by the storm. Are you heralding an even greater disaster now? Are you trying to tell me that what's to befall us is worse than the storm we hardly pulled through? Don't you see how calm and peaceful the sea and the sky are?"

The Grey took two more interrupted breaths without changing his posture and then suddenly neighed a few times more, the way he had done earlier. It was as if he had understood what Suleyman Pasha had said to him and he was replying. Looking at the mane of his horse in a slight sense of awe, Suleyman Pasha became concerned by his horse's reaction. He felt as if he was sensing a hand touch his skin, extended in his direction with the intent of strangling him. He

unbuttoned the top button of his shirt made of black Buldan[25] silk
with his large fingers, hoping that he would be able to breathe easier.
Opening his top button neither eased his mind nor helped his
breathing. He unbuttoned a second button. A harsh and cold breeze
blew into his shirt from his unbuttoned collar all the way down to his
body, as if it had been waiting for him to unbutton his shirt. Feeling
cold, Suleyman Pasha did the buttons of his shirt back up. In order
to not be reminded of worse things than the incessant rainfall which
had confined him and his men to their tents for days, he turned his
Grey's head towards the castle. Watching him from afar, the *serdengeçtis* also turned their horses' heads towards the castle and
began to wait. When Suleyman Pasha spurred his horse they did so,
too. The path, coiling between gardens for a considerable distance,
suddenly came out to the neighbourhood outside the castle. The
neighbourhood was buried in quiet resentment as it had been completely emptied. Despite the neighbourhood's morose silence, the tall
and thick walls of the Gallipoli Fortress that had been besieged and
showered with arrows and stones for three days were still standing
with a pride of impassability. Casting his winning hawk gaze on the
high-rising castle, Suleyman Pasha muttered, "You will get over that
unflagging great pride and throw yourself at my feet. The tunnels
dug by the miners are filled with water. The new tunnels are also
about to be completed. If the stones and cannonballs my catapults
don't destroy your walls, I will get heavier stones and cannonballs
and erect bigger catapults. Even if you survive for days and months I
won't leave you in peace. You will open your gates sooner or later. If
you stop being stubborn not even a single stone of your castle walls
will be harmed but if you keep insisting on struggling against me, I
will level you to the ground. It's best if you give in voluntarily. If you
don't open your gates to us and we run out of cannon balls and

---

25 T.N, Buldan is a type of fabric that has been produced in the Denizli Province
of Turkey for centuries. It was once favoured by Ottoman sultans and princesses
as well as other wealthy families of the Ottoman court.

stones to throw at you, we will lay siege to you and force you to submit. To tell you the truth, I don't want the people living in the castle to perish because of hunger and thirst. Do you have any other choice than to surrender in the face of all that I will inflict upon you?"

Suleyman Pasha now identified the castle with its commander and as he observed it he thought about his miners, infantries and horseback *levends* who, with body and soul, had been waiting ready for days to undertake a mass attack. Suleyman Pasha called out to the castle commander, "We haven't caused you harm until now but as of this moment you will be hurt severely" and spurred his Grey once again.

Hacı Ilbey had turned one of the vacant houses into a headquarters. When the horse stopped in front of the spacious headquarters he immediately leapt down from his horse. He briskly entered his office that was lit up by large oil lamps. Inspecting the castle plan drawn on Praenetos paper and laid out on the massive table, Hacı Ilbey smiled subtly when he saw the prince enter the room. Pointing to the castle plan on the table, he said, "The castle is so fortified and has internal and external walls on all sides. In between the walls, there are only devil's passes. It's even stronger than Antigone Castle. It might take more time than we anticipated. When aid arrives from the sea, Evrenos Bey and Akça Kocaoğlu's barges will block our way and this will result in an even longer attack."

While listening to what Hacı Ilbey had to say, Prince Suleyman Pasha was also bent over the rough draft of the castle. In a slow tone of voice, he asked, "How did you draw this plan?"

"One of the envoys Fazıl Bey detained is quite knowledgeable about such matters. When he told me that he was prepared to work with us, I asked him to draw it. This is the rough draft he drew."

"I hope he is not tricking us."

"My Bey, life is sweeter than the Emperor's wealth and Gallipoli Fortress. He is clever enough to know that when we enter the castle and find out he tricked us he will lose his life. So please don't have any doubts about the precision of his draft."

"Hacı Bey, I want us to capture this castle more than any of the ones we previously besieged. We must do all we can to capture it as soon as possible. We need this castle in order to have control over the peninsula, to stop the aid that will arrive for the enemy and to safely advance further into the peninsula. If we can't capture it in a short period of time I am afraid that the Byzantine armada will run to their aid. For now, we don't have the power to fight against their naval forces. Moreover, we can only get to the opposite shore from here. If their land forces from the north join forces with the naval forces they will annihilate us before we can make it across the shore. In the meantime, we can't ask for help from my father as he is advancing to fight the *Germiyanids*."

"My Prince, I don't think we will need to ask him for his help. If our remaining forces manage to get here we will have as much power as the Byzantines in Rumelia. That is, as long as the Byzantine armada don't have any knowledge of our arriving forces. Our irregular light cavalry units have already begun to survey the borders of the Duchy of Aenus and Hadrianopolis. As far as we can tell, Byzantium doesn't have much power in these lands. Those who have power over these lands seem to have been exhausted because of looking out for attacks from one another. Fazıl Bey has turned his gaze to the north and continues to advance. It is obvious that there will not be any powers to deter him from continuing his campaign. One of these days he will perhaps send news that he has reached the Black Sea coast."

"Just like the way deceased Akça Koca moved to the capture the peninsula opposite?"

"Fazıl Bey must do exactly the same and must touch the tip of the Ottoman wedge against the Black Sea. However, before that, we must take hold of Gallipoli so that there aren't any safe harbours where the Byzantine armada can anchor. After Gallipoli, we have to blockade Aenus. According to the rumours, the new Duca doesn't like to stay put. Apparently, he is recruiting mercenaries from the north in order to cast us out. That is why it is crucial for us to capture this castle in the shortest period of time. If we can invade this castle we can lay siege to his forces on all fronts. Then, let alone recruiting mercenaries, he won't even have time to breathe."

Looking at Hacı Ilbey, Suleyman Pasha spoke slowly, "For now we don't have any units to spare to fight them but, if my father's campaign to the *Germiyanids* is complete, by then we could ask him for a few divisions of his *müsellims*[26]. When they reach here we can get their *Alps*[27] to start dealing with the Duchy of Aenus."

"He will certainly know what it means to recruit mercenaries when he is confronted by the *müsellims* of Orhan Ghazi."

Hacı Ilbey then turned back to the castle plan laid out before him. He nodded a couple of times, with his head seeming as if it was buried under its shadow with the effect of the rubescent light from the oil lamps. Then looking at Suleyman Pasha he said, "We must make a move together on all fronts at dawn."

After letting a frozen smile wander on his lips, Suleyman Pasha spoke in a tone more emphasised than his previous, "At the break of dawn we can send one last envoy. If they don't decide to surrender, we can attack."

"We should send the priest of Tzympe Castle along with our envoy. I think he might be able to convince them to surrender. As you know the priest is willingly spreading propaganda about us in surrounding villages. Apparently everywhere he goes he tells people, "My brothers, if you want to stop paying tax to the Byzantines every day, join the Ottomans and assent to paying tax once annually."

---

26 T.N, "Müsellim" is a word of Arabic origin and means "one who hands over". Persons who were responsible for the administration of regions as commanders of *müsellim* soldiers in the name of the central authority were given this title.

27 T.N, "Alp" was a title given to those soldiers who were especially brave and valiant

"Hacı, that is very good news. Despite the fact that I feel something akin to disappointment, hearing this news has made me happier."

As Hacı Ilbey liked to analyse every word to its core he wanted to find out the reason behind the prince's disappointment, "My Prince, is there something that worries you, or causes doubt?"

After swaying his head to either side, Suleyman Pasha said, "I have complete faith that we will capture this castle. I don't pay much attention to superstition but the fact that my horse exhaled towards the sea and neighed successively got me concerned."

"Is he sick?"

"No there is nothing wrong with him. It's just that he has a very strong sense of instinct and becomes uneasy whenever he anticipates danger."

"Animals have great instincts but it is also possible for them to be mistaken."

"Yes, perhaps he is... But after his neighing, I got seized with fear."

"Tomorrow is another day. I hope that the danger he anticipated was only for tonight. The Grey was perhaps heralding our victory tomorrow. Now it is time to rest. We can wake up in a few hours and begin the attack. Everybody is waiting for your orders at their posts. Ece Bey's most trusted cavalrymen are watching the gates. We have cautioned them to not even let a bird fly out of the castle. We will advance as soon as the miners light the gun powder."

As Suleyman Pasha turned back and walked towards the door, Hacı Ilbey tried to assuage him, "The worst-case scenario is being confronted by an onslaught. However, as you see we have also taken precautions against that. Don't you worry, My Bey, all will be fine."

Suleyman Pasha left the room and walked down the path with abandoned houses that led to his marquee. He kept thinking of his neighing Grey, which had already been taken to the stables by his groom. As he shook his head to either side, he muttered, "He has never been mistaken until now. I know that a bad omen will befall us."

CHAPTER TWENTY-EIGHT

Two advance guards in service of Emperor Kantakouzenos VI rode their horses to the gate that was being opened. As they pulled back their horses' reins and brought them to a halt they carefully inspected the vaulted, tunnel-like entrance. When they couldn't see anything suspicious they turned back to their commander who was approaching them from a distance of a few horses' lengths. When the commander signalled for them to proceed they rode their horses into the vaulted entrance.

Silence prevailed for some time. There wasn't a single sound other than the echoing sound of clapping horseshoes on the stone-paved path under the vault. When they reached the square on the other side of the vaulted path the imperial guard commander sent another four of his advance guards after them. As he listened to the clapping sound emanating from the horseshoes he sent two knights to investigate the staircases leading to the top of the castle walls. Once all those who had proceeded to the castle signalled back to convey that there was no danger in sight, the imperial guard commander rode to the vaulted entrance with all his knights.

While waiting for news from his imperial guard commander, distressed Emperor Kantakouzenos watched the blue horizon extending behind Chrysopolis slowly turn crimson. He was frustrated at his ever-more accentuated distress. As he turned his head and cast his gaze on the vaulted entrance over his driver's shoulder, he recalled how fiercely he scolded his guard commander. He muttered, "What if he doesn't return?" He thought, "I suppose I was in the wrong" as if he regretted getting angry with his commander. Seeing that his commander was returning from the vaulted entrance he felt relieved. He watched how his driver cracked his whip on the horses' backs. Just as the first horses reached the square inside the castle, he distinctly heard the lead castle gate shut. He quickly turned back, drew back

the rear curtain of his imperial carriage and looked out. Seeing that
the carriage carrying his servants and the rear guards behind them
were proceeding down the arched entrance he felt at ease and sat
back.

The inner space, onto which the vaulted entrance of the castle gate
opened out, was as quiet as the pier square outside the castle. Unable
to make sense of the stillness Emperor Kantakouzenos repeatedly
muttered, "This silence bodes no good." He thought about the
strange sound that emanated from the heavy gate that was shut
upon their entrance. As his hair stood on end he asked, "Why haven't
the watchmen come out?" Then he timidly looked at the square once
again. As he lent an ear to the silence, he momentarily thought of
getting out of the carriage and disappearing into one of the side
streets. Just as he reached out for the knob of the carriage door he
changed his mind and pulled on his bushy beard with his meaty fingers. He slowly tilted his head upwards and looked at the age-old,
high-reaching maple tree in the middle of the square. He tried to
overcome his fear and suspicion by cupping his face with his hands.
He thought hard to make sense of the deathly silence that embalmed
his Constantinople, the city he finally returned to after an entire
week's yearning. As he examined the square once again he loudly
said, "Is there not even a single vassal of God that remains here?"

He watched the advance guards and armoured guards slowly proceed towards the opposite street. His eyes, which for days had been
wedded to seeing infinite shades of green, were fearfully directed at
the stone houses compassing the narrow streets. The only thing he
was heard to be muttering was, "How strange!" What was so strange
to him was how Constantinople, which he referred to as the most
beautiful and affluent city in the whole world, looked so poor and
quiet. As if that wasn't enough, the fear of silence that had been
groping his body since the moment he went through the gates wafted
an unbearable breeze onto his skin. When his tangled beard stood on

end, a sentence that shook his mind to the core appeared, "What is this tortuous, fear-filled silence? This is a paragraph I hadn't added to my stories of arrival." He felt even more suffocated inside. As he looked at the narrow streets, he thought the walls of the buildings would close in on him and that the guards at the front would encircle him, the horses, and the carriages turning them all into a gooey paste. As his fear soared he yelled at his driver, "Go faster!"

His screaming was rendering the fear he felt all the more apparent. In fact, his fear was so blatant that both the driver and the head servant sitting beside him turned around and gave him a strange look. He didn't pay any attention to their looks. He yelled again, this time in a hastier tone of voice, "Faster!"

As he struggled against the fear of the quiet restlessness, the long-distance horses finally came to the end of the narrow path in between the houses and arrived at a small square near the mansion. Realizing that he was finally close to home, Emperor Kantakouzenos took a deep breath and muttered, "Not even a single person looked out their window to welcome me back." After the horses completed half a tour around the young maple tree in the middle of the little square they turned onto a street that wasn't any wider than the last one and the Emperor started feeling claustrophobic once again. Despite the fact that the roof of his hill-top mansion was already visible he still thought he wasn't going to be able to make it there. Just as he pondered on one of his self-fabricated stories becoming real, he saw the walls of the two houses across from each other further down the street sway towards each other. Seeing that the walls were crumbling down in front of them, the long-distance horses began to pelt as if, due to fear, they had forgotten just whom they were carrying in the carriage harnessed to their torsos. However, it wasn't only the horses pulling the imperial carriage that were panicking, the guards' able-bodied horses, the artillery horses pulling the servants' carriage after the imperial carriage, and the horses of the rear guards were all pelting and neighing. There was such havoc that it was as if the wheels of the carriages weren't even touching the ground anymore. Emperor Kantakouzenos VI was so shocked that his face was as white as chalk. The only thing he was capable of doing was holding onto the seat with both hands. As loud booms were heard in the direction of the narrow street they passed by just a little while ago and the horses arrived at the steep slope leading to the mansion, the Emperor's carriage was rocking like a cradle. Quivering with fear, the Emperor was hesitant to do anything. Then he heard the sound of walls toppling in the back street. At that moment, when the sound of human screams mixed into walls crumbling down, he became startled by someone's touch on his arm. Shaken by the Emperor's startled state of mind, his head servant Nikidis wailed, "Your Majesty, it's only me, Nikidis."

Kantakouzenos VI slowly turned his head and vacantly looked at his head servant. Witnessing the fear roaming his pupils, the head servant opened the small door of the built-in closet at the front of the carriage and served water to the Emperor from a silver tankard. Noticing that the Emperor's fear hadn't subsided, Nikidis gently held the water to the Emperor's lips to assuage him. The Emperor came back to his senses after taking a few sips of the cold water and asked, "Nikidis, what happened?"

As if he had caused what had happened, Nikidis replied under his breath with the timidity of a child, "Your Majesty, there has been an earthquake."

As Emperor Kantakouzenos slowly got out of his carriage by holding onto his servant's shoulder he turned his glance to the garden gate of his mansion. A cry lingered in his nostrils and before he could stop himself, tears began to run down his cheeks. As he stepped down onto the ground and crouched down, he sarcastically said, "What could be more fitting as an end to an earthquake-like journey?"

Then he looked at Nikidis and gave his orders, "Inform the servants in the mansion of my arrival at once, they all should come out."

As the servants and the guards ran to the mansion, Emperor Kantakouzenos VI spoke in a sad tone of voice and as if Co-Emperor John V Palaiologos was standing across from him, "Andronicus's son, I knew it wouldn't bring us any good fortune before I set out on this journey. Yet, every time that sad image of you appeared in my mind it told me you would blame me if I hadn't gone. So, I went. But, what difference has it made? Not only did I fail to achieve the results I had in mind but all this trouble has also befallen our Constantinople."

Just as he finished his sentence, he felt the ground under him quake. As he fearfully tried to stand up, he yelled, "One of you, help me!"

Needless to say, there wasn't anyone in sight. As he vacantly looked around, his tears began running down his cheeks as if they weren't done with their day's work. While his face was covered in tears, Empress Irene ran out to the garden in a state of panic. She ran to Emperor Kantakouzenos as soon as she spotted him. Trying to make sense of their panic, the Emperor smiled wide. He wiped his tears, stood up and took Empress Irene into his arms. In that moment of embrace, they both shed all the tears they had hidden in their pride all their lives. Seeing that they were crying while embracing each other, the servants looked at them as if they had seen a creature descend to earth from the skies.

The Emperor felt as light as a bird after crying as much as he needed to and thus finding some relief. Even though he agreed that the earthquake was a warning, he muttered, "There is no need to think any more about this" and began to walk towards the mansion. Just then, his head servant appeared beside him. The Emperor told Nikidis, "Nikidis, first take a look around the mansion with your men and see what needs to be fixed. After that, inspect every street in Constantinople."

Then he turned to his chief guard and said, "Send for the castle commander, all the units in the castle should run to the aid of those who are in need of protection and help."

Then, he turned to his wife, Irene, "This mansion was built by the greatest architect of the Palaiologos. I doubt that it has been affected by the earthquake but we should still go and sit in the gazebo just as a precaution."

Looking at her husband's face sadly, Empress Irene replied, "I have been watching the garden gates for days. I haven't slept a wink in days. I only dozed off for a short while just before the break of dawn."

Then she fell silent for an extended period of time. She tried to talk a few times but her suppressed crying made her change her mind at every instant.

Sitting on the cushion in the gazebo, Kantakouzenos VI thought that the last half an hour of his life felt longer than his entire life of over half a century. Then he spoke, "Irene, it never occurred to me that the humankind is so powerless in the face of nature. I came to fully understand that when the ground I was sitting on began to move from under me. I wish I had known the power of nature before."

Then Constantinople was suddenly cast over with a cloud of dust. Noticing that her husband was exhausted, Empress Irene replied, "John, you look exasperated."

"Yes. I am tired and stink of sweat."

For a while, they sat at the gazebo and waited for news from the city. The first news that was delivered dictated that there wasn't an overwhelming amount of damage. Though the Emperor was happy to hear the good news, he was also falling asleep in his seat. Empress Irene immediately sent the servants to prepare the Emperor's bath.

When she was informed that the Emperor's bath was prepared, Empress Irene got hold of the tired emperor's arm and accompanied him inside.

CHAPTER TWENTY-NINE

The sun was yet to sweep the moon into the vastness of the sky and appear on the horizon to pierce the morning twilight as Suleyman Pasha got out of his marquee, mounting his Grey brought to him by his groom. Feeling a light spur on his flank, the horse trotted between the quiet houses of the neighbourhood outside the castle walls and then began to gallop when they reached the north wall of the castle. This was the final field survey before the battle drums were beaten. As soon as the field survey was completed, the battle drums would be beaten and the attack would be commenced all together. The miners would first collapse the tunnels they dug. Then a fire would be started in the castle and embers slung in with the use of trebuchets and arrows of fire shot in the direction of the enemy. Subsequently, the roofs of houses would be shattered by the shot cannonballs and the heavy stones that were slung. Shortly before this initial moment of terror that caused panic among the people subsided, the taut bowstrings would be arched and death would prevail in the castle. As those in the castle tried to save themselves from this unexpected moment of flailing life, the climbers, *serdengeçtis* and the *delis* would climb to the top of the walls.

When Suleyman Pasha raced his horse against the morning-fresh sea breeze to complete his survey and arrive in front of the house they had established as their headquarters, Hacı Ilbey was already waiting for him. Noticing the arrival of the prince, he got on his raven-black horse that was darker than the darkest of nights. He first looked at the mountains hiding the slowly rising sun and then at the *levends* beating the battle drums. Then he raised his whip, which was made by the loriners of Hüdavendigâr province and looked more like a strand of plaited hair rather than a plain whip. He then looked at Suleyman Pasha one last time. Perceiving the decisiveness on his bright and wide face turned towards the horizon, he cracked his whip. As the dawn broke behind the distant mountains the sound of battle drums roistered.

During such attacks, each and every soldier knew exactly what they had to do. The only thing the commander had to do was to yell, "Come on my brave men", in order to help his brethren-in-arms assaulting the castle to keep up their courage. Watching out over the coastline and the harbour, the units under the command of Akça Kocaoğlu and Evrenos Bey had also begun their assault at the pier simultaneously with the units at the northern front. Stones, arrows and javelins were raining down into Gallipoli Fortress from every imaginable direction. The castle gates that opened out onto the seafront were blockaded. The attack gradually became more violent. The castle commander and his guards were defending the castle selflessly. When a guard got hit by an arrow in the bastions, another guard quickly took the wounded guard's place and, with just as much skill as the man before him, began shooting arrows in the direction of Suleyman Pasha's *levends*. As arrows were shot to-and-fro, the climbers were busy climbing up the high walls of the castle. As it happens, the higher they climbed the harder the guards positioned on top of the castle walls were trying to deter them from reaching the top. When the swords of the first climbers collided with first rays of the rising sun and began to shine in the bastions, a great wave of joy spread through the trenches. The exuberant drummers began beating the battle drums harder. With the power of that joy, tens of climbers managed to climb up the walls after the first unit. The *yaya serdengeçtis* followed them into battle, with *delis* reaching the top of the castle walls last.

The attack gradually gained momentum between daybreak and sunrise but it also had an effect on the men fighting in the castle. The arrows shot from outside the castle had brought those in charge of pouring tar and hot oil to a halt, except the ones posted above the main gate. The battering rams of the *yaya* units had also moved closer to the gates. As if such a brutal attack wasn't sufficient for invading the castle, the miner's tunnels which were fired at the start of the assault had also begun to collapse one after another.

Sitting up straight on his horse, Suleyman Pasha rode his Grey around the front, yelled out encouraging battle cries and constantly swung his sword towards the castle. When he noticed that the battering rams were beating down the gates, he rode his horse towards the tall gates, above which those in charge of pouring tar and hot oil were posted. Seeing him ride his horse towards them, the *yayas* in charge of the battering ram shielded themselves from the scorching oil and continued beating down the gate with renewed power—with the power of joy. If they kept at it, the gate would not stand for long but they were unable to undertake their task to the fullest of their capacity because of all the tar, boiling water and oil being poured onto them from the spaces above the gate. They kept beating the gate by pulling back those who were burnt and replacing them with new, uninjured *yayas*. Just when Suleyman Pasha approached the vulnerable *yayas* using the battering ram, a very loud noise was heard. As Suleyman Pasha looked around him to determine the source of the noise from atop his horse, he saw that the piece of land a few metres away from him was torn apart down the middle, like a piece of cloth. The awful noise was a result of the soil mixing where the earth was torn. Suleyman Pasha screamed desperately and looked at the *yayas* running to their positions in awe. At that moment the Grey suddenly came to a halt and he tumbled down. If he hadn't held on to his horse's neck he would have fallen into the deep crevice a few footsteps away and disappeared into the quaking ground. When his Grey cautiously retreated step by step and distanced both of them from the crevice before them, Suleyman Pasha took a deep breath. Then, he gratefully caressed his horse's head. He tightly embraced the bitterly neighing horse. For a while, he remained still with his arms around his horse's neck. When he opened his eyes, he noticed he was exhausted and his legs were shaking.

He looked around in disbelief. The ground had swallowed so many *yayas* who were alive and walking ahead of him just a little while ago. He thought about how powerless humankind is in the face of nature. He paused until he felt he was less vulnerable. Then he slowly squatted down, sat on the ground and cast his gaze in the direction of the castle. The rift that turned the ground almost upside down had also caused a massive crack under the castle walls, destroying the thick outer walls of the castle as well as the inner walls. Unable to avert his gaze from the dilapidated castle walls, Suleyman Pasha came to his senses when his horse nudged his shoulder with his nose. Seeing that one of the *serdengeçtis* fortunate enough to be alive was extending his water-filled leather canteen to him, his face lit up with a sense of indebtedness. He took the canteen and drank a few gulps of water. The ground shook once again. As the voices of *yayas* and *serdengeçtis* who had disappeared into the ground still echoed, he felt a gradually increasing desire to cry but it was lodged in his throat and was burning the back of his nose. Realising he wouldn't be able to hold himself back much longer, he hastily stood up and began crying his heart out as he put his arms around his horse's neck.

Crying from the depths of his soul felt good for a while. He removed his arms from his horse's neck and slowly squatted down again. As he looked at the castle the sun was rising in the horizon, caressing his face. Gradually raising his voice he muttered, "My God, you have opened gates for us all around the castle where we have been struggling to enter for days. Is this a favour you have bestowed upon us—or cruelty at the hands of which we suffer? It is impossible for me to comprehend such a turn of events because I will not forget the screams I heard for the rest of my life. How will this human body of mine get over the favour you did at the expense of such pain?"

He cupped his face with his hands and remained silent for a while.

After shedding his last few tears he stood up. It was when he felt a bit better that he came to realise the time and his location. He was muttering, "We'd only started the attack early so that the people living in the castle wouldn't wake up and we would only cause harm to the guards behind the bastions. Now, the whole castle is torn apart. The only thing we can do now is to help those in need", when Hacı Ilbey appeared beside him. Seeing the prince gazing around with eyes wide open and talking to himself, Hacı Ilbey became alarmed. He immediately got off his horse and gently touched the prince's shoulder. Despite the tenderness of his touch Suleyman Pasha flinched.

Hacı Ilbey said, "My Bey, it's only me."

Suleyman Pasha looked around with vacant eyes as if he hadn't heard Hacı Ilbey. Unable to hold himself back, he embraced Hacı Ilbey and began to weep from the depths of his heart as if to complete his previous cry.

As Hacı Ilbey tightly wrapped his arms around Suleyman Pasha, whom he loved like his own son, and listened to his quiet weeping, he noticed the existence of another kind of sensitivity in his own character. He stood still without finding it strange that this man who defied death on the battlefield was crying for those who died for no reason, other than an unexpected natural disaster. While standing still, he thought of ways to save him from the bosom of sorrow. He held Suleyman Pasha's hands, took a step back and looked at his face. He blinked and softly nodded a few times to show that he felt Suleyman Pasha's pain. When Suleyman Pasha finally calmed down he said, "My Bey, it's no use being sad about something you have no control over. What we have to do now is to help those who are still alive rather than cry over those we have lost."

After falling silent for a short while, he looked at the *serdengeçtis* and *yayas* around him and shouted, "Come on my brave men, let's save those friends of ours whom the earth is trying to swallow and

who are struggling against fate. And then we shall run to the aid of
those awaiting our help in the castle."

He then lowered his voice and added, "It's good that we vacated
the outer neighbourhoods, or most of those living there would have
been stuck under the collapsing roofs."

Suleyman Pasha calmed down as he listened to Hacı Ilbey. He left
his crying and emotional state behind and helped some of the *yayas*
who were buried in soil up to the waist to be saved. He asked the
cavalrymen, who were waiting for the castle gates to be opened, to
retreat immediately, hand over their horses to the groom and run to
the rescue of *yayas*. After cautioning the head *yayas* to save all the
soldiers they could, he walked over to the partially collapsed castle
walls with Hacı Ilbey and a few infantry units. He climbed into one
of the enduring bastions and viewed the inner castle. Then he addressed the infantry behind him that was awaiting his orders, "My
brave men, it was only a short while ago that each and every one of
you was a warrior. I'd told you not to have pity on anyone who op-
poses you. Now, with the grace of God, there remains no one to defy
you. Thus, you will rest your swords in their sheaths and you will
help those who are awaiting your aid under the ruins. Some of you
should assume the post of guardsmen with their swords at hand as
there might be those who panic upon seeing you. Be cautious as you
try to save those under the wreckage. And remember, there shall be
no looting or taking captives. Take the casualties to the physicians
and gather those who are not injured in an open space."

Once he finished his speech and fell quiet, the infantry split into
groups and rushed to the ruins. Watching them run to the help of
those affected by the earthquake, Hacı Ilbey spoke in a soft and sad
tone of voice, "We raided an island on the Aegean Sea with a small
fleet of the Karasids. It was as if the island was waiting for us to raid
it. When we stepped foot on land the island began quaking just as it
did here today. We were all frozen with fear, completely still. Once

we came back to our senses we deemed the island to be ill-fated and ran straight back to our rowing boats. After that incident, the island was never raided again."

Preoccupied with other thoughts, Suleyman Pasha replied, "I used to tell myself that there is nothing sturdier than the land I set foot on every morning after getting out of bed but today I witnessed how wrong I was to think so."

Trying to conceal his wisdom, Hacı Ilbey thought it would be more beneficial for him to motivate Suleyman Pasha to work rather than waste time on chit-chat, "My Bey, now is not the time for a chat, it is time we saved those buried alive in the ground. We will have to undertake this task with the infantry we have, rather than waiting for those who will come to our aid. I am going to supervise the infantry. You should place guardsmen at the castle entrances and gather the casualties on the streets in an open space so they may be treated. May our endeavour be gainful!"

Hacı Ilbey departed with a group of infantry.

Suleyman Pasha, who at times of battle, looked like a storm on the back of his Grey, was trying to do as Hacı Ilbey urged. Nevertheless, he was not able to dismiss the recent sight of *levends* being buried in debris with rocks falling on top of them as the castle wall caved in.

CHAPTER THIRTY

After waking up, Emperor Kantakouzenos VI felt as like a lizard that had been lying down for its final sleep of death for months. As he pushed the duvet to the side with his foot, he muttered, "Why not a tortoise or a snake, but a lizard?" Sitting on his bed, he added to his previous muttering, "Whereas, at this age, I look more like a languid tortoise as I try to carry the weight on my back. Even though I am old I am not that heavy. In fact I trail like a snake... When defeated by my ambition, I am even more like a snake because I bite and poison anyone who sets foot on my path. If that's so, why do I feel like a creature that I am not alike? Perhaps there was something that replenishes the human in the water we drank the other day from the spring near Praenetos. That's why I must have likened myself to the most agile of reptilians. Or perhaps, it was that earthquake I witnessed before falling asleep..." With a smile on his lips he shook his head to either side before finishing his sentence. He then decided to change the subject. "I didn't do anything tiring on the way there but I was so exhausted by the time I stepped out of the carriage. I think it was fatigue caused by the fear that pervaded my body."

He suddenly paused. When he recalled the earthquake he had forgotten about in his sleep, he continued with awe, "How could I have forgotten about the earthquake? Yes, it must have been fatigue created by the fear of witnessing an earthquake." For a while he tried to remember what had happened in the morning in detail. His lips quivering, he repined, "The cradle-like quaking of that ground I stood on reminded me once more that nothing really matters in this life. I used to think that everything belongs to the Emperor, but it is not so." Looking in the direction of the bathtub now with its curtains drawn, he kept on philosophising, "We consider our ambition as a virtue but the two have nothing in common." Then he delved into thinking about what the wise men he could recall said about life. Although he couldn't remember much of what the philosophers, whom he was very eager to learn the teachings of in his youth said, it still felt good to ponder in broken sentences. Coming back to his senses a little while later and finding himself sitting on the bed half-naked, Emperor Kantakouzenos VI experienced a moment of bashfulness that mixed into a smile. He stood up when his smile vanished.

Worried that her husband fell asleep as soon as he got into bed after returning from his journey, Empress Irene resolved in immediately calling the physicians. Once she found out that her husband had nothing wrong with him other than a deep and peaceful sleep, she left him to sleep and went out on an expedition of discovery around the mansion with her servants to check whether the mansion had been harmed by the earthquake. After investigating for a while, she returned to her chambers, knowing that there wasn't any serious damage to the mansion. As she waited for her husband sleeping in the room next door to wake up, she started conversing with the very young handmaidens sent to the mansion by the newly appointed Duca of Aenus as a gift as well as the skilful handmaidens whom she bought from the previous Genoese market. As soon as the young servants, trying to answer the questions posed by Empress Irene, heard footsteps in the adjoining room, they looked deep into Empress Irene's eyes for instruction. When the Empress implied that they should go in, all four of the handmaidens entered the Emperor's bed-chamber. Empress Irene also joined them. As she entered the chamber, she addressed the Emperor who was treading towards the Venetian-made spelter bathtub, "John, the messengers Empress Anna and our son-in-law sent have been waiting for you for days."

Slowly plunging his body into the warm water infused with a thousand and one flower essences, the Emperor took his time replying to the empress. As he tried to surrender himself to the youthful touch of the young handmaidens he felt his senses, which had been asleep for days, surge. He became startled as if there was a pinprick on his buttock. As he looked at the scrub mitten being applied onto his heel, he said, "Why is there..." Before he could finish his sentence, he dazedly mumbled, "I was going to tell you something else—I have no idea why I am concerning myself with the sensation on my buttock." He further resigned himself to the touch of the handmaidens' fingertips. For a while he lay back in the bathtub quietly, before looking at Empress Irene and replying, "I will see them after my bath."

Looking at the young handmaidens, Empress Irene replied in a sarcastic tone of voice, "I doubt you'll get out of the bath today—if you like you can see them tomorrow..."

Emperor Kantakouzenos VI seemed to feel the pinprick he felt shortly before once again on his buttock. As he smiled he murmured, "Gosh!" Hearing his exclamation, Empress Irene replied as she walked towards the door, "There is nothing to be astounded at by my darling... The Duca of Aenus has sent truly beautiful handmaidens... As if that wasn't sufficient I also bought two just as skilful as them..."

The Emperor briefly thought about the word that escaped his lips and the meaning his wife assigned to the word he uttered. As the empress was about to walk of out the door he elaborated on his previous sentence, "Even if it takes me a bit of time, seeing the messengers will be the first thing I do..."

As Empress Irene shut the door behind her, she didn't hear the end of her husband's sentence but she had understood that her husband would take the matter at hand seriously because she placed importance on it. She knew that he would even cut being skilfully caressed by the young handmaidens short and accept the audience of the messengers. And that was exactly what happened. On his way to-and-fro Nicaea, the Emperor had thought long and hard about the doubtful loyalty of those who referred to him as "usurper emperor." He had decided that the empire would not stand without the Palaiologos family. He had also concluded that he had to bring John Palaiologos

V back to Constantinople at once to sign an agreement that would benefit both parties and begin co-governing the empire. Thus, he considered it a great opportunity to see the messengers Empress Irene told him about. He left the servants, who were drawing him further and further into a well of lustfulness with the touch of their warm fingertips, by the bathtub. He got dressed quickly and went to his study in the mansion to meet the messengers sent by the Palaiologos.

Two messengers and his old and faithful head servant Nikidis who had been his confidant many times were all waiting for him in his study. When they saw the Emperor enter the room they respectfully bowed their heads and greeted him. Impatient to deliver news about the earthquake, Nikidis addressed the Emperor as soon as he sat in the chair behind his desk, "Your Majesty, according to the news sent by our men inspecting our beloved Constantinople street after street there have fortunately been no casualties in the city. Some of our citizens whose houses have caved in were saved with minor injuries. The houses that have been damaged will be repaired by your loyal and wealthy friends. However, we have received news that many of the Greek houses situated on the Sikodis[28] Quay and almost all of the Jewish dwellings extending out on the hills of Pera have been completely destroyed..."

Emperor Kantakouzenos asked precipitately, "Has anyone been sent to their aid?"

Nikidis turned his tongue around in his mouth as if he had said something wrong. He remained quiet. Then, he turned his tongue around in his mouth again and gulped. Looking at him, the Emperor thought that he might have swallowed his tongue. Though after doing the same and gulping again, Nikidis suddenly uttered, "Your Majesty, aid was sent to Sikodis immediately. However, as you know, those on the hillsides of Pera have been considered to be cursed by

---

28 T.N, Referred to as "Sikodis Quay" is the current-day Karaköy quay.

the castle people since the Romans. Thus we can't send anyone to help them. They can only be aided by the Genoese of Sykai upon your orders."

The Emperor's face became taut with fury and his lips twitched. After shaking his head to either side he explained his decision, "Look Nikidis, if we are still claiming to be an empire we must send help to them immediately because they are a part of this empire. The fact that they are Jewish, does not forbid them this right. What now? Should we treat them as the Romans, who confined them to the hill-side of Pera after expelling them from the castle and who forbade them to even purchase horses to harness to their carriages? Shall we, in their time of need, leave them alone and helpless? No, we don't have the right to do that. Inform the castle commander at once, he should form a recovery unit from our guards and send it to the hill-side of Pera. I will immediately write a letter to the mayor of the Genoese neighbourhood so that he can assist the process of recovery and start rebuilding all the houses that were destroyed. Go to our castle commander at once and tell him that these are my direct orders. I will write the letter as soon as I am done with what I have to do now. I now want to hear from the messengers sent by the Palaiologos. I hope that they also wish to end this game that has been going on between us for so long. In any case, I am tired of this game."

Before leaving the room, Nikidis approached the messengers of Palaiologos who were waiting by the door. He took the scrolled letter written on Praenetos paper from the messenger's hands. He gazed around as he gently touched his tongue on the letter and swallowed his spit. Realising that there wasn't any numbness on his tongue, he held the scroll with both hands and extended it to Emperor Kantakouzenos VI before leaving the room. Upon his departure he sent his auxiliary into the room to provide security for the Emperor. The Emperor opened the letter and began to read. When he got to the end of the letter, the Emperor sighed deeply and looked at the messengers with teary eyes. He gazed at the door handle as he always did when he was about to make an important decision. Then, looking at Nikidis' auxiliary—referred to as "very diligent" by Nikidis but of whom the Emperor was not fond—the Emperor spoke to the messengers through trembling lips, "I suppose you have rested well while waiting for an audience with me. You can set out immediately... I order you to return to the island with the speed of wind. Upon your arrival, inform Andronicus' son, Co-Emperor John Palaiologos that he can prepare to return to Constantinople. Once you have left, I will be sending the news to the navarch so that he can personally sail to bring them back here. Go on now, God speed..."

With the joy of being able to convey such elated news to the young Co-Emperor in Tenedos, the messengers immediately headed towards the stud farm where they'd left their horses. Watching the door shut after the messengers' departure, the Emperor perused the letter from Palaiologos that lay open on his desk and loudly mumbled, "Can any father's heart endure his daughter's misfortune? How can my heart endure it? Matthew will blame me for being cowardly, but I don't care. I am my daughter's father just as much as I am his..."

CHAPTER THIRTY-ONE

Suleyman Pasha rushed to the aid of those buried under the landslide, dressed in his princely outfit. He was now just another yaya, the same as all the others··· He had forgotten about being a prince while helping those trapped in the spaces between the collapsed roofs and walls, those trying to salvage the remaining parts of their bodies by leaving their broken limbs behind, those dredging up the soil of death covering them except for their hardly moving fingers reaching out towards the surface, the lifeless bodies squashed and folded under thick wooden beams, and the injured whose bones had broken through the skin. As he removed one body from under the ruins and laid it on top of the soil to go back and help another one, those who were saved, be it a child, an adult, a man or a woman, were all crying and screaming due to the immense pain coursing through their flesh.

The cries were tearing Suleyman Pasha's heart apart—he wanted to sit with those who were weeping and join them in their pain and sorrow. But, as soon as he saw another person waiting to be saved, he quickly forgot about the weeping of the injured and rushed to help those still buried under debris. So many injured people had been carried to the open spaces next to the remaining castle walls that there was no space to place those who were still being brought out from the ruins. Before returning to his work, Suleyman Pasha ordered the cavalryman to join the relentless *yayas* in dedicating their efforts to clearing new spaces for the casualties. Inspecting the skilful rescue work of miners who had arrived after the cavalryman, Suleyman Pasha thought, "Whoever said, 'Give your dough to the baker even if he eats half of it', was so wise." As he looked at the castle guard, dressed in armour from head to toe being lifted out of the ruins, he murmured, "Just yesterday, both he and those who saved him were referring to each other as enemies." He then turned his gaze to the walls of the inner castle and the dwellings, half of which had been destroyed by the earthquake. When he tilted his head upwards and set his eyes upon the sun, he said, "We didn't even notice the day slip into the afternoon", to the *serdengeçti* beside him. Then, seeing the head servant beside him carrying a wounded person he said, "After admitting the casualty to the physician's care, announce that we will be taking a break to eat."

For a while, he returned to helping those working beside him. After his servant announced what he had told him, Suleyman Pasha, too, began eating the food he had brought. He hadn't even eaten a few bites when he noticed that he had a knot in his throat. He said to himself, "How odd it is that I thought about eating something amidst all the smell of blood and screams!" He suddenly wanted to tread towards those awaiting help but when his hunger overrode that impulse, he forced himself to eat. His mind went blank until he had finished eating. Then he got up and walked amongst the ruins as if nothing had happened.

He had walked past a few caved in walls when he heard unified wails and screams. As he tried to figure out the source of the sounds, he saw that the castle church had been partially destroyed. Approaching the demolished building, he noticed the voices were getting louder. He muttered, "Those trapped inside must be able to see me." Examining the ruinous building he shouted, "Send the miners over here now!"

Hearing his orders, the serdengeçtis immediately called out for the miners. When they arrived at the double, he ordered, "Go on, this is not the time to hesitate. First take precautions and then save them all."

Suleyman Pasha had just delegated tasks to the miners when Evrenos Bey, a lanky man, arrived and woefully said, "My prince, please accept my condolences."

Seeing Evrenos Bey, Suleyman Pasha suddenly felt stronger and better equipped to deal with his emotions, and replied, "My condolences to you too, Evrenos Bey." He inspected his plain and swarthy face, and continued, "Today, I saw the land we stepped foot on fill with more blood-thirst against us than any enemy. If it wasn't for my Grey, I would have been swallowed by this land... This land I've risked my head to conquer. We should be glad that we are still alive. At first, I was hesitant whether we should pray for the souls of those who are buried under our feet or help those who need help. Then without a single thought in my head I came to help the injured. How did you manage to get away from this disaster?"

"We were at the pier when it happened. I suppose that was the steadiest area. It quaked a lot but it didn't cave in. The waves rose so high that I thought the water would swallow us and the world. A few seconds later, I nearly jumped out of my skin when I saw the corpses floating on the water—I could have been one of those corpses. After the waters ebbed, I was just as puzzled as you were, I wasn't sure whether to pray that I was still alive or be sorry for all that I had witnessed. As I wandered like a crazy person, the physicians ran to my aid and saved me from that blanked out state of mind...

" Just then Evrenos Bey's physician, who always followed him wherever he went, joined them too. After smiling at the prince covered with dust, he said, "I hope you'll recover soon, my bey." Then he walked towards the nearby open space that was being cleared by the miners. Upon his arrival, he told his helpers to assist him in examining those who were being taken out of the ruins of the church.

As he stood on a pile of rocks and observed the recovery work, Suleyman Pasha's eyes lit up when he saw that they were able to reach those confined in the church through the path the miners had skilfully cleared. His grateful gaze was focused on the miners when he saw that the infantry, who were attempting to lift the rocks that were once a wall, cried out, "Ach!" in unison and retreated. Startled by their cry, Suleyman Pasha uttered, "I wonder what happened?"

In the meantime, after a few strides, Evrenos Bey arrived by the infantry. He must have been just as terrified as the infantry so that he also yelled out, "Ach!" Deeply concerned as to what had happened, Suleyman Pasha also ran in their direction. Evrenos Bey spoke in complete disbelief, "This must have been the building where the castle guards were posted. They got crushed under the ashlars that fell on them."

For a while Suleyman Pasha was left speechless as if all the thoughts on his mind had been wiped clean. Evrenos Bey's physician, who came to them as they waited tongue-tied, immediately asked his helpers to bring water. When the water arrived, he washed the prince's face with his own hands. Slightly coming back to his senses with the effect of the cold water, Suleyman Pasha swayed his head to both sides in mourning, "What kind of a victory is this? We didn't exsanguine our swords, but we are covered in blood up to our elbows."

As he cast his gaze on Evrenos Bey, a group of the infantry roistered, "They are all alive!" With the joy of the moment, they hugged the children who were near them and ran to where the physicians were. Evrenos Bey saw that the miners, who had supported the trees that might have fallen on them and cleared away the jagged rocks around the church, were trying to open the jammed door of the church.

He ran to their aid, telling the miners, "If you break the door the walls could come crumbling down."

He told them to retreat and knocked on the door. With all the power left in him, he called out to those trapped inside the church in Greek, "Can you hear me?"

A voice-like sound emerged from behind the door. Evrenos Bey repeated himself, "Can you hear me?"

This time a piercing voice was heard from behind the door, "Yes, we can hear you."

Evrenos Bey put his mouth closer to the door, "The door is jammed we can't open it. If we break the door the walls might cave in. We are going to make a hole in the roof and save you from there. Just be patient···"

The miners immediately started working. They borrowed the ladders of the climbers and leaned them against the few remaining sturdy walls of the church. Tens of miners climbed up onto the roof of the church at once. Shortly after they reached the bell tower, where once a bell ringer had pulled the bell-ropes, from the holes they now made in the roof. Reaching the top, Evrenos Bey walked to the stone steps and yelled below, "Holy Father! Are you there?"

The piercing voice from before answered, "We are here. We are here, my child."

Evrenos Bey replied, "First you should climb up here by using the staircase."

The priest insisted, "The others should climb up first, I can climb up later."

Evrenos Bey persisted that he climbed first. The priest didn't object and slowly ascended the staircase. Evrenos Bey saw him approaching and reached out his hand to help him climb on top of the wall. The priest, who had never seen Evrenos Bey in the castle before, looked at him with kindness. He turned around, looked at the wrecked houses and the countless injured people lying down by the wall. Tears welled up in his eyes. As they ran down to his long and white beard, he crossed himself. He turned his gaze at the skies and said, "We humans, the children of God, must show the patience of acceptance." He looked at Evrenos Bey again. He must have felt the impatience of those trapped inside to climb the stairs so that he hastily called out below, "Children should be the first to climb."

When their gazes met, Evrenos Bey bowed his head and greeted the priest, "Holy Father, I am Evrenos, one of the Beys of Orhan Gazi, son of Osman. We laid siege to your castle before the earthquake. Now you and the entire castle people are under the protection of Orhan Gazi. Those who are injured will be healed in the shortest time possible and the dead will be buried with the ceremonies you shall arrange. The destroyed castle walls will be fixed as soon as possible and the castle will once again be the way it was. We should go down now and wait in a safe location. Our *levents* will help all those who are trapped in the church to come out.

The priest grasped what had happened after a while, "We thought that the Ottomans had come to wipe us off the face of the earth, but they turned out to be our saviours. This must be a blessing from the saints."

He then climbed down the ladder leaning against the church wall towards where Suleyman Pasha had been waiting. When he reached the last step of the ladder, Suleyman Pasha extended his hand to him and helped him step onto the ground. He greeted the priest in Greek words he had learned from his mother. Distinguishing that this was an important person, due to the reverse-wrapped turban on his head, the priest kindly greeted Suleyman Pasha.

Suleyman Pasha briefly looked at Evrenos Bey, who was now beside them, and said, "Evrenos Bey, tell the Father that as of this moment their lives, goods and properties are in our safekeeping. Both the church and the castle will be brought back to their previous states as soon as possible and the people will once again go to the church for worship using these streets covered with ruins."

First Evrenos Bey introduced Suleyman Pasha to the priest and then he translated everything Suleyman Pasha had said to the priest word for word. As Evrenos Bey talked, the old priest was looking at Suleyman Pasha. He comprehended the reality better with each passing minute and felt that their old style of living had been buried under the rubble with the earthquake. Thinking that nothing would ever be the same as before he said, "My God, he who grants life to humankind even from disasters, my only wish from you is that you don't allow humans to be enemies of each other. Erase the memories of those who presented others to us as enemies and re-fill their minds with beauty."

He looked at Evrenos Bey and asked, as if he was doubtful of what Suleyman Pasha had told him, "Will we be able to keep our church open from now on? Will the sons of Osman allow us to worship in our own way?"

Evrenos Bey looked at the old priest and smiled, showing his pearl-white teeth, "Father, from now on you will be able to worship in your church as you wish. Suleyman Pasha, son of Orhan Gazi, told you that rest-assured you may practice your worship in peace. The only difference is that, as of this moment, the castle people will be under the governance of the Beylik of Osmanoğlu instead of Byzantium.

When the priest looked at Suleyman Pasha with doubtful eyes once again, Suleyman Pasha grasped the priest's dilemma. He wet his lips with his tongue and said, "Holy Father, the beliefs of those under the protection of the Beylik of Osmanoğlu have never been meddled with. You will be allowed to carry out your prayers according to your beliefs. It is now time to help the suffering people who are captured under the ruins. You should sit and rest a while. If you suffer any complaints, our physicians can take care of you while we go and help those in the church and under the landslide.

CHAPTER THIRTY-TWO

Emperor Kantakouzenos VI had solved the Palaiologos problem that had been nagging him for days by deciding to accept Palaiologos V as his Co-Emperor. He brought him back from Tenedos, who he had, in his own opinion, exiled to Tenedos to "rest and gain maturity," with a sumptuous ceremony. The situation in Constantinople was better than he anticipated but he simply couldn't feel at ease. In order to calm his restlessness, he was, on the one hand, sending letters of advice to his son Matthew Kantakouzenos who previously sent him reproachful letters, and urging him to be contented with the imperial partnership he gave him if he wanted to become Co-Emperor after him. On the other hand, he devoutly attended the Sunday services which he referred to as "old age salve."

After attending the last service at Hagia Sophia, he helped the poor with the mediatorship of his men and got into his carriage and set out towards his mansion. He recalled that the priest giving the sermon was repeating what the Patriarch had said. He thought about the subtle criticism the priest directed at him during his sermon. As he tried to forget about the criticisms he thought about consort emperorship and the rumours that had been spreading about him from one mouth to the other since his return from Nicaea. The rumours all concluded that he was inauspicious. He muttered, "If I could, I would turn the whole world upside-down to suppress all hear-say but let alone turning the whole world upside-down, I know that people don't even have the power to turn a handful of soil upside-down." He looked out from the carriage window in the direction of his mansion. As the horses advanced up the slope that lead to the hill the mansion was located on, he noticed a familiar fear grip hold of him.

He looked towards Balat[29] to defeat his fear. His sad gaze moved away from the vicinity as if to escape it and focused on the Genoese neighbourhood across the sea. As if they were the source of all his problems he exclaimed, "To hell with the Genoese! Clouds of sorrow descended upon our Constantinople with the arrival of those inauspicious Genoans!" He kept quiet for a while. Just as they approached the mansion he continued his rant, "The past emperors couldn't notice that the Genoans would take ten times of whatever they gave because they concealed their true faces. Back then, they weren't showing their dark side the way they do now. First they erected an observation tower and then built a wall around it. They won't even suspect the game I am going to play against them. It will be a game that suits the name the Arabs bestowed to the Genoese neighbourhood, "The Sublime City." Then he tilted his head down as if he regretted all that he had said. When he became tired of this posture he turned his head and cast his gaze on the hills of Apostolon[30]. As he aimlessly viewed the hills he recalled the words of the priest, a representative of the Patriarch, "The woodworm can never tell when a huge tree is going to topple over, until it's uprooted by powerful winds. The woodworm knows that its actions will also harm itself but there is no turning back when the tree is uprooted." He waved his hand as if to chase away the priest's words from his mind but the voice in his head didn't quieten down. As if the priest and the patriarch were beside him, he said, "Don't fret priest, I am preparing such a poisonous concoction that I will vanquish all who desire to pick on our aged sycamore." As he viewed the detached houses surrounded with gardens on the opposite hills he said, "All these are the words of the Patriarch. Even if it is someone else who utters them I always

---

29 T.N, Balat is the traditional Jewish quarter in the Fatih district of Istanbul. It is located on the European side of Istanbul, in the old city on the historic peninsula, on the western bank of the Golden Horn. The name Balat is probably derived from Greek *palation* (palace), from Latin *palatium*, after the nearby Palace of Blachernae.
30 T.N, Referred to in Turkish as Fatih, Apostolon encompassed the peninsula coinciding with historic Constantinople.

know whose words they really are." His restlessness soared. The carriage felt claustrophobic. He hastily got out of the slowly moving carriage without even warning Empress Irene, who was sitting next to him. Seeing him precipitately leave the carriage, his servants also got out of their carriage. Watching the Emperor delve into deep thoughts and suddenly get out of the carriage, Empress Irene prayed that her worries, which had been gnawing at her recently, were not real. She too got out of the carriage as they were close to the mansion. As she tried to catch up with Emperor John Kantakouzenos VI she muttered, "When worries go hand in hand with old age..." She couldn't complete her sentence. She silently walked to the mansion. She didn't utter a single word until she changed her attire in her bedchambers. Then she appeared before her husband, looked at his pensive face and said, "You don't have to be so resentful... We are now considered old. All that you have done until now was for Byzantium and our children. If you were to leave it all to them I suppose it wouldn't be the end of the world... You should either defeat your doubts or retreat to a corner and pursue tranquillity. Perhaps that's what the priest was implying. There is nothing to be resentful or angry about. From now on you should think about yourself as much as you think about Byzantium..."

This speech by his wife, who had submissively accepted everything he had done for years, who pretended not to be worldly, who never let go of his hand when he tumbled down from the cliffs of hopelessness in the face of life, was like a boring summary of their recent mundane life and it hit him like a slap of fire. With the effect that slap created in his mind he said, "It's now time to talk about everything", and decided to convene with the Co-Emperor at once. The cart transporting the letter carrier of Co-Emperor Palaiologos V who had arrived from Tenedos stopped in front of the mansion. The messenger walked briskly and appeared before Emperor Kantakouzenos VI.

"Your Majesty, your Co-Emperor and venerable son-in-law has ordered me to inform you that, if you wouldn't mind, he would like to meet with you at the imperial palace. If you accept, he will be waiting for you there."

He respectfully bowed down, saluted the Emperor and began to wait for the Emperor's reply. Co-Emperor Kantakouzenos VI placed the goblet containing wine from Nicaea on the walnut table. As he stood up he told the messenger, "What a great coincidence, I wanted to see him too. Inform my venerable Co-Emperor that I will be at the palace shortly."

Empress Irene entered the room shortly after the messenger's departure. Looking at her, Kantakouzenos VI said, "Our dear son-in-law sent a messenger to inform me that he would like an audience with me. I also want to talk to him. I hope he won't talk about anything that will hurt my feelings. I suppose I have become very soft lately, it doesn't take much for me to become resentful. Even though his call doesn't seem to be very auspicious I will still go and listen to what he has to say. After all, we have to make a decision sooner or later."

Empress Irene took care not to hurt her husband's feelings, "John, you have really become suspicious and fragile lately. The rumours that have been spreading have deflated you. You have served the empire all this time, I am sure the young emperor has much to learn from your experiences. I am certain that he is probably asking for an audience with you so that you can counsel him. I think it is irrational for you to be suspicious of everything."

Co-Emperor Kantakouzenos VI left his mansion in a hurry after listening to what the Empress had said and got on the imperial carriage that was waiting for him. Despite the fact that he wanted to get off the carriage pulled by well-groomed horses, the moment they started trotting he immediately listened to his inner voice that said, "Whatever may happen will happen" and sat back in his seat. After muttering to himself, "I shall caution the lead guard to be careful and to come to the palace gates if he doesn't hear from me within the hour", he fell silent. As they got closer to the palace he listened to the sound of clapping horseshoes. In his mind Antiphon's words lingered, *"Life is filled with an astonishing level of destitution, there is nothing exciting, noble or sacrosanct. Everything is small, weak and short-term and it all depends on deep sorrows and toils"* and then he remembered the great conflict between the Athenians and Spartans. As a bitter smile spread across his lips, he said, "All of it was for the sake of sovereignty, just as everything we do..."

He bit his lower lip with his upper teeth as if he hadn't finished what he was going to say. It had nothing to do with the subject on his mind but loudly and suddenly he said, "Who knows, perhaps there are as many bodies decaying in the depths of the Aegean Sea as the sands that cover the seabed of Helle. Then he muttered, "What difference does it make if one John Kantakouzenos joins them or not," and his mind shut down. He was unable to think. He felt drowsy even though they were about to arrive at the palace. This state of sleepiness had begun to happen frequently since his return from Antigone. He constantly felt like napping regardless of the time of day. That was also partially why he didn't go to visit the imperial palace. Most of the time he accepted the mesazōn sent by his son-in-law in the study of his mansion and informed the Co-Emperor of his decisions with the mediatorship of the mesazōn. He spent most of his free time with his expecting daughter Helena who frequently visited him. During her last visit he'd discovered a difference in her gaze but he couldn't really put a finger on it. However, because he trusted his daughter, he thought that if there was bad news, Helena would definitely tell him. As such he had refrained from prying.

When they reached the imperial palace, he forgot about his inner conversations as he walked past the courtyard and entered the palace. He repeated his previous sentence, "Whatever may happen, will happen... After this age I am not..." As he usually did in recent times he once again left his sentence incomplete. Seeing the worry in the young Co-Emperor's face, who greeted him standing up, the aged Co-Emperor said, "Son of Andronicus, you seem very anxious..."

Co-Emperor Palaiologos V replied in a sour tone of voice, "On the one hand I am trying to speak sense to the church, those in government and to our dissociated supporters and on the other hand, I'm having to deal with the cumbersomeness of my dear brother-in-law, your imperial partner Matthew Kantakouzenos..."

Co-Emperor Kantakouzenos VI didn't get on well with his son Matthew either, but he would never let anyone speak ill of him. In an attempt to defend him, the Emperor said, "My Matthew would never do anything to upset my dear son-in-law. If there is something he didn't do, it's probably because it was out of his hands."

Co-Emperor Palaiologos V replied with a sense of maturity that Kantakouzenos VI didn't expect, "My dear imperial partner and venerable father-in-law... We must never forget that your son-in-law, and my brother-in-law Suleyman, son of Orhan, has intentions to settle in our peninsula. All this time neither Matthew nor the Duca of Aenus has done anything to stop him from expanding his lands. I warned them to do whatever it takes to stop the Ottomans. However, as you can see they have informed me that they will not leave their castles, let alone stop the Ottomans. Now, the Ottomans have not only mended the walls of Gallipoli Fortress but they are also telling people not to pay their taxes to Byzantium. Moreover, they convinced the people who became homeless after the earthquake to voluntarily immigrate to the opposite shore. And, now their irregular light cavalry forces are advancing towards the Black Sea. This is against all the agreements they have made with us and in my opinion, this on its own constitutes a reason to start war."

Co-Emperor Kantakouzenos VI paused briefly before responding, "Yes, that is a reason to start war. All that you say is fair, son of Andronicus. But are we strong enough to go into battle against them? You see, they have transferred thousands of cavalrymen and infantry to our peninsula in the blink of an eye. All this indicates that they are here to stay. They are raiding our lands to provoke us into battle. I suppose what they want, is for us to declare war on them because if we do, they will no longer be considered as invaders. They will use that as an excuse to attack us on all fronts. I wish we had the power to fight them on all fronts, I would then say that we should declare war against them as you say. You now grasp the situation better than I do. There is no one who will aid us. Those in the west don't give anything for free. When it comes to Pontus, they are dealing with their own internal problems. We can't expect aid from a few fortresses on the Black Sea who could potentially help us, because they are also in pursuit of trying to get on well with the dynasties surrounding them to sustain their existence. We can't throw them in the fire by asking them to help us. There is only one thing we can do. We have to meet Orhan, accept his terms and convince him to maintain peace. Later, we can underhandedly come to an agreement with our neighbours and find a way to repel the Ottomans from Thrace."

"I'm not sure which neighbours you're referring to..."

"I mean the ones to the south and north of Didymóteicho, or perhaps even those that are further away."

"I understand about the north, but do you mean the Catalans who have settled in the south, in Athens?"

Co-Emperor Kantakouzenos VI made a wry face upon hearing the name of the Catalans, "No, no, to hell with the Catalans! I mean the native Despotēs there. We can tell them that if they don't help us their turn will come sooner or later."

"And the others?"

"Serbians, Croatians and Macedonians. We could even stretch

this as far as the Vatican and Avignon."

"All this would take very long, I mean for us to procure their help. We don't have any time."

"I said it before and I'll say it again, they are forcing us to declare war. It's best if we don't hurry and make it easy on them. Winter is ahead. They can't advance quickly in Thrace in the winter. Even if they advance a bit now, inclement weather will stop them in their tracks. As they deal with the harsh weather we can try to attain peace and complete the preparations for the big move we will make on them in spring. We can renew the armada from top to bottom and keep a sharp lookout on the Dardanelles."

Co-Emperor Palaiologos V scratched his shaven face with his fingertips as if to claw it and said, "I will discuss this matter with members of the church and the government. Also, we must do something to suppress the rumours about you. If you like, I can talk to the Patriarch and you can meet with your supporters. We should gather the pontiffs, knights, counts and government officials. Talk to them in unison and eradicate the disunion among them. Otherwise, it is a matter of time before fires spread in Constantinople."

Co-Emperor Kantakouzenos VI shook his head to either side as he looked at his son-in-law's face. He decided that his son-in-law wasn't intending harm or trying to push him into a corner. He thought, "If he wanted to do me harm, he wouldn't say such things," and replied, "I am fed up of hearing these rumours, too. It would be great to meet with all the concerned parties and finalise this situation for once and all. Everyone should get rid of the disillusionment that we have unresolved issues amongst ourselves. As long as we don't achieve that, we can neither attain peace amongst us nor become strong enough to go into battle with the Ottomans. We should delegate tasks. We should write to the Serbians, Bulgarians and Hungarians to explain the enormity of the danger we are facing in Thrace. We should also inform our castle commanders, dukes and Despotēs of the situation in detail. I will warn Matthew not to make any moves on his own."

Co-Emperor John Palaiologos V replied in a low tone of voice as he cast his gaze on the floor, "We will also send a letter to Prussia informing them that we want to come to a new agreement with Orhan. We can imply that we will give whatever is necessary for him to retreat from Thrace."

"That's a good idea but what if he demands a sum we cannot pay?"

After a sly smile, Emperor Palaiologos V continued expressing his train of thought, "As long as we can afford paying the initial part of the sum, we won't have to concern ourselves with the latter."

CHAPTER THIRTY-THREE

S tanding on the pier with the stately body he inherited from his father, Akça Kocaoğlu looked at the last departing ships and barges and smiled with the joy of having fully completed another task that was delegated to him. Meanwhile, Suleyman Pasha was standing near the castle gate that opened onto the pier and watching him from a distance. He addressed Evrenos Bey and Hacı Ilbey who were also beside him, "Beys, the fact that the homeless have abided by my father's suggestion and immigrated to the opposite shore has made our work here a lot easier as we pondered on how we were going get the people of Gallipoli to accept our terms. Akça Kocaoğlu has been very efficient in sorting out means of transportation. What we have to do now is to rebuild the dwellings of those who have left, before arrival the people from the opposite shore. In order to achieve this, we need competent and skilful craftsmen. Send word to Fazıl Bey so that he can send us all the craftsmen among his captives. We should also send word to my father so that he can send us immigrants who are skilful craftsmen.

As the three beys talked among themselves in a language he didn't understand, the priest of the Gallipoli Fortress, who had been following them everywhere for the past three days, was watching the voluntary immigrants set out on barges. When the departed immigrants gained a distance from the Gallipoli Fortress and reached the pier of Lampsacus[31] he stopped watching them. He turned to Evrenos Bey as if he had understood what Suleyman Pasha told them and asked, "Will they be allowed to return when they want to?"

After briefly thinking about his reply, Evrenos Bey said, "Saintly father, once they spend the winter where they are headed they will be asked whether they wish to return in the spring. Those who wish to

---

31 T.N, Lampsacus was an ancient Greek city strategically located on the eastern side of the Hellespont in the northern Troad.

return will surely be allowed to do so but those who want to stay there will also be given land."

The elderly priest briefly delved into his thoughts. Then without hiding his suspicion he asked, "My son, Evrenos, will they have a church where they can hold mass?"

Evrenos Bey looked at the old priest with soft eyes. In a tone as soft as his eyes he explained that the Ottomans never laid a hand on the churches of the castles they invaded and that those who wish to pray can continue to pray in their own places of worship. Despite his persuasive explanation, the old priest didn't seem to believe in what he was told. Nevertheless, he never asked another question on this subject after that day.

As hasty days chased one another and winter approached, Suleyman Pasha left the governance of the recently invaded castles on the southwest of the Gallipoli peninsula under the care of Hacı Ilbey, and was busy consigning new *yaya* and *akıncı* units. Meantime, he was sending the captives sent by Fazıl Bey to Bursa. In turn, Fazıl Bey was delegated with the task of advancing to the northeast of Thrace. The people of the invaded castles who co-operated with the *akıncıs* usually remained in their castles and, in fact, they even became the new governors of the castle. Fazıl Bey, the brain behind this method, was very content with how things were going. Thanks to his method he had managed to conquer many small castles in the blink of an eye and closed in on the castles perched on the coasts of the dark seas without causing any casualties.

As Fazıl Bey captured the small castles with the implementation of such a simple method, the beys of *akıncıs* were continuing to annex the villages outside the castles as Ottoman lands with Ahiyan-i Rum, Ghaziyan-i Rum and Baciyan-i Rum[32] units under their command.

---

32 T.N, "Ahiyan-i Rum" refers to the *Âhis* or *Akhts* which was a fraternity and guild which for more than half a century was also a *Beylik* in 14th century Turkey. The "Gaziyan-i Rum" was defence units formed by Turkmens settled in the Aegean coast. The "Baciyan-i Rum" was an order of female warriors who were highly trained in archery.

The literate villagers who spoke several languages were talking to those who had small lands and convincing them to emmigrate to Bursa with the promise that they would be given vast lands. The houses that became vacant after their departure were given to the nomadic Turkmens leading the units and as such, permanent settlement was achieved in newly conquered lands. The immigrants who voluntarily departed for Bursa were settling in the fertile lands of Anatolia and teaching cultivation methods to the nomadic Turkmens. Thus, that was how balance and order was attained, and no one was treated unfairly.

Advancing through Thrace bit by bit with his *akıncıs* and implementing unconventional methods, Suleyman Pasha set up his marquee near Plajar Castle[33] on the brink of winter. He referred to this place as the "location of the most beautiful sunset". Suleyman Pasha usually watched the consignment of the units that arrived recently sitting atop his horse from dawn until dusk. On bright days he returned to his marquee set up on the hillside of the Plajar Castle early so he could watch the sunset. Sometimes he watched the setting of the sun while sitting on the back of his Grey, and sometimes he dismounted, leaned back against a tree and cast his gaze on the sun gliding down the horizon. As if to show him his skills, the sun first painted the horizon deep ochre, and then swallowed the blue moirés of flames created around the huge ball of fire beside the deep red horizon. Watching the sunset in admiration, Suleyman Pasha asked, "Were there others before me who watched this beauty from the same hills?" while the blue sky, jealous of the sun's exquisite show, cast its darkness over the horizon and instantly devoured the flaming blue moirés and the sun.

The locals called this small castle "Plagiari" while Suleyman Pasha and his beys referred to it simply as Plajar. It was from there that Suleyman Pasha watched the sun's play of light at sunset with a re-

---

33 T.N, Plajar is current-day Bolayır, a town situated on the Gallipoli peninsula.

newed enthusiasm every day. One of those days he thought, "It is time to watch the sunset," left his marquee and slowly walked towards a nearby meandering tree. He sat down and leaned back on the thick trunk of the tree. Squinting slightly he began to watch the sunset. On the horizon, there were white clouds that looked as if they had been slashed with a knife. The sun looked crimson because the clouds refracted the light. As the sun quickly closed in on the clouds, as if he was angry with them for destroying his rubescence, the clouds advanced towards the sun like fearless warriors. Their aim was uncertain—were they trying to swallow the sun or claw the sky? Suleyman Pasha smiled whilst watching them and muttered, "If I were you, I would quickly run away from him." The clouds surely couldn't hear him, so they swallowed the red moirés of the sunset after trying to claw the face of the sun, knowing that they would vanish if they came into contact with it. Meanwhile, Suleyman Pasha turned his head and looked at the Tzympe Castle visible beyond the small observation tower located at the south of Plajar Castle. His gaze extended out to the blue waters of the Dardanelles. When he became restive with the shapeless contours of the opposite coastline, which looked like a line on the horizon, he turned his face to the north. This time his glance met the waters of the Aegean Sea furtively flowing into Thrace. A light beam percolating up from the waters pierced the scattered clouds and reached the sun. His gaze wandered on this light beam between the land and the sky. The clouds, jealous of Suleyman Pasha's eyes seeking the sun, slithered towards the sun like hasty children. A reflection of the sun appeared above the clouds when his light was veiled. Suleyman Pasha further leaned against the tree and said, "You are not going to give it a rest this evening," as if he was cross with the clouds. When he noticed that he was likening the jealous clouds shaped by the light play of the sun to various animals, he remembered that he hadn't been out hunting for a long time. As he looked at the sun, who was finally winning his battle against the clouds, he said, "Ece Bey is right to refer to this place as the waist of the peninsula." He was just about to get ready to watch the sun slide between the mountains in the horizon when he heard footsteps. He turned his head and looked in the direction of the sound. Seeing that Ece Bey and Evrenos Bey were walking towards him he muttered, "They know that this is my moment of seeking shelter in my loneliness. If what they had to say wasn't important they wouldn't disturb me." He stood up. As he looked at Ece Bey, whose beard had completely turned silvery in the light, he thought, "The heirloom of my father, my treasured Ece Bey seems to have grown old in these lands..." Just as his gaze lingered on Evrenos Bey's ranginess, he reiterated his previous thought, "There must be an important reason as to why they have come."

CHAPTER THIRTY-FOUR

Emperor Kantakouzenos VI jumped out of his bed in distress as soon as his head chamber servant left. He began traipsing around the room swaying his silk robe and looking at the tapestries hung on the dark purple walls in his stately bedchambers, the washroom in the corner of the room separated with a curtain and the huge bed in the middle of the large room. He wandered around the room for a while without thinking about his exhaustion. Then he suddenly stopped, put his hands together, clasped them into a single fist and started punching the feather pillow he laid his head on every night. When his arms felt weak and he stopped, he thought about the strangeness of his fist—the fist he had never looked at before. His gaze wandered between the pillow and his fist. He smiled as he shook his head. Then, in a scream-like tone he shouted, "They have nothing to do other than bothering me!" His own voice scared him so much that he briefly remained still. He looked at his fist in embarrassment once again. He instantly freed his fingers from the fist. He put his open hands into the pockets of his dressing gown. He thought his voice must have been heard from outside the room and that the servants would run into the room at once. He thought that they would assume that the head chamber servant who recently left the room had harmed him in some way and decide to question her. They could perhaps even detain the innocent girl and accuse her of something she didn't do. But because the walls of the spacious room were covered with tapestries from Persia, Philadelphia (Alaşehir), and Felek Abad (Lycia) his scream was absorbed by them and those on the other side of the walls hadn't heard a thing.

That's why none of his strange expectations actually came to fruition. This somewhat caused a breeze of lethargy to course through his body. After a while, his lethargy turned into exhaustion. When all traces of his previous vitality vanished, he literally dragged his old body back to bed. That morning he sent his wife to Helena, who felt heavily pregnant with every passing day. Regretful that Irene was not with him he muttered, "Perhaps I should call the servant and take another bath." He himself was shocked that his brain, contrary to his exhausted body, was functioning promptly and that his thoughts were changing swiftly. Just as he covered his face with his hands and resigned himself to the motion of his thoughts he repined, "To hell with them all... I will go to Didymóteicho after I take my grandchild into my arms. I can decide what my next move will be while I rest. This way, in my absence, son of Andronicus can have a taste of how difficult it is to govern the empire all alone. What I resent bitterly is that despite all my service and all the great endeavours I have undertaken, Patriarch Kalekas still bothers me instead of getting on with his errands. When I was mesazōn I voiced to the Palaiologos that he didn't even possess a mansion. The Palaiologos gave me such a hard time until the mansion he resides in now was built. Nevertheless, he is disturbed by my mere existence, as if he has forgotten all that I did for him. If only I had worked towards uniting the church by reaching consensus with Andronicus! If I had done that I could now ask for the help of the popes from Rome and Avignon. Surely the popes wouldn't write us off so easily. I didn't trust the mesazōn because he sided with the Palaiologos but what have I ever done to the Patriarch?" He looked at his large bed as if he was ashamed and fear, like a cold breeze, cruised over his skin. He felt his heart grow cold at the same time as his skin. As the shivering encased his entire body he yelled out "Ach!" This time around, his voice came out piercing and the servants who heard it from the room next door entered his bedchambers. Seeing them enter the room, Kantakouzenos VI said, "Fill the bath with hot water again. In the meantime, prepare me for my bath."

Then he repeated himself in a commanding and harsh voice, "Make sure the water is nice and hot."

The servants who helped him take his morning bath first looked at each other in surprise upon hearing the Emperor's command and then quickly began to prepare his bath.

As the chamber servants of Kantakouzenos VI got him ready to bathe in the Venetian-made spelter bathtub filled with steaming hot water, young Co-Emperor John Palaiologos V was lazing in his bed, enjoying his day off in his mansion. When, at some point, he momentarily dosed off he began to dream about one of his long walks when he was on exile in Tenedos. He was walking at the front with the prime minister behind him. The prime minister was talking incessantly. Tired of the prime minister's constant and never-ending monologue, young Emperor Palaiologos V suddenly turned back and shouted, "All you ever want is blood to be spilt, nothing else!" After a short silence, he said, "I don't care what it is that *you* want! I no longer wish for blood to be spilt in Constantinople. When I return home I can't tell my beloved Helena that I have to get her father murdered... or that I got her father murdered. The Patriarch and a member of your delegation should go and reason with the Emperor. Perhaps he will consent and no blood will be spilt in our Constantinople. The streets will perhaps then not be washed with the blood of the supporters of the Kantakouzenos and the Palaiologos. We are not emperors from Rome, the Council of Athens or the Spartan Senate. Nor are we the Latins. We are children of Byzantium. We cannot let each other's supporters be killed. You should all come back to your senses. When you reach Constantinople, tell the Patriarch what I just told you."

The stubborn mesazōn was tired of talking at length and walking behind the Emperor. However, he thought he would try his luck one last time. "Your Majesty! Your Majesty, there is just one thing you should know. The Palaiologos are both the rightful owner of Byzantium and the protector of Byzantium against the Latins. The struggle between you and your father-in-law is nothing like the struggle between the Athenians and Spartans. Their fight was about which of their city states would be superior. The struggle between you and your father-in-law Kantakouzenos VI is an entirely different story. Yes, John Kantakouzenos has dedicated his life to Byzantium and he is a relative of the Palaiologos from his mother's side but this cannot be a reason for him to demand imperial rights. Because, before and after him, there have been people who have served our empire just as much as he did and none of them wished to be Co-Emperor in our Byzantium in exchange for their services. This is an ethical legacy that has been bestowed upon us throughout history. It shouldn't be the Kantakouzenos who change this legacy. I don't even want to know what will befall our Byzantium if that happens."

He paused to catch his breath and also to see the effect his speech was having on the young emperor. He wiped the sweat dripping from the tip of his red and round nose with his handkerchief made of Laodiceia and Mora silk. When he felt that his body, wrapped in black clothes, was shaking to the bone he thought that the Emperor's silence lasted far too long and accepted that this was another way of dismissing what he had said. He then, with all his courage and in a cold tone of voice, decided to say his last words which he presumed would influence the Emperor's decision, "Sire, you have to do something for the future of Constantinople, for you and for our princes who are to be born, and for the happiness of our people. Otherwise, you will only become half an emperor by accepting the demands of usurper Kantakouzenos. Or even worse, you will spend the rest of your days on this deserted island."

Emperor Palaiologos V was young and full of youthful energy and as such, his ambition occasionally took precedence over his mind. However, because he had matured since his arrival at the island, he ignored all that his mesazōn told him. He responded, "Oh, my faithful mesazōn, you and my other wise counsels have tirelessly been telling me the same things over and over again since my arrival at the island. I am grateful to you for confirming my thoughts but I assume I will also have to wait for my body to also be strong. All that I wish you to do for now, is to send news to our supporters and to inform them that they shouldn't break the peace in our Constantinople. We will not be any different from the Kantakouzenos if our supporters disturb the peace, will we? Then what will happen to our nobility as the Palaiologos?"

He had just completed his sentence when his dream became hazy. He was surrounded by a dingy light. The image of his mesazōn disappeared in that light. Gladiators wearing glimmering armour began to charge towards him. He screamed, "Ouch" in a very high tone of voice upon feeling the pain caused by the sharp tip of the first gladiator's sword touching his skin and leapt on his bed.

Empress Helena, deep in sleep due to her pregnancy, also woke up to her husband's scream. She told the servant, who had entered the room upon hearing a noise, to re-light all the colourful oil lamps in the dim room. As the servants renewed the wicks of the oil lamps situated in the corners of the room, she caressed her husband's back with her soft hands. When she realised that the young emperor's body wouldn't stop shivering, she held his hands and placed them on her tummy. Startled by feeling the baby's kick, with trembling hands Palaiologos V escaped the clutches of his dream. With his gaze, he caressed the hands of the empress positioned on his hands. Sensing the happiness in his eyes, Empress Helena caressed her husband's hand and said, "My father is sending my mother here today. He suggested that she should stay with us for a while as I am nearing the end of my pregnancy. Perhaps she's already arrived. It would be best if you let go of your judgments about my father. You see, we are in our Constantinople, as we wanted. I am going to give birth to my child here, at the imperial palace. These days my father doesn't think about much else other than seeing his grandchild. You must be a bit patient and resolute in the face of rumours. You know that my father doesn't agree with what my brother Matthew has been doing, but he can't cast him aside either because he is his son. Please, John overcome your night terrors and get a proclamation written to be read in church. Specify clearly that the Palaiologos and the Kantakouzenos families are governing the empire, that this will continue to be so for a while and that no one has the right to involve himself in the governance of the empire. This proclamation should be read by the priests and announced to the masses by town criers so that no one throttles each other anymore."

The young emperor asked the time of day to the servants in the room. One of the servants informed him that it was afternoon. As the Emperor got out of bed and plunged himself in his bath he said, "Helena, it's too late, I am going to go to the working palace after breakfast."

Her servants helped her as Empress Helena exerted herself to get out of bed. Looking at her husband, who was bathing with the help of very young handmaidens she said, "You are right, it is quite late. Mother must have arrived, or she is about to arrive. I suppose we can have breakfast all together when she arrives."

The warm bath felt good to young Emperor John V Palaiologos who woke up from his dream sweating blood. As he played with the water like a child, he felt that he was slowly being stimulated by the fingertips wandering on his young body. As Empress Helena left their bed-chamber, he said, "I'm going to resolve everything today, dear Helena."

CHAPTER THIRTY-FIVE

The news delivered by Fazıl Bey's messengers made Suleyman Pasha and the other beys happy. Their gazes became deepened. Suleyman Pasha looked at the faces of Hacı Ilbey and Ece Bey, growing grey like their hair, and said, "Beys, both God and the people living in the heart of the peninsula want us to remain in these lands. This is exactly what we desired since the first moment we stepped foot here. The plans we make from now on must be in accordance with the idea of our permanent existence in this land."

After remaining silent for some time, acting as if he was hiking to another realm within himself and with his gaze fixed on the floor, he continued, "I say we have to spend time thinking about all this and devise a plan on this irremediable matter in the best way possible. For this plan to be permanent we have to include my father in our deliberations."

Hacı Ilbey pushed down his woolly skullcap, which he wore when he was not on a campaign, with one hand and then trailed over the fingertips of the same hand on his forehead as if he had a bright idea. He then spoke softly, "My Bey, so what you mean to say is that we should put a hole through the pearl in a single attempt to increase its value."

Suleyman Pasha smiled, first directing his questioning gaze at Hacı Ilbey and later at Evrenos Bey. Evrenos Bey had to have understood the question lurking behind Suleyman Pasha's gaze as he, in an all-knowing tone of voice, said, "My Bey, a pearl that is drilled twice is not desirable."

With his gaze fixed on the beys, Suleyman Pasha shrieked with laughter and his broad shoulders jerked. His heart burst with joy and he replied, "So that's what we shall do, drill a single hole into the pearl that has been given to us so it shall be desirable and valuable. However, before we drill a hole in this beautiful pearl we should arrange a hunting party to find it. We haven't been able to go out hunting to our hearts' content for the last two years."

With the self-esteem of his old age Hacı Ilbey cut in, "My Bey, I think we should transfer our harems to this coast and then we can go on that tremendous hunting party."

Evrenos Bey showed his support, "My Bey, Hacı Ilbey is right, I also think it is time we transferred our harems here."

Looking at his beys with a smile on his face, Suleyman Pasha replied, "If the heirlooms of my ancestors say it is time I won't object. The hunting can commence after we transfer the harems here. In any case, there is no one to scare away the wild animals in the forest across from us, at least for now.

After listening to his beys wishing him "a long and prosperous life" he continued, "We shouldn't make hasty decisions. I say we should go to the marquee of our headquarters and talk to the others. I assume Ece Bey has arrived or he is just about to."

Then he walked towards the marquee of the headquarters.

Seeing them enter the marquee, Akça Kocaoğlu and Ece Bey, who had just arrived from Gallipoli, and Kara Hasanoğlu who had arrived from Bursa with his *yaya* units stood up in respect and greeted them. Then, upon the hand signal from the Prince, they all sat back down on their cushions. Kara Hasanoğlu addressed Ece Bey as if he wanted to finish a half-spoken thought, "It is also Orhan Ghazi's wish that *yayas* are settled in the castles before winter bears down."

Hacı Ilbey, who had already dispatched the *yayas* in the direction of the *akıncıs*, and predetermined where the newly arriving *yayas* were to be sent, looked at troubled Kara Hasanoğlu and tried to assuage him, "Do not fret Kara Hasanoğlu, there are plenty of large castles in Thrace to accommodate your *yayas* and our cavalry. Before your arrival we decided that it would be best if the *yayas* and the *akıncıs* are settled in close proximity so that when they need help they can quickly run to aid each other. We'd sent our previous *yayas*

so they can provide support to the akıncıs of Balabancıkoğlu. Your
infantry will be posted near to the *akıncıs* of Fazıl Bey who is advancing towards the Black Sea coast. You will spend this winter settling
in the castles that you capture over there."

Kara Hasanoğlu smiled wide with his pearly white teeth showing.
After getting his smile that spread from his greying beard to the hair-
less skin of his cheeks under control, he replied, "My Bey, we are
grateful for what is bestowed to us. We will do what we can to capture the castles that are bestowed to us and to avoid being stranded
in tents during the winter cold."

Ece Bey looked at Suleyman Pasha and said, "If our Bey sees fit,
Akça Kocaoğlu and I are thinking of over-wintering near Aenus. We
have received news that the Duca of Aenus is undertaking secret
measures. We will lay siege to Aenus and keep the peninsula under
control. As he is the new Duca we might end up in a tough situation
if he decides to get in the good graces of the Emperor. For now it
doesn't seem as if he is going to attack but we think that in such situ-
ations we must be cautious and always be on the lookout."

Hacı Ilbey had already discussed this matter with Suleyman Pasha
and Evrenos Bey and had asked Evrenos Bey to settle in that area.
Suleyman Pasha approved the decision but he also stated that the
subject should be discussed in the Beylik council. That's why when he
heard Ece Bey's suggestion he was a bit overthrown. He made a sour
face and fell silent until he came to terms with the idea that Ece
Bey's train of thought was right in his own way. Then he responded,
"We discussed this matter yesterday evening. You are right, Ece Bey.
I also agree that we shouldn't leave that region unattended. As you
say we can never know what the next action of someone who has just
become worthy of a title will be. Especially if we keep in mind that
the wealth of this new Duca has become a byword, we can also figure out that he could also put together an army of mercenaries and
attack us. If, in the north, Kantakouzenos wasn't concerned about

his own dealings they would have marched on us long ago. However, since our *akıncıs* have been able to infiltrate the areas surrounding Hadrianopolis we can say that Kantakouzenos neither has the time nor the power to bother us. Considering all this we can conclude that the new Duca and the Emperor won't be attacking us for now."

After Suleyman Pasha's speech ended, Evrenos Bey said, "You are both surely right. We should consider all possibilities and take caution accordingly. I think that we should first take the coastal castles on both sides of the strait under our control. The Byzantine armada is currently the most powerful in both the Aegean and the Mediterranean Seas. Thus, we should have control over all the ports that the Byzantine armada will use as harbours. I think it will be best to keep control over arrivals from sea by capturing coastal castles and to advance in Thrace with our *akıncıs*, taking over lands piece by piece. I am in support of Ece Bey guarding the harbours of Gallipoli and Maydos. I also agree that Akça Kocaoğlu should raid the coastal castles to the north of Plajar. Meanwhile, I can advance between Hadrianopolis and Aenus with my *akıncıs*. It would be very beneficial if we could buy barges and galleons suited to our requirements from either the Genoese or the Venetians."

Suleyman Pasha's gaze wandered on the faces of his beys. As it grew darker inside the marquee, he watched the servants light the oil lamps hanging on stakes. When the servants were done with brightening the marquee he said, "I am also in support of Evrenos Bey's plan. Our *akıncıs* should continue their advances in the north, east and west. The *yayas* should also back them up. Keeping the ports under control is the wisest move. We can buy barges and galleons with the treasures we plunder during our raids. However, we should at once inform my father, Orhan Ghazi, of these decisions with a letter. That way we can also find out if he has any suggestions."

The chief messenger of the command marquee who had been waiting by the entrance for some time waited for Suleyman Pasha to finish his speech, and then bowed down to greet him. Then he announced, "My Bey, the private messenger sent by Orhan Ghazi has arrived."

When Suleyman Bey looked at Hacı Ilbey, Hacı Ilbey hastily gathered himself together as he was responsible for managing such duties, and said, "Don't keep him waiting, show him in."

CHAPTER THIRTY-SIX

Fed up with the hearsay and gossip in Constantinople, Co-Emperor Kantakouzenos VI had already handed over his duties to his son-in-law and retreated to his palace, which he referred to as the mansion in Phanari[34]. He didn't meet with anyone other than the mesazōn sent by Co-Emperor Palaiologos V. As he dreamed about holding his third grandchild-to-be-born, he consoled himself by thinking, "Everything will change after my Helena gives birth." Meanwhile, in Constantinople, an endless thread of rumours spread about him. According to the rumours, the streets smelled of blood more and more each day. On one hand the supporters of Palaiologos were being provoked by the supporters of the Patriarch and on the other hand, the followers of Kantakouzenos were pouring oil on the fire, and flaming the anticipated conflict by producing as many rumours as they could. At times, when Kantakouzenos VI distanced himself from dreams of having another grandchild, he muttered, "Everything will change after my grandchild is born. I have never meddled in anything until now but after the birth I am going to speak in a way they will understand. And if I don't, Matthew, who won't let go of his imperial partnership, will not pay heed to anyone when he hears this news. I hope that for the time being he won't hear these rumours because if he does, he will come here at once. Let alone sanguining the streets, he will even kill the baby in his sister's womb and cause a bloodbath in the palace. I don't want that. What I wish is that our Byzantium is governed the way we govern it now, in partnership with Andronicus's son. In the future, they should pull together and govern Byzantium as uncle and nephew. The Ottoman

---

34 T.N, Referred to here as "Phanari," Fener is a neighbourhood midway up the Golden Horn within the district of Fatih in Istanbul, Turkey. The streets in the area are full of historic wooden mansions, churches, and synagogues dating from the Byzantine and Ottoman eras. The wooden mansions between the main axis and the shore were often used for importing wood from Pontus or the Black Sea area.

grip on Constantinople is tightening every passing day. If Orhan hears that we fell out, he will enter the castle with the excuse of aiding us never to leave again. Neither my son Matthew nor the Patriarch or my son-in-law Palaiologos are able to anticipate this. Whose lifetime is ever long enough to know everything?" His recent soliloquy had reached such a level that the servants who entered his chambers usually found him talking to himself. Even though they didn't like the Emperor's lethargic speech, they couldn't confront him. They sometimes interjected, "Your Majesty, we are as much in the right as Justinian's Greens were... Your followers will take action upon a single command from you. Constantinople will not attain peace before the Blues die off."

Kantakouzenos VI never got angry no matter who spoke to him, instead, he just sighed and quietly replied, "I used to assume that I could see what was happening in the Genoese neighbourhood by just looking out the windows of my mansion. Howbeit, I couldn't even see what was going on in my own palace." After uttering such broken sentences, he usually got up and resentfully sought peace in his bed-chamber. He wasted some time and plunged himself in the lukewarm bath prepared by the handmaidens.

That day Arakos, one of his most loyal men, who had also grown old, told him all the gossip he had heard in a trice and said, "Your Majesty, it is time you elucidated your supporters."

Co-Emperor Kantakouzenos VI didn't say anything. He merely headed for his bed-chamber after looking at Arakos and those who were there at the time with previously unequalled anger. The handmaidens in the adjacent room heard him shut the door of his bed-chambers and immediately came to his chamber and prepared another lukewarm bath. After being idle for a while, the Emperor undressed and got into the steaming bathtub. He had just let his body relax with the soft caresses of the handmaidens when Arakos, the only man who was allowed to enter his bed-chamber, hastily walked into the room. Seeing him from behind the half-open bath curtain, emperor Kantakouzenos VI said, "Arakos, did you forget to tell me something?"

With his gaze on the floor, Arakos said, "Sire, I didn't forget anything. As someone who experiences everything beside you, I know you are right in your decisions. I don't wish to talk more about this matter but I have to inform you of the news that has just arrived."

Looking at him curiously, Kantakouzenos VI replied, "I suppose what you call news is a new thread of gossip."

Arakos, who wasn't at all fond of beards, scratched his closely-shaven face with anxiety, "I don't know but the person who sent the news is one of your most trusted men. According to what he has heard, if you remain silent or get on your horse and abandon Constantinople, the supporters of Palaiologos are going to exile us for helping the Latins, just the way the Jews were. Upon hearing this news your men have begun preparations, they are swearing an oath to exiling them before they get exiled themselves."

Kantakouzenos VI understood that the situation was serious. However, he remained in his lukewarm bath and replied, "Fine, Arakos now go and gather the palace servants at the drawing hall. It is time that I talked to everyone."

Old Arakos walked to the door, without turning his back to the Emperor or tilting his head up, and exited the room. With his gaze following him, Co-Emperor Kantakouzenos VI immersed his body in the water and resigned himself to the soft caresses of the handmaidens. He muttered, "There must be an end to this just as there is an end to everything."

After staying in the bath for a long time, John VI Kantakouzenos got dressed with the help of his handmaidens. He held the hand of the handmaiden who was combing his beard for a while. His eyes smiled brightly in response to the laughter of the young girl. He looked at his other handmaidens for a while. Then he walked to the drawing hall with them. All the servants bowed down to the floor to greet him. Then, in an unruffled tone of voice, he began talking, "According to the news I received from Empress Irene, my daughter Empress Helena's birth pains have begun. If not tonight, by tomorrow morning my grandchild will be born. This will be one of the joys bestowed upon me by God. I have been happy many times before. In fact, after the death of Andronicus, I enjoyed great happiness as the king's regent. If it wasn't for Empress Anna's ambition, nothing would have turned sour. However, mesazōn Alexios whom I raised, and Patriarch Kalekas have hindered the Empress's ambition by continuously creating malice. A conflict of many years began because she couldn't face reality. It was vouchsafed that I was to become Co-Emperor with the help of my son-in-law, Orhan. For a while, everything was great but the cauldron of unrest was lit as it still is now. I thought that I could overcome these troubles by exiling them to Tenedos, but I was mistaken. Once the cauldron of unrest is ignited it boils regardless of whether it has any water in it. I am old and tired. Andronicus's son doesn't want siblings to throttle each other in Constantinople any longer. I believe that he will succeed in attaining peace, therefore..."

During this point in his speech, a sensation of lament knotted his throat. The silence that spread made the servants' ears ring. Looking at the servants huddled around him Emperor Kantakouzenos VI continued, "I have decided to leave here until the flame under the cauldron of unrest in Constantinople is extinguished. I have resolved on setting forth towards Didymóteicho after I take my baptised grandchild into my arms. All those who want to can come to Didymóteicho with us."

Then he walked to his study. He paused in front of the door and told Arakos who was following him, "Arakos, send word to the commander of the guards that I expect him at once."

CHAPTER THIRTY-SEVEN

Shivering with the chill of the breeze from the sea exceeding Mount Ganos that loomed like a dark cloud in the horizon at the break of dawn, Fazıl Bey turned back on his horse and looked at his cavalry following him in rows of two. They were followed by the *yayas* and rear guards. He laid his eyes on the valley that had been causing them hardship for days. As he turned and looked at the *akıncıs* ahead of him he muttered, "Taking over this valley has been unexpectedly hard. Byzantium seems to be powerless but you can't judge a book by its cover. Small castles surrender of their own volition but the guards of Peristasi Castle[35] defended the castle until their last breaths." As he looked at the gloomy clouds that looked like they were holding onto the zenith of Mount Ganos, he wrapped himself in his caftan with its thick lambskin lining. After positioning his red turban, which he styled in a distinctive way on his head, he leaned forward on his horse to shield himself from the harsh wind and trotted towards the *akıncıs* heading east.

Forces under Fazıl Bey's command were advancing towards the north-east of the peninsula by wiping out Byzantine knights at Uğraş Valley, who upon the Ottoman conquest had escaped from Peristasi Castle. Meanwhile, Suleyman Pasha and Hacı Ilbey, who were yet to find out that the castle had been captured, had set forth towards Peristasi Castle from their headquarters in Plajar with new forces that arrived from Bursa. Suleyman Pasha, riding his Grey right behind the leading *serdengeçtis*, got cold in the morning gales. Fazıl Bey was also cold. Suleyman Pasha, who hadn't encountered such cold weather since their campaign in Ancyra before they crossed the Dardanelles, was unable to think about anything on the back of his horse other than the cold that almost paralysed him. He let the reins of his horse loose and rubbed his numb forehead for a while. He

---

35 T.N, Peristasi Castle was near current-day Tekirdağ.

placed his hands under his armpits and leaned forward. He watched
the breath coming out of his Grey's nostrils as the horse ambled.
When he forced his mind to think, the first sentence that appeared
was, "Don't even try, the wind says 'I am the true proprietor of
mountains.'" He leaned further down his horse's neck. He had just
pushed his turban down to his ears and put his hands back under his
armpits when his thoughts took him back to his childhood days in
Bursa when his mother, Nilüfer Hatun left his younger brother Halil
at the mansion and took them to the gardens by the Nilüfer River...
He remembered mostly playing with his brother Murad. Despite the
fact that he got on quite well with his brother Kasım, he was erased
from his memory almost immediately after his death. Oddly enough,
he couldn't even remember his brother's face. It was as if, in compar-
ison to the memory of his sisters, Murad's and little Halil's faces, his
memory of Kasım had gone astray and risen up to the heavens.

Their mother, who always watched them play in the garden, was a
quiet woman but with a smile imprinted on her lips and her gaze,
turning meaningful by blinking her eyes, her face would tell much
about what she had on her mind. Though, when necessary, she sat
her children beside her and told them all she thought they should
know. She explained things to them in such a sweet and sour way
that no one of the children repeated the same mistake again. At
times when he sought shelter in such memories, he first and foremost
recalled the games they played in the garden, and then he would take
off on a long journey among the fruit trees in the gardens with the
male servant in charge of him and his brothers and the other servants employed to serve the children. That was also exactly what
happened this time. Leaning forward on his Grey ambling forward,
Suleyman Pasha set forth on a long journey down the path of his
memories that began with his mother and continued with the male
servant who was in charge of his care during his childhood. They
were advancing and watching the colourful flowers amidst the fruit

trees by the Nilüfer River. All of a sudden the flowers and his male servant began to talk to each other. In unison, the flowers said, "We are the most beautiful flowers in the world."

Suleyman Pasha's male servant looked at them and laughed, "You don't have to be so arrogant. Do you see those mountains surrounding Bursa?"

The flowers amidst the fruit trees replied with one voice, "Yes, we see them."

Suleyman Pasha's male servant smiled bitterly and then, looking at the flowers, he said, "Yes, but you only see one side of the mountains, if you could see them from the other side you wouldn't even call yourselves flowers."

When both his male servant and the flowers fell silent, Suleyman Pasha returned back to the times when he and his siblings used to visit the gardens with their mother. He tried to remember the games he played with his siblings as he strived to overcome the joy in his mind. He remembered his brother Kasım falling from the tree that he climbed up to hide in one day when they were playing hide and seek. As he could hardly restrain himself from laughing, the cool sea breeze blowing from the zenith of Mount Ganos went through his clothes and wandered over his skin. As his entire body shuddered, he muttered, "It wasn't as cold as this on our way back from Ancyra." He wrapped his sleeveless top made of lambskin tighter around his body. He looked at the mane of his Grey that swayed from side to side as if to play with the cold wind and smiled, as he tried to stop himself from shivering. He caressed the neck of his horse with one hand and with the other he did up the mother-of-pearl top button of his *buldan*[36] shirt sewn by Greek tailors from Bursa. He leaned forward once again and listened to his horse's intermittent breaths. As he strived to return to his memories and as they suddenly became

---

36 T.N, Buldan, a town and a district of Denizli Province in the inner Aegean Region of Turkey, was famed for a thin handwoven cheesecloth-type fabric, with laced edges and used chiefly for bed covers and tablecloths called "Buldan bezi" (Buldan clothes) after the name of the locality.

vivid, the voice of his conscience began talking, "On one of the days when the rumour that Geyikli Baba[37] had gifted my father a syca-more sapling spread from mouth to mouth, we'd bombarded mother with questions. As we waited for answers to our questions my mother said, 'Come on, I shall take you to the riverbank... Don't forget your questions because, as you walk under the fruit trees in the gardens, you will find the answers to your questions yourself.' Assuming that my mother was stalling us because she didn't know the answers to our questions, I insisted. My poor mother reached the end of her tether and finally in a soft tone of voice said, 'Dear Suleyman, I am not sure if Geyikli Baba ever visited your father or which sycamore he gifted to him but as you can see, there are tens of sycamore trees in the gardens of our mansions and the harem. Geyikli Baba might have brought one of the trees as a sapling. However, all the syca-mores are planted in rows and none of them takes a stroll in the gar-dens at night to chat with the other trees. I want you to know that sometimes people want to reach something they cannot attain in reality through their imagination. So the rumour that the sapling brought by Geyikli Baba walks the gardens at night and talks to the other sycamores must be a tale created by the imagination of those who believe in it. The tale is real as long as you believe it. You can also ask your father when he returns. Perhaps he can enlighten you further in this matter.' When we got into our new carriage and set forth towards the gardens dowsed by the Nilüfer River, I saw my mother looking at me resentfully and gathered that I'd insisted far too much on an answer. As I looked at her face apologetically, she held my hand and did not let go until we reached the gardens beside the riverbank. When we reached the gardens and got off our car-riage, she said, 'See my dear Suleyman, what is real is right in front of you' and pointed to the Tike Castle on the hill opposite. I looked

---

37 T.N, Geyikli Baba was a dervish who departed from Azerbaijan for Anatolia in the initial years of the establishment of the Ottoman Empire. It is rumoured that when the Ottomans settled in Bursa he participated in a war on the back of a deer and with a huge sword, scaring away the Greeks.

at the castle and told my mother that I hadn't understood what she meant. She sighed and said, 'My son, instead of trying to prove to me that you are growing you should just grow.' I was lost once again. My mother became slightly agitated and said, 'When tomorrow, or the day after, your father returns from his campaign he will tell you to gird yourself with a sword and ask you to prove yourself. You will have to do something to prove yourself to him. If you can't put your mind and power together and do something, you cannot make anyone believe that you have grown...' When my mother fell silent without looking at me in the face I suddenly uttered, 'What if my father doesn't return from his campaign?' Then quickly thinking about what my mother was trying to tell me, I came to the conclusion that I need to grow up before long."

The memories in his mind slipped away from him as suddenly as they'd appeared. When he realised his hands were under his armpits while he was on the back of his horse he had difficulty keeping himself from laughing. He spoke out loud, "Now I understand what my mother was trying to tell me as she looked at me with her dark blue eyes. That day was the day when I felt I had grown up. The pleasure of playing with my siblings had subsided. I constantly thought, 'This must be what growing up feels like...' Then I walked over to my mother, where she was sitting with her odalisques. They were all singing a song with the chorus line 'Hey Odryses[38], Odryses.' When the chorus line of the song my mother sang in Greek came up again, I clapped my hands and joined them, repeating, 'Hey Odyrses, Odryses.' That was the last time my mother took me to the gardens to play with my siblings."

That day Suleyman Pasha's memories appeared in his mind like a heavy downpour of rain. He sat up straight on his saddle. Viewing the slowly rising sun from behind Mount Ganos, he recalled his father's return from the campaign. His internal monologue contin-

---

38 T.N, Odryses is thought to be the first king of the Odrysian Kingdom, a state union of Thracian tribes that endured between the 5th and 3rd centuries BC.

ued, "What wonderful welcoming ceremonies we had! When my father entered the castle from the north gate the castle rejoiced, jugglers did somersaults in front of the trotting horses, swordsman clashed their swords, and wrestlers beat down their rivals." He suddenly became agitated and loudly commanded, "Giddy up!" The commanded blue-blood horse came to a halt instead of going forward. Confused about his horse's behaviour Suleyman Pasha looked ahead. When he saw the thick walls of the Peristasi Castle magnificently rising before him he muttered, "I must have been daydreaming" and turned back. He looked at Hacı Ilbey, who had been following him at a distance. As he muttered, "We got here so quickly" in surprise, he saw cavalrymen approaching them in full gallop from the castle. He tightened his horse's reins. He turned back and looked at Hacı Ilbey once more.

CHAPTER THIRTY-EIGHT

J ohn VI Kantakouzenos, always referred to by the Patriarch as usurper emperor, had been playing with his beard for hours. His wife, Empress Irene, was yet to return from his son-in-law's palace. Despite the fact that he had little time left, Kantakouzenos VI was determined to wait for his grandchild's birth. He was adamant on not leaving his mansion until Empress Irene returned with good news. He still thought that with the birth of his grandchild a rain of blessing would pour down on Constantinople. He also hoped that the Patriarch could at least bring the ugly propaganda about him to an end before his grandchild's baptism ceremony. That is why he had retired to his drawing-room. He didn't want to listen or talk to anyone. However, despite his wishes, those brave enough to talk to him came to his drawing-room, repeating that it would be too late if he didn't make a move at once. Co-Emperor John VI Kantakouzenos did everything he could do to ignore them but in the end, when another person walked in he turned around and looked at the Church of the Holy Apostles from the wide window of the room. When he saw that dusk had slowly filled the room and drowned the scenery of the neighbourhood opposite with darkness he said, "I thought the sun would never set today." He waited in silence and then muttered, "No one can do anything in this moonless night." The castle commander who had just entered the room and heard him talking to himself, looked at the deputy mesazōn behind him and then, leaning forward, he asked, "Your Majesty, did you want something, or perhaps you have an order for me?"

With the crestfallenness and exhaustion of waiting in insidious silence, Kantakouzenos VI remained with his back to them and said, "No, what could I order you to do now? What I was saying was that no one will be able to go out in the impending darkness and that means our Constantinople will have another easy and eventless night."

After watching the darkness swallow the houses in the neighbourhoods located on the hills opposite, he turned and looked at the
castle commander and the deputy mesazōn, whom he appointed as
the assistant to Demetrios. The deputy mesazōn understood what the
Emperor's gaze, which he knew very well and now was seeing in the
light of oil lamps, meant. In a bothered, sad and vulnerable tone of
voice he said, "Your Majesty, the messengers we sent out to various
neighbourhoods are probably on their way back now. There is still
no news from the messenger we sent to the Palaiologos mansion at
noon. According to our sources, the followers of Palaiologos have
surrounded the periphery of Vlakerne with twice as many guards because they know how loyal you are to the empress. But worry not—
Empress Irene is with your daughter. Co-Emperor Palaiologos
ordered, 'If even a single hair on my mother-in-law comes to harm
all the guards posted around my palace will be held responsible.' In
any case, this afternoon we sent her two of her handmaidens disguised as nuns."

Kantakouzenos VI was deeply saddened by the events that had
been taking place in Constantinople for the last two days. He felt
bound hand and foot because he couldn't do anything in the face of
the events. He could no longer believe in what anyone said because
the news that arrived changed from one minute to the other. He
feared that his mansion could be raided at any moment and that he
would be taken to one of the dungeons of the Blachernae Palace.
Whereas he and Co-Emperor Palaiologos V had come to an agreement and sent a definitive proclamation to all the neighbourhoods
and military units explaining, "No one has the right to make decisions in the name of the Emperors or to kill anyone. If anyone, who
does not have written orders from the Emperors, takes action in the
name of the Emperors, provokes supporters and causes the death of
anyone, they will themselves have prepared their own death sentence
when the Emperors find out." Although, not even this hard-edged

proclamation had extinguished the fires burning under the cauldron of gossip, the unrest spread by the men of Dowager Empress Anna and the Patriarch continued to wander from one house to the other. Thus, both the Emperors were doing all they could to avoid a new slaughter from taking place in the city but the danger surged. Emperor Kantakouzenos VI felt as if he was about to suffocate in the room. He took a deep breath and heaved a deep sigh—a sigh that carried within it everything pertaining to sadness. The commander of the guards and the deputy mesazōn, whom the Emperor considered to be his most loyal men, were crushed under the sadness of his voice. They began to feel guilty as if they were the ones who had done wrong. As they tilted their heads in sorrow and looked at each other out of the corner of their eyes, usurper Emperor John VI Kantakouzenos stopped playing with his scruffy beard. He then spoke, "My friends, this has to come to an end. I have been blessed to work with you over the years but I don't want our Constantinople to endure anymore pain. The time to retreat is upon us. Last week I told those under my service that they can, if they wish, come to Didymóteicho with us, and asked them to start preparations for the move. I assume they have made preparations even if it is unwillingly. I am not asking you to come with me. You will remain in Constantinople as my representatives and appease our followers. I have talked about this with my son-in-law and imperial partner John Palaiologos. He also trusts you. I was hoping to hold my grandchild in my arms but I now see that everything is getting worse by the hour. I will consider myself a victim of the circumstances and leave Constantinople before dawn. Now, I kindly ask one of you to go to my son-in-law and the other to the gossip jug that is the Patriarch and to inform them of my decision. If you receive good news from the palace of the Palaiologos deliver it to me immediately and safely transport Empress Irene to outside the city walls..."

Seeing that the Emperor was adamant in his decision to leave Constantinople, the deputy mesazōn, who had been in service of the Kantakouzenos family for years through good and bad times, said, "Your Majesty, I assume this is a temporary decision and that you are taking this action to calm the city?"

Referred to by the Patriarch as 'usurper' Emperor, Kantakouzenos replied, "This surely doesn't mean that I am withdrawing from my rights as Co-Emperor. But I don't want the blood of Kantakouzenos on the throne which will one day be taken over by one of my grandchildren."

The castle commander, who observed the way the deputy mesazōn, bowed his head in response to the Emperor's decision, said, "Sire, will your son Matthew approve of this? What if he turns this into a matter of honour for the Kantakouzenos? What will happen then?"

Co-Emperor Kantakouzenos hadn't even thought about this aspect. He felt an immense weight position itself upon his shoulders, which he tried hard to keep straight. From his men's comments he gathered that they had a good relationship with his son Matthew, an imperial partner, just as they did with him. He shuddered at the thought of his son arriving in Constantinople immediately after his departure. He turned back with worry and viewed the Genoese Quarter where oil lamps brightened houses. Everything seemed to be calm and ordinary in the Genoese Quarter. In any case the life inside the castle on this side of the Golden Horn didn't affect or interest them much. As he viewed the serene living on the opposite shore, he remembered how they used to go to the basement taverns behind the port long before he was appointed as head consul to Andronicus. As he shook his head to either side he said, "They all had secret exit doors... In fact, some of them even had two secret doors. Someone who discovered the first door would be faced with a thick wall, most people never discovered the second door hidden deep inside the wall," as a sad smile vanished from his lips. He remained with his back to his men who were still waiting on him to say something to them and continued, "Once, when I thought I would encounter my youthful fantasies in a half-dim corner I'd seen that Slavic beauty sitting across from me. First our eyes met. Then we sat beside each other... I held her hand as we sipped our blood-red wine. As her warm hand moved inside mine a shriek was heard outside. Those who frequented the tavern did not pay attention to it as they were used to such ruckus but the voices gradually became louder and eventually turned into a scream. When the screams were heard closer to the door everyone dispersed. The Slavic beauty pulled my arm and took me through the first secret door and that famous wall appeared before us. As I thought we would be trapped between that door and the wall, the wall split and an invisible hand pulled us both into the darkness of another room. When the door in the wall was closed the bitter screams in the tavern became louder. When we managed to escape to one of the back streets I anxiously told the Slavic beauty, "The others are still stuck inside."

The Slavic beauty, whose height complimented mine, replied, "We should be grateful that we could save ourselves, I am sure they can take care of themselves."

I couldn't see her face buried in the darkness of the street but I was still looking at her hoping I could catch a glimpse. Panting I said, "But their screams!"

"Most of those screams are to scare those escaping."

"Who are they? Are they from the castle or from elsewhere?"

"They are those who remain of the Catalans of Pigasi. They come now and then, rob those who are in the tavern, take the women they can lay their hands on and leave..."

"And then?"

"Nothing... The things they take with them become theirs. Or they will return another day and sell them back to the tavern owner."

Our conversation ended there. I couldn't work up the courage to go back to the tavern. I had to wait on the street for the morning because the castle gates were shut. The Slavic woman took my mind away. I frequently remembered that night during the first years of my emperorship but with time I forgot about it because pain remains with the one who suffers it." After his long reverie he stood aghast at his internal monologue. When he strayed himself from his memories, he muttered, "The reality of Matthew stands tall before me like a mountain. He has, just as I had done, given into the greed for power. Even if he doesn't get involved in these issues now, all the ill that will be committed later will be committed in his name..." He felt as if someone was strangling him. He had just lifted his foot up to stamp the ground when he spoke his mind, "Matthew cannot leave Hadrianopolis now and come here. If he does, the Ottomans will find out he is no longer at the castle and will invade it at once. Matthew cannot risk that, because he knows that if Hadrianopolis is lost to the Ottomans, he will never be able to get rid of being blamed by the supporters of Palaiologos." He felt a bit more at ease. With that sense of calmness he said, "I can go to him before he comes here and convince him to remain there." Then looking at his men standing in front of the door he continued, "I told you that one of you should go to the Patriarch and the other to the palace of the Palaiologos. Why are you still here? I know that you trust Matthew dearly but it is impossible for him to leave Hadrianopolis now. If he leaves his castle when Orhan's son is ceaselessly closing in on him he will be the one who loses. That's why you should not set your hopes on his arrival. I talked to my imperial partner and son-in-law, Palaiologos, about all this. He, like me, doesn't want the blood of brothers to be spilt in the streets of Constantinople. Moreover, he doesn't want our Byzantium to be involved in any internal conflict while the Ottomans grow stronger with each passing day and continually push against our borders. For now, he can't do anything more than what I have done but we both have much we can do together. I cannot let Orhan advance into our lands despite the fact that he is my son-in-law. If it comes to that, I will ask for aid from the Vatican or Avignon to repel the Ottomans from Thrace. Their existence in Thrace will always pose a threat to our Constantinople."

Kantakouzenos VI, who completed his speech in a tone of voice that grew colder towards the end, met the cold gazes of the castle commander and the deputy mesazōn standing by the door. Their gaze, as cold as his own tone of voice, gave the Emperor goose pimples.

CHAPTER THIRTY-NINE

Suleyman Pasha and Hacı Ilbey arrived at Peristasi Castle to convene with Balabancıkoğlu, left behind by Fazıl Bey to keep order at the castle, and the *subaşı* appointed by him. They also visited the priest of the Peristasi church and met with the dignitaries of the castle. Then they left two *yaya* units at the castle and set out in the opposite direction towards Fazıl Bey who was campaigning in the north-east of Thrace. After they advanced through the region, a natural trap with its small hills and streams, and crossed the endless flatlands they arrived at the castle, referred to by the Byzantines as Dyme. There, they saw that the new cavalry and *yaya* units sent by Ece Bey were waiting for them.

As Suleyman Pasha waited for his marquee and the headquarter tent to be set up, he found out that most of the *yayas* and the cavalry were from Ancyra. This spread a smile across his wide face. Before attending the meeting in the headquarter tent, he shortly retreated to his marquee where he drank a cool beverage to refresh himself. As soon as he lied down on the thick cushion spread on top of the felt floor of the marquee and rested his head on his pillow, he recalled his last campaign to Ancyra before crossing over to Thrace. Just as his tired eyes were about to close, his thoughts raced, "The *Âhis* were watching us from a distance as we advanced towards the east from the lands of the Gerede beys. We didn't attack them because they didn't attack us. As we ceaselessly advanced towards the east, the heat of the day fried our brains and the cold of the night made us shiver to our bones. It was impossible to understand the wisdom behind the change that happened within the space of a few hours. We took the necessary precautions and reached the outskirts of Ancyra in the evening. The next morning, we woke up to milk-white frost. Let alone stripping down to our waists and training our swordsmanship, we couldn't even hold our swords until noon because of the

cold. The *Âhis,* who hadn't attacked us until then, suddenly man-
oeuvred and attacked us. They knew how vulnerable we were because of inclement weather conditions. We were stunned because
they kept attacking and retreating. We were happy that the Gerede
beys joined the Ottomans but the unexpected attacks of the *Âhis* deflated us. As we thought hard on the kind of precautions we could
take, the rope traps of Karasid beys saved our skins. We caught almost all of those who left the castle with the rope traps we set up in
a single night. When we beheaded the leaders of the *Âhis* we captured in front of the castle, the castle surrendered. However, the *Âhis*
rose up in arms after being provoked by the *Karamanids,* who found
out that we had crossed to this side of the Dardanelles, causing great
damage to those we left behind at the castle. If we hadn't crossed to
this side we could have gone back to Ancyra and brought both the
Âhis and the *Karamanids* to their knees but I still have much to do
on this side of the Dardanelles. If I can invade this side of the Dardanelles all the way up to the Black Sea coast, the first thing I am going to do will be to go to Ancyra and make the *Âhis* pay for the
blood they spilt on behalf of Karahan Bey." He lost his sleep. Just as
he fixed his gaze on the ceiling of the tent made of goat hair, Karahan Bey's sunburnt face appeared in his mind's eye. He was the one
who taught him how to use a sword. They looked at each other for a
while as the image of Karahan Bey smiled at him. When he got tired
of looking at him in his mind's eye he muttered, "Say something instead of looking at me vacantly, Karahan Bey!" He lay down on the
floor cushion staring into the void. The image of Karahan Bey, hurt
by Suleyman Pasha's subtly angry words, his bulky body, his wide-
bladed sword, and the silhouette of his sunburnt face appeared before Suleyman Pasha shortly before he completely disappeared into a
land of nothingness. Startled by his disappearance, as sudden as his
emergence, Suleyman Pasha shook his head to both sides as if he regretted all that he had said. Just then he heard Hacı Ilbey's voice in

front of his marquee. He suddenly stood up and walked outside. Seeing him emerge from his marquee, Hacı Ilbey addressed him melli-
fluously, "My Prince, most of the cavalrymen are good men trained
by Gerede beys. The infantry is also formed of the *Âhis* of Ancryra
whom we have taken captive. Orhan Ghazi clearly convinced Sultanshah Bey during his campaign to the lands of the Gerede after our
campaign. According to the bey of the Gerede cavalries, as of now
Sultanshah Bey and the other Gerede beys are going to be on our
bey's side. According to what the Gerede beys say, your gradual advance through Thrace has generated excitement amongst the beys of
Anatolia. The large beyliks are afraid that the small beyliks under
their hegemony will soon join our judicious Beylik. The small beyliks
are overjoyed with the idea of becoming a part of the hegemony of
'Ottoman justice'. My Bey, the existence of such antagonism signifies
the fact that the order your uncle Alaüddin Bey, may he sleep in
heavenly light, and his viziers intelligently established, persists and
that before long, it will also be adopted by others. Believe me when I
say that this has been my dream since my time at Karasid Beylik. As
you can see, Orhan Ghazi, may he live long, has already gently informed the furthest Beyliks of Anatolia of our gradual progress in
Thrace. Regardless of how much this situation plagues the *Karamanids* it is a golden opportunity for the Osmanoğlu Beylik."

Suleyman Pasha looked at Hacı Ilbey, who was talking as if he
could read his mind, with a smile on his face, "Hacı Ilbey, I also previously thought that the *Âhis* should pay for rising against us in arms
and massacring our brave men like a herd of sheep after we left
them there, but then I remembered a conversation I had with my
father. During that conversation my father said, "Unripe fruit not
only has no benefit but it also upsets the stomach. That is why you
have to patiently wait for fruit to ripen. Sure, it's not easy to patiently watch that fruit change colour and ripen more each day with
your mouth watering but you must curb your desire and wait pa-

tiently. If you are considering taking a Beylik under your governance, you have to show the same kind of patience as you do when you wait for fruit to ripen so that the Beylik can mature enough to enter your empery willingly, so that they don't gag you once they are under your rule. The fact that Sultanshah Bey joined my father's sovereignty proved that my father was right all along. Not even a single drop of blood was shed and now, their swords have also become ours. Recall- ing these things also brought to mind another memory. One day when I went to see my father he was in a conversation with my uncle Alauddin Ali Bey. When I headed towards the door to leave the room so I wouldn't interrupt their conversation, my uncle asked me to stay and pay heed to their conversation, during which he said, 'Secrets of the state are more whimsical than all other secrets. If you cannot preserve them they quickly lose their charm. If you wish your Beylik to be great, wealthy and enduring, you should have secrets that you keep even from yourself. Moreover, your men have to know how to keep secrets just as well as you do. Know that a man who cannot keep secrets will also have a yielding wrist and a deserting sword. Let alone protecting you, men like that cannot even defend themselves.'

"My father, listening to him with utmost attention, turned to me once my uncle stopped talking, and asked, 'My Suleyman, have you heard what your uncle said?'

"Acting as if I were playing a game and not really grasping what was being said, I replied, 'I heard, father.'

"He dismissed me with a wave of his hand. I walked backwards and left his presence and ran to my mother's harem. Seeing me run to her, my mother realised my panic and swiftly noticed the bewildered apprehension on my face. She got me to sit by her side as if she wasn't aware of any of it. As she caressed my head on her lap she first asked what I had done since the morning. I told her all I had done one by one and felt increasingly at ease and recovered from my worries. It seemed that my mother was just waiting for that moment. She pulled away her hand from my hair and told me to sit across from her. As I sat across from her without an inkling of what was happening, she slowly began to talk to me in an imperious tone, 'Just then, I could see a bewildered sense of apprehension on your face. As you know, apprehension is a sign of ignorance. If you are knowledge-able you won't be anxious about not understanding what is being said to you.'

"When my mother spoke as if she could read my mind, I responded, 'Oh, my dear mother! When I cannot understand what they were telling...'

"My mother turned her soft gaze at me after blinking her eyes boasting fine and long eyelashes. Noticing that I had directed my gaze on the floor, she said, 'It is not a good habit to look away when you are in conversation. Don't do that again.'

"Then she attempted to complete her previous thought, 'It is im-possible for a person to understand everything and there is no shame in not being able to understand something you have heard for the first time but if you hear the same thing twice and cannot under-stand it, that is shameful. That is why you should first find out the reasons underlying your incomprehension and then learn to under-stand what you have heard. Did you know that when I came to Bursa I had to learn almost everything from scratch?'

"I looked at her face and asked, 'So what happened to all that you had learnt before?'

"Before sending me to my room, my mother smiled half-heartedly and replied, 'All that I'd learnt before was confined by the walls of Yarhisar Castle. When I ventured outside those walls, I understood the boundlessness of knowledge. Right now I am only knowledgeable within the bounds of our Beylik but I should widen my knowledge to extend beyond the borders of our Beylik. That is how it should also be for you. For, life is more comprehensive than everything that I, your father and your teacher can teach you.'"

After telling Hacı Ilbey this childhood story Suleyman Pasha fell momentarily silent before continuing, "God bless you, Hacı. You have distanced me from myself with the few words you spoke. That day, when I was listening to my mother something strange happened. Thinking that I couldn't hide my ideas from my mother, I threw my arms around my mother's neck saying, 'My mother! My mother! My sultana mother' as if to express the first thought that popped into my head. Then I kneeled before her once again, and said, 'Tomorrow I will ask my father's permission to join his beys but first I want to receive your consent.'

"Then, as if she had forgotten all that she told me, my mother looked at me with sorrowful eyes and opened her arms so I could hug her."

Suleyman Pasha quietly travelled between his memories almost every moment he had alone, whether it was riding somewhere on horse-back or watching a castle he arrived at. However, this time round, he had dipped into his memories out loud while talking to Hacı Ilbey. When he finally realised this, he began to laugh and when he stopped laughing, he said, "You have enabled me to dive right into my memories with the few words you said. I usually never talk about my memories. It must be that I've missed my mother dearly."

Hacı Ilbey replied, "Valuable things are always missed, My Prince. I noticed you travel back to your memories even though you haven't told me them before. Today we shall set out on that journey you usually take alone. We should be glad that we have memories we can share."

Kara Hasanoğlu approached them as they chatted. He bowed his head and saluted them before saying, "My Prince, the archers, climbers, *yayas* and the cavalry are all in position and are awaiting your orders."

Suleyman Pasha responded, "May you live a long and prosperous life Kara Hasanoğlu, I see you have quickly put things into order..."

"My Bey, the Gerede beys had already began their preparations before our arrival. Everything was completed when I posted the cavalry units to their positions."

Suleyman Pasha viewed the tranquil castle in front of him before looking at Mount Ganos in the background. As he turned his gaze towards the sun hanging in the sky like a purple oil lamp he muttered, "Is it shining its light on us or on those in the castle?" After a moment of silence, he looked at Kara Hasanoğlu who was standing across from him and said, "We don't need to wait for the *yayas* to catch up to us. We can try out the *Âhis'* courage until they arrive."

Kara Hasanoğlu, following him two steps behind, turned around immediately upon hearing Suleyman Pasha's order. He called his head messenger and told him to secretly send word to Akça Kocaoğlu positioned on the north side of the castle, to Kuloğlu Hasan Bey posted on the west of the castle and to Ese Bey on the south informing them that they should get ready for the attack. Then the head messenger left at once. The three messengers, who were waiting for him at a short distance, rode their horses in the direction they were ordered to deliver the messages. After a short wait, long enough for the messengers to deliver their messages, Hacı Ilbey looked at the military drummers and shouted, "Beat the drums!"

Hearing his command, the military drummers began to beat their drums and arrows of fire began falling down on the tranquil Dymne Castle from all sides. After the second downpour of flaming arrows, the archers retreated. They were immediately replaced by long-distance archers. As the arrows fired by the long-distance archers tore up the sky glowing purple with the last rays of sunlight, the *yayas* formed of *Âhis* from Ancyra charged towards the next emplacement. Arrows were sporadically shot from the bastions against the second

attack of long-distance archers. Thus, Suleyman Pasha and Hacı Ilbey thought the castle didn't have any power left to defend itself any
longer. They ordered the shielded *yayas* and the battering rams to
advance towards the castle gates. The moment the infantry began
marching towards the castle gates an unexpected shower of arrows
poured down on them. Seeing this, Suleyman Pasha got on his Grey
and said, "Keep shooting, don't stop!"

In that moment both the arrows of long-distance archers and arrows of flaming arrows poured down on the castle. Watching the
events unravel, Hacı Ilbey addressed Suleyman Pasha, who was yet
to ride his horse further towards the front, and asked, "My Prince, do
you see how the sun is shining for you?"

CHAPTER FORTY

John Kantakouzenos VI assessed the news that had been arriving all day in great detail before making a final decision. He paid gratitude to darkness, the most beautiful blessing the night could present him, and left his mansion. He got on the plumed imperial carriage that was always ready for his use. He looked at the small palace that had been his mansion for years one last time. Unable to see much in the dark, he gave his driver the order to move. When the imperial carriage harnessed to well-fed horses began to move, he muttered, "Years ago I'd also entered the castle by making use of the dark of night." It wasn't apparent whether he was proud or sad about what he said. As he inhaled and exhaled deeply, he slowly mumbled under his breath, "And now, I am taking shelter in darkness to..." He couldn't manage to complete his sentence but simply sat down on the seat inside the carriage without even casting a glance upon the deserted streets. As the Emperor sat biliously, the commander of the guards posted in front of the carriage, the knights following the Emperor's carriage and all the servants who got on the servants' carriage in the last minute were hoping, "The Emperor will regret leaving the castle before us. He himself knows full-well that he cannot live away from Constantinople." Yet the old emperor was determined. When the imperial carriage left the castle from the Gate of Charisius, the hopes of all concerned parties were shattered. Almost all of them now accepted that the old emperor was leaving Constantinople for good. They had just left the city walls behind when the commander of the guards said, "Your Majesty, my men will accompany you until Hadrianopolis. I will be waiting for your return in Constantinople in service of the castle commander."

Leaving behind a few knights with the old emperor's carriage, the commander of the guards returned to the castle before the gates were shut. Then, a few of the servants asked the Emperor to dismiss

them from his service. He looked at them calmly, as if he was expecting all that, thinking about Empress Irene who was staying with his
daughter. He thought, "If only she'd arrive soon and we could continue on our way." He recalled the succinct letter his son-in-law and
Co-Emperor Palaiologos V sent to him the previous afternoon,
"Your Majesty, I now fully understand that the surroundings of our
mansion as well as the streets are girded with adversaries who only
see red. Empress Irene leaving the mansion could have dire consequences, thus I will not be sending her to the mansion. Since you
are determined to go to Didymóteicho, leave the castle from the
Gate of Charisius and wait for me there. I will bring Empress Irene
to you with my own carriage..." He muttered, "They will feel at ease
if they find out I am leaving Constantinople," before catching sight
of his loyal vassal Atantos who was standing in front of the open
door of the imperial carriage waiting at the small square outside the
castle gates. Upon hearing the Emperor's muttering, Atantos replied
hastily with the last bit of hope he had, "Did you say something,
master?"

Kantakouzenos replied in a whispery tone of voice, "Do you think
we have anything left to say, Atantos? We couldn't even realise that
we couldn't win the hearts of the people because we were preoccupied with not causing harm to anyone since our first day in the
castle. What I bitterly resent is the Patriarch's behaviour as it doesn't
at all suit a spiritual leader of his standing. They'd been thrown out
on the street since the Latins. At the least I gave them the monastery
so they wouldn't have to be out on the streets. But his highness, the
Patriarch, did not fall short of picking apart the Kantakouzenos
even when he was absolving people of their sins in the holy space I
gave him so he could keep his position."

"I think you shouldn't leave Constantinople like this, master. The
Co-Emperor is your son-in-law, and perhaps you think he won't
harm you but as you can see he is not sending Empress Irene to you

unattended. There is only one reason for that, it is so that he can bring her here himself and see with his own two eyes that you are leaving the city. In fact, if he anticipated that Empress Anna will cause great distress to him, as of now on he would have never consented to your departure."

Co-Emperor Kantakouzenos VI replied as if he was speaking his last words on the matter, "How did you come up with that, Atantos?"

After sighing softly Atantos replied, "My master, don't you see that the Empress has the same greed and rage as Theodora?"

"Theodora's greed and rage were towards the Romans who renounced her. She got her revenge through that greed and rage after the death of Justinian. Empress Anna's rage is meaningless. Is she going to take out her revenge on her own son?"

Shrugging his shoulders in the dark Atantos replied, "I suppose she is vengeful towards the Kantakouzenos."

"Well, now that I have withdrawn from my position, there is no reason for her vengeance. I have no other wish than to leave here as soon as Empress Irene arrives. Didn't you just see how the servants who are willing to stay here got up and left us?"

"I assume they have some hope left."

"And, for what?"

"In my opinion, they are waiting for your son Matthew."

"Perhaps... Maybe they are in touch with Matthew."

Pretending not to know as he did before, Atantos replied as if he were imitating Kantakouzenos, "Perhaps..."

Then looking at the Emperor from the dark, Atantos thought, "Everyone waited for you to shine a light on them. You can no longer blame anyone. I will only come as far as Hadrianopolis with you, after that you are on your own. A single sign or a single word from Matthew, the imperial co-partner, is more than enough for me to return."

Waiting inside his carriage, Kantakouzenos VI was unable to think of anything else other than his wife, Irene. Then, as if something suddenly appeared to him, the Emperor addressed Atantos, who was quietly looking at him from the open door of the carriage, "Atantos, we rode through the neighbourhood of our supporters on our way here but as you could see there was no one in sight. They have all withdrawn to their houses as if to say, 'You are the one to blame for all that has befallen us. You brought your bad omen with your arrival and now you are leaving us with that bad omen.' They were willing to die for our cause, what of that now?"

"No one knew about your decision to leave. Everyone was out on the streets until the night set in."

"I am not just the Emperor of the people residing in Constantinople but the Emperor of the whole of Byzantium. If it was only the people living here who would suffer the consequences of what happens here, I would remain and fight until the end. But you fully know that the suffering that will be endured in this place will not just remain here."

Having finally understood that the old emperor had fully quailed, Atantos raised his voice slightly, "You might have as well have stayed in Constantinople until your son's arrival. I am sure that the news of his mother being kept by the blues has already reached him."

Kantakouzenos VI jumped out of the carriage and with great fury said, "How could you do that without my permission?"

Atantos replied in a deep tone of voice, "You were resting when the imperial mail arrived..."

At that moment Kantakouzenos VI realised that he was an overthrown emperor instead of an emperor who left Constantinople of his own will, replying, "Oh you mindless buffoons, do you know what will happen now?"

Atantos gathered all his courage and replied with the air of a commander giving orders instead of acting like a head servant, "Your Majesty, it is of no use to bewail any longer. Now, the reign of Matthew Kantakouzenos will commence."

Trying to see Atantos' face, intentionally hidden in the dark of night, Kantakouzenos said, "I now see that you were eager to fight. I see that I have been wasting my breath. However, remember that my son will not look fondly upon your disobedience to me. Pray that I reach Hadrianopolis before Matthew sets forth."

CHAPTER FORTY-ONE

Suleyman Pasha arrived in Bursa in order to attend the Imperial Council meeting upon his father's call, following the siege of Dyme Castle, but the cold breeze blowing from Mount Ganos was still in him despite the fact that he spent two days at his harem renewed by his mother's choice of concubines. And, regardless of the excitement he felt when he entered the large chamber where the Imperial Council had convened, he was still cold. He couldn't figure out the cause of the shudder that shook his body to the bone—was it the excitement or was it simply because he was cold? When he entered the chamber and greeted his father by kneeling before him and the old heroes, most of whom were his grandfather's peers, the beys of his father moved to stand up. Seeing this, Orhan Ghazi moved his arms that seemed as if they had been sewn onto his broad shoulders, putting his hands in the air in order to stop the old heroes—who knew not only him as a child but also his son—from standing up. For some reason, he couldn't find it in his heart to get them to stand up to greet his son. Then, when he realised that he had previously never responded in such a way, he thought it best to make sure his beys didn't misunderstand him. He addressed them with a deep voice emanating directly from his larynx, "My heirloom heroes and My Beys who are older than me, I agree with your respectful sentiments in view of the Imperial Council and its participants. However, I cannot find it in my heart to allow you to stand up for Prince Suleyman for he was raised by you. The fact that you are attending the Imperial Council and offering guidance bestows us great power. Thus, please do not stand up to greet us, as that will only burden us."

Orhan Ghazi's speech was followed by a brief silence. Hacı Ilbey, who had good manners and previously served the Karasid Dynasty for many years, gathered that none of the heroes or the viziers wanted to take the floor. He gently sat up straight on his knees and said, "My Bey may you live long. If I may be so bold, we are a part of our Beylik, our respect is not merely to our bey or to our prince. Our respect is for the perpetual order of the Osmanoğlu Beylik. That is why our respect will always remain verdant regardless of our ageing bodies..."

Softly looking at Hacı Ilbey who always spoke his mind, even on the toughest days when he was all alone against Demir Bey, the black sheep of the Karasid Dynasty, Orhan Ghazi replied, "You are right, Hacı Ilbey. Our respect is to the order of our Beylik. However, I wasn't jesting when I recalled our old age to mind..."

Samsa Çavuş, the oldest bey in the chamber, and Aktimur laughed at Orhan Ghazi's words as he never ever joked during Imperial Council meetings. After mutual chuckles and an exchange of sympathetic words, Aktimur said, "Orhan Ghazi, may you live long, you've put a smile on our faces. Old age knows very well how to re- mind itself regardless of you or Hacı reminding me of it."

They briefly talked about old age, after which Orhan Ghazi real- ised it was time to commence the meeting. First, he exclaimed "Destûr!"[39] Then, looking at Suleyman Pasha, who had cast his gaze back on him, kneeling down at the other end of the room, he said, "Suleyman Pasha, both our Beylik and our Imperial Council are grateful to you for the services you and your beys have undertaken with reason and logic. Thanks to you, we now know that we can ad- vance even further than the Dardanelles. With your campaigns, the existence and amity of our Beylik have shone. We would have liked to reward you for all your efforts but we don't have a reward great enough to give you, as you are giving yourselves the greatest reward our Beylik has to offer by advancing step by step across the strait. There are perhaps those who don't consider it important to capture a few castles beyond the Dardanelles but rest assured that you are opening the gates of the enormous Balkans to our Beylik. Reaching

---

39   T.N, "Destûr" means "allow me".

those lands was at first Kalem Bey's dream, and it later became mine. Thank you for making this dream a reality. From now on it will be there that we will welcome those arriving from the old continent and bid farewell to those departing."

Orhan Ghazi fell silent for a while as if he had said all that he wanted to. Then, he cast his gaze on Saltuk Alp, the heroes and Sultan Şah Bey[40], who had adjoined Gerede Beylik of the former lands of Bithynia into the territory of Ottoman Beylik without even having to gird a sword. Looking at his son Suleyman Pasha and the beys sitting behind him, he continued, "When you were on the other side of the Dardanelles our beys proceeded towards Ancyra. Realising that we were adamant on getting our revenge for Karahan Bey, the *Âhis* of Ancyra have come under our hegemony once again but as it stands, *Karamanids* and other powers unknown to us are continually inciting the *Âhis* against us. Our beys heading towards Ancyra had just arrived in Bursa when the *Âhis* started a revolt in Ancyra and put three of our *uç* Beys[41] and soldiers fighting our holy war on behalf of Islam to the sword. This is the greatest offence committed against us. It is now time to punish them. The *Âhis* in Ancyra have but two choices. They will either be loyal to us or to the *Karamanids*. If they opt to stand with the *Karamanids*, when the time comes they will have to accept the hegemony of our Beylik under the *Karamanids*.

"The agreements we have come to with the *Germiyanids* have solidified in peace in our Beylik in the south. The Venetians and Greeks residing on the islands in the Sea of Marmora have been showing their loyalty to our Beylik at every chance. As it now not the season for campaigning, we should focus on the reconstruction of the castles we have captured. The castles on the other side of the Dardanelles surely need reinforcements despite the repair work under-

---

40 T.N, Sultan Şah Bey was the only known ruler of Gerede Beylik.
41 T.N, *Uç Beyi* is a title given to sanjak beys who are responsible for overseeing civil and military matters in bordering territories.

taken after the earthquake. It is my wish that the reconstruction of castles on both sides of the Dardanelles is completed this winter."

Orhan Ghazi finished his speech with those last words. He asked the heroes and beys who wanted to take the floor to take turns. Hacı Ilbey's eyes met Suleyman Pasha's before he started talking about the opposite coast just as they'd agreed. Noticing that Suleyman Pasha wanted to take his turn to deliver his thoughts, Hacı Ilbey gave courage to his bey with a gaze. Suleyman Pasha greeted him by nodding and began his speech, "My Bey father, may you live long, your commendation has given both me and my men heart. The campaign we initiated with nearly a hundred brave men across the Dardanelles is now extending beyond the Dardanelles. Once the winter is over and as soon as the campaign months begin our borders might be extended all the way to the shores of the Dark Sea. This will not be as easy a task as we anticipate but the reconstruction of the castles and the aid we supplied to the Gallipoli Fortress after the earthquake has spread to all the castles in Thrace by word of mouth. They no longer put up walls behind castle gates when they hear of our arrival. In fact, the feudal lords of some castles secretly sent news to Fazıl Bey inviting his forces to their castles. We are not faced with difficulty when we capture new castles but the weather in Thrace is so bitterly cold that let alone campaigning there in the winter, even stepping outside is impossible."

The beys in the Imperial Council chamber all smiled subtly. Suleyman Pasha saw the smiles on everybody's faces. It was as if they were trying to imply, "if our prince finds it cold then we shall freeze" with the smiles on their faces. When they stopped smiling Suleyman Pasha repeated, "My last words put a smile on your faces but the weather across the Dardanelles is nothing like the weather here."

When Suleyman Pasha, who didn't like to talk long, finished his sentence, Hacı Ilbey said, "My Prince is utterly right. The cold air that blows from the Balkans is not like the cold breezes that blow here from the Mysian Olympus. Even our *yayas*, who during their training at the headquarters in Bursa are covered with snow, complain about the cold weather there."

Hearing these words, the smiles on the faces of beys vanished. Just as they were about to propose changing the subject, exchanging timid glances, Aktimur sitting next to Saltuk Alp said, "The cold season is upon us. We were also very cold when we were approaching the Ancyra Castle."

Trying to keep his wide shoulders straight, Orhan Ghazi replied, "If so, what we have to do is to advance the *yayas* and the cavalry towards the borders with short and continuous journeys until the spring. We should also start minor reconstruction work at the castles as and when the weather allows it. It would also be beneficial to organise races and hunting parties with neighbouring castles."

Upon receiving the approval for his last suggestions from his heroes, viziers and beys, Orhan Ghazi turned to Suleyman Pasha and continued his speech, "According to the news we received from Kostantiniyye, my father-in-law has proclaimed he is no longer an emperor and departed for Didymóteicho but he finds it too confining there. Now, he is planning on joining our brother-in-law Manuel Kantakouzenos, who he appointed as the Despotēs of Morea. However, in my opinion, my father-in-law will not remain there, he will advance to Avignon and Rome. That is why I assume he has left Kostantiniyye. Moreover, according to some other hearsay that reached us, Matthew, our brother-in-law and the co-imperial partner in Hadrianopolis asserted his co-partnership and asked his uncle Palaiologos for his imperial rights to become Co-Emperor in his father's place. However, Palaiologos does not seem to be budging an inch. As things stand, a great deal of conflict and reckoning is about to begin between them. I think their dispute will be of use to us."

Seeing that his father was looking at him, Suleyman Pasha responded, "My Bey father is right. The dispute between them benefits us because the people of the castles are sick and tired of this double-headed empire. It doesn't matter to whom they pay their taxes, the party that doesn't get taxes always wants more. This frustrates the people. Their state of confusion is an advantage for us. When we send messengers to the castles to inform them that they will not be required to pay taxes if they enter the hegemony of the Osmanoğlu Beylik, everyone, including the feudal lords of the castles and the priests, rejoices. This makes our work easier. However, we have to guarantee that we will be everlasting. That can only happen with the arrival of new forces."

When Suleyman Pasha finished his sentence and took a step back, Orhan Ghazi took the word, "He naturally claims to be a partner to the throne of Kostantiniyye now because he was declared as the imperial co-partner by his father. However, this time we are not on the same side as the Kantakouzenos. We are now supporting Emperor John Palaiologos who has made us promises. Therefore, we should send him presents as a show of our friendship and remind him that his imperial partner John Kantakouzenos VI is headed to Morea and from thereon to Rome. I will also express that we are closely follow-ing the developments in Byzantium and inform him that we don't approve of old Kantakouzenos' doings. I will remind him that we are neighbours who share borders and ask him whether he has any knowledge of this Byzantine game that Kantakouzenos is playing ac-cording to his own rules. This letter we are going to send will also have to implicitly specify that this situation can one day give way to a war between us. If we don't have our reasons, the Beyliks may not approve our unexpected entry into their lands."

The Imperial Council meeting, during which opinions were voiced about Byzantine campaigns and their costs and the approval of opinions and suggestions were motioned, came to a close towards the evening. Trying to hide their exhaustion, the heroes set out towards their mansions as soon as the meeting ended. Meanwhile, Suleyman

Pasha remained in the meeting chamber with his beys to briefly talk to his father about the work they would be undertaking beyond the Dardanelles during the winter. Then he said, "If My Bey father allows it, My Beys will be advancing to Thrace with their harems at their earliest convenience. During this time, I would like to visit the Yarhisar Castle for a few days and spend time with my mother and siblings who I haven't seen in a long time."

Orhan Ghazi looked at his son with questioning eyes as Nilüfer Hatun had not mentioned anything about this visit, to which Suleyman Pasha replied, "When I was conversing with my mother yesterday she talked about her childhood and Yarhisar at length. Therefore, I decided that a journey might be good for her because she was reminiscing about her youth. If you allow it, I would also like to see the state of the structures that have been built in my and her name in İznik."

Orhan Ghazi felt deeply saddened that he hadn't thought of creating such an opportunity for his beloved wife for years. As he looked at his son with gratitude, he informed the beys and viziers in the chamber that they were free to leave. He asked his son to approach him. When Suleyman Pasha moved closer to his father, Orhan Ghazi said, "I am glad that you thought of doing that for your mother. It will be good for you to spend a few days with your mother and siblings. I wish I had thought of this before so I could visit Yarhisar with all of you. Alas, I don't have any time. It will also be good for you to visit İznik and check on the state of the construction of the social complexes being built in your names. If only Halil, who we have just sent to Nicomedia, could have joined you as well. If you send him a messenger before your departure, he might still be able to come and join you in İznik. I am also very curious about the soup-kitchens in İznik. I will have to wait for your safe return to find out. Regardless of the state of the constructions, tell the officers in charge that I will definitely visit there after the first campaign in spring. If all the buildings are not completed by then, someone will have to answer for it."

Then he stood up to leave the spacious Imperial Council chamber. Looking at his son Murad, who had until then not uttered a single word, he advised Suleyman Pasha, "I will be entrusting my Murad to you in the spring. It would be good if you could tell him about the lands beyond the Dardanelles on your way to Yarhisar."

Looking at his younger brother Murad, Suleyman Pasha replied, "My brother is always welcome to join me. I will make sure to tell him everything I know."

He respectfully bowed and headed towards the door after his father. Orhan Ghazi, who was just then about to get out of the room, uttered a final sentence without looking at his sons, "Who knows when we will be able to sit face to face at the Imperial Council chamber again..."

CHAPTER FORTY-TWO

Overthrown Emperor Kantakouzenos VI was feeling quite washed out when he arrived in Mystras after a long sea and land journey. He had retreated to his chambers as soon as he arrived at his middle son, the Despotēs of Morea Manuel Kantakouzenos' chateau surrounded by high walls. Those who had accompanied him through his journey weren't as tired as him since they were younger and were seated around the long dinner table set up for them in the courtyard of the chateau that seemed to defy history. These walls surrounding the courtyard were the walls of the only castle in the Peloponnese lands that had managed to stand against Athens for decades. Mystras did not have agorae like Athens but it had chateaus and squares that were connected to one another with indoor pathways. When required, the doors that opened from one square to the other were utilised to pass from one chateau to the other and the enemy was led to the small spaces, before the doors were closed and the enemy was trapped between the high walls and killed. The Athenian commanders who knew Mystras' reputation for such tactics, also known as Sparta's unobtainable castle, mostly attacked the castle from the outside.

Agesilaus, the advisor of the Despotēs of Morea Manuel Kantakouzenos, raised his glass filled with Morea's famous mulberry wine in honour of those sitting around the feast table, "Friends, let's raise our glasses in honour of the famous ephors of beautiful Mystras and our guests."

After taking a big gulp from his mulberry wine that was poured into a goblet decorated with a figure of Minos, he continued his speech, "My friends, one of the renowned ephors of Istria was my illustrious grandfather, Agesilaus, who was a Spartan commander and whose name I share. He was one of the ephors who gathered in this courtyard the day the Achaeans' envoys arrived. The Achaeans had nominated one of their own as the speaker before their arrival at the courtyard. When they were welcomed to the courtyard, their speaker appeared before the ephors and the people's assembly. The speaker began talking with a tone of voice much more powerful than thunder, much like that of Zeus whose voice recalled streaks of lightning in rain. He said, 'O' Spartans! O' the people who stopped Athenians in their steps! O' ephors, the honourable men of Sparta! O' members of Sparta's people's assembly that delivers justice! We are the envoys of Achaeans with whom you have cast your lot. We speak in the name of Achaeans today. The people of Achaea are in dire straits. As you know we are always ready for your orders and we accompany you in all your campaigns. We go wherever you consign us. However, despite the fact what we are besieged by the Acharnians and their allies, Athenians and Boeotians, you have not taken any steps to provide us with aid. It is almost impossible for us to keep our heads above water under these circumstances. Thus, we are either going to sever our relationship with the Peloponnese war and run the risk of going to war with the Acharnians and their allies after we deploy all our forces across the gulf, or try to attain peace at any cost.' Even though our people initially objected to their decision because they were implying that they would break their agreement with Sparta, they later reconsidered the situation with a presence of mind characteristic of Spartans and settled on helping the Achaeans. Thus, following their decision and watching the sunset that appeared in all its glory the assembly speaker said, 'O' Agesilaus the Great this is now your task. Under your command, the army of Sparta and its allies will defeat the armies of Acharnians and their allies Athenians and Boeotians' and inform the joint decision of the ephors and the assembly to my great grandfather whose name I carry.' That great commander left this courtyard with a ceremony and headed to the headquarters of the Spartan army waiting outside the castle walls. Perceiving the smell of new war booty, the soldiers and their com-

manders greeted him with joy. They all began celebrating their victory before they even set forth because back then there was no power
which could resist against the Spartan hoplites. Above all, when the
Spartan powers united their forces with that of the Achaeans they
became undefeatable. Despite all the joy and cheering, Agesilaus had
not forgotten about the former entrapment of the Lechaion battalion. Therefore, he was being cautious and also honing his warriors
to take revenge for the entrapment of the battalion. When the army
crossed the lands of the Achaeans and arrived at the gulf, the numbers of hoplites and armoured cavalry doubled with the participa-
tion of Achaeans and other allied powers. Agesilaus was overjoyed.
As he led his army towards the gulf on horse-back he had so many
soldiers behind him that the trees and mountains of fertile Peloponnese seemed as if they were walking with them. When the
hoplites got carried away and clashed their heavy shields against one
another to excite themselves and their fellow soldiers, the whole
place roistered. Accompanied with the yells of the cavalry the commanders could hear the ground and the sky rattling. So when that
glorious army crossed the gulf and stepped foot on the lands of
Acharnians, the Acharnian villagers left their crops in the fields,
their elders in their villages, their sick in their beds and escaped to
the north with only their herds. However, the cavalry and hoplites,
who had for days been dreaming of the booty they would be taking
from the Acharnians, tracked them day and night and invaded their
lands bit by bit. And of course, as they invaded it, they made sure
that they caused as much suffering to the Acharnians as they, the
Acharnians, had caused them before. They seized everything they
could, both people and goods, as booty. They set bed-ridden sick
people on fire with their mattresses for fear of contagious diseases.

"The advent of the cavalry and hoplites created such fear in the un-
traveled parts of Acharnian lands that the inhabitants cursed the
cowardly Athenians and Boeotians, abandoning their houses and

seeking refuge in uncharted mountains. Brave Spartans who received word of this immediately set out to hunt down the fugitives. However, as the fugitives knew their way around the mountains they were able to hide out for days. Reaching their limits of tolerance, the brave Spartans closed in on the fugitives when their animals were grazing by a lake between the mountains in the north. The illustrious Spartans took them as booty with their animals and captured all the castles on their way back. They took the castle people captive and looted their animals and commodities. They also set fire to all the unripe crops.

. "The Achaeans were overjoyed by the incredible success of their ally, the Spartans, because they were returning to their lands with their freedom and booty that would last them for years. It was during that campaign that my great grandfather Agesilaus, the triumphant commander of the Spartans, frequently gathered with the polemarchs, the three Equals and his marquee fellows and discussed the course of the war. He also appeared respectively before the cavalry, the hoplites and allied soldiers after every victory in order to render their desire to fight continuous and repeatedly told them, 'My brave men! This is how we take our revenge on the Athenians and their allies who killed hundreds of our brethren in arms by laying an ambush on the Lechaion battalion. We will not have any mercy on them as long as our campaign goes on, just the way they had no mercy on our fellow soldiers, and we will not grant them their wish of peace until we have taken our revenge upon them. If we make peace with them now will they give us back what we have lost because of them? No! In that case, we will bury those who killed our friends next to our friends so that the brave and holy souls of our brethren can find happiness. We will give out a large part of the booty we have collected to their orphans so that their children do not live in destitution.' When the final booty was collected and they had just set out towards the south, they were suddenly attacked by a peltast of the Acharnians. The place where the attack took place was a narrow passage but the brave hoplites of Agesilaus immediately counterattacked and drove the peltast to the summit of a mountain where Athenian and Acharnian cavalry and hoplites were situated. When the Spartan hoplites attacked them, the Acharnians who were in position at the summit of the mountain, rejoiced but shortly after they saw that the cavalry of Agesilaus surrounded them from behind, the wind was taken out of their sails. Thus, the last Athenians and Acharnians who were quickly defeated by two forces were taken captive. Most of the captives and booty were sent to Sparta while, with ten percent of the booty collected, Agesilaus erected a monument of victory at the summit of the mountain in memory of his brave men who lost their lives fighting there. He then continued on his campaign but he did not invade any castles. The Achaeans considered this decision to be risky for them so they proposed that at least some of the castles were besieged. In return, Agesilaus responded that winter was near and he would no longer attack any castles. The Achaeans told him, "We should at least set fire to the granaries of some castles and prevent them from sowing crops before we leave." However, Agesilaus, a very intelligent man, stopped them in their steps and said, 'O' Achaeans, let their granaries be. We should let them sow their crops. This way when we come here with the first spring, their crops will have turned green, and their fields will be overgrown with grass. The animals they have managed to hide from us should breed, and their women should give birth to healthy children so that they can once again be one with the land. When we arrive here again and begin to burn their fields they will no longer have any seeds to sow, their animals that bred will not be able to find food to eat, and desperate mothers will become your slaves to save their children's lives. That is when the Acharnians will accept to agree on our terms.' After saying these things, wise Agesilaus crossed the gulf with his army to return to Sparta.

"The Achaeans did not trust the promise they were made but brave Agesilaus kept his promise. When the crops had turned green and were knee-height he crossed the gulf and attacked the Acharnians who had just recovered. The Acharnians, who saw that the enemy army burned down all the villages they came across and that all produce from their last seeds had turned to ashes, informed Agesilaus that they would accept all his demands, asked for peace and became allies of the Spartans. From then on, no wars were fought in the south of the Peloponnese and in the north of the gulf for a long time."

When Agesilaus finished his story, Manuel Kantakouzenos, the Despotēs of Morea, looked at him with gratitude and said, "Oh great commander Agesilaus' grandson, Agesilaus the Wise, it is now time to see reality. Beautiful Istria now has neither ephors nor commander Agesilaus. The name of these lands is no longer Peloponnese. It is best if you complete your journey through the past centuries and come back to today. Don't you see what has become of our Byzantium with Co-Emperors? What will we do if the Ottomans head towards here from Thrace? Wouldn't you agree it is time we pondered on this for a while?"

Agesilaus of Istria, who was still thinking about his great grandfather's famous victory in the ancient times, looked at the Constantinopolitan Despotēs condescendingly and replied, "Do not fear our dear Despotēs Manuel Kantakouzenos, our mountains always desire to be referred to as the Peloponnese. That is why they have always had the power to protect themselves for centuries."

Just then, overthrown emperor Kantakouzenos VI who had rested well took his place at the table. He first looked at his son Manuel and then at the courtyard of the chateau surrounded with walls. In order to have taken part in the conversation of which he caught the last few sentences, he said, "Dear Agesilaus, you should also know that it didn't even cross my mind to leave my imperial throne just a few months ago. But, as you can see I am here now. My son-in-law, who gave me assurances to leave Constantinople, now seems to have forgotten all the promises he made. However, that really does not matter. I am resolved on doing whatever it takes to make sure our Byzantium remains Byzantium forever..."

———

CHAPTER FORTY-THREE

Evrenos Bey and Hacı Ilbey, who briefly stayed in Bursa, had crossed the Dardanelles with their harems and settled in the headquarters to the north of Gallipoli. Suleyman Pasha, still residing in Bursa, was also going to cross the Dardanelles after the Imperial Council meetings where he would be informed about the new order of the Beylik. The prince had retreated to his harem for a while following the journey he went on with his mother during the first days of his stay in Bursa. He spent a considerable part of his days in Imperial Council meetings, and the rest of his time at the military training headquarters near the Fortress of Lüblüce[42]. Now and then, he trained with the beys at the headquarters, and at other times, he watched the races at the field of contest and decided which of the soldiers should be appointed as *çavuş*[43] and *çavuşbaşıs*[44] with his beys. Orhan Ghazi had entrusted him the running of the headquarters during his stay in Bursa.

Time in Bursa passed by so quickly due to all that he had to do that Suleyman Pasha couldn't believe how fast an entire winter had elapsed and how the cool breath of the soaring mountain, referred to by the locals as the Mysian Olympus and as the 'Mountain of Monks' by Turkmens, had warmed up. Thus, he was rather baffled when he received news that whole battalions of cavalry and *yayas* were ready to cross the Dardanelles. However, despite being so baffled, he was also overjoyed that the days of the great campaign had finally arrived. He immediately informed his harem that they should begin preparations. The day he found out that the harem, which his mother had adorned with new concubines, was ready to set forth

---

42 T.N, The Fortress of Lüblüce was located on the western slope of Mount Olympus (Mysian Olympus, present-day Uludağ).
43 T.N, *Çavuş* was a title given to the officials of the Palace who were often sent to the provinces to convey and execute orders.
44 T.N, *Çavuşbaşı* literally means "head-çavuş."

with him, Suleyman Pasha first bid farewell to his mother. Once he set out with his harem, he went to visit his father Orhan Ghazi. Seeing that his son was ready to set forth on his campaign, Orhan Ghazi stood up and, looking at his son with pride said, "Come on son, let's ride to the headquarters together and we can bid farewell there."

As they got on their saddled horses, Prince Murad also joined them. Orhan Ghazi was at the front on his roan, Suleyman Pasha's Grey was behind him, and Prince Murad was following both of them on his chestnut-brown horse. Rows of cavalry and groups of *yayas* who saw them enter the headquarters exclaimed, "Oh! praise be!" Then, Yahşi Bey approached them and said, "My Bey, both our cavalry and *yayas* are ready to set forth on our campaign."

With this statement, Orhan Ghazi understood it was time to part. He got off his horse and kissed his son on the forehead. He said, "Son, may your horses be agile and your holy war blessed."

Suleyman Pasha kissed his father's hand and replied, "My Bey father, I hope to send you word of new victories as soon as possible."

Then he embraced his brother Murad who was standing right behind Orhan Ghazi and said, "I will need your help beyond the Dardanelles, my brother. I will be waiting for your arrival once you have fulfilled your duties here."

Orhan Ghazi cut in after Suleyman Pasha's words to his brother, "I will send your brother to you as soon as we return from the Germiyan campaign. We can easily preserve peace in our Beylik with your presence over there, while I continue our work from here."

Orhan Ghazi got up onto his horse as soon as he finished his sentence. Realising it was time to leave, Suleyman Pasha also mounted his Grey and rode northwards. Orhan Ghazi and Prince Murad waited for the *yayas* to move after the cavalry battalions and when they did, they steered their horses towards Bursa. After the departure of the beys and the battalions, the flat area dedicated to the

headquarters in front of the Fortress of Lümlüce was suddenly transformed into a quiet cavern. Remaining there with his beys, Yahşi Bey
watched those departing disappear into the distance and then
walked towards the *acemî*[45] units posted at the south end of the
plains.

Suleyman Pasha arrived at Plajar with his new forces after a three-
day journey. He left the cavalry and *yayas* under the command of his
beys at the headquarters and retreated to his quarters for a few days.
During those days of rest, he sat under a small canopy of trees situated on the hillside to watch Plajar's grasping sunset almost every
day. He arrived at this special spot and sat down. He watched the
setting of the sun to his heart's content. Watching that scenery reminded him of the winter days when he conversed with his mother.
He laughed to himself when he was reminded of the few days they
spent in Yarhisar and their trip to Nicaea, which his mother referred
to as İznik. After bursting into laughter, he delved into his memories,
"On the first day when we arrived in İznik from Yarhisar, which my
mother recalled as a 'place where very little remained from her childhood', my mother disappeared from sight. When I sent word to find
out where she had gone, I found out that she was taking a walk by
the lake with my nurses. Taking advantage of their absence I went to
the hill nearby and began watching the sun slowly glide in the horizon and shimmer on the lake. I wasn't even going to notice the fall
of night when I became engrossed by the play of the sunset and the
lake. If the *serdengeçtis* hadn't cautioned me I would have sat there
all night dreaming of the play of the sun and the lake. When I returned to the castle and arrived at the guest mansion readied by the
subaşı, my mother welcomed me with laughter. Her eyes sparkled
with a sense of happiness I had never seen before. I was delighted to
see her so happy. She immediately took me to her guest room and
said, 'My Suleyman, today I saw the most beautiful girl in all of

---

45 T.N, *Acemî* was a title given to conscripts who later joined the Janissary corps.

Nicaea... I thought that the beautiful daughter of Kara Ali Bey, one of your father's beys, would be worthy of your harem.'

"I replied in a way that wouldn't hurt my mother's feelings, 'If you think she is worthy of my harem and it is her kismet, it shall happen, mother.'

"I don't know why I spoke without thinking but when the words came out of my mouth I felt a stir in my heart that I had never felt before. As if the concubines she acquired for my harem weren't enough, she was now looking for a girl who could take her place in time to come. Sure, it was an innocent enough wish that could not be turned down. Thus, I didn't turn her offer down but I told her that I first wanted to capture the Fortress of Hadrianopolis and that, if she agreed, I could marry her upon my return from the autumn campaign."

Suleyman Pasha directed his gaze on the horizon as if he didn't want his memories to be slowly erased from his mind. He picked up a broken branch as he shook his head to either side connoting his frustration with his mind and distanced himself from his memories. As he stirred up the ground with the twig he looked at the setting sun and loudly said, "You are gliding behind the mountain the same way you did when I left you previous autumn. One of these days, when we set forth on our campaign, I will perhaps no longer be able to watch you to my heart's content but you will always race behind the mountains with the same intensity and at the same hour. I will no longer be here but know that I will climb up to the highest bastion of every new fortress I conquer and watch your glorious glide into dusk from there. Perhaps you won't set as beautifully there as you do here but I will always watch you set by remembering your beauty at this moment, here and now. And don't forget that no matter how much you try to escape my attention I will be chasing you tirelessly until the end of my life. I don't know how you set elsewhere but the way you do it in Plajar is special. That is why I am going to tell Hacı Ilbey this evening that they should not take me back to Bursa but bury me right here at this spot if I give my last breath during this campaign. For, I can watch you from here forever."

As soon as he finished his sentence he shuddered. He recalled that he had shuddered in exactly the same way when he and his mother watched the fish swim in Lake Askania during their trip to Nicaea. He asked himself "What in heavens is that?" and in fear, he jumped up on his feet. He got goose pimples when he felt the cold sweat trickling down his back. Then he said, "I think that was the time I was so scared for the first time in my life. I suppose what I was afraid of was death itself. But, what could be more absurd than being afraid of death? Yet, you cannot command the heart, the heart fears death. If only everyone could be as fortunate as Geyikli Baba and could live beyond the age of one hundred. Having heard so much about Geyikli Baba as a child, I had told my father that I wished to visit Geyikli Baba. In turn, my father replied, 'Neither should you go and get the secrets of your life revealed nor should you go looking for secrets in his life. Even if you went to see him you wouldn't get an audience with him. If you perhaps sent word to him, he might accept a visit from you. However, I think your best bet is to meet him like you meet other wandering dervishes who pass through Bursa if and when he comes here.'"

"Would he come to Bursa?"

"Just wait and see. What renders him esteemed is that everyone anticipates his arrival. The opinions of others do not matter, what is important is the judgment you pass on him and what you think of him. Remember, whatever attributes we may ascribe to him, in the eyes of God no man is more superior to another."

"After talking to my father that day I was able to distinguish better between right and wrong in everyday life. I waited for Geyikli Baba to come to Bursa for a while, but he didn't come. As time passed by I forgot about him."

Walking and muttering to himself, Suleyman Pasha had unwittingly arrived at the headquarter marquee. When he tilted his head up and looked at the entrance to the marquee he saw that Hacı Ilbey was waiting for him. Hacı Ilbey put his hand on his heart and saluted him. Emphasising each word, Hacı Ilbey said, "My Bey, both Fazıl Bey and Evrenos Bey are advancing day and night. They have both sent word that we should send new *yayas* to leave behind at the fortresses they captured."

Suleyman Pasha entered the spacious hall of the headquarters lit up with oil lamps and sat on the mat at the far end.

"Is there a certain reason as to why they are able to advance so swiftly?"

After scratching his neck with the tip of his finger he replied, "Certainly there is, My Prince. According to the hearsay we received, upon Co-Emperor Kantakouzenos's withdrawal from his imperial duties, his son Matthew Kantakouzenos has asked Emperor Palaiologos in Constantinople to announce him as the Co-Emperor and that if he refuses to do so, Matthew himself will arrive at Constantinople to announce his own emperorship."

"Is it true that Emperor Kantakouzenos has withdrawn from his imperial duties?"

"The news and hearsay we received point to that. It is said that he has gone into seclusion at a monastery in Didymóteicho."

Suleyman Pasha smiled. Looking at Hacı Ilbey sitting across from him cross-legged, he said, "During the first years of his emperorship, I was a guest of Kantakouzenos in Constantinople for about a week. Every time I saw him I caught hold of a different expression on his face. He is not the kind of man to give in to old age and go into seclusion. I wonder what plans he is conjuring up now. This is not the time to think about him. We should continue with our campaigns while they struggle against each other. We should first clear the Uğraş River of the knights who have been rising up in arms against both emperors. Afterwards, we should advance by capturing the coastal fortresses to the south of Mount Ganos with the forces at our disposal and reach Rodosto. Thus, we will be able to have control over the aid that will be sent by land from fortresses in Kostantiniyye as well as being able to prevent aid from coming into fortresses in Kostantiniyye by sea."

Hacı Ilbey responded as if to add something he had forgotten to say, "Meanwhile, we shouldn't forget about Aenus. According to the news we received, a large section of the Byzantine armada is anchored there. We have been informed that if Matthew Kantakouzenos marches towards Kostantiniyye, the hoplites from the armada are going to advance towards Hadrianopolis."

Suleyman Pasha briefly glimpsed at Hacı Ilbey and replied, "Perhaps this is a chance for us. As they wait and observe each other's moves, we should expedite our campaigns."

Hacı Ilbey seemed a bit more distressed than before, "However, My Prince, we need *subaşıs* who are competent in managing the fortresses and *kâdis*[46] who will manage and be in charge of the immigrants we will settle there. The *subaşıs* of Fazıl Bey and Akça Kocaoğlu are not very good at managing the fortresses. Orhan Ghazi, may he live long, informed us that the grandsons of Kalem Bey in Yahşi Province would be competent *subaşıs* and that he would dispatch them here, but they are yet to arrive. It is my opinion that it would be beneficial if we sent a number of the voluntary migrants from the newly captured fortresses to the Yahşi Province. They can settle in the lands of beys who are due to arrive from there. This way the lands of the beys will not be vacant and the beys can easily settle the migrants in the fortresses. As such, we can establish balance both here and there."

Suleyman Pasha replied, "Before we do anything else, we ought to lay siege on Dyme Castle once again as it still remains as a bone of

---

46 T.N, *Kadî* is a judge administering both şerîat and kânûn and chief administrator of a kâdîlik.

contention on our way up north. We should show them what it means to reclaim the castle upon our departure. They need to be taught a lesson on what it means to draw the sword against the Ottomans."

Hacı Ilbey replied, "I suggest we first deal with the deserters residing near the Uğraş River, capture the fortresses on the coastline of Hellespont and then direct our attention towards Dyme."

Suleyman Pasha approved of this suggestion by nodding. Hacı Ilbey continued, "If so, I will call the unit sergeants and beys for a meeting and inform them of the decisions we have made. Once the preparations are completed we can set forth."

As Suleyman Pasha stood up from his seat he said, "May our holy war be blessed, Hacı Ilbey."

With his broad shoulders tilted and his steps limber, he walked out of the headquarter marquee and walked towards his harem marquee pitched between the small fortress and the encampment.

CHAPTER FOURTY-FOUR

Tired of waiting for the cold winds blowing towards Mystras from the Aegean Sea to the east and from the gulf to the north after uniting in the forests of Morea, as if it was exhaled from between the lips of a giant, to subside, Kantakouzenos VI ordered his men to prepare to set out on their journey even though his son, Manuel Kantakouzenos, the Despotēs of Morea, insisted that he remained put. Despite the fact that his men were hard at work preparing for the journey, Kantakouzenos was unable to make his mind up on leaving his wife, Irene, in Morea. His wife would surely be safer with his son but he couldn't find it in his heart to leave her behind when he had just saved her from the clutches of Emperor Palaiologos V by giving up his imperial position. As he waited undecidedly, he was trying to anticipate what awaited him in Rome. He was weighing the worst possibilities against the best in his mind's eye and, after much consideration, he seemed to have made a decision. But just at that moment, he changed his mind again and began to reason from the beginning all over again. He couldn't recall being in such a state of undecidedness in all of his life and he frequently muttered, "Perhaps this *is* my most difficult and final decision?"

The evening his men informed him that the preparations were complete and that they were ready to set out, the usurper emperor climbed on top of the castle wall that separated the inner courtyard of Mystras from the surrounding neighbourhoods before nightfall. For a while, he walked on top of the wall aimlessly and came back to the point where he started. He stood on top of the staircase. As he looked to the north he saw that a dark cloud was approaching Mystras. As he looked at it in a disgruntled manner, he muttered, "A herald of the last days of winter", in order to console himself. Just then, he felt like crying, the sadness enveloped him gently, and seemed to mock him. This troubled emotion gradually climbed up from the pit

of his stomach and approached his heart. It was as if first his large
intestines and then his small intestines had been severed from his
stomach and were all advancing upwards like a snake. He was so
startled that the fear he felt could be seen in his eyes. He began
shouting at the guard posted at the bastion closest to him in the
loudest tone of voice that his throat permitted. Even though he was
making such a great effort to be heard, the guard gazing into the distance couldn't hear him. Kantakouzenos VI began waving his walking stick with its gold-gilded handle at the guard. The guard just
couldn't see any of the commotion. Realising that the guard wasn't
even aware of his presence, the overthrown emperor of Byzantium
leaned on his walking stick and sat on the top step of the ladder. Just
then, he heard the guard whistling. Breathing deeply Kantakouzenos
VI shuddered at the thought that crossed his mind, "I can hear him
whistling so why can't he hear me shouting?" He looked in the direction of the guard once more. Even though the guard seemed very
powerful, with his upright posture as if to show off the armour on his
arms and torso, he didn't seem to have a head. Thinking that he was
mistaken, Kantakouzenos VI first wiped his teary eyes with the back
of his hand and then closely observed the guard. He knew that the
melody he remembered from his childhood was emanating from
between the lips of the guard but he somehow couldn't see his head
or his lips. He thought that his eyes were misguiding him when he
saw that the headless guard dressed in armour was charging towards
him with his spear directed at him. Seized with fear, Kantakouzenos
VI let himself go and began tumbling down the staircase before the
headless guard could get to him. He rolled down to where the steps
met the ground. After crashing on the ground, it took him some
while to come back to his senses. He thought of getting up and leaving immediately but he didn't. He kneeled down and began waiting
for the headless guard who would climb down the ladder. As he
waited he said, "Before he stabs me with the spear I will ask him,

'Did Manuel send you?' When I give my last breath, I want to find
out if Manuel also accuses me of being a coward like his older
brother does." He didn't know why such a string of thoughts came
into his mind at such a dire moment but he knew that finding out
whether Manuel also despised him would give him peace. As he
looked towards the ladder with fear in his eyes, he realised that there
was neither a guard descending the ladder nor anybody else around.
Just as he was about to force himself to speak, tears streamed down
from his fearful eyes. He couldn't stop the tears that kept rolling
down until there were no more tears left to shed. When the tears
ceased, he wiped them off his face with the back of his hand and
stood up at once. He first turned his head to the courtyard and then
at the staircase. His gaze ascended to the top of the staircase and became fixed on the helmeted head of the guard posted at the highest
bastion of the castle. The guard was still whistling and viewing the
dark cloud up in the sky. He looked at the guard, at the cloud and
then at the spacious inner courtyard. Shy of itself, his gaze hid behind his eyelids. Supporting himself with his Baghdad-make gold-gilded walking stick, he began walking towards the small chateau
which his son used as his residence and headquarters. He muttered,
"Matthew has taken a fancy to power and does not believe me but
my Manuel has served me for days without fail and also repeatedly
assured me that he would be beside me come what may. I will have
committed a great sin if I doubt his sincerity."

Then, he momentarily stopped walking. His gaze became fixed on
the inscription on a wide and flat stone on which he was about to
step. The letters had almost become indistinct due to the cracks in
the stone but it was clear that they were letters, that they were once
made for decorative purposes or to symbolise a victory. He crouched
down to try and read the inscription. Worn out with time, the shapes
were tangled and almost indecipherable. He tried linking the letters
he recognised to make sense of the text but he failed. Taking deep

breaths, he muttered, "I thought I was knowledgeable, but there is so
much that I also don't know. I suppose the reason why I tumbled
down the ladder and why I didn't know why I couldn't see the
guard's head are also amongst the things I don't know. What fear
blurred my memory so much? Is this the fear caused by our experiences en-route, or the fear caused by my experiences in Constantinople after Andronicus?"

He felt his body grow stronger when he came closer to the small
chateau. He waved his Baghdad-make walking stick in the air and
tried to ease the bothersome thoughts in his mind by saying, "This is
all Andronicus's fault." Then, as if Andronicus Palaiologos was right
in front of him, he said, "As you may know Protagoras of Abdera
said, 'Of all things the measure is Man, of the things that are, that
they are and of the things that are not, that they are not.' As you
may also know, the ambition of power was not one of my feelings
until your death. I was infected with that by your death and after
you, I also had to live by shouldering all that pain. You might say,
'Why do you dwell on the outcome constructed by Protagoras's own
dogmas? Just forget it all, let go of it.' It is easier said than done. My
life now includes everything in it, how could I possibly forget it all? I
will not forget anything until the end of my life. I will not forget any
of the harm they have caused me even though they are my sons in
law. However, for now, I am going to set the things I will never forget aside and will do whatever is required by my Byzantium. Once
my Byzantium is rid of all this mess I will make sure to ask them
both to account for their actions. My wish is to not return empty-
handed from this journey. I will even accept the union of the
churches if it is necessary for me to do so." As he walked through the
doors of the small chateau, the inscriptions he thought he had forgotten appeared in his mind. He exclaimed, "We couldn't decipher
it!" as if to resent himself. He took a few steps towards the inner
rooms. He hadn't yet approached the chamber where he stayed with

his wife when he muttered, "Some Iawolic letters look like ours but I couldn't read the ones that looked foreign. I assume they were the letters of a language spoken by their ancestors..." Then he took a few more steps, muttering, "Who knows how many languages were spoken here before Iawolic?" and entered the inner room.

CHAPTER FORTY-FIVE

Fazıl Bey was unable to contain himself and he kept turning around and looking eastwards and westwards. He walked and continued looking to the east and the west until everything on earth was clearly visible after being shadowed from the darkness with the first rays of the rising sun. The moment he saw the first light he ran to his horse and rode him towards the *yayas* who were closing in on the castle walls. He encouraged them by shouting, "Come on my lions, come on!" at the top of his voice. He listened to the deep sounds of the battering rams beating on the castle gate. He changed position and looked at the *yayas* who were ever closer to the castle. When he saw that the armoured *yayas* were in formation under their shields and approaching the *koçbaşıcıs*[47], he yelled once more and louder than before, "Come on my lions, you're almost there!" Hearing his yell, they displaced once again without regard to the arrows hailing down on them from the castle. Noticing the arrows falling on the *yayas*, Fazıl Bey rode his horse to where his archers were while he exclaimed, "Displace all the archers in the cavalry to the front!"

As the messengers rode their horses to deliver what he had said to the cavalry commanders, Fazıl Bey reached his fire archers and told them to fire all their arrows and to take aim at the top of the castle walls.

After receiving his order to fire, the archers began to incessantly fire their arrows, which they set aflame in the wink of an eye, towards the Byzantine guards atop the castle wall. The sky became invisible due to the sudden surge of flaming arrows. As if the continuous firing of arrows wasn't sufficient, the newly erected trebuchets began showering the Byzantine guards with stones wrapped in flaming rags. The mutual firing of arrows lasted for a while before the ar-

---

47 T.N, *Koçbaşıcı* was a title given to military officials who supervised the use of battering rams.

rows fired from the castle stalled. Attempting to take advantage of this, the *yayas* sallied towards the castle gates while the climbers, the *serdengeçtis* and the *delis* ran to the climbing points of the castle walls. When the first ladders were propped against the wall, the climbers effortlessly climbed on top of the walls. Then with the ropes they suspended, the *serdengeçtis* began climbing up the walls. In order to keep up with the *serdengeçtis,* the *delis* also climbed up the castle wall. As the fierce conflict that started on top of the castle walls continued, the flaming arrow archers were lobbing flameless arrows into the inner castle.

Fazıl Bey first fired up the archers who had encircled the castle from atop his horse. Then, as soon as he approached his cavalry unit he commanded them, "Bear down on the gates!"

He rode his horse towards the main gate and dismounted when he was near the *yaya* emplacements. He had only taken a few steps towards the *yayas* when he surmised that the ground was shaking. He paused and looked around. Seeing that the ground was solid he sneered and muttered, "This land shook many brave men, who are you to shake the ground Fazıl?" Noticing that the *yayas* were charging towards the castle gate, he observed them without a thought in his mind. He got back on his horse when the first *yayas* entered through the main gate. Fazıl Bey became excited when his horse, accustomed to keeping pace with the *yayas* approached the gate. He incessantly shouted, "Come on my brave men! Come on my lions!"

When the Ottoman *yayas* quickly began entering the castle through the broken down gate, the feudal lord of Malgara[48] had cast his gaze on the castle guards over half of whom had suffered burn injuries. Despite the fact of being defeated was written on the cards, he kept muttering, "We will withstand as long as we can. We sent messengers to both emperors, aid should arrive any minute." He also exhorted

---

48 T.N, Malgara was derived from the Persian name ('Margaar' meaning 'cave of snakes') given to current-day Malkara, a town and district of Tekirdağ Province in the Marmara region of Turkey.

the commander of the guards, "Do what you must and endure as long as you can." But the commander of the guards was slightly wounded and replied, "We don't have any power left." Having given up all hope on the commander of the guards, the feudal lord was in a state of bewilderment. He charged towards the top of the castle walls. After encouraging the clashing guards for a while, he approached the guards minding the hot oil and tar cauldrons above the main gate. As soon as he realised that the main gate under the arch had been broken down he shouted at the guards, "Don't stop! Keep tipping the cauldrons over the wall!"

The guards were just about to fulfil the lord's orders when an enormous rag-wrapped stone thrown from a catapult landed inside one of the hot oil cauldrons. Spattered with hot oil the guards were in shock. *Akıncı delis* suddenly appeared out of nowhere and surrounded them. The feudal lord witnessed how the delis were slicing the guards alive with their swords and surrendered in fear. As he did so he also commanded the guards standing by the cauldrons to surrender.

The Ottoman cavalry units retreated when a white flag was hoisted upon the highest bastion of the castle before noon. Fazıl Bey entered the castle behind a small cavalry unit and *yayas*. When they arrived at the square between the main gate and the church, he commanded the *yayas* marching before him, "Gather everyone here. Ensure that not a single person remains indoors."

The head *yayas* separated their men into groups and sent them into the narrow streets to fulfil Fazıl Bey's orders. Meanwhile, not knowing where the castle commander and the feudal lord were, Fazıl Bey delegated his *serdengeçtis* to search for them. The *serdengeçtis*, who spoke the language of the castle people, found and brought the wounded castle commander after a brief search. Fazıl Bey noticed that the castle commander was in a lot of pain due to his burn injury and told the physicians to treat him, whilst another group of *ser-*

dengeçtis brought the feudal lord of the castle captured by the *delis* at the top of the castle walls to the square.

Looking at the captured feudal lord, Fazıl Bey asked the head of the *delis* why he had been taken captive. The head of the *delis* bowed and saluted Fazıl Bey before explaining, "My Bey, he was caught when he was ordering the guards to tip the cauldrons over the castle wall. He has been proven guilty of this offence."

Fazıl Bey couldn't think of anything to say. After a brief silence, he replied, "He is your captive—take him to join the other captives. We have nothing left to do with him."

Then he called one of the old people brought to the square by the *yayas* and asked him to take him to the priest. Fazıl Bey got off his horse and followed the old man on foot with his beys following him. The priest watched them walk towards the church of Malgara Castle and glanced at Fazıl Bey's turban in awe. Fazıl Bey saluted the priest by nodding and addressed the interpreter behind him, "Tell the saintly priest that there is no need for fear or worry. Nothing will change in his castle. Everyone will be able to continue to pray in accordance with his or her beliefs. My men are gathering the castle people in the large square. We will also head there with the saintly priest. Together, we will tell the castle people not to fear and worry. I wish that they will understand that their castle is now under the hegemony of the Osmanoğlu Beylik and that they are in the safekeeping of our Beylik."

When the interpreter translated Fazıl Bey's words to the priest, his face lit up. The priest gently bowed and saluted Fazıl bey. As he followed him towards the church door he promised, "I will do whatever you want in the name of God, as long as nobody suffers any pain."

İskender Bey, assuming the role of interpreter, conveyed the priest's words to Fazıl Bey who, in turn, smiled and replied in Greek, "Saintly father, we don't want anyone to suffer either."

They reached the square after walking down the small street in silence. Fazıl Bey climbed on top of the arch above the castle gate with the priest. He first looked at the hot oil cauldrons and then at the people gathered in the square, "People of Malgara... Today is the day your castle has been conquered by the forces of the Ottoman Beylik. As of this moment, your castle is in the safekeeping of our Beylik. No one, except those who shot arrows at us and swung their swords against us, will be punished. If there are those of you who fought against us that remain here and surrender themselves to our forces of their own volition they will only be treated as captives. If you do not surrender willingly you will face harsher punishments. And, if any of you know of such persons and do not report it to us, they will face even more gruelling sentences."

İskender Bey first cast his gaze on the priest and then translated Fazıl Bey's words to the people gathered in the square. When he was done interpreting, Fazıl Bey looked at the priest and said, "Saintly father, the Ottomans have never changed the order in the castles they captured until now. The same will be applied to Malgara. You will continue the life you had yesterday tomorrow, as long as you co-operate with us and accept the sovereignty of Orhan Ghazi and pray for the victory of the Ottomans during your ceremonies. If, despite all that, there are those who willingly want to leave the castle we will help them reach where they wish to go in safety. If there are people who want to migrate to Anatolia, our judicious bey Orhan Ghazi will give them enough land to sustain themselves. As of this moment, you will pay your taxes to the Osmanoğlu Beylik annually. You will be able to receive further information from our *subaşı* who will be appointed to your castle."

Unable to believe all that had been happening, the priest was listening to the interpretation of Fazıl Bey's words and thinking, "So all of the information included in the letter sent by the priest of the Gallipoli Castle was true." Trying to overcome his suspicion, he asked İskender Bey, "Will we be able to hold mass in our church?"

Understanding his question, Fazıl Bey smiled and replied in Greek, "Of course you will continue to hold mass in your church. And if other people settle in the castle they will also be able to carry out their religious duties in their own places of worship."

İskender Bey interpreted Fazıl Bey's response regardless and assured the priest who was looking at him in surprise, "Father, our Bey has been very clear. You will continue your life as if nothing had changed except that you will also have new neighbours settling in your castle."

Noticing that İskender Bey was looking at him, Fazıl Bey addressed the people gathered in the square, "You may now return to your homes and continue your day's work."

Listening to the interpretation of his last words the castle people remained silent for a while before heading back to their homes. Fazıl Bey addressed İskender Bey, "Dispatch the messengers so that the couriers waiting at the headquarters can inform our Bey that Malgara is now part of the Ottoman lands."

As the messengers set forth, Fazıl Bey was drinking the water brought to him as he had a dry throat after his speech. The head courier, who never left the headquarters unless there was an urgent matter, approached Fazıl Bey in a great hurry. As Fazıl Bey handed the silver tankard to his servant, the courier said, "My Bey, you have a letter from Orhan Ghazi."

Then he took the letter from his sash and handed it to Fazıl Bey who quickly opened the folded letter placed inside wax cloth. He read the concisely written letter in one breath, and grouched, "This shouldn't have happened! If their aim is to stop us advancing in Thrace, then they shouldn't have done that! And if they did this so it could benefit Thrace they are yet to find out that they have done the worst possible thing they could have done!" as he handed the letter to İskender Bey.

CHAPTER FORTY-SIX

Overthrown Emperor Kantakouzenos VI had delayed his journey to Rome several times due to the bad weather conditions. He was spending most of his time with his grandchildren at the modest mansion of his son, Manuel Kantakouzenos the Despotēs of Morea, in Mystras where he stayed throughout the winter. He was telling his grandchildren about Byzantium and the Peloponnese without ever mentioning Athens or the Athenians. After spending the entire winter between his son's mansion and the Church of Istria, the overthrown Emperor decided to leave his wife Irene with his son when spring arrived. By the time he set forth on his journey, he had reached the end of his tether. Thus he had informed his men to have short breaks en-route to their destination from the Peloponnese lands, which he referred to as Messenia. Advancing for days with few and short breaks the guards, the drivers and the servants we exhausted when they arrived at the nonchalant Pylos harbour. If the overthrown Emperor allowed it, his men could have perhaps slept for a week. However, Kantakouzenos VI had slept a lot in his royal carriage and thinking that his men could get rest once they were on the ship he immediately ordered them to find a ship to take them to Rome.

The loyal guard commander and two of his men got to work at once and before long they found a sizeable Genoese ship that was being loaded en-route to Rome, negotiated with the captain and returned to the Emperor. Remaining at the Pylos Castle[49] until the day the ship was to set sail, Kantakouzenos VI was amazed by the size of the sailing ship that looked like a round pool on the sea when he boarded it. When he entered his spacious cabin he muttered, "The Genoese don't sail in the Aegean Sea with such large ships because of their fear of being spotted." He spent some time in his cabin be-

---

49 T.N, Pylos Castle is also known as Navarino Castle.

fore climbing up to the deck and realising that the ship had sailed
far from the harbour he couldn't stop himself from exclaiming, "In
such a short period of time!" He had just about lent an ear to the
yells of the oarsmen on the superimposed levels of the ship, as they
pulled on the oars, when he noticed that they were quite far from the
coast and that the Pylos harbour was almost invisible. As he looked
at the distant coastline and the clear blue waters of the sea that
gradually seemed more like it was going to swallow the ship, he recalled the foamy waters of the Bosphorus visible from the window of
his mansion in Constantinople. He thought, "Perhaps these are the
same waters as the ones that accompanied me on my way out from
Constantinople." A bitter chill coursed through his body with the
coolness of the mellow wind that caressed his skin as he tried to visu-
alise his Constantinople in his mind—the city that had not slipped
his mind even for a moment in all the months he had been away.
The more the chill lingered in him the more it travelled to his core.
He abandoned thinking about Constantinople and fixed his gaze on
the coastline that was gradually fading into the distance. He was astonished that the coastline, extending abruptly at the mountain skirt,
was deprived of trees. With the same astonished look in his eyes, he
viewed the verdant copses at the zenith of mountains now so distant
and hard to see with the naked eye. He muttered, "They seem as if
they are cross with one another." After taking a few deep breaths he
repined, "Neither these coasts look like those of Hellespont nor do
these trees look like the trees I saw on my way to Antigone... The
clearings I travelled across in Messenia en-route from Mystras are
not fertile like the lands of Antigone. It's as if what looks like soil
isn't soil but rock and it's been sprayed with red dust. Chuckling at
the metaphor he thought of haphazardly he mumbled, "Why did the
Spartans and Athenians cause such a fuss over these arid lands that
don't bear any fruit other than mulberries? The innocent people of
Megara, Mantinea and Argos shed their blood for no reason. The

lands for which they sacrificed their necks still stand but neither Pericles defeated by the plague nor any other general stands tall. Now we are looking for ways to stand up to the Ottomans but we fail to consider what time will bring, what it will take away from us."

A sense of relief appeared on his face as if his idea had reached a certain level of maturity. When he turned his gaze towards the coast-line that was disappearing in the horizon, once more he felt as if it wasn't the ship that was moving away but the coast but with the coast, life. He felt exceedingly powerless and vulnerable in the face of that life that was feeling ever-more distant. As he searched for somewhere to take refuge he stumbled on the sight of the partially armoured sentry. Casting his gaze on the blue waters anew, he thought of his wife Irene whom he referred to as his "True Empress." He had left her, his entire harem and almost his entire treasury be-hind in Mystras. When he momentarily thought that his wife might tell their son about the imperial treasury he had left behind he felt tightness in his chest. He got goose pimples on his round face covered by his long beard. His previously cold body became warm. He unbuttoned his coat. He turned his face in the direction of the cool wind. As the wind was caressing his long beard, he repined, "My God, how can existence make one feel so alone?" As he tried to brush away his woes something unexpected happened. A wave of yearning came over him for Morea, the lands he previously thought to be without charm. Lovingly looking at the coastline extending in the ho-rizon like a line out of reach, he said, "I wish I could step foot on those lands now." While gazing at the coast longingly, the image of Empress Anna appeared out of nowhere and slowly started pacing in his mind. As if it wasn't enough that she was occupying his mind, she was laughing sinisterly and mocking him, "You still dare to think of yourself as Emperor and you are heading to Rome on behalf of the empire. I suppose you will be heading to Avignon from there? You think that you can pay your debt to Byzantium by doing so. But your debts match your sins. You cannot lessen either no matter what you do!" She laughed loudly and consecutively repeated, "If you knew how happy you made Byzantium and Constantinople by leaving, you would retreat to your corner and not overshadow their happiness." Kantakouzenos VI waved his hand and shooed her away "Go away, Anna! My sins do not exceed yours! It is you who should retreat to her corner and leave her son be so that both our Byzantium and our people can finally be at peace!" Overhearing the Emperor's monologue, the partially-armoured sentry addressed the Emperor, "Did Your Majesty want something?"

Startled by the sentry's voice, Kantakouzenos VI came back to his senses. He looked at the sentry with a smile on his lips. Before heading towards the door of his cabin, he said, "It's best I return to my cabin before I catch a cold."

The largest cabin of the sailing ship advancing on the blue waters like a round pool was reserved for him. His servants, guards and a few loyal men he never left behind were staying in adjacent cabins. Upon entering his spacious cabin, Kantakouzenos VI felt like sitting on the armchair fixed to the floor and thinking but the moment he sat down, he realised that the hefty bed on the other side of the cabin was calling him. He looked at the knee-high boots on his feet. He wanted to call the servant to take them off but he changed his mind. He stood up and lied down on the bed with his boots on. The moment his body surrendered to the bed, he noticed how much his body ached. He had just begun to think about the pains coursing through his body when he realised that they were gradually becoming unbearable. Scared of the pain, Kantakouzenos was riddled with the fear of death. He jumped up from his bed and rushed out of his cabin. Seeing the sentry in front of his door gave him a sense of relief but he was embarrassed to leave his cabin in such a hurry so he walked back inside. Unable to make sense of the Emperor's sudden exit from and return to the cabin, the sentry lifted up the spear in his hand a couple of times. He waited awhile. He felt suspicious. He decided to look inside the cabin through the round window on the door of the Emperor's cabin. When he approached the door to do so he thought, "I have never looked out from my window or through anybody else's" and refrained. As he turned his face towards the sea he muttered, "If he had some kind of discomfort or if he had a request he would have told me." Then he continued to stand guard with his spear as he always did.

After returning to his cabin, Kantakouzenos lost his bearings when his fever gradually went up and caused his strength to dwindle away. The only thing he could think of doing was pulling up the duvet. The fear of never opening his eyes again if he shut them wandered in his mind again. He began to stare at the ceiling without a single blink. But a few invisible hands mounted a huge mirror on the ceiling of the cabin, right above his bed as if they were waiting for him to stare at the ceiling. First, the image of himself appeared on the mirror, then his son-in-law Palaiologos'. He was looking at Palaiologos in the mirror and the Palaiologos in the mirror was looking back at him. They stared at each other for a while. His son-in-law Palaiologos had just opened his mouth to say something when he saw Orhan Ghazi standing right across from his image in the mirror. The entire Kantakouzenos family, except his daughter Theodora whom he referred to as 'my intelligent daughter', was standing behind Orhan Ghazi who was scratching his round nose with the back of his hand. Quavering his lips parched by high fever he asked Orhan Ghazi, "Where is my Theodora?" When Orhan Ghazi idly continued scratching his nose, Kantakouzenos yelped in a tone of voice brimming with yearning, "My intelligent daughter! My Theodora! Will I be able to see you one last time before I die? Your gentle footsteps never leave my thoughts." Then, smiling he said, "My Theodora, is it true that Holofira[50] is jealous of your beauty? If it is so I will not be

---

50 T.N, Referred to in this instance by her birth name "Holofira" is Nilüfer Hatun, wife of Orhan Gazi.

surprised, my beautiful daughter, for all women are jealous of the woman who is more beautiful than themselves. Wait for me, if I manage to return to Constantinople I will also come and visit you in Bursa. I wish Orhan had brought you to Nicaea..." He felt his body abandon itself except for his eyes and mind. As he tried to endure living with his gaze, he saw his imperial carriage in the mirror. It was being drawn by six horses. There weren't any advance guards or commanders in front of the carriage. The driver of the imperial carriage, which he reproached, was dressed in rags. As he viewed the carriage and the driver that smelled of poverty, he muttered, "I cannot visit the Pope with this carriage."

As if the mirror had been waiting for him to utter these words, the idiosyncratic image of the Pope's cherub-like face appeared on the mirror. Looking at Kantakouzenos sitting in his destitute carriage the Pope called out in a deep tone of voice that did not suit his old-age, "Welcome, mesazōn John Kantakouzenos who opposed Andronicus' idea of uniting the church!" Kantakouzenos stepped out of his carriage timidly.

As he stood across from the Pope and viewed the mosaic ceiling, he said, "Yes, saintly father? I pray that the sin I committed be forgiven." Looking deep into Kantakouzenos' eyes, the Pope replied, "The absolution I can provide is of no use to you, my son. You should repent to God for forgiveness."

He continued gazing into Kantakouzenos' eyes with his shimmering eyes for a while and then said, "We are listening. Tell us, what can we do for you?"

Kantakouzenos VI replied hastily, "Saintly father, we want your help not for me, but for our Byzantium, for our Constantinople. In return for your help, I and Andronicus Palaiologos' son, my Co-Emperor John Palaiologos will do all we can to unite our church."

The Pope's smiling image leaned on its walking stick. This time, the Pope replied in a crestfallen tone of voice encased in old-age, "Dear son, we had been waiting for this moment for years. The Vatican will rejoice upon hearing your good tidings. We are not sure what those in Avignon will think of this, but you should know that the Vatican is on your side. We want you to know that all those of Catholic and Orthodox faith will not forget your good doings for centuries to come. Dear son, go and rest now. We will prepare the letters we will be sending to kings and princes and inform you. Once you are sanctified and have reached peace, we will send the letters."

Hearing the Pope's soft and soothing voice Kantakouzenos' eyelids slowly became heavier and heavier. He was buried so deep inside his high fever that he was sweating blood before he knew it. When he awoke to his men's voices he looked at the mirror at once. Upon seeing that the mirror was no longer there above his bed, he uttered, "Thank God!" As he looked at the men around him he shouted out the first word that appeared in his mind as if he was scared of the voice that emanated from his throat, "Sentry!"

CHAPTER FORTY-SEVEN

Gathered in Prince Suleyman Pasha's headquarter marquee, the beys were trying to explain the reason behind the icy weather to each other by exchanging glances. Suleyman Pasha sat up straight with his legs crossed and leaned back against the backrest. Realising that his beys were impatiently waiting for his speech he took a deep breath and filled his lungs with air as he always did before delivering a speech. As soon as he let out the breath he had kept in for a while, he spoke in the softest tone of voice, "My Beys, we are conquering lands bit by bit on this side of the Dardanelles and capturing Byzantine castles of different sizes one by one. However, we don't have authority over the seas yet. According to the news we received, my father, may he live long, has left Antigone with his army and is heading towards Kostantiniyye. He must have gotten as furious with the kidnapping of my brother Halil as with the incompetency of the Byzantine emperor. Think of an emperor, who doesn't even have any influence on his *levends*..."

Then he looked at his beys' faces to signify that he had said all he wanted to.

Hacı IlBey sat up straight on one knee and took his turn to talk, "Beys, I participated in a couple of marine expeditions with the small armada of the Karasid Dynasty for the conquests of lands in Thrace and Urum. It was during these expeditions that I learned that the seas are nothing like the land. You should know that water is not suited to people of the land. Soil fills all gaps whereas water empties out what has been filled in with soil. What I mean to put across is that people of the land are strong when they step foot on trusted land. If they step foot on a surface that swashes like water, they become taken aback. As such, we should not even dream about setting out into the seas before we train *levends* who can feel as powerful as Phocaean pirates when they set foot on water. From this point of view, there is currently no way for us to get Halil Bey back from the clasp of the Phocaean pirates. We also must not believe the Emperor who says Phocaea belongs to Byzantium, because it is impossible for anyone to know on which island the pirates are holding Halil Bey captive. The only way for Halil Bey to be released is to pay the ransom the Phocaean pirates are demanding. I don't think Byzantium is capable of paying that ransom."

Evrenos Bey took the floor when Hacı IlBey finished, "Hacı IlBey is right. Byzantium bent over backwards in order to get rid of the Latins. As they fought against the Latins they didn't really kick up a fuss about the pirates dividing and sharing the Aegean Sea amongst themselves. At present, the Phocaean pirates are the second most powerful group of pirates after the Jesuits. They know full well that the double-headed Byzantium will not come after them."

When Evrenos Bey fell silent, Topal Hasan Bey—Hacı IlBey's second in command from the neighbourhood of el-Hac Yahşi who joined the Council of Beys a short while ago—took the floor, "Beys, both your descriptions of the seas and your thoughts about the Phocaean pirates are correct. But I must remind that the Phocaean pirates are neither like the Genoese nor the Venetians. They consider everything in the seas as their own and think that they have the right to seize everything across the coastlines. As Hacı IlBey so aptly put it, there is no other choice than to pay a hefty ransom at present. The Phocaea Castle is not strategically convenient for attacks from land. Both Latins and Catalans have laid siege on the region but they couldn't even close in on the castle. The castle is very sheltered and the ships of cornered pirates advance out to the sea with the speed of the devil. According to rumours, Umur Bey once drove them into a corner and when he thought they had defeated them, he realised they'd managed to slip through his fingers. However, we could perhaps still cooperate with the neighbouring Aydınids and have an advantage."

As Suleyman Pasha listened to his Beys, who were more experienced than him, he became overwhelmed about learning new things regarding the seas and the Phocaean pirates. Then he noticed that Akça Kocaoğlu—known as the conqueror of Bithynia and as Akça Koca Bey—was getting ready to take the floor. While waiting for him to start his speech, his eyes met Fazıl Bey's anxious gaze constantly directed at the door. As he pondered about what made Fazıl Bey so uneasy he heard Akça Kocaoğlu's deep voice, "According to the hearsay we have received, Emperor Palaiologos is currently more concerned about his brother-in-law Matthew's fantasies of becoming the Emperor rather than Halil Bey staying alive. I think that the only reason why he cannot leave Kostantiniyye for Phocaea is that he fears his brother-in-law Matthew Kantakouzenos capturing Kostantiniyye. He is right to fear this. The city is bubbling with trouble. If we can get to the coastline of the Black Sea as soon as possible we will have intercepted all the roads Matthew Kantakouzenos will be using to get to Kostantiniyye. Thus, with no fears left, Emperor Palaiologos can easily leave Kostantiniyye."

As Suleyman Pasha and the other Beys who had been dealing with state affairs for years looked at Akça Kocaoğlu with astonishment, Hacı IlBey added, "Akça Kocaoğlu is right. The Emperor doesn't want to lose his throne again. When he sees that Matthew Kantakouzenos is no longer a threat he will get to the pirate's castle in no time flat. Byzantium does not have much power over the land outside Kostantiniyye but the vast seas are still under their control..."

After laughing up his sleeve, Evrenos Bey cut in, "The fertility of Thracian lands has illuminated us all so much that we have come to say better things about the future more than one another. I agree with Akça Kocaoğlu. The best way to deal with this situation is to intercept Matthew Kantakouzenos's journey to Kostantiniyye."

Topal Hasan Bey added, "You are all right, Beys. If we intercept Matthew Kantakouzenos's journey, Orhan Ghazi will send the Emperor to Phocaea without delay."

As Suleyman Pasha calmly listened to the other Beys' brief
speeches he felt a sense of exhaustion for the first time. He gazed at
his Beys' faces one after another and before he stood up, he said,
"Beys, we have been able to defend the castles we besieged throughout spring and summer. We should now prepare for winter and unite
our troops. Before winter is upon us we should depart for the Black
Sea coast in order to intercept Matthew Kantakouzenos. Tomorrow
the cavalry of Akça Kocaoğlu and Hasan Bey will set out towards
the north after the *akıncı* units—Fazıl Bey and Balabancıkoğlu will
set out towards the north-east—Evrenos Bey and the forces of the
Gerede beys will head towards the west. The cavalry units arriving
from Bursa will be sent to Aenus to get the north of Aenus under
their control. Once they have secured this area they will join Evrenos
Bey's forces. With our central forces, Hacı IlBey and I will advance
towards Hadrianopolis where Matthew Kantakouzenos is currently
residing. All the castles that are under our command will be placed
under the authority of *subaşıs* sent from Bursa by Yahşi Bey. I hope
that the forces of Akça Kocaoğlu and Hasan Bey will settle in the
castles on the Black Sea coastline and Fazıl Bey's in the castles surrounding Kostantiniyye before winter is upon us. We will begird
Hadrianopolis to prevent Matthew from doing something insane. If
we have the opportunity, we can corner him in the castle. If we need
it, we will send for your help. May our Holy War be blessed!"

Fazıl Bey, who spoke the least that evening and constantly watched
the door of the marquee, had almost lost all of his hope when he
stood up with the rest of the beys. Just then he saw the chief messenger of Suleyman Pasha enter the marquee. He smiled when their eyes
met.

CHAPTER FORTY-EIGHT

J ust as Young Emperor John Palaiologos V had managed to establish peace after extraordinary efforts to deter his supporters in Constantinople and the supporters of his father-in-law, usurper Emperor John Kantakouzenos VI from mercilessly throttling one another like the greens and blues did during the reign of Eastern Roman Emperor Justinian, he had found out through a letter from Orhan Ghazi that Halil Bey of Nicomedia, his cousin from Princess Asporsha the second wife of Orhan Ghazi, had been kidnapped. In the letter, Orhan Ghazi was asking for his help to find and save his son. However, Emperor Palaiologos V didn't respond to Orhan Ghazi's letter immediately due to the rumours he was receiving that the internal problems in Constantinople were still ongoing and that his brother-in-law Matthew Kantakouzenos was heading towards Constantinople from Hadrianopolis. Even if he had responded to his letter immediately, it was impossible for him to leave Constantinople at such a critical period and search for Halil Bey in all the coves of the seas.

Nevertheless, in his rather late reply, he had informed Orhan Ghazi of all that had been going on in Constantinople and that, as it was impossible for him to leave the city, he had instructed the commander of the navy to find Halil Bey at once.

On the days that the delayed letter of the Emperor reached Orhan Ghazi, the Byzantine armada had visited the Pigas Castle. Once they had found out that the Ottoman princess was still living in the castle and had never left, despite the lawless Catalans who had laid their claim to the castle, they had set out towards the Aegean Sea. The armada sailed through the Dardanelles and advanced towards the south, searching the small and large islands and the coastline castles in the Aegean Sea which they came across on their way, asking about the whereabouts of Halil Bey of the suspicious castle commanders.

In the afternoon of one of those days, the ambassadors from Phocaea wanted to see the commander regarding Halil Bey. The commander ordered that the ambassadors be boarded onto the command ship at once. The spokesman of the ambassadors boarding the command ship stated that Halil Bey was in fact in Phocaea and that the leaders of Phocaea demanded a hefty ransom to deliver Halil Bey back to them. Enraged that the Phocaean pirates demanded such a large ransom, the commander of the armada angrily ordered the captain of the command ship to reroute towards the Phocaea Castle.

The captain had just ordered the crew to steer the ship towards Phocaea when a mutiny started on the deckhead ship with its two rows of oars—the second largest ship of the armada. The rioters, who firmly affirmed their allegiance to Matthew Kantakouzenos, were refusing to attack the Phocaean pirates.

For a while, the fleet commander attempted to appease the deckhands and to prevent the mutiny. When he realised that he couldn't, he ordered for the ship to be burned down together with the warriors and oarsmen. When the deckhands of the ships and barges heard his order, the deckhead ship was assaulted with Greek fire and arrows of fire from all sides. The warriors on the deckhead ship, who realised they would be burned alive, responded with the same level of rigour and fire swarmed almost all the ships of the armada.

While the fire on the other ships was quickly extinguished, the fire on the deckhead ship gradually spread. The flames spread throughout the ship in a very short period of time. As the deckhands surrounded by flames drew their final arrows of fire and got buried in the deep waters of the sea, they also took the lives of hundreds of other sailors posted on the other ships.

Fleet commander Archiados, who watched the deckhead ship sink and the half-burned corpses from the other ships being thrown into the sea, kneeled down as he gazed at the peninsula of Chalkidiki across the water and repined, "My God, why did you allow me to see this atrocity? Look at this! I have suffered more loss than Teleutias, whose army suffered severe casualties during their expedition to Chalkidiki while trying to suppress the mutiny in my own fleet."

Due to the buzzing in his ears, Archiados heard neither the yells of the sailors who were trying to put out the fires swarming the ships nor the "plop" sound emanating from corpses being thrown into the sea. When he came back to his senses a good while later and stood up, the first thing he saw was the fine smoke rising from the ships. He addressed his helper standing behind him in a sad tone of voice, "Carry out a damage assessment immediately. Reinforce the ships with decreased numbers of oarsmen with oarsmen from the command ship. We cannot attack Phocaea Castle in this state, we have to get our armada to Constantinople. Get going! Prepare for our return journey. Make sure that the messenger boats are ready. They are going to inform all the castles en-route that the Ottoman princess is at the Phocaea Castle."

Byzantium's young emperor was upset beyond measure when he realised that the Byzantine armada had returned to Constantinople empty-handed after the mutiny. While he was still wallowing, he found out that Orhan Ghazi, who alleged that the search for his son had not been conducted to the highest standards, had furiously set out from Bursa to Constantinople.

The young emperor fully understood that Orhan Ghazi's arrival was not an auspicious one and forgot about all his woes, the health issues of his newly-born child and even his beloved wife Empress Helena. Instead, he began to think about Orhan Ghazi.

On the one hand, he was trying to find a way of easing his fury and on the other hand, he sought the foreclosing of the passage of all ships arriving from Morea and the Aegean Sea through the Bosphorus in order to prevent Orhan Ghazi's arrival in Constantinople. He ordered for the ships waiting to load and unload goods off the shore of Genoese harbours to anchor in the sheltered bays of the Golden Horn.

After taking all these precautions, he began brooding over how he was going to come up with the ransom the Phocaean pirates demanded. He kept adding together his personal treasures with the treasures remaining from Kantakouzenos VI but this was not enough to cover even half of the ransom that was demanded.

Unaware of all that was happening, Orhan Ghazi first arrived in Nicomedia with the cavalry under his command and the *yayas* under the command of Yahşi Bey and set out towards Constantinople. Before leaving Nicomedia, he had appointed the landlord of the Iznik Castle—referred to by native Greeks as Antigone or Nicaea and referred to by Turkmens who settled in the vicinity after the conquest as Iznik—and the kadî of the castle as ambassadors and instructed them to pay a visit to the Byzantine Emperor Palaiologos V by sea. Orhan Ghazi's advance cavalry had reached Chalcedon, situated on the shore across from Constantinople, in the midnight of the day when the two ambassadors arrived in Constantinople with a forty-oar Venetian ship.

The next morning Orhan Ghazi had already settled into his marquee and was resting while the young emperor of Byzantium was having an audience with the ambassadors sent to him by Orhan Ghazi.

As the five *levends* who were accompanying the ambassadors waited in the courtyard of the palace, the landlord of Nicaea and the kadî were in the presence of the Byzantine emperor. The landlord, who spoke both languages fluently, was appointed as the chief ambassador. Instead of presenting the Emperor with gifts, the chief ambassador handed the vitriolic letter sent by Orhan Ghazi to mesazōn Alexios Apokaukos standing beside him.

Apokaukos broke the seal of the letter and placed it on the desk of the Emperor. Sitting on his throne-like armchair behind the desk

Emperor John Palaiologos V slowly read the letter written in his mother tongue. The lines of anxiety on his face became more apparent and deep. Tired of the Emperor's silence the chief ambassador spoke out loudly, "Your Majesty, it is Orhan Ghazi's wish that his son Halil Bey is saved before something ominous befalls him. If you can appreciate the woes of a father whose son has been kidnapped and help Halil Bey to be found and saved I assume Orhan Ghazi will be able to overcome his fury and return to Bursa."

Emperor Palaiologos leaned back and forth in his armchair a few times and then looked at his mesazōn and at the archpriest of the Hagia Sophia—the most trusted person in Constantinople after the patriarch who accompanied the Emperor at almost every reception. For a while he gazed around the room vacantly before swallowing his silence and responding in a languid tone of voice, "The request of Orhan Ghazi, the inimitable commander of the Ottomans, my sister-in-law Theodora's and my aunt Princess Asporsha's husband and my brother-in-law, is reasonable in our eyes. I understand and appreciate his impatience and fury. He displays the behaviour of any good father and wants his son to be rescued. I am doing all I can to rescue my cousin Prince Halil but I haven't informed Orhan Ghazi because we have not yet reached a solution. As he mentions in his letter to me, I am deeply saddened by the fact that I have not been able to keep my promises to him—not even to the extent that my father could. Prince Halil might have already been saved from the clutch of the Phocaean pirates if this disaster had not struck our fleet. If I can match the ransom that they demand, I will personally go and retrieve my cousin from the Phocaea Castle."

Upon hearing the last sentence of the Emperor, the chief ambassador thought, "Finally some good news of which we can inform Orhan Ghazi" and smiled, but then he suddenly realised that the Emperor had said, "if I can match the ransom". The premature smile on his lips withered. Looking at the kadî of Iznik he tiresomely muttered, "Congratulations *kadî* effendi! His majesty, the Emperor has ascertained that Halil Bey is in fact in Phocaea."

Appointed as an ambassador for the first time, the old *kadî* could not decide whether he should rejoice at the information presented to him. Then, in an excited tone of voice, he took his turn to speak, "Once he knows where his son is, Orhan Ghazi will definitely be able to rescue him."

The Emperor asked for the kâdis words to be interpreted. When he came to have an understanding of what the *kadî* had said, he drifted into a daydream of sorts. Turning his gaze at the mesazōn he said, "I have no doubt that if Orhan Ghazi knows where his son is he will rescue him. But the Phocaean pirates are like no other. As soon as they realise they won't be receiving the ransom they demanded, they will take Prince Halil to a remote island in the Aegean Sea and hide him in a castle unknown to us. If we attack them and don't leave them with any route of escape they will kill the prince. The only way of getting the prince back alive is to pay the ransom they have demanded."

When the chief ambassador interpreted the Emperor's words to the *kadî* of Iznik, the lines on his smiling face transformed into lines of grief. Mesazōn Alexios, who had been idly lending an ear to their conversation until then, began talking as if he had a solution, "Master, I think it is best to inform Orhan Ghazi of the situation and to ask for his help."

When Emperor Palaiologos vacantly looked at the ambassadors with a sense of despair shadowed by his pride, the chief ambassador realised how powerless he felt in the face of this dilemma. The chief ambassador urged the Emperor, "Your Majesty, I agree with your mesazōn. As soon as Orhan Ghazi is informed that his son is still alive, he will do everything in his power to help you."

Upon hearing the chief ambassador's words, Emperor Palaiologos became hopeful, "We will explain everything in our letter to Orhan

Ghazi. If he decides to aid us, I will set sail as soon as our ships are fixed. Our Byzantium will be indebted to you Antigonians once more for all the efforts you will make in order to get us help."

The chief ambassador smiled gently as he picked up on what the Emperor was saying in between his lines and replied, "Your Majesty, our Antigone is a castle that has always created its own peace. If I can have a small contribution to the peace that will be attained in this regard I will be overjoyed about it on behalf of the people of Nicaea. I hope that everything will be set straight once I take your letter to Chalcedon and hand it to Orhan Ghazi to relieve him."

Despite the chief ambassador's calming reply, the Emperor couldn't shake off his worries. After a brief silence he replied in a soft tone of voice, "You should rest until we have written our letter. We will write a detailed letter to Orhan Ghazi without further delay."

When the ambassadors left his presence, Emperor Palaiologos summarised the situation in a grief-stricken tone of voice. Looking at the mesazōn and the archpriest of the Hagia Sophia he said, "You have done many good deeds for our Byzantium until now. Our empire is grateful to you both. Now I want you to do one more thing for our empire. Please write such a letter that Orhan Ghazi completely understands he has no other choice than to help us."

CHAPTER FORTY-NINE

Akça Kocaoğlu approached Fazıl Bey ebulliently, opened his long arms that looked like the branches of a great big tree and wrapped them around Fazıl Bey's stocky torso. In return, Fazıl Bey also wrapped his arms around Akça Kocaoğlu as far as his arms could reach. They stayed silent for a while before they saw Hacı Il-Bey looking at them with a smile on his face. Fazıl Bey explained, "Hacı, time has rasped us so much that our hearts have become paper-thin. In the past, we used to part thinking we would return in the evening and never thought otherwise. But now we say farewell before each time we part."

Scratching his goatee Hacı IlBey replied, "Do you remember the time before we got to Bursa, Fazıl? I am not sure whether you are trying to explain how fast time elapses or that time makes us become emotional as we age. But if there is one thing you should know it is that we have been fortunate enough to see the many brave men we raised become beys. We committed many of our beys and hundreds of brave men to the ground with our own hands. As we thought that we had seen and experienced so much throughout this time we realised that time never gets old. What has become old are our hearts. When we recently crossed Mount Rhaedestus and reached Uğraş River, casting our gazes on the round white pebbles at low tide on the stream's bed where we had taken a break, I thought, "Are we like these pebbles?" At first I asked myself why I had thought of such an analogy. Then, as I continued viewing the pebbles I thought, "In the past these pebbles were a part of a massive rock high up on Mount Rhaedestus. Those who saw it thought that the massive rock would never crumble. But one day, the ground under the rock shook and rumbled down into the abyss. With nothing to hold it in place, the massive rock began tumbling down and as it did so, it crashed into other rocks and split into pieces. Then, those pieces split into smaller pieces so that they became so small that even rainwater was capable of dragging them further down. The stones dragged by the waters became softer around the edges as they rubbed against one another in muddy waters, their shapes changed and they turned into pebbles that can roll in any direction. Being aware of being alive, maturing and ageing is as such too. Neither leaving nor returning are in fact easy."

After a brief silence, he continued, "I remembered something as I was telling you all that. Yesterday evening, I mentioned the sailing boats and the barges I saw as I viewed the vast Sea of Marmara from Mount Ganos. I mentioned them to Suleyman Pasha this morning. After listening to me he responded, 'I suppose we had the same dream last night.' He fell quiet and I didn't dwell on it. However, a little while later he began to talk of his own accord."

Fazıl Bey stroked his short and blond beard that looked as if it had been glued to his chin and that made his long face look longer. Then he eagerly asked, "What did he say?"

"He wants to talk to Ece Bey first and then share his thoughts with Orhan Ghazi."

"I also think that's the best course of action. Ece Bey knows the seas. He learned much about seafaring during his time in Gallipoli. I am certain that he will inform Suleyman Pasha in the best way possible. The most suitable port for the initial phase is Ece Abad."

Noticing that his brothers in arms were becoming excited when everything was still in the air, Hacı IlBey observed their faces carefully and said, "Beys, I am as excited as you are but remember that impatient chickens lay twice as many eggs in order to incubate them as soon as possible. However, when the time comes, chicks don't break out of those eggs. We should not make the mistake they make. As you know, the Karasids had previously set out into the seas with makeshift boats against massive galleons and galleys and was not able to reap anything. It was then that we learned the sea does not accommodate pleasantries and the meaning of Kalem Bey's words, 'To dally with the sea one has to be like Achilles with hidden secrets.'"

For a while, Fazıl Bey pondered about what Hacı IlBey had said and asked, "Hacı IlBey, do you think that Hector would have come out of his castle if Achilles' secret had not been revealed?"

"I don't know!"

"I think he wouldn't have and Achilles wouldn't have become such a legendary hero."

Joining them shortly before, Evrenos Bey recalled the legend of Troy which he had heard in the initial years of his adolescence as he lent an ear to their conversation. He tried to remember from whom he had heard the legend for the first time. Although when he realised his memory didn't reach that far back he quit straining his mind and smiled at his brothers-in-arms. When he stopped smiling he said, "Beys, you are right, but I neither think what made Achilles legendary was Paris' knowledge of his secret nor Hector appearing before him. What made him become such a legend was that he opposed the most powerful tyrant of the time, 'Are the sons of Atreus the only men in the world who love their wives? Any man of common right feeling will love and cherish his wife' and took off. Then sitting across from old Priam whose son he had killed he said, 'We'll let our grief lie quietly in our hearts' and cried with him side by side."

Looking at Evrenos Bey with a smile on his face and incessant admiration for his wisdom, Hacı IlBey responded, "Both the stories of Achilles and Hector remain on the opposite coast and in the past. If you like we should now talk about what the Achilles and Hectors of this coast will do."

Despite Hacı IlBey's desire to change the subject, Evrenos Bey's heart was brimming with the zeal of telling stories of the past. After casting a gaze in Hacı IlBey's direction as if to say, "Don't attempt changing the subject", he continued with his soft tone of voice, "Yes,

today we are the Achilles of these lands but the fact is these lands
have not always hosted good-hearted Achilles such as us. There have
also been malignant Achilles such as the Latins and the Catalans
who threw out the grandchildren of Thracians from their castles."

Hacı IlBey cut in, "Both sides of the Dardanelles are full of hearsay
and legends, so you say Evrenos Bey. However, before hearing any
new stories I would like to ask a question. How come our hearts hurt
for Hector when we should be identifying more with Achilles as
strangers of these lands?"

Smiling, Evrenos Bey replied, "Despite the fact that we identify
with Achilles as strangers of these lands who fight with their minds,
our hearts side with Hector because his castle was turned to ashes
with the unrighteousness of an underhanded battle."

As Hacı IlBey bit his lips due to the appeasing response he got, he
agreed with what Evrenos Bey said by nodding approval. Fazıl Bey
became impatient to hear a new story as they glanced at each other.
Looking at Evrenos Bey he said, "We have never come across a Hector in any of the castles we have conquered. That is why neither I nor
Akça Kocaoğlu has felt like Achilles. So that is to say, our task is
easy. However, who are these Latins and Catalans who have taken
the Hectors of these lands before us and made our task easier?"

Evrenos Bey replied, "The history of these lands stretches far beyond them. If you look into these lands in detail you will see the footsteps of the Achaeans, the Goths, the Cimmerians, the Huns, the
Macedonians and the Persians."

Looking at Evrenos Bey with transfixed eyes, Fazıl Bey said, "I
hope that nobody else's but our footsteps will remain after us."

Hacı IlBey responded, "Fazıl Bey, if you recall I was trying to say
that time is the master of all of us..."

They all fell silent for a while. They looked at Prince Suleyman
Pasha who was once again watching the sunset with his back to a
mighty plane tree a few hundred metres away. They couldn't really

guess whether he was thinking about his brother Halil or conquering the lands in the distance where the sun was setting. Akça Kocaoğlu, who had previously joined in such conversations very seldomly, took a guess as to what the beys were thinking, "I think he is thinking about his brother as much as he is wondering about the lands beyond the horizon."

Without waiting for an answer to his previous question, Fazıl Bey continued, "In all honesty, I had not suspected the pirates. I thought that this was a game between the *Karamanids* and the Byzantines, but I was mistaken."

Hacı IlBey said, "At first I thought it was an accident but then I suspected that it was the Kantakouzenos' doing in order to create conflict between Orhan Ghazi and the Palaiologos."

Evrenos Bey added, "I said it before—it is either the doing of the Knights of Rhodes or the Phocaean pirates. It also crossed my mind that the Catalans of Pigas might have kidnapped him. Since we now know where he is it will be easier to save him... In any case, Palaiologos must have been so scared of Orhan Bey's arrival in Chalcedon that he set forth without waiting for the completion of repairs on the burnt ships. In fact, even Matthew Kantakouzenos sent news to Orhan Ghazi informing him that he will aid in saving Halil Bey safe and sound."

After watching the sun disappear into the horizon, Hacı IlBey said, "Another evening is laying down upon us. We will depart at first light. We should all retreat to our marquees and prepare. We shall meet at the council after dinner."

Then he walked towards his marquee which was much larger than most dwellings in the Plajar Castle and which also included his harem.

A cool breeze blew inside the beys upon hearing Hacı IlBey speak without mincing his words. They took courage from his departure and quietly headed towards their tents. Suleyman Pasha came back down to earth from his magical state of mind once the sun had set and turned his head to quietly watch the beys walk towards their tents. In a tone of voice which could easily be heard by the beys, he muttered, "See you at the council." The beys, who had never had such a calling from Suleyman Pasha before, paused suddenly but instead of turning around and responding to him, they continued on their paths.

Suleyman Pasha stood up as his beys got closer to their tents and watched the final trace of rubescence in the horizon mix into the blue of the sky. He turned around and looked at his marquee. He felt that he was yearning for his tall Greek belle with slender fingers and skin softer than velvet and who he had engaged since the day they conquered the Tzympe Castle and whom he found to be more beautiful with every passing day.

As he hastily walked towards his marquee he mumbled, "A woman whose intelligence matches her beauty gradually becomes..." He swallowed the last words of his sentence. His hasty footsteps and the thoughts in his mind became momentarily entangled. In order to defeat his palpitating heart, he talked to himself, "We will talk about most things at tonight's council meeting but this time I will spare my last thoughts until we part tomorrow..."

When he suddenly found himself in front of his marquee he was surprised by how quickly he had got there. He gazed around him with a smile on his lips. Realising that no one had noticed his hastiness he took a breath of relief and entered his marquee. He had turned towards the harem of his marquee when his feet steered towards the chamber of the Thracian beauty from Tzympe.

CHAPTER FIFTY

The ambassadors who had gone to Chalcedon returned at dusk. Waiting for their return with the archpriest of the Hagia Sophia and his mesazōn Alexius, Emperor Palaiologos V summoned the ambassadors for an audience with himself in a tired, heavy and timid tone of voice. Entering the Emperor's study, the landlord of Nicaea and the *kadî* of Nicaea bowed down at the same time and saluted those in the room. The landlord of Nicaea wanly turned towards the guard commander standing behind the Emperor and said, "Your Majesty! Orhan Ghazi is grateful to you for finding out who kidnapped his son. However, he is deeply saddened by an incident of this nature taking place in Hellespont and the Aegean Sea, which are under the protection of the Byzantine fleet. Thus he considers the Byzantine fleet, the ruler of the seas, to be as guilty as the Phocaean pirates who kidnapped his son. However, he hopes that you will atone for the situation as soon as possible and that his son will be saved and delivered to him."

Curious as to where the conversation would lead, Emperor Palaiologos V interrupted, "We will do all we can in order not to disappoint him."

Pausing to hear what the Emperor had to say, the landlord of Nicaea continued his speech once he realised the Emperor had said what he wanted to, "Your Majesty, Orhan Ghazi wanted us to inform you that upon considering the situation explained in your letter to him, he will pay half of the ransom demanded from his own treasury to aid you and that he accepts your wish to aggregate the Byzantine and Ottoman committees so that they can reorganise the reciprocal agreements that have been made until now after Halil Bey is delivered to them. However, you have to set forth to Phocaea before dawn tomorrow so as to save Halil Bey at once."

Acting as if he hadn't heard the last sentence the Emperor tried to get rid of his heavy mood and walked towards the landlord of Nicaea. He stood in front of him and said, "I thank you for your help. I understand Orhan Ghazi's anger and pain. We have been given very little time but I will complete my preparations tonight and will board my ship before dawn. Once the sum sent from Orhan Ghazi reaches the boat I will set sail immediately."

Then the Emperor sat in his throne-like armchair. The landlord of Nicaea replied confidently, "Your Majesty, the sum promised by Orhan Ghazi will be handed over to you as soon as it reaches the ship."

Emperor Palaiologos V replied without delay, "In that case I will be setting sail at dawn with my mind at peace."

When the ambassadors who completed their task left the Emperor's presence to head back to the opposite shore, Byzantine emperor Palaiologos V briefly waited for the chief guard, who had left the room to see the ambassadors off, to return. When the chief guard returned the Emperor instructed him to personally visit the navarch at once and to tell him to ready all the substantive and repaired ships to set sail before dawn. As the chief guard left the room to fulfil his task, the Emperor ordered his chief messenger waiting in front of the door of his study to urgently summon the deputy mesazōn in charge of the treasury and the castle commander for an audience. Shortly after the chief messenger left the room the deputy mesazōn in charge of the treasury entered. Looking at him, the Emperor spoke in an undeniable tone of voice, "I want to know about all that you have spared for hard times because there couldn't be a harder day for Byzantium than today."

The deputy mesazōn in charge of the treasury went on a short journey in his mind with his experience of many years, deducted the cost of running the palace for a few months and said, "Your Majesty, I am deeply sorry but I have to tell you that we only have ten thousand stavraton."

After a bitter smile, the Emperor said, "Semerisius, the Phocaean pirates demand one hundred thousand gold coins. Orhan, son of the Ottomans, says he can send fifty thousand gold coins without batting an eye and you tell me that the great Byzantine Empire has only ten thousand gold coins in its treasury."

Following a brief silence, he bitterly said, "Tell me what there is left in my personal treasury."

This time deputy mesazōn Semerisius cast his gaze on the floor. Understanding what his silence meant, Emperor Palaiologos V quietly said, "So nothing, eh!"

Semerisius felt a sense of guilt, "I am sorry master... If you wish, I can add the few hundred gold coins that are in my treasury to the imperial treasury."

The Emperor looked at him and believing his sincerity replied, "If we must we shall also add that to the imperial treasury. Put together all that we currently have. For now, we shall wait for news from the Genoese. If they don't send us the sum we asked for, we will start borrowing from personal treasuries. In the meantime, find out who has well-stocked treasuries that can be of use to us."

After leaving the Emperor's study, Semerisius put his men to the task of counting the ten thousand Byzantine coins that the treasury could afford and placing it in a trunk and made a list of the people whose personal treasuries could be made use of. The first name on the list was Empress Anna. The second name was that of the navarch. The third was the mesazōn's and the fourth was that of the archpriest of the Hagia Sophia. The treasures of Patriarch Kalekas and the other names on the list, which followed the top four names, didn't amount to great sums. Semerisius took the list he prepared and the trunks full of Byzantine gold to the reception room of Emperor Palaiologos V. The commander of the Constantinople Fortress and the assistant of the archpriest of the Hagia Sophia who had returned from the Genoese Quarter had also arrived at the reception room. Semerisius saluted the Emperor before handing the record of the counted gold coins and the list of emperor's personal treasures to the Emperor. Emperor Palaiologos V briefly perused the list given to him by Semerisius and said, "Thank you Semerisius."

As Semerisius respectfully stood near the door and cast his gaze on the Emperor the assistant of the archpriest sought to continue his previously interrupted speech, "Your Majesty, as I mentioned, the Genoese claim that the Venetians have far too many privileges and that their income has plummeted because of this. They say that they can only get together the sum we have asked for in two months time."

As Emperor Palaiologos V looked at the assistant of the archpriest like a beggar whose dream has been stolen because he couldn't receive the handout he had wished, he went weak at the knees. His legs shook, he felt drowsy. He gently leaned his chest against the desk without having the others notice as he thought he was going to fall off his chair. Noticing that the Emperor was shaken by what he had said, the assistant of the archpriest of the Hagia Sophia glanced over at the archpriest in surprise. The archpriest took his turn to speak, "Your Majesty, the Genoese are not within their right to drag their feet. It is obvious that they have not yet understood the severity of the situation at hand. I assume their reply is due to the fact that they can't stomach Venetians being spoilt under the wing of the Ottomans. If we promise them that they will be given as much a share of our customs as the Venetians, I think they might hurry up in gathering the amount of money we asked for..."

Emperor Palaiologos V smiled bitterly. Then looking at the list in front of him he began to express himself, "Saintly father, you know as well as I do that these days and the recent years have been very sorrowful for our Byzantium and Constantinople. However, neither the Genoese nor you understand the graveness of the current situation. Orhan Ghazi's ambassadors visited me a few hours ago. They informed me that they will provide half of the ransom demanded by the morning and requested that I set sail at dawn to save Halil Bey. I sent word so that the substantive ships in the armada can be prepared to set sail in the morning. In the meantime, you are telling me about the scheme Genoese vultures have put together to benefit from our misfortune..."

The Emperor fell silent. His silence ushered in an ice-cold and quiet breeze. The Emperor looked at the list in front of him once more, but this time with an animated look in his eyes. His gaze became fixed on his mother's name at the top of the list. He thought, "I can't ask her" and continued reading the list. He muttered, "The Patriarch is not in the list." He paused and muttered, "He must have forgotten" and then called Semerisius. He whispered that the name of the Patriarch was not in the list and Semerisius whispered back, "The Patriarch's personal treasury is much smaller compared to the others. The holy patriarchate has a treasury but I did not consider it suitable to include it in the list."

As Semerisius returned to his space near the door, Emperor Palaiologos V looked at the archpriest of the Hagia Sophia, the mesazōn and the castle commander and said, "Sirs, I don't want to delay this journey. It is obvious that the Genoese will not lend us money in such a short frame of time. We have to cover the total sum by borrowing from Empress Anna's and your treasuries and adding it to the rest of the ten thousand gold coins which we have kept in our treasury for a rainy day."

The faces of those in the Emperor's presence turned as red as beetroot. The archpriest of the Hagia Sophia replied hastily, "Your Majesty, if you like we can explain the urgency of the situation to the Genoese once more. Perhaps they can create an opportunity."

As the archpriest looked at the mesazōn, the castle commander cut in, "Your Majesty, if you like I can pay a visit to the Genoese. If they don't have the required sum they can perhaps borrow from the merchants at the ports."

Emperor Palaiologos V ironically smiled at the three old men who were still treating him like a child. He leaned back on his throne-like chair. He reached out for the handle of the small bell atop his desk. The messenger appointed during the reign of Kantakouzenos entered into the room as soon as he rang the bell. "Atantos, summon the guards who are on duty at once. They will be accompanying Semerisius to the Genoese Quarter."

As soon as the messenger left, the young emperor looked at Semerisius who was standing by the door and said, "Semerisius, you will go to the Genoese Quarter and inform them that unless they pay the sum they can afford to pay at once they will be arrested. If they don't want to be arrested, they will pay up and you will bring that to me. You will cover the rest of the demanded sum from the personal treasures of the names on the list. I will be saying farewell to Empress Helena and my children as you fulfil your duties."

As Semerisius left the room with the joy of having gained the Emperor's trust, those remaining in the room were flushed. The archpriest of the Hagia Sophia thought, "I wish I hadn't taken the mesazōn's advice" as mesazōn Alexius blamed the archpriest of the Hagia Sophia and thought, "That rapacious Anasta." Unaware of the secret glances between them, the castle commander was fretting and fuming, "I managed to save my treasure from the Kantakouzenos only to hand it over to the Palaiologos..." Gathering much meaning from their silence, the young emperor surprised them all by consoling them, "My friends, Byzantium will never forget you for your help during such hard times. Your confiscated treasures will be returned to you as soon as possible."

The ice-cold breeze roaming the room became colder when Castle Commander Atantos entered the room. Atantos addressed the Emperor without paying any attention to the surprised look on the faces of those in the room, "Master, your orders have been conveyed to the commander on duty as we have not been able to locate the navarch despite our detailed search. They have presently begun preparations. The navarch will be brought to you as soon as we find him."

Atantos took a step back towards the door. Instead of bursting with anger like Atantos and the others expected, the Emperor laughed insidiously. He looked at the list in front of him. In a tone of voice that had never been heard before he said, "Atantos, you will retrieve as many guards as you can and pay a visit to the mansion of the navarch. If we cannot find him, we shall seize his treasury."

Atantos did not notice the faces of those remaining in the room turn to ash as he left the room at once to follow the Emperor's orders.

CHAPTER FIFTY-ONE

Having rested well during the long winter days, the Thracian conquests of the Ottoman forces continued throughout spring and summer and did not slow down during the autumn months. On the one side the *akıncı* units formed of *Âhiyân-i Rum* and *Bâciyân-i Rum* were charging towards new fortresses and on the other side the dervishes were temporarily establishing order in the newly seized fortresses. They then passed the torch to the *subaşıs* appointed to respective fortresses and continued on their campaigns following the other *akıncı* units. Some of the *akıncı* units had reached Byzantine castles on the Black Sea coast and others had closed in near enough on Constantinople on horseback to be able to see the city walls. The *akıncıs,* who approached Peristasi Castle on the south-east of the peninsula for the second time after Malgara and Visa Castles, had formed circles around the castle in order to prevent aid that could be sent to the castle overland and blockaded the port. They had been impatiently waiting for the siege day for a long time when the special messenger sent by Suleyman Pasha arrived. When the *akıncı beys* were informed of the news that the messenger had arrived they exclaimed, "Hurrah! Our Bey surmised we were running low on patience once again!"

Then they shouted out in unison repeating, "Hurrah! Hurrah! May you live long Suleyman Pasha!"

Suleyman Pasha's messenger, who looked like he would blow away even in the slightest breeze, was shown inside the headquarter marquee. He took out the letter enveloped in leather from his sash and began to read it out loud, "The courageous and patient *akıncı beys* of our Beylik, I know that you don't like to remain in one place for such a long period of time and desire to watch new horizons at every dawn. The most important reason as to why I asked you to patiently wait near the Peristasi Castle was because I was waiting for the

yayas sent from Bursa. As you know we have lost hundreds of men at
the Peristasi Castle that has changed hands twice already. Given the
situation, I never want us to lose another soul or to give back the
castle we are going to besiege. Thankfully the *yayas* we have long
been waiting for have arrived in Plajar. When my messenger who has
brought this to you sets out, I will also be setting forth with the
newly-arrived *yayas*. All being well, I will be with you in a few days.
Until then I wish for you and the people of the castle to try your patience and to wait for me. Ghazi Suleyman Pasha."

Hearing the words "Suleyman Pasha" part from the lips of the messenger the *akıncı beys* exclaimed once more, "Suleyman Pasha! Suleyman Pasha! May you live long, Suleyman Pasha!"

On the afternoon of the third day after the arrival of the letter, Suleyman Pasha and his beys were welcomed to the Peristasi Castle by
pelting rain before the *akıncıs*. Nobody could see beyond the tip of
their noses due to the rain that became heavier in the evening. They
beys who were summoned to Suleyman Pasha's travelling
headquarter tent erected hurriedly arrived only wearing sleeveless
felt cardigans. When Suleyman Pasha saw that all the beys,
yayabaşıs and *akıncıs* were sitting on the mats across from him he
kneeled and saluted them. He felt a sense of joy when he saw the lu-
minous eyes of his beys in the flavescent light of oil lamps made in
Lycia and sent to him by the Beylik of Teke for all the victories he
achieved in Rumelia. For a while he watched impatience on his beys'
calm faces challenge the suppleness in their gazes. As he viewed their
impatience he recalled his own impatience in his younger years. He
thought of how he had given up hurrying up after Hacı IlBey illuminated him. Listening to the sound of the large raindrops hitting
the tent the way water cascaded down the Nilüfer brook appeared in
his mind. He remembered that one day, when he was walking beside
the brook with his father, his father suddenly held him by the arm
and stopped him and pointed to the water lilies that had recently

shed their leaves and how he said, "Son, one has to sometimes go beyond the reticence of patience in order to see hidden beauties." As he directed his gaze at the faces of the beys, *yayabaşıs* and sergeants once more he said, "They went beyond the reticence of patience long ago." He was just about to start talking when his father's sentence "They don't call this the pharaoh flower for no reason" quickly passed through his mind. After a hardly visible smile, he continued his speech, "My Beys, our beys who have departed from Plajar some while ago are heading towards the east, the west, and the north of Rumelia. You have been waiting in front of the city walls of Peristasi for a long time. In my letter, I explained the reasons for your long wait. You have patiently waited for us. Thank you. I'd hoped that as you waited, the castle people would come to their senses and open their gates to us voluntarily. However, this did not happen. Moreover, may he live long, my father had sent us news so we wouldn't be stabbing Byzantine Emperor Palaiologos in the back while he is on a campaign to save my brother Halil Bey. This was one of the reasons for this long wait which I couldn't explain to you in my letter. I kept the promise I made to my father. I tried your patience all this time but neither you nor I have any more patience left. If the news we received is accurate there is no reason for us to wait any more. I would like to talk to you about how and when we will be attacking the castle tonight. If you all join in the conversation and make your opinions known, we can make the best plan of attack."

Sari Yumni Bey, who had taken the place of Topal Hasan Bey, one of the beys from the Yahşi province who had recently the joined Suleyman Pasha's forces, in the campaign because of his sickness bowed a couple of times and saluted the beys, "My Bey, you know when the best time is better than I but think that the best time for attack is when we decide upon it."

Hacı IlBey, who until then had not made his presence felt, looked at Sari Yumni Bey whom he referred to as the handsome lad of

Yahşi province. He thought that Topal Hasan Bey must have had a reason behind choosing him for Suleyman Pasha's service out of all the beys he had under his service. Looking straight into the eyes of the narrow-faced, hook-nosed lad who quickly grasped what was desired of him and expressed his ideas courageously he said, "Yumni Bey, I don't really understand your suggestion."

Yumni Bey immediately grasped what was wanted of him. He tilted his head down slightly and, as he looked at the rug depicting traditional Nicomedia motifs that was spread under the mat he had been sitting on since he had been accepted to the council. As he glared at the colourful motifs that looked a lot paler in the yellow light of the oil lamps, the vivaciousness of the droopy blood-red rose embroidery drew his attention and thought "Hiding something that shines is to no avail." Without averting his eyes from the blood-red rose embroidery he said, "My Bey, I know we can't see beyond the end of our noses outside. Nevertheless, I wanted to point out that such moments are the best for initiating an attack. Because those in the castle won't leave their homes in this weather and they won't suspect that we will attack. I think that the climbers should start climbing the walls before the rain ceases."

Looking at Sarı Yumni Bey in surprise, Suleyman Pasha noticed Hacı IlBey's thin lips curled up in a smile. Just as he was thinking about why he had asked the question he posed to Yumni Bey he saw the other beys exchanging concerned glances. As Suleyman Pasha cast his gaze on the beys Hacı IlBey coughed intermittently as if to signal he had received the reply he was after and backed Sari Yumni Bey's suggestion by replying, "I also think tonight is the night."

After stretching his wide shoulders to either side, Suleyman Pasha said, "But as far as I know we are unprepared for an attack tonight."

Hacı IlBey cut in, "My Bey, if our *akıncıs* have set up headquarters in front of a castle it means they are ready for attack at any moment."

Sarı Alaüddin Bey, one of the *akıncı beys* added, "We are ready to attack the castle but the sea rocks like a cradle. There are two armada ships and a cargo boat that rock on that cradle. I am not sure whether we can occupy them with the boats we have..."

Overwhelmed with surprise, Suleyman Pasha asked, "I don't understand. Can you please explain this to me, Alaüddin Bey?"

Hacı IlBey cut in again, "My Prince, our *akıncı beys* have not been vacantly waiting here, they have taken all precautions to lay siege to the castle. Thinking that they would need to attack from both sea and land to lay siege on the castle they seized all the ships they captured and anchored them in safeguarded bays. They took the oarsmen on the boats captive. Sari Yumni Bey's *levends* are apt at sea. If they can quietly close in on the enemy fleet with these boats they will capture the castle in a few hours. Albeit, the ships cannot move from their locations in this weather but it would still be to our advantage to by-pass them. Then we will also have an additional two galleons in our port. If we sort out our defence in the sea, we will only have to lay siege on the castle from the land. The newly-arrived climbers and *yayas* from the Taurus Mountains are cut out for this task."

Gündüzay Bey, one of the *akıncı beys* said, "My Bey, the castle commander has turned out to be very cautious. He didn't even let the farmers who left the castle to work in their fields in the morning back inside in the evening. Thus, we haven't been able to get the vanguards in multifarious disguises and the volunteer polyglot scribes into the castle."

Shaking his head to either side Suleyman Pasha voiced his suggestion, "If they haven't allowed even just a few of us into the castle, we will enter the castle all together tonight."

A warm breeze of excitement blew inside the cold headquarter marquee after Suleyman Pasha made his decision known. A sincere smile appeared in Suleyman Pasha's eyes when he saw the breeze of joy wandering amongst the faces of the *akıncı beys*. Seeing Suleyman

Pasha's jovial gaze, Hacı IlBey exclaimed, "Beys, may your holy war be blessed!"

Standing up altogether after Hacı IlBey's words, the beys, *yayabaşıs* and *akıncı* sergeants placed their right hands on their hearts and in unison said, "May our holy war be blessed!"

They left the headquarter marquee in order of their entrance. The attack that began after the beys went to attend to their units was finalised just before midnight. Climbers from the Taurus Mountains were at the forefront of the attack that commenced upon Suleyman Pasha's order. They were followed by *akıncı serdengeçtis* and *delis*. The *yayas* were right behind the shielded men in charge of the battering rams who were advancing towards the castle gates step by step.

Making use of the loud rain, the climbers from the Taurus Mountains suddenly appeared by the thick walls of the castle. They had just propped their ladders against the walls when the *serdengeçtis* and *delis* immediately behind them climbed to the top of the walls in leaps and bounds. When the climbers fulfilled their duty successfully and reached the top of the walls, the deep sound of battering rams pounding down on the gates was heard. In shock, the bastion guards were taken captive even before they could attempt to use their spears. Owls' hoots rose from the top of the castle walls. Hacı IlBey said, "The grandsons of the Galatia did away with them very quickly. They precede their honour." After inhaling deeply, a couple of times he ordered the long-distance archers, "Discharge the bows!"

Hearing Hacı IlBey's deep voice the archers discharged their bows all at once and for a moment the sounds of the arrows suppressed the sound of the rain. The *yayas* collapsed their circular formation and closed in on the castle. When the *serdengeçtis* announced that they had taken all the guards in the bastions captive, news that Sari Yumni Bey and his *levends* had set sail arrived. Suleyman Pasha dismounted his Grey in that moment and reached the *serdengeçtis* and the men in charge of the battering rams positioned behind him. The men in charge of the battering rams were cautiously and slowly approaching the gates behind their shields but when they saw their prince beside them they enthused and gained speed. Suleyman Pasha carefully looked at the arch on top of the gate as he continued encouraging his men. When he couldn't spot anyone on the arch he yelled with all his might, "Go on my lions, break the gate."

Seeing Suleyman Pasha lunge towards the gate, the *yayas* got even more worked up and began pounding on the wooden gate with the battering ram. They had only pounded on the gate a few times when muffled voices were heard from behind it. As Suleyman Pasha approached the gate to determine the voices, it was broken wide open. The *serdengeçtis* surrounded Suleyman Pasha and formed a wall of flesh around him. When the surprised men in charge of the battering rams retreated to either side of the gate, the *yayas* weighed those trying to get out of the castle gate down. Furious with his lack of caution, Suleyman Pasha retreated back a little with his *serdengeçtis* and suddenly paused. He drew his sword and began marching and yelling towards the gate with the *yayas* around him. Finding encouragement in his yells, the *serdengeçtis* also drew their swords and attacked the castle guards positioned on either side of the gate. Before long, corpses were piled on top of each other in the clearings in front of the castle gates.

Suleyman Pasha stood under the arch above the castle gate at daybreak and addressed Hacı IlBey as he pointed at the corpses piled on top of each other, "They gathered all their forces at the main gate."

As Hacı IlBey looked in the direction of the corpses pointed out by Suleyman Pasha, he said, "Perhaps they considered sortie as the last resort."

CHAPTER FIFTY-TWO

Emperor Palaiologos V was fed up with shuttling back and forth between the deckhouse and his chamber for days, reading the manuscripts he had taken with him, and resting. As he stood in front of one of the round windows of his spacious chamber with several partitions he was thinking of something to amuse himself with in order to shake off the boredom that weighed him down after breakfast. He viewed the waves chasing each other in the Aegean Sea. He became curious when he spotted a dark green mass on top of a wave. He squinted. He couldn't liken the mass in the distance to anything he had seen before. He went to the deck to be able to see it better. After listening to the sound of the juddering sails in the zephyr for a while he leaned his chest against the thick wooden handrails of the deck and took another glance at the green mass that was now quite close to the fleet. Seeing it change shape as it rode the waves he recognised it and said "Seaweed". He continued watching the mass of seaweed drawing closer with the waves for a while longer. Smiling as if he had thought of something witty he muttered, "Are the waves gibing or is the seaweed trifling?" When the smile glued to his lips vanished he said, "You were the one doing the tricking until you got defeated but now the waves are gibing with you" as if he was attempting to make the mass of seaweed that was nearing the command ship hear him. Smiling again, he added, "It seems they have also tired you out to cut you off from your roots as they did to our Byzantium." Seeing the seaweed break into pieces after being stroked by the waves colliding with the command ship he said, "I hope that the end of our Byzantium won't be like yours" and tried to relax. He looked at the peninsula extending to the middle of the sea like a hand and the Phocaea Castle on top of it. He shouted with rage and as if to make his voice be heard by the castle people, "Ye, the people of Phocaea, I will enter your bay with my galleons come what may, even if you come to me with a new proposal today."

Yet, as the hasty winds carried his voice that mixed into the sound of the sails far away he couldn't even hear his own voice. As his weary and lazy eyes scanned the surface of the sea once again, he couldn't stop himself from bursting into laughter when he saw torn pieces of seaweed riding the waves towards the shore. When he ceased laughing, he commented, "It's like the troops of Bacchus going to wake up Eros." He watched the seaweed disappear from sight and walked back to his chamber.

He silently marched between the two windows until his feet tired. Then he turned around and headed towards his privy. The door of the chamber opened by itself. He lay down on his large bed as he smiled at the odalisques from Lesbos standing behind the door. He shut his eyes at once with the desire to sleep. As the odalisques took his boots off his eyes opened involuntarily. Humane but "factious thoughts" roamed his mind as his heartbeat quickened. He tried turning his back and falling asleep as if to chase away his thoughts but it didn't work. He lied on his back, first looked at the odalisques and then at the ceiling. As the odalisques slowly approached his bed he recalled his departure from Constantinople—a memory that hadn't left him alone for days. Trying to avert his gaze from the odalisques holding his hands he muttered, "I was tempted by damned Alexius and acted as if I were setting sail in Hellespont with fleet ships as I saluted the Ottoman Bey in Chalcedon. I didn't understand much at first but as I got off the ship across from Ayastafanos and got closer to the shore I felt smaller. As if that wasn't enough I entered the castle I rule hiding like a thief." Without looking at the odalisques who were rubbing his hands he loudly said, "My only consolation in those days when I hid my shame even from myself was my little Manuel. I was trying to forget everything looking at the way he wiggled his little toes. I could neither forget nor console myself but I had already given the Genoese an inch and they had taken a yard. I was only going to depart when they sent the aid they promised. When I realised that they had given me false hope I could only do what I last thought initially before departing. Unable to save their treasures, my mother and Alexius filled with rage but what else could I have done?" The odalisques were startled by the Emperor's loud speech as they stood up and tentatively observed his face. The Emperor raised his voice more as if there was no one else in the chamber and said sadly, "They consider all the decisions I make to be wrong. They don't even approve of the decisions I make on behalf of my pre-pubescent daughter..." His sadness swelled and his eyes brimmed with tears. But for a while, he couldn't cry and he couldn't defeat that feeling of wanting to cry. His desire to cry clogged his throat like a fist. He turned from one side to the other when he found it difficult to breathe. He tried to conjure up his nephew Halil in his mind as he continued speaking without looking at the odalisques, "Helena and I were wed young for the sake of our Byzantium. That's also what her aunt Asporsha and her mother's sister Theodora did. I hope that our Irene will understand the need for this when she grows up." He muttered, "If my nephew is wise..." but he couldn't complete his sentence because the image of Halil Bey that appeared in his mind was forlorn. His clothes were torn to shreds, his eyes were blue and black and his half-naked body had been scratched as if he had been attacked by a lion. That fist clogging his throat became more powerful in the face of the image of the young man in his mind. Emperor Palaiologos V gasped for breath. His heavy eyelids shut. His hands slipped out of the palms of the odalisques and fell onto the bed. The odalisques were momentarily flustered before they listened to the Emperor's breathing. They covered him with a duvet and retreated to their own chamber.

Tired of waiting and idling around Emperor Palaiologos V was wakeless until the afternoon. If he hadn't instructed the commander of the guards Atandros, he wouldn't have woken the Emperor. However, because the Emperor had cautioned him, "Inform the moment any news or messengers arrive from Phocaea" the commander of the guards got to the Emperor's chamber in no time flat when the envoys from Phocaea arrived. The head servant of the Emperor woke up the Emperor upon Atandros' arrival at the chamber. The well-rested emperor immediately got out of his spacious bed as soon as he found out that a delegation from Phocaea had arrived. He yawned a couple of times while waiting for his odalisques to put on his boots. As he opened his arms and stretched he said "Antiphon says, 'the mind is what gives direction to man's body in both good health and sickness'" as if he was advising his odalisques. As the odalisques from Lesbos looked at each other in surprise the Emperor smiled, and as he made a move to stand up he said, "How would you know anything about Antiphon, a man who became ancient as did the ancient age." He kneeled down a bit to help the servants place the crown on his head. After taking a look at his attire, brushed by the odalisques, he left his chamber.

When he saw Atandros waiting in the larger, hall-like chamber he asked, "Did you send word to Alexius?"

Dressed in semi-armour, Atandros, the Emperor's childhood friend whom he trusted with his life, lightly leaned forward and replied, "Master, the mesazōn is with the delegation."

Mesazōn Alexius saw Byzantine Emperor John Palaiologos V enter the audience chamber above the lowest section where the oarsmen toiled and exclaimed, "Your Majesty!"

Waiting on foot in the audience chamber, the knights of the Duca of Phocaea bent and saluted the Emperor. When the Emperor sat down on the throne-like armchair in the spacious audience chamber of the armada vessel, Mesazōn Alexius continued before slightly bending forward and waiting, "Your Majesty, the spokesman of the delegation sent by the Duca of Phocaea has news for you."

Emperor Palaiologos V looked at the aged knight at the front who, with all his mannerisms, looked very much like a spokesman would and with a modicum of temper said, "I am listening to you."

The aged spokesman tried to smile brazenly but noticing that the anger in the Emperor's gaze thickened he assumed a humble attitude and listed the new demands of the duke one by one as he had done on previous days. The Emperor didn't even hear his last words because of his flaming rage. "Phocaeans! If you weren't envoys I would have ordered my men to make mincemeat out of you! Go to your duke at once and inform him that if he doesn't deliver the prince to us by sundown I will burn your castle down with Greek fire and if any of you survive I will capture them and deliver them to the Ottomans by my own hand."

The Emperor left the chamber. The envoys realised that the Emperor's anger could not be quelled and looked at the mesazōn with fear in their eyes.

Mesazōn Alexius said, "Venerable knights of Phocaea you have enraged the Emperor because you have been stalling him for days. Our emperor is absolutely right to be angry. I now wish that you go to your duke at once and convince them to deliver the Ottoman prince according to the terms that were previously ascertained. If you cannot succeed in doing so you will all burn inside your beloved castle."

As the envoys walked towards the staircase of the galley to board their round rowing boats, the mesazōn raised his voice and said, "Should anything befall Prince Halil be sure that the Ottomans will seek revenge from both you and us."

The boats of the Phocaea delegation, which seemed to advance on the surface of the sea turning round and round without looking back, suddenly disappeared from sight as soon as they entered the mouth of the bay. The Emperor became suspicious of their sudden disappearance and summoned the fleet commander whom he had appointed before setting forth on his campaign and ordered him to get the ships in formation at bay's mouth. The fleet commander immediately informed the ships of the Emperor's orders. Ships of different styles and sizes shut off the bay's mouth by advancing forth in formation like a chain. They had just anchored when they saw a rather magnificent boat carrying the order of the Duchy of Phocaea, Genoa approach them. The Emperor was overjoyed thinking that they were finally delivering Prince Halil but his hopes were broken when he saw the spokesman of the envoys standing at the front of the splendid boat approaching their command ship.

The spokesman climbed up the rope ladder in one breath, reached the Emperor, saluted him and exclaimed, "Your Majesty! I have been given the duty of conveying to you the final decision of our Duca and our venerable Phocaea council."

For a while, the Emperor quietly assessed how he should respond and then replied in a moderate tone of voice, "Go on, tell me, what is the final decision of your Duca and venerable council?"

The spokesman worked up his courage, "The last wish of our Duca and the venerable council is for our emperor to visit our castle and to bring the sum that has been agreed upon to retrieve the prince..."

Emperor Palaiologos V burst with anger inside, but thinking that the smartest thing to do would be to keep his poise, he calmly informed the spokesman that he accepted the terms and that he would visit the castle as soon as possible. The spokesman was content with the Emperor's decision. He asked for permission to convey the good news to the castle and left the Emperor's presence. He walked towards his sublime boat and just as he had climbed down the rope ladder and stepped foot inside the boat, Emperor Palaiologos V ordered that the Venetian-style large assault boat (a back-up ship for the command ship) built by Pontic foremen and which carried the imperial coat of arms be prepared to set sail. He also ordered the sealed chests of ransom money to be carried aboard. He boarded the rowing boat with his guards in full and half armour as soon as the preparations were completed. Once the rowing boat carrying the im-

perial coat of arms began moving towards the jetty to the east of
Phocaea Castle, the small barges carrying spare munitions with the
assault boats that served as tugboats for the other ships formed a
long chain behind them. As the Emperor aboard the imperial rowing
boat quickly nearing the jetty looked at the castle for a split second,
he muttered, "Antiphon, don't you see, the mind cannot always show
the way." He turned his gaze on the captain showering the oarsmen
with orders as the imperial rowing boat advanced around the island
while drawing an arc towards the south on the surface of the sea.
Then he turned around and looked at the armada at the mouth of
the bay and the boats that formed a chain behind them. He looked
at guards who formed a shield of flesh around him. Looking at
Atandros Avokavos, the commander of the guards, the Emperor
said, "I'd thought of sending Alexius into the castle with the ransom
money but if those at the castle want..." Before he could finish his
sentence all the bells in the castle began to ring as if to alert the
castle people to an attack. Trembling at the sound of the bells, the
Emperor momentarily lost his bearings. He caught Atandros's eye.
He was just about to order the armada to retreat when he saw the
half-naked people running towards the jetty trampling each other
from the castle gate that opened out onto the jetty. Looking at them
the Emperor whispered, "They look as if they have emerged from the
other side of the world." Most of those running from the castle to the
jetty really did look as if they had emerged from some invisible side
of the world. The strange sounds they made as they ran was like
proof that they did not belong to any world.

As the imperial rowing boat drew up to the jetty made of rough
wooden planks, the Emperor was looking at the pirate ships of the
Phocaean Genoese camouflaged between the south of the little island and the shore. "That's all they have. If..." He couldn't finish his
sentence because the imperial rowing boat crashed into the jetty and
he careened. As the rowing boat was tired to the jetty with ropes he

muttered, "If they..." His sentence was once again interrupted when the commander of the guards pointed to the small portable ladder leaned against the jetty. Slowly stumbling towards the ladder, Emperor Palaiologos V hesitated about getting off the rowing boat when he couldn't catch sight of the delegation among the half-naked people on the jetty. The commander of the guards climbed up onto the jetty in a breath and waited for the Emperor to do the same. Looking at him, the Emperor thought, "I suppose they didn't anticipate I would arrive so quickly." He climbed up the steps of the wooden ladder held tight by a few oarsmen and arrived beside Atandros. Some agitation took place at the front of the crowd when he stepped foot on the jetty. As both the guards and the Emperor looked in the direction of the ruckus, a squad of pirates squirmed out of the crowd and surrounded the Emperor and Atandros. The spokesman of the pirate squad at the ready with arrows loaded in their bows said, "Not another soul climbs up on this jetty. If anyone attempts it, they will be sorry."

CHAPTER FIFTY-THREE

The beys gathered at the portable headquarters immediately after chest to chest and knuckle to knuckle combat to capture the Peristasi Castle and decided that the guards taken captive would be sent to Bursa as soon as they were recorded. They also came to the conclusion that those who voluntarily wanted to leave the castle would set forth towards Plajar with the principal forces that would retreat there, that the Turkmen immigrants from Sultanönü would settle in the vacant castle, and that one of the subordinate beys of the Ottoman Bey who first entered the castle would be appointed to the command of the castle as was the custom. All this was decided upon so that the castle would not change hands again. They also appointed one *subaşı* and one *kadî* recommended to the post by the *akıncı beys* to oversee the castle. Noticing that order was achieved in the castle a few days after the meeting Suleyman Pasha and Hacı IlBey were convinced that their work there had come to an end and set forth towards Plajar Castle with the principal forces. Upon their arrival at the military camp near Plajar, they began to prepare for the winter. While they prepared their camp for the winter, they also sent news to all the holy war beys scattered across Thrace informing them the campaign period should be brought to a close and that they should retreat to the castles that had been designated to them.

The holy war units that retreated to their winter camps upon receiving the news from their beys had just completed preparing for the winter when the grim and dry cold weather seized control of Thrace and heavy snowfall that would last for days began. Suleyman Pasha couldn't even drill the forces in his military camp during the long periods of snowfall. On the few days when the snowfall ceased, he and Hacı IlBey visited Ece Bey posted at the Gallipoli Castle and did not much else. The holy war beys also seemed to have been stuck in the castles where they set up camp. As they all became alarmed at their decreasing provisions they were praying for the swift arrival of the campaign months. This gruelling wait continued until the heat fell in succession from the sun to the air. With the weather steadily warming up campaign preparations were started. Seeing the thin streams of steam rising from the slightly visible soil after heat fell on the ground, Suleyman Pasha said, "Time to campaign" and immediately sent long-distance messengers to the four corners of his lands to invite his beys to their meeting point. Three days after the messengers left he set forth towards the meeting point with Hacı IlBey.

Suleyman Pasha liked setting out in the early hours of the morning. That day he set forth on the back of his Grey with the joy of spring and going on another campaign, too. The Grey noticed he was overjoyed the moment the Pasha mounted him. As he galloped with his mane fluttering around, the horse was increasing his speed without his rider noticing it. Suleyman Pasha and his milky grey horse had a strange emotional communication between them. This communication based on intuition was so powerful at times that they both did the same thing at the same time without each other's knowledge. It was the same once again. Just as they were about to set forth they'd both turned around and looked at the prince's marquee one last time with eyes of sadness.

The gallop of the Grey that had such an emotional relationship with Suleyman Pasha was like that of no other horse. While other horses ran faster after being smacked on the croup, the Grey became restive when he was smacked on the croup, slowed down and even came to a halt. Suleyman Pasha had to nudge the Grey on the abdomen with the front of both his feet in stirrups on either side for the horse to gallop. The Grey that loved the caresses of his rider leaning forward on his neck either trotted or cantered depending on the speed of the scratching on his neck. When he galloped he usually craned his neck forward like an eagle gliding over its prey. However, in the battlefield he always galloped bravely with his head held up high because by doing so he helped his rider achieve balance and also protected himself better. The Grey transformed into a completely different horse in the battlefield. When he encountered Suleyman Pasha's rival he always eyed the rival's horse and resisted in his opponent's weakest moment with a reverse turn. Both the poor horse and the cavalryman would fall flat on their faces not knowing what hit them.

The Grey which behaved differently on the road and on the battlefield, also did not like any horses to be galloping in front of him during long-distance journeys. If there were horses in front of him, he would increase his speed until he passed them by. However, at such times, regardless of how fast he would be galloping, he would always come to a halt soon after Suleyman Pasha lightly smacked him on the croup—as if a magical brake had been installed.

The grooms knew about the emotional relationship between the Prince and his horse. They doted on him and made sure he was always fed and watered on the dot. Suleyman Pasha held his Grey dear and almost never delayed his daily visit to the stables. If for any reason he couldn't visit him, he would make sure to send him water in the silver bowl from which he watered his horse every day.

The emotional relationship between his horse and the cavalry had been continuing as such for years. Trotting along after casting its gaze on the prince's marquee at the same time as the prince, the Grey tried very hard to catch up with the advance cavalry in the distance but failed as the distance between them was far too great. When the day slipped into evening, the Grey looked at the Uğraş River in the distance. As he struggled to catch up to the advance cavalry he neighed intermittently as if to voice his concerns. He became bad-tempered because of the cold and sharp wind that blew into his eyes as he climbed up the slope. A bitter smile spread across Suleyman Pasha's lips when he noticed his horse's agitation. He spoke in a whispered tone, "I think you're trying to remind me of our first conflict here..." Looking at the distant hills that looked like traps chained to one another he said, "Sansaoğlu gave his life to save mine." Hearing his horse neigh again while looking in the direction of the field of the previous conflict he got enraged and voiced his reproach at the river once more, "Grey, I know! What happened at the Uğraş River cost us dearly!"

Just then Hacı IlBey caught up with him and said, "My Prince, if you like we can rest awhile and pray for the brave men who lost their lives for us."

Prince Suleyman Pasha replied, "Hacı IlBey, we have to forget about the men we have lost if we want to win new victories."

Hacı IlBey continued in an excited tone as if he was reliving that first conflict at the Uğraş River when they lost a lot of men, "I thought about why the men fighting on our behalf that day were so brave but I was not able to find answers to any of my questions until I encountered the priest of Firece. When I was telling him about our conflict in this valley, I explained to him how the enemy refused to surrender, how they attacked us more vigorously every time we thought we had defeated them. After listening to me calmly and holding my hand, the old priest spoke in a tone of voice as soft as his hand, 'That's because they are the grandsons of Isaurians who did not accept defeat'."

Suleyman Pasha sneered, "Who are the Isaurians, My Bey?"

"That was exactly what I asked the priest."

Impatient for a reply, Suleyman Pasha hastily slowed down his horse and asked, "What did he tell you?"

"They also came to these lands from Anatolia but not instinctively like us. They were a people who lived in the coves of desolate highlands, currently in the province of Karaman. But they weren't like the other tribes. They always moved from one place to the other regardless of the time of day and seasons. They unexpectedly appeared out of nowhere as if to rise from the ground, set fire to the fortresses and villages that came up their way, put people to the sword and pillaged every single house. And what's more, they didn't even fear their rulers. They neither paid tax nor served any man. It was as if they owned these mighty mountains. In fact, they were the only people who dismayed the Goths who ripped apart Rome and ended up in Anatolia. However, time eventually played its trick on them, too. Becoming ever-stronger in the east, the Roman army surrounded the entire tribe. Those who resisted their rule were put to the sword and those who gave in were taken captive. All those who were taken captive were brought to Kostantiniyye where all the men were hung, drawn and quartered. Women and small children were settled in these valleys. So, according to the priest, the enemy fighting against us could have been the great-grandsons of those Isaurians who were fearless in the face of death."

After listening to him intently, Suleyman Pasha said, "Hacı IlBey, this leads me to think that it is not correct for us to call every living soul we come across in these lands as Thracians or Greeks. These lands are worldlier than we assumed. That's what I initially thought about our enemy, too. I thought that those fortresses belonged to us long before. But after travelling to this side, I realised these castles belong neither to us nor to those who protect this castle against us. I think that sometimes it's both ours and theirs, sometimes it's ours, sometimes it's theirs, and sometimes it neither theirs nor ours."

"Yes, My Bey, you are right but I think there is something missing."

A humble man, Suleyman Pasha smiled and said, "Sure, it might be. Would we even dare say everything accurately? What is it that you think is missing?"

"I think you could have said that sometimes it is as much theirs as it is ours and vice versa, and sometimes it is as much ours as it is our predecessors... And it belongs to those after us just as much as to us."

"There is room for elaboration."

"All aside, the way the Uğraş River cascades down is something else. It's as if the rotting hearts of those resting in these hillsides are wailing..."

Falling silent with the effect of Hacı IlBey's words, Suleyman Pasha attempted to change the subject, "Will we be able to get there before night falls?"

"We can get there by then with the cavalry but the *yayas* following us will only be able to get there by the morning. However, this River is quite treacherous. We have to caution the advance troops and the sentinels to keep their eyes wide open so nothing bad befalls them after we leave."

They brought their horses to halt and waited momentarily. They told the messengers to caution the *yayas* and high-ranking cavalry-men to secure the road they were to take and to leave behind guards on their path. When both of the messengers left their place to their aids to inform the high-ranking cavalrymen, Suleyman Pasha loosened the reins of his horse and muttered, "If we can clean out Thrace before winter, we can probably move the headquarters to the north..."

Listening to him in a dazed state of mind, Hacı IlBey replied, "We have to move both the headquarters and the harems. Since temper-atures will be lower up north we have to find a mansion in one of the newly captured castles to accommodate the harems."

Suleyman Pasha pursed his lips as if they were forcing him to do something he didn't want to do.

"You are right, Hacı IlBey but I am not thinking of moving my harem from Plajar before we capture the Hadrianopolis Castle. If it is vouchsafed to us, we can move the harems once we capture it. Evrenos Bey's *akıncı* units should check out Hadrianopolis first. Fazıl Bey should approach from the east. Meanwhile, rovers should act as if they are escaping from us and seek shelter in Hadriano-polis... We can make our move according to the news we will receive from them."

As they advanced talking amongst themselves first the Grey came to a halt and then Hacı IlBey's sorrel. As the beys looked at each other without being able to make sense of why the horses stopped, the Grey pricked his ears and began listening intently. When Hacı Il-Bey's sorrel did the same Hacı IlBey looked at Suleyman Pasha and became all ears in order to determine the origin of the noises. He reminded, "My Bey, did I not tell you that this River is auspicious?"

Then he dismounted his horse after Suleyman Pasha, who made a move to dismount his horse before him.

CHAPTER FIFTY-FOUR

Walking majestically towards Byzantine Emperor John Palaiologos V standing at the pier square, Dionysus, Count of Phocaea Castle, paid special attention to seeming as daunting as possible. As he kept pace with the rhythm of the thundering doomsday drums hanging from the drummers' necks following him he frequently turned back and glanced at the grey-bearded priest and his guards armoured from head to toe.

Waiting for Count Dionysus, who was walking ceremoniously to arrive beside him at the pier square, Emperor Palaiologos V didn't fail to recognise that the show they were putting on was a manifestation of their fear even though he himself also felt a shiver of fear course through his body. His nerves eased when he realised that the fact that his guards were not permitted to step foot on the pier was another tell-tale sign of the same fear. He looked in the direction of the ships forming the most well-equipped fleet of the time lined up next to each other in the shape of a half-moon at the mouth of the bay opening up to the Aegean Sea. He turned back towards the count when he couldn't see anything other than the poles of the galleys and sailing boats. He considered taking a few steps towards the count who was approaching with ceremonious steps but quickly changed his mind in the name of showing him he was more powerful. He looked at the bollards lined up haphazardly. As he thought that fear prowled wherever Phocaea's name was uttered, he deduced "It seems the rumours are not true since the pier is in a state of disorder." Just as he turned back again and looked at those approaching, a colossal wave rolling in from the Aegean Sea and stirring the calm waters of the bay crashed onto the pier with a "whassss!" The sound of the wave crashing onto the pier first mixed into that of the wind and then entered through the very narrow castle gate. And as it did so, it transformed into a sound that evoked the howl of a wolf. As the Em-

peror thought about the reason behind the change in the sound
Count Dionysus arrived beside him, slightly bent forward and saluted him.

"Son of Andronicus the Sovereign of Great Byzantium, Emperor
John Palaiologos, you honour our castle with your presence. The
people of our castle are delighted to host you."

As Emperor Palaiologos V had never been welcomed with such a
ceremony he looked at Count Dionysus in surprise. He smiled gently
when he saw the soft look on the face of the priest dressed in black
and standing immediately behind the count. He squared his
shoulders in order to present himself even stronger than he was. He
responded in a tone of voice peppered with a sense of huffiness, "I
too am happy to visit your castle. However, I cannot say I am happy
about the reason for my visit. I would like you to acknowledge that
you left our Byzantium in dire straits against the Ottomans."

The guards who were unable to step foot onto the pier from the imperial caïque carrying the magnificent coat of arms of the empire
yelled out, "Long live the Emperor! Long live the Palaiologos dynasty!" to give him courage as soon as they overheard the Emperor's
stalwart speech. Looking at them with an indistinct smile on his lips,
Dionysus, renowned as the noncompliant Count of the Phocaea
Castle, took a couple more steps towards the Emperor. The Emperor
was baffled when he noticed that the count with one hand on his
sword and his body turned towards him was looking at the sea. He
smiled when he realised that the count was extremely cross-eyed. He
thought that it would be no use for him to display a show of strength
or raise his voice. In a tone of voice softer than his previous he said,
"I desired to visit your castle before and under different conditions
but as you know, the Kantakouzenos caused our Byzantium much
trouble. Thank heavens, our Byzantium has now rid themselves of
their wickedness. However, we get on well with our surrounding
neighbours for now so that our empire can regain its strength. That

is why we have promised to hand over the Ottoman prince to his father Orhan Ghazi at once. I am sure you'll aid us in keeping our promise."

When he fell silent he tried to assess the effect of his words on Count Dionysus and the Phocaeans gathered at the pier square. He became irritated when he realised that those on the pier were also quiet. As he restlessly looked at the ground, the old priest took a few steps towards the Emperor, despite the armed pirates' attempt to inhibit him, gently bowed his head and saluted the Emperor. Then he said, "Noble Emperor of Supreme Byzantium, welcome to our castle... As believers of the castle, we tried to host the prince to the best of our capability under the patronage of our esteemed Count. We hope that you won't be sparing with compensating our services and that you will not demand at least a part of the taxes we pay to the esteemed count in your name."

Cross-eyed Count Dionysus looked at the priest but the Emperor felt as if he was looking at him. Picking up on the anger hidden in his cockeyed eyes, the Emperor gazed at the deep hollow on his forehead and oddly wondered, "I wonder what his real name is?"

The Count turned his head to the sea, "Your Majesty, the priest has voiced the wishes of our church. I am also in support of you returning the tax paid to the patriarchate. Moreover, the castle council wishes that the treasury tax deducted from our castle be delayed for some time. We would also like to take the fishermen we caught off the shore of our castle captive."

Emperor Palaiologos recoiled from his daydream and looked at Count Dionysus in the startled manner of someone who awoke from a deep sleep. As he tried to restrain himself from getting angry he tried to focus his gaze on the priest and replied, "Father, we will not expect taxes from your church just as it is with other churches in the Byzantine Empire. I will discuss this matter with the Patriarch."

Then, he turned to Count Dionysus and said, "Esteemed Count Dionysus, despite the fact that your men who kidnapped the Ottoman prince put us in a very difficult situation, your castle is under the protection of our empire's loving wings. Your castle will be held exempt from Byzantine tax for a period of two years but the fishermen taken captive will be under the protection of our empire from now on as it has been previously."

After looking at the ships of the Byzantine fleet of which only the poles were visible, Count Dionysus turned his gaze to the Emperor and spoke in an assertive and angry tone of voice, "Your Majesty, in return for the Ottoman prince we demand payment and the right to keep the fishermen caught offshore captive in our castle as per the final decision made by our castle council."

Even though he didn't have much bargaining power, the Emperor persevered, "I accept your wishes on the condition that we will come to a new agreement in Constantinople in six months."

Holding onto his petulance, Count Dionysus responded, "Your Majesty, we will only agree to review the agreement in a year."

Observing the Emperor's unyielding gaze and knowing Count Dionysus' stubbornness, the priest intervened to avert further disagreement, "Master, in the name of God, please don't give offence to the Count. You can see how impoverished our castle is."

Then he looked at the Count with a sense of respect mixed with fear. The Emperor's gaze tracked the priest's and caught the boss-eyed count's eyes reeling. He felt his previous mischievous smile course through his mind again. However, he also noticed the grisly look in the count's eyes. Looking at the priest pitifully he said, "Father, I accept the count's wishes. We will come to a new agreement regarding the fishermen in a year's time."

Upon hearing the Emperor's words, Count Dionysus signed his archers lined up on the pier to point down their arrows. When the archers pointed their arrows to the ground and loosened their bows, the Phocaeans gathered at the pier square all yelled out in succession, "Long live our supreme Emperor, Long live Count Dionysus."

When the crowd fell silent, the Emperor turned his gaze to Count Dionysus and before saluting him in a graceful way befitting of his position, he said, "Esteemed Count, our agreement will be valid as of the moment you deliver the Ottoman prince to us."

Count Dionysus appreciated the Emperor saluting him. He bowed and saluted the Emperor in a manner that would not be expected of him. He then told his archers to retreat and permitted the Emperor's guards to embark on the pier. As he watched the imperial guards, who were more majestic than him, slowly embark on the pier, he asked, "Your Majesty, would you care for a glass of our castle's wine as you wait for our treasurer to count the payment in return for delivering the Ottoman prince?"

Wanting to receive Halil Bey and depart as soon as possible, Emperor Palaiologos V seemed to understand that the only way to get rid of the pirates was to act like he accepted their wishes even if he didn't. Looking at Count Dionysus he said, "I would love to taste the famous wine of Phocaea as I wait for the prince's arrival."

Then, he turned his gaze to his armoured guards standing behind him in a vee.

CHAPTER FIFTY-FIVE

With their horses' hindquarters turned to the cold wind unbecoming of the season and blowing from the north, Suleyman Pasha and Hacı IlBey tried to figure out the source of the indecipherable sounds that were gradually becoming louder. And, as they did so they looked at each other blankly. When they inclined their ears and listened carefully they realised that the sounds were emanating from the near-by streambed. They turned their horses' heads towards the stream at the same time and began riding them down to the streambed drawing large zig-zags on the steep downward path. The *serdengeçtis* waiting for them on the main road were alarmed when they disappeared from sight after suddenly riding their horses towards the hill. As both *serdengeçtis* were riding their horses together, the hillside wrapped in the cold wind became enveloped in a cloud of dust and earth. Oblivious to the *serdengeçtis* state of anxiety, Suleyman Pasha and Hacı IlBey's faces connoted a sense of disbelief when they saw what they saw upon their arrival at the streambed after their ride through the sparsely forested hillside. Hacı IlBey's gaze plied between the prince and the scribes and the dervish who were reciting hymns on the streambed. Looking at Suleyman Pasha, who was just as puzzled, he asked, "When did they get here?"

Riding his horse towards the convoy, Suleyman Pasha replied, "I have no idea. But what puzzles me is why the hymns they are reciting can be heard crystal-clear here and completely muffled atop the hill?"

Hacı IlBey answered, "I am not an arithmetician but what I heard from some of them is that sound becomes dispersed because the wind on the higher ground blows faster."

Suleyman Pasha looked at Hacı IlBey, who knew what to say and how to say it very well, with a smile. Noticing that he wasn't paying much attention to him, he didn't attempt to ask another question.

Instead, he whipped up his horse and arrived next to the convoy
leader who was positioned in the middle of the convoy. Those at the
front were walking in groups dressed in various colourful outfits. Suleyman Pasha had previously seen dervish convoys formed of ten to
fifteen people in Bursa but he had never seen them walking together
in such large and different groups. The dervishes recognized him because of his turban and saluted him bowing down in their learned
order before continuing to recite their hymn. After finishing every
hymn, they repeatedly chanted the lines:

Swords are bloody,
Their soldiers, veterans,
Like flying birds,
Soldiers like hounds.

Watching them continue their walk in an orderly fashion for a
while, Hacı IlBey approached the elderly convoy leader who looked
like an Indian merchant and asked, "Saintly fathers, where do you
come from and where are you headed?"

The convoy leader, with his hair brimming over from his quilted
turban, saluted them from the back of his horse and replied calmly,
"We are headed towards Evrenos Bey's protection with the zeal of
Orhan Ghazi."

Suleyman Pasha realized that there was no need for him to speak
further. He didn't want to pose another question but when he
couldn't tame his curiosity he said, "Saints, I am curious about the
colourful caftans of your dervishes."

Riding his horse, the convoy leader realised that he was a prince
because of the way his turban was wrapped. With a smile on his lips
he explained, "My Prince, each group comes from a different dervish
lodge and castle. They all want to be recognised with their own colours. See those walking in front of us dressed in black and red? They
are from Termez. Those in front of them dressed in yellow and green
are from Herat. The large group behind us wearing crimson caftans

are from the castle of the Caliph. Those in plain black robes are from Tabriz and those in white are dervishes who entered Orhan Ghazi's service in harmony from Karaman. As we all wished to join our *akıncıs* on this shore, Orhan Ghazi, who hosted us throughout the winter, told us, "If your wish is one, you can all depart once it's warmer" and sent us on our way here. When he heard that you would be campaigning in Gallipoli we set forth at once to catch up with you. We all come from different places. If you place us under the command of the *akıncı* units you deem appropriate, we will take to different directions."

Suleyman Pasha looked at the old dervish, who spoke every single word with caution and care, and smiled. A messenger arrived beside them just as he was looking in the direction of Hacı IlBey as if he had said all he wanted. As they cast their gaze on the messenger, the messenger dismounted his horse and saluted Suleyman Pasha. Then he said, "My Bey, they asked me to inform you that there is half a day's journey between us and the cavalry."

Watching the dervishes and scribes wend their way dressed in their colourful caftans, Suleyman Pasha and Haci IlBey noticed that they lost a lot of time when they rode down to the streambed. Without replying to the messenger, they chanted the lines:

Swords are bloody,
Their soldiers, veterans,
Like flying birds,
Soldiers like hounds.

in unison with the group of scribes passing by them and spurred their horses...

That day, the cavalry advancing with short breaks under the command of Suleyman Pasha arrived at the meeting place just as the sun set into the horizon and disappeared behind the mountains. When Suleyman Pasha and Hacı IlBey entered the temporary marquee set up by the advance units most of the *Alps* and holy war beys were already there. Once the beys fulfilled their longing for one another the council *Alps* sat down on the diwan to the right and the holy war beys on the one to the left. When Suleyman Pasha looked at the ranks of beys as if his eyes were searching for someone in particular, Evrenos Bey asked, "My Prince, are you looking to see Ece?"

Suleyman Pasha replied with the ease of knowing that these beys with whom he had shared the same common fate for years, "Yes, Evrenos Bey, has he not arrived yet?"

"My Prince, his messengers informed us that he will be delayed in order to bring us good tidings."

"Let's hope for the best, Evrenos Bey."

As the joyous and cunning gazes of the two beys smiled at one another, Akça Kocaoğlu, ebullient and looking like an over-sized baby, took the floor, "My Bey, I don't have any patience left. I would like to start telling you what I have to say."

When Suleyman Pasha cast his gaze on him it was as if the joyous gaze glinting from the rosy great-big-baby-like-mannered Akça Kocaoğlu's large eyes fell onto the ground in embarrassment. As he plied between lifting or not lifting his embarrassed gaze from the ground, Evrenos Bey's voice came to his rescue. "What's Akça Kocaoğlu's joyous news overflowing from his great heart?"

Prince Suleyman Pasha looked at Akça Kocaoğlu in a manner that strengthened Evrenos Bey's question. Akça Kocaoğlu had to explain, "My Bey, I shared my overflowing joy with almost all of the beys before your arrival."

Seeing his child-like enthusiasm Evrenos Bey murmured, "Just like his father" and continued, "The night Akça Koca sent Rahman to Aydos Castle I was with him. That night your father was just as joyous as you are now."

"Evrenos Bey, our joy cannot really be compared."

Evrenos Bey's curiosity was growing, "Come on then, don't get us more anxious! What is greater than that feudal landlord's daughter's love for Rahman?"

Looking at Suleyman Pasha, Akça Kocaoğlu said, "My Bey, our *akıncıs* entered three castles on the shores of the Black Sea on the same day last week. The castles are small but their locations are important."

Taking advantage of Suleyman Pasha's silence after he had exclaimed, "Divine!", Evrenos Bey said, "You are right to be joyous Akça Kocaoğlu. I actually wanted to initially tell you that our first raiding convoys took shelter at the Didymóteicho Castle as refugees escaping from us. But what you had to say was more important than what I had to tell."

Then, looking at Akça Kocaoğlu and Evrenos Bey, Suleyman Pasha responded, "You have made us happy with your news. May God deem you just as happy."

He then looked at Hacı IlBey to find out the subjects that would be discussed in the campaign headquarters that day.

The meeting continued late into the night after a break for dinner. As the meeting came to an end towards midnight, Suleyman Pasha's head messenger entered the headquarters. After bowing and saluting the beys inside, he spoke in a thunderous tone of voice, "Ece Bey arrived at his marquee a little while ago and informs that he will be joining the meeting shortly."

CHAPTER FIFTY-SIX

Despite the fact that he had returned from Phocaea days ago, Emperor John Palaiologos V had not been able to rid himself of the effect those nightmarish days had had on him. Every time he was reminded of that time he came unglued with fear on the one hand, and on the other hand, he was remembering those illness-ridden days, which he thought he had forgotten. On one of the days when the weather was warmer and a soft spring breeze wandered the Constantinople Castle, Emperor John Palaiologos V remembered that time again. Fearing that he was going to suffer a feverish seizure, he left his study and arrived next to his imperial carriage. As he got onto the carriage he ordered the driver, "We are going to the mansion."

The horses reacted to the driver's whip and began trotting accordingly towards the imperial mansion, referred to as the little palace by Empress Helena and as a mansion by the Emperor. The Emperor lied down on the seat in the rear section of the carriage and waited for the next seizure. However, this time the incubus he expected did not arrive and in his heart, he felt a sense of joy, the reason for which he did not know. As he revelled in that joy, he somehow saw Prince Halil piteously walking towards him. For a while he watched him walk weakly as he did at Phocaea Castle. As he tried to recapture the vision that disappeared with the shrill voice of the driver his memories took hold of him and his inner voice began to talk, "When I saw him in that bedraggled state I thought he had got a nasty disease at the castle and remembered my mother's words, 'Since your childhood, you've drawn disease to yourself like a magnet.' I felt anxious. I tried to keep my distance from the prince after our initial greeting, with the idea that I could contract his disease by the time the ship arrived. Once I left the prince alone with physicians in his chamber I sought refuge in my tiny little inner chamber as if to hide from my fears. I wanted to lie down as soon as I entered into the chamber as I did most of the time but I took my crown off first and placed it on the bed. As soon as I took my cape off I soaked myself in the doweled wood tub that looked like a carved cask. The odalisques from Lesbos ran to my aid when they saw me getting in with my clothes on. As we blankly looked at one another, the chief odalisque asked me, 'Would his Majesty allow us to undress him?'

"I got out of the cask-shaped tub in embarrassment. The odalisques took off my clothes and boots. They changed the water and added St John's wort extract into the warm water and asked me to get in again. When I had slowly recovered myself with the touch of the odalisques' soft finger tips, I took deep breaths to fill my lungs with the scent of the extract. Then I said, 'I see now that the Romans aren't all bad.' The odalisques from Lesbos looked at my face vacantly and I felt the need to elaborate, 'What I mean is, if Attalus, King of Pergamon, had not left his lands to Rome, the Romans wouldn't have built the baths and the blossoms of St John's wort added into the bathwater would not have been the antidote to the wear and tear of the human body. If that was the case, we would still be thinking that these blossoms were only good for Eros to smell.' When I had completely sobered up with the soft touches of the odalisques I told them that I was ready to get out of the tub. A master of her domain, my chief odalisque and the others helped me get out of the tub and dried me with sizeable fluffy towels. As they dressed me in my silk pyjamas my hand brushed against the fabric. I said, 'I think I am really right about the Romans. They are really not that bad. If that foxy Justinian had not told the fortune-hunter Persian monks, 'You will receive the weight of the silkworms, you bring in red gold' as he handed them staffs, we would still be waiting for the Chinese silk to be brought by Sogdoit merchants. When the odalisques, which I likened to the Muses in the light of colourful oil lamps, stared at me stupidly, I thought of telling them about the Muses but then the pale face of Prince Halil on the pier re-appeared before my eyes. As he walked towards me with his lacklustre posture I thought, 'He must have contracted a nasty disease at the castle.' However, when I realised that he had been in dark tunnels for months without being able to bathe I stood up again and told them to dress me. As I went out onto the entrance to my chamber I told my chief odalisque, 'Prepare the tub again as you just did.'

"When the chief odalisque looked at my face vacantly, I explained, 'Dear Perominos, prepare the tub as you did for me so that you can bathe the prince.'

"They all smiled upon hearing my request. When they realised that I was being serious their smiles froze. When they bathed him and dressed him in the clothes his aunt Helena provided, I was faced with a different Prince Halil compared to the one a few hours before. As I looked at his pinkish face I thought, 'My Irene is only a few years younger than him but he will grow older soon.' The prince's body, relaxed with the bath he had had for the first time after many a month, seemed to come to terms with his fatigue. Seeing that his sleepy eyes were about to close I told him to rest in his chamber. He respectfully saluted me and joyfully headed towards his chamber. When he left my chamber, I stepped out onto the deck to watch the sun painting the Aegean Sea in a setting red. My gaze cast on the sea sparkle delved into the distance. I loudly murmured, 'Ye philosophers who bathe Athens with their light of wisdom, did you have to take all your wisdom and leave? Couldn't you have left some of it here on earth? And how about you, Antiphanes? You say, 'Humans assert that they look more like gods than animals?' Does this also apply to Dionysus, Phocaea's curse? If it does, you should know that you are mistaken. Something moved in me. My heart rejoiced. I had just begun to pace the deck whistling with joy when something unexpected happened. I thought I heard Antiphanes tell me, 'Ye son of Palaiologos, remember that trouble is not far from where there is joy.

For, joy and happiness do not arrive on their own...' from the shimmery phosphorescence in the distance. As I looked into the distance, I heard approaching footsteps. When I turned around I found the fleet commander I appointed when we set out towards Phocaea right in front of me. He wanted to tell me something but it seemed as if he couldn't. When I carefully observed his face, he averted his gaze and said, 'Your Majesty, we will arrive at the mouth of the Dardanelles before midnight. But the captain says that we will be caught in a storm before we reach there...'

"Pointing to the blue skies, I asked him, 'Can you see a storm brewing in this blue sky?'

"'Your Majesty, I don't. But the captain knows the blue sky as well as he knows the blue waters. I only wanted to inform you of what he said.'

"I told the fleet commander that he should relax and not let anything, including the storm, stop us until Constantinople. Then I went to my chamber and penned my letter to Orhan Ghazi to give him the good news, 'It should be known to Orhan Ghazi, Sovereign of the Osmanoğlu Beylik, that Prince Halil is safe and sound under our protection. As of now, he is also our son because we, I and his aunt Empress Helena, decided to engage him to our daughter Princess Irene. Thus, Prince Halil will be our guest at our palace for some time when we arrive in Constantinople. Later, I will accompany him and my daughter to the Nicomedia Castle, where the prince will be the commander of the castle. We only wish them happiness. Orhan Ghazi, illustrious Bey of the Ottomans, I hope that we will have the opportunity to talk face to face in Nicomedia.'

"I ended the letter with my signature 'Emperor of Byzantium, John Palaiologos V.'

"I had just finished writing my letter and thinking about having dinner with Prince Halil when the captain's forecast turned out to be correct. The massive waves of the suddenly angry sea began to rock our great big ships like a baby's cradle."

When the carriage arrived at the small palace and stopped so did Emperor Palaiologos V's inner voice.

CHAPTER FIFTY-SEVEN

Ece Bey dismounted his horse as soon as he arrived at the beys meeting place. He took off his embroidered woollen socks knitted with zephyr yarn that looked like a part of the white felt rawhide sandals, which he wore when travelling long distances on horseback, and instead put on his white socks and calf boots. As soon as he briefly rested in the tent that was his temporary marquee and drank something cold, he climbed up the side of the little hill where the military camp was set up. He straightened out his quarter length salwar of blue twill and his bolero with brocaded silk before he entered through the flap of the military camp tent. When he thought to himself, "I don't want them to say that I am wretched now that I am old" he chuckled. Suleyman Pasha stood straight on his knees out of respect for his old age when he entered into the tent with a smiley face and saluted him, "Welcome, Ece Bey. "

Ece Bey gently bent forward with respect and replied, "I'm glad to be here, My Bey."

He then walked past him and sat on the vacant floor cushion between Akça Kocaoğlu and Evrenos Bey sitting on the right of Prince Suleyman Pasha. He turned his gaze to Suleyman Pasha saying, "We are all curious to hear all that you have to tell us, Ece Bey."

Ece Bey straightened up on his knees and began to talk after gently bending forward, "Forgive me for making you wait, My Prince. It was a force majeure. A reckless galleon of Emperor Palaiologos V's fleet sank one of our barges while cruising across from Gallipoli. Fortunately, the sailors from other galleons ran to our help and we didn't suffer any loss of lives. Also..."

He didn't finish his sentence, as he cast a quiet glance. His eyes with shimmering whites circled the tent. Noticing that the attendees were getting impatient he continued, "We also waited for the strangely dressed new *yaya* convoy, keepsake of the late Aladdin Ali

Bey to our Beylik to cross the sea in order to set out from Gallipoli."

Prince Suleyman Pasha informed him that he was pleased with the news Ece Bey delivered. After a moment of silence, he responded, "Ece Bey, thanks to you, everything is in magnificent working order from Eceabad to the coasts of Tristasis. The news you have delivered has made us rejoice. The new *yayas* from Bursa also arrived just in time. Because we really need them in the castles within our boundaries widened by Akça Kocaoğlu and Fazıl Bey. We also have good news to share with you in return for yours. As of this moment, the Ottoman dagger lodged in the heart of the Black Sea there is now also lodged in the Black Sea here thanks to our advance cavalry."

Ece Bey turned his head to either side, greeting Akça Kocaoğlu and Fazıl Bey, the beys of the fronts in charge of those territories. Silence took over after his greeting. The silence meant that there was nothing more to be discussed. Gathering that the session was at an end, the old *Alps* left the divan after receiving permission to be dismissed. However, the beys who had captured new castles stayed together until it was gone past midnight sharing their memories with one another. As he enjoyed the company and the conversation, Suleyman Pasha hadn't left the military camp tent either. Though, as midnight turned to the early hours of the morning, Hacı IlBey said, "As we stepped foot on this side of the Dardanelles I thought that we would remain here. This, however, is no longer just a thought. We will capture many more castles as long as we continue being forgiving and not killing or plundering in the castles we capture from now on, as we have done so far. May our forgiveness be lasting, our wars bloodless and your justice equitable."

The meeting in the headquarter tent ended with his final words. When all the beys bowed, saluted and left the tent, Suleyman Pasha also got up and headed towards his traveling marquee. Before entering, he listened to the raucous human voices that mixed into the hoot of owls and eagle owls trying to pierce the silence of the night.

He was surprised upon entering his marquee. He tried to make sense of the mystery hidden in the misty darkness lit up by colourful oil lamps as he breathed in the scent oozing towards the entrance of the marquee, which was separated from the inner sections with layers of drapery. When he pulled aside the first curtain of a series of curtains that separated the chambers from one another and entered inside he came eye to eye with Antiope, a belle from Tzympe who was waiting for him. Suleyman Pasha had taken Antiope to Bursa in the previous year and Nilüfer Hatun had educated her for her son as she did with all the other odalisques.

Antiope had organised a farewell night for the prince on the occasion of his first campaign of the year with all the other concubines and odalisques, the way she was taught how to by Nilüfer Hatun's head concubine. Suleyman Pasha didn't feel such irresistible passion for her but somehow nurtured an endless sense of gratitude for this woman who was the only one capable of consoling him during those unbearably sorrowful days in Gallipoli. That is why he had appointed her as the forewoman of his travelling harem. Antiope, who was accustomed to settled life, at first found it difficult to get used to Suleyman Pasha's nomadic living.

However, she gradually understood that this was the only way of being close to Suleyman Pasha, so much so that when she stayed at the castles she had begun to feel abandoned. Thus, in order to stay close to Suleyman Pasha, she had dedicated her life to complement his. She was content, but not even such a degree of happiness could make her forget her parents, who were first hacked to pieces by the Catalans and then thrown out onto the street from the windows of their house like bloody rags, and her husband who was lost at sea. She attached a handkerchief of red silk, which she had sewed and embroidered herself on her girdle, so she would remember them at all times.

From time to time she dabbed this handkerchief on her face and felt a strange sense of happiness to remind herself of her family. She did want to get used to their absence but it was as if that treacherous serpent that enticed Eve was hidden in the handkerchief and perpetually called her to revel in that peculiar happiness. She must have understood that she had no choice but to live with this strange feeling that she fantasised, "I am not nearly as lucky to give birth to twins as my namesake Antiope but I wish Suleyman wanted to have a child with me" as she consoled herself by saying, "What fools me is not the lies of the serpent but the chasteness of my heart." As she welcomed him from behind the drapery of the bed-chamber this thought had crossed her mind like a soft zephyr. She held Suleyman Pasha's hands as he looked at her and took him to the inner chamber where a massive cube-like tub made in the style of Minoan ceramic masters from the time when the most splendid Greek palaces were built.

Separated from other chambers with thick velvet drapery, Antiope's room was lit up by harlequin Cretan oil lamps while assorted scents effused from censers. Slowly inhaling the pleasant scents that tingled his nostrils, Suleyman Pasha had timidly surrendered himself to Antiope's hands like a house sparrow that got away from the claws of owls severing the dark of night. As Antiope helped him undress, he was inhaling the rose oil scent which he likened to his mother's scent and that evaporated with the warm water inside the tub. Suleyman Pasha had just immersed himself in the warm water when the drapery on both sides of the chamber was pulled aside and two beautiful odalisques taller than Antiope entered the chamber. Smiling at Suleyman Pasha who was looking at the odalisques he had never seen before in surprise, Antiope said, "The servants Evrenos Bey obtained in Aenus for your harem. They have been taught all our customs by the ladies in Evrenos Bey's harem."

Then she prompted the new servants to begin their work. They were carrying out their tasks excellently under Antiope's guidance and by paying heed to the sentence that was taught to them at the palace, "If you obey the esteemed ladies of the harem your life will be easier." They were scrubbing Suleyman Pasha's body covered with arrow and sword scars as if to gently caress him.

Exhausted from the heat and the constant motion involved in bathing Suleyman Pasha, the servants took off the fine tulle veils covering their faces. As Suleyman Pasha mumbled, "The beauties Evrenos Bey sent" the two odalisques sent by his mother Nilüfer Hatun a short while ago to join him on his campaign also arrived by the side of the bathtub. Introducing them to Suleyman Pasha, Antiope snapped her fingers. Immediately afterwards, the tapestry that separated the living quarters from the smaller chambers was taken off its wall hooks. Once the tapestry partition was moved, the water in the tub was refreshed with hot water to avoid it going cold. Unable to see much through all the steam, Suleyman Pasha heard the sound of the musical instruments serenading him.

Once the steam dispersed, he saw the musicians in the living quarters and smiled with joy. Antiope said, "I purchased them from the Gallipoli market last autumn because they are nimble-fingered. They practised together on long winter days and now they are brilliant. This is one of the things your mother Nilüfer Hatun taught me before our departure from Bursa. When she found out we were going to leave the city she pulled me to a corner and said, 'A harem without musicians is one that's incomplete.' So I did this without seeking your approval in order to complete it. I hope that we can repeat this tradition for many years before you set out on your campaigns."

Suleyman Pasha got out of the warm water, dried his body, put on his night-robe and sat on the large floor cushion across from the musicians. As he leaned against the thick cushion behind him he signalled Antiope to sit beside him. Seeing that the prince was happy, Antiope smiled at him with her entire face and green-blue gaze. Looking at the tray of food placed before him by the servants, Suley-

man Pasha held the hand of Tzympe's most beautiful woman. Gazing at the odalisques seated across from the musicians and ready to
sing he said, "Thank you for beautifying this moment of our lives. I
hope that your wish will come true and we will experience many
beautiful moments such as this throughout many years."

CHAPTER FIFTY-EIGHT

Byzantine Emperor John Palaiologos V was sad that his flashback mired down when he got off the carriage in front of the small palace but happy that he wasn't going to experience those moments of fear again. He greeted the servants who welcomed him at the garden gates. He got startled when he arrived by the door leading to the great hall. It was as if one of those humongous waves crashing against the galleys and sailing boats had lashed the walls of the small palace. He paused and turned back to look as he stepped foot inside. There weren't any waves lashing the walls. He entered the hall hastily, thinking that the fear that possessed him earlier was coming back. Even though he thought he could, as always, overcome his fear by taking shelter in Empress Helena's arms he changed his mind and headed towards his bed-chamber for solitude. He thought he could be alone there. However, the odalisques and chief chambermaid quietly entered his bed-chamber when they heard him. Watching the young odalisques take off his boots, the Emperor grasped he wouldn't be alone, reverted back to the first solution that occurred in his mind when he realised he couldn't bear the anxiety and ordered his chief chambermaid, "Summon Empress Helena."

As the chief chambermaid left to summon Empress Helena as soon as the order parted from the Emperor's lips, the other odalisques also quietly retreated back to their chambers from the side doors of the Emperor's chamber. His fears elevated together with the momentary silence that permeated the bed-chamber. Emperor John Palaiologos V invited Empress Helena to lie down next to him. Then, he began to talk rapidly as if he wanted to share everything with her and to empty out all of the thoughts that had accumulated inside his head, "Helena, on our way back from Phocaea we went through such strife until we entered the Dardanelles from the Aegean Sea and reached Gallipoli. I frequently thought that we would all die drowning. Once the seas calmed down and I came back to my senses I wrote a letter to Orhan Ghazi first thing and sent it to Ece Bey, the Commander of the Gallipoli Castle. Perhaps the old Ottoman Bey jumped on the back of his horse with the joy of finally receiving the good news he had been awaiting for months and rode all the way to the coast of Chios and yelled from Hellespont towards Constantinople, 'Oh, son of Palaiologos, I am grateful to you for sending me this news—even if it is a bit delayed. I will keep all my promises to you. I will first send for my son Suleyman and tell him to give Matthew Kantakouzenos a lesson he will never forget. Let alone dreaming of becoming emperor, he will never even be able to turn to look at Constantinople again.' Then he perhaps took the letter and went to your sister Theodora. Who knows? How happy do you think your sister was to read the letter I sent?"

With sadness on her face upon hearing her sister's name, Empress Helena gently held the Emperor's hand and looked into his eyes, and repeated in a whispery tone of voice, "Who knows?"

Seeing the sadness on the empress's face, the Emperor also felt sad. In order to hide his teary eyes from her, he first turned his head towards the wall and then to the carved door of the bed-chamber that opened into the great hall. He was all ears when he heard the footsteps approaching from the great hall. He pulled himself together on the bed. As the footsteps which he listened to for a while, leaning against his pillow, became distanced he carefully looked at Empress Helena as if he had just seen her, "Let's not filibuster any longer. I want the preparations to be started no later than tomorrow. We can ship out as soon as we meet with your father's partisans and sign the agreement that will bring peace to Constantinople. I know it will be hard for you to get our little Irene, whom you named after your mother, engaged at such a young age but we have to make this sacrifice for our Byzantium. As you know, this is not something only we have had to deal with. My paternal aunt Asporsha and your older sister Theodora have both agreed to be wed to Orhan Ghazi who was much older than them for the good of our Byzantium. Not only so but tens of Roman princesses were wed to princes at a young age from other countries to benefit Rome. Sure, our Irina is too young. We would like her to remain with us for a while after the engagement. What's important is that our daughter is the first fiancée of Prince Halil."

Listening quietly to him, Empress Helena snuggled the Emperor and exclaimed, "She is so little!"

She sighed deeply and continued, "I hope, John, I really hope that they will let our daughter stay with us for a while longer."

Hearing his wife's trembling voice, the Emperor put his arm around her waist and said, "Even if they don't allow her to stay with us, our daughter will become your older sister's daughter-in-law. She will be just as protective of her niece. Aunt Asporsha is also there. My mother tells me that Nilüfer Hatun has a great influence on her husband and sons. If all else fails, we can entrust our daughter to her until she grows up and becomes mature enough to get married."

As Empress Helena felt a feint and lingering ache in her heart with the image of her little daughter in front of her eye, the Emperor kept a forced smile on his face, seeming to empathise with her. After a deep and long breath, he quietly said, "I explicitly wrote this in my letter to Orhan Ghazi because we decided on this together before going to Phocaea. He knows we agree to the engagement of our daughter to his son. There is no turning back now Helena. The only thing we can do now is to take our daughter and the prince and go."

Watching Empress Helena leave the room, with a snap decision the Emperor said, "You have every right to be sad", in a tone of voice that could only be heard by him.

As the Emperor and the empress, who didn't mention this subject again after that day, quietly prepared for their departure, Orhan Ghazi's letter informing that he wanted to see his son as soon as possible and that he was waiting for the Emperor in Antigone, not Nicomedia, arrived in Constantinople. After reading the letter carefully a few times, Emperor Palaiologos V wanted the preparations to be completed when he met with the notable supporters of the Kantakouzenos in Constantinople so there wouldn't be any trouble in his absence. He frequently visited churches and monasteries with the pontiff of the Hagia Sophia and the Patriarch to tell young students that the only heirs of the imperial throne were the Palaiologos. However, no matter how hard he tried, he couldn't stop disjoined corpses from being dumped into the depths of the Bosphorus at night. Even though he wanted it to be concealed, the fishermen of Sycae collected the human remains that washed up on shore and constantly informed the public of the nightly murders. The Emperor had been thinking day and night about how to lessen the effects of these events on the public when he finally stumbled on the subtle idea of spreading the rumour of 'The corpse of another Moor who didn't know how to swim has been found' through his men. By explaining the appearance of the corpses in the Bosphorus as such, he was cushioning public reaction and getting his men to apprehend Matthew Kantakouzenos's supporters inside and outside the castle in Constantinople one by one. Until the day the fleet commander informed that they were ready, many supporters of Matthew Kantakouzenos who had arrived from Hadrianopolis had either been thrown into prison or exiled from Constantinople. Seeing that the good days were slowly but surely approaching, the Emperor informed the fleet commander that they were ready. As he waited for the barges and the imperial caïque that was sent to the Balati Pier by the commander, he approached the commander of the guards at the castle, son of the mesazōn having summoned him to the mansion, cautioning him, "I invited most of those who caused unrest in Constantinople to the engagement ceremony. I will take them with me. Keep a watchful eye on those who remain here."

Then, accompanied by Empress Helena, his daughter Irene, Prince Andronicus VI, Prince Immanuel II and Prince Halil, he set off in the direction of Balati Pier. As the Emperor and his entourage got on the large caïque carrying the imperial crest, those invited to join them on the journey were being transferred onto the barges together with their sprung carriages one after another.

The Emperor felt a sense of happiness seeing his son who was watching the ship of the mayor of the Genoese neighbourhood, the showiest boat after the imperial ship, stand next to Prince Halil. He turned around and looked at the sun rising from behind the hills that canopied Scutari. Then, he turned to Empress Helena saying, "The rising sun heralds the happiness of our children."

When the imperial galley dropped anchor off the port of Heleno-polis in Bithynia, which the Ottomans referred to as "Yalak-abad", people of the entire castle had gathered at the pier. There was a great deal of excitement among the castle people gathered on the pier when the large caïque carrying the imperial crest diverging from the galley and the barges carrying the carriages pulled up to the Hel-enopolis pier. When the Emperor stepped foot on the pier all hell broke loose. The joy heightened when the flashy carriages used by the imperial family all moved at the same time. Surprised at the level of enthusiasm the castle people were showing, the Emperor couldn't contain himself and signalled to his treasurer seated in the carriage before him to remunerate the people. Upon the Emperor's signal, the treasurer and his helpers scattered gold and silver coins to the rap-turous crowd.

The inventory of the Ottoman guides leading the imperial convoy and the guard cavalry following the convoy was more abundant than the Olympian guards of the Emperor and they had as shiny helmets, armours and saddled cantering horses as the Byzantine knights. Watching the carriage that was carrying Helena and their children, he murmured, "The condyles must have a specific purpose" when he saw the bones fixed in place of the dowel rod at the end of the spears which some of the Ottoman knights were carrying in their hands, and he remembered how respectful the *subaşı* of Helenopolis was to Prince Halil. Even though he found the exaggerated sense of respect the *subaşı* displayed to Prince Halil, merely a boy, laughable he thought, "Perhaps this sense of respect with which we are unfamiliar is what renders the Ottomans so successful." For a while, he went over the same thoughts. He suddenly felt sleepy either because he was overthinking or the carriage was cradling him. Even though he tried to vacantly watch his surroundings for a while he succumbed himself into the arms of sleep and delved into dreams as he laid on the back seat of the carriage. As soon as he did so, nightmares descended upon him. He was at the zenith of a mountain spurting fire from its mouth. He was wallowing on hot ashes and for some reason, those hot ashes weren't burning his feet. However, when he continued walking, he felt that the lava he was walking on was getting hotter and hotter. He was alarmed. "Soon my feet will melt away," he thought and with that thought, his toes began to melt. When the heat enveloped his feet all the way up to his ankles the scared emperor screamed, "I can be saved if I can roll down the zenith before my knees melt." But a voice from deep within him replied, "You won't be saved if you roll down but only if you throw yourself into the flames." The Emperor didn't want to believe in the voice much but when he got himself to the most suitable point he threw himself into the centre of the crater. As he dreamt himself disappear into the flames he woke up to the sound of his helmet banging against the floor of the carriage.

CHAPTER FIFTY-NINE

Suleyman Pasha was delighted that his beys were capturing castles of various sizes on the peninsula of Thrace—named after the Thracians—one after another but when he reached the magnificent Hadrianopolis Castle on the back of his galloping horse his excited heart throbbed in tune with the heavy breathing of his horse. He excitedly watched the castle for a while before noticing swordsman Sungu Alp catching up to him. He said, "This will be the largest castle we besiege on this side."

"The largest castle of the Byzantines after Constantinople."

"Just as Byzantium's vein reaching out to Anatolia was severed after the conquest of Nicomedia so shall the lifeblood that connects Byzantium to Europe once Hadrianopolis is conquered."

Sungu Alp took off his helmet and changed the sweaty kerchief under it. "May he live long, Orhan Ghazi dispatched the forces of the Umur Beylik just in time—they know this castle well."

Looking at Sungu Alp's calm face, Suleyman Pasha replied, "I hope that we will take control of the castle without the loss of many lives."

"My Bey, keeping the castle under our control is more important than taking control of it as this is where all the roads leading to the east, the west, the south and the north meet. According to Evrenos, this is the castle that has changed hands the most since Orestia[51], the first settlement of the Thracians."

Looking at Sungu Alp, conversation friend of Evrenos Bey and Hacı IlBey, Suleyman Pasha asked, "So would you say that the masons who laid the foundations of Orestia prayed 'May no castle built in this region remain under the control of a singular entity'?"

Sungu Alp replied with another question, "What other meaning could we derive from the explanations of Evrenos Bey, a wise man of this region, and the priests?"

---

51 T.N, Oresteia is the old name of current-day Edirne, a city in Turkey.

Suleyman Pasha continued, "My tutor took interest in the past of Thracian castles after the siege of Gallipoli Castle."

Sungu Alp, "The information he has found is quite useful to us My Bey. Both Hacı IlBey and I like to spend time with him when we can."

Suleyman Pasha counted the bastions between the surrounding pinnacles with still lips as he looked at them with squinting eyes and quietly said, "There are twelve bastions between two pinnacles..."

Hearing him but failing to understand him, Sungu Alp asked, "Did you say something, My Bey?"

Realising he had verbalised his thought, Suleyman Pasha felt the need to explain, "I counted the bastions between the pinnacles. They are all an equal distance from one another. I didn't think that the castle was so sheltered and large. I always imagined it the way Evrenos Bey told us about it as 'the tiny little village of Thracian people'. Now stands before us the Hadrianopolis of Roman Adrian. It's undergone significant change since its first construction and become larger. As if the height and width of the castle walls weren't enough there were also several moats around it. If God grants us the conquest of this castle, it will mean that all the land from here to the city walls of Constantinople is ours."

Sungu Alp smiled inconspicuously as if he was holding onto something he couldn't say. He adjusted his helmet a couple of times as he usually did when he was not holding his sword and said, "My Bey, don't look to the east of the castle only, as it also has a western façade. Perhaps this is where our journey to the old Roman realms will begin."

Suleyman Pasha replied, "A journey that will not be so easy..."

Sungu Alp urged him, "Yes, My Bey, our journey will not be so easy but we should take on one challenge at a time. We should concentrate on the castle before us. I am sure that tens of commanders who arrived here thought that laying siege to this castle is not an easy ordeal as they explored the castle and later, they probably reconnoitred to determine the weaker pinnacle."

This was the first time Suleyman Pasha had talked to Sungu Alp for so long except during the headquarter meetings. He thought to himself, "If he didn't think highly of his intellect, Hacı IlBey wouldn't have been such close friends with him." Diverting his gaze from Sungu Alp, he asked, "Which pinnacle do you think is our vantage point?"

After considering all the options in his mind, Sungu Alp replied, "The two pinnacles to the north are very close to one another. The moats in front of them are much narrower. If we can erect timber bridges above the moat at night and position the *yayas* and climbers by the castle walls and gates we will have a better chance."

"Yes, it might seem so at first look but they could also be concealing a trap..."

"Yes, My Bey, there must be a reason for the proximity of the bastions."

Looking at Hacı IlBey, who caught up to them with his sorrel, Suleyman Pasha asked him, "Hacı IlBey, you rode around the castle before our arrival, do you have any ideas on the siege? Almost all of the castles I have seen until now had either curved or rectangular walls. I have never seen a castle shaped like a trapezoid such as this one."

Feeling Sungu Alp's gaze on himself, Hacı IlBey unbuttoned the felt waistcoat he was wearing on top of his robe. Looking at Sungu Alp and Suleyman Pasha, he explained, "My Prince, regardless of how impenetrable it might seem, the castle besieged by our forces will fall in the end. I think we first have to determine the side where defence is weakest from a distance with our archers. Then we can bear down on that side and enter the castle. However, what I fear the most is that the castle will change hands when we leave to attend the engagement ceremony..."

"Hacı IlBey, I have not laid siege on such a big castle until now. I cannot attend the engagement ceremony of two children while the Hadrianopolis Castle awaits us. We can send our gifts for now and attend their wedding ceremony later, in person."

"But, My Prince, your father might take offence."

"My father will understand the emotions that hinder me from attending the engagement. Since Emperor Palaiologos summoned Matthew Kantakouzenos this won't be an issue. They will both be content—especially if we send Matthew Kantakouzenos along with those taking our gifts."

"But the greatest dream of the Emperor is to send us back to the coastline across the sea."

"Hacı IlBey, he can dream all he likes, we need to capture this castle... Us capturing Hadrianopolis will suit his book, as Matthew Kantakouzenos won't have anywhere to take shelter in once this castle is off his hands. This will serve the Emperor. Let's stop thinking about him and start considering how we will capture this castle. Why is the distance between those two pinnacles so short?"

Hacı IlBey responded self-assertively, "There could be two reasons. One of them is that the walls were built at different times by different people, and the other is the condition of the ground on which the pinnacles rise above. It's very hard to be certain on this before capturing the castle. Perhaps Hadrianopolis was shaped in such a peculiar way because it is where the caravans arriving from both continents met."

"Could it also be about defence?"

"It doesn't matter even if it is about defence because there weren't explosive experts when these castle walls were built."

"Regardless of why it has been built as such, this is a highly sheltered castle."

"The castle with the powerful defence is the one that is hard to take control of, not one that is sheltered, My Bey. As you know the climbers reached the top of Peristasi Castle in one breath but we seized the castle with great difficulty due to its defence."

"So how do you think we should attack?"

"My Prince, the headquarter marquee is being erected, soon our war council will gather. Our attack strategy will come to light when we receive the opinions of the beys of all our forces. Crossing these moats doesn't seem easy but our beys have captured many castles encircled with numerous moats. They'll know exactly how we can cross them."

Scanning the distance as he listened to Hacı IlBey's words, Suleyman Pasha said, "Hacı IlBey you should go and start the meeting once the marquee is ready. Sungu Alp and I will be joining you shortly."

Hacı IlBey replied, "I located some areas but it would be good if you could identify suitable places where we can set up the trebuchet. Perhaps?"

"Perhaps what?"

"Perhaps, My Prince, Matthew Kantakouzenos who has just recently returned from near Didymóteicho will begin his work before he completes his preparations and..."

Suleyman Pasha interrupted, "Is there something I should know?"

Hacı IlBey looked at Suleyman Pasha sincerely. As his faraway gaze extended beyond the wide walls of Hadrianopolis concealing the pomp of Rome and Byzantium behind them, he smilingly tried to ease Suleyman Pasha, "My Prince, life is too short for us to be able to learn everything. The castle walls which we look at now were previously viewed by the Thracian Odrysians, Achaeans who turned both sides of the Aegean upside down, trickster Persians, Macedonians irritated with the Athenians, breeze-like Galatians, Goths who considered it an art to scatter people's ashes out to the wind from above castle walls, Romans who massacred their commanders and the Catalans of Roger de Flor who entered the castle alive and left it dead and just like us, there were many things they didn't know. Even if we are similar, there is something that we have learnt..."

Suleyman Pasha patiently listened to Hacı IlBey's long-winded and seemingly never-ending explanation. Then looking at Sungu Alp, he asked, "What is it that we know, Hacı IlBey?"

Looking at Sungu Alp, who was generally not a talkative person, Hacı IlBey replied, "What we have learnt in the last few years we have spent in Thrace is that there are no longer any strong castles that can resist us."

Spurring his horse, Suleyman Pasha replied, "Hacı IlBey, we haven't entered Hadrianopolis yet... We can lay down the law once we enter it."

CHAPTER SIXTY

Byzantine Emperor John Palaiologos V arrived in Nicaea with his magnificent imperial carriage and his entourage, settling in the old palace by Lake Ascania. He told his prime minister that he would be returning a visit to Orhan Ghazi who had, with great hospitality, welcomed him and his entourage at the Constantinople gate of the castle. The prime minister immediately summoned messengers and got them to deliver the Emperor's message to Orhan Ghazi's men. Receiving the news while going over the plans for the engagement ceremony that would take place the next day in the spacious hall of Nilüfer Hatun Külliye, Orhan Ghazi exclaimed, "Certainly! If his highness the Emperor is not tired, I am heading to the Senatus now and I can wait for him there."

Waiting for Orhan Ghazi's reply Emperor Palaiologos V was sitting under the gazebo in the large courtyard of the old palace and watching the clusters of various flowers and roses. He recalled the infantile face of his daughter while looking at the rosebuds covering the wall. His sadness could be read from his face as a forcedly whispered, "She's like them" sounded out of his lips. Imagining his daughter's woeful face, he said, "Emperor's tears don't pour out, my Irene." At that moment the empress arrived next to him. Seeing that the Emperor was in a daze and hadn't noticed his bleeding finger she pointed at it and said, "John, your finger is bleeding!"

Looking at it, Emperor John Palaiologos V replied, "It happened when I wanted to hold the rosebud by that wall there."

And he pointed to the roses by the tall wall surrounding the courtyard. The empress took the Emperor's hand into hers with compassion. Casting her gaze on the floor she said, "If we prolong our daughter's engagement period she will grow up by the time she gets married. It is best if you accept that we can no longer change anything. According to the feudal landlord who is an interpreter, oil lamps have been lit in churches and mosques and preparations have been underway for the engagement ceremony for days."

"I am trying to come to terms with it but I somehow can't. In fact, I want to be happy that our daughter will get engaged in this castle that carries the name of Nicaea with whom Dionysus had fallen in love at first sight but I can't. The fact that our daughter is still only a child spreads a strange throe across my body."

After a groan-like sigh, Empress Helena replied, "John, don't forget that you were also at a very young age when we were getting married. I had only just become a young woman. Regardless of her age, our daughter will always be a little child to us. As you know there are hundreds of girls who want to marry the prince. Marrying Prince Halil will make her happy. In any case, Nicomedia commanded by Prince Halil is at the most a day's journey from Constantinople. When you miss her you can easily pay her a visit. This way my sister Theodora will also be able to protect them.

Looking at the roses by the wall the Emperor replied, "My Helena, I also want to think like that and feel at ease but it's not possible for me to influence my heart. I know there is nothing we can do."

"John, you can't imagine how much I want my brother and my father to overcome their greed and for us all to be together in Constantinople once again if it's only for once. But I know that is also impossible. Since we cannot experience this happiness with them we should at least hope that our children will be happy."

"Helena, you know that our hearts have beaten to the same rhythm and our minds have mostly thought the same for years. I hope that I can come to terms with all that you have said in time. I think it bodes well that Orhan Ghazi welcomed us at the castle gate because last year he didn't even come to see your father when he visited Antigone."

"This place could be the Antigone of Persian satraps but it's first and foremost the Nicaea of the Byzantine Empire, don't forget that John."

Emperor Palaiologos V looked at the beautiful face of Empress

Helena, who was almost twice as knowledgeable about the past than him, decorated with a slightly flat nose and bluish-green eyes. As he caressed the long and well-kept fingers of the empress with his bleeding finger he tried to change the subject, "While we are here we should pay a visit to the graves of our ancestors at this castle that served as the capital of our Empire for years. Also the grave of the empress who carried your name and took Nicaean painters under her wing and the furnaces where the red ceramics were made."

Just as Empress Helena replied, "There is no reason why we can't visit them all...", the messengers hastily entered into the courtyard from the exterior door. The prime minister stepped out of one of the rooms near the door and talked to the messengers. Then he walked towards the gazebo where the Emperor and the Empress were sitting side by side. He bowed gently, greeted them and said, "Your Majesty, Orhan Ghazi is waiting for you at the Senatus Palace."

Emperor Palaiologos V stood up at once and walked towards the interior chamber of the old palace to put on his ceremonial outfit and Empress Helena followed as she loudly said, "It would be good if you informed them that we would like to tour the castle during our visit to Orhan Bey."

The prime minister and his men loaded onto the carriages the gifts that would be given to Orhan Ghazi, the groom's father, Nilüfer Hatun, the first lady of the Beylik, Teodora, the mother of the groom, and Asporsha, the paternal aunt of the bride. At the same time, Emperor Palaiologos was putting on his ceremonial attire and walking down to the courtyard. After saying goodbye to Empress Helena he headed towards the imperial carriage waiting for him in front of the gates. The regimental bugles were heard when he left the courtyard. There seemed to be some hustle and bustle inside the castle when the bugles that sounded like the owl song of Afrasiab were heard. Almost everyone left whatever they were doing and poured out onto the streets. Those who didn't go out into the street were watching the events from windows.

As the imperial carriage drawn by eight well-groomed horses and
guarded by cavalry at the front and rear slowly wend its way down
the narrow streets of the castle, the Nicaean people were saluting
and applauding the Emperor with great joy. The Emperor momentarily felt as if he was in the streets of Constantinople when he was
greeted with such warm interest and Romaic praises. Seeing the happiness in the faces of the priests waving at him as they passed by the
Hagia Sophia chapel he thought, "They are not at all as unhappy as
the Patriarch made it out to be". He looked at the well-fed horses
that made the imperial carriage look even more majestic. As the carriage went past the Monument of Cassius, in the shape of a triangular prism with five stones placed on top of each other, he muttered,
"Was it a lie that everything was destroyed and set on fire?" He stood
up in his carriage and saluted the stalwart warriors who greeted him
by raising their spears atop the cove of the south gate of the castle.
Leaving the castle from this gate, the imperial carriage made its way
down between the gardens outside the city walls. When the walls of
the Senatus Palace by Lake Ascania appeared, the ceremony bugles
were heard to raise a cacophony. The Emperor stepped out of the
imperial carriage accompanied by the sound of bugles in front of the
entrance gate of the Senatus Palace and cast a furtive glance on the
horse carriage of Orhan Ghazi who was standing in the distance. He
murmured, "It seems so humble yet it's not any less magnificent than
ours". His eyes met those of the feudal landlord of Nicaea whose
gaze spoke volumes as the Emperor walked towards the door of the
Senatus Palace where the first and the seventh council were
gathered.

CHAPTER SIXTY-ONE

The arrows and stones thrown at the four-turreted Hadriano-polis Castle which had been under siege for days had formed heaps in the streets but those in the castle were continuing to with-stand as if it was the first day and refusing to hoist their white flag of surrender. The castle commander and Co-Emperor Matthew Kantakouzenos who were in the know about how the smaller castles in the surrounding areas were defeated had strategised a perfect sys-tem of defence. The moment a bridge would be extended over the moats filled with water the enemy would immediately be forced back with Greek fire and those who managed to escape the fire became targets to marksmen. Suleyman Pasha had lost a lot of men in the first days and changed his mind about erecting bridges on the moats. The arrow shower that began in the early hours of every morning continued into the night with fire arrows. The trebuchets that were set on fire with Greek fire in the day were being replaced by new ones that were built almost every night.

The castle commander and Co-Emperor Matthew Kantakouzenos, who had been doing a very good job of defending the castle, were aware that they were losing hope with each passing day but would not even dream of surrendering because he had nothing left other than the castle he was fighting to keep. While on the one hand, he awaited help to arrive from his brother Manuel Kantakouzenos, the Despot of Morea, as his only other hope, he was asking for the sup-port of his neighbours to the west, the Bulgarian king and Serbian Voivodships, via the envoys he sent from passages opening out to the Maritza River. Meanwhile, he was also helping the castle people who had locked themselves in their homes and whose conditions were get-ting worse by the day, as they couldn't leave their homes in fear of the arrows and stones raining down on them and the foul smell ooz-ing out of the animals that died in the stables due to hunger and thirst was fanning out into the castle. The feudal landlord, the priest and commander Matthew Kantakouzenos set up meeting after meeting in order to find a solution to this problem and in the end decided on the idea of demolishing the joining walls of terraced houses in order to allow access from one house to the other. Work had immediately begun on the night the decision was made. Some of the people who were imprisoned in their homes moved to the church and some others to the spacious underground battlements through these gateways. As the stray livestock was butchered and the flesh stowed in cool cellars the rotting animal carcasses were also piled and burnt. This boosted up the castle peoples' morale to some extent. However, when the Ottoman explosive experts found out that there was no shortage of water in the castle despite the fact that the water supply to the castle had been cut for days, those in the castle began to experience water shortage because the Ottomans dug around the castle and discovered numerous tunnels leading to the river. Seeing that the water levels in the cisterns had decreased considerably, Co-Emperor Matthew Kantakouzenos felt as if he had fallen into an abyss. He first banned people to wash and then gathered all the sick into one place and put them all to the sword so that the healthy could live longer. The priest of Hadrianopolis, the most respected priest in the Balkans after the priest of the Hagia Sophia, rose up against Matthew Kantakouzenos and yelled, "The sin you are committing is unforgivable in heaven!"

The feudal landlord of the castle intervened to separate the priest and Matthew Kantakouzenos. The priest found it hard to contain himself, "Hoist up the white flag at once!"

Matthew Kantakouzenos insisted, "The Bulgarians and the Serbians won't leave us alone. You'll see, the Ottomans will be caught in a cross-fire in just a few days."

The priest softened when he heard that help was on its way. He told him that he would wait patiently for a few more days and headed to the church. However, days passed by and neither a message nor any help came from the Bulgarians or the Serbians. Concerned about the situation, Matthew Kantakouzenos started a rumour that the forces sent by his brother Manuel Kantakouzenos, the Despot of Morea, would reach their castle soon in order to get the castle people to help themselves.

The castle commander and Co-Emperor Matthew Kantakouzenos did not lose hope for days. One evening, just as they retreated to their chambers in the stone building where the doors to the tunnels leading to the river, after wandering on top of the castle walls and bolstering the morale of the guards, Suleyman Pasha received news that the Roman-made ninth gate of Hadrianopolis had been opened. The climbers immediately stepped into action upon the orders of Suleyman Pasha and Hacı IlBey to check whether it was a trap. A few volunteers quickly advanced down the stone path leading to the ninth gate with extension ladders in their hands and extended the three ladders across the three canals. The *serdengeçtis* and *delis* ran over the extended ladders as if there wasn't a moment to lose and in leaps and bounds arrived by the pointed stakes, the final barrier to reaching the ninth gate. The *yayas* who were waiting for them to reach it after squeezing in between the pointed stakes ran across the ladder bridges as soon as they heard the first owl hoot and pounded against the ninth gate. They put back the wooden bridges that had been removed from the canals by Matthew Kantakouzenos and took the stakes off of the gate. Suleyman Pasha and Hacı IlBey rode their horses towards the ninth gate once the bridges leading to it had been erected and the *yayas* began entering the castle.

The sky was bright but the moonlight that dispersed from a genteel crescent was not enough to light up all the darkness of the earth. Hence the reason why the guards in the other turrets had seen neither the ninth gate being opened nor the quietly erected wooden

bridges of the *dalkılıç*[52], the *serdengeçtis*, the *akıncı delis* or the *yayas*.
In any case, exhausted from the siege days, most of them were sleeping at their posts. Those doing the rounds had retreated to the
guards' burrows in the turrets after midnight as they thought that
the canals brimming with water, which could not be traversed during
the day would not be at night. The quietly advancing *serdengeçtis*
took advantage of their carelessness and besieged the castle in a
short period of time. When the *dalkılıç* and the *delis* came to know
that the *serdengeçtis* had surrounded the guards' turrets they began
to clear the arches above the gates. The *yayas* separated into groups
and advanced into the streets but making way was difficult as most
of the narrow streets were blocked with the stones that had been
thrown.

As those inside the castle were experiencing the last moments of
deep morning sleep, those outside the castle had opened the eight
gates outside the north gate and set up all the extending bridges in
front of the gates above the canals. Not a single Byzantine guard remained on top of the castle walls or the turrets lit up by the first rays
of sun. Only the guards' unit holding down large stone buildings on
either side of the north gate of the castle had not surrendered. As armoured guards were guarding both doors of the stone buildings, the
yayas who managed to get inside were being turned into mincemeat
and thrown back onto their comrades. Hacı IlBey arrived by the gate
just as the *yayas* who watched their fellows being injured were about
to lose their courage. He recoiled when he saw the corpses with
severed arms and legs. He first thought of getting his men to throw
hot embers inside but he changed his mind at once and immediately
commanded the explosive experts to make a hole in the roof. There
was a great calamity when the explosive experts made a hole in the
roof and threw in bundles of flaming dry weed and fresh thicket
which caused a great deal of smoke. The clashing of metal was heard

---

52 T.N, *Dalkılıç* were soldiers who enlisted in the Ottoman army to dive right into
the enemy with a bare sword.

for a while and later, all was buried in silence. Hacı IlBey got his soldiers to strip the few guards who made it out of the castle alive of
their armour and allowed the *yayas* to slaughter them just as they
had done to their comrades.

Waiting for the heavy smoke to disperse from the stone buildings
with connecting chambers, Hacı IlBey and his *yayas* were surprised
when they entered the castle. They thought they would encounter
suffocated guards lying on top of one another but there was no one
in sight. Dumbfounded that there was no one in the building from
where such noise emerged shortly before Hacı IlBey cautioned the
yayabaşıs to look at the walls carefully. Just then he saw that the
building was adjacent to the castle and the battlement hatchways
opening into the castle. Realising that the tightly shut hatchways
that were locked from the inside would be a challenge to open he
summoned the battering rams.

Just as Hacı IlBey endeavoured to get the hatchways open Suleyman Pasha and Evrenos Bey had dismounted their horses in the
church square and were looking at the *yayas* searching the houses
that opened out into the narrowest of streets. Unable to catch sight
of anyone, Evrenos Bey turned back, looked towards the door of the
church and said, "My Bey, let's take a look inside, perhaps they took
shelter there."

Evrenos Bey entered through the half-open door easily but when he
wanted to push open the second door leading to the body of the
church, he couldn't open it. He pulled back and gave way to the *serdengeçtis.* They also attempted to open the door but the door did not
open. Looking at Suleyman Pasha, Evrenos Bey told the *serdengeçtis*
to step aside and slowly approached the door. He leaned on the door
and whispered in Romaic, "Can you please open the door? If you
don't open it, we will have to break it down."

He waited a little while. Not a single sound was heard. This time he
banged on the door a few times with the hilt of his sword and waited

a little more. Then, in a higher tone, he said, "Saintly father, Matthew Kantakouzenos has abandoned Hadrianopolis. You are under the protection of Ottoman Bey Orhan Ghazi as of this moment. If you open the door not even a single hair on you will be harmed."

First indecipherable noises and then intelligible ones were heard. A terrible smell spread out when the heavy walnut door was opened with a massive creak. They all walked back out of the door and left the church. Knowing full well the reason why they walked out in a rush the grey-bearded priest said, "We have been with the dead for days, my sons. This is the reason of the foul smell."

CHAPTER SIXTY-TWO

Orhan Ghazi was standing beside a rose bush in the court-yard of Suleyman Pasha Külliye, a complex commissioned by his son Suleyman Pasha and still in its stages of construction, and looking at the purplish roses situated between the pink and red ones. After performing his prayer at the house of prayer—something between a masjid and a mosque—for some reason he didn't feel like going to the new mansion reserved for his harem. As he looked at the roses and thinking, "I wish I could have breakfast here looking at the roses" he felt a swelling pain on his waist slowly taking over his body. He was worried. With the aim of dismissing the worry that was try-ing to settle in his mind, he murmured, "My Suleyman planted these roses the day the foundations were laid." And as he scratched his wide forehead, the wrinkles on which deepened ever more with pain, with his fingertips he said, "Not long has passed since then, I wonder why this rose bush looks so old." The pain spreading from his waist increased. His thoughts scattered due to the increasing pain and he momentarily lost track of his line of thought but as soon as the pain alleviated, the flow of thought returned.

After exhaling the breath from his lungs through his puffed up cheeks he changed his course and walked towards the low wall between the courtyard and the garden. When the breeze created by his caftan moved the flowers on the grass it looked as if the flowers were walking behind him. Sitting on the low wall he recalled Nilüfer Hatun saying, "I miss my sons, I wish they could all be here" during the previous evening. As his gaze wandered across the colourful flowers scattered on the grass of the courtyard he said, "I miss them, too". Remembering the engagement gifts sent by Suleyman Pasha he continued his spiel, "My Suleyman hasn't come. He must be trying to get organised in Hadrianopolis if he has captured it. It's nothing like the smaller castles. I know it well from Nicomedia, how exciting it is to capture a large castle. Like taking a large bite from an apple, the more you eat the wider you open your mouth. But one must not fall prey to the magnificence of the grand and forget about the grander..." As the journey that was taking in his mind deepened so did his unrest and worry for a reason unbeknown to him. He stood up with agility that would not be expected of someone his age so that his worry wouldn't turn into lethargy and turned his face to the northeastern mountains which he called Yellidağ and the locals called Arganthone. After unbuttoning his caftan, he said, "Ye Yellidağ! See how I worry! Send me your healing breezes so that my chest can cool." Taking deep breaths, for a while he couldn't believe that these words dipped in emotion had departed from his lips. As he chuckled at the thoughts that carried him away he mumbled, "My tongue is a part of my body, why shouldn't it say strange things now and then?"

Yellidağ sent him breezes caressed and cooled by the face of Sangarius[53], in which Nicaea bathed to cool down once upon a time, as if it had heard Orhan Ghazi's wish. After cooling his chest with the fresh breeze, Orhan Ghazi buttoned up his caftan and as he did so saw that the red sun slowly swallowing the blue sky reared its head behind Yellidağ. He heard a messenger's bugle from the northern side of the castle as he smiled in the realisation that the secret to how the dark green forest on the hillside turned to a purplish yellow every morning and evening like the leaves of cyclamen was a trick that the sun and the forest played on the eyes. He set out once again on a journey to the sea of thoughts in his mind awakened by the high-pitched sound of the bugle. He thought of who he was waiting for. Tilting his head down he murmured, "It could be İsfendiyaroğlu Beys, Germiyanid Beys or one of our beys from Bursa". Remembering that there were sufficient mansions and marquees prepared for all the guests who were due to arrive, he calmly watched the morning

---

53 T.N, *Sangarius* is the present-day Sakarya River.

sun sheer off the bosom of great Yellidağ and rise. He was just about to stride towards the old mansion prepared for himself and his harem when the bugles heralding the arrival of guests at the Constantinople gate of the castle were heard. When the bugles quietened down, the bugles heralding the arrival of guests at the Lefka gate to the east of the castle were heard. This was followed by a high-pitched bugle signalling the arrival of a caravan at the same gate.

Right after the sun was freed from the bosom of Yellidağ and had risen an incredible sprightliness took over the castle. Just as Orhan Ghazi changed his mind about heading to the mansion due to his curiosity about the arriving guests and began waiting for announcements, Empress Helena, wife of Byzantine Emperor Palaiologos V, who was a guest at the old palace, jumped out of her bed unable to make much sense of the bugles and looked out of the window. Unable to see anything on the street, she had run to quieten Manuel, her son, who woke up because of the bugles and was crying. She was wearing her light yellow nightgown made of silk from Morea, embroidered with Turkmen motifs on the chest and gifted to her by Holofira Hatun. Seeing her enter the chamber, the dry nurse moved aside, "My empress, the prince does not awake at this hour. He must have been scared by the sound of the bugles."

In response to the soft tone of the dry nurse, Empress Helena said, "They also scared me, Maria."

She kneeled down next to the Turkmen cradle commissioned by Asporsha of Byzantium, wife of Orhan Ghazi, as a present for her son. When she took his tiny hand into hers and caressed it the boy felt safe and quietened down. He began to smile ebulliently. As the dry nurse left the son and mother in the room, she realised that the Emperor was nearby as she could hear him coughing. Waking up to the sound of the bugles, the Emperor noticed that the empress was not in bed and had gone to look for her. Seeing the dry nurse exit his son's chamber, Emperor Palaiologos V asked, "Maria, where is

Helena?"

Maria Minosaia had been a servant in the imperial mansions for as long as she could remember and was given the duty of looking after her son's children by Empress Anna because she was the most trustworthy servant. As a result of this connection, she had become a part of the imperial family. She enjoyed a privileged position because she had a vast knowledge of the empire and could find joy even in the hardest moments. However, what really set her apart was that she was as well informed about children as a paediatrician. She had an immaculate sense of smell. She fulfilled her position as a nursemaid fondly and also volunteered as the chief taster of the Emperor. Instead of providing a verbal reply to the Emperor, she pointed to the nursery with her hand. As Emperor John Palaiologos walked towards the nursery, she walked towards the kitchen where breakfast was being prepared.

As the Emperor and the empress took their little son and headed towards their own bed-chamber, bugles could be heard from near the Senatus Palace opposite the old palace where they were staying. The Emperor looked at the street that could be viewed from the window of the mansion that was referred to as the old palace and which he knew was the largest mansion in existence at the time. The roads between the little Hagia Sophia church with its bell tower already in sight despite the newly rising sun and Uzbek Mosque with its minarets were alive with people. There were also drummers marching towards the Lefka gate. The drummers suddenly paused while beating their drums and continued marching and keeping beat after exchanging words with one another. As the Emperor took his little son into his arms from the embrace of the empress beside him, he said, "Let's get ready and go down to have breakfast."

Empress Helena replied, "Yes, we barely have enough time to get ready."

As they prepared to have breakfast, the multitude of the guests arriving one after another put Orhan Ghazi and his men in a flurry. However, when they realised that most of those who had arrived were from their own Beyliks, they breathed a sigh of relief as a majority of them had come with their own tents and all they needed was to be shown where to set themselves up. The envoys of beys who had come a long way were attentively settled in the mansions. The envoy that enjoyed the most care and attention was the one sent by the *Karamanids*. Nevertheless, the breakfast trays of the guests staying at the old palace had not been forgotten about in all of this racket. On such days of celebration, the daily fare of all guests from breakfast to supper was covered by Orhan Ghazi. No one knew when this custom was adopted but it had long been a tradition of the Ottomans. The Emperor was amazed when the breakfast tray arrived at the old palace. After ordering for the breakfast prepared by his own cooks to be sent to Orhan Ghazi's table, he beckoned chief taster Maria Minosaia to taste the food sent by Orhan Ghazi. There were so many varieties of food on the round metal tray that chief taster Maria Minosaia was full after eating only one bite of each dish. As the Emperor and the empress sat down for breakfast, Orhan Ghazi was also having his breakfast around a large metal tray with Nilüfer Hatun who he addressed as "the divine light in my eyes", his son Murad—who had just arrived from the guard post on the day before —Ibrahim, Kasım and his youngest son Halil who he referred to as "the little man". Asporsha, Theodora and her daughters were gathered around the metal tray next to them. Needless to say, this was a togetherness they had all yearned for. Experiencing the happiness of having his entire family united except for Suleyman Pasha but also feeling the perpetual ferment of not having his oldest son present, Orhan Ghazi said, "Those outside are just as much family as those gathered around this tray." He stiffened the previous smile on his lips and continued eating his breakfast. He tried hard to avert his gaze from Nilüfer Hatun whose true happiness could be read in her eyes. He knew that the little authoritarian sternness he had in his heart would dissolve if he looked at her soft and emotional eyes. Trying to concentrate on his breakfast and struggling against his emotions he said, "This is the stuff of Beyliks and beys". He then dismissed all thoughts and had his breakfast. Once breakfast ended he revisited the garden of Suleyman Pasha Külliye. After idling around for a while, he walked to the square by the Lefka gate where fair and entertainment tents had been set up. All of the guests staying at the castle were watching the shows in high spirits. It was in these tents and open spaces that conjurers, acrobats, tamers, horse-back performers and entertainers were bringing the house down with all their buffoonery.

CHAPTER SIXTY-THREE

Suleyman Pasha was mesmerised when he turned his face to the setting sun after looking at the graze on his horse's chest. His head was askance, seeming larger than it was due to his long hair falling on his broad shoulders. Without averting his gaze from the rotund ball of purple fire he murmured, "How come you set so beautifully in all corners of Thrace, ye old Sun!" Just then, when he was buried in silence, he heard a hearty sound from the depths of the world. It wasn't certain whether the sound was trying to tell him something or simply scare him away but its requiem-like timbre was bringing a lump to his throat and making his hair stand on end. At one point he thought that it was coming from the graze on his horse's wide chest and approached his horse again. He put his ear on the graze and listened hard but heard nothing. When he stood straight again he looked at the branches of the surrounding trees slowly swaying in the evening breeze and the verdant fields on the hillside across from him. Viewing the closed and tall sunflowers, he exclaimed, "It's not coming from the horse's chest, the trees, the sunflowers! There is no one in the fields!" For a while he tried to figure out the source of the sound but before he could come to a decision the repeating sound spontaneously slowed down and died off after a while. When it was all quiet again he looked at the tortoises—one young, the other old—which came out from the grass around a nearby tree and walked towards the fields before the sunset. A common raven hastily perched on the branch of one of the trees beside him and cawing at the tortoises drew his attention. "You are calling your friends to help you because you know you are not strong enough to lift them. Meanwhile, you want me to leave so that you can get your claws on the smaller tortoise. But even if I leave, it's not a hatchling you can have. Even if you manage to lift it, it won't break like the cubs of other animals. It has a shell of scutes so that you cannot get into it. Your hard and pointy beak won't help you this time," he said, and as he looked at the blue sky, he continued with sorrow, "As long as the hatchling doesn't fall on its back." The raven flew away as if it understood what he was saying and Suleyman Pasha watched it depart. He saw that black clouds were fast approaching the castle to the north. Smiling, Suleyman Pasha murmured, "Wherever and whenever he sees a black cumulus, Hacı IlBey calls it a rain cloud." He felt like waving at the raven and the clouds. Chuckling to himself, he mounted his Grey with one swift move and spurred him. He commanded, "Let's get to Hadrianopolis before the clouds!"

The Grey had just approached the north gate of the castle, after depleting the distance as if it had crossed a few hills in three gallops, when Suleyman Pasha saw the crowds coming out of the gates. It seemed like they had been kicked out. Almost all of them were on horseback. Looking at them Suleyman Pasha muttered, "All of the horses in the castle were confiscated after what happened, I wonder where they got these horses. The secrets of this castle never seem to cease. Doors that open from one house to the other, the hidden passages between the turrets, the underground tunnels that connect battlements to one another..." He suddenly caught sight of the riding knights following the group that left the castle on a gallop. He steered his horse in their direction. The chief cavalryman who saw him approaching them rode his horse towards Suleyman Pasha. Recognising Aktimuroğlu Bey, the Bey of the Bâciyân-ı Rum units of Evrenos Pasha, "What's the matter Aktimuroğlu? Where are you headed?"

Aktimuroğlu, the *akıncı* Bey of the *Bâcıyân-ı Rum* unit, replied, "My Prince, we're no longer of any use in Hadrianopolis. We have Evrenos Bey's permission. We are headed to Didymóteicho."

Suleyman Pasha, "Are you the only ones leaving?"

Aktimuroğlu, "No, My Prince. The *Âhiyân-ı Rum, Gâziyân-ı Rum* and *Abdalân-ı Rum* are also leaving soon. We are the vanguard so we are going to determine the billet."

After a brief pause, Prince Suleyman Pasha asked, "Is Evrenos Bey also setting out today?"

Aktimuroğlu paused to think a little in order to provide accurate information and replied, "Evrenos Bey will be setting out with the new *yayas* that are due to arrive in a few days."

Suleyman Pasha replied, "Ghazis, may God speed you, may your horses be swift and your booty plenty."

After saluting them with a nod of his head, he gently spurred his horse on the flank. When the Grey arrived at the castle gate Suleyman Pasha turned around and watched the *Âhiyân-ı Rum* ride into the distance. Seeing that they were quite far from the castle he asked, "Tell me Grey, when will we blend into the horizon like them?"

CHAPTER SIXTY-FOUR

Both Orhan Ghazi—who arrived at the Nilüfer Hatun Külliye where the engagement ceremony was going to take place, after getting changed at the new palace reserved for him and his family following his visit to the street fair—and Byzantine Emperor Palaiologos V were dressed in their most exuberant attires. As they both passed through the entrance gate and quietly walked in the courtyard towards the building, they were praying for the realisation of all that they had talked about at Senatus Palace the day before. They were treating each other with as much kindness as they could so that nothing unfavourable could cause the magic of this beautiful moment to be ruined. Walking a few steps behind Orhan Ghazi and Emperor Palaiologos V, Empress Helena and Lady Theodora were holding hands as if to defy all rules. Nilüfer Hatun was happy to see them hold hands with such sisterly love. Looking at them in admiration, she muttered, "If only everyone could experience the happiness of motherhood and sisterhood like them." As she looked ahead she spontaneously took a trip down memory lane. She felt the resentment of not being able to experience such a sense of love with her own siblings. In order to dismiss that feeling she muttered in a tone of voice only she could hear, "I couldn't experience such love to my heart's content but I am a bit like Holofira and a bit like Nilüfer." Wanting to suppress the swelling yearning for her sisters, she added, "Furthermore I am both Theodora and the others. And that's enough for me". But that resentment fueled by sisterly yearning did not let her go. As she walked with that feeling rooted deep within she looked at the külliye named after her. As she smiled bitterly she muttered, "My name will be recalled in these lands just like Aphrodite and Nicaea who wandered these places." The resentment that enveloped her, dissipated when this last sentence warmed her heart. She thought of turning around with a crazy desire and embracing the

sisters holding hands. Just as she was about to turn towards them
and open her arms she saw Orhan Ghazi walking beside the Emperor, beckoning her to come closer. As she walked faster and approached him she saw that Orhan Ghazi—featuring a round nose
that complimented his wide face—was alternating between smiling
and laughing. She was a little surprised, as she knew that when he
had such an expression on his face, it was usually because he was
thinking of a joke. She thought, "He won't joke with the Emperor,
will he?" Sensing the change of speed in her stride, Orhan Ghazi
said, "My Nilüfer, tell our child's father-in-law that despite the fact
that we are both sovereigns, there is another sovereign who doesn't
leave us alone.

Despite the fact that she didn't understand much of what she had
been told she interpreted what he had said to Emperor Palaiologos
V who was curiously waiting, word for word. Possessing a quick
mind, Byzantine Emperor Palaiologos V first looked at Orhan Ghazi
with curiosity and then turned to Theodora, his sister-in-law and his
wife Helena and said, "They have stopped being Kantakouzenos
since the day they knocked on the Ottomans doors and arrived in the
mansion of the Palaiologos."

Hearing the interpretation of this sentence, Orhan Ghazi looked at
Emperor Palaiologos V shrewdly and thought, "He is young but not
at all naïve". After taking a break for a while he continued, "Oh my
Nilüfer! You didn't really understand what I said but he did. In any
case, I couldn't have expected a different response from him. However, although they are our wives they are still the daughters of our
father-in-law, the great Kantakouzenos. That is why his sovereignty
will always exist in our households."

Listening to Nilüfer Hatun's interpretation, Emperor Palaiologos
V thanked Orhan Ghazi, who acknowledging his quick mind, replied,
"The great Kantakouzenos certainly played a great role in my educa-
tion and the continuation of my life. I always acknowledge the sover-

eignty of Helena's father but he has made a lot of mistakes in recent years. Appointing his son as Co-Emperor was his greatest mistake."

Lending his ear to Nilüfer Hatun's interpretation with admiration and patience, Orhan Ghazi replied, "I agree with the Emperor. A heavy stone is not easily moved."

When Nilüfer Hatun stood up straight with her beautiful body, which was showing the first signs of age, and continued to carefully interpret every word that left Orhan Ghazi's lips, Emperor Palaiologos V said, "Orhan Ghazi is right, Matthew is not cut out for the imperial crown."

Hearing this interpretation, Orhan Ghazi looked as if he was surprised as to how quickly the young emperor understood what he had said and caressed his white beard with his meaty fingers. Looking at the young emperor he said, "Byzantium would have perhaps not even witnessed the fights between siblings had your great grandfathers sustained the friendship between Kaykhusraw[54] I and Laskaris[55] before taking shelter in Nicaea because they were too scared of the enormity of the Romans. Thus, the Kantakouzenos wouldn't have pursued an old dream."

When he fell silent he seemed as if he regretted what he had said. As he harkened to Nilüfer Hatun's interpretation he thought, "A peaceful Byzantium wouldn't have suited our book". He looked at Korkut Tekin Alp standing by the door. Korkut Tekin Alp knew the meaning of his gaze well. Approaching him, he said, "My Bey, we will start the ceremony as soon as you take your place."

As Emperor Palaiologos V considered how he should interpret what Nilüfer Hatun said, Orhan Ghazi walked towards and entered through the main door. Emperor Palaiologos followed suit without giving much thought to it. However, as he walked he was trying to

---

54 T.N, *Kaykhusraw I* was the eleventh and youngest son of Kilij Arslan II, was Seljuk Sultan of Rûm.
55 T.N, *Laskaris* was a Byzantine Greek noble family whose members formed the ruling dynasty of the Empire of Nicaea from 1204 to 1261 and remained among the senior nobility up to the dissolution of the Byzantine Empire.

muster the most suitable response he could provide to dismiss rumours. Once he walked through the dipterous inner door held open by nonvisible servants he felt mesmerised by the walls of the hall decorated with predominantly Nicaean red glazed tiles. Seeing how amazed he was by the glazed tiles, Nilüfer Hatun said, "Your Majesty, the glazed tiles of this building erected in my name were baked in the kilns of Nicaea and installed on these walls by the master tilers of Nicaea."

The Emperor suddenly began to sweat as if he had experienced a rude awakening. The reason for his flash of sweat was the quick succession of the idea that he had still not built anything for his Helena who had given him three beautiful children. After taking a few steps towards the centre of the külliye hall, lit up by the sizable colourful oil lamps situated in the corners, he first turned his gaze to Empress Helena and then to little Irene and Prince Halil sitting behind the partition separated from the rest by a tulle curtain. Irene seemed to be playing a game while Prince Halil was sitting idly in boredom. The groom was accompanied by a young man, who seemed a few years older than him, and the bride was next to a lady dressed like Lady Theodora. He was curious as to who they were. His eyes searched for Nilüfer Hatun so he could ask her. However, as Nilüfer Hatun was experiencing the joy of hearing many historical subjects— previously taught to her by Byzantine historians when she was the daughter of a feudal landlord from Orhan Ghazi and the fervour of the superiority bestowed unto her by her mother tongue which had been of no use until now—she didn't even see that the Emperor was looking at her. Just when she started walking towards him, upon realising why Palaiologos V was looking for her, Orhan Ghazi had taken his seat on one of the thrones prepared for him and the Emperor and was inviting Palaiologos to do the same. She realised that it was now her and the Empress's turn to take their seats. She took a seat behind Orhan Ghazi and the Emperor, with Empress Helena on one side and Lady Theodora on the other. Orhan Ghazi's *Alps*, beys and those accompanying the Emperor all took their places after them. As the Emperor glanced at Orhan Ghazi's beys who were standing up he thought, "Even though the friendship between Kaykhusraw I and my great grandfather Theodore Laskaris seems to have been initiated at the right time the friendship between the Turkmens and the Akritai of Byzantium had begun long before. If only that friendship could have been rendered continuous with the Persians. Then perhaps there wouldn't have been any need for the Battle of Manzikert. He gently turned back and glanced at Empress Helena and Lady Theodora. He turned to the other side and looked at her daughter behind the fine tulle curtain. He felt as if his gaze was falling before him. He became disheartened. He only had the courage to briefly look at his mesazōn who was standing across from him with his men. After that, he just looked downwards. He was about to delve into deep valleys of thought within himself when Orhan Ghazi said, "Do not worry Your Illustrious Highness. The friendship initiated by the Turkmen ghazis at the Persian border and the Byzantine Akritai will be immortalised with this engagement."

Realising that the Emperor who was listening to him keenly hadn't understood a word of what he had said, Orhan Ghazi smiled at him reassuringly and summoned Korkut Tekin Alp with a thunderous voice. Upon Korkut Tekin Alp's arrival by his side he said, "Korkut, commence the ceremony."

Upon Korkut Tekin Alp's return, the sound of earth-shaking drums emerged from the main gate. When the drums quietened, the envoys of neighbouring beys began to enter the castle one by one, according to the distance they had covered to get there, accompanied by concubines carrying trays of gifts.

Once the envoys presented their engagement gifts the Ottoman beys took over. Kara Hasanoğlu, margrave of Hacı IlBey, was the first to present Orhan Ghazi's oldest son Suleyman Pasha and his beys' gifts. As the servants left the tent after placing the gifts in the gilded walnut chest in their allocated place, Kara Hasanoğlu took his place behind Prince Murad seated to the right of Orhan Ghazi. Then, Lala Şahin Bey presented the gifts of Prince Murad in a magnificently carved chest made by the renowned masters of Gerede. As the servants left with it, Lala Şahin sulkily took his place next to Kara Hasanoğlu. After the Beys' and Beyliks' gifts were presented in order of status during the presentation of Byzantine Emperor Palaiologos V, it was announced that many Byzantine castle commanders and despots had sent their gifts to Nicomedia. That day Orhan Ghazi's gifts were presented last as a matter of courtesy. Afterwards, Orhan Ghazi expressed his gratitude to the Emperor and the envoys at length and, turning to his son Halil, said, "Halil Bey will continue his role as the Bey of Nicomedia Castle. We hope to organise his wedding at Nicomedia."

The ceremony came to a close with Emperor Palaiologos V's brief speech that followed Orhan Ghazi's. Empress Helena—enthralling everyone with her beauty as well as intelligence—held Nilüfer Hatun's hands tightly when it was time to leave the ceremony and asked, "My Irene, named after my mother, is still only a child. Can I entrust her to you rather than to my sister Theodora after the wedding?"

Nilüfer Hatun's eyes brimmed with tears. Wiping away Empress Helena's tears with her motherly and warm hands she softly replied, "My empress, no one has ever witnessed princesses to be children."

CHAPTER SIXTY-FIVE

It momentarily seemed as if the clusters of neighbourhoods scattered on the small hills surrounding the Hadrianopolis Castle encircled by tiers of channels formed of tall, insurmountable walls were smiling at Suleyman Pasha who was viewing them from the Macedonia Tower. As he tried to smile at them he muttered, "Each and every one of them is like a different footprint." He turned his head to the south and said, "the Odrysians". He turned to the west and muttered, "the Macedonians." Looking up towards the north he said, "The Romans." As he made a move to stand up he said, "I suppose my tutor's love of history seems to be contagious." He headed towards the former mansion of Matthew Kantakouzenos, transformed into military headquarters by Hacı IlBey. As he walked, he recalled that the castle was still only theirs during the day time and others' at night.

When he arrived at the military headquarters he had just come to the end of a long train of thought, "We easily entered the castle through the Gate of Rome with the help of the priest's men. Both the priest and the people helped us. Together we took out those who were opposing us in the inner part of the fortress. We let those who wanted to leave, leave, helping those arriving to settle in their new homes. We must have been wrong to allow the forward units to leave the castle by thinking that everything was fine when the *subaşı*, the *kadî*, the feudal landlord and the priest all began to work together. The men who had been hiding for days and observing them took advantage of their departure and attacked us. We forced them back but our misjudgement cost the lives of hundreds of warriors. Since that day it feels to me as if the castle belongs to us during the days and to others at night." Looking at the mansion he muttered, "They must be led by Matthew Kantakouzenos." Hacı IlBey, who had gone to inspect the work of exploring the battlements, arrived in front of the

mansion. He immediately said, "My Bey, we have located a few battlement hatches. The *serdengeçtis* have climbed down and explored
the tunnels but they didn't come across anyone. However, according
to the information they provided there are passages that connect the
tunnels. This has made our work a lot easier. If we start fires at the
mouth of the battlements we located and smoked out the tunnels, we
can locate the tunnel exits and force that ominous Matthew to leave
his lair."

Suleyman Pasha had relaxed a good deal with Hacı IlBey's news
and ordered the *yayabaşıs* near him to start work immediately. As
the explosive experts removed the stones in front of the located battlement hatches, the *yayas* took precautions against any possible attack. As they prepared in the inner part of the fortress, the cavalry
units outside the castle spread out into the field and took measures
to prevent the Byzantine guards from escaping through the tunnel
exits once the fire was started.

By the time the explosive experts had completed their preparations
and lit up the wood fire smothered with plenty of oil, Suleyman
Pasha had climbed up the Byzantine Tower—the tallest tower in the
fortress—with Hacı IlBey. He had been informed that the fires had
been lit in all four battlement openings and was intently watching
the events that would take place. They waited for a long time and
failed to see any rising smoke, looking at each other hopelessly. Hacı
IlBey caught sight of the gradually increasing worry in Suleyman
Pasha's gaze and tried to assuage him, "Do not worry, My Prince.
Smoke will soon find its path. Matthew is clever and perhaps he has
blocked the passages with walls. But no matter what he has done
smoke will find its way and rise up to the sky. Neither he nor his men
can endure being underground much longer."

Just as beautiful Antiope of Plajar was about to appear in Suleyman Pasha's mind as he listened to Hacı IlBey's confident talk,
smoke began to come out from the tunnel exits on all four sides of

the castle. As the cavalry formed circles around the tunnel exits and waited for those inside to come out, Suleyman Pasha began to laugh as he looked at Hacı IlBey. Hacı IlBey joined him with laughter and said, "We are creatures with the flimsiest lungs against smoke, My Prince. Watch and see how Matthew's men will crawl out of there one by one."

Hacı IlBey had not yet finished talking when his last sentence became reality. The guards of Hadrianopolis hiding underground began to exit the tunnel one after another and the cavalry started to catch them. The chase lasted until the mid-afternoon. Watching them from the tower, Suleyman Pasha climbed down from there and walked down the narrow streets paved with stones, arriving at his mansion located next to the church and reserved for his harem. Dressed in his princely attire, he retired to his spacious room at the mansion. Noticing the change inside the room, he carefully inspected the walls. He muttered, "Antiope has been busy at work again." He caressed the velvet side of the thick woollen cushion with his fingertips and viewed the deer with antlers embroidered in all shades of brown onto the red Tbilisi tapestry hanging on the wall opposite. After inspecting the deer from its hooves to its antlers and vice versa a few times he said, "It's aged". This thought was followed by his memory of his Beys and *levends* crossing to Tzympe with fishermen's caïques and rafts. Turning his eyes from the deer he hummed, "Almost none of those Beys are alive now." He recalled his uncle Alaeddin Pasha who loved him very much when he was a little boy. When Prince Suleyman Pasha thought of him, Pasha, who didn't much care for tender-minded combat fields, he recalled his brother Kasım, who had died very young for some reason he couldn't make sense of. When such unwarranted recollections followed one after another he became stressed. When he forced himself to relax he remembered his *levends* who got injured during combat. He mumbled, "They were saved from being weary of life by being deployed in the garrison of

the *yayas* of my late uncle." Those who lost their lives and those who
became disabled did not know what a gentle soul he had because he
never shared his feelings. Neither did he want them to know. His
gaze coursed over the deer with antlers once again and became fixed
on the raven-black bird-figure embroidered on the Mamluk rug. He
muttered, "It must a blessing of the Ottomans that my uncle Alaeddin never really liked combat." He continued looking at the bird figure without batting his eyes for a while and grumbled, "The Çandarlı
family is also due some recognition." He knew that he was canon-
ising his uncle but it wasn't in his hands. Wherever he found himself
alone he seemed to hear his uncles voice that said, "Be the salve of
all those broken-hearted with whom you cross paths." He felt at ease
when he heard his uncle's voice in his head as he looked at the
raven-black bird on the Mamluk rug. He loudly said, "I need this." As
he stood up he thought, "I hope that the Kantakouzenos are among
those who have been detained. If he has been caught I no longer
need to stay here. Hacı IlBey can take care of the remaining work
while I head to Plajar to prepare for the great campaign." He left the
room looking at the crested bird motif on the small Gerede tapestry
hanging beside the door. His heart rejoiced as it did every time he decided to set out campaigning. He went to the Roman fountain featuring a central basin with constant flowing water and performed his
ablution. He arrived at the small building nearby that was used as a
masjid. He turned to Hacı IlBey, who had arrived before him and
was waiting for the prayer time, and said, "I miss my mother dearly."

Even he was surprised at the sentence that departed from his lips.
Smiling back at him Hacı IlBey replied, "My Bey, you can spend the
winter in Bursa again if we complete the preparations for the campaign in good time. We have moved our harem to this side and have
no thought of crossing to the other side. I suppose we have enough to
do in Hadrianopolis. Evrenos Bey has Didymóteicho in his sights.
Fazıl Bey and Akça Kocaoğlu are planning to overwinter on the

coastline of the Black Sea. If we can get rid of Matthew Kantakouzenos there won't be much danger left in these lands."

Suleyman Pasha was disgruntled, "It seems you have all decided where you will spend the winter long before its arrival. I suppose I should leave, too. I will go to Bursa but won't remain there for the entire winter. I will return quickly."

"We can ready a mansion suitable for your harem until your return. The mansion of the former feudal landlord is beautiful but it is not fit to serve your harem."

"You are right, we hardly have enough space there for even a few people."

"You can deliver more information to us about the way the great Çandarlı govern their castle when you go to Bursa. In fact, it would be much better if it's in writing. We can replicate it and send it to all the *subaşıs* at the castles so that we can prevent each governing according to their own judgment. Oh, and before I forget, keep your distance from Prince Murad's tutor..."

Suleyman Pasha believed that Hacı IlBey possessed great wisdom and didn't question his judgment. Instead, he smiled and said, "Hacı, I have long had a wish. I want to set forth as soon as possible and make that wish into reality."

"With a slight tone of curiosity Hacı IlBey replied, "I cannot wish to lay down the law for you but you have got me curious."

Suleyman Pasha replied, "I want to remember the *levends* we have lost until today by shouting their names from the tallest bastion of Ece Bey's Gallipoli out towards the Dardanelles. I promised myself that I would do so the first day we crossed the Dardanelles. But if you don't consent whole-heartedly I won't go."

"I consent whole-heartedly, My Prince. Go and return in peace. We don't have much left to do here other than capturing Matthew Kantakouzenos. That beggar was not amongst those captured today. But sooner or later we will capture him and the castle commander."

"Or?"

"Or, what?"

"Or, Matthew Kantakouzenos who likes the plays of Horatius, will return with an army..."

"My Prince, you know better than I do that no suppository heals the wound caused by an Ottoman dagger."

They smiled at each other. After looking at each other with mutual understanding they both stood up and performed Salah.

CHAPTER SIXTY-SIX

Byzantine Emperor John Palaiologos V was sitting on the deck of his magnificent armada galley, watching the coastline in the distance and looking at the other vessels and barges following them. However, he was seeing neither the blue sea nor the oarsmen in the galleys or the sailors running around on the barges. He was only vacantly looking at the coastline of Pelekanon and thinking about the engagement ceremony that he had not been able to erase from his mind for days. In his mind, he was replaying how much respect the Beys had for Orhan Ghazi. The way they united their hands at the front and bowed down to Orhan Ghazi with respect, the way they addressed him in a soft tone of voice with their heads slightly tilted down, the way they saluted him in Romaic once they were done addressing Orhan Ghazi... All these respectful manners were repeatedly playing in his mind. The gifts brought by his Beys were so valuable that his daughter Irene and his son-in-law Halil already possessed a fortune that almost matched his. On top of all that, Orhan Ghazi had given his son the duty of governing the former lands of Bithynia—the people of which caused problems when their ancestors escaped the evils of Romans and took shelter in Antigone—which he referred to as the lands of Akça Koca and Aygut Alp. The fact that Prince Halil was now a neighbour of Byzantium made him very happy as this was an assurance for the Byzantine Empire. Even if he was over the moon when he heard of Prince Halil's new role and did not wish him any harm, a strange sense of reflection coursed through his heart and moved up towards his mind as soon as he had departed from Nicaea. His reflections usually only set forth towards his heart when they had already matured in his mind. However, that wasn't the case now. It had first materialised in a flash in his heart and flowed into his mind, returning to his heart again without staying in his mind for long. Emperor

Palaiologos V noticed this retrograde flow of reflection that was unfamiliar to him and fearfully asked himself repeatedly, "Is this the
beginning of ill or good luck?" When he realised he couldn't come to
a conclusion he decided that he should talk to Empress Helena. But
let alone talking to her he had not even caught sight of the empress
since they set out from Nicaea towards Helenopolis. Empress Helena
saw the Emperor delving into abstraction with a vacant gaze on the
deck of the galley. She told the odalisques to ready his bath with the
flower essences that Nilüfer Hatun gave to her as a present. When
they left to prepare the Emperor's bath she stepped out onto the
deck. She approached the Emperor with quiet and slow steps. She
held the pensive emperor's hands and as she perused the same coastline as he, she asked, "Why are you so absent-minded, John?"

"Helena, if it wasn't for your brother Manuel's presents which arrived at the last minute we would have felt so small next to Orhan."

Squeezing the Emperor's hand purposefully, Empress Helena
replied, "I thought that Matthew would have also sent a present to
his niece but I now see that his heart has been blinded by his imperial ambitions."

The Emperor looked at his empress, of whose intelligence he was
always proud, and said, "My Helena, governors have always been
like Sparta in Sparta since the day Solomon spoke..."

The empress sensed subordination in the Emperor's tone and
asked, "Was taking a stand against contemptuous Athens easy back
then?"

Instead of answering her question, Emperor Palaiologos V looked
at his Helena's whiter than snow skin. He had always admired her
wisdom. As his gaze extended to his fantasies the empress held his
hand. Their eyes met. She prompted him in the direction of their
cabin without letting go of his hand and the Emperor followed her
quietly without a single thought. As Emperor Palaiologos V and
Empress Helena stepped into the bath infused with flower essences,

Nilüfer Hatun had immediately retreated to her chamber upon her arrival in Bursa and was looking at Orhan Ghazi's tired face. She murmured, "Time doesn't only put years on somebody but it also tires one." She turned to him and said, "You look tired."

"The tiredness of the body heals quickly as long as our hearts are young, my lady. I wouldn't normally be so tired but I wanted our guests to leave Nicaea with fond hearts."

Looking straight into his eyes, Nilüfer Hatun replied, "If it's your body that's tired I will get the servants to prepare you bathwater infused with the essences of a thousand and one flowers from the Bithynian Olympus and the petals of roses from Constantinople given to me by the Empress. You'll feel good as new after that, my Orhan. It is time you tried the odalisques brought by the Emperor. It would be good if they are accompanied by Theodora."

As she walked towards the door she thought that he had deserved to experience the happiness of his son's engagement.

Smiling at Nilüfer Hatun's allusive speech, aged Orhan Ghazi said "exhorter" as she walked towards the door. When this word appeared in his mind he remembered his brother Alaeddin Pasha. Looking at the door shut by Nilüfer Hatun he murmured, "He was a true exhorter. He delivered great speeches during ceremonies. He loved to squabble with Âşık Pasha. I was always jealous of their bickering. He used to respond to Âşık Pasha's couplets with Yassawi's. I never saw him squabble like that with anyone after Âşık Pasha's death. He always repeated Yassawi's line "At sixty-three, with years of carefree living" as if he meant it for someone else. Each time he said it I tried to demystify this couplet as he retreated to his reading room which he referred to as "the dervish convent" with a strange sense of joy. I saw him in such a joyful mood on two occasions—when he was retreating to that room and when he was going to visit the Çandarlı family. As he prepared for a long period of silence he noticed a sense of peace replacing the sadness that sunk into him when he usually recalled his brother. He stood up and started walking up and down the room. He began a long conversation with himself, "I understood why you repeated those lines when I aged. Now as I repeat those lines, I will call my Suleyman and tell him all that you told me. He is the one who will rise to the throne after me. You see, it was enough for him to just show his sword in Ancyra. Regardless of the fact that the *Âhis* are restless, the fact is that the fear that penetrated them has had such a long-lasting impact. I could get Murad to attack them but this is not the season for a campaign. I want to sit and wait for the games *Karamanids* will play. In any case, the *Karamanids* are our target, not the *Âhis*. They want us to remain without any holy victories because they are not campaigning themselves. But according to the information I have, the raiders of my Suleyman have long reached the shores of the Black Sea. It is because they heard of our holy victories that the ghazis and raiders of the Seljuk province have joined our Beylik and Suleyman Shah accepted our patronage. Which ghazi, cavalry, raider, *Âhiyân-ı Rum* and *Bâciyân-ı Rum* stays without a holy war for long?" He turned his gaze to the tall stone wall of the building where the servants' quarters were located. He rested his eyes on the chiselled surface of the ashlars. When he began to stride across the room he imagined being across from Halil of Karaman—a man with a black goatee and a round face, boasting a colourful turban—and continued his grunt, "Now you are caught in between. You intend to start a battle by provoking the *Âhis* of Ancyra because you know you don't have enough power to fight against the Mamluks in the south. But you should know that your power is no longer enough to beat us either. If it continues like this, you won't have any allies left in the battlefield. It doesn't matter... You can waste time provoking the *Âhis* for now. If I can come to an agreement with the *Germiyanids*, *Sarukhanids* and *Aydınids* I have a lesson to teach the Phocaean pirates before I come after you. Nilüfer Hatun had been standing by the door and listening to him for a while when he paused. She said, "You don't want to accept that you are getting old but it is you who always says, "People talk to themselves more when they get old."

Orhan Ghazi looked at Nilüfer Hatun with a slightly crestfallen and embarrassed gaze. Noticing how sheepish he felt, Nilüfer Hatun decided to change the subject, "I think that this engagement wasn't so suitable since our older sons are still single. Nevertheless, this could be a good beginning."

Orhan Ghazi got excited, "Oh, may you live long... Why hadn't I thought of that before?"

"Forget about all that for now. The odalisques have prepared the bathwater. We can talk once you have rested your bones."

As he left the room Orhan Ghazi repeated, "Why hadn't I thought of that before?"

CHAPTER SIXTY-SEVEN

Highly fond of travelling on horseback as if to pierce the silence of the night when the birds were asleep, Suleyman Pasha told his groom to put on felt boots on his horse so he wouldn't make any noise while leaving the castle. He also helped his groom to put them on the hooves of his Grey. Although the horse disliked wearing the boots and got up on his hind legs, it became calmer when he began competing with the wind. When Suleyman Pasha bent towards his neck it went into a trot that raised dust from the earth road. The *Alps* and Beys behind him and the cavalry following them began to trot in order to keep pace with the Grey. However, as all the horses were equipped with felt boots there wasn't a single sound that could pique the dawn. His steed was trotting more freely, as he competed with the early morning wind that seemed to be blowing harder and harder while paying attention to his stride as if to show its gratitude for the cavalry that granted him the freedom of the gallop.

The morning star shone brightly when the sky covered the earth with the final darkness that was pregnant with the dawn. That yellowish brightness in the sky reached the earth and the Grey began to shine as if it was an earthbound star. Meanwhile, all the morning birds woke up and began to sing hastily as if to usher in the dawn. When the late-rising nightingales and skylarks joined them, Thrace's endless rolling hills became flooded with a riot of birdsong. The neigh of the steed mixed into the sweet-voiced choir was overwhelming as the horizon began to turn purple.

Looking at the slowly brightening horizon, Suleyman Pasha's gaze extended out to the bubbling waters of the narrow brook flowing with a wild purl between the two hills near him and stopped at the distant Uğraş River. A bitter smile that fractured his thoughts spread upon his lips. He turned his wry gaze downwards. As the smile on his sunburnt face disappeared he murmured, as if to call out to those he left in the horizon, "I am leaving now to keep my promise to you. I won't make it to Tzympe or Gallipoli in time today. But tomorrow morning I will yell out your names as the sun rises." He dismounted his horse and walked down the hill towards the brook he had been hearing for some time. He caught sight of the deer and gazelles drinking their morning water across the brook and saw them arrive by the riverbank after passing by bushes bearing wild berries and pine trees. A few roe deer who had not seen them yet had just cantered towards the water when they raised their noses and began to smell the air. Their timid gaze was first turned to the deer and then to the approaching cavalry. The deer seemed to be seeing humans for the first time and were intent on keeping their eye on the cavalry across the brook. It was obvious that they were going to sprint away with a subtle movement and hide among the trees even though they didn't look scared. Suleyman Pasha and his entourage stood still for a while as if they were rooted to the spot in order to keep the herd at ease. The deer and gazelles first took a few strides back and then suddenly turned back and began to run uphill into the woods. They were followed by the timid roe-deer. The last to leave the riverbank were a few hares.

Once they disappeared into the woods Suleyman Pasha felt that he was getting hungry. He immediately ordered his men to take a break for breakfast. The service company found a suitable plain, spread the ground cloths, placed the round metal trays on top and prepared breakfast. The silver ewers were filled with water from the brook where the deer were watering shortly before. While breakfast was being prepared for the cavalry, the felt boots on the horses' hooves had been taken off, the reins had been removed and the horses had been let loose to graze. Saddle horses didn't usually graze during campaigns and journeys but the grass on the riverbank was so appetising that almost all of the horses were catching their breath and feeding.

After breakfast, Suleyman Pasha drank a few handfuls of cool water from the silver brook and addressed his Beys, "My wish is to be on
the Gallipoli coast at sunrise tomorrow. I made a promise to myself,
I need to keep it. Though I really like the water of this brook. When
we set forth we should follow it and see if there are any villages
around here. If there aren't, we can inform Ece Bey and he can settle
his first nomadic convoy here. This valley is ripe for settlement. Animals can be kept and agriculture can be carried out."

Upon hearing Suleyman Pasha's viewpoint the Beys stayed behind
and sent cavalry to the surrounding areas to investigate. When they
realised there weren't any nearby settlements they put markers in the
name of Suleyman Pasha, Bey of Hüdavendigâr Vilayet. Once all the
cavalry was gathered together they set out towards the Tzympe
Castle once again. However, the horses were advancing slowly despite being spurred. Not sharing the negative comments of his Beys
who didn't interpret the situation favourably, Suleyman Pasha
thought the horses might be sluggish because of the fresh grass they
grazed on and the water they drank and left his Grey to its own
devices for a while. When he tired of the lazy stride of his steed he
pushed his heels into its barrel so he would pick up pace. When the
Grey, which usually competed with the wind at this signal, ignored
him he spurred him harder. The animal paid no attention again.
This time he pulled in the gag-bit and dug in his heels harder on
both sides of the horse's barrel. It became bad-tempered at first and
then began to trot unwillingly. The other horses had just started
keeping pace with him when they saw a mob of deer appear out of
the woods up ahead and sprint across the road. They pulled in their
reins to slow down their horses but the deer saw them and instead of
crossing the road they began to run alongside the cavalry timidly and
wildly. As they disappeared into the distance Suleyman Pasha's appetite for hunting was whetted. As he nocked the arrow he took out
of his quiver onto his bowstring he spurred the barrel of his horse

again. But it slowed down. Unable to make sense of his horse's behaviour puzzled Suleyman Pasha for a while. He grumbled, "If you
won't speed up..." and pulled back the reins and brought his horse to
a halt. He dismounted. As he caressed his horse's head he said, "If
you don't want to walk behind me" and walked on. With the horse
reins around his arm, Suleyman Pasha mumbled, "The grass was en-
ticing but perhaps there were some weeds that were not fit for con-
sumption." Continuing to walk without looking at his horse tagging
along after him he murmured, "My Grey, is this your way of warning
me against a bad omen?" He momentarily thought about the cleav-
ing ground in Gallipoli. He shuddered at the thought of being buried
under again as he was that evening. When he repeated the lines, "If
Venus had seen what this Yunus has seen/Leave aside her harp and
forget her saz, she would," he was taken aback. He laughed to himself, nodding his head. He turned back on the spot and shouted out
to the *Alps* and Beys, "Now that we have seen this mob of deer we
have to hunt. Ready the ropes now, game meat will enrich the food
of our harems this evening!"

He turned to the front and looked at the valley where the deer were
scattered. He turned back again and told his Beys and *Alps*, "I have
been wanting to battle for some time now but haven't had the opportunity. This will help quench our gusto..."

Hearing what he had said Şirmend Bey and his Beys got excited
and yelled, "Hurrah! Live long, Suleyman Pasha!"

Lassos were hanging on the saddles of almost all cavalrymen except the servicemen. They all grabbed their lasso ropes at once. Just
then Suleyman Pasha mounted his horse, untied the knot and
propped the rope up with his elbow and spurred the Grey. This time
the horse started a more submissive trot and pricked up its ears. Regardless, he suddenly stopped again after a short while. In fact, the
horse had come to a halt so suddenly that Suleyman Pasha was
about to fall off. He glowered at his horse like never before. When he

deduced that it had no intention of moving, he turned his gaze at the long road unwinding before them. At that moment he caught sight of the large snake that had been squashed under the hooves of the deer that sprinted down the road shortly before. He winced. He caressed the mane of his Grey with his gaze fixed on the snake. Looking at the horse he said, "So this was the reason why you refused to go forward?" Şirmend Bey arrived beside them and looked at the snake. He dismounted his steed with agility and pushed it to the side of the road with the pointed end of his spear. As he mounted, the Grey was spurred heavily and began to gallop as fast as it could. He caught up with the herd of deer soon afterwards.

Suleyman Pasha eased down his horse and told the cavalry to spread out into the widening valley. Şirmend Bey and the *Alps* immediately performed the task and spread their cavalry across two sides of the valley. Şirmend Bey slowly rode up hills with thinning woodland and then advanced down the plain by the streambed. He waved his sword in the air so that everyone could see it. Everyone was watching him with bated breath. He looked back at Suleyman Pasha who was mounted on his Grey. When Suleyman Pasha signalled with his head, Şirmend Bey rested his sword and cried out, "May your hunt be blessed!"

When the echo of his voice was heard on both sides of the hillside, all the cavalry party in the hunt spurred their horses. When the horses began to race a battue had begun. They didn't have dogs running before them but the wild animals that heard the clop of the horses were rushing out of the bushes and running towards other bushes for their lives after seeing the horses that were chasing them. Some of the more skilful cavalry, who saw that the deer were too far from the lassos' reach, were putting the ropes on their shoulders and shooting arrows at them. The animals that had taken a momentary sigh of relief were falling flat on their bellies. However, none of the cavalry were speeding down to collect the game that had been hunted as was usually customary. The valley was soon outrun by the cavalry. They rode into a plain adorned with orchards that had produced the most delicious fruits once upon a time. The soil was as soft as ashes. The horses that had gone astray from the main road were sinking into the soil up to their pasterns. Trees with dried up branches had randomly toppled down and were lying on top of the mushy ground. The baffled deer were jumping over these dead trees with a little difficulty and acrobats' agility but the cavalrymen who were chasing them were having to ride around this lifeless grove. Thus, they were gradually falling behind. Suleyman Pasha had not managed to hunt down even a single deer. He spurred his Grey so hard that even though the poor animal was sinking into the ground up to his pasterns he managed to jump over a few dead trees. Just as Suleyman Pasha was ready to throw his lasso at a deer he saw, getting ready to jump over the bushes in front of them, a grunting wild boar rushing out of the same bushes and the Grey suddenly changed its direction, causing it to lose its balance. As the horse tried to regain its stance, one of its forefeet got stuck in a mole hole and Suleyman Pasha fell on top of the dead tree his horse had just jumped over. The steed rolled over on its back and fell on top of its master.

CHAPTER SIXTY-EIGHT

Orhan Ghazi—whose father aided Andronicus Palaiologos III during the Bulgarian and Serbian uprisings—had sided with his father-in-law John Kantakouzenos VI, who had condoned the Ottomans' landing of Thrace. However, he had also finally seen sense and promised him that he would help him in his struggle against Matthew Kantakouzenos. They hadn't signed a written agreement but Byzantine Emperor John Palaiologos V was at ease because he believed that Orhan Ghazi would stay true to his word. Thus, after his relaxed return from Nicaea, the Emperor set himself the task of improving the order in the castle as soon as he arrived in Constantinople. He immediately summoned his supporters and the counts, dukes, ecclesiastics, merchants and all other important vassals of the Empire known to be supporters of the Kantakouzenos to the meeting at the prayer hall of the Hagia Sophia. Talking to them at length, they went over what could be done together one by one, making the necessary decisions. The Emperor was happy when those attending the meeting decided, "As of this moment we are and everything we do is for our Constantinople." He ordered that entertainment should be organised at the arena, dating from Roman times, so that the castle people who had disintegrated for years could mingle. The poor castle people who were used to such bloodthirsty entertainment quickly left their resentments behind with the effect of the wine they consumed.

The only thing that caused Emperor Palaiologos V—who noticed that the order in the castle was improving day by day—to lose his sleep was how he was going to keep his promises to Orhan Ghazi in return for his help in capturing and handing over Matthew Kantakouzenos, claiming the title of Co-Emperor with his authority. Every time he looked out over the Bosphorus from the window of his spacious chambers at the mansion or the administrative palace he recalled the promise he made, "The day you deliver Matthew Kantakouzenos to Byzantium will be the day you will start receiving tax from many of the Pontus lands on the coast of the Black Sea." The more he thought of it the more he felt an unbearable sense of pressure. In order to extenuate his doldrums, he first tried to console himself by thinking, "You need to give a little to take a little. As they waste time with their newly gained territory, we can complete our preparations and retrieve what we gave to them and more," and then he contradicted himself when he mumbled, "We can't really trust the castle people of the Pontus..." Unable to get rid of his angst no matter what he did, he found solace in frequently turning his gaze to the Genoese quarter across the water and trying to forget about the Black Sea coast. However, when he did so, he began thinking about the Genoese in a huff, grunting, "All this is because of the concessions my father and those before him allowed them... As if it isn't enough that they are evading taxes they have renamed the hillsides of our Sykai as Pera. But I am not sad about all that because I know that no land helps to germinate an unfamiliar seed," and begun to pursue his dreams. On one such afternoon, Erasinides—who was acting as Deputy Mesazōn due to the illness of Mesazōn Alexios Apokaukos—hastily entered the Emperor's chamber. Suspicious of his unannounced arrival the Emperor stiffly said, "For the love of God, Erasinides! What's the hurry?"

Erasinides felt embarrassed because he always announced his arrival at the Emperor's chamber in advance. With a sad tone of voice, he replied, "Your Majesty, the news we received..."

He couldn't continue. The Emperor looked at the chalk-white face of the old man, whose father had been deputy mesazōn during his father's reign, walked around the large table and showed him to the chair in front of the table. He sat across from him and said, "I hope you don't have any health problems Erasinides because I really need your wisdom these days."

After taking a deep breath, Deputy Mesazōn Erasinides spoke, "Thank God, I am healthy. The news I bring to you does not concern myself."

"If not you, who?"

"It is regarding Suleyman Pasha, son of Orhan Ghazi."

"Did he capture another one of our castles or Matthew Kantakouzenos?"

"Neither, Your Majesty."

"So? What is it?"

"According to the news we received he is dead. A part of me wants to rejoice about Thrace... But..."

Emperor Palaiologos V interrupted the Deputy Mesazōn, "How did this happen? When did it happen?"

"According to our source, three days ago, when he was hunting..."

"Hunting? How could that be? He spends his life on a horse..."

"His horse foundered while galloping and lost its balance..."

"This must be a joke... A man who spends his life on horseback died because his horse foundered?"

"We don't have any more information about the cause of his death, Your Majesty. But, there is one more thing..."

Erasinides turned a lighter shade of white. The Emperor waited for him to gather his thoughts but he lost patience. He yelled, "Erasinides! What has come over you?"

"Your Majesty, I wouldn't want to be the one giving you this news but Matthew Kantakouzenos heard of Suleyman's death. Without a moment's delay, he began marching on the Ottomans with the Bulgarians and Serbians. Apparently, he is claiming to take back both Hadrianopolis and Thrace... Worse still..."

The Emperor shook his head in disbelief and paused. Erasinides mumbled a few words but the Emperor couldn't understand him. In a more raged tone of voice, he exclaimed, "For God's sake Erasinides! Speak man! What could be worse than all of this?"

"What's worse still... Your Majesty..."

Growing impatient the Emperor shook his head and yelled, "Are you trying to drive me mad, Erasinides!"

Realising that he was enraging the Emperor even though he didn't intend to, the Deputy Mesazōn replied, "Your Majesty, Matthew Kantakouzenos has been putting the Ottoman advance units he captured on his way to Hadrianopolis to the sword and..."

The Emperor gathered that the Deputy Mesazōn was lacking the courage to say what he had to say. Emperor Palaiologos V softened his voice to encourage him and said, "Erasinides, tell me what happened so we can take the necessary measures."

Deputy Mesazōn Erasinides took courage from the Emperor and finally uttered those unutterable words, "Matthew Kantakouzenos has declared himself the new King of Thrace."

"We knew that this was his ambition all along. What you told me is not something I didn't anticipate..."

"Yes, Your Majesty, it is not unexpected but Matthew Kantakouzenos has apparently been saying, "Now that I am the King of Thrace I will punish the invaders like King Diomedes."

"What does that entail Erasinides?"

"This means that Matthew Kantakouzenos is going to mince his captives and add it into his horse's feed, Your Majesty..."

CHAPTER SIXTY-NINE

T he Beys under Hacı IlBey's command had finally managed to take a break as the mysterious happenings that took place at Hadrianopolis Castle at night diminished. They had just reached the end of their meeting in the spacious mansion chamber—where Hacı IlBey and Suleyman Pasha convened the day before—when two messengers arrived from Evrenos Bey who was advancing towards the west with his units. One of them was Şükür Agha, Evrenos Bey's renowned dispatch rider. Once he appeared before them, swung his head and bowed, he spoke in a tone of voice that chased away sadness, "I bring you the compliments of Evrenos Bey who has added Didymóteicho and the castles to its north to the lands of the Osman-oğlu family. Our Bey has asked me to inform you that Didymóteicho and the castles to its north have been captured with very few casualties and that some tribes which came to these lands before us and speak our language helped us capture the castles. These tribes, which are merely our supporters, for now, will be settled in Rumelian castles."

As the dispatch rider was about to walk back and leave the room, Hacı IlBey motioned him to remain and asked, "You have made us happy with the news you brought to us Şükür Agha. Is there nothing else Evrenos Bey has said about the tribes that arrived there before you?"

Şükür Agha replied with a hoarse and grinding voice, "Evrenos Bey believes them to be Central Asian tribes who came here with Attila who marched so close to Rome he could even see the city lights."

Scratching his short-trimmed goatee, Hacı IlBey replied, "Evrenos Bey is a wise man and if he says so, he is probably right. The news you have brought will be conveyed to our Bey, Suleyman Pasha, at the earliest opportunity. Our Bey will be spending this winter in Pla-jar and we will be overwintering here in Hadrianopolis. It seems that

Evrenos Bey will be taking Didymóteicho as his winter base. Deliver
our compliments to him. You can leave once you've rested. God
speed..."

Hacı IlBey had just finished talking and Şükür Agha had headed
towards the door again when Suleyman Pasha's chief messenger
entered the chamber. Upon seeing him Hacı IlBey's bearded face
turned yellow like beeswax. Recognising Suleyman Pasha's blood-
stained hunter's vest in the messenger's hands he exclaimed wailing,
"My Suleymaaaan!"

His voice echoed so much in the spacious chamber that even the
thick stone walls vibrated. As his tears spontaneously poured out of
his eyes he cried out, "We shouldn't have underestimated
Kantakouzenos! We should have sent our Bey on his way with a larger force... How did this happen?"

The blood-drenched hunter's vest in the messenger's grasp explained everything perfectly well but the *Alps* and the Beys wanted
to hear it all from the messenger. When the messenger had finished
talking, Hacı IlBey stood up and said, "Come on, we are leaving."

Evrenos Bey, Fazıl Bey and Akça Kocaoğlu had received the dire
news shortly after the Beys at Hadrianopolis Castle and they were on
their way to the scene of the accident. The first to arrive were Ece
Bey and Kara Timurtaş Pasha. Seeing Suleyman Pasha covered with
blood, the sadness on Ece Bey's sea salt-burnt plain face emerged
through his voice and mixed into his tears. Had Suleyman Pasha
been massacred in a field of combat he could have had all those who
were there beheaded to take the edge off but these were such unusual
circumstances that he could salve neither his rage nor his pain. As
string-like tears poured out of his old eyes, he reproachfully looked at
the Grey lying beside his Bey. However, seeing that the horse's belly
was ripped from one end to the other like a towel his reproach subsided.

All of the Beys rode their horses to the point of exhaustion and gathered at the location of Suleyman Pasha's mortal remains the next morning. Meanwhile, Ece Bey had completed all the preparations to transport Suleyman Pasha's lifeless body to its final resting place. The Beys held each other tightly for a while and cried on each other's' shoulders, and then the whole convoy set out towards Plajar. As they walked behind the horse carriage carrying the corpse of Suleyman Pasha's, who had once been their comrade in arms, they were all replaying their memories of him in their heads. None of them had any memories of him that offended them. They could only expostulate about him, "You shouldn't have left us alone in these lands we stepped foot on together."

It was midnight when the convoy arrived on the hill at Plajar which Suleyman Pasha had referred to as the "Best place to watch the Thracian sunset from", where he bequeathed to be buried and kept his harem. The sad news reached Orhan Ghazi as the morning prayer was recited.

Upon receiving the news, the feeling that his mansion had crumbled on top of him overcame Orhan I as he gasped for breath. He struggled out to the gardens as he realised that his body couldn't bear the pain he felt between the four walls of his room. Once outside he let out such a yell that even Mount Olympus, leaning her shadow over Bursa, would take two steps back in fear at the extent of this pain. As soon as she overcame her fear and saw that this painful scream was none other than the outcry of a helpless father she approached warily to console him with her shadow. Realising that consoling this hurt father would take more effort, she yelled to all the trees adoring her hillsides and peaks, "Cast all your remaining green leaves." All trees except the wayward pines shed their last remaining leaves when they heard the mountain's command. With no other consolation to offer, Olympus bowed her head of shadow before Orhan Ghazi. Feeling the magnanimity of the mountain, Orhan Ghazi forgot his pain even if it was for a brief moment, and with his

fingertips caressed the wayward pines on the skirts of the mountain
that extended his head of shadow. He said, "It doesn't matter if your
name is Olympus or Mount Monk. From now on you are my sublime
mountain." As these words departed from his lips, he sobbed his
heart out once again. Extending her hand from between her shadows, Olympus caressed the silky white hair on Orhan Ghazi's bare
head and said, "O! Orhan Ghazi, the man with the mightiest heart!
Sob louder if it shall dull your pain!" before taking her shadow and
giving into the morning sun.

Orhan Ghazi gave some of the pain in his heart to the cool morning breeze that blew from Olympus. As he searched for ways to accept his son's death as he had accepted many others' over the years,
he discovered that the Beylik carriage was ready to depart. Orhan
Ghazi got into the carriage with Nilüfer Hatun and those of Aktimur
Alp, Deli Rüstem Agha and Korkut Tekin Alp followed.

CHAPTER SEVENTY

As the inner castle sunk into darkness, Deputy Mesazōn Eras-inides had long started a meeting attended by his auxiliaries, commander of the troop of guardsmen and the commander of the armada who hadn't done anything other than sailing into Hellespont, with the chief commander of the castle, sick Mesazōn Alexios and the patriarch who was accompanied by his clergy. However, he had already run out of things to say and the small hall where the clergy of the Hagia Sophia had gathered was buried in heavy silence. Perhaps he had got to this point a little too early but the others weren't saying anything either because they were all very crafty at keeping silent. The great Patriarch of Constantinople who usually wouldn't stop talking during meetings had also only said a few sentences before buttoning his lips. Noticing his unusual silence, the Deputy Mesazōn tried to prompt him into talking more, "Is that everything you wanted to say, Father?"

"I contemplated before coming here that my mouth will not overstep the mark in these hard times."

As the Patriarch's words rove around in the Deputy Mesazōn's head in those silent minutes, he was thinking about where to begin telling what had happened upon the Emperor's arrival. Surely he had to begin with the news conveyed by the newly arrived messengers but he couldn't keep together the sentence that loitered in his mind and his other thoughts. He couldn't decide on his starting point. He saw one of the Egyptian granite column feet that seemed as if it was shouldering the arches on the ceiling while it was dismally looking at the open-plan inner chamber where the clergy were performing worship. When his thoughts visited every nook and cranny in his mind and began to wend their way back to the time of Justin II he mumbled, "It was our Belisarius who brought him into existence. If it was up to the Roman commanders—the Latins wouldn't have been so successful. Perhaps it would have been better for our Byzantium that way and these lands wouldn't have witnessed such tyranny. Regardless, our Byzantium will always whet others' appetites as long as it has such fertile lands. If they hadn't marched from the west, someone else would have attacked from the east. It's best to leave time to its own devices. It can somehow or other sort out everything in its own time. Just as it sorted out Justinian the Younger[56], who brought these granites from the land of the Pharaoh..." He suddenly remembered Empress Theodora. Her name was in many of the historical records he had read a short while ago. He was just thinking, "Theodora was the one who was truly powerful" when a second thought appeared in his mind, "But the force that strengthened that power was the love between them." Whenever he pondered on politics he always dismissed such thoughts from his mind but this time he made up an excuse, "Perhaps thinking about them will help some ideas fill my empty mind." Right then a competing thought passed through his head with the speed of a knight riding his horse with his red cape flapping in the wind, "Justinian bestowed him with the name *Iustinus Iunior* but he didn't match the diminutive adjective by which he was named. Instead of sufficing with the name given to him, he acted bravely enough to be called 'great'". As he hadn't realised that he had spoken the last sentence out loud, he was surprised when he tilted his head up and met the gaze of all those sitting opposite him. He tried to purify himself from the thoughts in his mind while perusing those who were looking at him. At that moment the Patriarch asked, "Who has been acting bravely?"

Making no effort to conceal his surprise, the Deputy Mesazōn replied, "Saintly Father, I recalled Justin II while looking at that granite column. The Emperor named him *Iustinus Iunior* but I think he was great."

"If you are talking about him in relation to the Hagia Sophia, you

---

56 T.N, Also known as Justin II, Justinian the Younger was Eastern Roman Emperor from 565 to 574.

are right."

Despite the fact that the Deputy Mesazōn had known the Patriarch for many years and admired his wisdom, he could neither make sense of why he only referred to Justin II in relation to the Hagia Sophia nor liked his contemptuous tone of voice. In order to make his disgruntlement known he responded, "Saintly Father, as you very well know, even wanting to change rooted traditions have cost the lives of many emperors. But let alone changing the deep-seated traditions, Justin II also changed the desire to change tradition."

"Oh, you mean what he did for Theodora?"

"Yes, if he hadn't gotten those laws changed for Theodora, Rome couldn't have survived in the west or in the east."

"So if they had not been enacted, Theodora couldn't have been empress and given her speech that provoked his supporters. So, you mean that if all that hadn't been, the Eastern Roman Empire would have been short-lived?"

"Yes, father. Had Theodora not empowered the Emperor who had lost power against the rebels by saying, 'May I never see the day when those who meet me do not call me empress.' If you wish to save yourself, my lord, there is no difficulty. We are rich—over there is the sea, and yonder are the ships. As for me, I agree with the adage that the royal purple is the noblest shroud...'"

The Patriarch sighed lightly as the Deputy Mesazōn kept quiet and waited for the others to come up with ideas, continuing, "If only she hadn't empowered him and thousands of our brothers hadn't strangled each other in the arena in a single day..."

The Patriarch was interrupted by a voice, "Saintly Father, the Nicaean were already waiting for the opportunity to kill one another, just as the supporters of Kantakouzenos who we are currently hardly keeping under control."

Everyone turned in the direction of the voice and saw that the young emperor was leaning on the door frame of the open wooden

door of the clergy room—built by Justinian and still standing in perfect condition—and listening to their conversations. Almost all of
them stood up except the Patriarch, who shuffled around, but young
Emperor John Palaiologos V motioned him to remain seated and
started to walk. Sitting on the marble seat next to the Patriarch, he
said, "Forgive me for interrupting your insightful debate. You may
continue if you wish. Both Helena and I have recently read much on
Justinian's period. What drew our attention the most was the dura-
tion of his reign and that his period was as tumultuous as our current day."

The Patriarch gently straightened his headpiece adorned with gold
crucifixes, sighing with rage, "Your Majesty, Roman Emperors are
not very exemplary because they covered up what the Latins did to
our Constantinople with thick drapes of blood. However, if you wish
to have a good grasp of Justinian's period..."

As the Patriarch plied between finishing his sentence and leaving it
as it was, Emperor Palaiologos V insisted, "Yes, Father... To have a
good grasp, I should..."

Neither of them wanted to leave their sentences half said but for
some reason they did. Looking at the Emperor, the Patriarch said, "If
you want to have a good grasp of his period, you should go and stay
at the Heraeums across the water in the spring."

"Oh, Father! You are suggesting this to me knowing that it can no
longer happen... It is obvious that you don't know the new masters of
Chalcedon. I got to know them very well on my trip to Nicaea,
saintly father. Their commanders, Beys, the clergy in their mosques,
and even the priests of the churches in the castles are endlessly loyal
to Orhan Ghazi, while we can't get even just a few of our castle commanders to obey our orders. That was what we saw in Nicaea. I am
not scared of them growing stronger or increasing in numbers but
their respect, saintly father. We could easily make them sorry for the
day they stepped foot on these lands with naval assaults but their fi-

delity and the loyalty of our men to them worry me. This is what stops me from making a decision."

Deputy Mesazōn recognised the Emperor's concerns, "The Emperors of our Byzantium were dreaming big before the Roman arrival. Some of them dreamt of moving beyond the Indian mountains and reaching Chinese silks. When the Romans stripped them of their dreams they tried to make do with less ambitious plans in Nicaea. Their sleep-nurturing small dreams lasted for years but they never forgot their great ambitions. However, if there is one thing we now know it is that that great vision will never be seen again. It turned into an endless reverie with Diogenes of Sinope. I gather that the saintly father is still in pursuit of that old unattainable dream. We no longer have time to pursue great visions. It is best if we embrace our old peaceful sleep when we can be content with our little dreams and ambitions."

The Patriarch seemed hurt by the words of the Deputy Mesazōn and replied with rage, "Erasinides, everything you see is deceptive, just as your status. But we, as believers, have never lost our dreams because we have never stopped believing in our emperors and our Byzantium. The Romans came here so we could grow our aspirations but they never thought that those who came with them would be predatory. Had they have come here with the noble commanders of Ancient Rome and their warriors, our troops would have already reached beyond the lands of Afrasiab."

Krilinados, the castle commander of Constantinople and the commander-in-chief of all the castle commanders said, "Saintly Father, as you know, the efforts of the noble commanders of Rome, who were captivated by the riches of Anatolia, didn't amount to much most of the time. If it wasn't for our honourable Belisarius, the Romans couldn't have even stepped foot in Anatolia."

Seeing that the atmosphere in the hall chilled after his speech, Deputy Mesazōn thought that he had never been so reckless until this day. His deductions from the recent news came into his mind and he felt the impulse to interrupt, "Ah! My dear friend Krilinados... We have castles which surrender at the sight of the Ottoman cavalry at their gates..."

The Emperor felt uneasy that the Deputy Mesazōn was taking on the commander-in-chief and the Patriarch at such a critical time. He decided to change the subject, "Saintly Father, dear Krilinados and cordial friends of the Palaiologos family, the main reason why we summoned you to this evening's meeting is not to talk about the Ottomans who are invading our coasts, but the situation that has arisen in Thrace following the death of Prince Suleyman, son of Orhan Ghazi. Of course, we want the Ottomans to retreat from Thrace. However, at this point what concerns us is that Matthew Kantakouzenos likens himself to the Thracian king Diomedes and acts like him too. Should Matthew's violence be met with violence of a similar force, we won't be able to stop the Ottomans in Constantinople. It is now time for us to talk about what we can do to re-establish brotherhood in our Constantinople and what measures we can take to stop Matthew from getting more support. If we don't do something to stop his cruelty, we should be aware that the Ottomans' mourning will be brief."

The Patriarch cast his gaze upon the bright lights of the recently lit oil lamp and replied, "Your Majesty, you are right. The situation is dire. Matthew Kantakouzenos' cruelty is unacceptable. We should treat them with the same compassion and mercy they treat us with when they capture our castles. There is not a single religious text that portrays God on the side of the tyrant."

Looking happy that his last thoughts had been taken notice of, Deputy Mesazōn said, "Father, you should know that you are the only one who can penetrate his heart. You are the only person we can send to him."

The commander-in-chief of Byzantine forces looked down on the

Deputy Mesazōn who had criticised him harshly shortly before and said, "This is a matter of diplomacy, saintly father. I think that the Deputy Mesazōn is the one who should be sent to Matthew."

The subject was discussed at length until the late hours of the night after the commander-in-chief's suggestion. When the Emperor noticed that most of the elderly participants were exhausted, he said, "I am grateful to all of you for your attendance. We haven't made any particular decisions today but I strongly suggest that we convene again tomorrow evening."

He then stood up and walked down the ramped path leading to the ground floor accompanied by the old Mesazōn, the Deputy Mesazōn, the commander-in-chief and the guards. As their footsteps echoed in the rear courtyard, the others stood up and left the hall one by one.

CHAPTER SEVENTY-ONE

Nilüfer Hatun had not been able to get her son out of her head for months. She had been crying quietly night and day. She was even barely talking to Orhan Ghazi who held her hand and tried to console her now and then. Despite the fact that Orhan Ghazi was also very sad, he was spending most of his time beside her so he could give solace to her. He walked from one side of the room to the other with his gaze fixed on Nilüfer Hatun who was staring at the wall and crying, before approaching as if he had thought of something. He told her to stand up. Then, he looked at her face as she stood up, "My lady, you know that I am also deeply in sorrow. I never thought that he would end up buried in the ground when I sent him to conquer and incorporate the lands on the other side to our Beylik. I buried a part of my heart in his grave with him. If it was possible I would like to be the one buried instead of him but unfortunately, they don't accept another in his place. We have to compose ourselves and work on our Beylik to try and forget our pain. We need to hold onto life."

Looking at Orhan Ghazi's tanned face with her deep gaze she replied, "My Bey, you are thinking about the Beylik while I am still thinking about my son. Nothing can give me back my Suleyman..."

"I know how your heart hurts. I am trying to understand you but please remember that death is the only truth. What causes us immense pain today is what will take us away tomorrow."

Nilüfer Hatun gently shuddered and understood that she was putting a strain on her husband. With a soft tone of voice, she said, "I understand all that you have said, my Orhan. But as luck would have it, I cannot seize control of the mutiny in my heart."

Observing her face and holding her hands, Orhan Ghazi replied, "Time cures all ills, my Nilüfer."

Looking at Orhan Ghazi's face as if she had regained her levelheadedness, Nilüfer Hatun said, "I am sorry, My Bey. I couldn't hold sway over my feelings even though I bid him farewell as if it's the last time whenever he leaves."

"Which mother would surrender her child into the embrace of death? I have been trying to be the sultan and the sovereign all this time but I now see that I am as mortal as all the other mortals. The only difference between me and them is that I am responsible for protecting the lives and goods of those who are in my domain until my last breath. Don't you see that there are those who want to take advantage of our pain? The *Karamanids* on this side and Kantakouzenos' son on the other have already mobilised. While one of them is provoking the beys in Anatolia against us, the other has declared his kingship and is mincing our ghazis who he has captured and is feeding them to his horses. Now both you and I have to forget our pain so that we can take our Murad under our protective care and protect the lives of the unfledged in our lands."

Nilüfer Hatun softened the sadness in her pale and beautiful face that had few wrinkles in spite of her age, replying, "I know that it will be our turn one day but what has really shaken me is the fact that it suddenly became our son's turn before it was ours. You can take care of all the things you have to take care of as of today. I will be fine."

Orhan Ghazi walked towards Nilüfer Hatun, kneeled down and kissed her on the forehead. After pondering for a while as if he was remembering something he said, "Ah, my dear Nilüfer, I have known that the business of death is unpredictable since our Kasım's death and the death of all my young warriors who jumped in front of swords that were meant to slit me in battlefields. I can never forget Shayyad Hamza's statement, 'Fate holds an enormous goblet in its hand, a goblet filled with destinies.' If you like, you can also make use of this statement."

Nilüfer Hatun felt that she could find more solace in human

warmth rather than his words. She approached him with shy and quiet steps and placed her head on his chest. Sighing softly, she said, "I will try to remember it, my Orhan. I hope it will help me."

Holding Nilüfer Hatun's shoulders, Orhan Ghazi embraced her tightly and encouraged her, "Come on, my dear Nilüfer, gather your handmaidens and head to the river. Listen to how the sound of the birds and insects mix into the sound of the water and sing along with your handmaidens whose voices are reminiscent of nightingales. I will come and join you immediately once I am done with my work at the beys' council."

Upon finishing his sentence, he kissed Nilüfer Hatun on the forehead and walked to the door.

As Orhan Ghazi left his harem and headed towards the building where Grand Vizier Sinanüddin Fakih Yusuf Pasha's drawing-room and the spacious chamber was located, Asporsha Hatun and Lady Theodora arrived in Nilüfer Hatun's morning room. Nilüfer Hatun showed her fondness to her fellow ladies by embracing them with all of her warmth and crying on their shoulders. Wiping her tears, she said, "Come on, call your handmaidens and we can go to the riverbank. Perhaps the sound of water will do us some good."

As Asporsha Hatun remained behind embracing Nilüfer Hatun, Lady Theodora left the room. As they talked to one another they heard Theodora clap her hands. Shortly after, Lady Theodora came back into the room and informed them that the carriages were ready. Just as they got into the carriages without much preparation, Orhan Ghazi was attending the council meeting and had just finished his speech and it was now old Grand Vizier Sinanüddin Fakih Yusuf Pasha's turn to deliver his speech. The way he used his voice so expressively always had an effect on the council. However, this time it seemed as if every word that departed from his lips weighed tons. Acknowledging this, he was grinding the words in his mouth before they departed from his lips in order to increase the weight he ascribed to them. He slowed down his tone of voice so much without bringing his train of thought to a conclusion that the entire council was all ears. Feeling that they were all hanging on his every word, Sinanüddin Yusuf Pasha suddenly raised his voice, "Beys, in order to be able to remain within our range we need to eliminate the distances between us and succeed in standing shoulder to shoulder. You have all set your heart on Orhan Ghazi's cause and leagued together. You have buried many a brave man in battlefields to enlarge his state. However, your harmony also increased the number of your rivals. While our forces that crossed to the other side of the Dardanelles have acquired new lands, the friendly Beyliks in Anatolia have joined forces with us. Yet, some Beyliks whom we have considered as our brothers-in-arms noticed our increasing power and are decided on interrupting our mourning for Suleyman. As if it wasn't enough that the *Karamanids* provoked the *Âhis* of Ancyra and recaptured the castle, they are now inciting the *Âhis* to attack the lands of our Gerede beys. Moreover, they are trying to provoke the *Germiyanids* against us even though they know how close we are with them. If they hadn't made this mistake, we wouldn't have even found out about their seditiousness. Orhan Ghazi and I talked about this subject on our way back from our Suleyman's funeral. I'd explained to him that it was time to give a lesson to Halil of Karaman who has named himself the last representative of the Seljuks. We revisited this subject with Orhan Ghazi yesterday and came to a decision. If you approve our decision, our first campaign in the upcoming spring will be against the *Karamanids*. Our continued presence on the other side of the Dardanelles depends on this campaign."

He turned his gaze to Orhan Ghazi. The words of the old Grand Vizier had sufficient effect on the council. No one wanted to talk for a while. The heavy atmosphere in the room became heavier with the effect of the quietness. With his white beard shaking, Sinanüddin Yusuf Pasha said, "There is nothing more natural than for you to feel anxious upon hearing all of this. We are also concerned about the events developing at the borders but we have to discuss and we have to make decisions. So don't keep quiet. Talk if you wish to. As the poet says, "what can I do on my own?" So if you keep to yourselves we cannot achieve anything on our own dear aghas, beys and *Alps*."

Taking courage from his words Kara Halil of Çandar, a well-respected member of the council, replied, "I have no doubt that the decision you have made is befitting. We will be honoured to join our bey, Orhan Ghazi's holy war. Our beys in Rumelia, beyond the Dardanelles, are in dire straits. I think it is best if our forces that will set out to help them depart as soon as possible before the campaign to Anatolia begins in the spring. If what we heard is true, Kantakouzenos' son is spreading fear and terror in the area."

Deducing that his protégé Kara Halil had learnt diplomacy well from the way he adjusted his tone of voice and his choice of words, Sinanüddin Yusuf Pasha continued, "Halil Pasha expressed his thoughts very well. We must send new forces to Hacı Ilbey, Evrenos Bey, Fazıl Bey, Akça Kocaoğlu and Ece Bey so that they can stop Matthew Kantakouzenos' attacks. If he can't be stopped, the Kantakouzenos in Constantinople will raise his hopes. If they nurture the aim of driving us out of Thrace we will have our work cut out for us."

Lala Şahin Bey—Prince Murad's tutor—dismissed a devilish grin from his lips and said, "I think that Hacı Ilbey on his own is enough to take on Matthew Kantakouzenos and the Emperor. According to hearsay, he strives to absolve recklessness."

Sinanüddin Yusuf Pasha was the only person who had insight into Lala Şahin Bey's sarcastic remarks. Turning towards Orhan Ghazi, he said, "It makes us happy that Lala Şahin Bey has faith in Hacı Ilbey's forces. However, John Kantakouzenos has almost convinced the Bulgarians and Serbians to join forces with Matthew

Kantakouzenos. If they join Kantakouzenos' powers, it won't matter if they are against Hacı Ilbey or Lala Şahin Bey, as we will be powerless. That is why Hacı Ilbey has not been giving Matthew any chance to get back on his feet and has dispatched Fazıl Bey and Akça Kocaoğlu to the castles in advance. As you know, the cavalry is not of much use in sieges. Now what we have to do is to send them more *yayas.*"

Then he looked at Orhan Ghazi as if to prompt him to speak. Orhan Ghazi realized it was his turn to speak and gently recapped everything he and Sinanüddin Yusuf Pasha had spoken about before continuing, "My *Alps*, My Beys, My Viziers, My *Kadîs*, My Lords and *Ghazis*... Thank you for your support, for not hurting the ones who have not hurt us and for always staying by my side in good times and in bad times. As Yusuf Pasha said, as our lands expanded and our subjects increased in numbers so have our enemies. Even some beys whom we assumed to be our brothers played tricks of sorts on us. However, no matter what those beys think we know that all the scout troops in the east, west and the south are on our side. Most of them wait for our signal. Perhaps even some of the beys want to join forces with us but they are leery of the more powerful neighbouring beys. We must first give them power and get them to trust us so that we can receive their power. We must start preparations no later than today to march on the *Karamanids*. Prince Murad and Lala Şahin Bey should set out at once with their forces and head towards Ancyra. They should recapture the castle that my Suleyman laid siege to. As the new warriors sent by them from Ancyra and other castles are trained in Bursa, our trained *yayas* should quickly mobilize to join Hacı Ilbey's forces. Meanwhile, we will campaign to the south with our forces. It would be beneficial for us to put in place some agreements with the *Germiyanids*, *Sarukhanids* and the Beylik of Menteş as well as to come to an agreement to march on the Genoese in Phocaea. It would be good if we can manage cleaning up Phocaea from the Genoese and Ancyra of the *Âhis*, supporters of the *Karamanids*, by spring. Thus we will have attained sufficient power at the borders and closed in on the Karamanid lands. As soon as the spring has blossomed, we can unexpectedly organise raids to their lands.

"When my Suleyman voiced his wish to cross the Dardanelles to me he had also told me how much he wanted to add those lands to ours. Unfortunately, this deplorable accident stopped him from doing so. As of this moment, it is Prince Murad's duty to add those lands to ours. As soon as our campaign to the *Karamanids* is complete, Prince Murad and Lala Şahin Bey will cross the Dardanelles and finalise the conquest with the forces posted there."

Prince Murad looked at the council with a surprised facial expression as a result of the succession of duties that were given to him. He stepped forward as soon as he pulled himself together and kneeled urbanely. After kissing Orhan Ghazi's hand, he said, "I won't let my older brother Suleyman Pasha's legacy be forgotten. I will fulfil the duties you have given to me even if they cost my life. My exemplary father should know that the *Âhis* of the Ancyra Castle will recognise the sovereignty of the Ottoman Beylik at the earliest."

Orhan Ghazi usually communicated with his son Murad through the messengers he sent from one battlefront to the other. He was surprised to hear his younger son speak with such power and intelligence. He had never thought that his eldest son would die before him and thus never shared anything about the governance of the Beylik with his younger son Murad. When he recalled this, he said, "We forgot about life itself while thinking about battlefields. Then looking at his son, he murmured, "He grew up so much without me even noticing." Looking at him, he went on a personal journey in his mind, "It's still not too late. It's not essential for him to immediately set out with his forces. He can depart a few days after his *yayas* and cavalry. It will console his mother if he stays here a few more days. Meanwhile, I can create an opportunity to share my thoughts on the governance of the Beylik with him and Nilüfer Hatun can teach our daughter-in-law, Gülçiçek, the customs of our mansion. Happy with his decisions, he looked at his son with a smile on his lips and said, "May your tongue and your wrist always be strong. Lala Şahin Bey can depart at once but you should stay here in Bursa for a while. Both your mother and I need you here these days."

Lala Şahin Bey gently bent forward on the cushion on which he was sitting and said, "We also need a few days so that the beys who will join us can ready their units. I can send forth the advance units tomorrow and we can follow them in a few days. Prince Murad can catch up with us later."

Seeing the dusk percolate into the room subtly and slowly, with his old and wrinkly eyes Grand Vizier Sinanüddin Yusuf Pasha spoke in a tired tone of voice, "All that we had to talk about for today has been covered. Now everyone knows what their duty is. The meeting of our great council attended by *Alps* and Beys has come to an end. The decisions that will be made in the gatherings of our small council attended by viziers and the ulema will be communicated to all of you. May your wrist be strong, your spoils abundant and your wars blessed."

As Orhan Ghazi told his beys, "May your holy war be blessed" he remembered the promise he made to Nilüfer Hatun. As he hastily left the council and waited for his horse, he murmured, "I didn't presume that the meeting would last so long."

CHAPTER SEVENTY-TWO

John Palaiologos V didn't utter a word to those following him until he arrived at the guest reception room in the Palace of the First Ministry. His face seemed more matured in the yellow light of the oil lamps. As the Palace of the First Ministry was closer to the Hagia Sophia than this own mansion, he had arrived there after the council meeting as the sick mesazōn, the deputy mesazōn and the commander of the land forces. He had tried to put into order what he was going to do in his head on his way to the meeting—both during his journey on the hardtop horse carriage and while walking to the Palace of the First Ministry from the Hagia Sophia—just as he had done all day long. He thought, "I can share everything except thoughts that I must reserve to myself with the mesazōn, the deputy mesazōn and the commander of my land forces this evening and give them the chance to speak their opinion. Then, tomorrow night I can listen to the clergy and the public representatives and receive their suggestions. I can make the wisest decision based on all of that. This is the chance to get the better of the Ottomans before they set sail. If we cannot succeed now we will never be able to get rid of them. If we can act in an organised way and I can convince the Kantakouzenos, we can quickly remove the Ottomans from Thrace.

The staff at the Palace of the First Ministry was stumped when the mesazōn, the deputy mesazōn, the commander of the land forces and the Emperor all arrived at the palace unexpectedly. They had, however, managed to sufficiently brighten the corridor and the reception room by lighting the oil lamps that had recently gone out. Moreover, they poured red wine made of Thracian grapes—kept in the carved wooden cupboard embedded in the masonry of the reception room—into gilt glass goblets for the esteemed guests. Once they were finished with serving the guests they quietly left the room. As the Emperor and commander-in-chief sipped on their wine from Chinese glass goblets and stared at each other, the mesazōn was sitting in his official seat and watching the deputy mesazōn ready the inkstand and the scribe. After taking a second sip from their goblets of wine altogether, Emperor John Palaiologos V swirled the wine around his mouth and swallowed it before asking, "And what about the state of our fleet, Krilinadis?"

As the commander wasn't anticipating the first question to be directed at him it took him a while to respond. Looking at the high ceiling and doing some sums in his head he thought, "Why did he only ask about the sailors and not about our entire forces?" In the end he replied, "It is currently split into three but one of our squadrons is currently visiting the castles of Pontus situated on the coastline of the Black Sea. Our principal forces are currently moored at the port at Golden Horn. One part of our fleet is in Pigasi and another in the Aegean Sea."

Emperor Palaiologos V knew that this rounded up response was caused by a lack of information but he acted as if what he had been told was sufficient to make a decision.

"How long would it take for all of them to join together at Hellespont?"

In spite of his young appearance, the commander had begun to suffer from forgetfulness. He cast his gaze on the ceiling again to try to come up with a reply, "The galleys and galleons can get there in two days but the row galleys and barges might take longer. Counting in the time for the orders to reach them and for them to undertake the necessary preparations, all of them except those being repaired can be in Hellespont within two weeks, Your Majesty."

Taking notes, the deputy mesazōn asked, "How many castellans and cavalry do we have in total in Pigasi?"

The commander-in-chief looked at the mesazōn as if to say, "You should know this" and replied, "As the Catalans have not been allowing our castellans in their castles for a while I cannot give you an exact number, Sire. We have been sending fewer and fewer castellans to take over temporary duty."

The mesazōn held the floor, "How about the sailors?"

"There might be two or three hundred if we count in the rowers who have been given permission to go home. But we haven't had a headcount in a long time. Many of those who have been given leave might not want to return."

Emperor John Palaiologos V looked at the mesazōn and said, "You may remember the times when our fleet could hardly fit into the Aegean Sea but as you can see we are lost in that same sea. We must restock our fleet even if it is at the cost of increasing the ship money of the Genoese."

As the Emperor waited for the deputy mesazōn to make notes, the commander-in-chief spoke in a resentful tone of voice, as the Emperor had not really brought up the land forces and castellans, "If we need to strengthen our fleet it would be good to seize some of the Genoese ships, Sire."

The Emperor briefly looked at the commander standing up straight and replied, "Seizing their ships would be the most mindless thing to do. You know as well as I do that they suspect on which way the wind blows before everyone else. If we seize their ships, those in other colonies, if not those across the sea, will immediately hang the Ottoman marker on their ships."

The mesazōn replied slightly timidly as he had lately been running counter to the Emperor, "His Majesty is right. The Genoese smell the wind before anyone else."

The commander-in-chief didn't expect the mesazōn to back him up but he felt uneasy. He turned his gaze shifting back and forth between the Emperor and the mesazōn to his goblet and as he drank the wine remaining in it, he thought, "If only I can get out of here without raising suspicion..." He refilled his goblet with wine averting his gaze from them, as he was scared that they would read his mind.

Just as he raised the goblet to his lips once again he saw the Emperor and the mesazōn looking at each other and became even more suspicious. He couldn't swallow the wine he was holding in his mouth. As he couldn't spit it out he swirled it in his mouth. He first looked at the window and then to the door. He gulped again but it was as if the wine had solidified in his mouth. He was incapable of swallowing it. As he tried to gauge the thickness of the bars on the windows and the width between them he thought, "I can't leave out of the door. The guards will swoop down on me as soon as I step over the doorstep. If I vanquish one, ten will come for me and if I vanquish ten, a hundred will attack me. There is no escape through the door but if I can leave out of the window I can perhaps find an escape route from the rear garden. Actually, the window is not a good solution either... But a path of hope might open up if I can make it to the garden. Neither the mesazōn nor his deputy are armed, but the Emperor has his sword on his waist." As these thoughts coursed through his mind he felt the wine become softer in his mouth and hastily swallowed it. Ironically, his strange feelings disappeared the moment he swallowed the wine. He suddenly smiled, and consoled himself with delusions of grandeur, "The Emperor's wrist power will not match mine even if he has grown into a man. The poor thing does not know any sword tricks. If he uses the tricks I taught him against me I can pull him down so quickly." Then he constructed an infinite sentence, "And, if I cannot do anything..." because the Emperor was looking at him carefully.

The Emperor was young but what he had seen had brought him experience and his gut instinct had grown stronger. It was as if he had read the commander-in-chief's mind. His gaze seemed to say, "Now I don't want anyone to do anything silly because they are thinking of themselves. Alexius and Krilinados... I want you to end the meaningless race that has been going on between you for years. It is now time to become allies and be strong. While Matthew Kantakouzenos takes advantage of the death of Suleyman Pasha we should also step into action so that we can come down on the Ottomans and send them back to the other side of the Dardanelles. This will benefit us in two ways. Firstly, the people will understand that we are also against the Ottomans who are closing in on Constantinople step by step. And secondly, we will get rid of them by helping Matthew Kantakouzenos. As the commander of the armies lined up these words that never departed from the Emperor's lips in his head, the Emperor addressed the mesazōn with jittering lips, "If you feel well, I want you to return to your duties at once and to find three ambassadors who can depart for the Karamanid lands. We will send them there one after another and each will be aware of the next one's arrival. They will determine their meeting point. They will find out what is going on and indulge the *Karamanids* accordingly. However, the road they decide to take is crucial. It would be best if they didn't go through Ottoman territory. Although nothing bad would befall them if they went through there but the ambassador to depart last should travel across the lands of our ally, Isfendiyar Bey."

As soon as the Emperor finished his speech, the mesazōn cut in, "I think that sending them separately one after another for sake of cautiousness is the most dangerous thing to do. I suggest that they should all follow the same course. We can form merchant caravans for each of them. Three merchants who are transporting the goods they bought from the Genoese to Baghdad. They can arrive in Ancyra together. As the two of them sell their goods one of them can reach the *Karamanids*. If he doesn't return the remaining two can try to get there."

The Emperor replied, "Fine, plan it as you suggested and inform your ambassadors fully before bringing them to me. The *Karamanids* have been sharpening their teeth for the Ottomans for a long time but they cannot bear the consequences of getting their teeth into them. I think that once they hear about us stepping into action they will also march on the Ottomans without further delay. If we can come to such an agreement with them, we can also come to an agreement with Matthew Kantakouzenos until the Ottomans have withdrawn to their past confines. First, find the ambassadors that will go to the *Karamanids* and then get ready to set forth. You will be going to pay a visit to Matthew as soon as we receive news from the *Karamanids*. Nobody other than you can convince him."

The commander-in-chief was sitting in an agitated state of mind because he had not been able to express his thoughts. His gaze was shifting between the deputy mesazōn who was taking notes and the Emperor. Comprehending that he had prepared an environment in which the commander felt empty, Emperor Palaiologos V said, "Commander-in-chief, it is now time to live down what we did before and to empower the empire once again. We must send away the Ottomans from Gallipoli with our fleet on one side and our land forces on the other. You must start preparing your battle plan at once."

Hearing the last sentence, the commander-in-chief surmised that his thick neck—which appeared like a continuation of his waist—was getting thinner. Holding his goblet in one hand he touched his neck with the other. Confirming that his neck remained unchanged he heaved deeply.

When the goblets were all empty they stood up together. As the deputy mesazōn walked the Emperor and the commander to their carriages in front of the gates, the mesazōn waited for his deputy's return with tremors coursing through him.

CHAPTER SEVENTY-THREE

The conifer trees that decorated the northern shoulder of Olympus were graded into shades of green towards the mountainside. They thinned out as they got closer to the castle and gradually left their place to deciduous trees which became wide apart as they descended down to the large plain embracing the Nilüfer River and mingled with the fruit trees in the gardens. Both sides of the road leading to the banks of the river with silvery water were adorned with haughty chestnut trees and sweet and sour cherry trees—branches of which were bent and broken by the weight of their scarlet fruits in spring. The chestnut trees were jealous of the colour of their fruit and condescendingly said, "Our little siblings who remind us what time of the year it is." However, because the sweet and sour cherry trees knew that the chestnut trees were good at heart and were only mocking them because of their pride, they started giggling at them like little girls with white teeth.

As Orhan Ghazi speedily wend his way down the road besieged by haughty chestnut trees on either side towards the Nilüfer River on the back of his trotting blue Roan, every now and again he saw the golden head of the sun in the horizon. The buildings in the castle met with the evening earlier because the castle walls were tall, yet the sun was still playing with multi-coloured leaves outside of the castle. Orhan Ghazi delved so deep into his thoughts while looking at the sunset that he had begun to spur his Roan. He didn't even notice that he had been spurring his horse so hard that he had gained great speed and began to totter. Coming back to his senses upon feeling the struggling horse, Orhan Ghazi extended his hand and caressed the combed mane of his steed. Picking up on the signal of his rider, the Roan slowed down a little.

Just as Orhan Ghazi, who was riding his horse with his *serdengeçtis* following him from a distance, were about to arrive at the thermal springs—built by Justinian, the great Emperor of the Eastern Roman Empire, for his wife Theodora so that she could come here from Constantinople and rest now and then—Nilüfer Hatun had just clapped her hands and was summoning the odalisques and handmaidens. As they were gathering around her slowly, she dazedly watched the colour of the silvery waters of the river named after her look like red silk with the crimson of the setting sun and then turn to a dark emerald green. Listening to the boundless quiet of nature with her slender and long fingers covering her face, she muttered, "Orhan is late but listening to this silence alone has done me good. It has given my mind power and quelled my rebellion." She turned her gaze to the thermal springs—where Theodora, Rome's empress of legendary beauty, experienced the tales of one thousand and one nights—as if she anticipated Orhan Ghazi's arrival. Just then she heard the Roan neighing and, for some unknown reason, she got excited. Her heart beat as if it was about to burst out of her ribcage and she murmured, "As excited as I was when I saw him return from a campaign for the first time..."

Then she spoke out loud, "Orhan Bey is coming."

The odalisques and handmaidens who had gathered around her upon hearing of Orhan Ghazi's arrival stood still. At that moment everything was frozen and became buried in shimmering mystery.

Orhan Ghazi appeared from among the trees with his horse and rode towards Nilüfer Hatun. As the blue steed approached the ladies, odalisques and handmaidens of his master's mansion waiting around on the riverbank, the *serdengeçtis* and watchmen disappeared from sight among the tall trees where a galley was set up.

Finding out about Orhan Ghazi's arrival, the head chef ran to Nilüfer Hatun and asked her whether dinner was going to be eaten under the moonlight. Nilüfer Hatun approached Orhan Ghazi who was talking to Theodora and Asporsha, asked him, "Would like to eat dinner tonight under moonlight or shall we return to the mansion?"

Orhan Ghazi had not thought of this at all on his way back. Caressing his short-trimmed grey beard with his long fingers he replied, "Nilüfer Hatun, I am not sure what you would prefer but I will be setting forth on another campaign soon. I don't know how the weather will be when I return. Let's eat tonight's dinner here..."

"We were waiting for your arrival, otherwise we would have returned long ago. But if you so wish, we can accompany the moon tonight."

Nilüfer Hatun then turned to the head chef and said, "Prepare a dinner tray and bring it to us."

As the head chef ran into the distance, Orhan Ghazi was sitting on a ground cloth spread upon the grass. He said, "I suppose Asporsha won't deny us the pleasure of listening to that beautiful voice of hers which we have not heard in a long while."

Nilüfer Hatun had nurtured and brought up both Asporsha and Theodora so well that if something befell her, Asporsha and Theodora could manage the mansion flawlessly. During her first days at the mansion, Asporsha had kept her distance from Nilüfer Hatun but in time she had got to know her and had become a part of her. She had come to accept Theodora as if she was one of her own daughters. She had perhaps had the biggest shock of her life when she heard that Kantakouzenos wanted to wed his young daughter Theodora to aged Orhan Ghazi—even though it hadn't even crossed his mind—but in time she had to come to terms with the fact that this was a part of the beys' life. To start with, Asporsha said she likened herself to a dirty handkerchief when she saw Theodora who had come from the Byzantine palace, like herself. With time she had come to accept Theodora just as Nilüfer Hatun accepted her. They had become confidantes.

Nilüfer Hatun's mental journey back into the past started when Orhan Ghazi said he wanted to hear Asporsha's voice and continued further into the earlier times as she listened to Asporsha singing. She was listening to the song played by odalisques and sung by Asporsha while reliving the day she married into the Ottomans. With smiling lips, she remembered, "Orhan was also on a blue Roan when the wedding procession was surrounded by people. I was just as excited when I saw Orhan's face as I was startled when I heard Osman Bey's nasal voice. Both my gaze and my heart had begun to shift towards him when Osman Ghazi said, 'Son, this beautiful bride compliments you much more than the old feudal landlord she is promised to. Take her, she can be your lady.' Orhan never questioned his father's judgment and thus, he obeyed. When we returned to the marquee of the Beylik, Malhun Hatun was delighted. Festivities continued for exactly forty days and forty nights." Nilüfer Hatun continued listening to the touching voice of Asporsha Hatun. When she turned her gaze to the river she seemed to hear it whisper, "I replaced my name of all those years, Odryses, with your name since the day you built that bridge." Just as moonbeams transformed into moonlight she joined Asporsha Hatun in her singing when she heard her sing a Greek song from the past. Hearing the beautiful harmony of their voices, Orhan Ghazi rejoiced and wanted to join in but he changed his mind when he thought that his low-pitched voice would spoil their accord. He took Nilüfer Hatun's into his palms and caressed them. As they held hands, the full moon rose from behind Mysian Olympus, hastily followed the Nilüfer River and positioned itself above the vineyards where they took delight in the beauty of the night. Mesmerised by the beautiful voice of Asporsha Hatun mixing into the sweet gurgle of the Nilüfer River the moon stayed with them until there were no more songs to sing. Just as the full moon was about to disappear from sight, Orhan Ghazi held Nilüfer Hatun's hand tightly and stood up. When all of the ladies, odalisques and handmaidens also stood up he told them, "You should all follow us."

Then he walked in between fruit trees and reached the edge of the water. For a while, he listened to the purl of the waters polished into silver white and dipped into golden yellow by the moonlight. He said, "Go on, sing a couple of songs for the waters."

He sat on the grass. Sitting beside him, Nilüfer Hatun delved into memories again, "We were both in our thirties. We had reached the waterside on horseback all in one breath. We tied the horses to trees and walked to the edge of the water hand in hand. It smelled of water lily just as it does now. It was as if water lilies had rained onto the river from the sky that year. Orhan took off his boots and went into the water. He picked a flower from among tens of water lilies stretching to the middle of the water from the edges and returned to me. Looking at me he jested, 'Let me see, is my Nilüfer[57] or the water lily more beautiful?' Then he looked at the flower and at me for minutes on end. Giving the flower to me, he said 'You can have this, my Nilüfer is more beautiful.' I held his hand and put it on my belly. When I whispered into his ear, 'I am expecting.' My Orhan was mad with joy. In order to join him in his mad joy I said, 'I want to commission a bridge to be built on this crazy river after I've given birth'."

Holding Nilüfer Hatun's hand as she retreated into silence, Orhan Ghazi had also delved into his own thoughts, "I couldn't spend any time with my Nilüfer in those first years when I was riding from one castle to the other with my father. I didn't have time to get to know myself—let alone her. I was adding my grandfather's advice to the duty given to me by my father and trying to take lessons from them. But no matter what conclusion I arrived at, the result was always the same. Sheep, horses and cows multiplied when they were inseminated but castles didn't, they had to be besieged. I took great pleasure in capturing those castles that didn't multiply unless they were invaded. In any case, I had no other choice. All of those around me were telling me I had been chosen to capture the castles, fuelling my joy.

---

57 T.N, *Nilüfer* literally means "water lily".

Especially my grandfather Sheikh Edebali was always beside me and I was spending most of my time, except when I was campaigning, with him instead of with Nilüfer. In those earlier years, I never wanted to leave my mother's side. I didn't realise back then that my mother was training Nilüfer with work and my grandfather was getting me ready to be a man with his words. Sometimes, when I sat beside my mother, she told me, "Not ready yet." I didn't know what it was that I wasn't ready for but I didn't challenge my mother. When one day my mother made me sit across from her and told me, 'You will spend less time with me and more time with Nilüfer from now on', I had understood what was meant by 'ready'."

He gathered that Nilüfer Hatun was remembering the day she told him that she was pregnant with their son Suleyman. He pulled her up and, looking at her face, he said, "We wish you well, my God who has bestowed upon us the greatest pain, for giving us the opportunity to test our patience. Let's leave, my Nilüfer."

CHAPTER SEVENTY-FOUR

The clouds above Constantinople were gradually darkening despite all of Emperor John Palaiologos V'S precautions and the situation was amplifying his concerns. He was disgruntled that the messengers he sent to the Pigasi Castle across the Sea of Marmara and the Heraclea Pontica Fortress on the coastline of the Black Sea still hadn't returned. He was constantly clamping down on his mesazōn with that vexation. Meanwhile, the mesazōn who had to resume his duties before he was fully recovered from his illness was sick and tired of looking for the commander-in-chief who had constantly been making excuses whenever he was summoned. Wherever he sent messengers, he only discovered that the commander-in-chief was elsewhere—if the messenger were at sea, the commander would be on land and vice versa. He deeply regretted not derailing him perforce at the ministerial palace on that evening but since the damage was done, there was nothing he could do to revert the situation. Even though he found temporary solace in himself when he decided to tell the Emperor about the fact that he had got himself into difficulties, the thought of how he would respond to the question of, "What have you been doing all this time?" was fettering him and he somehow couldn't explain the situation they were in to the Emperor.

Waiting for the mesazōn's arrival every day, the Emperor got impatient and alighted his horse carriage, which always waited for him in the courtyard of the palace, telling the driver of the carriage to take him to the palace of the mesazōn.

The driver had a really good feeling for the horses and brought the horses to a halt in front of the palace of the mesazōn with only a few cracks of his whip. The Emperor immediately hopped off the carriage and swiftly walked to the drawing-room of the mesazōn. In the meantime, the messengers of the mesazōn had informed him of the Emperor's arrival. The mesazōn was prepared, as he had known for a long time that he would bear the brunt of the situation. He stepped out of his drawing-room calmly and with the experience of years, greeting the Emperor in the corridor. As he did so, he ordered the servants to bring them the most mature of their wines from Tristasis.

The Emperor was walking down the corridor hurling the air around him. As if it wasn't enough that he was breathing heavily through his nose, it was as if he was setting his exhaled breath on fire with his rage. Realising fully that his arrival didn't bode well, the mesazōn was waiting for the Emperor with the patience of Paris waiting for Achilles. The only thing he had learned from Kantakouzenos VI was how to behave at such times. Even though he lashed himself into a fury by recalling Kantakouzenos, he thought, "The idea is good, it doesn't matter who thought of it." While bending down and greeting the approaching emperor, he showed him into his office with a polite hand gesture. The Emperor—who was acting with rage rather than rationality—somehow softened up upon seeing that hand gesture. As he walked towards the door he thought, "It wouldn't be nice of me to scold him in front of everyone." As soon as he stepped over the threshold he noticed there was a servant with his back to the door. Hardly able to contain himself not to shout at the mesazōn who was closing the door he muttered, "I should wait for the servant to leave." However, the servant was moving so slowly that it felt to him as if he was killing time instead of finishing his business in the room. Realising that he had no patience left, the Emperor was about to tell the servant to leave the room when the servant turned around with a silver tray and presented it to him. Seeing the gilt goblet full of wine in the middle of the tray, Emperor Palaiologos V thought, "A little wine will make me feel good" and took a few sips from the goblet. He liked the taste and drank all of it. Seeing that his goblet was empty, the servant refilled it and walking backwards, disappeared behind one of the side doors that opened to other rooms. Waiting for him to leave the room, the Emperor drank half of the wine in the goblet, realising that he forgot about half of his rage with the wine he swallowed. Looking at the mesazōn's face with regard, he murmured, "You know exactly how to soften my rage" and then took another sip of his wine before asking, "Alexios, what's happening? Where is the commander-in-chief? You answer each and every question I ask with the explanation that you are waiting for news from your men. Do you not know how crucial each passing day is?"

The mesazōn wiped his exhausted sagging and swollen eyes with the back of his hand and took a sip from the goblet that was always half full on his desk. Then, in a soft tone of voice, he replied, "Your Majesty! I have not slept for days but the conditions are such that I cannot do anything but to writhe in despair. As if it wasn't bad enough that we suddenly encountered inclement weather when we set the ships sailing, I have not been able to receive any news from any of the messengers we dispatched."

For days, the Emperor had been storming through in his study and into Helena's chamber but he hadn't once thought of the sea storm. Looking at the black attire of the mesazōn in surprise, he sat at the wide chair in front of the desk, turning his gaze to the ground, "I hadn't thought of the storm at all."

The mesazōn took a deep breath with the ease of softening the Emperor's anger through his initial explanation. Putting on an even more concerned face he said, "We have another malady, Your Majesty and I don't know how we can fix it."

"What's the matter? What's this malady?"

"The commander-in-chief... I don't even know where he is. I was going to pay you a visit to tell you but you have done me the favour."

"I see... He is not reporting his location despite me telling him that he had one last chance to prove himself worthy."

"Rumour has spread like wildfire... According to my sources, he is in communication with Matthew. I fear that something bad will happen, Sire!"

"All right, don't you worry. I will get them to find him. Let's see if
he will figure out what has happened once he no longer has an army
to command!"

The mesazōn had finally found a sense of peace with the ease of
turning over the issue of the commander-in-chief to the Emperor. As
he swallowed the wine slipping across his tongue with great gusto, as
if he was drinking in honour of the business he concluded, he wanted
to let out an "Ah!" but he couldn't. Smiling without looking at the
Emperor he said, "We have completed our preparations to be able to
make the adequate payment from the treasury as per your orders.
Thank God for the riches of Byzantium. Thank God for the riches of
Constantinople. Thank God for the magnanimity of our people."

The Emperor raised his hand, "It doesn't matter what the people
do. Alexios, as I said before, we must benefit from this as well."

The mesazōn understood at once what was being implied. In any
case, he wanted the conversation to follow in that direction. He added hastily, as if his previous speech was incomplete, "Thank God
for the riches of our empire. Thank God for the magnanimity of our
castle commanders and loyal counts. Thank God for the earnings of
our tradesmen. Thank God for the fertility of our seas. Thank God
for the one who sends abundant winds to the Genoese ships..."

The Emperor smiled when he noticed that the mesazōn kept mentioning others and never himself. He muttered, "Or is this matter of
the fish right, despite all our precautions?" Looking at the mesazōn
who diverted the conversation from his own treasury, "I suppose a
little piece of the riches you speak of will find their way to our treasuries?"

The mesazōn replied brazenly, "A quarter of the mesazōn's treasury will certainly be added on top of this sum... However, if we seize
the commander-in-chief's treasury we will not need to touch your or
my treasury, Your Majesty."

"Does the commander-in-chief have that much?"

"That's why he's escaped and in hiding. If he feared for his life instead of his riches, he would have long joined Matthew. Sure, he wouldn't want to fall into Matthew's clutches but nobody has ever died of lying, Your Majesty..."

The Emperor looked at his half-full goblet as if he regretted how quickly his anger had subsided. With the tranquillity of the wine he was drinking he replied, "I will go and get them to find the commander-in-chief. I will dispatch a messenger to you as soon as they find him. Come and join us at once when you are finished with your business. We should first find out what has been going on before we do what we must."

The mesazōn looked at him as if to say, "You won't find him and I won't finish my business and come to you" and saw the Emperor place his goblet on the table. Thinking that the wine was doing its job, he hastily said, "Wouldn't you like some more wine, Your Majesty."

He moved to fill the Emperor's goblet even though it wasn't his custom to do so. The Emperor stopped him with a sign of his hand, "No, I am leaving. I have to get my men to find the commander-in-chief before night falls. We must find out about the state of our fleet and our castles. We don't have any castles in Anatolia other than Pigas and Heraclea Pontica. We also have Philadelphia but it's like an island between the lands of the Beyliks. We could actually ask them for help."

When the Emperor stood up to leave, so did the mesazōn. The mesazōn walked him to the gates and returned to the drawing-room with a bitter smile on his lips. Two tears rolled down his eyes just as he started working at his desk again. He was trembling through and through. Looking at the teardrops falling onto the paper atop the walnut desk, the question of, "Are these for Byzantium, the Palaiologos or for myself" lingered in his mind. Realising that he couldn't work more that evening, he quickly gathered his strength and walked to his mansion. He had only walked a few steps in the side courtyard of the garden when he returned with hasty footsteps as if he had just thought of something. He ordered the messengers waiting in their quarters that he was going to be at his mansion and that they should inform him as soon as possible if there was any news from the Emperor. Then, walking towards his mansion, he recalled the Emperor's son, a commander of the guards, and his daughter, the wife of the commander of the guards of the Heraclea Pontica Castle who had two children and who he hadn't seen in a long time. As he muttered, "I need to talk to them so much right now. I wish they were at the mansion with me at this moment and we could talk" he recalled the mother of his grown children and muttered, "It is her to whom I need to speak." When he arrived at the mansion he felt very dirty. With the hope of washing the dirt off his body, he told his servants to fill the brass tub—his new favourite. He immersed himself in the water as soon as it was full of water.

While the mesazōn spent his time in the warm waters of the tub, Emperor John Palaiologos V had summoned the commander of the imperial guards and ordered him, "I want you to find the commander-in-chief within the next two hours. Dispatch your men in all directions and bring him to me before midnight."

The commander of the imperial guard, who had never received such a high order, sent word to all of his men and ordered them, "Find the commander-in-chief no matter where he is."

The knights delegated tasks between them. Erymanthos, a commander of the guards and the mesazōn's son, was given the duty of searching the commander-in-chief's house. Erymanthos set out to Commander Krilinados' mansion as soon as he received his orders. Before riding away on his horse he told his knights, "Behead anyone who tries to prevent you from entering the mansion!"

CHAPTER SEVENTY-FIVE

Orhan Ghazi wasn't interpreting the suddenly gusty weather favourably. He was thinking that the campaigns before winter would be delayed and that such delays wouldn't be beneficial for his Beylik. When he was alone he kept fixing his gaze on a certain point as if he was seized by fear. He had been in this state of mind for days, repeating, "Everyone says the wind blows hard on high ground but no one knows it reserves its real power for the lowlands." Almost every time he said that he was deploring his old-age by saying, "The things I have to do have become fewer even though I have much work to do."

Murad Bey was getting really bored on the days his father spent lamenting. He wanted to set forth as soon as possible to catch up with Lala Şahin Bey, who had departed from Bursa with his forces, but his father was just not giving him his consent. During the last small council meeting, which he attended in his father's place, he was finally allowed to leave. Joyous about this decision, Murad Bey went to the mansion as soon as the meeting was over. Seeing his father gaze at the lacklustre sun, which had almost disappeared over the horizon, he said, "I wouldn't want to disturb my father."

He then placed his hands together and kept silent. Orhan Ghazi turned to him and said, "Thank God for the day you were born, my son. You'd have to do much wrong in order to disturb me. Since when is visiting your father a wrongdoing? Do you know what I was thinking about while looking at this lacklustre sun?"

Prince Murad replied, "Who can know my father's secrets unless he tells them?"

Looking at his son proudly, Orhan Ghazi continued, "I was thinking about that first day when I met your mother. I was beside my father who was postured on horseback like a piece of marble and looking at the castle with all his ambition. Our *levends* had entered

the castle and it was ours but my father's rage fuelled his ambition
so much that he couldn't calm down and tell his brave men to stop
plundering. The *Alps*, my uncles and the beys were all praying for my
father's rage to subside. However, none of them could work up the
courage to tell him to stop his men from continuing to plunder.
When my eyes met the eyes of your mother behind her veil, I noticed
that she was feeling sorrowful for the people of the castle. The grief
in your mother's look must have given me the courage to approach
my father, whose tanned face boasting eyes like lighthouses with
large whites, and said, 'Without wishing to lay down the law among
all of these *Alps* and Beys but I believe my father, who considers
Lady Holofira worthy of being his daughter-in-law, will not find it in
his heart to upset her further. And since all of the feudal landlords,
commanders and guards who attended the wedding and were in cahoots have been taken captive, I wish that you would forgive the remaining women, the children and the elderly for her sake.' I thought
that my father would explode with fury but I couldn't believe my eyes
when I saw the lines of rage on his face soften. When he rode his
horse a step closer to mine I was thinking, 'This is how he ap-
proaches his enemy, with a soft and gentle face, and then he suddenly thrusts his sword into his enemy's chest...' when my father
replied, 'Son, rage is like a hard wind. You have to wait for it to
leave or you will suffer instead of others. Right now, I wish to have
the walls of the castle of Yarhisar demolished from its foundations
upwards. But not long ago, I have given you a soul I have saved from
there. Now the people of this castle have also become our family.
Thank you for reminding me of that. Go now, and tell the cavalry to
leave the castle.' With the fire of my youthfulness, I felt as if my
blood was about to spurt out of my veins and got so excited that I
could have touched the sky. Immediately after bowing to him and
leaving his presence, I spurred my blue Roan. My first horse was a
blue roan just as my last. When I arrived by My Beys, I informed

them to sound the bugles so that the plunder could come to an end at once. As the bugles were blown, Akça Koca's men yelled, 'Seize the plunder' from the bastions of the castle. When our brave men abandoned the castle, the inhabitants who were gathered at the squares were told to return to their homes. Then, the feudal landlord —who was also my father-in-law—vowed to never betray us again and the castle was placed under his control. But all of the guards who resisted and the other feudal landlords who were at the wedding were taken into captivity together with their men. Later, many of those who were capable settled in Bursa with us. The people of Bursa rejected this at first but when their lives became easier due to their crafts and trade it became easier for them to accept their existence among themselves. Son, what I mean to say with all of this is that should you wish to establish a great state you should win the hearts of the people living in those lands. I have strived to do so in the castles I have captured to this day. However, I now realise that time —the master of all of us—is whispering to me to tell you this. Because establishing a state requires not one but many lifetimes."

Understanding his father's message thoroughly, Prince Murad affirmed his father with a subservient motion of his head, "My dear father knows better than I do that the lifetime of many a man is no more than a drop in the ocean. But my dear father's life is a vast lake that is apart from the ocean."

Orhan Ghazi was struck in admiration of his son's words. Looking at him with awe, he replied before sitting on the floor cushion in the main corner of the room, "You are right, my Murad. No matter how much I seem like a lake that is separate to the ocean, the flood of time will one day arrive and add me to it."

"My dear father, today the council decided that I can set forth towards Lala Şahin Bey. I would like to capture Ancyra before the winter comes down and build winter quarters for our cavalry. If you approve, it is my wish to catch up with him before he besieges Ancyra, and after we capture the castle, to establish our friendship with the Jandarids."

Observing his son's excitement, Orhan Ghazi thought he had to caution him, "Son, you should know that the greatest issue is that the *Karamanids* still think they are the owners of both Kilij Arslan's sword and lands, whereas they are nothing more than a segment of the Seljuqs who have been divided up into shreds. As they are ignoring this reality, 'Their rage and ambition equal one another', as my father always used to say. Don't forget that we will have to reckon with them sooner or later."

Prince Murad could make neither head nor tail of what his father was telling him, "What does my dear father think about this for the future?"

Orhan Ghazi scratched his short-trimmed beard, featuring hardly a black hair in sight, with his large fingers. He looked at his son's face and thought, "How clean and beautiful" before turning his head and looking at the last bleary light beam percolating through the window and being reflected on the opposite wall. Keeping his gaze fixed on the beam of light, he continued, "I am certain that my Suleyman also watched another day's sunset just as I am right now. He had also thought of, in fact dreamt of, many tomorrows. However, the truth is that he has left his tomorrows to you and I. I would have liked to see him go beyond the Dardanelles and you beyond Anatolia as far as you could. Though, it is no longer even worth dreaming of these. You should know that as my oldest son, it would be unfair of me to want you to realise my dreams after I am gone, but I would be happy if you always kept my dreams close to yours. I never thought that anything could sadden me as much as my father's illness until your older brother's death. But the pain of losing my sons has covered that great pain. One thing I have never forgotten about my magnanimous father, who didn't care for riches, is his failing voice speaking into my ear, "Son, as I depart for the infinity of my fate which has taken me into its grip since the day of my birth, my soul finds peace in your existence. In these final moments, as I prepare to depart from you, I am leaving no desire unaccomplished because I am handing over my place to you. May all evils and worries be far from you." He spent so much energy to tell me this, that he was exhausted. He slowly placed his head on the pillow. I was scared when his grip loosened. I leaned over him. When I felt his breath on my skin I recovered. My father opened his eyes again. It was as if his large hand had sprung to life and was taking shelter in my palm. As I caressed his hand with my fingers I thought, "You cannot be the Osman Bey who used to roar in battlefields..." His breath quickened. He looked at me as if to prompt me to get closer to him. I put my ear close to his mouth. In a tone of voice just about louder than breathing, he said, "Son, steal your gaze from cruelty. Do not shelter those who tyrannise. Be just. Listen to those who know better than you. Don't waste your time. If you can succeed in these, my soul will rest in peace and you will be dear to God..." I couldn't make out the words he said after these. Since then, I have tried to guess what he said but I could never get rid of the feeling that none of those were my father's words. I don't have much to add to what he said. You will be campaigning soon. I am an old man. We can't know what the future holds but I hope that you will live a long life. Now go and receive your mother's blessings and bid farewell to Gülçiçek Hatun. Watch out for Lala Şahin Bey's rage during the campaign.

Orhan Ghazi extended his hand to his son. Hearing his father's last sentences, Prince Murad's clean and handsome face had turned red. However, when he realised that it was his father who had said that everything was part of life, he noticed that curtain of embarrassment sliding off his face."

Prince Murad kissed his father's hand. Orhan Ghazi held his son's hand tightly, pulled him towards himself and embraced him to his heart's content. Then, in a sonorous tone, he instructed, "Capture

Ancyra for your brother Suleyman. Don't keep us in the dark here.
Send us news of your success..."

CHAPTER SEVENTY-SIX

The Emperor was not angry but because he couldn't calm down, he could neither sit in his chair for a long time nor write the letters he wanted to write. All that he had managed to put down on paper in hours was a couple of short paragraphs. He failed no matter how hard he tried to rewrite them. Walking up and down the room and trying to gather his thoughts, he thought, "The first letter has to be written in a diplomatic language and should hint to the prince that there is an impending second letter so that he is not surprised when he receives it". When the fantasies that suddenly filled his heart began roaming in his head, he joyously ran to the pen and inkstand waiting for him on his desk. He dipped the pen into the ink but realised that not a thought remained in his mind. It was as if in that shortest period of time, the words had splintered and taken to flight.

Sitting in his chair, he slowly realised that he wasn't going to be able to write anything at that moment. He placed the pen in the inkstand and leaned back on his chair, looking at the empty space that was once occupied by the throne that Kantakouzenos VI had used during his reign. He had arranged for the throne to be removed and cast off into the old furniture stores upon his return from Constantinople. He talked as if Kantakouzenos was sitting across from him, "Wouldn't it have been good if you hadn't attempted to take the empire from me and we were working together again? See how much I need you and your thoughts now? If you were beside me, we could have perhaps found a way out much easier. You returned empty-handed from Rome. You knew better than I before you set forth that the Vatican and Avignon don't give anything without receiving more. Your journey has been of use to neither you nor to Byzantium. On top of it all, your son has destroyed our forces here but yet this moment in time poses an opportunity for us. If you help us it

will be easier to throw the Ottomans out of Thrace. But regardless of
what happens, we will succeed in sending them to where they came
from, whether you help us or not. When I ordered Krilinados to the
ship I doubted my actions but then I saw that I had no other way
out. In any case, he is not liked by the other commanders anymore
because he doesn't get on well with the mesazōn. His focus on saving
himself during that strange event that befell us on our first return
from Phocaea had already cast enough doubt about him in my heart.
This time I told him that he is only the commander of the small ship
he is boarding. I cautioned the fleet commander, who I appointed as
the commander-in-chief, to keep a close eye on him. If he attempts to
join forces with Matthew once again he will have to pay with his life.
Perhaps this will be his last campaign." When his ruminating spiel
ended, he recalled that Kantakouzenos VI wasn't actually there with
him. Laughing with a void smile that only appeared on his lips, he
got carried away with the desire of writing and took the pen into his
hand once again.

He felt mentally alert as he dipped the pen in the inkwell, smiling
again and saying, "You are very far my dear father-in-law but you
are still a source of inspiration to me. I really want to see you but
perhaps it will never again be possible." A sense of bitterness came
down upon him. As it dissolved, he felt even more mentally alert and
began to write, "My dear son, you should know that you are our most
precious entity amongst all the Ottomans. I believe we can achieve
much together through collaborating with you. Keep trustworthy
people who give good advice close to you—people who will always
be behind you when one day you stand up on your own two feet. Let
me give you an example. Last night I ordered the arrest of my commander-in-chief, who was the commander of our armies before my
time and summoned him. My guards must have knocked him around
a bit as his clothes were ripped. I asked him why he had been on the
run for days and instead of telling me the truth, he said, 'I come from

a tradition of commanders who, like Agesilaus, attack the enemy from the frontline. I never run and hide or evade my duties. But I deeply resent being assigned to the mesazōn. I would rather die than receive orders from him because I am the commander-in-chief of the imperial army.' When he talked to me as if the mesazōn was not my representative I told him, 'My mesazōn, who has been working for me with obedience for many years, is also the chief representative of our empire when and where I cannot be present. He represents me under my authorisation. If and when necessary, I also listen to his advice. If you cannot accept working subordinately to him today, to-morrow my orders will offend your feelings too. Thus, I discharge you from your duties as commander-in-chief and pardon you so that I can benefit from your past experiences. From now on you will be the commander of a small ship and you will not disembark it until you set forth for the campaign.'

"His eyes opened wide. If he had a sword on him he would have at-tacked everyone in the room including me. His rage was apparent, no matter how much he tried to conceal it. But he had lost heart be-cause he was defenceless without a sword. The tone of his voice was proof of his weakened will, 'Your Majesty, at least allow me to go to my mansion to see my wife and children.'

"However, I didn't allow him that because I knew that he would head towards Matthew Kantakouzenos as soon as he got into his carriage. I told him that a commander who has not been fulfilling his duties for months and who doesn't obey his emperor doesn't have the right to see a Byzantine woman. He must have understood his wrongdoing as he replied softly, almost as if to test my mercy, "I couldn't fulfil my duties as they should have been. I am guilty, Your Majesty. However, I wish that you will give another chance to your commander who knows the seas with Zeus's cough better than any-one and ask for your forgiveness.'

"I looked at his face at length and said, 'Ye, Krilinados! I equipped you with important duties in both the evening of our last meeting and the evening before it, and gave you a final chance. But just as you didn't keep your word, you also prevented our messengers from going where they had to go. You are giving Zeus's cough as a pretext for the envoys who will be setting sail but what do you have to say about the fact that our messengers who are on horseback have not yet returned? Be grateful that I am not handing you over to the hangman, despite the fact that I know exactly what you and your men have been up to. As of this moment, you should report to our new commander-in-chief Demeksinos.'

"In order to intimidate him into doing what I said, I told him, 'Don't you dare leave your ship. If you do, remember that your wife and children are under the watchful gaze of my guards.'

"My dear son, I told Krilinados all of this within the space of a few minutes. But I am not merciless." The Emperor looked at the page as if he couldn't believe he had written it. His gaze became fixed on the inkwell and then on the water jug on the round meeting table. He dipped his pen in the ink, adding, "Dear Prince, I trust you more as my son-in-law. I take pride in you. With this trust, I would like to tell you the good news that the days when we will be able to walk across the Aegean Sea with our ships lined up alongside each other are not in the distant future—as long as you don't reject the demands I am outlining in this letter." The moment he placed the full stop he felt as relaxed as if he had completed the hardest task in the world. As he dipped his pen in the ink to begin writing his second letter he muttered, "I hope you will the gist of this." All of a sudden he jumped up as if someone had pricked him on his thigh with a needle. The thought that made him jump out of his seat was, "What if he gives the second letter to his father?"

He ran to the window on the double. He viewed the Genoese Quarter across the shore for a while. Then, sitting back in his seat, he continued to talk to himself, "Siellus Xenephenos, an envoy for many years, will masterfully tell him that his own head will be in danger if he gives the letter to his father. He doesn't usually consider me as a good diplomat but I think this time, he will appreciate my approach. He always mutters, 'I have come to exist with the Palaiologos but when the day comes I will cease to exist with them' to emphasise his loyalty. This way he can have another opportunity to exist." His words seemed to suddenly run out. But they hadn't. He wanted to continue his internal monologue but his mind got muddled when his gaze, perusing the walls, got fixed on the earthenware wine ewer. There was a flower motif with long and twining branches on its light brown ceramic. When seen from a distance and a certain angle, it looked like an octopus but when he moved slightly, that view suddenly disappeared and an orchid branch replaced it. When he stood further away from it, the orchid branch looked like a nautilus. Surprised about his mind's ability to come up with such images, he recalled his father-in-law John Kantakouzenos VI once again, "He was sitting across from me on his fake throne. When I turned my newly adolescent gaze to this ewer he looked at me and smiled. After scratching his greying beard, he had told me, "Son of Andronicus, I don't know what you think there is in that ewer but there it will be a long time before you can consume it. If you start drinking that now, you won't have any power left to reign as you grow older. But, if you are thinking about the motifs on it... They change according to the angle you look at them. It is a present from the noble Minos to those living in the Mediterranean and Aegean Seas. Even though it is said that they learnt these motifs from the people living on the continental coast and painted them with pigments they had brought from there, the plants from which these pigments are derived do not grow anywhere else other than Crete, the land of the Minos. See this purple colour, you cannot see it on any ceramic other than on that made in Crete."

He paused briefly and then continued, "The Minos gradually decreased in numbers when the Achaeans set foot on the island before mixing with them—so much so that they couldn't be distinguished at all. It is to no avail to say anything about them now. But what remains from them is the truth before you. Come along, let's go. We wouldn't want to be late for the engagement ceremony. I have never made my Helena wait, neither should you as of this moment.

"On that engagement day, I sought his advice every time I was unsure or stuck. I need him now as I did then. My mesazōn manages imperial matters well but he doesn't know how to manage people like he did. If I knew that my father-in-law was in Didymóteicho I would send some men and meet him wherever he wishes to but I am not even sure if he is there. He has been in fear of his life since he left here. The reason why he wanted to go to Rome was so that he could save himself from his son. Otherwise, he would have never gone to ask for help from the Catholic pope, even though he is a devout Orthodox, knowing full well that neither the Serbians, the Hungarians or Bulgarians can bear the consequences of fighting against our armoured knights. Matthew doesn't need to be looking for a supporter at all..."

This time his desire to continue his internal monologue waned just as his desire to write had previously. For a while he cast his void gaze on the walls and looked at the ewer on the small table. Looking at the drawings hanging on the wall bearing the imperial coat of arms he stood up. He took weak steps and sat on the chair behind his desk. He took his pen and submerged its tip in the ink. He read the final sentences he had written on the paper. With the courage he received from the lines he read, he began adding a closing paragraph to his second letter, "My dear son, be ready for the victories of tomorrow so that you can deserve to be victorious." He re-read his sentence and muttered, "That'll do." He ended the letter with his signature. Placing the letter in his desk drawer, he muttered, "We can wrap them in wax cloths and seal them once Xenephenos has read them" and hastily left his drawing-room.

CHAPTER SEVENTY-SEVEN

As his son Prince Murad left the room after receiving his blessing and before setting forth on his campaign, Orhan Ghazi looked behind him and said, "He will fill your shoes." He momentarily regretted that he was being a bit emotional while talking to his son but a while later he felt a sense of relaxation knowing that he had talked to him about everything he considered to be his legacy. The peace that coursed his heart while sitting in the room alone until dark gave him a great sense of joy. When night fell he left for his harem. The peace he felt could be seen on his face when he entered Nilüfer Hatun's room. Seeing Orhan Ghazi in the light of the oil lamps, Nilüfer Hatun said, "Orhan, are you trying to seem peaceful to console me?"

With a new smile that added even more tranquillity to the peace on his face that looked tanned in the light of the oil lamps, he replied, "Does the inner peace I have reached after many months, now show on my face, my Nilüfer?"

"I don't understand."

"There is nothing not to understand. After the death of my Suleyman, I became unable to see my friends because of my sorrow. I always concealed it so I wouldn't be adding more pain to your pain. Now it's all gone. I think that, as someone who has been in so many battles, my mourning has to end. That's why I have been able to reach inner peace and that's what you see on my face. The only thing is, after my Suleyman, I deplore being reminded of my old age and feeling cold in even a gentle breeze. I am a bit scared. But I will overcome all of this."

"You don't fear anything easily, my Orhan. You will surely overcome that as well."

"I seem fearless from the outside my Nilüfer but lately a strange fear roams my heart. That's what makes me shiver I think. In the old campaign days, I used to sleep in burrows made of snow and never felt the cold. But now, even the gentle breezes nip my old wounds. Until now, this wasn't what scared me but the thought that my Murad hadn't matured yet. I know that when the time comes we will pass over to the other side without resenting our fate. That's why I had talked to my Suleyman, whom I wanted as my successor, about everything relating to the Beylik when he was here last year. But I had never talked to Murad about all of that. God sent me his breezes and gave me a chance. I was able to talk to my son about everything. When he visited me this evening to receive my blessings and I told him all I wanted to tell him, peace coursed through my heart. I now feel peaceful enough to even prepare myself for death."

As he fell silent and looked at the oil lamps, he muttered, "They will keep burning as long as the wicks soak up oil and give out the same light without a care about who lit them." Looking at Nilüfer Hatun he continued, "Do you remember the day I went to visit Geyikli Baba? I'd returned from that visit with such peace as well. Did I tell you what it was that made me feel so peaceful that day?"

Turning the two fallen grey strands of long hair over and over again between her fingers, Nilüfer Hatun replied, "No, you didn't tell me. The only thing you said was, "I called him many times when I was a bey but he didn't come to visit me. When I wanted to visit him he declined my offer."

"True, no matter how many times I called him to my council he didn't come. I wanted to attend his council several times but he declined my offer by telling me it wasn't the right time. Then one day, he planted a sapling he was carrying on his back in the garden of our mansion, without asking for anyone's permission. Then, he turned his back and left without accepting any of the things I offered him. I got a little angry and made inquiries about where he was staying. When I found out that he was dwelling on the east versant of Bithynian Olympus I rode my horse there. When I arrived there, there was a massive ladle with its handle made of an antler in his hand but there was nothing in the cauldron in front of him. Looking at the empty cauldron, I said, "What use is it if your ladle's handle is made of an antler when your cauldron is empty?" He looked at my face. I paused so he could speak but he kept quiet for a long time. Then he turned his tall and thin body towards me. Stirring the empty cauldron with his antler ladle, he said, "We fill up on heart, not on meals, My Bey. This cauldron always seems empty but never stays empty because our friends of the heart always fill it. Looking at him, I replied, "Wouldn't it be better if you put something in the cauldron instead of waiting for your friends of the heart to do so?" He seemed slightly cross with me. He turned to the side and gently said, "How?" I replied, "Ye, dervish, you have such a big heart and you have all these dervishes with you... I donate the environs of İnegöl to you. Instead of waiting for your friends to fill your cauldron, cultivate this land so that you can always have something to boil. After weighing my words in his head he said, "My Bey, thank you, may you live long but we are not domestic people." I became curious and asked, "Who are?" He replied, "Beys like you." I insisted, "How so?" He replied, "Because what makes you a bey is your earthliness. We have no desire of possessing land and thus, we have nothing to do with the earth. Your land can be yours, those who come to me can make do with what I have." When I told him that making mention of God's name on an empty stomach would not be acceptable to the Almighty, he smiled. Looking at my face, he pointed to a small hill just a little further from the mountainside where the dervish lodge was located and said, "If you insist, we won't break your heart. Let the lands beyond this little hill become the yard of the dervishes and they can cultivate it in their free time." I gave the land he spoke of to them and came back. The peace I felt that day was dependent on the fact that I could give that yard to him. After then, neither he visited me nor I, him until his death. I could only preserve his grave. Shall we go and visit him before snowfall?"

Seeing her husband so peaceful, Nilüfer Hatun thought that the mansion that had been shrouded in mourning for a long time had to cheer up. She stood up from her floor cushion and sat beside Orhan Ghazi. She held Orhan Ghazi's bony and wrinkly hands and held them against her chest, "If it shall fill us with peace we should go and visit him tomorrow. But let us bury our sadness into the depths of our being tonight because what we are sad about today will one day befall us. I think we should feed more orphans from now on."

"Yes, we should. Let's find peace by looking after orphans for the rest of our lives."

"Murad is setting forth on his campaign tomorrow but he is leaving Gülçiçek behind. This means that our son will return as soon as he has completed his goal and spend the winter here."

Looking at a strand of cotton white hair that slipped from his lady's headscarf, he thought to himself, "Oh, my Nilüfer, you wouldn't say that if you knew that the *Karamanids* have a game in every bag. Who knows if one will return from a campaign?" He was startled and so was Nilüfer Hatun. Looking at Nilüfer Hatun's face again, Orhan Ghazi said, "He has to return, otherwise my heart cannot take it..."

In order to re-embrace the sense of peace he had when he entered the room, he said, "Let us go to the harem. We will spoil the little peace we have if we are left alone."

Nilüfer Hatun clapped her hands and told the servant who entered the room, "We will be having dinner in the living room. Summon the instrument players and singers. Call Lady Theodora and Lady Aspor-sha."

The odalisque was an efficient woman. She had been serving her lady for a long time and knew exactly what each task entailed. She left the room in an elated mood grasping that the mansion shrouded in mourning was finally going to be cheerful. Nilüfer Hatun held Orhan Ghazi's hands again, they stood up together and hand in hand walked to the living room through the long corridor brightly lit up with the yellow glow of the buzzing oil lamps. When the entertainments began, Orhan Ghazi noticed two new odalisques amongst his odalisques and turned his inquisitive gaze to Nilüfer Hatun.

CHAPTER SEVENTY-EIGHT

Emperor John Palaiologos V was unable to contain himself when the campaign preparations were complete. There were two reasons for his joy. The first reason was that he had managed to establish a new order in Constantinople after Kantakouzenos and the second was that he was collaborating with the *Karamanids* against the Ottomans. However, his joy was short-lived. The messengers conveyed the bad news to him when they were getting ready for the Sunday service at the Hagia Sophia, a day before they set forth on the campaign when he would unexpectedly eradicate the Ottomans from Thrace. Angry with Zeus in the early hours of the morning, Poseidon had overflowed Hellespont with his exhaled breath and sent her raging waves to the ports where the fleet was located. Some of the ships anchored in the ports had become unable to set forth on their campaign because they were colliding against each other while others were crashing against the coastline. Palaiologos V knew very well that he couldn't campaign without his fleet and postponed it by saying, "It seems that God doesn't consent to us campaigning in this season." However, not even this misfortunate managed to stop him. On the one hand he was getting the damaged ships of the fleet repaired and on the other he was sending envoys and gifts to his allies, despite inclement weather conditions, in order to strengthen the cooperation between them.

On ever-longer days of winter, mostly dedicated to writing diplomatic letters, Emperor Palaiologos V spent his day-to-day life between his mansion and the imperial palace where he worked. As spring approached, he was getting restless about still having pre-campaign preparations to finalise but he was doing all he could to make sure everything was on time. When he tired of working in his drawing-room, he opened the window to get fresh air and inhaling the scent of seaweed brought to him by the sassy north wind, he

voiced his longing for campaigning by muttering, "Smells of victory."
News of support brought by his newly appointed commander kept
whetting his appetite for campaigning. On those days when his appetite was whetted to the greatest extent, the envoys he had sent to
Nicomedia and Konya returned with good news. The only envoy who
hadn't returned was the one he sent to the Eretnids. Thinking that
he would return in a few days he kept saying, "All will be complete in
a week. I will first march on the Kantakouzenos to keep Orhan
Ghazi unsuspecting and then on the Ottoman units who are campaigning in the south of the peninsula."

As days passed by and the scent of spring spread to every corner,
Emperor Palaiologos V ordered his fleet commander, who he had
appointed as commander-in-chief, "Complete your preparations.
Our campaign begins next week" but the envoy sent to the Eretnids
had not yet returned. However, all of the ships of the fleet that were
overwintering in the ports on the coastline of the Black Sea had
joined the fleet anchored at the estuary of Chrysókeras[58] that opened
to the Sea of Marmara and were waiting for the day when they
would set forth on their campaign. The ships that were due to arrive
from Pigas were going to join them at the mouth of the Dardanelles.
The ships that were to arrive from various islands of the Aegean Sea
were going to convene with the fleet in Aenus.

One Sunday when the warmth of spring rejuvenated the earth, Emperor Palaiologos V waited on the coast until the last barge of his
fleet departed after the church service. After waving at the ships in
the distance for one last time, he walked towards the imperial carriage drawn by eight strong horses and turned around to look at the
hills of Constantinople. Then, as if his father was beside him he
spoke out loud, "Ye Andronicus Palaiologos, who didn't allow me to
live my childhood with his hasty death, raise your head from where it
rests and watch our fleet. Look how magnificently it sails in the Sea

---

58   T.N, Byzantines used to call current-day Haliç (Golden Horn), Chrysókeras.

of Marmara. I will also set forth on land tomorrow to meet that magnificent fleet. Once I clear the Kantakouzenos from the face of the earth without Orhan noticing it, I will send everyone who doesn't belong in Thrace to where they came from."

The driver who was ordered by the Emperor to drive to the imperial palace of the mesazōn steered the horses passing through the stone-paved ceremonial road towards the building where the mesazōn was working. Noticing the mastery of the driver in steering the horses, the Emperor courageously said, "We will no longer idly sit in the palace. Others come upon us as long as we stay in the palace. It is now our turn to walk over them." Looking at the guards stationed in the back and front of the carriage with a smile on his face, he exclaimed, "These unique warriors will accomplish everything."

During the days when the Emperor was preoccupied with campaign preparations, the responsibility of managing state affairs was on the shoulders of the mesazōn but he wasn't disgruntled about it. In fact, he was so delighted that no one was sticking their nose into his business that he had buried himself deep in his affairs. He had forgotten about his old age, his afflictions and even Sunday sermons. The only thing he hadn't forgotten was how new wealth would be added to his treasury. He had come up with a thousand and one ways to collect tax. If one of them didn't apply to a certain situation another one did. That is why he never objected when the Emperor said, "Let's add a little from our own treasury" with regard to the pending expenditure. Instead, he immediately took the necessary measures and sent his officers to the Genoese Quarter across the Golden Horn to collect "Campaign Tax".

As the Emperor was getting closer to the mesazōn's imperial palace, the mesazōn was hosting a guest in his drawing-room, even though it was a religious day. The Genoese of Sykai were suspicious of the tax collection that had become more frequent recently and had found out from their supporters in the palace that the Emperor had no knowledge of these levies. Thus, they had sent their mayor to meet with the mesazōn. The mayor of the Genoese Quarter appeared before the mesazōn with the confidence of the sovereignty bestowed unto him by the Emperor and said, "We know that the Emperor is not informed about the taxes you are collecting from us."

The mesazōn replied in a soft tone of voice as if he hadn't heard him, "It seems that the honourable Duca is still in trouble with the new neighbourhood located behind Pera... Or are the Jews who were expelled from the castle years ago causing you a headache?"

The mayor of Sykai looked at the mesazōn, who was acting as if he hadn't heard him, in surprise and said, "Esteemed mesazōn, we haven't had any problems with anyone in a long time."

Mesazōn Alexius replied, "So you are having trouble with the Polinormions[59]. We will immediately take the necessary measures, honourable Duca."

Knowing full well that "taking the necessary measures" meant giving an order to plunder the neighbourhood, the mayor of Sykai replied, "Sir, we know that you will take the necessary measures but we haven't any issues with the Polinormions. Our only problem is..."

The mesazōn interrupted, "So you have a problem with making too much money?"

"Sir, tax was also previously collected without your knowledge."

The mesazōn put on the appearance of someone who was face to face with great injustice and looked at the mayor as if he was looking at a stone, "Of course I know about it! As you know, our emperor is preparing for a campaign. So the Sykaians are complaining about the taxes they have to pay when even I am emptying my treasury for this campaign. But those who are disgruntled today should remember that they have to pay these levies so that our emperor can return from his campaign victoriously. If they don't pay their dues they can forget about making five times what they paid when our armies re-

---

59 T.N, People living at the Port of Galata were referred to as such by the Byzantines.

turn with glory. Go and tell this to those who sent you here."

When the mayor of Sykai realised from the mesazōn's tone of voice that the matter at hand was complicated, he moved to leave the room at once. Watching him leave, the mesazōn spoke out just before he stepped out of the door, "Tell them that they will pay to aid our emperor's campaign so that when they return with a victory they will be able to have the cheek to ask for what they want."

The two-horse carriage waiting for the mayor of Sykai in front of the garden gates of the mesazōn's imperial palace had just set out when the Emperor's eight-horse carriage pulled up. Getting out of the carriage in his ceremonial attire, the Emperor summoned the commander of the guards. When he had dismounted his horse and approached the Emperor, he commanded him, "Send word to the castle commander. All of our knights within the city walls should depart from the gate of Hagios Romanos with their men and convene at our headquarters outside the city. Our campaign will commence at sunrise tomorrow."

When he had said all he wanted to, he walked through the garden gate and headed towards the drawing-room of the mesazōn.

CHAPTER SEVENTY-NINE

Despite his broad shoulders, Lala Şahin Bey was tall and slim-waisted. It always seemed as if he looked down on people because he sat up straight on his horse. He disguised the ugliness of his long nose that resembled an eagle's beak with his curled up bushy moustache. There was always a sense of slyness in his greyish blue gaze that adorned his flat and long face. It was as if it had become flat just to complement his face. He always placed one of his hands on his sword whether he was walking or riding his horse. He didn't take his wide sword with both sides as sharp as an open razor out of its sheath very lightly but when he did, he wouldn't put it back in its sheath without exsanguinating it. He never yelled in the battlefield until he got furious but once he did, he yelled and regardless of who his enemy was he either reaped him down or cut him across the middle. Due to his method, the beys who served him likened him to Saladin, who they had heard much about. He couldn't stand it when people didn't pay attention to what he was saying. Despite the fact that he wanted to bring up Prince Murad like himself, he only likened the prince—who had a gentle nature—to himself in the battlefield. In fact, he watched the prince closely in the battlefields, pulled him aside afterwards and told him his mistakes while they were fresh in his mind. He cautioned him, "Be grateful that you landed on your feet this time but also remember that next time you won't have time to be grateful."

Prince Murad unconditionally accepted everything his tutor told him and always saluted him by bowing whenever he finished talking, before replying, "Tutor, I promise I won't make the mistakes I made today so that I can come out alive from the next battle."

When Lala Şahin Bey departed from Bursa and advanced on his way waiting for the *yaya* units here and there, the weather suddenly turned stormy. As they progressed in the south of Bithynian Moun-

tains the cold breezes were replaced by a blizzard. Everything was
covered with a blanket of snow within a few days. Lala Şahin Bey
saved his units from freezing by settling some of them in the small
villages between the mountains and others in the large tents they
had set up. When the snowfall had stopped he dispatched messengers to Bursa. Prince Murad ran into them in Nicaea but sent them
to Orhan Ghazi because he couldn't make a decision. As he waited
for Orhan Ghazi's orders, he lodged in one of the large rooms in his
mother's imaret where construction work was still on-going.

Orhan Ghazi headed to the council to consult his Grand Vizier
Sinanüddin Fakih Yusuf Pasha and the *Alps* as soon as he received
the news. The councilmen all agreed, "Neither the good could do
anything good nor the bad could do anything bad under such inclement weather conditions." So Orhan Ghazi announced, "We shall
continue the campaign in the spring." In the aftermath of the meeting, the Grand Vizier got the *kadî* of Bursa to write two copies of a
letter. The letter briefly read, "You can advance to Gerede by making
use of the days when the Bithynian Mountains do not blow snow.
Find suitable winter quarters with the help of our friend Sultan
Shah. You will continue your campaign with Prince Murad who will
join you in the spring."

Prince Murad read a copy of the letter, returned to Bursa and
stayed there until the spring. As the weather warmed up he set forth
to campaign with new cavalry units. After a week's journey across
plains where ice had thawed and snow had melted, he settled in one
of Sultan Shah's mansions in Gerede. Just a few days before he arrived, Lala Şahin Bey had departed for the Ancyra Castle, known as
the land of the *Âhis*, with his advance units followed by his *yayas*.

Lala Şahin Bey went to visit Prince Murad as soon as he found out
that the prince had arrived and settled in Gerede. Upon entering the
spacious meeting room in the mansion, where the prince was staying,
and saluting him, Lala Şahin Bey allusively said, "Welcome, My

Prince. I see that staying in Bursa has done you well."

Knowing exactly what he was hinting at, the prince replied, "What has done me well must be the motherly love I have been longing for many years. And also perhaps Çandarlı's teachings during the days, and my father's advice in the evenings."

"My Prince, I am sure that both your body and your mind have benefited from the various nutrients you received. I hope that you have learnt much from Çandarlı because Sinanüddin Yusuf Pasha is training him very well in matters of the state. I am sure that your father's advice will be highly treasurable to you throughout your life."

Then, Lala Şahin Bey summarised the events of the winter but hardly mentioned any of the challenges they faced. Listening to his tutor carefully, Prince Murad asked, "I am sure you also faced some challenges throughout the winter."

Lala Şahin Bey squared his shoulders as he usually did on horseback and, looking at the prince who was almost as tall as him, said, "I can say that we didn't face many challenges here. We struggled a little until we got here and set up the headquarters but after that, we didn't want for anything, thanks to Sultan Shah Bey. His silver tongue and the pleasant conversation was God's blessing to us throughout the winter. I noticed that he was a bit concerned upon my arrival. When I inquired about it, I found out that the *Karamanids* are cooperating with the Eretnids and the *Âhis* and that by sending them envoys, they were asking them to opt for cooperating with the *Karamanids* rather than Orhan Ghazi. I told them to rest assured that we will capture Ancyra in the spring and that their borders will be safe with the great forces we will leave behind in the castle. They must have been so impressed by what I told them that they overcame their fear and informed us that they would join us in capturing the Ancyra Castle. So we trained their forces and prepared them for the campaign. I think that your arrival has given them additional power and encouragement."

Prince Murad looked at Lala Şahin Bey with a smile on his lips that showed he was satisfied with the news. After wetting his lips, which were chapped by the harsh winds of the Bithynian Mountains, with his tongue, he said, "May you live long, Lala. We have to teach the Âhis such a lesson that they will not only opt to cooperate with us but also sever their relationship with the Karamanids for good. They also have to pay their debt to my older brother, Suleyman Pasha."

Lala Şahin Bey dropped his bluish-grey gaze to the floor and said, "The Âhis are very stubborn. If they get help from the Karamanids we might have trouble on our hands. However, my real fear isn't them."

When he fell silent, Prince Murad understood that he had a much bigger reason to worry. In order to give some time to him, he turned his gaze to the walls of the room covered with colourful tapestries and the ceiling carved by master wood engravers. Seeing that the lines on Lala Şahin Bey's face were softening, he asked, "Are we lacking something? Is that what worries you?"

Glad that the prince, who had listened to him carefully, understood he was worried about something, he replied, "My fear is that the Karamanids will march to Ancyra in spring. Even that wouldn't be too much of a problem but..."

He had understood his tutor's concern about the Karamanids but he was very curious as to what was concealed in that "but".

"But what, tutor?"

Lala Şahin Bey thought that Prince Murad had finally reached maturity. He replied, "But, My Prince, even if the Eretnids, friends of the Karamanids, came I wouldn't care. But, if the Eretnids send upon us the Tatars of Çavdar, we will have serious trouble on our hands because everyone in these lands knows that they have a great thirst for blood. Our levends might be discouraged if they hear that we have been attacked by them. Even all of that is manageable... There are certain other signs of danger which we should talk about once you have rested..."

Noticing the fatigue in the prince's eyes, Lala Şahin Bey cut it short and stood up. He turned back before walking out of the door and said, "I'll come to visit you with the other beys before dinner. I will also be bringing a guest with me."

After Lala Şahin Bey's departure, Prince Murad immediately headed towards his bed-chamber and threw himself on the bed. He was exhausted after having been riding for days. He spent the whole afternoon sleeping. When they woke him up for dinner, he was quite well-rested.

All the beys stood up and saluted Prince Murad when he entered the spacious room where all of his beys were gathered. He saluted them with a nod and sat on the seat of honour reserved for him. His beys also sat down in order of their seniority one after another. Lala Şahin Bey pointed to a man who was dressed like a merchant and standing up by the door and said, "My Prince, remember I told you we would be hosting a guest. This man dressed like a merchant is he. He has been captured en-route to Byzantium from the lands of the *Karamanids* by the men of our Gerede beys. He told us that he was on his way back after delivering a letter of friendship to the *Karamanids* as an envoy of the Byzantine emperor. However, when we interrogated his men we found out other things. His reply hasn't changed even though we asked him once again what duty he was given by the *Karamanids*. During our search, we found a letter in the hidden compartment of his horse's saddle. The *Karamanids'* letter to the Emperor was of great interest to us, so we detained him for you. The decision of what we do with him is up to you.

"Tell me what is it that is of greatest import to you and I can quickly decide on our course of action."

"My Prince, the *Karamanids* swear allegiance to the Byzantines in their fight against Orhan Ghazi and clearly express that they will attack our Beylik from the east as soon as they receive news that the

Emperor has commenced his campaign in Thrace in the spring."

Prince Murad had really matured quickly. He listened cold-bloodedly and replied softly, "I understand everything except the *Karamanids'* hatred towards us, and why they are uniting their forces against us, knowing full well that the weak will be defeated. It is good that we have found out about their plan of betrayal. Let's invade Heraclea Pontica located on the coast of the Black Sea to send a message to the Emperor on our way back from Ancyra. The envoy can be our guest until then because when we take the castle we will need an envoy to send to the Emperor. If this envoy doesn't accept that duty, he will be beheaded."

Lala Şahin Bey told Topal Hasan Bey—who was fluent in Greek—to interpret everything that had been said to the envoy and he obliged. The envoy saluted the prince with the joy of being spared his life by kneeling down. Lala Şahin Bey addressed his men, "Hand him over to Sultan Shah Bey's men. They can host him in Gerede until our return from Ancyra."

When Lala Şahin Bey's men took the envoy outside, the beys in the room rejoiced as if they were already victorious and exclaimed in unison, "May you live long, Prince Murad."

That night the food prepared by Sultan Shah Bey's cooks was eaten and wines offered by odalisques from European provinces were drunk. Music was played and dancers were watched. When the preparations were complete and camp was broken the next day, they set forth towards Ancyra Castle, foundations of which were rumoured to have been laid by Hittite kings. Prince Murad ran into Lala Şahin Bey at their first resting place after a few days' journey and saw his worried face, The prince hastily asked, "Did you receive bad news, tutor?"

CHAPTER EIGHTY

B yzantine Emperor Palaiologos V entered through the garden gate of his mother's, Empress Anna's mansion with a swelling sense of joy. The garden of the mansion adorned with an assortment of flowers sent from Savoy, the birthplace of the empress, and ever blooming roses that appeared more beautiful than they were under the bright light of the sun, which seemed as if it was an overdue oil lamp caught in morning light atop the hills adjacent to the neighbourhood of Chrysopolis, located across the Bosphorus as if it was the only man-made paradise on earth. Since the warm weather set in, which the empress defined as the harbinger of the spring, she had been spending her days in the garden. She didn't sit around idly while keeping an eye on the gardeners but instead frequently helped to loosen up the soil around the trees with a gardener's fork.

When Emperor Palaiologos V entered her garden she was loosening up the soil around a cherry tree. Seeing that her son had arrived, she left the fork to one side and cheerfully walked towards him. She opened her arms with the gaiety of a mother who was about to embrace her child rather than an empress. Emperor Palaiologos V was the Emperor of great Byzantium and heir to the Palaiologos but he was still her son. Moreover, according to hearsay he was about to depart for his first campaign. As she had got to know her husband, who campaigned throughout his life, well over the years, she was anticipating her son's state of mind. That is why she welcomed him with an exalted sense of warmth, thinking, "may he desires to come back to me safely more than death and separation." After holding him in a pincer-like hug, she took two steps back to look at him. She approached him once more and hugged him again, kissing his cheeks. When tears started to fill her eyes, Emperor Palaiologos V said, "Don't do that beautiful Anna, chosen by the Savoy and sent to the Byzantine throne. It was you who gave my father Andronicus strength on his campaigns, please be the one who gives strength to his son John now. Because with this campaign, his son wants to beatify the almighty soul of Andronicus."

Noticing the excitement in the voice of her son from whom she had never been apart from since the day she gave birth to him, the empress pushed aside the sadness in her heart and tried to give him courage, "Like every emperor's mother I will also wait for the day of my son's glorious return. You will find me with my arms open here when you come back. I only have one thing to ask—that you don't take your armour off, except when you rest, and when you do take it off, make sure that your most trusted knights are in armour because war is war and every minute of it is dangerous."

Holding his mother's slender hands in his palms for a while, John Palaiologos V replied, "When I return I will come to your garden to spend more time. Pray for me whenever you step foot into this beautiful garden. Until now I haven't had such an opportunity to campaign. Matthew Kantakouzenos doesn't have any followers left now, not even in the backcountry. I will first do away with him. I will clear Thrace off his forces until Orhan Ghazi whose forces have gone to lay siege to Ancyra arrives. Then I will return to Constantinople at once."

Looking at his son with a bitter smile, Byzantine empress consort Anna of Savoy said, "Know that as you gain power, they will have no followers left. I don't want to get involved in the punishment you will decide on Matthew but if you take his father captive, remember that he is your father-in-law. I am the one who has suffered the greatest evil at his hands but I don't want to forget about his endeavours for you. We both owe our lives to him."

"Once he has given up settling his old scores with me I will have no trouble coming to terms with him, mother. I wouldn't do anything that would upset my Helena. If she wants it I will bring him back to his mansion."

A woman of wisdom, Empress consort Anna kissed her son's fore-head. This kiss expressed everything and in a way it meant, "You can now leave." Noticing it, Emperor Palaiologos V first took three steps back facing her, bowed his head and saluted his mother before turn-ing around and walking to his carriage waiting for him in front of the garden gate. He didn't forget to wave to his mother when the driver's whip cracked upon the backs of the horses.

The Emperor had two more matters to attend to before setting forth to join the units awaiting him. The first was to see his mesazōn one last time and the second was to bid farewell to Empress Helena and his children. When his carriage stopped in front of the imperial palace, he headed to his drawing-room, took the imperial coat of arms and handed it over to the commander of the guards. He in-quired about the arrival of the mesazōn as he walked towards the meeting room. Finding out that the mesazōn was about to arrive, he entered the meeting room and began to wait. Looking at the Gen-oese Quarter from the window with a smile on his face he muttered, "It's good that we came to an agreement with the Venetians, even if it's secret. Their appetite was whetted when they found out that the taxes they paid to Orhan Ghazi would be halved. If our son-in-law has an open mind this deal will be done." Just then, the mesazōn entered the meeting room. After saluting the Emperor, he said, "Your Majesty, you can go on your campaign with your mind at peace. Both the Genoese and the Venetians have done the best they can. All our units are waiting for you near Selymbria."

Emperor Palaiologos V felt like a real emperor for the first time in years. He thought that discharging the commander-in-chief had been very effective in ensuring the obedience of all of his forces. He turned to mesazōn Alexius Apokaukos and said, "As of this moment I en-trust Constantinople to you. I told the commander of our castle guards that your orders are mine. I will dispatch messengers and send you news of our progress, and you will send me news, too. Make sure that the empresses are kept satisfied. The letters I send to them must be delivered to them at once, and their letters to me must be dispatched as soon as possible. Keep the Genoese Quarter under control but don't put more pressure on it."

The mesazōn had understood the Emperor very well. He muttered, "Once or twice more" and then replied to the Emperor, "Your Majesty, don't worry anymore. If the Genoese want to send gifts out of their own volition they will, if not it doesn't concern us..."

The Emperor thought that he no longer had any duties to fulfil there so he bid the mesazōn farewell and headed to his own mansion. Just when his carriage arrived at the front courtyard of the mansion, Empress Helena was working in her garden, as was Empress Consort Anna earlier, but her garden had fewer flowers and roses.

Children who saw the Emperor enter the garden ran to him. He hugged and kissed them. As they walked towards Empress Helena together, the Emperor spoke out loud, "Kantakouzenos's daughter, is this what you call a garden? You should head over to the garden of Anna of Savoy and see the blossoming flowers and the budding roses."

Empress Helena turned her elegant and mature body to the side and watched the Emperor walk towards her. She responded, "Children see their mother's garden as beautiful even if there is nothing in it. I can't even imagine how beautiful my mother's garden in Didymóteicho is now."

"According to the most recent hearsay, your mother is with Manuel."

"I'm sure she's returned... She can't stay away from her garden for long."

"Your voice is filled with such longing... If God allows me victory I will bring her to Constantinople. I don't know how I will react when I come face to face with Matthew but if I come across your father I will just tell him how much you miss them..."

A bitter smile spread across Empress Helena's face, "Thank you, John. Though don't forget that my older brother Matthew is a great commander. I wish you could have the opportunity to collaborate with him. However, you should do what you think will benefit our Byzantium."

After chatting for a while longer, Emperor Palaiologos V spent time with his children until dinner. He frequently turned his gaze to his daughter Irene, Halil Bey's fiancée, who now looked more like a young lady than a child. A voice in him said, "My daughter, I wish you hadn't grown up so quickly" while another whispered, "Now that you are grown you must go where you belong so that our sunrises can be brighter than ever". Tired of the interchanging voices within, he sat down at the dinner table. He wasn't sure if it was the excitement of setting forth on a campaign for the first time or the trepidation of going on an ambiguous journey but he had been eating excessively for days. That evening, Emperor John Palaiologos didn't really feel like eating but he forced himself and ate a little dinner. After dinner, he walked his children to their rooms and entrusted them to his servants. He then went to his harem where Empress Helena had been waiting for him. He bathed in fragrant waters inundated with flowers that were said to have arrived from lands very far away. He discharged his chambermaids and lied down next to Empress Helena who had been waiting for him in their spacious bed. As he looked at her with love, Empress Helena said, "John, I would like to thank you for all the beautiful things you have made me experience despite the bad days we have been through. I hope that you will return to us before you forget tonight. I will be waiting for you here with longing in my heart."

Emperor John Palaiologos V took shelter in Empress Helena's insatiable and delicate body once more and said, "I don't know what to say to you because I have never set out on a campaign before. I don't know what will befall me. But, regardless of what happens to me and whatever befalls me, you shall not leave Constantinople. If I return, I want to find you here."

Then he stood up, got dressed and left.

The carriages, drawn by powerful draught horses, competed against the wind and arrived at Selymbria Castle at twilight. The young castle commander, who hadn't hosted an emperor in his castle since being knighted, welcomed the Emperor in the garden of his mansion overlooking Hellespont, which seemed like a blue bedsheet. There was not a thing missing on the breakfast table prepared in the garden. Joining his commanders for breakfast, the Emperor gathered from their smiling gazes that they had been longing for such a campaign during which they could have the opportunity to show their power and strength. He stood up as soon as he had finished his breakfast. After respectfully thanking the castle commander and his wife, he looked at his commanders sitting around the breakfast table and said, "This campaign which we will begin in Selymbria—the castle of Selis, which was given its name by Silenus—the son of Pan and a nymph with the gaze of a bull—will bring our empire strength and you, glory. Victory will be ours!"

The Emperor stood up and so did all of his warriors. In unison, they repeated, "Victory will be ours!"

Then, they all followed the Emperor and walked towards their noble Selymbrian horses.

CHAPTER EIGHTY-ONE

Prince Murad was galloping down the path between blossoming trees. This was already his third horse but it had started foaming at the mouth. As he cared more about looking at his surroundings than his horse he didn't even realise that his horse was foaming at the mouth. On the one hand, he was looking at the flowers on the trees and on the other, he kept spurring his horse. The poor horse knew he couldn't keep up much longer but kept galloping as if he was racing against the wind so he wouldn't betray his master's noble blood. Just then Prince Murad heard sounds of something scampering between the fruit trees with white and pink flowers that appeared as if they had sought shelter under the branches of massive chestnut trees. He pulled back his horse's reins to slow him down and saw that it was foaming at the mouth. He caressed his horse's head with gratitude and looked behind to see Lala Şahin Bey and the others. But he couldn't see anyone because he had ridden his horse so fast that let alone those who were immediately after him, even the advance cavalry in front of him had stayed behind. As he inclined his ear to hear the clap of the others' horseshoes amidst the whispers of trees swaying in the soft breeze, the sounds that caused him to slow down his horse became louder. Startled by the sudden noise, Prince Murad looked ahead and saw a herd of buffalo appear from between the trees and cross the path. In surprise, he rode down the path for a while and watched the herd disappear between the trees on the south of the path. When they disappeared, he dismounted his horse with agility and crouched down with his back to the trunk of the massive chestnut tree by the roadside. In the silence of that moment, where no one was in sight, he noticed that he wanted to do something that he hadn't been able to do for days. When his eyes filled with tears, he resigned himself to the arms of his sobs. He cried until he heard the very distant clap of horseshoes. Wiping his eyes, he felt energised, as his eyes searched for those arriving. He was surprised that crying made him calm down and feel so refreshed. He stood up as the advance cavalry and his messengers passed him by, galloping. He caressed the head of his horse that was waiting by his side and breathing intermittently. Looking at his horse, he said, "My tutor has been advising me to be harder than hard all this time but you see, I can't be as hard as he wants me to be. I think one should be so hard when he becomes a bey." He then bent down and looked back at the path again. He could see the hooves of the horses galloping down the road stretching flat between trees but he couldn't see the cavalry riding them. He turned his gaze to his horse once again and smiled. He wiped the sweat off his horse's chest with his hand. The horse was happy that his master was taking care of him and touched Prince Murad's shoulder with his chin, returning the compassion shown to him. Prince Murad spoke as if to respond to his horse's affectionate nudge, "They say beys don't cry but you saw just then that that is a lie. This should remain our secret. Don't think that I am embarrassed but this can be our mutual secret."

When Lala Şahin Bey and the other horsemen approached, Prince Murad looked at them and repeated, "I am so glad that I cried." After a breath or two, looking at a branch adorned with white flowers, he murmured, "Perhaps my father saw these flowers blossom last year." The others arrived before he could delve into his thoughts. He jumped onto his horse and positioned himself on the saddle. The rested horse was about to make a move when Lala Şahin Bey said, "My Prince, we haven't got long to go now. Your horse is rested but ours are exhausted. Let's let them rest awhile before we continue."

The cavalrymen, who were waiting for their horse's to catch their breath, drank water from their wooden flasks covered with embroidered leather. They moved their arms and legs. After talking about the remainder of the journey amongst themselves they got back on their horses. Lala Şahin Bey, who usually rode his horse next to his prince's was following him from a distance this time as he thought the prince might need time alone to cry. Looking at Prince Murad's back he kept murmuring, "The best cure for bad times is staying alone, My Prince" to himself. Then he was trying to put the things he had to do into order in his head. The thing that kept popping into his mind was who would become Grand Vizier in place of Sinanüddin Fakih Yusuf Pasha. Despite the fact that he frequently considered himself suitable for the role, he kept thinking, "For now, I have to be beside My Prince who will soon become a bey. I have to witness his victories just as I hàve seen him become a bey. I can become Grand Vizier when I've aged a bit more." Yet, the majority of the time he couldn't help but surrender to his ambitions as he thought, "If it is My Prince who is becoming a bey, then I deserve the highest rank."

Just as the Bursa Castle came into sight the sun was hanging down over Olympus like a fake pendulum, watching over the splendid vineyards of Bursa with its lacklustre light. Orhan Ghazi's voice hovered over the castle as if he was seeing the sun's resentful gaze, "You haven't done anything wrong. Don't be cross with each other. I am also like the other mortals."

Grand Vizier Sinanüddin Fakih Yusuf Pasha was with Orhan Ghazi when he gave his last breath. Not only was he sorting out the plans for the funeral ceremony but he had also gathered the council and was sending khutbah texts to all the *kadîs* so that they could announce on their first Friday khutbah that Prince Murad would be replacing Orhan Ghazi for peace in the Beylik. While dealing with these matters the Grand Vizier was waiting for the prince's arrival. Upon receiving news that his arrival was imminent, he went to the castle gate to wait for him. Standing up with support from Çandarlı who was beside him, the old Grand Vizier addressed Prince Murad who, upon seeing him, immediately dismounted and walked towards him, "My condolences, My Bey."

Not dwelling on the fact that the Grand Vizier, who usually called him "My Prince" was now addressing him as "My Bey", Prince Murad replied, "My condolences to you, Yusuf Pasha."

Then, the prince kissed his hand out of respect for his age. Grand Vizier Sinanüddin Fakih Yusuf Pasha was very moved by Prince Murad's behaviour. Adding the tears rolling down from his old eyes to his voice, he said, "My Bey, we should hold the funeral after the afternoon prayer."

When Murad Bey approved with a nod, they all got into Grand Vizier Sinanüddin Fakih Yusuf Pasha's carriage and headed towards the Orhan Ghazi Mosque. On the way there, Çandarlı told Prince Murad about his father's last moments on earth and what happened afterwards. When he was done talking he looked at the old Grand Vizier, who held Prince Murad's hand and said, "Your father's desire was for you to become the head of the Ottoman Beylik. We have in-formed our *kadîs* of the decision we made during the council meet-ing. Following the funeral, the ceremony of accession to the throne will be held and the first khutbah will be recited in your name. You might say that there is no need to rush but the Beylik cannot remain leaderless, my son."

As they got off the carriage in front of Orhan Ghazi Mosque, Prince Murad felt the entire weight of the Beylik on his shoulders for the first time. After delivering his condolences to his brothers, Ibrahim and Halil, who had arrived in Bursa and at the mosque be-fore him, he positioned himself in their midst and walked over to visit his father. All three of them kneeled down, placed their hands on the coffin and thought about their father in awe. When they left the side of the coffin, Sinanüddin Fakih Yusuf Pasha ordered for it to be carried onto the coffin rest. After that everything happened spon-taneously. When the funeral prayers were complete the beys carried the coffin to the grave on their fingertips. After looking at his father's earth-covered grave for one last time, Murad Bey took his brothers and headed to the council meeting held by Grand Vizier Sinanüddin Fakih Yusuf Pasha. When they entered the room where the council meeting was going to be held, the Grand Vizier showed him to the floor cushion where his father always sat. Prince Murad became so emotional that he couldn't walk. The Grand Vizier interrupted, "My Prince, your pain is our pain. However, the only way for your pain to subside is for you to become the head of our Beylik, which your father has left to you, and to put down the Ottoman plume beyond our borders. As of this moment, we will all be under your command as the bey of our divan, cavalrymen and *yayas*. May God make you triumphant."

Then, he bowed gently with respect. Meanwhile, Prince Murad overcame his emotionality and sat down in his father's seat. Once all the Beys, *Alps* and ulema who were waiting for him to take his seat sat down cross-legged, Murad Bey began to talk, "Esteemed viziers, *Alps*, beys, scientists, princes of my father Orhan Ghazi, I vow to do all I can to duly fulfil this sacrosanct duty which you have given to me upon my father's last will and to carry our Beylik from victory to victory. My brothers Ibrahim and Halil will remain as the beys of their castles. They will join us with their cavalry when we set forth on great triumphs. My tutor, Şahin Bey will head on to lead our forces near Ancyra following the enthronement ceremony. Once he is done with his duties there, he will set out towards Heraclia Pontica, the last standing castle of Byzantium on the Black Sea coast. I will depart to join them once my work in Bursa is finalised. Once we are done with our tasks on this side of the Hellespont, we will set forth beyond the Dardanelles in order to carry my older brother Suleyman Pasha's coat of arms beyond his dreams. May God grant me victories as he did to my father, Orhan Ghazi and my older brother, Suleyman Pasha. Pray for me and our Beylik."

Everyone stood up, placed their right hands over their hearts and repeated in unison, "Murad Bey, son of Orhan Ghazi, we will lay down our lives to add glory to your glory."

As soon as they had all sat back down, surah Al-Fatiha was recited for Orhan Ghazi which was then followed by the drinking of sherbet. Thus, the council meeting of the day was over. Prince Murad, who became a bey after the ceremony, joined his brothers and went to visit their mother. Nilüfer Hatun saw her son across the room as she sat in the large sitting room by herself. She became highly emotional and began to cry out loud. Listening to his mother's sobbing for a while, Murad Bey held her hands in his and said, "The matron of all ladies, my dear mother, my father's harem will remain under your control. I don't want anything to change there. You and my step-mothers can reside here or in any other castle of your choosing."

Looking at her son's clean-shaven face, "Son, thank you for coming to the mansion and cushioning our pain. From now on, my wish is to be near my son. I don't have any fears but your father's other wives might be sheltering some fears. I will get the servants to call them here so that you can tell them all that you want to say so that they can be at ease."

Looking at his stepbrothers seated on either side of his mother, Murad Bey approved her idea. Nilüfer Hatun summoned her servant with a clap and when she entered the room she ordered her to call Lady Theodora and Lady Asporsha. They were saluted by Murad Bey and his brothers upon their arrival. When they sat down opposite him, Murad Bey held his mother's slender hands in his palm and said, "Esteemed wives of my father, Orhan Ghazi. You should know that there won't be any changes in your lives. My brothers Ibrahim and Halil will continue their duties in their castles as before. You can visit them whenever you wish. As before, you will not want for anything from now on. The pious foundations and imarets you have commissioned will continue to be built, and foundations will be increased in numbers for their income. As heirlooms of my father, you will always be held in the highest esteem."

As the two young and elegant wives of Orhan Ghazi saluted their stepson with gratitude, they exclaimed, "May you live long, Murad Bey."

CHAPTER EIGHTY-TWO

When Emperor John Palaiologos V's imperial carriage—one door of which was decorated with a figure of Dionysus walking side by side with Satyr and Maenad carrying vine stocks, and the other, with a relief of bolt upright Artemis drawing his golden bow on his carriage drawn by deer—departed from Perinthus Castle and headed towards the military headquarters in the north, knights who were dressed in armour from head to toe and renowned Byzantine hoplites, wearing leather kneepads and shields, saw him and began to let our yells of victory. When the Emperor approached them and saluted them standing up it was as if all the thunderbolts struck Thrace. The Emperor was waving at the warriors positioned in orderly lines while squinting at the proud Perinthus Castle. Seeing the castle defy time, he murmured, "You seem to have forgotten how you surrendered to both Phillipo and his son, how Darius transformed you into his headquarters and how Septimus turned you into his playground." As his carriage, drawn by powerful Odrysian horses, turned back from the unit at the furthest end, he mumbled, "If you have no one to protect you the stones in your walls won't protect themselves." After looking at the castle one last time, he raised his hands and yelled out to all of his units, "May victory be with you!"

He told his driver to go slowly so he could wave at the units again. When the imperial carriage drawn by powerful Odrysian horses arrived in the middle of the units the Emperor told his driver to bring the horses to a halt. Dressed in armour, Emperor Palaiologos V put his hands down and quietened the crowd. He viewed the units spread in orderly fashion across the sloping field. Deep silence took over. The Emperor waited for a while as if he was listening to the silence, and then roared at the top of his voice, "My dukes, counts, knights and hoplites! Byzantium's unbending wrists! With this campaign, we

will once again show the power of great Byzantium to both friends
and foes!"

Just then, in the distance, he saw some cavalrymen galloping towards his units. Watching them out of the corner of his eye, he continued, "This my first campaign with you. I trust you wholeheartedly
and I want to gallop from one victory to the next with you."

It was as if the connection between his mind and his tongue had
been severed. When he realised that what he meant to say wasn't
coming out of his mouth he desperately repeated thrice, "Long live
the triumphant knights of Byzantium! Long live brave hoplites!"

When his units repeated what he said, the Emperor gained the time
he needed and summoned the commander of the guards who was sitting on his horse with the patience of a sculpture a few metres behind the imperial carriage. When the commander of the guards approached him, he pointed to the approaching cavalry and asked,
"Who might they be?"

The commander of the guards sent his messenger towards them
with a signal and replied, "Your Majesty, I am not sure but they
might be messengers dispatched by our land forces."

Feeling lonely amidst the cheerful yells of his knights and the wait,
the Emperor tried to rid himself of his loneliness by talking to the
commander of the guards but he didn't succeed.

As the chief messenger of the commander-in-chief, Demetrius dismounted his horse and walked towards the Emperor that same silence spread throughout the land. The messenger respectfully gave
the letter which he took out from between his sash and which was
wrapped in wax cloth. Reading the letter that he removed from the
wax cloth in a hurry, the Emperor suddenly became excited. He
didn't know what to do. For a while, he tried to gather his thoughts
by looking at the commander of the guards. He gulped a couple of
times. As soon as he had overcome the excitement that enveloped his
heart he exclaimed, "My dukes, counts and hoplites! I wanted our

next stop to be Rodosto but Demetrius, the triumphant commander of our land forces, is calling us to Tzirallum Castle because Matthew Kantakouzenos wants to face us there. Now is the time to catch him!"

He then showed his driver the way to Tzirallum. A great big cloud of dust began to rise when the cavalry saw that the imperial carriage was advancing towards Tzirallum with great speed and set forth. Shortly after, the hoplites had also disappeared in the dust cloud. It was almost evening when the cavalry units, which were advancing non-stop behind the imperial carriage, caught sight of Tzirallum Castle. Emperor Palaiologos V arrived at the headquarters of the land forces with his units, after advancing down streambeds in order to not be seen by the castellans, and immediately ordered the war council, comprising of the commanders who were present, to convene at the headquarter marquee. As he waited for the war council to convene, he dispatched his messengers with the message, "Make sure no one does anything that can be seen from the castle before night falls. Don't light any fires until I despatch my second order." Knight Demetrius, Commander of the Land Forces, delivered the inaugural speech of the meeting and gave information about the situation in the castle. Then he ended his words by saying, "In our imperial tradition, if the Emperor crusades he becomes the commander-in-chief of the entire army."

After a brief moment of surprise, Byzantine Emperor John Palaiologos V who didn't know about this tradition asked, "From whom did you get your information about the castle?"

"We captured the messengers Matthew Kantakouzenos sent to Constantinople, Your Majesty."

The Emperor looked at the faces of the commanders who were carefully listening to the conversation and said, "My esteemed knights, as you know, our Byzantium has suffered greatly at the hands of Matthew Kantakouzenos until now. You now have the chance to get Byzantium out of trouble."

He saw the messenger enter the room and whisper to the commander of the guards. He kept quiet and keenly watched them. When the messenger headed towards the door, the commander of the guards gently bowed down looking at the Emperor who had cast his gaze on him and said, "Your Majesty, forgive me for interrupting you. Our messengers who arrived from Constantinople have brought us news of the death of Orhan, son of Osman, the father-in-law of your daughter and Princess Asporsha's husband. This must be God's blessing of your rightful campaign."

Looking at the commander of the guards with anger, the Emperor said, "We shall rejoice at no one's death, Mentaros."

For a while, he fell silent and envisaged Orhan Ghazi's broad-shouldered, stocky body. When he realised that he too would one day fall into that endless desperation in the face of death he said, "God doesn't take anyone's life to create opportunities for others, Mentaros. We will talk about our course of action in relation to this after the meeting. We should now talk about our siege plan."

After giving each and every one of his commanders a chance to express themselves, the Emperor said, "With my cavalrymen, I will lay siege from the east and you, Demetrius, from the west. Knight Arkhlias, Duca of Perinthus, will hold down the north of the castle while the hoplites secure the south. We will narrow down this circle until the morning and close in on the castle. Meanwhile, trebuchets will be erected and slingers and fire throwers will be positioned suitably. At first light, we will send our envoy and demand that Matthew is handed over to us. If they don't abide, the castle will be stoned with slings and trebuchets while Greek fire commences. The attack will continue ceaselessly until lunchtime. We will then send another envoy. If they don't hand over Matthew again the archers will come into play and the assault will continue until Matthew is resigned to us."

Once the commanders in the council had learned the general strategy, they set out towards their units. The Emperor addressed the commander of the guards in a hard tone of voice, "Mentaros, despatch messengers for Constantinople at once. One of the aids of the mesazōn should immediately set forth to deliver our condolences. In fact, he should tell them that I am about to capture Matthew Kantakouzenos."

The commander of the guards quickly left the headquarter marquee. The Emperor followed him and pointing out the nearby hill to Demetrius and his councillor he said, "Demetrius, come on, let's take a look at the castle from that hill before it gets dark. Once it's dark we can advance with our units."

As they advanced, with the Emperor at the front and the commander-in-chief and his councillor at the back, on the earthy side of the hill, the old councillor said, "This must be one of those Odrysian tumuli."

The Emperor didn't know much about the subject, so he asked, "How do you know?"

"The stubby trees, Your Majesty. Trees don't grow tall in such places."

"So, were the Odrysians hiding something here?"

"The ashes of their dead kings and their horses, Sire."

"So, are we walking on the ashes of a king and his horse now?"

"If this really is a tumulus, it must be one of a king or a commander who exhibited great heroism because only hills where their ashes are buried are so high."

The Emperor replied as if he was talking to himself, "Whether you are the unstoppable Odrysian king or an Ottoman bey, the earth takes you under."

The old councillor thought that the Emperor was asking him a question, "The most unstoppable Thracians are not the Odrysians but the Astias, Your Majesty. Their tumuli are on the skits of the mountains further north."

Emperor Palaiologos V interrupted so the old councillor would keep quiet for a little while, "Was it their king who added the flesh of his captives to the feed of his horses?"

"No, Sire. That's Diomedes, King of Thrace."

The old councillor kept quiet when he saw that the Emperor who had reached the top of the hill had cast his gaze into the distance and was no longer listening to him.

CHAPER EIGHTY-THREE

Prince Murad received the news of his father's death when he departed Bursa for Ancyra to begin laying siege to Ancyra Castle which he attempted last autumn but failed to finalise because of harsh weather conditions in the winter. When he received the news he changed his mind about the siege of Ancyra and he commanded that his units retreat to the lands of Gerede Beylik as the *Alps* and his tutor Şahin Bey departed for Bursa. However, the *Âhis* who were watching them from the castle left and stealthily approached the units on the periphery by advancing down the bends of the river flowing down the plain they were very familiar with and began waiting for the evening. When night fell and the units were resting, they slaughtered and killed almost all of the brave warriors of the periphery unit with a sudden raid. A few warriors who survived this carnage left the scene as fast as the wind and rode their horses hard to inform their beys who had already left. As they tried to catch up with the units who were approaching the lands of Gerede Beylik, the *Âhis* took the horses of the periphery unit and returned to the castle.

The beys of Lala Şahin Pasha were close by when they found out about the raid and thus sent Kara Sungur Bey to help the periphery units. Kara Sungur Bey and his men arrived at the scene in the early hours of the morning. When they saw the corpses spread out across the plain they couldn't believe their eyes. Kara Sungur Bey, who had until then been in many conflicts, had never witnessed such terrifying deaths. Looking at the shredded buck-naked bodies he broke into tears. When he stopped weeping, he looked at Ancyra Castle and muttered, "Even an enemy should have some chivalry." Then looking at the beys who were by his side, he said, "The *Âhis* wouldn't do this."

Looking at the scattered body parts, Ortanca Tekin Bey grasped his

face a few times and wiped his eyes before replying, "If they have
been provoked by the vindictive men of the *Karamanids...*"

Kara Sungur Bey averted his eyes to the castle so he wouldn't see
the guts and bowels scattered across the ground and replied, "No,
son. The *Karamanids* wouldn't do this, only the Çavdars of the
Eretnids. Investigate and see if there is a casualty they left for dead.
That's the only way we can find out who did this."

Ortanca Tekin Bey and his cavalry immediately went on the hunt
to find a casualty. They were relieved when they found four critically
wounded casualties who were left for dead on the way to the castle.
Two of them were about to give their last breaths. They left them to
die in peace and questioned the other two. One of them could
neither understand what he was being asked nor tell them anything
decipherable. They took care of the wounds of the last remaining
casualty before asking him what had happened and said, "If you tell
us the truth our bey will spare your life."

Hearing that his life would be spared, the Ahi from Ancyra told
them exactly what had happened. He told them that the *Âhis* were
provoked by the Çavdar Tataris of the Eretnids who had long been
in their castle and that they raided the Ottoman units. The Ahi who
appeared before Kara Sungur Bey, told his story to him once more
and appealed for mercy. Kara Sungur Bey replied, "Your sins will not
be erased just because I have forgiven you. It is best if we swiftly send
you to hell so that you can begin paying for your sins."

Then he handed over the Ahi to the swordsman known as the
headsman. When Kara Sungur Bey arrived at the marquee of Kara
Timurtaş Pasha, son of Kara Ali Bey and grandson of Aygut Alp,
who had been commanding the forces in Lala Şahin Bey's place, and
told him all that had happened, Kara Timurtaş Pasha felt very sad
that he hadn't taken the necessary precautions. He immediately des-
patched messengers to Lala Şahin Bey who was in Bursa at the time.

Lala Şahin Bey was fuming upon receiving the news. He began to

writhe with the desire of immediately setting forth to join his unit
and to wipe Ancyra Castle off the map until Murad Bey's arrival. He
opened the subject of Grand Vizier Sinanüddin Fakih Yusuf Pasha
before talking to Murad Bey. When he harnessed his anger with the
advice Sinanüddin Fakih Yusuf Pasha gave him, he spent his days in
Bursa roaming the streets and thinking, "We should allow our beys'
sadness to subside and then we can make them pay dearly for what
they have done." However, since Murad I's priority was capturing
Heraclea Pontica Castle on the coast of the Black Sea, Lala Şahin
Bey sent word to Kara Timurtaş Pasha, commander of the forces in
Gerede, and ordered him to immediately set forth for Heraclea
Pontica. He too set forth shortly after Murad I's enthronement cere-
mony.

After sending his tutor to lead his forces, Prince Murad began his
pursuit of learning everything he didn't know by talking to Grand
Vizier Sinanüddin Yusuf Pasha and his protégé Vizier Çandarlı Kara
Halil Bey about the governance of the Beylik in order to get used to
being a bey, governing the Beylik and fulfilling his duties to the best
of his capacity. Sinanüddin Yusuf Pasha was very old. One day,
when Kara Halil Bey wasn't with them, he told Murad Bey, "My Bey,
you have been entrusted to me by Orhan Ghazi."

Murad I interrupted him hastily even though he hadn't finished his
talk, "My father has also entrusted you to me."

Sinanüddin Yusuf Fakih Pasha was delighted. Then, looking at him
he replied, "Murad Bey, I wish to die serving the Beylik but as luck
would have it my knees have started betraying me. I am suffering a
lot when I walk and sit down. Perhaps this is not the right time but I
would appreciate it if you could excuse me from council meetings
from now on. I will always be with you in my thoughts."

Murad I was caught unprepared and didn't know how to reply. He
already felt lonely after the consecutive deaths of his older brother
and father. Now his Grand Vizier Sinanüddin Fakih Yusuf Pasha,

whose experience he needed the most in matters of the Beylik, was also leaving him alone. Looking at the Grand Vizier with shock, Sinanüddin Yusuf Pasha continued with poise, "I have been thinking about this for days. Concealing my pains, I was waiting for the right time to tell you. It is now time, My Bey. But you should know that my successor is Çandarlı Kara Halil Bey. He is well-versed in matters of the Beylik. He is as virile as I am in his knowledge and thought. This duty should be passed to Lala Şahin Bey who trained you but he is tactless in matters of the Beylik and doesn't know how to keep his ambition and anger separate. For now, his angry ambition is only of use in the battlefield. He can only become vizier when his mind harnesses his ambition."

Grand Vizier Sinanüddin Fakih Yusuf Pasha managed to explain everything he wanted to with this short talk. Shortly after, he voiced his request at the great council meeting. The viziers and beys, who saw his discomfort and pain with every movement he made, considered his request and agreed with him. They also agreed that Çandarlı Kara Halil Bey should chair the council meetings as his successor.

Lala Şahin Bey received news that Çandarlı Kara Halil Bey became Yusuf Pasha's successor when he was observing the thick stone walls of Heraclea Pontica Castle, the foundations of which were built by the Megarans who were escaping the cruelty of the Athenians, who defined everyone other than themselves as barbarians. There were seven turrets above the walls painted crimson by the evening sun that glided into the distance over the Black Sea. Arrows had been ceaselessly raining on them for days. Although, for some reason, those arrows hadn't managed to lace Lala Şahin Pasha's ambition with anger. However, shortly after the news he received, he felt his anger overtake his ambition and his mind succumb to his anger. As he waited for his anger to inactivate his mind he recalled what the envoy he had taken captive the previous evening had said, "Bey, these fertile lands will host you just as it hosted the tyrants of Athens, the insurmountable knights hospitaller of Alexander, the flaming cavalry of Prusias I of Bithynia, the storm defying sailors of Mithridates VI of Pontus, the Galatians who knew no limits and the wall-destroying Latins of Roman Emperor Aurelius." He knew that if he kept gazing at the sun his heart would soften. He changed his mind about watching the horizon and thinking. He yelled, "Attack!"

The castellans could only resist the full-on attack of the archers, slingers, trebuchets and climbers for two days. Shortly after the surrender of the castle, Lala Şahin Bey entered the castle through the main gate on his Sorrel. As if reciting a poem which he had long forgotten, he said, "The shelter of Saint Aghios Theodoros you are now the property of the Ottoman Beylik. You are now the property of My Prince, Murad Bey, with all that you have. You are now under his protection. I am sorry about the destruction. If we could have found a David like Kaykaus I, we wouldn't have done all of this. But you couldn't send us such a David from your castle. Moreover, we paid with the lives of our *levends*. Once those responsible for their deaths are punished everything will return to how it was." He dismounted his horse with a leap and climbed up the nearby stairs and got to one of the turrets. Looking in the direction of Bursa, he spoke as if to reproach Prince Murad, "My Prince, it is tradition that the tutor whose prince becomes a bey, also becomes a vizier of the Beylik. Even though you withheld this from me I am handing over a castle to you. May it bring good omens!" Then he quickly climbed down the staircase and headed towards the castle square where the *levends* of Pasha Yiğit Bey gathered the captured castle guards.

CHAPTER EIGHTY-FOUR

Emperor John Palaiologos V entered Tzirallum Castle through the south gate with the pride of his first victory on his milk-white, noble Selymbrian horse gifted to him by the castle guard of Selymbria Castle instead of his imposing imperial carriage. The noble steed gathered that this was a ceremonial march from the slow and orderly paces of the guards and began to keep his pace according to that of the horses in front of him.

Until the Emperor entered the castle on his horse, the castellans had known him as the "child emperor" due to the propaganda of Matthew Kantakouzenos's men. But when they saw him on the back of his horse with his crown and armour they were all shocked. He was a real emperor, not a "child emperor." Old Nikephoros was the first of the prominent castellans who composed himself and ran to the Emperor. He embraced the Emperor's foot placed on the silver stirrup. Not used to having his feet being embraced, Emperor Palaiologos V immediately bent down and held the old man's shoulder. He looked at his face with a smile and waved at the castellans gathered in front of the church near the castle gates. He dismounted his horse and walked towards the old priest standing by the door of the church. The castellans who took courage from his respectful saluting of the priest began to chant one of the hymns of the admired Monastery of Stoudios in Constantinople. The Emperor joined their chorus and after they finished singing the hymn, he addressed the people of the castle, "I didn't want to enter your castle after an assault but Matthew Kantakouzenos sought refuge in your castle and poured arrows over us. Those who have suffered due to this imperative assault will be immediately compensated. I hope that God will not make me besiege my own castle again. Now go back to your homes and continue your lives."

When he had finished talking, the priest started singing another

hymn but louder. After they all joined in and sang it the people of
the castle started heading home. As they walked into their homes,
the Emperor chatted to the priest in the church. After getting information on the castles Matthew Kantakouzenos might seek shelter
in from the priest, the Emperor went to the opening at the entrance
of the north gate where Kantakouzenos's knights and infantry were
gathered. He was startled when he saw a greater number of kneeling
knights and foot soldiers than he anticipated but he tried to compose
himself. He climbed the stairs and stood above the gate arch. Looking at the kneeling knights and foot soldiers he said, "I know that
none of you wanted to fight against your Byzantine brothers. However, Matthew Kantakouzenos, who professed himself as Co-Emperor, has perhaps made great promises to you and you believed
him. So you shot arrows at your Byzantine brothers. You injured and
killed a great many of them. Thus, you defied the laws. You all know
what this means. I am giving you one last chance as your emperor. If
you appeal for mercy and desire to join us, you will be demoted to
other services. Those who don't accept their new positions will be
punished accordingly."

When the Emperor stopped talking, the majority of the captured
knights and guards accepted to appeal for mercy and take on the positions given to them. However, those who considered being demoted
humiliating remained in their places like marble sculptures. After
looking at them with heartbreak, he commanded his own commander of the guards, "Listen to them one by one and punish them
accordingly."

After establishing order in the castle that evening, all the artisans
of the imperial forces were put to repairing the castle the following
morning. After two days of labour, there was neither a sling stone
nor a burned down house remaining in the castle. When the artisans
completed their work and returned to their units, the imperial court
established in the castle had listened to all supporters of

Kantakouzenos and reached the verdict to punish them all with the death penalty. But it wasn't the men of the Emperor who were going to kill them. The captured knights would kill each other and so would the hospitallers, the guards and the castle commanders. Those that remained last would be forced to jump off from the highest turret of the castle. Since none of them expected such hard sentences on their way to trial they all thought, "I'd rather suffer in the dungeon for a while than to accept a job that has no virtue." However, when the sentences were delivered they were all broken under the weight of the punishment for rebelling against the Emperor. Only the last hospitaller saved his skin because he appealed for mercy and accepted demotion. All of the others were buried fully-dressed in a flooded hole in the streambed near the castle after their armours and weapons were confiscated.

Emperor John Palaiologos V appointed old Nikephoros, who previously appointed knight Erymandhos—the son of the mesazōn in his own guard regiment—as the castle guard of Tzirallum Castle, as the landlord of the castle. Then he sent forth all of his hospitallers towards Hadrianopolis Castle under the command of Demetrius, the Commander of Land Forces, and immediately left Tzirallum as he had decided to head towards Rodosto with all of his cavalry.

The Emperor got some rest during the days he spent in Rodosto. One night, he received news that some units, which had come to aid Matthew Kantakouzenos in Hadrianopolis, were gathered in Cypsela and immediately left Rodosto. He sent word to the fleet commander and the commander-in-chief of the imperial forces in Aenus and told them to set forth towards Cypsela from the west with marine hospitallers as soon as they reached land. Meanwhile, he also sent messengers to Demetrius, the Commander of the Land Forces, who was headed to Hadrianopolis and commanded him to split his hospitallers into two groups to send some of them to besiege Hadrianopolis and the others to immediately depart for Cypsela.

As Matthew Kantakouzenos—who had proclaimed himself as the Emperor of Didymóteicho, the Dardanelles, Aenus, Hadrianopolis and surroundings—had no idea that the fleet had reached the port of Aenus, he had ordered his forces to meet in Cypsela and had set forth towards it after leaving behind a few of his trusted commanders in Hadrianopolis with their units. His aim was to advance to the southeast with his supporters gathered in Cypsela and to ambush and annihilate the imperial units in the Uğraş Valley that he knew like the palm of his hand.

CHAPTER EIGHTY-FIVE

After appointing Çandarlı Kara Halil as grand vizier, Murad I addressed him as "My Halil Pasha" during council meetings while Çandarlı Kara Halil, successor and deputy of the grand vizier, called him "My Sovereign". The title of "Khan" which was used by viziers as courtesy had more or less the same meaning but Çandarlı referred to him as "My Sovereign" because as a result of their conversations, he had understood that Murad I believed he could keep the lands he captured by the power of his sword with his mind. That is why the newly appointed grand vizier thought, "One who deals with the mind is better suited to be called a sovereign rather than a khan". Yet he couldn't rid himself of his concerns and tell him that the Ottoman lands, which had exceeded the borders of the Beylik, could no longer be governed as they were during the period of Orhan Ghazi. He had the qualm that Murad I might tell him, "Halil Pasha, let us not teach new tricks to old dogs". However, as soon as he received news that the surrounding beys and Byzantine Emperor John Palaiologos V, who had swiftly taken action following Orhan Ghazi's death, were planning an assault on the Ottoman Beylik from all sides, he planned on talking to Murad Bey and then delivering his thoughts on the subject to the ulema, the viziers, the *Alps* and the beys in Bursa during a council meeting. He started thinking about the most suitable place and time for such a meeting. When the Roman baths, which he frequented every week, popped into his head, he thought, "Roman and Byzantine emperors come all the way here from Constantinople to refresh their minds and complexions. Why wouldn't Murat Bey go there when it's so close to him?" and began to walk towards the Beylik mansion where the meeting hall of the council was also located. When he arrived in front of the mansion, after saluting the people who saw and saluted him on his way, he saw that the chief messenger of Murad I was waiting outside the mansion. Seeing Çandarlı Kara Halil walking towards him, Eseoğlu Kara Ali Bey said, "My Bey is waiting for you in his reception room."

As the Grand Vizier saluted Eseoğlu Kara Ali Bey, whose face always seemed to harbour a smile, he replied, "Thank you, Ali Bey."

Approaching the hand-carved door of Murad I's magnificent reception room, he murmured, "This is a good chance, I can also talk to him about the Roman baths." He entered through the door opened for him by Eseoğlu Kara Ali Bey. Murad I was sitting on his throne which seemed pale beside the august room adorned with tapestries. After receiving the grand vizier's salutation, Murad I said, "My Halil Pasha."

Then, he heaved a sigh that revealed his simmering worries. The grand vizier took his turn in his silence, "My Sovereign, have you received upsetting news? I hope that our prince does not have any health problems."

Murad I was still shaken by the news he had received at midnight and didn't know where to start but he replied at once, "Thank God, our prince is in good health, and so is Gülçiçek Hatun but I am devastated by the news I received last night."

Then he took out the letter sent to him by the *subaşı* of Nicomedia Castle from his sash and handed it over to Çandarlı.

Çandarlı Halil Pasha read the letter all in one breath. His face became dull for a while. Murad I was looking at him and growing impatient to hear what he was going to say. Çandarlı straightened his thin and short beard with his fingertips and his single layer, yellow and white turban that looked good against his tanned face. Then, in a soft tone of voice replied, "My Sovereign, if someone didn't make their young blood boil they would never dare this. However, it seems they have an inclination. We are face to face with an urgent subject. At this moment in time when the *Karamanids* are provoking the *Âhis* and the other beys are lying in wait to take back their lands, this attempt by your brother is not something that can be forgiven. If we don't act quickly in the face of this threat, we will run into greater threats in the future. You can rest a little while I summon the council. We can decide on a course of action together."

He then bowed and saluted Murad I before walking backwards and leaving the room.

Shortly after, Murad I received news that the council was ready and waiting for him and joined the meeting in a calmer state of mind. As soon as he took his seat, Grand Vizier Çandarlı Kara Halil Pasha took the floor, "Sarı Sungur Bey, the *subaşı* of Nicomedia Castle, has sent us a letter in which he informed us that Prince Halil, Bey of Nicomedia, and Prince Ibrahim, the protector of our Beylik's property in Hüdavendigar have united against our Sovereign Murad I. He is awaiting our instructions for the course of action he should take.

Kara Timurtaş Pasha, a bey of Lala Şahin Bey who had come to inform Murad I of the successful capture of Heraclea Pontica Castle on behalf of the other beys, was also present. He had interrogated the captured Byzantine envoy and also spoken to him a few times. During some of those conversations, the envoy had told him certain things about Halil Bey whom he referred to as the "son-in-law of our Emperor" but Timurtaş Pasha didn't pay heed to it because he thought that the envoy was trying to save his own skin. Hearing what Çandarlı Kara Halil Pasha said, he held the floor and told the councilmen what he could remember from the envoy's story. He voiced his concerns, said that it was his mistake that he didn't take the envoy seriously and appealed for mercy because he had been reckless.

Most of the *Alps* and viziers listening to him responded, "It is necessary to "finish off" both princes for the future of our Beylik."

Murad I felt his heart break when he heard the words "finish off". As cold drops of sweat accumulated on his forehead, he felt nauseous as if he had seen blood for the first time. As he waited for that heaving sensation to pass, Çandarlı Halil's chief aid addressed the council, "We must hold to the way of thinking Osman Bey left to us

as his legacy in high esteem in our Beylik that has added new lands
and new castles to its existing domain every day. Instead of punishing the princes, we should first put them to the proof, find out who
they are cooperating with and prove that they have committed an offence. I think that the *subaşı* and castle commander of Kocaeli can
tackle this. But just so that it is all carried out in a just manner we
should also send a *kadî* appointed by the *kadî* of Bursa to the castle.
If it is true that they are in cahoots against our Sovereign, he can decide what to do on behalf of us."

Grand Vizier Çandarlı Kara Halil Pasha and Murad I said that
they agreed with this opinion. For a while, they discussed if they
should give the task of monitoring the princes to the *subaşıs* of the
castle or to Lala Şahin Bey. The beys wanted Lala Şahin Bey to be
given this task since he was considered to be the commander of all
forces due to his position as Murad I's tutor, while the viziers who
knew of Lala Şahin Bey's ambition and that he would finish off the
princes for his own prince without batting an eye, wanted the task to
be given to the *subaşı* and a *kadî* who would be sent to the castle
commander. In the end, Çandarlı Kara Halil Pasha intervened and
the task was delegated.

Murad I went straight to his mansion after leaving the council
meeting that had resulted in the decision to "finish off" his brothers.
Before dinner, he took newborn prince Bayezid into his arms with
the hope that it would console him. Looking at his prince's face that
was still flesh red and calm he recalled the words, "finish off". He got
upset that he couldn't find any consolation in holding his baby son.
He suddenly wanted to give him over to Gülçiçek Hatun but when
his son briefly opened his eyes and looked at him, he changed his
mind and continued to look at his son's face. The longer he looked at
him the more his disquietude increased. He wanted to forget about
the child in his arms and to leave the room. When he suddenly recalled what one of the old viziers had said, "If they need to be done

away with for the good of the Beylik then they should be. This was why Osman Bey finished off Dündar Bey, to preserve the order of the Beylik." He felt a bit more at ease. He envisioned his brother Halil's body when he had just become an adolescent. Remembering his slender neck, he looked at the neck of the prince in his arms. He didn't want to "finish off" his brothers but the letters had already been written and send to the *subaşı*, the castle commander and Lala Şahin Bey. There was nothing else he could do other than to wish that the rumours were unfounded. He suddenly thought of his older brother Suleyman Pasha and said, "Had he lived, would he have finished me off?" It was as if something was stuck in his throat. He handed his son over to Gülçiçek Hatun and quickly left the nursery in the harem. He paced his stone-walled mansion for a while. He climbed up high and looked at the green trees that rose up the skirt of Olympus. He surmised that the trees had fallen out of favour with him. He immediately headed to his bed-chamber at the harem and threw himself on his bed. He didn't want to cry but he was filled with sobs. He closed his eyes and struggled against himself for a while. He cried for a time, even if it was brief, and then got up and walked to the dining hall. Upon seeing his mother Nilüfer Hatun in the room he felt a black cloud clear away from him. His mother's emerald voice echoed in his ears, "Son, you have forgotten us since Sinanüddin Pasha left the council. We would be pleased if you came by now and then."

"Oh my dear mother, you wouldn't be too upset if I told you that I hadn't even been able to spare time for Gülçiçek Hatun until she gave birth? I have been trying to spend at least the evenings with her since the birth. Being the head of the Beylik is so hard that the weight of it crushes me. When my late father was alive I never had to deal with any of it, so I was never this tired. When they pointed at a castle we had to capture, I didn't think about anything other than riding my horse there but now I can't even march onto the *Âhis* who are trespassing our lands every day."

Chatting to his mother over dinner, Murad I wanted to tell her about what was going on at the council meetings but he didn't. After his mother retreated to her harem, he went to see Gülçiçek Hatun who hadn't left the nursery for days. Seeing his son and his wife sleeping together, he watched them in the light of oil lamps for a while. He gave presents to a number of servants who came into the room as quietly as a breath to check on the mother and baby and then retreated to his own chamber.

The days that followed that night were stormy, passing quickly and involving a cacophony of hardship. The start of every new day brought disturbing news from either Hacı Ilbey, who was leading the forces across the Dardanelles, or Lala Şahin Bey who was commanding the forces in Bithynia. Murad I sent word to Hacı Ilbey and instructed him to do nothing other than finding out which way Emperor Palaiologos V's forces were headed because the news Lala Şahin Bey sent him about his brothers was bleak. As if all that wasn't enough, the *Âhis* who were raiding the properties of Gerede Bey were attacking the advance units almost every night and taking lives.

Spending the entire summer by listening to this gruesome news, Murad I decided to set forth on a campaign the day his son's health improved. It was on that day that he received news from Hacı Ilbey that Emperor Palaiologos V—who pursued Matthew Kantakouzenos all summer long—had lost track of his opponent. Murad I had not yet decided how to react to this news when on his way to the council meeting he found out that the messengers of Lala Şahin Bey had arrived and that they want to hand over to him what they brought with them.

CHAPTER EIGHTY-SIX

Matthew Kantakouzenos advanced on the hills of Maritza after setting forth from Hadrianopolis and met with his supporters from Didymóteicho. He then immediately set out and arrived at Cypsela Castle. He had just arrived at the castle and was talking to his supporters when Emperor Palaiologos V was spotted on the east of the castle with his knights and cavalry units. Matthew Kantakouzenos began defence preparations inside the castle at once. He was overcome by fear that the Emperor arrived so soon after him. He thought that someone had informed the Emperor of his arrival. He gathered the prominent figures of Cypsela Castle with their families, except the old priest, at the squares and beheaded them all, including children. He also ordered his men to ransack their mansion. The castellans who witnessed this merciless massacre and destruction were shaking with fear. Everyone retreated to their houses. When Matthew Kantakouzenos's men came to their doors they didn't answer. Instead, some of them poured boiling water from their windows and scalded the men.

Realising that the castellans weren't going to help him or his warriors, Matthew Kantakouzenos decided to immediately abandon the castle. He left from the west gate of the castle with his knights and supporters as soon as the night fell. His aim was to reach Hadrianopolis as soon as possible but the west gate of the castle was blocked by the renowned marine hospitallers of the Byzantine fleet who had arrived from Aenus not long ago. Well-trained in defence and war, the hospitallers began to strangle Matthew Kantakouzenos's men with great barbarity as soon as they saw them leaving the castle. Seeing the hospitallers scythe his knights and cavalry together with their horses as if scything a field, Matthew Kantakouzenos was so scared that he didn't look behind him until he reached Hadrianopolis. When he got there and turned around he started to cry. Shortly after he composed himself and entered the castle through the secret passages so he could save the few men he still had. Once he got back to commanding his men, he vowed to take revenge and set Greek fire on the imperial forces.

John Palaiologos V entered Cypsela Castle as a triumphant emperor but when he found out that Matthew Kantakouzenos had slipped through his fingers he was very sad. However, a few days later he received information that he was in Hadrianopolis. He became distraught and yelled, "This game of hide and seek is now over Matthew Kantakouzenos, you shall not leave Hadrianopolis!" from atop his horse. Then he rode his milk-white steed to Hadrianopolis Castle.

Arriving in front of the castle, he saw that his forces that surrounded Hadrianopolis, a few times larger than Cypsela, were closing in on the castle in perfect formation. He looked at the castle from atop the hill from where Suleyman Pasha had viewed the castle a year before, and yelled, "This is the end of you, Matthew Kantakouzenos!" and let the wind carry his voice but Matthew Kantakouzenos didn't hear it. He was busy keeping the imperial forces away from the castle while he beavered away on the preparations for a great assault to whet the appetites of his supporters to ransack Constantinople.

Unaware of Matthew Kantakouzenos's promises to his men and his inconceivable traps, the Emperor was thinking that the moment when he would let out a scream of victory was near. He was riding his horse between the units around the castle and encouraging his knights and hospitallers with his roars. Overflowing with the courage he felt, the knights and the hospitallers kept closing in on the castle with incessant yells.

On the third day of the siege, before ordering full attack, the Emperor sent his messengers and told the immigrants living in the outer neighbourhoods and market vendors to go as far from the castle as possible. The biggest trebuchets were set up in the most tactical positions immediately after their departure. They flung stones and fire-balls at the castle to try out the trebuchets. This was actually a warning. At dusk some of the smaller trebuchets were taken closer to the castle walls. Archers and climbers dressed in armour head to toe were positioned around these smaller trebuchets.

The Emperor summoned the war council and suggested that an envoy be sent to Matthew Kantakouzenos at sunrise to give him the opportunity to surrender and that if he refused, a full-on attack would be started. The council agreed. The meeting ended with the decision to take precautions throughout the night so that there was no leak between the sides and that a sudden raid would be averted.

The Emperor hardly slept that night. At sunrise, he sent an envoy and demanded the surrender of Matthew Kantakouzenos after warning shots were fired. However, Matthew cut off one arm of the envoy and the two guards who accompanied him and sent them back. The Emperor was enraged and immediately ordered a full-scale attack. When they showered the castle with arrows all day and was not shot at even once, the Emperor thought that the guards in the castle were no longer following the orders of Matthew Kantakouzenos. He decided to send a group of three priests as envoys and ceased fire for the night. Matthew's supporters got out of the castle through the secret tunnels at night and massacred the service units behind the attack units. Seeing the corpses in the morning, the Emperor was so dismayed that he didn't know what to do. He even gave authority to his commander-in-chief so that he could retreat to his marquee for a short period of time. The surgeons realised that he was ill and mobilised. Commander-in-chief Demeksinos and the Commander of the Land Forces united their forces, found the tunnels that Matthew's men used and blocked them with earth and rocks. They left some of the tunnels open as a trap and positioned gladiators with unyielding wrists around them.

Emperor John Palaiologos V had fully recovered the next day. He ordered another full-scale attack. He ordered to set Greek fire on the castle, which he had been reluctant to do before because he didn't want his people to burn alive. After a whole day of Greek fire and storms of arrows, flames began to rise from all sides of the castle. The people of the castle were so scared that they caught Matthew Kantakouzenos's knights and began to throw them into the flames. It was then that Matthew Kantakouzenos realised he could no longer stay in Hadrianopolis. He immediately and quietly escaped from the castle with his most loyal men through a tunnel unknown to anyone and that opened to the coast of Maritza, just like the way he had escaped from Suleyman Pasha. As he crossed the river, reached the horses that were waiting for them and advanced towards Didymóteicho, Emperor John Palaiologos V, who had been waiting for the morning with great rage, entered Hadrianopolis with the sunrise. The Emperor only talked to the archpriest of the castle before addressing the people of Hadrianopolis gathered at the square in front of the church, "Since you protected Matthew Kantakouzenos who has taken the life of so many people so mercilessly all this time, you will also pay for what you've done!"

Then he departed the wrecked inner castle. After that day the Emperor never visited the castle again and assigned the task of establishing order in the castle to Demetrius, Commander of the Land Forces. He sent his fleet towards Aenus and headed towards Constantinople in a bad mood.

After two days of travelling, the Emperor wasn't happy to see the city walls of Constantinople in the distance. Looking crestfallen at the castle, he asked, "How can I be happy when I have returned empty-handed?" Gazing at the sky, he murmured, "I chased him for two seasons but..."

Looking around him pensively, the first drops of rain fell on the thick canvas top of his imperial carriage. Bitterly smiling he said, "Even the sky is mad at me". Rain poured down. It was as if the sky had split open in the space of a couple of minutes and rivers were gushing from the clouds above Constantinople. The eight horses that were drawing the magnificent carriage of the Byzantine emperor became restive with the sudden rainfall. The driver realised that he wasn't going to be able to keep them under control so he loosened the reins. The horses relaxed and sped up to a fierce gallop towards the city walls of Constantinople. As the carriage entered the castle through the gate of Hagios Romanos, the Emperor tightly held the handle next to his seat so he wouldn't sway. The driver couldn't hear him no matter how much he yelled. Fortunately, the road was wider and less bumpy inside the castle and the carriage shook less. However, the Emperor was still holding on tightly, so much so that his entire body was stiff. When he looked back he saw that his guards were far away in the distance. When the carriage approached distant houses with gardens, the road suddenly narrowed down and the horses slowed down. The Emperor took a deep breath and leaned back. He tried to stop the shudder coursing through his body but his mind had no influence over it. He looked at the calm houses with large gardens on the roadside. Listening to the sound of the rain that hadn't slowed down, he muttered, "The return from victory." A bitter smile spread across his lips. When he heard the sound of horseshoes behind him he turned around and looked. Seeing the commander of the guards dressed in chainmail armour, he thought, "A body imprisoned for a lifetime." He cast his gaze down and put his feet up. Undecided about watching the pelting rain, he thought of Empress Helena. He muttered, "Who knows how many times she imagined my ceremonious return..." When pessimism took over, he said, "The triumphant are welcomed with ceremonies. Let alone being triumphant, I have returned after turning my castles into a wreck." Looking outside with his eyes full of tears, he said, "I should be grateful for the rain. It has prevented this emperor from feeling even smaller." Then, he put his pessimism aside, and consoled himself by thinking that even returning alive is a victory. He then continued, "I will set forth on another campaign in the spring and wipe him off the face of the earth. It's either him or me. I hope that he won't fool the Serbians and the Bulgarians by the time of my next campaign. I should send envoys to them at once." He took a few deep breaths. After a long sigh, he muttered, "I have to settle my accounts with Matthew Kantakouzenos while the Ottomans have retreated to the tip of the peninsula. I hope that Halil will succeed." Just then he remembered the sparsely bearded, clean face of Prince Murad whom he saw at the engagement ceremony in Nicaea. His face was so clean and transparent that the Emperor could count the pearly white teeth in his mouth and even see his heartbeat through his ribcage. Emperor Palaiologos V was very surprised to see him like that. As he studied Murad I's face with awe, Murad I's transparent heart cracked open and all of the blood inside it splashed on Palaiologos's face. The Emperor was just about to wipe his face when an invisible hand caught his wrist. When the hand pushed him back inside the carriage he became startled and stood up. Looking around him, he thought about why he had had such a daydream. He murmured, "I must be doing something wrong." He looked outside and saw they were close to the mansion. He became excited. Just then he saw a few people cheering for him.

He got his men to scatter Byzantine coins at those applauding him all the way to the gate of his mansion, one of the most magnificent buildings in the city. Emperor John Palaiologos V hadn't announced his campaign so he was surprised that there were people welcoming him. He embraced his mother and Helena who welcomed him back in front of the mansion. He kissed his children. He chatted to Empress Anna and Empress Helena in the living room for a while. When he was about to leave to take off his armour and take a bath, his chief servant informed him that the mesazōn wanted to meet him urgently. The Emperor aversely instructed for the mesazōn to be shown to his study where he also went. Entering the room, old mesazōn Apokaukos said, "Your Majesty, welcome home. Your success in Thrace is great enough to ease our grief."

When the Emperor looked at the mesazōn's face with hidden meaning, the mesazōn continued softly, "Your Majesty, I am sorry to disturb you at the time of your arrival but what I have to say cannot be delayed. After the capture of one of the envoys we sent to the *Karamanids* and Eretnids, Murad Bey has informed us that you have gone back on your agreement with him and sent the Ottoman forces to Heraclea Pontica. Despite the fact that our castle commander defended the castle with his heart and soul, he could only save himself. Our only consolation is that the castle commander brought us everything that was precious in value and light in weight."

The Emperor replied in a slightly annoyed tone of voice, "Why didn't you inform me of this earlier?"

The mesazōn hastily replied, "You were running towards victory in Cypsela at the time. We didn't want to spoil your triumph. In any case, Heraclea Pontica is like an island in between different Beyliks. We didn't consider this news to be very significant."

The Emperor smiled bitterly and said, "So Alexius, if this is not important what's more important?"

"Your Majesty, we only received this news a few days ago. I considered delivering it to you after investigating the truth but I am grateful that you are back."

CHAPTER EIGHTY-SEVEN

Murad I felt empty after the deaths of his older brother Prince Suleyman Pasha and his father Orhan Ghazi but the birth of his son Prince Bayezid had helped him rid himself of that sadness and he settled down to managing the matters of the Beylik. He had especially completely dedicated himself to his work after hearing the golden words of the former Grand Vizier Sinanüddin Yusuf Pasha who had been continuing his tasks for the Beylik from his home. Together with Grand Vizier Çandarlı Kara Halil Pasha and Sinanüddin Yusuf Pasha, whom Murad I addressed as Sinanüddin Pasha when they were alone, carried it so far that they were talking about the governance of the Beylik until the early hours of the morning. They shared what they talked about at night with council viziers and wise men the next day. Grand Vizier Çandarlı Kara Halil Pasha, who frequently called Murad I "My Sovereign", was very content with this situation because Murad I agreed with him on the fact that the Ottoman Beylik could no longer be governed like a small Beylik. He also really liked it that Murad Bey valued formed Grand Vizier Sinanüddin Yusuf Pasha just like he did and repeated his words, "The castle captured with a sword is best kept with the mind."

Murad I stayed in Bursa longer than four seasons and dealt with the governance matters of the Beylik. One day he visited Sinanüddin Yusuf Pasha again and after getting his opinions, he attended a council meeting. At the end of that meeting he said, "My *Alps*, beys, viziers, wise men it is now time for us to set forth on our campaign. Our first campaign will be to the *Âhis* of Ancyra who have caused us and our friends a lot of pain. I entrust Bursa to Hayrüddin Halil Pasha, and Hayrüddin Halil Pasha to you. His word is my word, his decision is my decision."

He stood up and so did all of the *Alps*, beys, viziers and wise men and exclaimed in unison, "Godspeed Murad Bey..."

As of that day Murad I spent all his time preparing for the campaign. Every morning he went to the military headquarters near the castle his beys called Lüblüce, which looked like a pearl on the plain, joined the training and returned to the castle late at night. When he saw that the *yayas* trained by Yahşi Bey and his beys, and the cavalrymen trained by Sansaoğlu Sarı Bey and his men were like quicksilver Murad I was delighted. One day when the weather started to get warmer he told Yahşi Bey and Sansaoğlu Sarı Bey, "Yahşi Bey, send forth your most excellent *yaya* units to join forces with Hacı Ilbey who is waiting for our aid on the other side of the Dardanelles."

Then he turned and looked at Sansaoğlu Sarı Bey and said, "The *yayas* should be headed and followed by your outstanding cavalrymen. The remaining units should quickly prepare for the Ancyra campaign."

Murad I didn't go to the training camp on those last days when his beys began the final campaign preparations. Instead, he spent most of his time with his mother, son and harem. When the day of the campaign arrived, he bid farewell to his mother Nilüfer Hatun and his wife Gülçiçek Hatun and headed to his working palace. He looked at the walnut cupboard in the corner of his study before walking towards it and unlocking it. He grabbed the handle to open the door of the cupboard but he was hesitant. When he felt the tip of his nose tingle he pulled the door. He took the silk javelle he hadn't touched since he first saw it. He slowly placed it on his desk. He opened the layers of cloth one by one and took out the bloody shirts of his brothers. Looking at the shirts, he repined, "I promised my stepmothers that nothing would be any different. How will I explain this to them?" As his eyes started to water there was a knock on the door. He waited without making a sound. When there was another insistent knock on the door, he responded shakily, "Enter."

Grand Vizier Çandarlı Kara Halil Pasha entered the room and saw the bloody shirts on the table. He replied, "You can only quell your pain if you add your brothers to all the thousands of people who died for your Beylik. If you distinguish them as your brothers from the others your pain will increase and it will also be more difficult for you to forget about it, My Sovereign."

Averting his gaze, Murad I said, "Halil Pasha, when my father died I told my stepmothers that nothing would change. How will I explain this to them?"

Observing his face, Çandarlı replied, "This is something that had to be done for the good of this Beylik. It will hurt you to tell your stepmothers about this decision that has been made for the good of the Beylik but you have to fulfil this duty before the campaign because this is a campaign and you don't know whether you will return. You shouldn't keep this a secret before your leave."

As Murad I sat back down on the chair quietly, Çandarlı Kara Halil Pasha quietly left the room as he changed his mind about saying more. Murad I stared at the door through which he left the room and first thought of telling the mothers of the princes after the campaign but he then realised that it wouldn't be right for him to set forth on his campaign with such a heavy burden on his mind. He took the javelle with the bloody shirts and headed towards his mother's mansion. After telling everything in detail to his stepmothers summoned by his own mother, he said, "If something befalls me on the campaign I wouldn't want to die without telling you this personally. I ask that you give me your blessing and pray for me."

He then kissed his mother's hand and left the room."

On the days that Murad I departed Bursa with Yahşi Bey and Sansaoğlu Sarı Bey, Lala Şahin Bey—who had set up military headquarters in the lands of Gerede Beylik to the east of the Bithynian Mountains throughout winter—had left with his cavalry units upon receiving campaign orders and established headquarters where he first caught sight of Ancyra Castle. Murad I arrived at Lala Şahin

Bey's headquarters days later with his central cavalry units and decided to wait for the *yaya* units who were following him at the
headquarters of his tutor when news arrived from the advance units.
The news left them both speechless. They looked at each other for a
while before setting forth with their cavalry without further delay.
They crossed the field of Çubuk that took its name from Ziata Bey
who used his own Beylik as a shield against the Arab raids in one
breath. A dark curtain descended down Murad Bey's eyes when he
saw hundreds of severed bodies lined up next to each other where the
river that flowed down the middle of the field joined two other rivers.
His calm and composed face became laden with sorrow. As he
wanted to cry his eyes out he looked at Lala Şahin Bey. Seeing his
despair, he writhed in sadness for a while before expressing his anger, "My Beys, the offences that the *Âhis* have committed are now
two-fold. They will suffer the consequences of their doings."

Lala Şahin Bey looked at Murad I, who was his prince until a year
ago and whom he now called My Sovereign, with surprise, "They did
much worse to our units who remained behind last year. I suppose
they dared to do the same thing again because they were not punished for what they did last year."

"So why haven't our margraves who knew they would do this taken
any precautions?"

Lala Şahin Bey pulled a face and pointed at the small hills ahead,
"I suppose that they too were fooled by the flatness of the field like I
was."

Murad I turned his head and looked at the Phrygian hills Lala
Şahin was adamantly pointing at. He pursed his lips as if he didn't
understand much. Lala Şahin Bey continued, "We are not the only
ones fooled by the flatness of the field, My Sovereign. There were
many who were fooled before us. Like the Phrygian commanders
resting six feet under those hills."

When Murad I told him that he didn't know much about the

Phrygians, his tutor began to give him information on them as if he was lecturing him. However, while listening to him, Murad I remembered his visit to Sinanüddin Yusuf Pasha in Bursa before setting forth on the campaign and told him, "Son, it was your father's wish to capture Ancyra, the castle of the *Âhis*, because he considered it to be a trophy of war for his Suleyman. He left our realm during our preparations for the campaign last year. Now there are two scores you must settle. One of them for your brother Suleyman Pasha, and the other for your father, Orhan Ghazi. Go and capture Ancyra. This way you'll settle your scores and also teach a lesson to the *Karamanids* who have been causing unrest on the borders of our Beylik at every opportunity". He had then kept quiet for a while before continuing with a soft tone of voice and cautioning him with his hand in his, "May your holy war be blessed! My benediction will be with you." Noticing that Murad I wasn't listening to him Lala Şahin Bey was looking at his prince's face as if he had changed his mind about telling him about the Phrygians. Coming back to his senses too late, Murad I saw that his tutor was observing him quietly and responded, "Don't mind me tutor. I remembered that I listened to some of what you just told me from Sinanüddin Yusuf Pasha previously, so I recalled him. Ancyra deserves for us to wipe blood on its walls. They must be rather enraged since they have severed and killed two of our margraves. It doesn't matter if they've taken out their rage on the grandchildren of Midas, the Galatians or the Cimmerians because their rage will never match mine. I'm not Murad, son of Orhan Ghazi, if I don't hang the bey of this castle, that has not brought good omens to righteous Şahinşah Bey, together with his men where Muhiddin Bey was hung from with his two sons."

Then he mounted his blue Roan that he had dismounted a little earlier. Lala Şahin Bey was surprised that his prince, whom he had raised and who was influenced by his own rage, was defeated by his anger for the first time while also realising that he hadn't at all been idle in Bursa. As Lala Şahin Bey also mounted his horse, he shouted, "Murad Khan, wait! The *Âhis* wouldn't commit such cruelty if there wasn't a power that was provoking them. Let's first make a plan and then attack them.

He knew that his bey wouldn't stop until he arrived by the periphery forces but he had nevertheless tried to stop him. It turned out to be exactly how he envisioned it—Murad Bey didn't bring his horse to a halt until he arrived by the advance unit positioned at the periphery. Since his Roan predicted where he was headed, he went there without hesitation.

The advance unit at the periphery was beside the ghazis. The bey of the advance units recognised Murad Bey from the quilted turban on his head and immediately ran to him. As Murad Bey cast his gaze on the walls of Ancyra Castle situated up high like an eagle's nest, he asked, "How come you didn't manage to run to help your brothers, Yakupzade?"

Yakupzade Suleyman Bey, bey of the advance units replied, "Forgive me, My Bey. There is usually heavy fog in the prairie after midnight. They came out of the castle when the fog settled in. They were advancing from the north as we approached from the south. They must have been blindsided when their messengers were trapped on the streambed. There was no one other than a few casualties by the time we received news and rushed there. At least we managed to get there quickly and they didn't have the time to sever the bodies of our men as they did last year."

Lala Şahin Bey rubbed his long and thin moustache with the back of his hand as he listened to them. When Yakupzade Suleyman Bey finished talking he asked, "What is the current situation, Yakupzade?"

Looking at Cavvaloğlu Kerim Bey, the bey of the ghazis, who was beside him, Yakupzade Suleyman Bey said, "Kerim Bey and I recently talked about the news brought to us by our messengers. All of the castle gates are closed shut for now. We assume that they are telling the people of the castle about the raid they organised in order to give courage to their people. We guess that the castle people have no idea of our Sovereign's arrival. They think that they can discourage us by repeating what they did last year. That's why they might undertake another raid tonight."

Lala Şahin Bey turned around and looked at the plain behind him. The forces were still in the distance and were hardly visible. In any case it was impossible for the forces that were resting to be seen from the castle. Then he turned back and looked at Murad I, "I agree with the beys. We should close in on the castle with our cavalry as soon as night falls. As the *yayas* advance we can pull them into the corridors in between our cavalry. Then we can finish them off with a wolf trap. If they don't leave the castle as we suspect, we can complete all of our preparations tomorrow and undertake a full-on assault the day after. We can ask them to surrender before we unleash our *serdengeçtis* on them."

Murad I waited a while to defeat his rage and then nodded in approval of Lala Şahin Bey's plans. The messengers who were dispatched immediately delivered the news to the cavalry and the *yayas* by using the streambeds. Murad I and Lala Şahin Bey retreated to their units by monitoring the river beds. Deaf silence, which even surprised the people of the castle, took over the plain throughout the day. Just as the sun disappeared behind the Bithynian Mountains, campaign dinner was eaten all together as per the customs and deportment commenced immediately after. The renowned "relentless" cavalry of Kara Hasanoğlu approached from the north of Ancyra Castle which had almost become invisible in the dark, while the cavalry and *yayas* of Lala Şahin Bey and Kara Aygut Alp approached from the south and the central cavalry and cavalcade under the command of Murad I closed in on Ancyra step by step from the west. The advance units and the ghazis at the very front were under the command of Kara Ali Bey.

This quiet march, which lasted until midnight, ended with the news that Aygut Alp had taken the east of the castle under his control with his cavalry. Following this, the forces started forming open-ended chain formations around the castle towards the south and the north. Advance units were positioned at the open ends of the forma-tions. Their task was to herd in those marching towards them into the trap. Since Lala Şahin Bey trained his messengers really well, even news that was sent from the advance units who were positioned the furthest were received by the beys and Murad I in a very short period of time. It had long gone midnight when the mountains to the north began to blow fog towards the plain. When the fog swallowed the castle—only the silhouette of which was visible in the hazy moonlight—the units narrowed their chain formation.

At the break of day, the fog that covered the earth had begun to lift away with the morning breeze. Yakupzade Suleyman Bey's lookouts informed him that there were people coming out upon their secret signal, the hoot of an owl. Intermittent owl hoots continued on the streambeds for a while. Murad I, who was taking a nap at the time, immediately got up and got on his Roan. Both Lala Şahin Bey and Kara Hasanoğlu had also received the news and mounted their horses. However, there were so many cavalier units that left Ancyra Castle in such a short period of time that the owl hoots sounded by the messengers had become continuous.

The cavalrymen that left the castle were riding their horses like greased lightning in the direction of Kara Hasanoğlu on the north and Murad I's forces on the west. Lala Şahin Bey was informed that there weren't any more cavalry units leaving the castle. He dis-patched the "relentless" under the command of Uyuz Hasan Bey to hold the pass on the return path of the forces that had left the castle. The day had broken when the fog lifted completely. The dawn that the sun tried to drown out was now preparing to leave its place to

the rays of the sun. The units that departed Ancyra had not encountered the Ottoman units even though they had advanced considerably. They thought that the Ottomans had changed their mind
about capturing their castle as they had the previous year. They had
just begun to rejoice with the possibility of this thought when they
saw the Ottoman advance units running away from them. Taking
courage from their escape attempt, they decided to follow them.

CHAPTER EIGHTY-EIGHT

Despite the fact that the entire winter was rainy and cold, Emperor John Palaiologos V had continued the preparations of his campaign that was going to commence in spring and almost every day supervised the training of the volunteer knight units and the new forces that would be joining the army he left behind in Thrace. He had attempted capturing Heraclea Pontica Castle with his renowned marine hospitaller by sending a fleet of six galleons even though the weather conditions weren't much suited for sailing in the Black Sea, let alone capturing the castle. The hospitallers were showered with arrows as soon as they went ashore and had only been able to save their lives by jumping back into the sea. Thus, the fleet commander—who understood that it was even impossible to lay siege to Heraclea Pontica let alone to retrieve it—headed to Chelae Castle, the last remaining Byzantine castle on the coastline of the Black Sea, bought as many sailors as he had lost and returned to Constantinople. When he arrived in the city, he told the Emperor, "We couldn't even embark when they attacked us like rabid dogs. We can go and capture the castle with a larger fleet upon our return from the campaign, Your Majesty."

The Emperor still nurtured the hope that he would capture the castle at a suitable moment. He replied, "Be ready in the next couple of weeks. We first need to clean up Thrace. Once there is no one left to stick a dagger in our backs we can return and take back our Heraclea Pontica."

Emperor John Palaiologos departed in his imperial carriage the day after the fleet set sail in Hellespont. This time the hospitallers were appointed to the task of starting to clear out the enemy on the coastline of Aenus and advancing to Didymóteicho, while the Emperor would travel down south after clearing the north of Didymóteicho from the enemy, as soon as he finished his business in

Hadrianopolis.

The Emperor, whose infantry units were posted in Hadrianopolis, arrived in the city from Constantinople two days later with his mounted cavalry. When the few heavy armoured units who set forth from land before them arrived in Hadrianopolis a few days after him, all of the infantry and cavalry units began to advance towards the west. The news that made Emperor Palaiologos V the happiest was that the sailors who were in support of Matthew Kantakouzenos sailing around Aenus had decided to join forces with the Emperor, who was welcomed with joy in all of the old Byzantine castles he visited. The day he received this news, he told Demetrius, Commander of the Land Forces, "This is the first sign that our campaign will be concluded in our favour."

Without waiting for Demetrius' response, he turned around and looked at the units which were in perfect formation and following his imperial carriage. He was bursting with pride. He muttered, "You dealt with Prince Halil but you won't defeat me Murad Bey!" He turned back around and looked at the advance units and at his knights and cavalrymen who were racing with the wind on horseback. Smiling at Demetrius, whom he had asked to join him on his journey in the imperial carriage, he said, "If we can remove the Ottomans from Thrace no other power will be able to oppose us."

Demetrius, a man of few words, approved with a nod.

The Emperor moved towards the west for two days in Western Thrace where the advance units didn't leave them much to do before changing the course of his forced to the south. After getting his hands on Matthew Kantakouzenos, whom he suspected to be in Didymóteicho, he wanted to go all the way to Therma. On his way back from there he wanted to march on the Ottoman forces who had been posted on the south of Malgara for a long time. However, according to the latest news the Ottomans were headed for the north. Thus, he changed his mind about going to Therma and decided to march on the Ottoman forces as soon as he had caught Matthew Kantakouzenos. When they had just departed from their resting place he saw that the commander of the advance units was riding his horse towards the imperial carriage. While watching him he noticed that the spacious valley they were advancing down gradually narrowed. The commander of the advance forces approached him and saluted him from atop his horse, "Your Majesty, the valley is gradually narrowing. There is a passage but because it's so narrow it's like a natural trap. We would suffer great losses even against a small unit."

"If that's so we should immediately have the scout units climb up on the hillside while we wait here. Meanwhile, you can carefully advance down the valley as far as you can. Make sure to keep in contact with the half armoured hospitallers and cavalry units that will be following you."

When the commander of the advance units rode away the Emperor got out of his carriage and walked around the valley for a while. When he got to a fir tree he sat on the grass and leaned back on the thick trunk of the tree. The servants in the servants' carriage right behind his imperial carriage immediately brought him a cool apple sherbet mixed with ryegrass. The Emperor looked at the steep hillside as he enjoyed his beverage. He told Demetrius, Commander of Land Forces, "The hillside is really steep."

Demetrius liked to be prudent, "Your Majesty, it is because this is where Haemus took his first steps on this valley."

The Emperor didn't like to talk about things he didn't know much about so he nodded his head back and forth and looked at the scouts who had dismounted their horses and were trying to advance through the hillside.

All of the cavalrymen got off their horses and had them in tow because their horses were struggling to climb the steep hillside. When they disappeared in between the trees that thickened towards the peak the Emperor walked to the nearby stream. He stood on a stone by the side of the river and washed his face with cold water from the river. Then he set forth down a road that was a little wider than a track. He looked at the trees that increased in numbers towards the top of the hill. He started laughing for no reason at all when he saw the various wild fruit trees that seemed to climb the hillside all the way to the fir trees. Just as he turned his gaze to the snowy peaks in the distance he received news that the scouts had completed their exploration and that the cavalry was continuing to advance. But he still waited for the heavy armoured infantry to lead in case of any threat. Immediately behind them were archers who hunted even the flying high bird. After the halberdiers the procession of imperial cavalry units resumed. Once the infantry and cavalry units left in the passage were positioned on either side, the rear service carriages loaded with goods began to advance safely. The Emperor was able to breathe a sigh of relief and looked at the emerald green valley adorned with various flowers extending right before him.

There wasn't a single tree in the flatter than flat valley. Looking at the trees that emerged from the skirt of the mountains that surrounded the valley and it itself, where verdant fields stretched forth, the Emperor thought, "Why so much contrast?" He remembered the writings of natural philosopher Leucippus, which Empress Helena read with great pleasure and also made him read, "Nothing happens of its own volition, on the contrary everything happens for a reason and under exigence." He repeated twice, "Under exigence". He took a few deep breaths. His stomach became active with the effect of his breathing, it started grumbling and he felt hungry. He looked at old Demetrius. He signalled the guard closest to him and said, "Demetrius and I are both hungry. Tell the kitchen to prepare dinner before we arrive at the next village."

Emperor John Palaiologos V was scanning the trees on the hillside opposite and turning his gaze to the cultivated fields now and then.

When he arrived in the village at the bottom of the valley with his central units it was already dark. The servants had long arrived in the village by the time the Emperor got there and prepared a village house where he could rest while the cooks prepared all the food. The Emperor ate his dinner with Demetrius and he was overcome by sleep. As he slept, Demetrius did a little survey in the village and was surprised to find out that there weren't any men in the village who could work. He ran to the church at once. The priest was nowhere to be found either. Demetrius immediately summoned a few women from the village and learnt where the priest was. Suspecting of the fearful gaze of the old priest whom he found in hiding, Commander of the Land Forces didn't utter a word. He took the priest with him and brought him to the house where the Emperor was asleep. Since this was an urgent situation, the Emperor had been woken up. Seeing the priest's frozen gaze, the Emperor summoned his physicians. They examined him from head to toe but didn't find anything worth worrying about. They told the Emperor, "It might a shock of fear caused by violence, Your Majesty." The Emperor told his servant to prepare food for the priest.

When the food was ready he held the priest's hand and sat him across from himself before signalling him to start eating. But the old man only extended his hand and held the Emperor's hand. The Emperor was concerned for the priest so he extended his other hand and placed it on top of the priest's. For a while they stared into each other's eyes. The warm feeling of mercy in the Emperor's gaze must have warmed up the priest's heart so that he began smelling the delicious food in front of him. Recalling his hunger, his gaze gained meaning. He got back to his senses. He cried a little and then began to eat. Watching him eat, the Emperor asked himself, "I wonder how many days he has been hungry?" Once the priest finished eating and recovered fully, his tongue became loosened. After stroking his unkempt beard, he recognised the Emperor from the medals he was decorated with. Then he explained, "Esteemed Majesty, Matthew Kantakouzenos's men took away all the working men in the village three days ago. They threatened me regardless of my old age because I opposed them. Something happened to me after that day. When I see a crowd of people walking towards me I freeze up."

Emperor John Palaiologos V was very happy that the priest had recovered. Trying to make sense of the bitterness in his voice he held his hand again and looking at his face he said, "Saintly father, the end of the Kantakouzenos has come. We will all live in the lands of Byzantium without fear. Do you know which way they went saintly father?"

The priest felt confident once again and with the soft and comforting voice of a clergyman he said, "I think they headed to Didymóteicho."

Then he got buried in the deep silence of weeping.

The Emperor considered the information provided by the priest adequate and dispatched his infantry and armoured units towards Didymóteicho.

CHAPTER EIGHTY-NINE

Murad I had grown accustomed to most of his men welcoming him with the title of "Khan" since he set forth on his campaign. He kept turning back on his horse and looking at the castle of the *Âhis*. He was getting angry that the bey of the *Âhis* in Ancyra was making him wait, even though he had summoned him to talk before he punished the captives. His blue Roan was just as angry as him. It was as if he could feel his master's anger and constantly changing legs looking at the horses of the captives gathered in a circle. Once in a while, he hoofed the ground hard. His horse's state of distress drew Murad I's attention. He extended his hand and caressed his mane braided by grooms. As he did so, he spoke to him quietly, "I am as angry and enraged as you are but I am striving so that my rage doesn't overcome my mind as Sinanüddin Yusuf Pasha told me to do. If the castle commander arrives within the time I allocated all will be fine, if not I will ride you over them."

Then he dismounted his horse with a leap. He looked at the tall man who was standing behind two *serdengeçtis* armed with axes who were opposite Lala Şahin Bey and the other beys. He was said to command the *Âhis* and the Tataris of Çavdar who left the castle in the morning. One of the captured *Âhis* nearby noticed that Murad I was getting impatient. In a shuddery tone of voice, he said, "My Bey, our castle commander is very old. That's why he is late."

Murad I lingered around without looking at the captives and then took ten steps forward and ten steps backwards. He had reached the end of his patience when the news that the old Ahi bey of Ancyra Castle had left. Murad I turned around and looked at the castle. For a while, he counted the horses of the cortege riding downhill. He walked to the right and to the left. He looked at Lala Şahin Bey who was standing nearby. He was actually more enraged than him but he kept trying to conceal it. He constantly pulled on his moustache curved up and quivered it. He walked towards him and wanted to say a few things that examined the situation but it was as if the words had escaped him. He changed his mind about talking and spent a little more time walking until the old bey of Ancyra arrived. When the old Ahi bey slowly dismounted his horse with the help of his man, Sungur Bey approached him and pointed out Murad I to him, "Murad Bey, son of Orhan Ghazi the Ottoman Bey."

The old Ahi Bey who was well versed in rules and conventions approached Murad Bey. He kneeled down on one knee and bowed his head slightly. Then he spoke, "Welcome to our castle, Murad Bey. Forgive me for making you wait due to my old age."

For a while Murad I assessed the temperance of the old bey. His flaming voice was heard, "We would have also liked to be welcomed but I see that we are not as welcome as you say, the bey of *Âhis*."

The old bey of the *Âhis* slightly stood up straight and replied, "Since the day your older brother Suleyman Pasha entrusted the castle to us, our castle has been a castle of the Ottomans. However, because your forces left our castle quickly we agreed to the hegemony of the *Karamanids* and the Eretnids in order to be able to sustain our existence. When we heard that you were on your way to our castle last year we organised festivities but the death of your father extinguished our joy."

Murad I looked at Lala Şahin Bey as if he didn't know what to say. Lala Şahin Bey cut in, "How about the way our margraves and their men were slain last year? How about the massacre last night?"

The old castle commander replied bashfully, "Some tyrants who joined forces with the Tataris of Çavdar sent to our castle by the Eretnids planned that attack. The *Âhis* of Ancyra had nothing to do with it. It is also our desire to get rid of them, My Bey."

Then he turned back and pointed at the captured bey of the Tataris of Çavdar and the Ahi beys next to him and said, "These are the ones who wiped their cruelty on the walls of our castle."

Murad I understood it was time to pass judgment when the old man fell quiet. He told Lala Şahin Bey to carry out the decision made on the battlefield. Lala Şahin Bey turned back and looked at the broad-shouldered swordsmen standing behind a line of *serdengeçtis*. The swordsmen took a step forward and approached the captured beys in groups of three. Seven captured beys were taken to a platform where all the captives could see them and made to kneel. They had just been pushed down on their knees when seven swordsmen, known as the headmen—the most merciless of all of the swordsmen—walked towards them. With a single motion of Lala Şahin Bey's hand, seven heads were severed in seven directions.

The old bey of the *Âhis* was struck by fear and immediately kneeled down, "My Bey, God know we never betrayed the memory of your late older brother Suleyman Pasha. But we couldn't influence the beys who were just beheaded. All of the people of our castle except those seven await your justice. I would be happy if you wouldn't deny them Ottoman justice. But if you decide to punish them, punish me first so I won't witness the soul of our Çubuk Bey—whose name was given to this valley and is renowned from Mosul to Egypt to Yemen — turn in his grave."

Murad I was impressed by what the old bey of Ancyra said. As he muttered, "Our heart is not made of stone" he looked at Lala Şahin Bey as if to denote he had nothing to say. Lala Şahin Bey walked slowly, put his hands up so all of the captives could see it and in a loud tone of voice said, "Ye, the *Âhis* of Ancyra! Your lives are not worth much compared to the lives you have taken from us by being provoked but Murad Khan is merciful. If you resign yourself to us like the *Âhis* who previously joined the forces of Suleyman Pasha, you will join our *yayas* in Bursa and be sent to the aid of our battle allies in Rumelia. If you don't abide, you will be our captives together with your families."

He then turned to the Tataris of Çavdar who were like hedgehogs taking shelter in their thorny pelts once their horses were taken away. He opened his hands wide and talked louder and prouder than before, "Ye, Tataris! You have taken the lives of so many of our men by adhering to the Eretnids and *Karamanids* under the influence of your inner seeds of evil. You will be captives to our beys for life to pay for what you have done. If you don't accept enslavement your end will be the same as your beys."

The *Âhis* and the Tataris of Çavdar who were buried in silence had their eye on Murad I. Seeing them looking at him in such deep silence, Murad I approached Lala Şahin Bey, cast his sharp gaze over the *Âhis* of Ancyra and the Tataris of Çavdar and said, "You have heard what Lala Şahin Bey said. I won't tell you anything less or anything more than what he has said. Now you will all announce your allegiance to the Ahi Bey of Ancyra and then set forth towards Bursa with the forces of Pasha Yiğit Bey."

Picking up on the decidedness in Murad I's voice, the rebellious *Âhis* kneeled down and announced their allegiance to the old bey of the *Âhis* and they all stood up together and began to march in line. Lala Şahin Bey saw the Tataris of Çavdar talk amongst themselves in the distance and got angry. He looked at Deli Rüstem Agha and said, "Split those into two groups first, and then split them all in half."

CHAPTER NINETY

I t was as if the sun was rising over the snowy peaks early in order to dissuade the forces closing in on each other with rancour from fighting. But neither Matthew Kantakouzenos, partner to the empire, nor Emperor John Palaiologos V, both of whom on were burning with the desire of attaining power, intended to change their mind about spilling blood. On top of it all, Emperor Palaiologos had received a letter from the fleet commander who captured Didymóteicho Castle with the help of the Duca of Aenus that read, "Your Majesty, the people of Didymóteicho are happy to be waiting for you. We have captured the castle from Kantakouzenos's men and departed. If you approach from the north and we approach from the south and trap Matthew Kantakouzenos, he will have nowhere left to escape." This letter had sharpened his rage and ambition further.

The Emperor prepared his units for attack immediately after reading the letter. He got into his armour with the help of his servant in his imperial carriage moving fast down the hillside. He put on his helmet and then turned to the village priest who was travelling with the Emperor because he insisted that he voluntarily pray for the imperial army and said, "Saintly priest, it is time to rid ourselves of the Kantakouzenos. In the name of this beautiful and sunny day, pray in the name of God who has shown us this victorious day."

When the Emperor signalled the driver to slow down, the old priest of the village church began to pray. The Emperor got out of the carriage when it stopped and mounted his horse with the help of his guards. He saluted the priest one last time with his head, spurred his horse and rode further than his guards and mounted knights. When the other units were signalled with a white flag that the Emperor was on the move, the hillside was flooded with the sound of horseshoes. Matthew Kantakouzenos's forces on the opposite hillside saw them descend the hill in half-moon formation and took to action.

Since Matthew Kantakouzenos knew very well how to fight on the highlands he thought that instead of attacking them from one direction only, he thought he could defeat the Emperor's knights with the cavalry units he hid behind the hills before the hospitallers arrival. However, when the Emperor's knights attacking from the centre started retreating a little while later, Matthew Kantakouzenos got caught in the euphoria of victory and ordered his armoured cavalry to catch the knights. The Emperor's knights, who detracted his armoured cavalry from the forces under the command of Serbian princes, suddenly turned back and counter attacked and quickly annihilated the disorderly forces of Matthew Kantakouzenos who were following them. At that moment, the imperial archers who had crossed the stream between the two hills began showering the central forces of Matthew Kantakouzenos with arrows. Emperor John Palaiologos V saw that Matthew Kantakouzenos's forces were panicking and advanced his second heavy armoured and halberdiers in the centre. Seeing them charge towards them at full speed, Matthew Kantakouzenos pulled his forces back and retreated to the hillside behind them. Demetrius, Commander of the Land Forces, was alerted by the fact that the arrows shot on his cavalry were not aimed well. Almost all of them were aimless. He thought, "Either they don't want to shoot us or they are inexperienced." With that thought, he sent forward his shielded cavalry. Shortly after their attack Matthew Kantakouzenos's left wing forces left their positions and disappeared behind the woods. Seeing that they were defeated, Matthew Kantakouzenos ordered the reserve forces he left behind the hill to attack from both sides. He was crazed at the thought of defeat so he attacked the central forces under the command of the Emperor. First human cries that tore up the skies, and then the sound of shields being attacked by spears were heard. When small streams of blood formed and there were no colliding spears and shields left, the fight of the renowned imperial hospitallers, who were called the "Swords of Byzantium" founded long before the Roman times, commenced. Matthew Kantakouzenos witnessed the superiority of the Emperor's hospitallers before long and rode his horse towards the Emperor, surrounded by his bravest and most loyal guards. The Serbian princes who were following him attacked the central forces and an unprecedented scuffle began. Matthew Kantakouzenos's guards were befittingly and completely slicing up anyone who opposed them. Seeing that they were closing in on him, the Emperor was overcome by fear and had just about decided to retreat when he saw his commanders on both sides confine Matthew Kantakouzenos's forces into a half-moon formation. He felt courageous like never before, dismounted his horse and began to charge towards the guards of Matthew Kantakouzenos who were approaching his units. His mad courage encouraged his forces so much that all of Matthew Kantakouzenos's guards were slain in a moment. Seeing that he had lost almost all of his guards, Kantakouzenos spurred his horse to a gallop in order to catch up to the Serbian forces that had retreated. Shortly after, he dissolved into thin air leaving behind thousands dead just as he had done in Tzirallum, Cypsela and Hadrianopolis. He was so masterful in that, that it was as if his humongous body somehow shrunk and he was able to fit into a mouse hole or a mountain split open in front of him, keeping himself safe within.

Emperor John Palaiologos V couldn't decide whether he should be happy about his great triumph, and taking in prisoners who weren't Byzantine, or sad that Matthew Kantakouzenos had slipped through his fingers again. As he walked amongst the dead in that state of bewilderment, his driver, who always followed him wherever he went, approached him with the carriage. When he saw the imperial carriage he recalled the village priest whom he had left inside. He forgot everything at once and got into the carriage. He held the old priest's hands and said, "Matthew Kantakouzenos slipped through our fingers again, father. But we have achieved victory with your prayers.

Please do not withhold your prayers from us from now on."

The old priest lowered his head and replied, "My prayers will always be with you, Your Majesty. I know it causes you pain that all of our religious fellows have died because of an unjust power war but unfortunately there is nothing that can be done."

"Yes, father. I had no other choice but to fight against the power-hunger of the Kantakouzenos. I hope that he will be able to find neither a Serbian prince to fool nor a castle commander to seek shelter with."

The village priest placed his hand on the Emperor's head and recited a prayer. He crossed himself to bless the Emperor and then continued, "Your Majesty, I presume we will be going our own ways from here. If there are any of our villagers amongst those who were forcefully taken away by Matthew Kantakouzenos's men, please spare them to their wives and children."

The Emperor stood up and then the old priest, whose hand had given him peace, said all he had to say and stood up to get out of the carriage. Smiling at the old man who lived and defended a plain life, something the patriarch had long forgotten about, the Emperor said, "Father, you can come to Constantinople with me if you like."

"I can hardly go to Didymóteicho, Your Majesty. I am a person of small places and I would suffocate in Constantinople."

Then he got out of the imperial carriage and so did the Emperor. He told the guards nearby that they should accommodate all of the priest's wishes and for them to arrange a carriage drawn by the best two draught horses for the priest.

As the old village priest and the villagers who were saved set out towards their village, the imperial forces set the heaps of corpses on fire and headed towards Didymóteicho.

CHAPTER NINETY-ONE

Murad I went to Ancyra Castle with the old Ahi bey immediately after the Tataris of Çavdar had been finished off. He appointed Kara Hasanoğlu as the castle commander, one of the men raised by Sungu Alp as the *subaşı* and one of the *akıncıs* as the *kadî* of the castle. He took the families of all of the Tataris of Çavdar in the castle as prisoners and shared them equally among his beys. He left the command of the akıncıs and ghazis he left outside of the castle to Sarı Alâeddin Bey and Deli Rüstem Agha and departed from Ancyra Castle.

Two days after leaving Ancyra, Murad I entrusted his *yayas* to Lala Şahin Bey and set forth to Bursa with his cavalry. He looked even more gallant in front of the cavalry units because he sat up straight on his blue Roan that raced with the wind. Capturing and adding the *Âhis* castle to his lands in a period of time shorter than he anticipated had made him so happy that he invaded all of the castles that he came across in the Germiyanid lands, which his father referred to as the "Sultan's doorstep", that stretched like a peninsula from the south to the east of the Ottoman Beylik. Once he had established order in the castles and posted adequate numbers of akıncıs and ghazis he set forth towards Bursa once again and arrived at Kulacahisar Fortress, which his mother still referred to as "Krulla". The castle people who received news of Murad I's visit welcomed him to there with great joy. Even though he was in a rush to be reunited with Bursa, his mother, Gülçiçek Hatun and his son Bayezid when he saw the warm welcome of the people he decided to stay a night at the fortress where his mother spent her childhood. He held a meeting with the beys of the war units whom he was dispatching to the borders before attending the evening festivities organised by the castle landlord. He calmly explained that they should advance slowly without any hostility and said, "My Beys, because the *Germiyanids* have roots in these lands, for now they have more supporters than us. That is why when you organise raids you must act with justice. This way your supporters will increase in numbers."

The *akıncı beys* and the beys of the ghazi units, who were to head to the border with new forces, voiced that they understood Murad I's orders. Following the meeting, they all attended the evening festivities organised by the castle landlord.

The next day Murad I galloped towards Bursa in front of the cavalry units and didn't take a break until he arrived at the military headquarters near Lüblüce Fortress. He left his units at the headquarters and rode his horse to the castle. For a brief period, he fulfilled his longing for Gülçiçek Hatun and his son Bayezid before going to his mother's harem and kissing her hand. He asked about his stepmother's well-being and conciliated with them. However, when he saw them he remembered the bloody shirts of his brothers. He felt so uneasy that he sought refuge in his own harem.

The following day he left his mansion after breakfast. As he was walking to attend the council meeting he murmured, "They would perhaps be forgiving if they knew that their sons prepared their own funerals but because they don't know it, they will never forgive me and I will never be at peace. Every time I see my stepmothers those bloody shirts will appear before my eyes. It is best to tell them to move to castles of their own choosing. We might forget about it sooner if we don't see each other." Just as he was about to enter the mansion where the council hall was, he mumbled, "The castle landlord and the *subaşı* of Kulacahisar seemed rivalrous. We have to free them from this rivalry. I hope that Halil Pasha has worked on changing castle governance as we talked about before my departure." When he crossed the small courtyard and entered the council hall, Grand Vizier and Council Chairman Hayrüddin Kara Halil Bey and other members of the council stood up in unison and saluted him. They sat down after he took his seat. Grand Vizier Kara Halil Bey sat up straight on his knees and said, "May God bestow upon you many bright victories, My Sovereign."

"May God bestow victory upon us all."

After a brief silence followed by prayers, Murad I told them about all that happened throughout the campaign. Following the long talk, sherbet was served to celebrate their victory. Snuffboxes were sniffed, and once it was all quiet again, Murad I said, "After all, I have seen during this campaign, I say we need a better-organised army and methodical governance in our fortresses."

Then he looked at Kara Halil Bey as if to remind him of their conversation prior to the campaign. Hayrüddin Kara Halil Pasha, who had taken on most of the duties of the Grand Vizier which he talked to Murad I about several times throughout the previous winter, looked at the members of the council and said, "*Alps*, viziers and wise man who build and shoulder the Ottoman Beylik... There is no doubt that the late Alâeddin Ali Bey, Prince Suleyman Pasha, Ahmed Pasha, Hacı Pasha, and last but not least Sinanüddin Yusuf Pasha have all governed our Beylik, the boundaries of which have continuously enlarged since the Beylik of Osman Bey, to the best of their capabilities. We should first realise that their governance was made possible through the contributions of our beys and *Alps*. However, if you look at our early borders and people you can see that the governance of that time is no longer sufficient for our time. Prior to his campaign, Murad Bey and I decided that governance should be shared as it was in many kingdoms before us to preserve our gradually enlarging borders, our farmhands who work on our lands as well as our ever-growing armed unit. I researched this in detail while our bey was campaigning. I decided that we should bring back the ranks of *Kadı'asker* and *Beylerbeyi*. I was planning on telling you about this after talking to our bey but since our bey asks about it I can tell you about it now. The *Kadı'asker* will report to the bey of our *Beylik* and approve the decisions of the council in his name while he is campaigning. If our forces in Bursa have to set out on a campaign while our bey is campaigning *Beylerbeyi* will command our forces in the name of our bey and they will be the highest rank to which the *kadîs* in our castles will consult. In addition to this, as you know, our army is campaigning in both Anatolia and Rumelia. Since a *Kadı'asker* will command our forces in Anatolia as the *Beylerbeyi* of Anatolia in the absence of our bey, a Rumelian should act as Beylerbeyi as the commander of our forces when our bey is away from Rumelia. Whichever princes, *Alps*, viziers and beys our Bey considers being suitable for these roles, we can debate it in our council and come to a decision."

He then turned and looked at Murad I, who lightly stroked his short well-groomed beard. With an expression of peace and happiness, he replied, "So we can first talk about the position of *Kadı'asker* and then *Beylerbeyi* in detail, determining their duties, and begin to appoint..."

After discussions lasting for a few days, the council members considered the creation of these positions suitable. In the final council meeting, which was also attended by Lala Şahin Bey whom Murad I summoned to Bursa by sending his personal messengers, Murad I said, "I consider Hayrüddin Kara Halil Bey to be suitable for the position of *Kadı'asker* because I believe he will govern our Beylik righteously. I also think that it is suitable for our princes to be appointed as *Beylerbeyi* of Anatolia. However, since our prince is still too young to take on such a position, *Kadı'asker* Hayrüddin Kara Halil Bey will also undertake this post. When it comes to the *Beylerbeyi* of Rumelia, who will be the commander of our forces in Rumelia in my absence, I consider Lala Şahin Bey to be suitable because of his performance during the siege of Heraclea Pontica and later in his unique governance of our forces."

When Murad I's choices for the positions of *Kadı'asker* and *Beylerbeyi* were considered to be suitable by the members of the council, the kadî of Bursa Mahmud Efendi suggested, "Since our beys will be referred to with their new titles they should be considered as part of the Ottoman family and called Pasha from now on."

This suggestion was also accepted by the council. As they drank sherbet to celebrate the big change in the council governance, the chief messenger pulled aside the drape in front of the door and hastily entered the hall. After bowing and saluting the council, he said, "We received a messenger from Urum. He is growing impatient to be in your presence, My Bey."

Murad I got so excited for the first time since he became the sovereign of the Beylik that he felt as if his heart was about to come out of his ribcage. As he tried to defeat that sensation he replied, "Show him in at once."

Ince Sungur Bey, one of the beys of Kara Timurtaş Bey, respectfully saluted Murad I and the council before kneeling down and said, "My Bey, Ece Bey, Evrenos Bey, Hacı Ilbey, Fazıl Bey, Akça Kocaoğlu and Kara Timurtaş Pasha who joined them recently send you their greetings."

Hayrüddin Kara Halil Pasha, who had just become the Beylerbeyi of Anatolia and *Kadı'asker*, presumed that Ince Sungur Bey would prolong his introduction. He lost his patience and said, "Get to the point, son! Do you bring good or bad news?"

Ince Sungur Bey bowed his head without losing his calmness. After a moment's silence, he quietly spoke before falling silent again, "The news I bring is certainly good, My Bey."

CHAPTER NINETY-TWO

W hen Byzantine Emperor John Palaiologos V was informed that the castle people had pooled their resources to catch Matthew Kantakouzenos upon finding out that he was hiding in their castle and that Matthew Kantakouzenos had to escape from the castle, he rejoiced. He exclaimed, "My Byzantium is finally forever rid of usurper Kantakouzenos. My next task is to expel the Ottomans from the peninsula." He organised festivities to celebrate "Freedom from Kantakouzenos". He ordered that instead of water, wine is poured from the fountains of conical Didymóteicho Castle which looked like a funnel atop a hill. The people of Didymóteicho ate, drank and celebrated for days. After these wonderful days of festivity, the Emperor headed to Aenus with all of his forces. He couldn't get enough of the colour of the cherry flowers in this castle where the Maritza met the Aegean Sea. For hours, he watched how the river mixed into the sea from the turret near the magnificent mansion of the Duca of Aenus. The Emperor was very generously hosted by the Genoese Duca of Aenus Castle. After a few days of imperial luxury, he suddenly decided to order his fleet to set sail, and to anchor off the coast of Gallipoli after clearing the Ottoman forces from the northern coast of the Dardanelles. As soon as the fleet set sail, he too set forth with all of his land forces towards Raussia and Pozapa. His aim was to drive the Ottoman forces from the north to Gallipoli and to stop them from crossing the Dardanelles. Thus, he was going to be in a position to demand Heraclea Pontica in return for the lives of the Ottoman forces he would trap in Gallipoli. This way, with one campaign he would have gotten rid of Matthew Kantakouzenos, taken back Heraclea Pontica, and eradicate the Ottomans from Thrace.

Emperor John Palaiologos V set forth with numerous beautiful

servants, odalisques, musicians and gifts that overflowed from
chests given to him by the Duca of Aenus. When night fell, he set
up his headquarters in the wide and sheltered valley between the
Fortress of Raussia and Pozapa Castle. He ordered the commander
of the guards who was beside him to dispatch scouts towards the
south and the east and told him that the war council should be attended by all of the commanders that evening. Then he watched
the work of his servants who were busy setting up the large
headquarter marquee. When the unassuming but practical marquee
was ready he went in to cool down. He took off his helmet and
wiped the sweat off his brow. He took off his breast armour, which
squeezed his body like a mangle, with the help of his servants. Before he took off his kneepads, he told them, "Bring some cold water
and wash my head."

The servants weren't used to such a request, so they look at each
other in surprise before they hurried to the horse carriage loaded
with the water barrels. Their short-lived surprise made the Emperor laugh. He spoke out loud to himself, "They are surprised because this is the first time told them to wash my head with cold water." Swaying his gradually fattening body he walked out of the
marquee. He waited for the arrival of his servants, squatting and
scratching his sweaty hair with his slender fingers. The servants
were even more surprised when they saw him squatting and waiting. The Emperor saw their surprised faces and laughed out loud,
"You don't need to be so surprised. I am not used to it either but I
will be attending a meeting shortly. Wouldn't it be better for me to
go into the meeting with a cool head rather than with an itchy
head?"

The servants who were trained for such days began their task immediately and washed the Emperor's hair with chamomile soap.
Once they completed lathering and rinsing his hair, another servant dried his hair with towels from Philadelphia. Then another

servant combed his hair with a boxwood comb. When the Emperor stood up, entered the marquee and lied down on the floor cushions prepared for him, the servants took of his kneepads and heel cups. As he rested, the servants suddenly disappeared.

He wasn't sure whether it was because his head was cooler or because he was exhausted after his travels but Emperor John Palaiologos V relaxed so much that he lost himself in a sweet and cosy nap. The commander of the guards anticipated that he was tired and delayed the meeting so that the Emperor could rest a little longer. When they woke him up, he muttered, "Travelling on horseback with armour must have tired me out." He got up, got ready and immediately went to the meeting marquee. When he entered inside, the commanders gathered around a table made of interlocking timber, bowed and saluted him. Demetrius, Commander of the Land Forces pointed at the section between Raussia and Pozapa on the map scrolled out on the table and said, "As we have decided with our emperor, we will move towards the south-west by drawing a large arc in the direction of east and west. Our fast-moving light cavalry will be positioned on the outside, followed by armoured cavalry, then followed by armoured infantry and central forces, with guard cavalry and light archers and armoured infantry in the centre. We will advance towards Gallipoli in the south without leaving any spaces between our units. We will destroy any Ottoman forces that oppose us, hemming in the others like ants."

Emperor John Palaiologos V thanked the Commander of the Land Forces who explained the plan they talked about the night before and cast furtive glances at his commanders' faces to sense their joy of victory. He kept quiet for a while and revelled in that sensation. Then he stood up and said, "My commanders, counts, dukes, knights who saved our Byzantium from the wrath of Kantakouzenos! I am not asking you to exile Murad, who murdered even his own brothers, to the opposite shore. Our sailors will besiege Maydos and Sestos at dawn tomorrow. I hope that we will be able to meet our sailors in no longer than a couple of days. What I wish from you is that you take as many Ottomans as prisoners as you can because the more prisoners we have, the higher our chances of negotiating for Heraclea Pontica. We don't have any reliable information on how powerful they are on the peninsula but we guess that they are only half as many as we are. Now go to your units, rest until midnight and wait for our news."

The commanders joined their units as soon as the meeting was over and rested for a while. They had just retreated to their tents when the howls of a few wolves and a few other sounds that didn't belong to any animal were heard through the restless pitch-black night. Almost all of those who weren't asleep heard the noises but since it wasn't repeated nobody paid it much attention. However, the bending valley had tried to wake them up with a soft breeze in order to make the sleeping Byzantine forces sense what was about to happen.

Emperor John Palaiologos V had some light food after the meeting. When he noticed the breeze licking his marquee he stood up. The guards waiting in front of his marquee with spears moved aside and let him pass through the door. He had just stepped outside and turned his face to the northern wind when he heard a growl-like sound coming from near him. He looked around carefully. When the sound wasn't repeated he relaxed but seeing that a few guards were headed towards the origin of the sound he became suspicious and went back into his marquee. He put on his chest armour. As his servant helped him put it on, the news came that one of the messengers had fallen off a cliff because he couldn't see ahead. Emperor Palaiologos thought of taking his armour off and resting. He couldn't decide whether to lie on his bed. Just then, sounds similar to the previous ones were heard once again. He girded himself with his sword and put on his helmet. As he was about to walk out of the marquee, the commander of the guards entered inside. He told the servant to put out the oil lamps. Then he turned to the Emperor and said, "We can't get any news from the messengers we dispatched or the scouts we deployed. I think we have been raided, Your Majesty. I can't believe that this could happen while we are awake. The only thing that comes into my mind is that all of our advance units and messengers have been caught."

The commander of the imperial guard had not yet finished his talk when they heard sounds of swords striking shields nearby. The Emperor had no idea what was happening so he stepped outside of this marquee. The commander of the guards who surrounded him said, "Your Majesty, it is best if you go far away from here since we cannot see who is fighting us and who we are fighting in this darkness."

REFERENCES

Ahmedi, Alexandria, trans. Dr. I. Unver, TDK, 1983

Aiskhülos, Ancient Greek Tragedies, trans. Yılmaz Onay, Mitos Boy. 2010

Akşin, Sina, Ottoman State, Cem Yay., 1993

Akurgal, Ekrem, Anatolian Civilizations, Net Pub., 2003

Alexiou, Stlianos, Minoan Civilization, trans. Dr. E. T. Tulunay, Archeology and Art Pub., 1991

Alova, Anthology of Ancient Anatolian Poetry, K Library, 2003

Aprim, Frederick Assyrians, trans. V. İlmen Yaba Yay., 2008

- Assyrians, trans. V. İlmen, Yaba Yay., 2008

Arslan, Murat, Galatians, Archeology and Art Pub., 2000

Aristotales, Rhetoric, trans, M.H Doğan, YKY., 1995

Aydın, Mehmet, Articles on Islamic Philosophy, Ufuk Bookstore, 2000

Balivet, Michel, Sheikh Bedreddin, Sufism and Rebellion, trans, Ela Güntekin, History Foundation / Yurt Yay. 2011

Bayar Muharrem, Ahi Organization in Akşehir, Kırşehir-2007

Bayram, Mikail, Ahi Evren - Mevlana Struggle, Damla Ofset - Konya, 1991 and - Bacıyan-i Rum, NKM, 2008

Baytop, Turhan, Turkish Plant Names Dictionary, TDK Pub., 2007

Brendjes, Burchard-Sonja, Ibn Sina, trans. O. Özügül, Window Pub. 1978

Boratav, P. Naili, Nasrettin Hoca, Literature Association-1996

The Great Larousse, 24 Volumes, Milliyet Pub., 1986

Bostan, İdris, Ottoman Maritime From Principality to Empire, Kitap yay., 2008

Carem, C.W., Homeland of Gods Anatolia, trans. Esat Nermi Erendor, Remzi Bookstore, 1979

Carpelle, Wilhelm, Philosophy Before Socrates, trans. O. Özügül, Window Yay., 2006

Cevdet, Muallim, Islamic Futuwwww and Ahilik, Sign Pub., 2008

Cogito, Ottomans, issue 19, YKY, 1999 (532- 533)

Cogito, Byzantine, issue 17, YKY, 1999

Cokay, Sedef, Lighting in Antiquity, Turkish Ancient Science. Inst. Arrow., 2000

Cicero, On Obligations, trans, c.cengiz Cevik, Turkey Isbank Pub., 2013

Avalanche, trans. Muazzez İlmiye, Sumerians (Research), Kaynak Pub., 1996

Çiloğlu, Fahrettin, History of Georgians, ANT publications, 1993

Danishmend, Ismail Hami, Annotated Chronology of Ottoman history, Turkey Publ., 1971

Dinçol, Belkis, Music in Ancient Asia Minor and Egypt, Turkish Antiquity Knowledge. Inst. Yay., 2003

Dukas, Byzantine History, trans. VL.Muzeyroğlu, Istanbul Institute Pub. 1956

Ekremkoçu, Reşat, Ottoman Sultans, Main Pub., 1981

Er, Yasemin, Classical Archeology Dictionary, Phoenix, 2006

Ercan, Yavuz, Bulgarians and Voynuks in the Ottoman Empire, TTK, 1989

Erhat, Azra, Mythology Dictionary, Remzi Publishing House, 1978

- Blue Anatolia, İnkilap Aka, 1979 - K. P. Mavi Anadolu, Cem Yay., 1979

Euripides, Ancient Greek Tragedies, trans. Yılmaz Onay, Mitos Boy. 2008

Evliya Çelebi, Evliya Çelebi Seyahatname, İskit Pub., 1962, YKY, 2006

Eyici, Semavi, Late Byzantine Architecture, Istanbul Unv. Literature Faculty Pub., 1980

Faroqhi, Suraia, Production and Marketing in the Ottoman World, trans. GC.

Freud, Totem and Taboo, trans. Niyazi Berkes, Remzi Bookstore, 1971

Trust, Ö. Türesay, YKY, 2003

Gibbon, Edward, Byzantine History, trans. A. Baltacıgil, Archeology and Art Pub., 1994

Guilmartin jr, J.F., Galleons and Galleys, trans. A. Özdamar Book Publ., 2010

Hacı Bektaş-ı Veli, Makalat, TDV Pub., 2007

Halacoglu, Yusuf, State Organization and Social Structure in the Ottomans, TTK Yay., 2007

Ibn Battuta, Travelogue of Ibn Batûta, trans. A. S. Aykut, YKY, 2004

Ibn Sina, Ministry of Culture Pub., 1999

Inalcik, Halil, State-i Aliye, Turkey Business Bank Pub., 2009

Islamic Encyclopedia, TDV, 2004

James, Henri, Europeans, trans. Z. Copper, Golden Bilek, 2006

Kabaağaçlı, C. Şakir, Anatolian Gods, Bilgi Pub., 1983

- Anatolian Legends, Bilgi Publishing House, 1985 - Blue Voyage Information Pub., 1979

Kantemir, Dimitri, The Rise and Fall of the Ottoman Empire (1-2), Translation Özdemir Çobanoğlu, Ministry of Culture Pub. 1979

Karal, E. Ziya, Ottoman History (Organizations), TTK Pub., 1999

Kerovpyan, Keğam, Mythological Armenian History, Aras, 2003

Konyalı, İsmail Hakkı, Akşehir Historical Numune Printing House, 1945

Konyalı, İsmail Hakkı, Konya Historical Sample Printing House, 1942

Köprülü, M. Fuat, The First Sufis in Turkish Literature, Akçağ Pub. 2007

Xsenophon, Greek History, trans. Suat Sinanoğlu, TTK Pub., 1999

Küçüksöz, Sema, Tebe'a-i Sadıka, Tek Yay., 2006

Lamartine, Alphonso D., Ottoman History, trans. S. Bayram, Sabah Yay., 1991

Mabeynci Pavlos, Statement of Hagia Sophia, trans. S. Rifat, Istanbul Research Institute., 2010

Mantran, Robert, History of the Ottoman Empire I.II, trans. Server Tanilli, Turkey İşbankası Sagittarius. 2011

Marozzi, Justin, Tamerlane, trans. H. Kocaoluk, YKY, 2006

McEvedy, Colin, Atlas of First and Medieval History, trans. Ayşen Anadol, Sabanci Unv. Yay., 2005

McNeill, H. Wıllıam, World History, Trans. Alaeddin Şenel, Image Publishing House. 2002

Merçil, Erdoğan, History of the Ghaznavids State, TTK Pub., 2007

Onan, Necmettin Halil, Divan Poetry Anthology, Social Pub. 1998

Özçelik, Mustafa, Yunus Emre, Doğan Ofset, 1991

Özdizbay, My Love, Agriculture in Ancient Greece, Know Turkish Antiquity. Inst. Arrow., 2004

Roux, Jean-Paul, The Ancient Religion of the Turks and Mongols, trans. A. Kazancıgil, Kabalcı Yay., 2002 - Central Asia, History and Civilization, trans. A. Kazancıgil, Kabalcı Pub., 2006

Saltık, Gazali, Emir Sultan, Asa Bookstore, Bursa, 1959

Sevim, M., Engraving with Turkey (Palace Clothing), Ministry of Culture Publ., 1997

Shaw, Stanford, Ottoman Imp. History, trans. M. Harmancı, E Pub., 1983

Strabon, Ancient Anatolian Geography (I-XIV), trans. Prof. Dr. A. Pekman, Archeology and Art Pub., 1993

Sheikh Bedrettin, Varidat, Esma Pub., 1994

Sheikh-Sadi-i Shirazi, pleasure. İbrahim Ülgen, Berfin Yay., 2004

Sophocles, Ancient Greek Tragedies, trans. Şükran Yücel, Mitos Boy. 2008

Bricksci, Pars, Ottoman Cities, Milliyet Pub., 1985

Uzunçarşılı, İsmail H., Ottoman History (Organizations), TTK Pub., 2003

Uzun Çarşılı, İsmail H., Çandarlı Vizier family, TTK Pub., 1988

Walter, Gerard, Everyday Life in Byzantium, Uitgeverey Hollandia, 1989

Wilkinson, Philip, Legends and Myths, ALFA, 2010

Yesevi, Ahmed., Divan-i Hikmet Selection, Ministry of Culture, 1991

Yücel, Yaşar, Es'ar Notebook TTK Printing House, 1992

Yücel, Yaşar, Studies on Anatolian Principalities (I-II), TTK Basımevi, 1991

Zoroaster, Avesta, Kora Pub., 1998

Zinkeisen, Johann Wilhelm, History of the Ottoman Empire (7 Books), trans, Y. Jun. Erhan Afyoncu, Yeditepe Yay. 2001

Other Books by Murat Tuncel

Inanna

This book's title is taken from the ancient Sumerian god Inanna. It is set in the Ottoman Empire during the 19th century and is the story of Cemil, an educated man who, despite having studied in Baghdad, Istanbul and Paris, still hasn't found "himself" and lives in his father's shadow. During his search to find himself, he meets an Armenian girl and falls in love with her. Cemil is already married and the girl's father does not approve of his daughter becoming Cemil's second wife. His father sends Cemil from their village into exile. The story follows Cemil, his wife and the Armenian girl on their journey to find a place to live and the three men who try to protect them. Intertwined with Cemil's story is another about Bilal, a young man sent to become a Janissary—a soldier for the Empire. Following the Sultan's disbandment of the Janissary Corps, Bilal starts working for a Pasha. One evening whilst looking after hunting dogs, in the Pasha's mansion, he sees a girl. She's Nurhayal, one of the Pasha's concubines. Even though it's forbidden for them to meet or even look at each each other, they fall in love. Set during a turbulent period in Istanbul's history this novel explores the lives of its soldiers and people, their social lives, relationships and their struggles to live in the capital of the Ottoman Empire. It tells the story of several cultures that lived together in a single Empire on the soil of Anatolia, and looks at the daily lives of the people and their loves against the background of change during difficult times.

Hardcover ISBN: 978-3-949197-35-2

Paperback ISBN 978-3-949197-36-9

The Third Death

MURAT
TUNCEL

THE
THIRD
DEATH

This is the story of the life of a Hungarian man living through the most turbulent years of the twentieth century. Born the youngest of three brothers and one sister Galgoczy, was denied a normal childhood by the chaos of the first world war. His father, a sergeant in the Hungarian army, was absent throughout the war years and did not return home permanently after the armistice but returned to soldiering in the south of Hungary. Galgoczy's father could only return home for a few days at a time on rare occasions and the growing boy missed him and dreamt of his return continually. The nationalist movement in Germany rose to power during Galgoczy's adolescence. In the thirties Germans began to arrive in Hungary to buy large tracts of land as farms. One such farm was built near Galgoczy's home. His mother began working at the farm believing that it would bring a better future for her children...

Hardcover ISBN 978-3-949197-44-4

Paperback ISBN 978-3-949197-45-1

Lightning Source UK Ltd.
Milton Keynes UK
UKHW041022150121
377035UK00001B/1